DARK DJINN

THE DARKNESS OF DJINN

BOOK 1

TIA REED

For my uncle,

Paul

The Three Realms

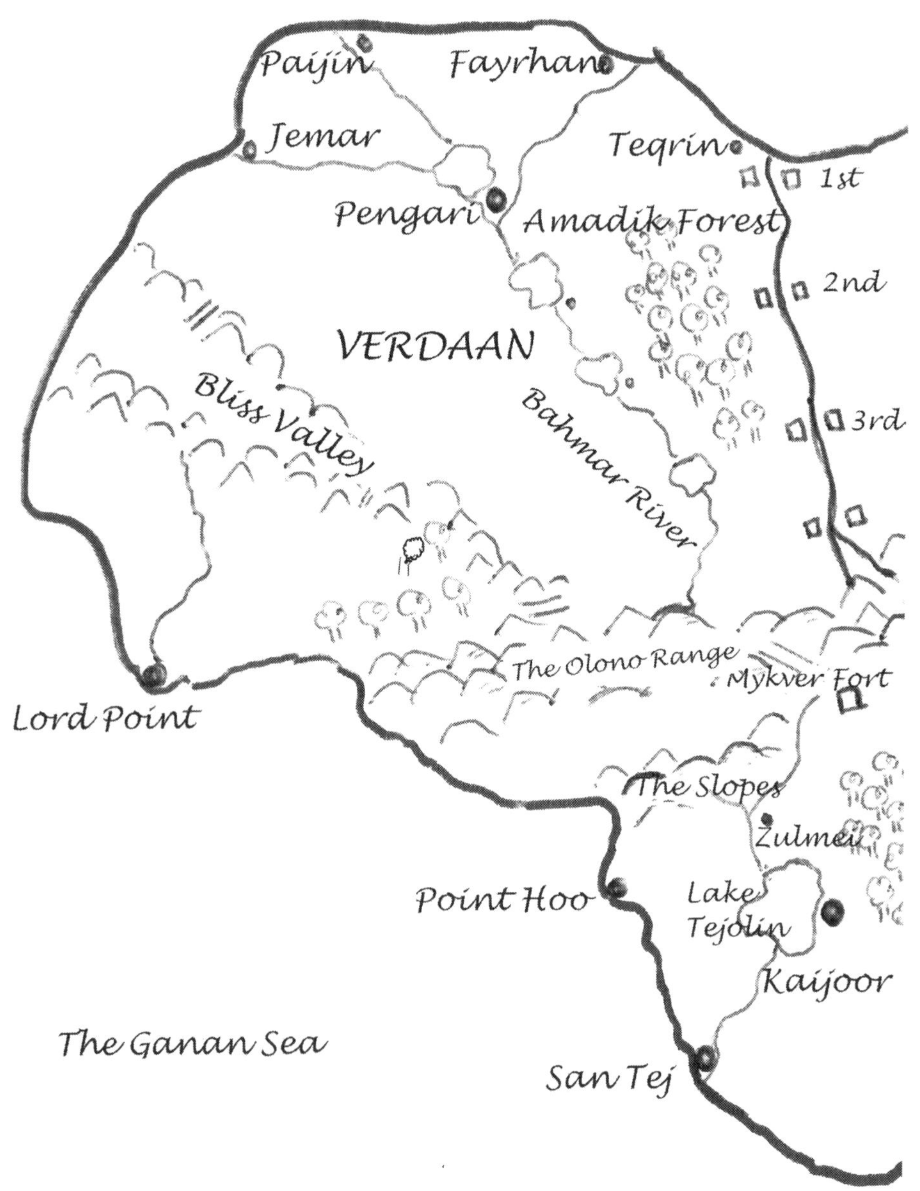

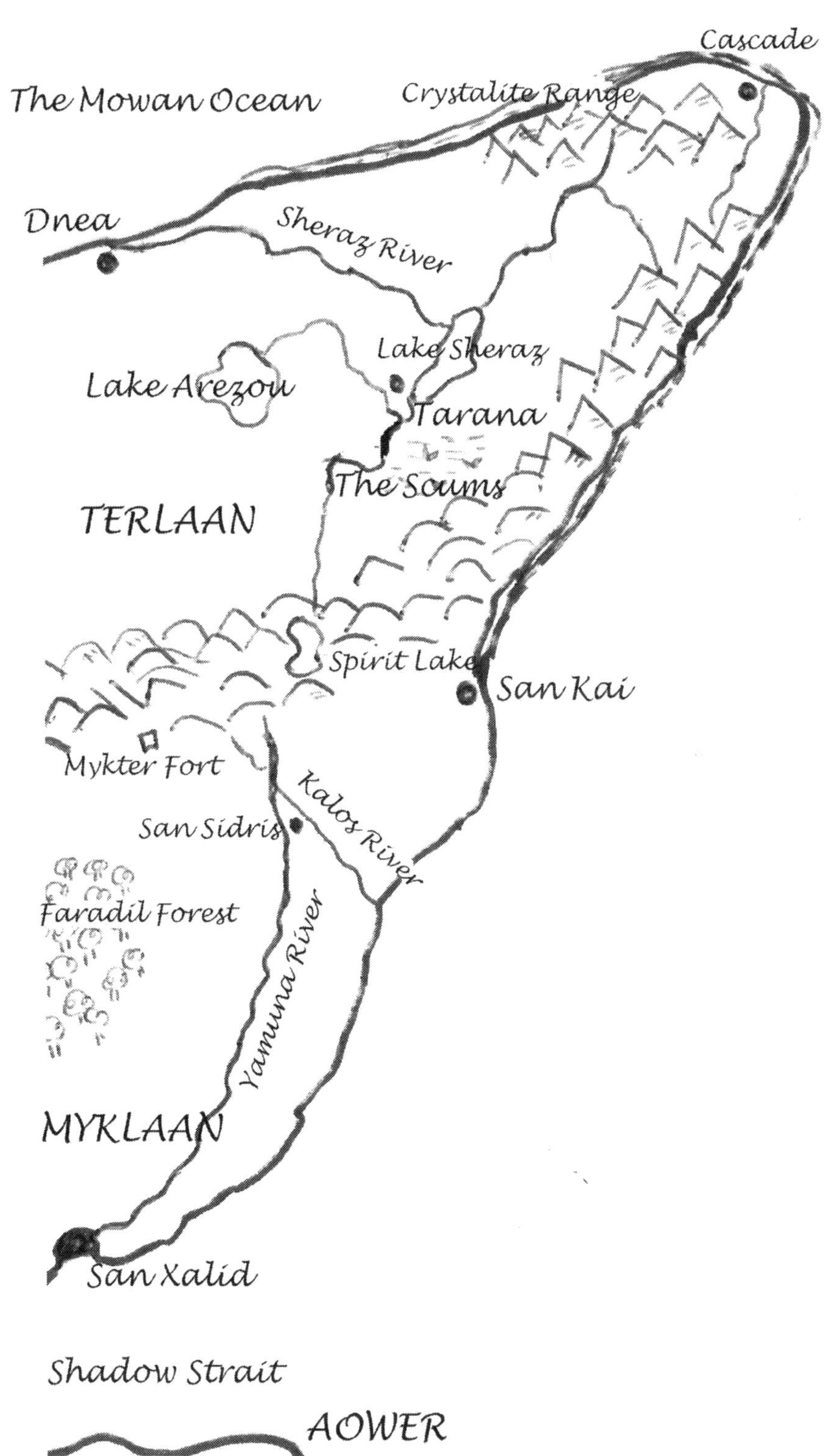

Cascade
The Mowan Ocean
Crystalite Range
Dnea
Sheraz River
Lake Sheraz
Lake Arezou
Tarana
The Soums
TERLAAN
Spirit Lake
San Kai
Mykter Fort
Kalos River
San Sidris
Faradil Forest
Yamuna River
MYKLAAN
San Xalid
Shadow Strait
AOWER

Chapter One

PRINCESS KORDAHLA THOUGHT IT best not to confide she found the ragged vendors selling battered pans scoured clean of burned rice bemusing. More bemusing than the tedious Verdaani guest they were riding through Tarana to meet, anyway. Her brothers had affected an air of tolerance for those downtrodden men, and for the tawdry merchants touting the virtues of tasselled kilims as vibrant as their kurtas. In their misguided wisdom, they might have decided the sweat-and-fish stink of the waterfront souk had affected her senses, and sent her straight back to the shackles of the palace.

If only she could have spent the entire sunny afternoon perusing the bewildering wares. Her freedom would have been perfect. The bloated pots fashioned in the likeness of the fearsome, swamp-dwelling bazwaeel were a novelty she would never tire of admiring – as she, the Terlaani orchid Father rarely permitted to bloom in public, was a delight to the cheering crowd. Not even her sombre escort, the black-robed, hooded mahktashaan, the soldier-magicians of her father's realm, could dowse her enthusiasm for the cloying bustle and persistent sell. Since they were enduring the onslaught with silent, good grace, she slid her veil onto her shoulders and tossed her walnut hair loose. The gesture set a skinny youth with narrow-set eyes to jumping as he waved a copper bracelet set with a green stone over his head.

"How much is that?" she asked the nearest mahktashaan.

Her guard needed only a pointed finger to part the throng from his midnight mount. The wide-eyed youth stilled his grubby hand in mid-air as he gabbled something to the mahktashaan before passing the trinket over with a vigorous nod of his head. Kordahla took it from the guard, careful to avoid his fingers, and slipped it onto her wrist. The smile she added to the boy's earnings had to be worth at least as many lek as the bracelet if his whoops as he danced his way through the clamouring crowd were anything to judge by. They were, at least, more welcome than the laughter chiming behind her.

Kordahla glanced over her shoulder, fixing Vinsant with a mock glare. Her tease of a younger brother poked out his tongue as he flipped his cloak over his head in mimicry of the veil. With an exaggerated roll of her eyes, she guided her horse to Mariano's side. The aloof detachment with which her older brother was surveying Lake Sheraz became the future Shah of Terlaan.

"Thank you," she said with a smile when he acknowledged her bare head with a raised eyebrow. It was ever a treat for her to escape the confines of the palace walls.

"Best you'd be thanking our little brother," Mariano replied, returning to his contemplation of the velvet waters. "You're welcome," he murmured a moment later. "But perhaps you should cover up?"

Grinning, Kordahla leaned across to place a playful hand over his. His purple turban tight over his dark hair, Mariano did not twitch a toned muscle but continued gazing at the skiffs plying the abundant lake. The fishermen wove around each other, rivalling the sequined dancers Father hired to entertain at court feasts for grace. The trout they hauled up in their nets, flopping and tumbling like acrobats, only added to the charm.

"Don't I have your permission, then?" she asked in a pitch that matched his and slew any opportunity for the mahktashaan to overhear.

"The value of my permission is moot. Levi will report your liberty to Father, and *his* permission is doubtful."

Kordahla chanced a look at the Majoria of the mahktashaan. Sure enough, he had turned his head toward her. As was the custom of the soldier-magicians, the hood of his cloak dangled over his face, obscuring his sharp features. Even so, his disapproval chilled the air between them. Kordahla suppressed a shudder, and only just forbore to make the warding sign. Whatever Levi might be, he was no djinn.

"You know this," Mariano continued, looking down on her now, his straight back testament to his expertise in the saddle. His sleeveless silk vest, supposedly the height of fashion in their neighbour, Myklaan, exposed his bronzed chest to the midriff. Mariano had pounced on the garments when the merchant ship docked from the liberal southern land. Why wouldn't he? Their tailoring displayed his glorious body to perfection. Father had not objected. But the skimpy choli and billowing skirt that barely hugged a woman's hips, the mere sight of which had rouged Kordahla's cheeks, the Shah had commanded burned. No woman of his realm would defile her body with such wanton exposure. For the audacity of introducing such filth to the land, the hapless merchant had suffered twenty lashes, his paltry life spared only when Mariano expressed a desire to expand his wardrobe with further shipments of the stylish garb.

The memory discomfited Kordahla. She fidgeted in the awkward side posture women were forced to ride, and pushed up her generous sleeves – the only concession to southern fashion Father allowed her – careful not to reveal her tainted elbows lest she antagonise Levi too far. "Perhaps we should find a more fitting diversion for the Mahktashaan Majoria's sensibilities."

Ignoring Mariano's warning shake of his head, she reigned her horse in and waited for Vinsant to catch her up. Her little brother was still laughing.

"What's so funny?" she asked with a mock frown, because nothing could rival his spiky, fair hair for comedy.

"You. You don't think Father's actually going to let you wear that piece of garbage, do you?" he asked.

Her momentary irritation dispersed on the ripples of her brother's mirth. This cloudless day of freedom was too gorgeous to waste with sour feelings. "He doesn't need to know I have it," she replied, twisting the bangle. She raised a hand to greet a group of squealing children skipping alongside the horses. As her generous sleeve slipped down her arm, exposing the indecent joint, she hastily lowered her hand, but not before Levi had turned in his saddle and fixed her with what she had to imagine was a stare of condemnation. It did not help that, unlike the masses, she had seen the face which scowled beneath that hood. It was the face of an ordinary, if austere, man, slipping past his prime. A man who might well have eyes in the back of his head. A man with a moustache and hair as black as the crystal around his neck.

"I don't believe you haven't gagged on this stench yet," Vinsant said, wrinkling his freckled nose.

"Actually, it makes a refreshing change from frangipani, sweet perfume, and the aroma of roasting goat," Kordahla said, twining the flare of her sleeve around her wrist, palming the end, and averting her gaze from the Majoria's hood.

"Surely you jest."

"Spend your entire life confined to Court and then tell me an earthy smell bothers you."

Vinsant tilted his head in agreement. "Yeah, well. There is that."

"Mariano said you are responsible for persuading Father to let me join you."

"It wouldn't be the same without you. Anyway, Mariano promised to defend your honour," Vinsant said. The djinn only knew how he managed to cast his face into a serious sort of mirth.

Kordahla sighed as she nodded. She should have guessed their older brother would have had to pledge blood honour before Father would even deign to think of letting his jewel of a daughter negotiate the cobbled streets. Sighing, she looked towards the tangled city, the spice of her privilege dulled. Overpopulated lanes zigzagged between sandstone houses before converging in cacophonous chaos on the fertile strip by the lake. Here Tarana's linear souk stretched in haphazard arrangement of every commodity available in Terlaan, from ripe plums to gold trinkets, hunting knives to caftans, glazed crockery to pots of rainbow spices which tickled the nose. She leaned forward, drinking it all in. Salted eel, candied figs and gaudy weavings plundered from the hill tribes at a fraction of the lek for which they would sell in the city were exotic to a princess interred behind palace walls.

She waved to a serious girl who had turned from the flat bread her father haggled over to watch them parade. The little one was sweet to dip a curtsey. Kordahla removed her copper bangle and bid a mahktashaan with a magenta crystal hand it to her. Vinsant was right. If Father ever saw it, he would toss it to a scullion.

The girl's father, a tall, lean man, frowned as his unsmiling daughter took the trinket. It was only natural he look for the source of the gift. Look at her, his face drawn in disapproval, no less.

"Vae'oenka's shame!" He grabbed the girl's arm and pulled her from the scene. The bangle clanged on the ground, trodden on, picked up, claimed. Kordahla could have died listening to his condemnation of the princess's bare head ring above the buzz of the souk.

Every vendor in sight turned to stare at her. Mariano too, one eyebrow raised in an expression that could mean nothing except *I told you so*. Her cheeks reddening, she flicked her veil back over her hair. The luxurious length of green fabric, embroidered in gold, was fraying in one corner, but it had been Mother's. However much she was loathe to wear the veil, this one honoured Mother's memory and love.

"Oh, you're not seriously thinking you've gone too far," Vinsant said, tugging it from her neck. He laughed as he flapped it through the air. She reached for it, but Vinsant hopped onto his horse's back and held it high, drawing a cheer from the black-toothed fruit sellers and sun-baked fishermen along the grassy shore. Unused to the attention, she averted her eyes.

"Vinsant," she hissed. "Give it back."

"Come and get it," he said, perfectly at ease in his precarious position.

"Vinsant!"

Ahead, Mariano had stopped his horse and turned in his saddle. He was a beast to wear such an amused expression. Since it was plain she would get no help from him, she edged her bay horse closer to Vinsant's, reaching across to pull him back into the saddle. He was a little monster, forcing her into unbecoming fidgeting. It was a wonder Majoria Levi did not demand an immediate halt to this folly, with it beginning to draw embarrassing murmurs from the onlookers.

"Vae'oeldin's rot," said Vinsant mildly, opening his hand to let the veil fly. "The God of the Sky has stolen your veil." The garment sailed over the heads of the mahktashaan and descended on a knot of startled onlookers. There was a sudden tangle of arms as they snatched at the prize.

"There," said Vinsant, sitting back down. "You can't get in trouble now. It's my fault you aren't wearing your veil, and I shall tell Father so."

Kordahla allowed the reins to slide off her fingers and crossed her arms. "That was Mother's! And besides, since when did I need my little brother to defend me?" she asked. In truth, the need for it was irking her more than the loss of the veil.

Vinsant turned his head aside. "Since Father kept this realm so backward," he muttered.

For once, she lacked the heart to offer even an insincere reproof. The day spoiled after all, she sighed.

Vinsant frowned. "You can't really like wearing that thing."

"That's not the point," she said, watching the lucky winner of her favour struggle free of groping hands. "They've stopped looking at Mariano." Mariano, whose handsome, chiselled features and exalted position never failed to entrance any who laid eyes on him. "They're all looking at me, like I've committed some heinous transgression, and in their eyes, and Levi's and Father's, I have."

"Nah, that's not it. Don't you get it? They're looking at you because you're beautiful. By the djinn, Kordahla, Mariano doesn't hold a candle to you."

Kordahla blushed. Vinsant might be prone to exaggeration, but he was never anything except honest with her.

"They've never seen you before, except from afar, or covered with a hideous veil. They didn't know. Look! Look over there!"

By a stall of linens, a wife was looking at her husband. He gently reached for her veil and with a few words tucked it behind her shoulders to reveal her glossy black hair. Kordahla gasped.

"You think because they're peasants they don't hear what Myklaan's like?" Vinsant asked.

Kordahla felt a flush of shame. That was exactly what she had thought. Who could blame her when she was denied excursions and prohibited the councils of men? It was selfish of her, but she rather wished the Shah had not begun to insist Vinsant attend those meetings. There was time enough yet for her little brother to grow up, and little enough in which she would retain some influence over him. She had never dreamed she might in some small way shape the future of the realm, but here they were, a handful of young men removing their wives' veils because she, the princess, had removed hers. It was a small triumph. The few unaccompanied women glanced about as though checking for acquaintances who might betray them to their husbands if they took the liberty. None did. No woman would ever have the nerve to remove it without permission. *Except me. And my doing so might have been rash.* One or two matronly types were tugging the veil further down their forehead. A bent, old woman even had the gall to spit a curse at her!

Kordahla threw a pleading look Mariano's way, but he was engaged in intense conversation with Levi. She edged her horse forward as the Majoria gestured to three mahktashaan, magenta, tan and teal of crystal. They left the escort and trotted to a withered meatball seller who was grinning with disbelief at the veil in his hand. Dear goddess, he did not even notice the mahktashaan dismount. Two of them gripped him, forcing him to his knees before he gathered the wits to see the danger. Beseeching the gods, he struggled against his captors, his faced blanched in shock.

"Vae'oenka, no!" Kordahla said. She pushed her horse between Levi and Mariano's. "It wasn't his fault," she said. "You can't."

Mariano raised an eyebrow. "I rather think your honour is at stake. Would you have him spread vile rumours about your attentions?" He assumed a cheeky smile. "And what in the Three Realms would Father say if he knew I'd permitted this indiscretion?"

Curse the blood honour, Kordahla thought, and nearly said aloud. She saw metal glint as the third mahktashaan drew his sword, felt sweat trickle down her neck, took a gulp of air.

"Hold," she called, and the mahktashaan's sword-wielding arm froze in the air above the babbling vendor.

Mariano's eyes turned dark.

"He will return the veil in exchange for his life," she said.

"It is not enough," Mariano replied, his cold gaze fixed on the doomed vendor.

She knew him well enough to see he was repressing a swell of anger. The Crown Prince could suffer no public challenge to his authority, and from his younger sister no less. The trickle of sweat turned to a rivulet, and ran down her spine. "There is a way," she said to him. He remained immobile, waiting. She licked her lips. "We'll take his meatballs as payment."

For three heartbeats, Mariano remained utterly still. Then he nodded, as she had known he would. Her elder brother was not given to wanton violence.

Levi needed no further instruction. He gestured to his man, who lowered his sword. The weeping meatball seller bowed his head to the ground, praising Vae'oeldin over and over. He rather had the wrong god, Kordahla thought. Vae'oeldin of the Sky, patron of soldiers and war, was prone to fits of rage. His triplet, Vae'oenka of the Earth, was the nurturing one.

"Get up," Mariano ordered. With anyone other than his siblings he was less than patient.

The meatball seller scrambled to his feet, snivelling the praises of the god. One of the mahktashaan pushed the man to his rickety cart, where he dusted off a bowl with his elbow. Satisfied by its gleam, he piled his choicest patties inside while another man, his grown son if their narrow noses and close-set eyes were anything to judge by, whispered in his ear. The vendor gave a vigorous shake of his head, shrugged the lad's hand off his shoulders, and turned. Bowl held out, he kept his head down as he shuffled toward her. The tall mahktashaan with the teal crystal blocked his way.

"Let him approach," Kordahla said. She would give this man back what dignity she could.

"Surely you don't intend to eat this slop?" Mariano asked.

"You bet!" said Vinsant, bringing a smile to both their faces. At thirteen he was still small despite a voracious appetite, while she, eight years older, had begun to watch every bite she took lest her full curves balloon beyond shapely.

Their hawk-eyed escort opened a narrow path to her. The man crept forward. His eyes darted over the mahktashaan as his trembling hand held out the bowl. She took a meatball. It was still warm, crusted golden with a tantalising, spiced aroma and the first bite melted in her mouth.

Vinsant had one in each hand and was inhaling as if they were a trained chef's masterpiece. "I'll have any that are left. And can you bring sauce for these?" he said as the vendor backed away, bowing repeatedly over his bowl. The withered man wriggled outside the circle of mahktashaan before offering the soldier-magicians his fare. The restraint required to wait for the condiment was bound to prove too much for Vinsant. Temptation was written all over her brother's face. She took another bite looking right at him, a tease to pay him back.

The world spun beneath her, giddiness overcame her, and her mind went floating over the surging crowd. Its roar became a muted murmur, the heat of the day a chill caress over every pore in her skin. She slumped in the saddle. Felt Mariano catch her against his strong chest, and knock the meatball from her hand. Heard Mariano bark at Vinsant to drop his food. Saw the vendor and his son flee the souk, her veil fluttering in his hand. Saw from way up above several mahktashaan in hard pursuit, each with a coloured crystal around his neck.

She flinched as Levi push his palm against her brow. His eerie words sparked his crystal, and its black light worked its way inside her, flowing through her body, imbuing her with strength.

"I cannot undo the effects entirely." Levi's mouth was close to her ear, but his voice drifted from far away. She tried to sit up straight, but Mariano kept his protective arm around her.

"Kordahla?" Vinsant squeaked.

"Will she recover?" Mariano asked.

"She will, my Prince. There will be no lasting damage with a dose this small."

Kordahla blinked. Forcing her way out of Mariano's arms, she wobbled on her horse's back. "I feel a little light-headed," she said, and her words sounded slurred to her ears.

"The meatballs contain porrin, Princess," Levi said, his gravelly voice bombarding her from all directions.

She giggled and wondered how the citizens would react if the Majoria's version of a veil was removed. As she reached for his hood, his hand clamped on her wrist. "I will forgive this intrusion because you are drugged. But do not ever take liberties with me again, Princess."

"Enough, Levi. She is not herself," Mariano said.

Kordahla shook her head when Levi released her. A tiny rational corner of her mind told her the porrin was altering her mood, but she really didn't care. She began to hum *The Curse of the Djinn.*

"Minoria Arun will take three men and escort her back to the palace," Levi said.

"I want to greet the boat," Kordahla said. Her face lengthened as she was struck by a thought. "Oh, Father." She giggled. It was odd to think of the punishment she would face as funny.

Mariano pursed his lips. "I think it better she remains with us. She is foolhardy enough when she is sober and in this state, she'll be a handful for even the entire escort."

"As you wish, my Prince," Levi said in a tone that made clear his disapproval.

"Mariano?" Vinsant said, his voice small.

"She'll be all right, Vinsant. Come, ride close to her."

"You're not going to tell Father, are you?" he whispered to Mariano.

"No. But I rather think he's going to find out anyway. Don't you?"

She really couldn't help the giggles. "If we convince him to nibble a meatball, he may forget about the rest."

"Look after her," Mariano said, moving towards the edge of the group so he could survey the dispersing crowd. Bareheaded women were hastily replacing their veils as they scurried after their nervous husbands.

"What's it like?" Vinsant asked her.

"Hmm. Like the day isn't a total disaster any more. Like I felt when we left the palace, only freer. Like I can fly. Did you have some?"

"Uh uh," he said with a wary look.

"You should. Do you think I can do magic, like a Myklaani mage?"

He shrugged. "You can try. How about turning Levi into a scumhopper?"

She flicked her fingers toward the Majoria, willing him to change form. "It didn't work," she said, affecting a pout. They both laughed.

Mariano looked up at the sound. "Maybe this was a bad idea. Minoria Arun, please."

Levi's second in command walked his horse to her other side. His elegant, lean stature identified the cloaked mahktashaan as much as the cerulean-blue crystal that hung about his neck. "Do not encourage her, Prince Vinsant. She will regret this enough on the morrow as it is."

Her little brother became sombre again. "I was just wondering if she can perform magic under the influence of porrin. You know, the way the Myklaani mages do."

The mahktashaan gave a slow nod. "It is a fair question for one of your age and so I will provide a considered answer. Porrin provides a conduit to the magical realm, but it takes talent and training both to perform the art under its spell. Many waste away, or even die, before they attain the skills. But this you already know."

"I know."

"And you will not be tempted to sample the poison?"

"No, Minoria."

Kordahla leaned inappropriately close to Arun. Her current state excused her. Vae'oenka, was his cedar scent nice. "Teach me. I've already tasted it."

Arun bowed his head in acquiescence. "If you still wish it on the morrow, Princess."

Vinsant looked aghast.

"As I have said, young Prince, the sane later regret porrin's bliss. Stay close now, for I do not think the Princess will bear well what is to come."

Arun backed up his horse, allowing Kordahla and Vinsant a view of the closest houses. Four mahktashaan were trotting their way, the meatball seller and his son lassoed between them. The prisoners' legs ran wild in a desperate attempt to keep pace with the horses. The father stumbled and, unable to regain his footing, he sprawled into the dirt, his body dragging, twisting, scraping until the mahktashaan halted their midnight horses before Mariano. From their exalted position, they gathered in the rope, tugging the man to his feet. It was ludicrous he yet clutched her veil, sullied by tears and snot.

"By Vae'oeldin, mercy," the seller cried, touching his fists to his forehead and extending them out to Mariano in obeisance.

Mariano's horse flicked its tail. The Crown prince regarded the meatball seller with contempt. "Mercy of the kind you showed the Princess of Terlaan?" he said. "Mercy of the kind you expected when you fled instead of facing the consequences of your actions like a son of the god?"

White-faced and shaking, the lad followed his father's example, repeating the gesture of obeisance over and over. His shalvar was wet in the most indecent of places. That humiliation was enough to induce another fit of giggles. Her humour sent him into a fit of incoherent blubbering. The sharpness in it cut right through her crazed delight. As did the force with which the guards shoved the prisoners to their knees. Swords grated out of scabbards, and a splinter of reason pierced her thoughts. In the blink of an eye, she was off her horse and at Mariano's side, gagging on the stink of urine.

"You can't," she said, unable to articulate the rest of her fuddled thoughts.

"I can," Mariano replied, as the mahktashaan sought his confirmation.

She had the presence of mind not to argue, but steadied herself by putting a hand on his leg. Mariano looked down at her, a fleeting compassion in his brown eyes.

"Come, Princess," Levi said, grasping her elbow. "You must mount. This punishment is exacted on your account, and our citizens expect to see you preside."

She shook her head as the Majoria pried her away from Mariano. His shadowed nose, sharp and long, was just visible beneath his hood. However responsible for her honour he might be, he had no right to mumble his magic words as he placed thick hands on her waist. It was a violation as severe as the meatball vendor's that she lost the will to resist. A violation that when he lifted her, she floated onto the horse. But he was Majoria of the mahktashaan, charged with protecting her person and preserving her honour. He was not a man to whom she dared voice her thought. She sought instead to turn her steed. Levi held the reins fast.

Arun walked his horse close to hers. "Hold brave," he said, eyes on Mariano.

The cruel masses were dribbling back, enticed by the promise of a bloody spectacle. Muted chatter passed back and forth as all heads turned to the prisoners. Eyes closed and shoulders slumped, the two men yet pleaded for mercy.

"For the crime of dishonouring Vae'oeldin with the filth you peddle, I would deal you an immediate death blow," Mariano said in the regal voice of the Crown Prince. "For dishonouring Her Highness Princess Kordahla you are spared my sword to face the judgement of the Shah himself." He grew quiet, thoughtful. "While I hold blood honour for the princess, it may be the Shah wishes to exact a lingering punishment on account of your double offence."

Her horse nickered and tossed its head. For certain, the Majoria had tightened his grip on her reins. Her anger at that cleared the last of the fuzziness from her thoughts even as her shoulders lowered with relief. She would plant a thousand kisses on Mariano's cheek for sparing her the bloody horror of an execution, however more wretched it would fall at Father's hand. The irony of the stay was not lost on the vendor. The veil slipped from his hand. He tottered, then fainted, slicing his chest against his captor's sword before slumping to the ground atop her veil and an indigo rag that reeked of rotten fish. In the hubbub to revive him, his son scrambled to escape. Quick as a djinn, the mahktashaan with the magenta crystal stepped upon the lasso still twined around his torso. He skidded as the rope snapped taut, and struggled to remove the loop from his chest as the mahktashaan reeled him in, an aging ram for the slaughter. The mahktashaan slapped a palm against his forehead, magenta light sparked in the crystal, and he became as docile as if he had ingested his own patties. Kordahla shuddered despite the beating heat, sure the prisoners' incapacitation would last beyond her own. Until the Majoria wished otherwise, no doubt. She looked around for her veil, and frowned when she noticed it gone. Vanished. Presumably tucked beneath a mahktashaan's robe, to be duly presented as evidence of her wrongdoing to Father. She shuddered again.

"Do you feel a still wind, sister?" Mariano asked, turning his horse to resume their journey.

"An ill one," she replied knowing better than to voice her distaste of the mahktashaan in front of him.

"It does seem the djinn have gifted you the diversion you so craved," he replied.

Chapter Two

BY THE TIME THEY reached the wharves, Kordahla could sit her horse without swaying, praise the Vae. The fact she had Levi to thank did nothing to improve her apprehension. When she sighted the docked galley, the five-lobed porrin leaf on the brash Verdaani pennant flapping at the masthead, she shuddered again. It seemed the cursed plant was to dominate the day.

The mahktashaan were busy clearing the area, an effortless task given their enigmatic reputation. At the mere sight of them, the riff-raff loitering around the docks melted into the curious onlookers. The crowd surged back and forth as the mahktashaan passed, eagerness for a glimpse of the foreign ambassador warring with their distrust of the magic-wielding guard.

"What did Father tell you of the visit?" Kordahla asked Vinsant. She had been so wrapped up in joyous freedom that she had forgotten their excursion served some political purpose. She watched a contingent of mahktashaan disappear down shadowed alleys and barge into warehouses, and wondered if they were always so meticulous when Mariano and Vinsant toured the streets.

Her little brother shrugged. "Not much. Lord Ahkdul of Verdaan is visiting next month, and his herald has arrived in advance with news of some import."

"No more?"

"Only what he told you, I expect. Ahkdul is coming to oversee the finishing touches to the royal barge his father commissioned. But

Mariano knows something more," Vinsant replied, narrowed eyes scrutinising their older brother. "I just can't pry it out of him."

His confounded expression made her chuckle. She was glad Vinsant had not yet outgrown his penchant for squirrelling out secrets. It meant he was still a child. As for her older brother, he sat astride his horse, facing the carpeted gangplank. She had little enough time to savour the sweaty flavour of the area before she must take her place at his side.

A flash of sun on metal drew her eyes to a stack of crates in front of an imposing warehouse. Some threat had induced one of the mahktashaan to raise his sword. His back to them, he swung it down. A sickening crunch churned her stomach. He must have had her under some spell to prevent her looking away, turning away. He was a brute to raise the bloody sword and step back. Her horse shied from the drip of blood, closer to whichever unfortunate their guard had deemed a threat, Vae help her. The gentle grey ignored the pull of her shaky hands on the reins, veering right at those crates, threatening to crush her legs. She kicked too hard, unnerving her poor mare further. Dropping the reins, she thrust a hand out to lessen the impact, to find Arun guiding his horse beside hers, nudging it away, settling it.

"It is not a sight you would wish to see, Princess." The lip of his hood had slipped back, revealing eyes glittering a cerulean so intense she was transfixed by their depth.

Kordahla tried to speak but all thought had fled. It was a relief Arun regretted his candour enough to bow his head. As his hood slid over his features, the hair on the back of her neck crawled. She forced herself to look over her shoulder. Levi was staring at her. Or his cloaked figure was. Had her baby brother not been striding towards the executioner, she might have fallen off her horse. Instead, she dropped to the ground and ran toward him. If she caught his hand, she could protect him from the grisly sight.

"Princess!" Arun's call was soft but sharp, and it stopped her.

Vinsant threw her a look blacker than the Majoria's crystal and kept walking. That hurt so deep she nearly cried out. By the djinn, he was too young to witness this. Hitching up her skirts, she took a step forward, prepared to scold him into obedience. She was prevented from going further when a hand clamped on her shoulder. Even through her kameez, the Majoria's grip chilled her to the bone.

"Vinsant," she said, his name rumbling with the low caution of the mother she considered herself to be.

He had a cheek to ignore her. A brutal execution was not an adventure. Bargaining with weathered fishermen for the overpriced crabs they were tipping out of nets and into buckets was an adventure. So was watching grubby children dodge sniffing dogs so they could kick a lopsided ball. Now, the fishy, sweaty smells were mixing with the metallic tang of blood to turn her stomach queasy. The Vae knew it should have done the same to him.

"He is not a baby, Kordahla," Mariano said, coming to stand beside her.

"Well he's still a child," she replied, watching Vinsant as intently as a scumhopper eyed a dragonfly. "And you should be protecting him."

"As I recall he has a father. One who feels he should take a deeper interest in the royal arts." Mariano frowned. "He's reaching the age he'll not miss having a woman to smother him."

Smother him indeed! She opened her mouth to point out that was exactly what Mariano was doing to her when Vinsant flinched. She tore free of Levi's improper grip. Nothing and no one stood between her and her little brother when he might have the slightest need.

It seemed he didn't have any need at all. Of all the heartless acts he could commit – laugh hysterically, even jab the sword through the dead man's heart – none could have shaken her more than his calm questioning of the mahktashaan executioner. Were it not for the grubby foot visible between the pair of them, she would have convinced herself she had imagined the whole ordeal. Five blistered toes beneath a tatty but brightly embroidered trouser cuff were incontrovertible proof, however, and she sidestepped the heartless little monster she loved beyond all words.

She was not prepared for an unimpeded view of the corpse. Her eyes travelled over bony ankles and wrists to the gaunt body and a bloody stump of a neck. The tribesman's head had rolled from his neck, a sickly-sweet puddle of blood the only connection between the two. Kordahla felt her stomach heave. She turned away, afraid she was going to disgrace herself and her brothers in public. It was fortuitous someone provided a steadying arm. The physical contact brought immediate calm. Strange that. Or perhaps not. The arm was cloaked in black. She twisted to identify her aide, expecting to see Levi's sharp nose and black crystal. She thanked the moons it was Arun. She knew even before she saw his crystal, though only the djinn knew how. The mahktashaan formed a starless sky, indistinguishable from each other save by the colour of the stone around their necks, their physique and voice, and then only with luck.

"Release me," she said, without conviction. It would not do for her to be in thrall of a spell.

"Princess, it is you who hold me," Arun replied.

She looked at her hand, which seemed to have grown a mind of its own. It rested on Arun's arm, and none too lightly at that. With grave effort, she retracted it and placed it upon her stomach. Arun immediately looked down. Beneath that hood, his expression was impossible to read. She might have sensed disappointment. More likely it was her own bitter regret she tasted. She had thought, of all the mahktashaan, he respected her despite her gender. Now here he was, taking advantage of her weakness. She would not have it. She opened her mouth to dismiss him only to have a drum interrupt.

"It was a mercy, Your Highness," Arun said through the brash musical phrases. He sounded troubled. "The tribesman was so far in porrin's bliss he was drowning in his own vomit."

Kordahla took a steadying breath and watched a teal paddle his family away from all the noise. It helped her push the gruesome image of the corpse from her mind. Father might conceivably forgive her the loss of the veil, but the one thing he would never tolerate was dereliction in matters of etiquette. Brushing past Arun, she went to stand at Mariano's side. Vinsant bounded up a moment later. As the last notes of the fanfare died, a stout, moonfaced man appeared on deck. His full beard tickled his midriff but was partially hidden beneath a blue woollen coat that, in Terlaan at least, was of a quality afforded by the merchants rather than the noble class. His eyes widened as he saw them. The royal offspring were a grand welcome for a messenger. He should not have considered himself privileged. It was only Vinsant's desire for an excursion on a clement summer afternoon that had brought them here this day.

"You are honoured as a guest in Terlaan," Mariano said, the formal words of welcome. "I am Crown Prince Mariano. This is my brother Prince Vinsant, and my sister Princess Kordahla."

Lord Ahkdul's messenger bowed low. "I am most grateful for your exceedingly generous hospitality," he said, exuberant in voice and manner. "I did not expect such illustrious hosts," he added, appraising Kordahla as her brothers might a horse.

His attention was not lost on Mariano. Her brother pursed his lips. "We are ever grateful for an excuse to ride the town," he said. The touch of frost in his voice was reassuring.

The messenger cleared his throat. His cheek twitched. "May I introduce myself. Baiyeed deq Ikher, personal attendant to Lord Ahkdul, son of Lord Hudassan, Shah of Verdaan, and currently Verdaani Ambassador to Terlaan."

"I was not aware Verdaan boasted royalty," Mariano said. His eyes were forbidding, his trademark courtesy barely on offer. Kordahla just wished deq Ikher would leave off ogling her. The grebes ruffling their brown breeding plumage out on the lake were less obvious than he. She folded her arms and stared right back. He seemed to sense her discomfort because he cleared his throat and began to make small talk with Mariano. After a few minutes expounding the trials of river travel in Verdaan, and the joys of the same in Terlaan, he blinked, mopped his brow, and woke up to the tediousness of his exposition.

"I take it your lord has sent details for his ship," Mariano said.

"He has," deq Ikher replied, removing a piece of parchment from inside his coat. "As well as some preliminary thoughts on the illicit porrin trade. To facilitate discussions on his arrival. If it so please His Majesty Shah Wilshem, to consider them."

"Huh?" Vinsant breathed as Mariano adjusted his stance. This was not what any of them had expected. Verdaan's production of the drug was decimating Terlaan. The trek of smugglers across the border had been an issue of contention since before she was born.

"And of another matter besides," deq Ikher continued. The right corner of his mouth twitched. The unfortunate timing made it look like he spoke in jest. "But I fear that one I must deliver to the Shah himself."

"If the news demands it, that is only right. Come. We will escort you to the palace."

"What other matter?" Vinsant whispered to her.

"It must be connected to the ship," Kordahla replied.

"I don't think so. Deq Ikher would just talk about that."

Which was true, since the lucrative commission had been the cause of much public excitement, in particular among the shipwrights. The galley's hull was complete in the dry docks across the lake, the carpenters awaiting Lord Hudassan's instructions for the cabins. The Verdaani dictator had insisted on sending his son to select the fittings and trimmings, and apparently to negotiate matters of state as well. When deq Ikher's vessel had been spotted, it had been something of a surprise. The messenger's reluctance to disembark only fuelled her suspicions. His eyes travelled to the prisoners, still bound and sedate next to two mounted guards. The meatball vendors had the gaunt frames of those long addicted to porrin. It was a wonder she had not noticed before.

What she did notice was deq Ikher avoiding a direct line of sight with the disconcerting mahktashaan. Levi had realised that too, because he had directed his men to fan around the royal party, to stand in a circle that opened at the gangplank.

"Your Highness is occupied with prisoners at present," deq Ikher said. Even at this distance Kordahla could see sweat shining on his brow. "Perhaps, I could approach the palace at a more convenient time." His cheek spasmed twice.

"The Shah has granted you an audience this evening," Mariano said. "And our guard must search your vessel before the appointed time."

Telling, how Baiyeed deq Ikher's nervous tic twitched a steady beat. "I'm afraid," he started, and licked his lips, "as part of Lord Ahkdul's convoy, this ship has diplomatic immunity."

Four mahktashaan glided into a row in front of the gangplank.

"I'm afraid you are mistaken," Mariano said. "Your arrival was not expected, and while you might represent Lord Ahkdul, you do not accompany him. However, should you wish to remain aboard while the mahktashaan search the vessel, I will understand."

"It is not customs who will conduct the search?"

Mariano did not deign to answer. Access to the royal grounds required a higher clearance than the mere lack of prohibited goods. When the first of the mahktashaan negotiated the plank, deq Ikher waddled down with alacrity. He stopped in such proximity to Mariano that Kordahla wondered just how much contraband he harboured on the ship.

The mahktashaan spread out across the deck, their unique talents enabling a thorough search in minutes. One emerged from below with paper packets stacked in his hands while another led three unblinking and docile sailors, tied at the wrists, off the ship. Kordahla held her breath. Undoubtedly, the mahktashaan had subdued their wills, but the dilated pupils, the clammy sheen on their skin and their lengthy breaths gave testament to their intoxication. Porrin, the staple diet of Verdaan, had extended its foul reach yet again. There was no end to its mischief this day.

Deq Ikher fidgeted as he looked from the sailors to Mariano. The salt and sweat of the journey had crusted so deep in his pores, they fouled the citrus scent he wore. "You cannot...these men are under Lord Ahkdul's protection," he said. His conviction had drifted away on the current.

"They are not," Mariano replied. "But they are your men. Do you wish to assume responsibility for them?"

Deq Ikher opened his mouth. Kordahla thought he might have missed the warning, but he clamped his jaw shut and shook his head.

"Since you have come to offer testimony to porrin's value, you should witness how seriously we take its threat."

At his words Levi drew his sword. Kordahla felt herself tremble.

"I would not think less of you if you looked away, sister," Mariano said.

She should have, but the gleam of sunshine along the blade entranced her. Her eyes fixed on Levi as he pressed a palm against the sailors' forehead and awareness returned to their gaze. It was replaced an instant later by terror so abject that she squealed.

Mariano pursed his lips. "Majoria, please remove those addicts from my sister's sight."

With growing horror, she watched the mahktashaan march the shouting sailors through the crowd scattering from the wharf. Her heart thudded as Majoria Levi escorted the protesting deq Ikher after them. Vinsant dawdled a few steps down. She reached an ineffectual hand toward him.

"Vinsant, you will stay here," Mariano commanded, with a frowning glance at her, knowing too well she would never stay put if their baby brother followed. Thank the Vae Vinsant listened.

At the corner of the warehouse, Baiyeed deq Ikher balked. His shuffles only delayed his turning. The merciless Majoria guided him to the cover of the stone building. The wharf was empty save for a one-footed gull pecking at discarded scales, and yet she could not look away. A scream drowned the lap of water. She started, had barely grounded herself when a spurt of blood sprayed across the wharf and into the lake. Her trembling hand flew to her mouth, but could not disguise her gasp. Blood drained from her face, and she was sure her knees would buckle. An execution was nauseating enough, but what malevolence lurked beneath those hoods that the mahktashaan would not grant the condemned calm oblivion as the blade slid home?

"It is the law, Princess. They must understand why they die, and must face the Vae with their wits," a low voice said into her ear. It was Arun again, and he had her elbow. Fear flitted through her eyes. Had he read her thoughts?

"No, Princess," he said, belying his words. "Your thoughts are plain on your face. Nor have I used magic to soothe you. I shall release you now, but take my arm if you have the need."

She nodded and placed an arm around Vinsant instead. Her little brother was staring toward the returning mahktashaan, a queer expression on his face.

"If they come to Terlaan, they must abide by our laws," Vinsant said.

It was Father's sentiment. Kordahla couldn't help feel a pang that Vinsant might embrace more of the Shah's values than even he knew.

"Oh don't look at me like that. I am not!" he said, not even bothering to phrase the entire thought. She knew him so well, he didn't need to. That he was growing like Father was a tease she oft employed when he voiced conservative views. If she had any hope the outdated laws which kept her chained in ignorance would crumble once Father passed on the crown, it was because her brothers doted on her. Vae'oenka knew, she took every chance to sow the seeds of change. It was never enough. These barbaric executions were testament to that. Oh, how she longed to visit Myklaan, if only for an eight-day, to be done with Terlaan's rigid rules and the harsh realities of womanhood. What ideas she would bring back and plant in her brothers' minds! It was no comfort the fairer sex fared so much worse in Verdaan.

She glanced at deq Ikher, who was waddling as fast as he could from the bloody executions. The Verdaani emissary stopped as close as he dared to them, and stared at her. Whatever Vinsant might claim, his expression did not suggest one awestruck by beauty.

"Do you find me so hideous?" she asked, annoyed by his rudeness and craving a distraction from the brutal images which kept intruding into her mind.

"Your loveliness is a gift from Tiarasae," he replied. His cheek twitched and Kordahla wondered whether to believe him. Not even Father had compared her to the Queen of the Genies, a daughter so beloved of Mahktos that the Old God had freed her from the bind of her name.

She scowled at Vinsant for snickering, more to turn away from deq Ikher than anything else.

"Then why do you address her as a commoner and feast your eyes upon her, as though she were a whore?" Mariano said, his countenance rather than his inflection revealing just how annoyed he was their guest paid her so much attention. "I would have you know I hold blood honour for her."

Deq Ikher jerked his head towards Mariano. "A thousand apologies, Highness. A hundred thousand for the transgressions of a besotted simpleton." Kordahla had to stifle a giggle herself when Vinsant poked a finger in his mouth. "It is only, you allow your noblewomen to wander in public without a veil?" he blurted. "Lord Ahkdul will not be pleased."

Kordahla frowned. Two of his men had been executed and this was what concerned him?

Mariano mounted his horse and looked hard at deq Ikher. "And what do I care for Lord Ahkdul's pleasure in the behaviour of my sister?"

Baiyeed's face coloured. His tic fired with unbelievable speed. "I only meant…it is not the custom for the high born in Verdaan, Highness."

Kordahla had a sinking feeling he had meant infinitely more than that.

CHAPTER THREE

WHILE THE JOURNEY DOWN the eastern arm of the River Bahmar had been tolerable, Lord Ahkdul of Verdaan, soon to be *Prince* Ahkdul of the *Kingdom* of Verdaan, was loathe to re-embark on the sea-going *Tenacity* without appropriate entertainment to take his mind off the pitch, the yaw or any other nuisance a competent captain should avoid while the second most important personage in the realm graced his vessel. The fact Captain Treme, though Nertese, would be Commander of the Verdaani fleet in more trying times did little to either boost his confidence or appease his distaste of the coming voyage. Unfortunately, the boy Ahkdul had selected to minister to his needs had bawled the entire first day and night, prompting the frustrated lord to grant him his wish to return home by tossing him over the gunwale. If the boy had any ability to swim, he might have sloshed as far as the bank before the jabberweis chomped him into morsels. Neither Ahkdul nor the crew had any illusions he made it back to his family, now living in unaccustomed style as recompense for the loss of their superfluous fifth son, but shortly to be hung, drawn and quartered for failing to deliver quality merchandise. Frankly, Ahkdul was glad of the resulting quiet.

The boredom, though, was vexing. So he had decreed they would delay in the overcast port of Fayrhan until he found an appetising replacement for the lad. In the sultry, salt-stained air, distant thunder rumbling, the task was proving wearisome. The Fayrhani boys they encountered cracked worldly jokes despite their tender years. Their eyes were wary, their faces grimy and their hands chaffed from work on the wharves. They might have been amenable if rewarded with a few lek, but their crass retorts rather dulled their appeal. Nor did the lass barely into her teens, who sidled up with a seductive hitch of her faded skirt, entice.

"Do you have a younger brother?" Ahkdul asked, more to deter the ragged whore than out of hope.

Her thin face fell as she shook her dusty tangle of red hair. The little fool ignored his dismissive wave, and titled her head toward the nearest guard. Scarred Kahlmed rewarded her with a brutish grope of her budding breasts. Before her thin lips could form a proposition, he pushed her onto the rain-dotted dirt and laughed in her shocked face. Ahkdul's men were well aware *their* pleasure was not to be indulged before their Lord's.

Since Ahkdul's satisfaction was currently less than assured, he stubbornly insisted they push deeper into town. The merchant mansions with their tender occupants sat well back from the dangers of the malodorous water, a belt of untamed but fragrant greenery setting them apart from the dilapidated dwellings of the rabble. They had the refined neighbourhood in sight when Ahkdul heard the clop of hooves on cobbles. Holding up a hand to stall the group, he peered through loose shrubbery, and licked his lips as he spied a father and son atop a rustic horse. Tired and travel-stained, dressed in drab kurtas, and wrinkled shoes, they nonetheless projected an air of decency lacking in the wharf-dwellers.

"Him," Ahkdul said to Kahlmed. The heavyset man stepped in front of the horse.

"Oi! You, man. Halt."

The father tensed. Alone, Kahlmed would have given a seasoned fighter pause. The jagged scars crisscrossing his face were testament to his survival skills. With men backing him, a lone rider stood no chance. The father's vigilant eyes assessed the guards, five with hands on hilts, one with an arrow nocked. Their tabards of Verdaani saffron bore the ruling insignia, a red sword through the mouth of a sharp-toothed, river-dwelling jabberwei. Their identity was plain, compelling the man to stop his horse and rouse his drowsy son. His dismount was precise, and he lifted the disoriented boy down with ease. Whatever Ahkdul may first have thought, this was not a common man. As guards blocked the retreat across the grass, the pair bowed. Ahkdul let them linger in the position so he could consider the virtues of the small body in front of him.

"You may rise," he said eventually. His gaze flicked over the man and would have passed straight back to the child had the black moustache and beard not held a trace of familiarity. He dallied over the face, pleasant but a little too long to consider handsome. The man could be nobody of consequence. The round-faced child, on the other hand, was a perfect age. Young enough to be pliable, old enough to be trained without him squalling Ahkdul deaf. His skin glowed with evidence of an adequate diet and his short, dark hair, while mussed, was untangled. That was just as well. Delousing the child would have proved difficult in the confines of the ship.

"Have you had occasion to greet me before?" Ahkdul asked the strapping man, examining what little of the boy's olive skin lay exposed.

"My lord, I am Rasheed deq Mekresh of the Third Watchtower, second to Captain Subhi."

"Ah." That explained both the hint of recognition and the horsemanship. "You are far from your post, deq Mekresh."

"The Captain has granted me leave. I received word my mother ailed and she would see her grandchild once more. She travelled to Vae'oenka at the setting of the moons, happy that he thrives."

The words were inconsequential. Ahkdul's blood was already stirring with desire. "And does this boy reside here?"

"In Teqrin, with his mother, my lord."

"He is decent to look upon. I will give you ten thulek for him."

Rasheed had the gall to purse his lips. "My lord, he is my only son. And he is young yet to be indentured. His mother would weep herself into the grave if he did not return."

"You ingrate. I offer you five times what he is worth."

The harsh words scared the child into huddling against his father. A plump raindrop fell upon his cheek, glistening with promise.

"I don't…I mean…" Deq Mekresh took a deep breath and dared

look him in the eye. "I cannot. Sons are priceless in the eyes of their fathers, as you surely know, my lord. I measure my worth by the –"

The upstart forgot to whom he spoke. "I am not a father," Ahkdul interrupted. His mouth twisted. "Nor do I have one who is overly fond of me. But I will lavish this child with affection, of that you can be sure." The boy was indeed fair of face, with solemn brown eyes he would enjoy kissing.

Rasheed deq Mekresh appeared stricken. "My lord, is there not an orphan you could take to your service?" He gripped the child's arm too tight. A bruise would blemish the perfect flesh, yet the child sensed danger and forbore to complain. That, thought Ahkdul, was encouraging.

"Enough!" Ahkdul was well aware innuendo preceded him. Well it was a subject's duty to satisfy his lord's every whim, and a soldier's doubly so. "Twelve thulek." He gestured to a guard, who advanced on the pair. "And that generous sum erases all claim of debt. The boy belongs to me."

The boy buried his face in his father's stomach. Ignoring the raindrops plopping on their heads, deq Mekresh smoothed the boy's hair. The fear showing in the whites of his eyes was unbecoming of a soldier. "I did not…I was not asking for more coin. I beg you!"

"It is just as well, or I would have left you with none. Ten thulek then. We are agreed."

Deq Mekresh enclosed his son in a tight hug. The guard took the boy's arm and pulled.

"No," the child said, struggling to keep hold of his father's kurta.

"For the love of Vae'oenka, allow me time to say goodbye."

"Be done, man. I have business in Terlaan, and Captain Treme is upset by the delay. The Nertese are not known for their patience."

The stubborn soldier refused to release the boy. Deq Mekresh's eyes pleaded with the weathered captain, but Treme remained impassive, Lord Hudassan's man to the last. Ahkdul gestured to Kahlmed, who set the tip of his blade towards Rasheed's eye.

"You gain nothing by forfeiting your life. I'll wager your wench is young enough to whelp a dozen more brats. If this one pleases me, I may even honour your family with another apprenticeship in a few years." Ahkdul smirked as Rasheed went down on a knee, turned his mouth to the clinging boy's ear, and whispered his farewells. It was touching really, if one believed in the bond between family. In any case, Ahkdul intended to make sure the lad did not miss his father's cuddles. The thunder had drowned the soldier's words, but he would discover later what the man had said. He nodded at Kahlmed, who slipped his sword along the side of the soldier's face, a warning that drew a thin line of blood. Rasheed deq Mekresh glared at the soldier, but delayed rising long enough for Ahkdul to understand the scratch was a mere annoyance. He released his son with a kiss on the forehead. Lord Hudassan would really need to speak to Captain Subhi of the Third Watchtower. His second's behaviour bordered on insubordination.

"Come here," Ahkdul said.

Kahlmed had to drag the boy over. He reached for his father but did not call out. Ahkdul was well pleased. The quiet ones always served him best. Delighting in the smoothness of the boy's skin, he ran the back of a finger from temple to chin while another guard counted out the coin. Rasheed spat to one side, but pocketed it all the same. Ahkdul's mouth twitched. No child could compete with wealth far beyond what his parent would earn in a lifetime. Still, he should not have allowed the doting father to shadow them all the way back to the derelict wharf where shrieking gulls swooped on trodden crumbs, and rats gnawed the corners of waterlogged sacks so they could scamper in and out of the spilling grain. The boy kept looking over his shoulder although Kahlmed's brawny hand clamped upon his wrist, forcing him to trot the creaking planks. When he saw the *Tenacity* looming in the choppy waters, he dug in his heels and screamed. It was not a scene Ahkdul cared to have witnessed. He should have ordered the rough labourers tossing sacks or lugging crates executed for their whistles and jeers. Since his retinue of eight stood no chance against the hundred, he would have to convince Lord Hudassan, his dear, despising father, to send the Verdaani army to do the job.

"Quiet, boy." With a callous laugh, Kahlmed hefted the boy over his shoulder, stepped past a rotting post stained with bird droppings, and boarded their rocking rowboat. Ahkdul ran a tongue over his lips. The curve of that tender body kindled a delicious arousal. As Treme ordered the crew to hoist the sails, he clamped his hands on the boy's stiff shoulders. Rasheed's eyes, he noted with a curl of his lip, were moist. What manner of soldier was he? Subhi required more than a lecture. He needed discipline. Only a poor captain would allow his troops to soften so.

Through the rumbles of thunder escorting the galley from the harbour, the sniffling boy remained at the bulwark, hands clamped on the gunwale, watching his father dwindle to a speck. Tears ran down his face long after gulls ceased to bob on the waves and land faded to a hazy line. Ahkdul let him be, practising swordplay with his men and counting the hours until the full moons cast their feverish glow. When green Dindarin was halfway to the zenith, when the sea had calmed to an oily sheen, he could bear the fire in his blood no longer.

"Come. You will learn to serve me," he said.

The child was nestled against the bulwark. He had eaten nothing but the salty spray, watching each step of their drills with those alert, attractive eyes. When he did not move, Ahkdul entered his cabin. The thick carpet on the polished floor was the only concession to luxury in this aging vessel. However the crew might snicker behind his back, the spicy perfume he splashed around was a necessity to cover the pervading stink of gutted fish and rotten seaweed. He only had time to lock his sword in his oak coffer before Kahlmed picked the child up by the arms and carried him in, pulling the splintering door shut behind him as he departed.

"What's your name?" Ahkdul asked.

Wary eyes watched him without answer.

"Would you prefer I call you Slave?"

"My name's Timak."

"Well Timak, you are mine until I tire of you, when you will be put to work in the porrin fields, a harsh, unforgiving occupation that will send you to an early grave. Learn your tasks well and you can live in comfort a good many years." He stepped up to the boy and stroked his cheek. "Perhaps, for the rest of your life."

Timak flinched at his touch. Ahkdul licked his lips. "You must have bruises. You were handled poorly, by your father and the guard."

Timak's eyes flashed. "My father wanted to keep me."

Good, thought Ahkdul. *There is some character there to spice the relationship.* "He took the money, Timak. I did not abduct you. He sold you to me."

The boy shifted uncertainly.

"Sit on the bed and remove your kurta. I will tend to those tender bruises."

Timak backed against the door, one hand rubbing his other arm.

"Do you need Kahlmed to help you? He is experienced with disobedient children, but none too gentle with those who displease me."

Timak locked eyes with him. Ahkdul felt a stirring in his loins.

"I have only to call. He is right outside that door."

The boy sidled to the bed, eyes never leaving Ahkdul's face. Ahkdul stood over him, so close he could smell honey-sweetened tea on the boy's breath. The gentlest he intended to be, he stroked a soft cheek.

"Come now. You must learn to do as I say. It will go badly for your father if you do not."

The boy sat. Slowly, he removed his kurta, and held it to his lap, rubbing it nervously over his shalvar. His upper arms were red. He had, Ahkdul noticed with a tremor, begun trembling. Ahkdul took the kurta and pulled. Timak refused to let go.

Ahkdul crossed to the simple table and poured a little water into a metal mug. It would not do to have the boy scream tonight. Not in the confines of this cursed ship when they were yet so close to shore. He removed a small paper packet from the top drawer of a bolted chest, and deposited two shakes of the red powder within into the mug. Swirling the contents until it had dissolved, he considered imbibing the drug himself. Later perhaps. This first caress would be that much sweeter if he revelled in each exquisite sensation. If he remembered every touch. Carefully, he rewrapped and replaced the porrin powder, careful to lock the chest.

"Here," he said, holding the cup to Timak's lips and dispensing two sips. "This will help." He set the mug on the chest of drawers and removed his kurta. The child's pupils had already dilated, his trembling eased. Ahkdul placed the boy's kurta aside and pushed him down.

❖ ❖ ❖

Timak stared without seeing at the ceiling. He was aware of only two things: his body throbbed inside and out, and the motion of the boat was making him queasy. Gradually he became aware of a third: Lord Ahkdul's bare limbs sprawled across his own. His tormentor's head was turned towards him. He could feel hot breath on his cheek.

His papa had known what horror lay in store for him. Those whispered parting words would remain forever in his mind. *Our lord will try to hurt you, little soldier. Escape if you can, but don't run home. I will not stop looking until you are safe in my arms again. Remember that. If you remember one thing, remember that.* Timak choked back a sob. His papa had allowed Ahkdul to take him. His papa, best swordsman in the Three Realms, had not fought for him. His mind played out the fateful ambush once, thrice, ten times. At the last, his father performed the legendary feats of bravery they enacted at play, besting the terrifying, scarred beast of a guard and the despicable, hideous lord without breaking a sweat.

It was cold comfort. Ahkdul's armed guards lurked in the background of every twisted scene. Deep down, in his heart of hearts, he knew Papa would have perished if he had so much as hinted at the slightest threat. Knowing didn't make him *feel* any less abandoned.

Vae'oenka spare him. Before today, he had not imagined a body could endure such agony. He tried to recall the comfort of his father's arms, but the memory of that last kiss made him shudder. All he could think of was his lord's lips moistening his body. His stomach heaved. He rolled out of bed and vomited a puddle of bile onto the carpet. The bitter stench made him retch.

So much pain.

As if in sympathy, timbers creaked.

Unbearable pain.

The mast groaned.

More pain than the time he had broken his arm when he flew off a horse. The physic had prescribed porrin to dull the edge of it. The drug had lulled him to drowsy oblivion. Today, Lord Ahkdul had forced him to ingest the powdered seed. It had deadened his nerves for a time. He wished it had not worn off before the torture was complete. Feeling like filth, Timak dragged himself up. The mug rested on the chest, the dregs of the liquid enticing and bright. He drained it, and slumped against the carved wood, knees pulled tight to his body, waiting for sweet release.

It came soon, eventually, too late. The room spun about him and his mind drifted free of his battered self, looked down at the broken body huddled on the floor, and the beefy grown up sprawled under the light covers. The lord's prominent brow, large nose and thick lips seemed cruel even in sleep.

Escape if you can. The words tumbled through his mind. Papa had not counted on him sailing on a ship, with water lapping all around and Vae'omar knew how many silver-grey sawtooths patrolling the water.

"Escape if you can." The words sounded muted, like the roar of Djinn Rage Canyon from inside his father's watchtower.

"I can't," Timak whispered. The voice needed to stop calling. He stretched an arm towards the porthole, imagined floating along Dindarin's green beams, free from Lord Ahkdul's whims.

"Where's he to go? Vae'omar's watery domain?"

"Oh, but I want him for my own. Escape. Escape."

Two voices. Were they Daesoa and Dindarin? Outside the portal, the green moon's harsh light defined every pitiless line on Lord Ahkdul's face. If only he could see small Daesoa's soft yellow glow.

"He's damaged. Choose another." The male voice. An insensitive tone.

"That's exactly why I want him. Oh, do escape. Escape if you can." This voice was younger, girlish.

"Who's there?" Timak whispered.

"Can he hear us?" the female voice asked.

"Don't be absurd. No mortal can," her companion replied. "He's intoxicated on porrin. Doesn't know up from down."

Escape if you can.

"Papa?"

Timak padded to the door and cracked it open. A breeze washed over the empty deck, freshening the stale, sweat-soaked cabin. He slipped outside. A figure worked on the tiller, and another stared over the starboard side. The moonbeams still beckoned, insistent, irresistible. Timak walked to the bulwark and climbed onto the gunwale. He could see Daesoa now, throwing him light like a lifeline. He would fly away from his torment, float among their beams.

"No. He can't. He'll drown." The girlish voice sounded upset. Timak couldn't think why.

"You wanted him to escape," the mean male said.

He stretched up, stood on tiptoe. He had only to lean and he would fly. For the briefest instant his body was surrounded by air. Then he thumped to the deck as a rough pair of hands dumped him back into captivity. A large boot landed on his chest, and Kahlmed's scary face bore down on him.

"Not leaving so soon?" Kahlmed inquired.

"Help me."

"I'll help you back to my lord's bed," Kahlmed said.

Timak extended an arm to Daesoa. "Help me."

"He *can* hear us," the female voice said.

"Impossible," her male companion replied.

"Please help." Serene Daesoa waited at his fingertips, though her pretty yellow light eluded his grasp. Below her, green Dindarin brushed the horizon.

"But he can," the invisible girl said.

Kahlmed frowned at Ahkdul, who had appeared on deck in nothing more than a loincloth. "I don't think he's talking to me."

"He had porrin. Ignore him. The drug has stolen his wit."

Strange, how the lord's words were sharp. Not at all like the muffled buzz Timak remembered of his last porrin daze. He had dozed in bed for a full day after a single dose for his broken arm. He would rather it were that. Too many of the motley crew had found tasks in the vicinity, counting him a diversion from the inky monotony of the silent ocean. Their sniggers sweated him cold.

"Daesoa, please help," he whispered, opening and closing his hand along her beam.

The twist of the boot over his ribs made him yelp. Kahlmed gave a nasty laugh. "The moon. The git's talking to the moon."

"Can you see us?" The soft voice was excited.

"No. Where are you?" Timak looked around. Wary faces stared down at him.

"Right here. Right above the ship."

Timak shook his head.

In the blink of an eye, the wind dropped. To a man, sailors and soldiers paused at their tasks. Real slow, several looked over their shoulders, peering into the night. In the lull, Kahlmed shuddered.

"A still wind blows," Captain Treme said, pressing forefingers and thumbs together in the warding sign. "Trim the sails and man the oars to boot. We're away from this haunted spot with all speed."

"He's cursed," a sailor said, copying Treme's gesture. "Djinn-touched. Capt'n, he canna stay aboard the ship."

"Superstitious fool," said Kahlmed, removing his boot from Timak's chest. But the seasoned soldier backed away.

"The boy's Lord Ahkdul's guest," Treme said. "Now back ter work, the lot of yer."

There were grumblings amid the "aye-ayes" as the sailors returned to rigging and ropes.

Timak lay on his back and listened. The voices had stopped.

"You are mine, Timak," Lord Ahkdul said, standing over him. "You please me too well for me to grant you release so soon." Slowly, the corners of his mouth broke into a smile. It fell far short of his formidable grey eyes. "You," Lord Ahkdul said, pointing at a sailor. "Tie him up."

The sailor leered at Timak with a mouth full of rotting teeth. Callused hands bound his wrists and threw the tether at Ahkdul. "He's trussed real good, yer lordship. Only yer leave him on deck, there's them as might take a fancy to 'is soft skin."

Kahlmed drew his sword. Timak closed his eyes, rolled against the bulwark, and curled up tight.

"Easy now," the sailor said. "There's no 'arm in a joke. We knows that piece of flesh is fer the Master."

"And the Master is not yet finished with him this night." Lord Ahkdul tugged Timak to his feet by the rope around his wrists. "You have grieved me, boy, and now you must make amends."

"No, please," Timak begged, as Ahkdul led him back to the cabin like a goat for the slaughter.

"He's so frightened. We have to do something," the young voice said.

"For a damaged human flea?" the mean male said.

"Take care, Yazmine. Our Court will not be pleased if you do something foolish," said a third, a woman, and kind.

They were barely inside when Lord Ahkdul dropped his loincloth.

"I can't bear it," the voice called Yazmine said.

"Come away, child," the woman called.

"No. No, I shall stay. He can hear me. I shall sing to him. Oh, I shall sing to you, little boy, through it all."

The sweetest melody lilted through Timak's head, its tenderness easing his pain.

❖ ❖ ❖

Yazmine couldn't look. Not while that beast did the unspeakable to a boy younger than she. An unbearable sadness had been eating her since she discovered Timak's plight. And what could she do about it? Nothing. She floated outside the portal, stared at the waves and sang to him, not sure if it helped. When he finally drifted to sleep, she sat on a moonbeam and wept, incredulous that she could still shed tears. One by one they fell, mingling with the salt of the ocean and achieving absolutely nothing. The waves did not swell, nor the fish alter their course.

Why? She wanted to scream. *What is the point?* What was the good of Mahktos planting her here if He forbade her to help? She might as well have stayed on the earth, where she could do some good. In human form, she could buy the boy, hire mercenaries to steal him, or assassins to kill that vile pretender. As a genie...*you may not interfere.* That was the only instruction the others had given before apprenticing her to a brusque couldn't-care-less who wouldn't even trust her with his name.

Who was she fooling? Brought up a baker's daughter, she would never have known of Timak's plight. She would never have collected enough coin to do any of the things she had just imagined. Frustration mounting, she kicked at the water, splashing spray against the porthole.

"There's fish a'flying," a sailor scrubbing the deck said.

"Yer be a fool," another replied. "There's djinn about. Don't yer feel that still wind?"

Yazmine kicked again, splashing the pair with water. She would buffet them with waves if they sat back while that brute tortured the boy. To the scums with the dreaded salt on her toes. What had she been thinking to say yes to the god? On earth, she could have helped others. Like the beggar she had given her ma's fresh baked loaf, or old Josar, whose cottage she had scrubbed when he lay abed with fever. What was the point if she couldn't interfere?

Frustration was building in her like a storm. It twirled her out over the ocean, faster and faster, until the water beneath was no more than a blur. Her fury dragged the waves from the sea, twisting them around her as she rose into the sky, weaving cloud through the water and moonbeams through the mist. At last, she collapsed on a moonlit wisp, shivering, though it was not from cold.

She blinked as a waterspout whirled past her, a school of fish rippling around its edge. Astounded, she forgot to concentrate. She fell into the ocean with a resounding splash. Salt water enclosed her, soaking, stinging, abrading. Draining her newfound magic from the rose-pink crystals in her joints. She thrashed for the surface, praying the ship was gone, using her last breath to cry for help. Salt water surged into her lungs. She splashed, coughed, spluttered when, "There!" the chilling shout came. "Tell the cap'n to heave to. We'll catch us our fortune t'night."

The ship listed as the tiller cranked the rudder. Yazmine dove. She would swim deep down before she would let those brutes capture her. She would drown herself, and go to Mahktos a different way.

The god must have guessed her intent. The waters parted, and a hand plucked her from the tainted depths.

"Dimwit."

She swallowed disappointment. It was only the indigo djinn who had saved her. He laughed as the galley tottered at the edge of the trough while she dangled at arm's length, the back of her pink bodice between his thumb and forefinger, coughing water from her lungs.

"Don't hurt them. Please don't."

He pulled his nose long in distaste. "Oh, very well." He flicked his free hand and the waters closed. The ship rocked in the turbulence, but the captain yelled, and the sailors lashed ballast, and it righted itself with a creaky shudder.

"Did I not warn you about salt, you tick on my behind?" Indigo said as she shivered and dripped. "I should throw you on deck just to teach you a lesson."

She closed her eyes tight, and pressed her fists into her face. Mahktos alone knew how lucky she was Indigo chose to toss her into storm clouds where the moisture rinsed her clean.

❖ ❖ ❖

For once in her dreary life, Kordahla was grateful the ride home presented nothing more diverting than mundane news of Verdaan's capital, Pengari. The day had certainly held enough excitement to satisfy her for an eight-day, and small Daesoa's rising had kindled a desire for home. When deq Ikher began to gasp at the palace walls, she tuned out and let her eyes rove over the city. As fabulous as the lofty barriers were, as formidable as the row upon row of iron spikes topping them stood, the giant carvings on the outer face mirrored those on the inner to a groove. A lifetime in their confinement tended to dull the wonder. For Kordahla, the ragtag streets adjoining the wide Royal Way, with its border of palms and generous footpaths, were infinitely more curious than the images of long past Shahs slaughtering at war, reclining in lush gardens and presiding over court. In the light of the two full moons, the whole area assumed a romantic ambience. She looked up. Small Daesoa was just brushing larger Dindarin. In all the fuss, she had forgotten it was a major moon. The first day of each month was the one moment in their perpetual journey across the heavens the two full lovers stole a glancing kiss. It was an auspicious time for courtship, if you were not a Terlaani princess forced to entertain a vile suitor. A princess could not help daydreaming about a dashing Myklaani Prince who would escort her about the livelier parts of town before asking for her hand. It certainly beat listening to the drivel spawned from deq Ikher's mouth.

So, when a fish dropped out of the sky and slapped into her lap, Kordahla could only stare in bemusement. The day was turning decidedly odd. The fish flapped about, gills pumping as it struggled to breathe. Delayed surprise set in, and she hesitantly tried to secure it, but the fish slipped to the paving where the poor thing continued to thrash. She barely had time to return Vinsant's startled look when another knocked him on the head. He looked about, as though seeking a prankster, fixed his eyes on the back of Levi's hooded head, and snorted when three more fish plummeted onto the Majoria's shoulder. Before Levi had turned, a veritable shower of fish assailed the party. Hands shot into the air to ward missiles from heads as the horses shied, their hooves treading on soft bodies, squishing scale, fin and guts into the paving. At the edges of Royal Way, the cheering commoners fell silent to stare in disbelief. Then one boy raced forward and dived on a large fish. He rose with it clamped triumphantly in two hands, no doubt anticipating a succulent dinner.

As abruptly as it started, the shower of fish ended. A number of the creatures yet flailed on the ground, grappers all she noted with surprise, dark tops delineated from light bellies by a reddish stripe. The hesitant crowd edged toward the saltwater treat and, at her suggestion, Mariano ordered the group pick their way out of the bounty so that the less fortunate might claim their windfall. Quite literally, she thought with no trace of amusement. She made the sign of the warding but dropped her hand when Vinsant scoffed, jumped off his horse and grabbed a wriggling fish.

Levi and Arun, she noticed, had already dismounted and were casting their glowing crystals about the clear skies. Around them, the crowd chanted haunting praise to Vae'omar and Vae'oeldin for their bounty, even though it was not the hour for prayer. Nor was the air chill. For all the utter madness she had just experienced, for all the magic the Majoria was spelling, she, the most sensitive of her family, sensed no still wind. Only when she caught the Majoria's slight shake of his head did disquiet seize her. Why that should be, she could not say; the absence of djinn should have been an unequivocal cause for relief. As the party covered the final distance home, the heightened attention of the mahktashaan to every deep shadow, to each faint sound, to every gust of wind, only served to intensify her foreboding.

Her brothers rode as subdued as she, Mariano assuring the gob-smacked deq Ikher that fish were not part of a Terlaani welcoming ritual but once. The Verdaani messenger's incessant questioning had worn on all their nerves and, in the end, they played deaf. Anyway, contemplating the oddity was far more entertaining than responding to the drivel from their irksome guest's mouth, even if Kordahla could conceive no explanation. No rational one at least. Mahktashaan and priests always preached that the ways of gods and djinn were beyond the figuring of mortals.

They rode over the moat into the palace gardens in silence. Never before had she been so appreciative of their confines, or the grooms who took her mount. She snapped a sprig of apple blossoms as they walked to the oak doors and breathed deep, letting the soothing lap of Lake Sheraz against the eastern palace walls wash her fatigue away.

"I'm sure the tale will make an amusing subject for one of these tap-estries," she said, as her shoe rang on the tiles. "You will excuse me," she added, deflecting Vinsant's demands to burst upon Father before dinner with the extraordinary tale and the salty proof that sat under his arm.

"Was that not the diversion you were seeking, sister?" Mariano called after her.

She turned to reply, walking backwards in a most unladylike man-ner. "May more fish klonk you on the brains," she said, not caring a hoot for decorum. Her reply drew a laugh from both her brothers. She joined in when she saw the scandalized expression on their guest's face.

Chapter Four

THE SUMMONS LEFT KORDAHLA apprehensive. Very much an incidental part of the Shah's court these days, she rarely received requests for her presence save at the odd dutiful supper and the obligatory royal event. Now a mahktashaan guard with a mauve crystal around his neck was informing her of His Majesty's demand for an immediate and proper audience, which could only mean one thing: a reprimand for yesterday's behaviour. Her hand hovered over the lilac veil her handmaid Karie had laid out on the curtained daybed, a shade lighter than her damask shalvar kameez, but she decided against donning it. The Shah had never insisted the women of the court wear the garment except at formal gatherings, a concession to her progressive mother she had heard tell. She had heard other whispers, too, of his desire to gaze upon the ubiquitous charms of the women under his thumb. Well, Kordahla was not about to admit to wrongdoing by meekly covering her head today. This particular veil could remain draped over the colourful woollen cushions she and her handmaids had spent countless hours embroidering.

She spent the entire walk down the vaulted stone passages fretting about her bare head. The elaborate corbels on the columns only served to remind her how stunningly a headdress could frame a figure. When she arrived at the double ironwood doors to the throne room, she was surprised to find Vinsant there, bright, cheery, and more spiky-haired than usual, yesterday's prize grapper tucked under his arm.

"I rather thought you would have had that for dinner," she said, wishing the smelly fish was far removed.

"Not a chance," he replied. "I'm going to ask the taxidermist to preserve it." He held it out to her, his eyes wide in mock innocence. "I'd like to gift it to you, to adorn your chambers."

"Prince Vinsant deq Wilshem, if you ever bring that putrid thing near me again, I'll make sure it's dished up to you for your evening meal and you eat every last scale."

"It's not that bad," he said, genuine again as he looked almost lovingly at it. She recognized that look. Here was a puzzle to keep his overactive imagination occupied. "I think I'll call it Errol."

The ordered march of four mahktashaan guards interrupted them. They were escorting the two hapless meatball sellers down the mosaic corridor. Fresh blood seeped through the bandage around the older man's ribs, staining it crimson. He paid little heed as he gawped at the detailed mosaic scenes laid over ceiling and wall in intricate retelling of the fables of old. Kordahla began to ask why Physic Nocrates had not attended to the wound. Then it dawned. There would be no reprieve for these men. The Vae forbid she associate herself with them further. A quick turn of the handle admitted her into her father's presence.

However much her appreciation of the palace walls might wax and wane, never, ever would she grow accustomed to the radiance of this room. Crystal *muqarnas* glowing every soft colour imaginable adorned the dome. Arches carved top and base with lotus flowers supported it, and framed small niches the entire way around the chamber. Within each alcove crystal statues of the most intricate workmanship shone from within, their radiance nothing compared to the diamond throne that stood upon a dais of black marble. The throne pulsed with a light that bathed the occupants, but none shone so resplendent as the seated figure in his turban of gold. Her father was a touch over average height, and well proportioned. Combined with the bearing of a long line of shahs, this allowed him to dominate any room he occupied, even in the company of sturdy men.

Kordahla and Vinsant passed Baiyeed deq Ikher, hands behind his back, his mouth agape and cheek twitching. The thick scent of geranium and lemon clinging to the odious man explained the expression. She held her breath. Vinsant sneezed. Mariano, her dutiful, steadfast brother, was standing at Father's right. He had chosen to proclaim his station by wearing a turban of royal burgundy. His nod as they mounted the dais was not the reassurance she had hoped for. Taking a steeling breath, she paid formal respects to Father – his choice of chamber demanded it – stepped to his left, and clasped her hands to still their trembling. This room was one of ceremony, whether joyous or solemn. Certainly, a simple messenger and the pair of unfortunate miscreants shuffling in did not warrant its use.

The prisoners fell to their knees just inside the door, bewildered beholders of a sight few in the Three Realms had witnessed: The Diamond Throne in its splendour. The Shah nodded, and the light dimmed to a gentle radiance which reflected from the gold-covered walls to lend the room an ethereal air.

"It seems you experienced a rather eventful day, yesterday," Father began with a wink at Vinsant and a stroke of his short, black beard.

Kordahla sighed. Father was incredibly lenient when in a genial mood. The prisoners caught his tone because they tried to look up, a mistake that earned them a clap on the head with the flat of the guards' blades.

Father wrinkled his nose and frowned. "I did not wish a second look at the fish."

"Errol. Its name's Errol. And I was on my way to see the taxidermist," Vinsant said.

"I'm afraid you'll have to catch another fish to stuff. I have asked Majoria Levi to examine it."

"It's just a fish."

"That fell from the sky."

"But..."

Mariano cleared his throat. "I'll take you fishing for swordfish, Vinsant."

Vinsant glowered, obviously unconvinced the elusive delicacy was more keepworthy than the grapper he cradled.

Father gave Vinsant a sympathetic look before bestowing a thoughtful one on her. Her nerves fluttered. Something was afoot, and it concerned her. She glanced at deq Ikher who was poised on the balls of his feet, his tic barely noticeable. His keen interest confirmed her suspicions. She took a deep breath and pulled a lock of her walnut hair over her shoulder, wondering what she could say.

"I have received a rather thought-provoking missive from Lord Ahkdul," Father said, relieving her of the burden.

Kordahla nodded. They had met deq Ikher's ship for no other reason than to accept it. "Is he pleased with the ship's progress?" she asked.

"He doesn't mention it. This concerns another matter entirely."

"Porrin smuggling," Vinsant said, rolling his eyes.

Father frowned but immediately returned his attention to her. "As it happens, no. Lord Ahkdul has expressed a desire to meet Kordahla."

Kordahla's heart beat more quickly. "If he intends on guesting here, our re-acquaintance is assured." She would *not* follow her thoughts to a logical if distasteful conclusion.

Father rose and took her hands. "His words imply he would like to cultivate a more serious relationship. He has even suggested you accompany him to Verdaan for a time."

She was trembling now, though Father's eyes were not unkind as they gauged her reaction. She shook her head in disbelief, glanced askance at deq Ikher, decked out in Verdaani saffron, and kept her voice low, though there was every chance he would hear. "You cannot be entertaining the notion of a marriage alliance with Ahkdul?" Years of forced propriety kept her from saying more. They all knew the rumours.

Father touched the back of his fingers to her cheek, an affectionate gesture from childhood. "Perhaps we shall allow events to run their course when he arrives? You will, naturally, avail yourself of his presence." His gaze held steady. "And it would be most fitting for you to don the veil while he is here. We would not wish him to think you uncouth."

The djinn stitched her mouth until Father had turned from her. "Since it is Ahkdul who will be the guest, shouldn't it be *he* who adapts to *our* customs?" She had meant to sound reasonable, to have the air of one asking for instruction in royal etiquette, but her trepidation had coloured the words with a touch of rudeness. As always, the hint of that tone, from a woman no less, wiped the cordiality from Father's face.

"Perhaps it is time the women of the court resumed the ways of old. I am told you caused quite a disturbance yesterday, and not one Vae'oenka's most ardent followers welcomed." His stare shamed her into looking at the green lines through the black marble.

"Umm, that was my fault," Vinsant interjected, with no trace of remorse. Even his most ill-conceived prank rarely drew more than a mild rebuke from father.

"Yes, and precisely the reason Kordahla will face no consequences. You presumed too far, daughter. This land will adhere to the old practices. We have been blessed with the mahktashaan crystals, and we will honour the god Mahktos for his gift."

Not fall in decadence like liberal Myklaan, you mean, Kordahla thought, wishing she was a princess of the south. She flashed a query at Mariano, at a loss as to why this intensely personal conversation was taking place before a messenger. Before *prisoners*, no less.

Her brother's eyes were as soft as Father's in pleading for her cooperation. "To protect Terlaan we must address the drug problem. By Vae'oeldin, Kordahla, you fell victim to it yourself."

Did he have to bring that up? Father would never let her leave the palace walls again, not in an eternity of eternities. "Lord Ahkdul is willing to negotiate an agreement," she said. "Isn't that the other matter to which you and Ambassador deq Ikher referred?"

Mariano took a half step. It was a movement of discomfort, not reassurance. "With a true alliance there would be more sway. Lord Hudassan has indicated he will commit resources to dissuading the smugglers if he has ties to our realm."

He had given voice to a shattering betrayal. What use did a woman have at court except to barter? What value other than to forge ties? Her hand flew to her mouth. She knew her eyes were wide. From the time she could toddle, she had counted on Mariano to help her fight for her limited freedoms. Without his support, there was nothing she could say.

"How will he succeed?" Vinsant asked. "Doesn't most of the porrin…Ow," he complained as she pinched his arm. Now was neither the time nor the place. They would not do this in front of the ambassador. The man was looking at her like a lost puppy, no more attractive for the absence of his tic.

A thud startled her into looking at the prisoners. A guard's boot was stomping the younger man's head into the floor. Merciful Vae'oenka, they had heard every word of this humiliating exchange. Could she be divested of any more pride?

As if in answer to her question, the doors behind the throne opened, admitting Majoria Levi. He glided across the floor in the eerie way the ranked mahktashaan employed when on official business. Had the hem of his robe not skimmed the marble, she would have assumed his feet floated.

"Majoria," Father greeted, resuming the throne. "I trust you have news."

"Majesty," Levi said, without deference or the slightest bow. Such was his esteem in the eyes of the court, the Shah took no offence. "Minekeeper Fenz located the writings of which we spoke."

"Then you have confirmed the legend," Father said. Beneath him, the Diamond Throne pulsed.

"The reference is obscure, but it is written in Shah Gustav's hand. Events herald a momentous occasion."

"Are we talking about falling fish?" Vinsant interrupted. "Because if you've found the reason can I keep him?"

Levi turned to Vinsant, his sharp nose shadowed by his hood. His decision to don it in the presence of the royal family reinforced her dislike of the man. "Prince Vinsant, Mahktos sent that fish. The mahktashaan must use it to determine the god's intent."

"Scums," Vinsant said, rolling his head back. "Here you go, then." He tossed the fish at Levi. The unruffled Majoria rotated his hand. Blackness flashed from the crystal around his neck. The fish slowed in the air before landing neatly along his arm.

"I thank you, Highness," Levi said, his sarcasm evident in a tiny bow. Had anyone else been the beneficiary of Vinsant's prank, she would have chastised her brother as he rubbed the freckles on his nose. She had, after all, taken it upon herself to raise him after their mother's accident eleven years back. But no prank, to her knowledge, had ever managed to ruffle the Majoria and, if she were to believe Vinsant's rambling tales of woe, Levi was not above revenge, prolonged, humiliating and painful. That said, Vinsant just did not seem to learn. She would need to have a word with him later. Father would expect it.

She fidgeted as a mahktashaan guard she had not noticed glided out of a recess and took the fish. Arun, she realised with lifting spirits and heated cheeks, though she could not fathom why it should be so. After yesterday's intoxicated conversation she should be happy if she never saw him again. Vinsant watched him carry the grapper from the room with an expression of loss akin to that of a child relinquishing a favourite toy. She dipped her head. With the Minoria gone she could count one less potential, if silent, ally.

"Cheer up, Vinsant. I'll ask the cooks to serve you grapper for dinner," Mariano said with a wink. The comment earned him a black look.

"Father, you mentioned a legend," Kordahla said because she wished to be done with this audience.

"It is for the Majoria to tell," the Shah answered.

Levi turned to face her square. "It concerns Shah Gustav, Prinncessss." His lingering over her title sent tiny shivers down her spine.

She nodded to show she understood of whom he spoke. The early Shah of Terlaan was depicted on the wall by the swimming area of the lake. Starting, she remembered he held a fish in his hands. A fish about the same size and shape as a grapper.

Levi placed his hands behind his back. He may have meant his pacing to unnerve her, but it served only to irritate. By the time he stilled, opposite her no less, she was regretting the asking. Her mood did not invite a saga. "Shah Gustav was blessed by a shower of grapper as he rode to welcome the Satrap of Crystalite and his daughter Lisabelle to Tarana. At his side was the king of one of the Eastern Kingdoms, and his daughter, Faromi, to whom Gustav was informally engaged. Assuming the fish were a divine blessing, Gustav ordered them served for dinner on the eve of their betrothal. What method the cook had used to prepare the fish we cannot say, but as the Shah cut into flesh, his knife struck metal. He was yelling for the cook, threatening to stuff the fish down his incompetent gullet, when the curious Lisabelle begged him to investigate."

"Well what else would you do?" Vinsant said.

"Behead the cook," Mariano replied.

Levi ignored the interruption. "The girl was a demure and tranquil beauty for whom the shah harboured feelings. Embarrassed by his outburst, Gustav felt unable to deny her. As he parted the flesh he found a diamond ring, a jewel the like of which has never been matched since. Faromi was abed with a stomach upset, so when Gustav slid the ring onto Lisabelle's finger, both she and her father assumed he proposed."

"A misunderstanding that would have led to embarrassment on all sides," Father observed. He was leaning over one elbow, intent on every word.

"Who did he wed?" Vinsant asked as Levi paused.

"Relations with a foreign king are far more delicate than those with a satrap under the shah's jurisdiction. Against the advice of his councillors, who thought grappers and ring a portent from Mahktos, Gustav married Faromi, promising Lisabelle their respective offspring might wed."

Kordahla stared at the lip of the black hood. The Majoria was not given to idle words, but the story failed to make a point. Either way, she did not like the direction the tale was taking. A royal marriage had taken place, and the Levi was looking at *her*, speaking to *her*, when Father was in the room. She kept her gaze direct, and her mouth closed.

When it became apparent she was not about to ask for the conclusion, Levi went on. "The day after the wedding, Gustav took Faromi boating on Lake Sheraz. A wild storm rose from calmness, and lightning struck the vessel. As you are aware, both Gustav and his bride drowned."

Butterflies fluttering in her stomach, Kordahla said, "This history entertains as much as it teaches. How is it we have not heard of the ring before?"

"After Gustav's younger brother and successor, Guntek, took Lisabelle for his wife, he forbade all present at the fateful dinner to mention the incident, on pain of death."

"Why?" Vinsant asked, crinkling his freckled nose.

"We speak of a time when the Shah was divine and the mahktashaan not yet in existence. It is likely Guntek wished his councillors to refrain from constant reminders of their insight," Father replied.

"Then you know of it how?" she persisted.

"A written record persists in the mahktashaan library, signed by Guntek himself."

She did not pursue her thoughts. The mahktashaan had come into existence under Guntek. Everyone in the room barring the prisoners would be aware of it. Her spirits sinking, she swallowed, and grasped at the only straw she had. "Guntek abdicated the throne after only a year. He was clearly unfit to rule."

The slight clench of Levi's hand unnerved her. "A mahktashaan serves Mahktos over all others. His abdication was a sacrifice that brought about a greater good – the founding of our order."

Shah Wilshem tapped a finger on his lip. "What is important here is the benefit to Terlaan when divine will was followed. Had Lisabelle not wed Guntek, mahktashaan might never have blessed this realm. What say you, Majoria?"

"It is as you say, Majesty."

Mariano asked, "Did fish ever again fall from the sky?"

"Not until yesterday, Highness," Levi replied.

"What happened to the ring? The one Lisabelle wore?" Vinsant asked.

"Lisabelle felt compelled to gift it to Faromi on her wedding day. Beyond that, the histories fail to give further mention of it," Levi said. He frowned. "Her father may have taken it east."

"Once, these fish fell upon a Shah and his divinely chosen fiancée. Now they fall on a Princess of Terlaan and the bearer of a marriage proposal," Father observed. "This bears thinking upon."

Not sure what that had to do with anything, Kordahla said, "You mean to take this as an omen I should wed? What of my feelings in the matter?" she asked.

"You will do as you are told, Kordahla," Father said. The throne he sat was altogether too bright.

"As you wish, Your Majesty," she replied with a bow of her head and complete insincerity. There had to be a way to avoid such a fate, but she was not about to argue in present company. Suddenly queasy, she swallowed. "Perhaps I may be excused?"

"Unfortunately, there is another matter of direct concern to you," Father replied.

She closed her eyes, not caring what any present might think. The Majoria knew her intimately, had witnessed her growth to womanhood and could, for all she cared, have one more indiscretion to hold against her. The Verdaani ambassador had already seen her at her most vulnerable. As for the prisoners, well, they were about to learn what their presence in this room meant.

"Street vendors," the Shah began. Again, the prisoners attempted to raise their heads and again the guards stomped their noses to the marble floor. Crimson spots of blood blemished its polish. "You are charged with the crime of peddling porrin in the guise of meatballs, and attempting to poison the royal children with those meatballs. By the testimony of Crown Prince Mariano and the Majoria of the mahktashaan, you are found guilty of said crime. According to the laws of Terlaan, which I am sworn to uphold, the punishment is death, to be executed immediately."

In the seconds of silence, butterflies whirling around her stomach, Kordahla found the audacity to speak. "Might they not be allowed to vouch for themselves?" she asked.

"Silence!" the Shah roared, making her jump.

Whimpers rose from the condemned, turning into pleas for their life.

"They are guilty!" the Shah said. "Any claim otherwise is false. Nothing they might say will alter that fact."

The Shah waved at the mahktashaan. They raised their swords, and lowered them in perfect unison, severing the heads of the luckless duo from their bodies. Kordahla covered her mouth and turned away as bile rose in her throat. It was inconceivable such a barbaric act be committed in this of all rooms, before the sacred Diamond Throne. Vae, most such executions took place in the square before the wharves or, when the glut of beheading had lost its appeal to the bloodthirsty public, in the dungeons of the palace. Kordahla stared at her father's feet, trying to blot out the stagnant image of two heads swimming in a congealed pool of red.

"I did not expect you to bear witness to this." Mariano had crossed to her side. She nodded, not sure what she was agreeing to. He lowered his voice to a whisper. "Perhaps next time you will see fit to accept my judgement."

The rebuke stung. She lifted her head and stared past Levi, defiant even as she fretted she might have lost her brother's regard.

"Relax Kordahla," Mariano continued. "I cherish your spirited ways, but all indication is that Terlaan is not ready for a woman such as you. There are repercussions to your actions, doubly so in these strange days."

Kordahla felt a surge of bitterness. "You don't need to lecture me, Mariano. I am well aware of the consequences I will face when Father thrusts me into Ahkdul's arms.

Chapter Five

LADY JORDAYNE DEL GIORDANO, niece to Shah Ordosteen and second in line to the Myklaani throne, was accustomed to needing no introduction and certainly no ushering when she set foot inside the Mage Guild. When the ignorant, carrot-haired apprentice who intercepted her in the airy entrance requested she wait in the empty front room until a mage could attend to her unannounced visit, she fixed him with a regal stare.

"My dear," she said, "my patronage pays for your tuition and the robes on your back, not to mention the amorous attentions of Master Magus Drucilamere. I trust you will remember that in future."

Having educated the scruffy lad, she strode down the green tiled passage into the heart of the guild. The shuffle of his feet as he followed sounded satisfyingly hesitant beneath the jingle of the metal ornaments adorning her skirt and cropped bodice. As was her habit, she paused in the back room to admire the breath-taking panorama of the rugged coastal rocks that swept around isolated Mage Cove on Lake Tejolin. Beyond the northern arm of the bay, Myklaan's neat capital, Kaijoor, nestled inside stone walls. Wyn deq Kaelor, whether one blessed him, cursed him, or most likely blessed and cursed in equal measure, had had the vision of a Myklaani when he constructed this guild on the slender promontory some three hundred years past. Backed by low cliffs and isolated enough to afford the mages the privacy they required, it nonetheless kept Kaijoor in their sight in times of unrest. Not to mention the spectacular views and extravagant fittings, every bit as sumptuous of those in the palace.

"This is a pleasant surprise," Drucilamere said, emerging from his study to the left end of the room. He was, she was pleased to note as he walked the length of the oak table which dominated the room, beaming at her. For that, Jordayne flung her arms around him and, standing on tiptoe, pulled his head down and pressed her lips hard against his, one hand sliding inappropriately low down his back as his found her bare waist.

She broke the embrace as abruptly as she had initiated it, running a teasing finger along the edge of his dark green kamarband, and trying not to breathe too deep of the intoxicating pine scent he wore. "The pleasant part will come later, Druce. We have business to attend to."

"That will be all, Brailen," Drucilamere said to the gaping apprentice without the slightest hint of shame. Jordayne stepped to the room-length window with a seductive tilt of her back. The irksome lad remained fixated on her bosom and midriff until Drucilamere cleared his throat. Remembering in whose company he dawdled, Brailen jumped and fled down the stairs like a hare pursued.

"Anyone would think the boy had never seen a woman before," she said, amused.

"None so brazen as you, I'm sure, Jordayne. Although, I must say I would have thought today's garb a little modest for your taste."

"I'll treat you to a spectacle of the flesh later, darling. I've rather missed your bold approach to lovemaking. Satrap Sorkel is far too gallant, and as for the palace guards, well, they do rather have to be put in their place." Satisfied she had kindled a spark of jealously, she walked along the glass. The green tiles of the passage continued as a border and central motif among the white tiles of this room, ensuring it remained light and airy on overcast days. The walls were plain but for a band of calligraphy quoting magical lore, directing the occupants' attention to lake and cove. She gazed out past the small dock, at the boat bobbing on the waves. Withholding her attentions from Drucilamere had nothing to do with their hectic schedules and everything to do with punishing him for his oversight with the guild's porrin merchant. Jordayne believed men were there to serve, in every way imaginable.

Her back to her favourite lover, she executed an artful stretch. "But to the dreary task of business first. I received a report from Mykver Fort that our dear porrin supplier Raj entered Myklaan eight days ago. He was searched, routinely of course, and found to be carrying a five-weight more than the agreed quantity of porrin. For once, the soldiers followed their orders and passed him unchallenged. Two accompanied him south on the pretext of having business in the city, but there's been no word they have arrived." Frustrating, since it was only a seven-day ride from the pass to Kaijoor. "The cheating scum of a man has to be lodging somewhere, most probably Zulmei."

Drucilamere's breathy attention as he absorbed the information brought a smile to her lips. As always, Jordayne was refusing to allow a business conversation to disguise her feminine charms. Their allure, she congratulated herself, was a significant accomplishment for one of modest looks, with straight ash blonde hair, and a boyish figure. The tilt of her hips, the pout in her lips were skilfully cultivated to disarm the men she dealt with by kindling their lust. Two minutes into a conversation the fools realised that not only did her station supersede their own and her intellect leave them stammering children, but they desperately desired a woman they were unlikely, ever, to bed. The tall Master Magus, while not as gullible or stupid as some, was no exception. Apart from their lovemaking, of course. Though starting to sport specks of grey in that distinguished moustache of his, he was probably the most pleasurable lover she had ever taken to her bed. She turned to find him openly feasting his eyes on her.

"Magus Trove scried Raj leaving Zulmei three mornings past. If he has not delayed further, our porrin merchant should arrive at the city gates late this afternoon."

"How is our dear senior mage?" she asked, watching a gull dive for fish.

"I'm afraid you will be shocked."

The gravity of his tone drove away her languid pretence. Fearing the worst but not daring to ask, she hastened down the stone steps to the lower level and the huge back room. The frieze of porrin leaves running along the three frescoed walls had, for centuries, proclaimed the status of Myklaani mages. With the populace under the ravages of the drug, it now mocked the plight of the realm. At the back wall, mages Santesh and Kaztyne bent over tasks at elaborately carved desks, taking the occasional moment to gaze out at the rocky landscape when spray pattered against the glass. On the far side of the room, Brailen and the serious older apprentice, Shom, looked up from the books they were pouring over as she entered, but hastily resumed their study. Jordayne almost missed Magus Trove dozing in a large armchair set in a narrow pool of sunshine in the centre of the room. She gasped when she saw him. In a matter of eight-days, the ancient fellow had shrivelled to skin and bone. Having forgone a kamarband, the green silk kurta the mages wore in deference to the ruling house swallowed him. At her chaste, fond kiss on the cheek, he opened his eyes.

"I didn't need porrin to see you coming, Jordayne. I could hear you approach from the other end of the cove," he said, his voice a raspy husk.

A swirl of her hips set the metal baubles on her skirt jingling. "One should never be without music," she replied, and sat on the arm of the chair.

Trove patted her hand. His translucent skin was parchment dry. "Your melody brightens my day."

"Indeed it does," Drucilamere said, exiting the stairs. He came to stand beside her.

Trove took a rattle of a breath. "You will forgive an old man for dispensing with the pleasantries but I grow tired and there is work to be done before I fall back to sleep. I believe you wish me to scry our merchant friend Raj." He coughed so hard he needed to grip her leg to prevent himself falling off the chair. Dear Vae'oenka, his breath held the stench of decay.

She flashed a concerned look at Drucilamere as she eased him into the armchair's depths. "Merchant turned smuggler, it seems. But I hardly think you are up to the task. Let Druce do it."

Between a smattering of coughs, Trove waved a hand to decline. “Why subject these healthy young bodies to porrin’s stress when mine is already ravaged?”

Standing drew the mages’ attention, though shy, dark-haired Santesh avoided her green-eyed stare by bowing his head and allowing his hair to fall over his eyes. The young mage was not yet adept, but Druce had said brown-haired, friendly-faced Kaztyne scried true. She should have acknowledged the journeyman’s grimace of disagreement with Trove but her voice settled on chill all on its own.

“The magician’s creed decrees you must share the burden. Need I be the one to remind you all of your code?” she said.

Trove shook his head and clutched her hand, urging her to reason. “Porrin is not entirely to blame for what you see. A growth eats at my innards and gnaws on my nerves. I take the seed gladly for it dulls the pain.”

She pursed her lips to digest the news. She had neglected this guild in favour of the hospice for far too long. Porrin’s blight had necessitated it. Drawing a deep breath, hoping it would hide her apprehension, she said, “Then take the porrin, Trove, but spare yourself the exhaustion of working magic.”

“My dear, you would surely not deprive an old man of the only worth he has?

“Vae’oenka bless you, Trove,” Jordayne said, planting a lingering kiss on his lips. “You know you will always be worth your weight in gold to Myklaan, and double that to me.” Tears welled in memory of all the times she had delighted in his acerbic company. His friendship with her father, and then his affair with her, had seen him lodge at the family estate with increasing regularity as she grew to womanhood.

“Is that an offer, Jordayne?” Trove asked with a cheeky grin.

“She is already spoken for,” Druce said, with a proprietary raise of his thick eyebrow.

“You are mistaken,” Trove said, shaking a finger his way. “It is you who are spoken for, am I not right Jordayne? And as yet, I am not. At least not at present.”

"An interesting notion, to experience what you *both* have to offer, but I am afraid the exertion may see the end of you, Trove," Jordayne said, running a hand along Druce's arm. His presence really was a comfort.

"But what a way to go, lass."

She laughed at that. "I could not bear the guilt."

"So I must make do with your company."

"Be grateful for it. I do not bestow it lightly."

Trove took her hand and brought it to his lips. "You are your father's daughter."

"Not truly, Trove, thanks to you. One might say I am as much your creation as his." The truths he had imparted about the world, as she sat on his knee and, later, lay in his bed, had primed her for the canny grasp of politics she possessed today.

As she got up, Brailen hastily buried his nose in his book. On the wall by the stairs, above a painting of brooding Faradil Forest, Drucilamere pushed a trigger hidden among the frieze. A concealed trapdoor grated open on a yawning space. The little fool of an apprentice immediately jumped up. Judging by his gawp, he had not known it was there.

"Quite the trusted one, aren't we?" she mocked.

"Jordayne," Drucilamere murmured. He took a candle from Santesh's desk and disappeared into the void. Pouty Carrot Hair made to follow until Kaztyne cleared his throat in prohibition. Jordayne sauntered over and through the opening, careful to rustle her skirts in a most provocative way.

"She's not even part of this guild," she heard the rude boy complain.

"Lady Jordayne is anything and everything in Myklaan, more so than Shah Ordosteen, and you had best remember that, my lad," Trove's distinctive rasp answered. The dear man had always known she would amount to more than a courtier, had lavished his knowledge and attentions on her when her father was too busy preparing her younger brother, Matisse, for the role of Satrap of San Xalid to bother with a daughter.

"Upsetting the apprentices, Jordayne?" Druce asked as she stood so close her hip touched his thigh.

"Would I be me if I didn't upset every male within arm's reach? You seem to have a reasonable stockpile of porrin."

The dark room was lined with shelves that stretched from floor to ceiling, about a third of them packed with earthy-sweet porrin leaves, fragrant dried flowers and jars of ground seed. She glanced towards the corner stairway that descended to a series of similar storerooms carved into the damp rock beneath the guildhall.

"This is it, I'm afraid," Druce said, following her line of sight. He set the candle on a dusty shelf. "The cellars are empty of porrin, although they are keeping some fine wine from your family's province in top condition."

This sparse supply was scarcely what Wyn deq Kaelor would have had in mind when he built the palatial guild. There were rooms enough for thirty mages, and storage space capable of holding more porrin than Verdaan produced in a year. The heady smell of the herb should have permeated the entire hall.

"How much is this, in practical terms?" she asked, watching the shadows of the plants leap over the shelves.

"For three mages, this supply would last eight-days. For five…they would be inadequate if Myklaan is ever threatened."

Jordayne frowned. For six major moons, the quantities of porrin delivered by the Verdaani merchant had been dwindling, and that in spite of the rather hefty price remaining the same. At first, her magical lackwits had believed Raj's rather improbable tales about production problems and border security. When the mages *had* chosen to report it, just two months past, she and her brother Matisse had taken a rather different view. Delivery of only two thirds of the usual porrin supply warranted investigation. Jordayne had ordered Raj followed. Unfortunately, their supplier had been on his way home and they had had to wait an entire month for his return, when surveillance of both the magical and ordinary kind revealed he stopped at a bordello prior to his appointment at the guild. He had emerged, hours later, with a satisfied smirk and a considerably lighter pack. The intriguing question was why. The mages, granted a heavy subsidy from the Shah, paid vastly more for the drug than the black market of commoners ever could.

She could have ordered the double-dealing merchant arrested that day while he basked in the throes of an imaginative passion. Instead, she had dared Drucilamere in his magical trance to witness it to the end and later replicate it in her bedchamber. But while she had no qualms convicting a man on the say so of a mage, the rulers of Verdaan, lacking access to any but the most rudimentary magic, might not be so favourably inclined. She was, after all, attempting to avert hostilities, not promote them. So, she had exercised patience, one of her few virtues, and plotted a trap to catch him in the act, because, so far, a plausible explanation for his behaviour eluded them.

"Do you think this is Verdaan's way to ensure we are on equal footing, in preparation for an attack?" she asked lightly, closing the door. She had already discussed the idea with Matisse. Their conclusions had been identical. More numerous, superbly trained, and better funded, Myklaan's soldiers could not only repel an attack from Verdaan but conquer their rustic northern-western neighbour without undue effort. It was holding the land they acquired, replete with hostile swamps, craggy hills, and dim forests, that would prove testing.

"It is not Verdaan I think we should be worried about."

That caught her attention. "What has this to do with Terlaan?"

"That I cannot say, except that Trove has been imbibing the porrin on a regular basis. It is the only way he gets any rest. He dreams the mage dreams, but they are tumbled visions without form. His eyes are haunted when he wakes, and all he remembers is the future shows no trace of the mages in Myklaan. The world is changing, he says, but the specifics elude him."

She grew quiet, contemplative, as she considered asking whether the disease tainted Trove's visions. It took a mere moment to dismiss the idea. She knew Trove every bit as well as she knew Drucilamere. Better even. "And since you cannot envisage Verdaan as a threat, you conclude the danger lies in Terlaan?" she said at last, shaking her head. "It is unfounded speculation."

"The mahktashaan outnumber and outpower the mages, yet Myklaan prospers where Terlaan ekes out an existence. I find it incredible they have not attacked before now."

"Our histories are full of less than amiable encounters. We have always prevailed, if with hardship. While Terlaan hardly struggles to survive, their resources are insufficient to wage a protracted war," she countered. With barren, rocky plains forming most of the realm's interior, they would run out of provisions before they inflicted any lasting damage.

"With a powerful mahktashaan army they could devastate us in eight-days. Sooner, if we have no porrin. And your patronage of those inclined towards artistic pursuits is depleting our stock of apprentices. Brailen was the best we could find, and he's shaping up to be a sorry specimen if ever there was one." He picked a packet of sterile porrin seeds off the shelf.

"You can hardly blame the young fools, darling. A lifetime of exacting study, wasting away under carefully meted out quantities of porrin can hardly compete with the romantic life of an artist struggling to achieve recognition, especially when the latter so casually imbibes the bliss for inspiration. But there is yet another possibility to consider." He frowned. She could tell his thoughts headed across the seas. It was not the direction she had in mind. She stood on tiptoes and kissed him. "Do try to think, darling," she said, knowing exactly what his mind would be on after her touch. "With no direct heirs to the Myklaani throne, I should have thought the mages would be looking in only one direction." She held a finger to his lips, shushing his words. "Trove is waiting for us. You can astound me with any further deductions tonight."

She brushed past Drucilamere as he released the catch of the hidden door.

"What were you doing in there," Trove said. "Leaving an old man to his imagination?"

"Trust me, Trove, your imagination couldn't even come close," Jordayne said.

The annoying Brailen had given up any pretence of reading. Unable to decide if his attention should rest on the porrin seed Drucilamere had withdrawn or Jordayne's bosom, he really did seem to be the disappointment Druce claimed.

"Attend here," Drucilamere called the apprentices, showing more than a hint of annoyance. He tipped the dark seed into a mortar and set

Brailen to pounding it to dust, admonishing him for sloppy work when the apprentice complained his arm was aching so.

"What in Vae'oeldin's name were you thinking by admitting that one?" Jordayne asked Trove.

"I can't remember," the mage replied. "It must have happened when I was under porrin's bliss."

Shom had the responsibility of mixing the powder with water.

"A perfect blend," Drucilamere praised, taking the red potion.

"Here, let me," Jordayne said, rolling her eyes at Brailen's jealous pout. The lad had to be at least sixteen years, yet he affected the mannerisms of one much younger. She reassumed her seat on the chair's arm, and held the cup to Trove's lips, dispensing small sips until her mage's head rocked back, his unfocused eyes opened wide and his limbs slackened. A small gurgle escaped his throat and spittle dribbled from the corner of his mouth. Tenderly, Jordayne wiped it away with the top layer of her skirt. Taking Trove's hands, Drucilamere and Kaztyne closed their eyes and hummed Raj's name. The focusing ritual drew her mind back to the one time she had persuaded a mage to use his magic to heighten her pleasure in bed. There would be no repeat of that particular ecstasy with porrin in such short supply.

She searched Trove's face for any sign of him slipping too far into the bliss. The mages knew their business, but her shrewd mentor was a shell of his former self. She felt a pang of grief that his time in this world was drawing to a close; forced herself to search instead for signs of the strain that indicated he was returning to them.

It was some minutes before he blinked, longer until he was able to stammer a response. "T-Raj has j-just left E-Emry Village. His p-packs seem lighter."

Which meant he had already unloaded porrin. For his growing audacity, the merchant deserved a special welcome this afternoon. "Can you scry him when he gets here?" she asked, loathe to place this additional burden on a sick man, but knowing if Druce was right about the threat to the mages they had no choice. They could not risk Raj evading the disguised guard Matisse had set at the gate to follow him. Nor could they wait another moon to try again. The porrin merchant must face the consequences of his deceit.

"For you, Jordayne, anything."

"He talks like one enamoured of you," Druce said, a slight frown visible beneath his amused smile. "And here I was thinking him the only one with influence over our wayward Lady."

"Mind your tongue, boy," Trove retorted.

Jordayne leant across Trove and kissed him on the lips. "Well aren't you? Weren't you always, right from the time you taught me the pleasures of the bedroom?

"You have no shame, girl. Nor a heart," Trove said, pulling her back for another kiss.

"Shame is akin to regret. Not something I like to waste passion on, but you shall always occupy a special place in my heart," she said, rising. "Now see if you can make things right with Druce. I wouldn't want him to miss the treat I promised. And do see he brings some of that wine he mentioned." And with that she walked right past Drucilamere and up the stairs with the tinkle of jewellery, leaving Brailen gawping, the other mages politely trying to pretend they had missed the exchange and Drucilamere standing dumfounded, opening and closing his mouth with undisguised desire in his eyes.

Chapter Six

TWO SEVERED HEADS, SITTING atop spikes high on the wall beneath the blazing sun, was not a sight Kordahla expected to have to endure. Twenty sleek crows pecking strips of flesh from flaccid cheeks was a nightmare which would torment her to the end of her days. As she turned away from the arched window, breath held to avoid a whiff of bloody decay, and fingers over her tight lips to keep the bile from rising into her throat, she realised she ought to have known better. Father, in his infinite generosity, liked to punish her mischiefs thrice over. Forgoing the fresh air she was craving after languishing forgotten in her rooms the entire afternoon, she lay on the plush daybed, hugged one of the embroidered cushions to her stomach and tried to imagine ways she might avoid being traded off as Ahkdul's brood mare. While her riotous imagination gushed scenarios, the only viable alternative seemed to involve death, unfortunately hers. As romantic a notion as a handsome Myklaani prince finding her sprawled on the flowery bedcover, her dying breath saved for a kiss, might be, she was not ready to enter Vae'oenka's realm. She pursed her lips. Neither was she prepared to spend the rest of her life as a chattel to the notorious pervert.

When the door to her rooms opened, she merely turned her head. The only two people who ever entered without knocking were Father and Vinsant. She smiled as her younger brother bounded onto the burgundy woollen rug, clutching something beneath a blue coat it was far too warm for him to be wearing.

"I hope you didn't see fit to bring the grapper into my apartment. I've suffered more than enough gruesome for a lifetime," she said, sitting up as he juggled his secret stash.

"So you looked out of the window then? I came to warn you not to," Vinsant replied. He wriggled three books out of the coat and deposited them on the low walnut table by the daybed. "Get rid of your maids, will you? I want to talk."

"I sent them to pick some flowers," Kordahla said, reaching for the top book, a weighty treatise on international relations. It looked decidedly boring, but she had to admit Vinsant had, as usual, chosen a relevant topic. "Their inquisitiveness would have made anyone think an execution was the height of entertainment."

Vinsant's guilty look near crushed her heart. He couldn't have intuited how she felt because he knelt on the bed to get a better look out of the window. "Awesome." The little monster had the decency to start when she squeaked. "Er, I mean gross. Father says porrin is destroying Terlaan. The mahktashaan arrest more and more addicts every day, but for every execution two more seek solace in its bliss."

"And what do you say?" she asked quietly, wondering if she had lost her only true ally.

He pulled the shutters closed, and shuffled on his knees to face her. The sun struck through the slats, striping across an expression more serious than she had ever seen him wear. "I heard Levi tell Father there is no winning the battle by fighting the visible enemy. Our army must strike at the traitor who allows our nemesis access to our ranks."

"Oh." Those sounded like Levi's words right enough.

"Father flew into a rage and ranted about sending troops to the borders and tripling the number of customs officers. But I don't think that's what Levi really meant."

"Is it that bad?" she asked, beginning to feel safe within the confines of the palace.

Remaining on his knees, Vinsant nodded. His stillness was uncharacteristic. "I think Levi meant we must discover why people desire the bliss so much."

"Isn't it obvious?" From safe on the ramparts, she watched the ragged poor queue for food, and the dazed sick beg for alms each eight-day. The drug was rumoured to transport people to Vae'oeldin's domain. Its influence over her had dwindled before she could fly to the moons, thanks to Arun, but for a wonderful, liberating minute she had sensed a vastness to the life she had never guessed existed. In a world of ceaseless toil, hunger and pain, was escape such a bad thing?

"But would you take it? I mean, knowing that you'll waste away under its sway or be executed as an example to all."

It was her turn to look abashed.

Vinsant paled. "Promise me you won't," he said. "You can never, ever take it."

The incongruity of that struck her. How many times had she said those exact words to him? "I can't live as Ahkdul's wife," she blurted. She winced and looked away, busying herself shaking the folds in the silk curtains straight. The last thing she had intended was to burden him with her fears, but if porrin's kiss was the only way to endure life in Verdaan, she doubted she would have the strength to resist, whatever horrors it might bring.

"I'll think of something," Vinsant said, sitting next to her and hugging a cushion in much the same way she had. "I'll find a way to stop it happening."

She took a deep breath and searched his face. "They whisper he prefers taking little boys to his bed." It near killed her, the need to have this talk with him. "When he's here, mind you are never alone with him."

He turned up his nose in disgust. "I'm not a child. Besides, he wouldn't dare."

Oh wouldn't he, Kordahla thought. The pleasure of his acquaintance had been theirs nine years back, at yet another of Shah Ordosteen of Myklaan's marriages. When Vinsant had disappeared during the celebration, she had spent a frantic half hour searching for him before spying him hand in hand with Ahkdul, who was heading towards the bedchambers. She had snatched him from Ahkdul with promises of a special surprise, and fled to the safety of the gathering. Convinced nothing untoward had happened and scared of the repercussions, she had remained silent, refusing to let Vinsant out of her sight for a moment during the remainder of their stay.

"I'm looking forward to his visit," Vinsant said with a frown. "Know your enemy, that's what Levi says."

"You seem to be paying a great deal of attention to what Levi says." It worried her. There was a self-serving streak about the man.

"He has an excellent grasp of politics," Vinsant said, sounding just like Mariano. "And he wields a great deal of power. He has to, doesn't he, to be Majoria."

"Yes," Kordahla said with a sigh and hugged Vinsant because they were alone so he would permit it. "I suppose he does."

"Why don't you like him?" he asked, batting her with the cushion so he could wriggle free of her arm.

"He's always staring at me."

Vinsant laughed. "I told you why."

"When his attention is on me, I feel like I've committed some treason." She shivered.

"Levi's all right, you know."

"But you didn't tell him you were borrowing these books."

Vinsant squirmed off the bed. Kordahla sighed again. It was luck she could read and write at all, and that only at her mother's insistence. Not for the first time she rued her reliance on Vinsant to smuggle in texts. What need had a Princess of learning, Father declared after Mother's demise. A level of education to converse on household matters, not one to flabbergast prospective suitors was most suitable for women of this realm. Barred the libraries, she had swallowed her pride and listened to her much younger brother talk of his lessons, gleaning what knowledge she could until, sensing her interest and the unjustness of her exclusion, he began tutoring her.

"I'm going to train as a mahktashaan," he said. He skidded around the room in clumsy emulation of the mahktashaan glide that saw him clip the corner of her curvy-legged dresser and brush the handle of her wardrobe. The creamy derral inlay sparkled all the colours of the rainbow in the shafts of sunlight poking through the slats.

Her eyes followed him. "Whose idea is this?" she asked, swallowing.

"Mine." He whirled to face her. "I've already discussed it with Father. He agreed I might apprentice to Levi directly. Ahkdul won't wed you for months, and by then I might have enough power to prevent it."

Kordahla stared at him, then patted the bed. He shrugged and hoisted himself onto her coffer. One finger traced the inlay.

"Vinsant, it takes years to become a mahktashaan. You couldn't possibly achieve that degree of power before Father arranges a wedding. You mustn't throw your future away on account of me."

He brought his feet up onto the coffer, and hugged his knees. "Why do you hate the mahktashaan? I'm the second son of a Shah. I'll spend my days overseeing some minor castle if I'm not married off to Lord Hudassan's niece and sent to supervise the destruction of the porrin fields. That would be a fate worse than yours."

Since he would be his own lord once Hudassan did them the favour of dying, Kordahla heartily doubted it. As an attempt to allay her fears, it was pathetic. "Pettina is only eight or so. You're in no danger of being married off to her any time soon."

He jumped off the coffer and squared his shoulders. "Anyway, if I have the talent, Levi's agreed to train me for the position of Majoria. Then I'd wield almost as much power as Mariano when he's Shah."

She had never thought of Vinsant as power-hungry. The allure had to lie in the mystery of those black-clad, hooded soldier-magicians. If unravelling a secret allowed him to assist her in any small way, he was unstoppable. She shivered again, and rubbed the goosebumps that had erupted along her arms. She couldn't be sick; Vinsant had belted his coat.

"A still wind is blowing," she said, her breath forming a white puff. She picked up a cashmere blanket from the daybed to toss around her shoulders. They both made the sign of warding. The temperature, if anything, grew chillier. She stood and turned about the room, fear prickling along the nape of her neck.

"Don't go," she said to Vinsant. Wide-eyed, he shook his head. Even let her take his hand when the flickering air in front of the door exuded the salted, seaweed tang of the sea. She gagged as it thickened into substance until a djinn floated before them, vermillion eyes blazing beneath a mop of black hair, indigo skin shocking beneath a shiny vest the colour of his eyes. Vinsant wrinkled his nose.

"You're real," Kordahla breathed, repeating the warding sign. For all the stories, superstitions and inexplicable chills, never had she thought to meet a djinn in the iridescent flesh. She would have fled to her bedchamber had Vinsant not wrenched his icy hand from hers.

The djinn snorted, and the curls on the end of his slippers rolled tighter. "Of course I'm real, impudent child. Do you think the *gods* waste their time toying with you foolish beings? Do you think the still winds a quirk of nature, or a figment of your piddling imaginations?" He flicked dirt as black as his shalvar from under his nail. She sidestepped it, dropping the blanket to make a grab for her impetuous little brother. To her horror, Vinsant dodged. Wrinkling his freckled nose, he began walking a wide circle around the shimmering creature, too calm to have understood their peril.

Kordahla folded her arms tight under her bosom. "What b-business h-have you with us?" It was unfortunate that, chilled to the marrow, she sounded insecure.

The query had the djinn bending over with hysterics. "Grubs on the earth!" He flew dizzying circles around the room, forcing Vinsant so hard against her wardrobe the solid thing rocked, its back thumping against the wall, its legs thudding on the floor. She spun to keep track of his blur, had to stop so she would not topple, and shuddered to think he lurked behind her. When he settled, he reclined in the air, head resting on a hand, one leg bent up at the knee. The indigo crystals which formed his joints pulsed with a muted glow. The utter strangeness of it caught her breath and sent her heart into an ill-timed gallop.

"A magical creature appears as you discuss your future, and the best you can think to do is ask why I am here."

She cringed at the whiff of fish in his breath. Lunged at Vinsant as he stepped forward. His sidestepping evasion was effortless. Dear Vae, what was he thinking, marching right up to the djinn.

"You're here to grant us a wish then?" he asked, eyes narrowed.

The djinn blew, and Vinsant flew across the room and landed on his behind. He looked more surprised than hurt.

"Name me flea, and I must do as you bid. Otherwise, you are my tools."

"But you can't compel us," Vinsant said, scrambling up. He had the good sense to keep close to the wardrobe. "You're forbidden to interfere."

"Rules change, flea." The djinn sat, his crossed legs level with Kordahla's head.

"We won't make a pact with you," Kordahla said. She swallowed. "Nothing you can grant is worth the price you would ask."

The djinn unfolded into an indolent stretch, arms high over his head. "A pity, since you have not yet asked the price. I knew you would be too pig-headed to deal."

"Then I ask again, what business have you here?" She retreated from his fishy stench, past her walnut dresser to Vinsant and the wardrobe. Her little brother was rubbing at the frost that had beaded over the handles. Vae'oenka preserve them, the djinn was drifting after her, his rotting teeth as hideous as his leer. His features blurred and shifted, melding, by the horrors, into the Ahkdul's thick prominent brow and large nose. A substantial hand groped for her breast. As she opened her mouth to scream, he grabbed her shoulders and kissed her hard. Vinsant lunged, but the djinn spun to the roof with a malicious laugh. Unable to stop, her brother careered across the rug, and went sprawling across the daybed.

Nauseated, Kordahla stumbled towards the door. She wanted the mahktashaan in here, though she was scarcely able to believe she felt that way. Quicker than lightning, the stinking djinn flashed into her path. Dangling upside down, he waggled a finger at her. She took a step back.

"Only a self-deprecating imbecile would allow herself to be molested by a swine like Ahkdul. Perhaps I am wasting my time."

On the verge of tears, Kordahla snapped. "Just what do you suggest I do? Give myself to you in exchange for protection?"

The djinn cocked his head and closed one eye, appearing to consider the ludicrous idea. "An interesting suggestion," he said at length. "But you lousy grubs hold no attraction."

"Touch me again and I'll spend my life uncovering your name. I'll send mahktashaan laden with salt to the ends of the earth to bind you."

"That, you annoying gnat," he drawled, sliding into the horizontal position he seemed to favour, "is the most sensible thing you've said since yesterday."

"You were watching me!" Outrage was beginning to replace her shock. The warmth it brought to her cheeks was welcome.

He drifted around her. "You do make an entertaining study. But where were we? What would any self-respecting princess do if about to be married off to a male-rutting boar? If she were condemned to a life of misery and subservience to ensure her elder brother had a prosperous rule? What, Princess, would she do if she had no hope of evading the inevitable in her father's domain?"

Kordahla shook her head and sidled toward the bedroom door. She wanted this creature gone. His truths were too confronting.

"What could a princess do if there was no escape while she remained in her father's house?" the djinn repeated.

"Nothing," she replied. "Nothing in this patriarchal country. Though, I suppose you would think running away a sensible option."

"Ahh," the djinn said.

She eyed him with suspicion. His devious manipulation had doubtless prompted her to arrive at this absurd solution.

"You can't," Vinsant said, voicing her own thoughts. "That's crazy."

"Very well, flea. Leave her for the swine, and take yourself along for company if you miss her so, though you are a trifle old for Ahkdul's taste."

Vinsant's worry as he regarded her made him look so young. Her mouth turned dry. Refuge in Myklaan would be a gift from the gods. Women were allowed an education. Vae'oenka's blessing, from all she had heard, they were valued members of society. There had to be a noble who would find her appealing enough to marry.

"They'd never," she whispered, running her sweating hands over her curvy hips. "They'd never harbour me. If father found out, or Ahkdul, it would mean war." Liberal their ideas might be but the Myklaani would not risk all for a single Terlaani woman, however noble.

The djinn backflipped until he was upside down, his clothing remaining in perfect place. “Indeed, you have nothing to offer. What could a *Terlaani* possibly offer Myklaan? There is nothing in this barren land of interest to thriving Myklaan, now, is there.”

When he put it like that, it was obvious.

“I’ll get you one,” Vinsant said. “I’ll have access as soon as Levi apprentices me.”

“I doubt it will be that easy. Or that one will suffice.” Until she spoke she had not realised she was actually entertaining the notion. At her side her hands were trembling. She cupped them in front of her mouth and blew.

The djinn tugged a corner of fabric from inside his vermillion kamarband. “Don’t disappoint me,” he said, teasing out the embroidered green rectangle and waving it in farewell. With a flutter of panic, Kordahla snatched at her veil. “That was Mother’s.”

The djinn winked. Before her hand had completed its arc, he disappeared in a puff of smoke and a whump of air.

She and Vinsant stared at each other, neither able to speak.

A tap at the door saw them both jump.

Chapter Seven

TIMAK COWERED IN THE corner of the cabin where he had been hiding the entire day. His tormentor seemed not to care his hands were idle. Aside from throwing him three pairs of boots to polish at daybreak, Ahkdul had ignored him. He held no hope that would last, so he had worked incessantly at his tether, rubbing the tips of his fingers raw until the knot unravelled enough for him to slip his foot free. Were it not for the sweet voice that chattered through the long hours, he might have smashed through the porthole and flung himself into the sea, diving deep until his chest screamed for air. She, whoever she was, cried aghast when he whispered of it.

There are sawtooths in these waters, she had said. *I've seen them. Maybe jabberwei too.*

That untruth coaxed a smile from him. The vicious, spiny relatives of crocs never left Verdaan's murky rivers.

And I'm not allowed to save you, she had finished.

Timak's smile died. That last implied that she could. "Who are you?" he asked for the fourth or fifth time.

A faint scent of roses rippled through the sandalwood perfume splashed over the aging timbers of the cabin. "A friend," was all she would say. From her artless turn of the conversation, to throwball, and syrup cakes, and secret hidey-holes, he guessed she was not much older than he.

"I know your name's Yazmine," Timak said.

Her sharp breath ended on heavy silence. He stood and strained for a sound, hearing nothing but the slap of water on the dipping bow, the flap of wind in the sail, the murmur of husky, unconcerned voices, and the cry of a faraway gull. The thought of her gone made him wobble. He could never bear it if she left.

Down into the sea, until water stole his breath.

He scuttled onto the narrow bunk, wrinkling the musty sheets. The magical Myklaani glass covering the porthole was cold against his hand. He squinted at the gold-streaked ocean, and the glare of the ailing sun

"Oh, don't, Timak." The voice was just a whisper.

He swallowed. The lengthening shadows threatened. When they reached the coffer, Ahkdul would force him to suffer the unspeakable on this creaky bed.

The door rasped against the floor planks. A hulk of a figure filled the doorway. Timak leapt off the bed, and pressed his back to the chest of drawers.

"Here, youngster." The deep voice and short words were all wrong.

Timak let out his breath. The grey-haired, pony-tailed sailor entering his cell was no one to worry about. He turned back to the glare. "What if the sun doesn't set?"

The sailor clattered a bowl on the table next to the coffer. "The sun always sets," he said. "Night always falls, and with it the greater evils of the world."

Timak was not talking to him. "The sun's not sinking."

"Timak, you're facing north," Yazmine said. "You can't see the sun."

"Then what's that?" He pointed at the white glare beyond the glass.

The sailor shuffled to his side. The sturdy hand had no right to seek his shoulder. Timak flinched, and ducked. The sailor settled his hand on his hip.

"You've been speaking to yerself all day. The lot of 'em is saying you're crazy, touched by the djinn."

"Well he is," Yazmine said through a giggle. "Sort of."

"You're djinn," Timak said, quiet awe in his voice. He had drifted to sleep on Mama's stories of the devilish pranksters. He couldn't remember any in which they acted like comforting friends.

The sailor made the sign of warding. "Vae'omar raise the wind to carry us away."

"Imbecile of a genie!" The deep male voice vibrated the thin planks. "Dimwit." A nail popped loose and bounced across the floor. The sailor started. "Next time you fall into salt, I will leave you for the sawtooths."

"Who is that?" Timak asked, staring into the glare.

"Have a care, lad." The sailor gripped Timak by the arms and thrust his face within a hand of Timak's nose. Timak went rigid, his eyes widening large as the sailor's. Under the man's chafed hands, his bruises stung. He couldn't help his eyes watering, or the tremble in his lips. "Not even lust will see Lord Ahkdul keep yer if yer spook him good. If yer be playing a prank, it'll see you thrust overboard to the sawtooths, and if yer not..." He trailed off, releasing Timak. "Ah, take heart laddie," he said, shaking his head and looking at the feather pillow with its imprint of Ahkdul's broad head, the knot in the wood above the coffer, the bolts on the slanting legs of the table. Looking everywhere but at Timak. "Your river ain't leading to no fishing ground, but there's plenty is worse off than you."

When Timak didn't move, the sailor stepped to the door.

"Do you have children?" Timak asked.

The sailor tensed. Timak turned his head a twitch, so the big man would know the question was for him and not some creepy ghost. "Aye," the sailor answered.

"Will you bring your son on this boat? In place of me?"

His only answer was a footstep, followed by the click of the door. He closed his eyes and listened to the silence. A tear trickled down his cheek. "Yazmine?" Another tear fell into the lengthening hush. "Please don't leave me alone...Yazmine?"

"YOU TOLD HIM YOUR NAME?!" The rage gusted through the cabin, rocking the bowl.

Timak cringed.

"Do you want to be hurled back to ground, to wallow in your miserable little existence for an eternity until the Court forgives you? If they ever forgive you!"

He heard Yazmine stifle a sob. It wasn't right she fell prey to some brute. "Stop it," he said. "You're frightening her." A gust whipped him up before he had finished speaking. He crashed against the wall and slid to the floor, bashing his arm against the coffer. Pain jolted through his elbow into his shoulder. He curled up, drawing his arm against his chest. It hurt so much it might have broken.

"You puny speck of creation. Do you DARE tell a DJINN what to do?"

He gritted his teeth, squeezing his eyes tight against the pain. "It's your fault. You spoke her name. Yesterday, you called her." He cowered into the corner. Wind moaned through the cracks in the planks and ruffled his hair.

"No, don't!" Yazmine pleaded.

The wind died. The djinn clucked. Timak let out his breath.

"He can hear us," the djinn said.

"Shouldn't he?" Yazmine whispered. "I mean if he's got a gift."

"Mahktos grants no such gift."

Timak risked a peep. The glare had gone, leaving the ocean to ripple until it met the hazy sky. "Maybe it was the porrin," he said.

"The porrin has worn off, you miserable insect.

"It started with the porrin," Yazmine said.

"And should have ended with it," the djinn snarled. His glare burst into the cabin. "The Court must hear of this."

A force tugged Timak to the tips of his toes. An icy breath slid across his face and down his body, chilling him to the bone. He shivered. For the first time in his ten years, he understood what a *still wind* meant. He wished he didn't when his breath puffed through the glare, heating it so he could see a creature with a hint of red in his blazing eyes and a touch of indigo in his crystal joints. He sobbed as the djinn shook him until his teeth chattered.

"If you ever have the fortune to cower in our presence again, you will address us as Djinn and Genie. You will never call Yazmine by name again and you will never so much as breathe it to another living soul, whether it be one of your inconsequential kind, or an insignificant scumhopper. Squeal, and I will allow a thousand like Lord Ahkdul to take their pleasure with you in a single night, insect. I will hack off pieces of your flesh and feed them to jabberweis while you watch, cockroach. Do you understand?"

Mute with fear, Timak could only nod.

"You had better," the voice said. The invisible djinn released him. Timak collapsed against the table. The bowl rattled, releasing the smell of onion and fish. He waited but the voices were silent. His stomach grumbled. He didn't think he was hungry, but Ahkdul and djinn had dug a big hole inside him. He slid onto the bolted chair and pecked at the cold meal to try and fill the emptiness.

The shadows in the cabin lengthened. The hull groaned. His tormentor scuffed the door open. Ahkdul breathed deep as his sight roved where it shouldn't. Timak slipped out of the chair, his eyes flicking to the frayed rope in the corner. He needn't have worried. Ahkdul had eyes for him alone. The monstrous lord stepped forward. Timak backed up, right into the narrow bunk. The contact forced him to sit.

"Shall we begin?" his tormentor asked.

A deep breath gave Timak the courage he needed to ask, "Please, may I take some porrin?" Papa would have flushed red to hear him ask. There was never a day they walked passed a wasted, rocking addict when Papa did not warn of its dangers. *Only the down and out, the rebellious or the foolish sample its delights*, the finest, fittest soldier in all addicted Verdaan would warn. Right here, right now, Timak was all three. If a life of torture lay before him, he would exchange his mind for numb release from his captor's filthy touch.

"Timak. Timak." Lord Ahkdul sat next to him, and placed a hand on his knee. "It is so much more enjoyable for me if you don't."

That was when he realised how truly evil Lord Ahkdul was.

Escape if you can, his father had said. He would, even if it were into the jaws of a sawtooth. Lord Ahkdul must have guessed why he eyed the portal. The monster retrieved the rope, bound Timak by the ankle and secured the other end to the table. The leash permitted him the bunk but strained short of the deck.

"Now," Lord Ahkdul said, "be a good boy, although I shan't really mind if you kick and scream."

The torture began, and with it a sweet lullaby that carried him away from this cruel world to the dream of Vae'oenka's comforting embrace.

Chapter Eight

THE SECOND KNOCK WAS urgent. Kordahla stuffed the books under the pillows while Vinsant, looking guilty enough to give their deceit away, dallied about answering. There was a short exchange, too low for her to hear. Then he admitted a black-robed figure. He faced her, unfathomable with his features obscured, deferential in holding his gaze lower than hers, in standing at the edge of her rug.

"I came to enquire after your health, Princess." When the white puffs of his breath dispersed, Arun slid back his hood. It was not often the mahktashaan deigned to unrobe outside Counsel. His golden-brown hair and goatee were longer than she remembered but his face was, as on every occasion he had chosen to reveal himself, open and honest.

"I am fully recovered," she said, a trace of annoyance in her voice. The mahktashaan had no business seeking admittance to her rooms. This one, though, she was not at liberty to order out. The Minoria was not just the superior officer of the guards outside her door, but also one of her father's most trusted advisers. If she were honest, she would add he was Arun for, whatever his rank, she would not have tolerated his spooky superior in her chambers for the sole reason of asking after her wellbeing.

"Do you still wish instruction in the magical arts, Princess?" His eyes gently teased before sliding around the room.

He was a beast to remind her. "Does it please you to mock me?" Despite the sting in her voice, her humiliation forced her to look away from those striking cerulean eyes.

He glided across the rug, the thick pile barely denting beneath his feet, and placed an embossed, faded leather-bound book on the table. *Tales of the Djinn.* The title made her shudder. Arun squeezed her arm, at which she looked up, not entirely aggrieved by his liberty, not completely comfortable either.

"On the contrary, Princess. It is my sworn duty to protect this family. In fact, I am amazed you remember."

She remembered all right. Every single embarrassing moment, thanks to Levi. No doubt she would bear the brunt of Mariano's teasing for long years to come. If she were not peddled to Verdaan before Dindarin was full. She looked away, which caused him to release her arm. She immediately folded it across her chest to stave off the cold.

"It is chilly in here," Arun said, a deep furrow on his brow as he noted her goosebumps. He picked up the cashmere blanket she had left crumpled at the edge of the rug, and handed it to her with a bow. She draped it around her shoulders, comforted by the softness of the fibres.

Gawking at the pair of them, Vinsant scampered to the window and threw open the shutters. "Um, closed the window so Kordahla wasn't upset by you-know-what."

"Vinsant, if you are to join the mahktashaan, you must not lie to either Levi or me, though with the unranked you may take your chances. This chill is not natural. A still wind blows in this room."

Kordahla forced her shoulders back as he held his crystal to the corners. Deep within, it glowed the colour of his eyes. "If he joins the mahktashaan, I shall hold you personally responsible for his wellbeing, his upbringing and his safety." Her heart thumped faster, willing him to follow the conversation onto firmer ground.

He let the crystal settle back on his chest. "Vinsant will be under my tutelage, and that of Majoria Levi. I assure you Princess, though Levi inspires dread, we are not the brutes you think us. Thanks to you, Prince Vinsant is intelligent and principled enough to make his own way without much further direction, and I shall be honoured to ensure he remains so."

The flattery worked on Vinsant, who stopped imitating Arun with the ruby he had plucked from her silver filigree jewellery box and stood tall. That alone told her Arun was premature in his judgement. She struggled to find good reason why he should delay his training. "The apprentices," she began, allowing the blanket to fall from her shoulders onto the daybed. "They are older." She paused. The sun was streaming false cheer through the window.

"Princess Kordahla," the Minoria interrupted. "May we revert to our previous topic? What business had a djinn within this room?"

The mahktashaan served Shah and Majoria without question: such was their code. Yet Arun was so calm and undemanding, she was in danger of believing him trustworthy. She swallowed. "I cannot say. We saw no djinn." Vinsant might be prohibited from lying but she was certainly under no such obligation, not to a soldier and certainly not when her happiness was at stake.

The Minoria glanced at Vinsant, who hastily reopened her jewellery box and nestled the ruby inside with exaggerated care. Arun bowed his head. "So be it. I hope you will not do anything rash. Perhaps you will consider the nature of the higher world as you enjoy those tales."

Her eyes fell to the book on the table. The title was legendary. She had read to Vinsant from it when he was a child. What she had not remembered was the subtitle: *duplicity and deception*. Kordahla took a deep breath. Arun knew something. Something she did not. Else why would he bring that particular book? As always, Vinsant was quicker than her.

"Why did you bring Kordahla a book?"

"For much the same reason you do, my Prince."

Startled, Kordahla's eyes flicked between the two of them. Vinsant's face was pulling through comical expressions as he struggled to come to grips with discovery.

"Have no fear," Arun said, with a half-smile and a slight raise of his eyebrow that suggested to Kordahla he used the last word in jest. "Your discretion, Vinsant, has been commendable. Neither the Majoria nor the Shah are aware the Princess is well-read, but then neither spends as much time in the libraries as I."

"But why *that* book?" Vinsant persisted.

"My answer remains the same. But tell me, Princess, have you retrieved your veil?"

Her *mother's* veil, cherished and worn more than any other. Her guilt must have shown. Worse, there was a gravity about the question that turned the casual enquiry into one of great import. She had to wonder if Arun suspected in whose possession it had landed.

Kordahla shook her head. "I have not. Nor do I wish it, sullied as it is." The lie cut her so deep, she almost missed the fleeting fear which passed across the Minoria's face. He concealed it well as he turned to her brother.

"The Majoria is about to examine the grapper. Would you care to watch, young man?"

"You bet!" Vinsant fairly jumped in his excitement. She couldn't help but smile.

"Then we must take our leave, Princess. While I am bound by the oaths of my calling, I hope you will consider me a friend, and call upon me should the need arise."

"I thank you for your kindness, Minoria," she replied formally. His warning about his loyalty, to Father, to Levi, did more to earn her trust than his gift.

He bowed, drew up his hood, and left her staring at the book until her chatty handmaids returned with bunches of frangipani they arranged in vases around the room. Enamoured of tales of love and betrayal, Karie and Samille had kept her secret through the years, begging her of an evening to read to them until the words swam in front of her watering eyes. With a sigh, she picked up the volume and began a story, her mind drifting over their squeals of delight and horror onto her own adventure of escape.

Chapter Nine

CAPTAIN EDARD DEQ LUNGO really ought to know better than to propose that Lady Jordayne del Giordano not abase herself by entering the gentleman's establishment. Really, did he think she was about to miss out on all the fun? When the ingenious scheme was her idea too! There was no limit to the cheek of these men. One would think their fathers raised them in patriarchal Verdaan instead of Myklaan.

"But dear Captain," she said, placing a manicured hand on the brass latch. "It cannot be that bad. I do believe there are a host of other women inside." And with that she pushed open the freshly painted door and entered into a haze of smoke and billowing silks, setting a dozen bells jingling in the process. Inside, elaborate settees piled with plump cushions of exotic design lined the walls, a delightful place to wait for the attentions of the escorts if one could reach them without becoming entangled in the swags.

"There is, I suppose, no dissuading you?" Matisse said, trying, but not too hard, to prevent a smile breaking across his face. She would bet her entire forearm of gold bangles his tanned complexion and fair hair attracted the first seductress out of the internal door.

"None, dearest," she replied, patting his arm. "So you had best see to my reputation before Captain deq Lungo feels compelled to defend my honour."

"This can only enhance your reputation, Jordayne," Matisse said, with a throaty laugh, "though I'm not sure our uncle will feel mine is unsullied."

"Big sister will own up to it being all her idea. But do see to the Captain, there's a good boy. He's going to give the game away before it's even afoot."

The Captain's scandalised expression, accentuated by the hard, angular lines of his cheek and jaw, was intensifying by the second. Surprising really, given he sported the odd grey hair. His men, Vae'oenka bless them, supposedly the finest in the palace guard, looked like children in a candy store who faced a spanking if they touched. And not a female yet in sight, herself excluded. That did rather need to be remedied. They could not expect their quarry to walk in on a room full of guards, who despite their neat civilian clothing looked every bit the trained soldier, and take the bait.

Jordayne took the bell on the dainty desk at the back of the room and, reclining on the blue brocade of the nearest settee, waved it above her head. Its tinkle drew the men's heads her way. Decked in gold, wearing a scanty beaded choli about her bust, and a chiffon skirt that exposed her toned midriff and revealed more than a hint of shapely leg, she delighted in their lusty grins. Cultivated them, in fact. When the solid, reinforced inner door opened, she affected a yawn. The summons had taken minutes, not a timeframe to which an establishment of good repute aspired if it hoped to attract a better sort of clientele. She wondered where the spy-holes were and how long it had taken the proprietor to appraise her unusual guests.

A trim, eastern-looking lady, white hair swept into a high bun bowed their way. "I sorry. Our rooms full," she said in a singsong voice that hinted of the eastern lands. Her slanty, dark brown eyes were a picture of nervousness, roving between Jordayne, the Captain and Matisse.

"Oh dear. I had heard this was the place to come for a romp. My brother and I did so want to try a room." She saw a spark of colour in Matisse's cheeks. He was never as much fun as she hoped. "Not the same room, of course," she clarified. It would not do to take things too far. Yet.

"Sorry, Lady. All full. This place not for you. You go West End."

"This early in the afternoon? These men are not after liquor, madam."

"What you want? What palace guards and shah heir and lady want?"

Oh dear. Were they really *that* obvious? Well she was, and Matisse was getting to be, but the guards?

"We want admittance," Matisse said, taking charge. He dropped a bag of gold on the desk. "We want anonymity." His sky-blue eyes grew hard. "And we want your complete cooperation or we will shut this porrin den down and raze it to the ground before tossing you in the dungeons."

The woman bowed three times in rapid succession. "You come. Come. Many exquisite girls waiting. What you like? Blonde, brunette? Even redhead here. What you like?"

"You wouldn't happen to have a dark-skinned gladiator by any chance," Jordayne said, delighting in the madam's blink. Her grey shalvar kameez, tailored to the eastern style and embroidered in the same shade, only served to accentuate her elegance, something the years of her profession had failed to dull. "Never mind," Jordayne said, taking the woman by the arm. "This is what we want."

Less than two minutes later, the proprietor, her demeanour more stilted but no less alarmed, led the way through the maze of curtains to a room stuffed with settees and alabaster tables. Through the bittersweet haze of burning porrin leaves and the scarce privacy afforded by the silk drapes, Jordayne surveyed the patrons, a remarkable number given the early hour. Well-to-do men and women, the plump and the slim, the bald and the smooth-chinned, flamboyant all, reclined in various stages of a porrin stupor, spiked drinks on the table before them, while paramours of both sexes, modelling tasteful if flimsy garb, draped over their arms or laps.

"Open the windows, there's a dear," Jordayne said, moving into an unoccupied area. It would not do to have the men intoxicated before the smuggler arrived. "And find these men someone they like." She sighed as the woman executed a short bow.

"My lord," the captain said, addressing himself to Matisse. "I hardly think that is appropriate."

"You are not paid to think, Captain," Jordayne purred, sinking onto a gold-leaf settee with fabric the green of her eyes. She drew up her legs, ensuring a thin ankle was visible to all. "We must have the appearance of authenticity and I dare say the men would welcome a reward after a job well done."

If there had been any lingering resentment among the men at having a woman command, in a bordello no less, that sentiment dispelled it. They fanned into the room, one or two immediately beckoning to the girls streaming from the back. Not so Captain deq Lungo. From the strain on his reddening face, he could barely control his anger.

"My lady, they are men. If you want them to do their job, you cannot expect–"

"They are professionals," Matisse interrupted. He slid onto the settee opposite Jordayne and blew the smoke from his face. "They will not imbibe porrin and they will perform their duty when needed. And if we catch the culprit, Lady Jordayne's reward will be well-earned. It has certainly been paid for twice over."

The captain gave a short bow and sat next to Matisse, straight-backed and tight-jawed. His eyes might be reddening from the smoke but Matisse's word was certain law. With the exception of deq Lungo, who had assumed his position a few months past, her adroit brother had led these men for many a year. Such was their regard for him some had even followed him home to their estate in San Xalid when he had tired of Kaijoor, and back to the capital when their dear uncle declared him heir. Devilishly handsome, in a rugged but clean-shaven kind of way, and full of integrity despite a laidback, mocking manner, there was no finer choice for the throne. With the possible exclusion of herself, of course.

The proprietor returned with a harem of girls, some carrying trays of colourful drinks, others shimmying before the men until someone's fancy claimed the right to tug his desire onto his lap. For someone whose income in the next few hours would be more than she earned in a month, the silvering woman looked decidedly unhappy.

"Do join us," Jordayne invited, leaning back. "Be a gentleman and give the lady your seat, Captain." The fool bowed again before vacating their corner. It was luck the customers were too stupefied to notice. Matisse might consider deq Lungo a skilled fighter and able strategist, but she had laboured over this scheme too long to forfeit it to a man with morals. She leaned across to Matisse, who looked quite at home as he perused the flesh on offer. "Do something about that captain before I do."

"What you have in mind would probably do him the world of good."

A brief twitch of an eyebrow accompanied her closed lip smile. "You do give me ideas."

The proprietor watched the exchange with a bemused expression.

"Please." Matisse indicated the settee.

"Must see to girls," the woman said with a bow.

"Madam Yinmae," Matisse said. Jordayne raised an eyebrow at his familiarity. It seemed her brother still had his surprises. "I'm afraid we must insist on your company. I cannot take the chance our prey is forewarned."

Jordayne ran a finger along her skirt and twirled it into the hem. "Now I understand how we were recognised."

"On the contrary. Is there anyone in Kaijoor who would not recognise you, Jordayne? I can't take you anywhere anymore."

"Not so, dear brother. I insist you take me to all those fun places I don't seem to find out about until after the fact. You will sit, Madam." She sprawled out, leaving Yinmae no choice but to take a seat beside Matisse. The woman moved with a grace that belied her staccato words to sit prim and proper on the edge of the seat.

"Why you think we have crime here?" Yinmae asked.

"You mean aside from the porrin haze and drug-laced drinks?" Jordayne reached for her glass and took a sip. The alcohol and tart juice cocktail went down a treat. She waved an arm, setting all the bracelets jangling. "An incidental discovery. A chance finding, really. But one of these men just happened to be here last month." Assuming a more serious demeanour, she leaned forward. "He recognised the dealer."

The truth involved more than that, of course. Nothing *just happened* where Jordayne was concerned. Not even, despite what the vast majority of Myklaan might believe, her passionate flings. Prudence dictated she did not let that titbit slip, so Jordayne continued to sip her cocktail, much to the frowning disapproval of Matisse. His instigation as heir really had dampened his spirit. One drink was hardly enough to intoxicate someone of her fortitude.

A girl with teased hair parted in the middle idled by and whispered in Yinmae's ear. Matisse pulled the proprietor's shoulder back before she could reply.

"Let us hear what you have to say."

Jordayne sighed as Yinmae spoke to her charge in an eastern tongue. Before the unfortunate girl could turn, Matisse had taken her wrist. That was all the coaxing she needed to begin lavishing unthinking attention on him.

"Addicts hold little appeal for any man," Matisse said, no sympathy at all. He ushered the courtesan to his other side. "Now send another of your escorts for our mutual friend, and mind he arrives."

Jordayne set her drink down. "I do hope you intend to look after this wench," she said, as Yinmae signalled to a willowy redhead. Both girls were too thin by far. Even in the muted light, she could see this one's skin had turned sallow and her hair was dull.

"Look after all my girls. But girls no allowed porrin. They know no allowed. She do wrong."

"With such bounty around them, do they stand a chance? Not all have your resilience, Madam Yinmae," Jordayne replied. Porrin was a problem of which even she could not make light.

"Which is exactly why its trade is banned." Matisse said.

The poor, blank girl beside him looked like a lamb in a jabberwei's jaws as her hands kneaded his shoulders. Matisse allowed her just enough liberty with his personage to fit into his surrounds.

Movement caught Jordayne's eye, and she turned to watch a wiry Verdaani man weave through the sheets of silk in search of Madam Yinmae. If the number of clients surprised him, he gave no indication.

Madam Yinmae rose. "Must go. Must greet guest." She hesitated, on pretence of seeking their permission, no doubt. Since that hesitation alerted the newcomer, it had to have been a calculated gesture. Quick as a devious djinn, the Verdaani leapt over the nearest settee. The couple entwined along its length never looked up. Grabbing a sheet of pink silk, the smuggler swung across the table, over the opposite settee and ducked out of sight.

Matisse was already halfway to the door as Jordayne settled back to enjoy the show, sparing a cursory glance for the girl who had ended up on the floor and Madam Yinmae, who was standing proud. Everywhere guards were emerging from ardent embraces, some more promptly than others, all tugged back by their escorts. A pragmatic rather than passionate display, Jordayne thought. For all they knew, their home was about to fall into the hands of the Crown.

She caught a glimpse of the smuggler, crouching between two settees, his head poking up to assess the situation. It did rather elicit a pang of disappointment. Swords drawn, the guards were surrounding him, about to end his bid for freedom before it had fully fledged. But then, *oh clever man*, the smuggler leapt onto the back of the settee, and from there onto a curtain, climbing his way up, as agile as a monkey. He rested at the top, slowly swaying, as the guards advanced. With immaculate timing, he jerked the curtain into motion and flew to the next, just outside the circle of guards. The momentum carried him on, swinging him toward the door with graceful art. The feat deserved a round of applause, and Jordayne, patron of the arts in this fabled city, obliged. The little man paused long enough to acknowledge her with an extravagant flourish of the arm and beaming smile before resuming his circuitous route across the room. His impeccable choice of curtains kept him just out of reach of the flailing guard until, hand outstretched, he realised the yellow drape for which he had aimed was sailing downward. His hand closed around air and he tumbled to the floor, landing on the curtain at deq Lungo's feet. Her estimation of the captain grew. The balance he had maintained while standing on the back of the settee, and the precise timing of his slash, demonstrated an innate appreciation for performance art. She awarded him a clap as Sergeant Rokan, a broad fellow with narrow eyes, a brown beard, and one scary smile dragged the prisoner to his feet and escorted him to Matisse, who was leaning on his sword.

"An artful manoeuvre, Captain," Jordayne said.

The disagreeable man failed to flush at her compliment. "My lady, it is a soldier's job to wield a sword well."

The smuggler looked from her to Matisse and back to her, and dropped to the floor, kowtowing before them.

"Oh do stand up. I'm hardly royalty, although you do know how to make a lady feel special," Jordayne said. The man wisely obliged. "That *is* better."

"Lord Matisse, Lady Jordayne, I bring you the smuggler Raj, the most elusive of the double-crossing dealers that curse our realm," her sergeant said with deadpan cheek.

"Really? How disappointing. I mean, I hardly make a habit of entering these sorts of establishments, although I must say it might turn out to be terribly entertaining if we could just persuade the proprietor to throw a few muscly, dark-skinned men into the fray. Yet here you are, netted by a complete amateur, and a woman at that. You can't be good at all."

The Verdaani looked like he was about to choke on his tongue.

Jordayne folded her arms. "Oh do speak up. Life is so dull when everyone's deferring to you. And you never know, your life could depend on how well you amuse me."

The man bowed but turned to Matisse. "I am trader of twenty-five year. I supply this inn with fabric."

"I'm glad to hear it," Matisse said. He nodded at two guards, who held the prisoner while another unceremoniously ripped his shabby, mustard kurta from neck to waist. The fabric parted, exposing a number of packets tied to his lean torso. The guard used a knife to prise them free. Deq Lungo opened one, tilting it so they could see the noxious red powder within. At his gesture, the guard yanked the prisoner's shalvar down. More packets were taped to his spindly legs. Raj, not at all discomforted to have his modesty dependent on a mere loincloth, beamed at her.

"Not quite the male specimen I was after," Jordayne remarked. She was pleased a smile formed on Madam Yinmae's lips. "Do you have anything to say for yourself, Raj?"

"Perhaps your lordship aware I am registered merchant, granted right of trade with magus guild," he said to Matisse.

Matisse shook his head, a clear indication he was game for some fun. "It was the Lady who addressed you, not I. Despite her sharp tongue and rather wicked sense of humour, she is lenient where I am not. I suggest you aim to ingratiate yourself with her."

The prisoner turned to her, lips pursed and colour spreading across his dark neck. He stared her directly in the eye, a Verdaani response to a female in authority if ever there was one.

"Then you check with mages. They confirm it."

The man had no idea about the balance of power in Myklaan if he thought she was about to be put in her place by a man. "What they tell me, dear fellow, is that you have been cheating them for many months. Of course, when you deliver this month's goods gratis, my brother and I will be prepared to overlook your indiscretion. What we cannot possibly forgive is the distribution of this toxin to our people. Your Verdaani drug is decimating our reputation as a centre of culture and refinement."

"Your people choose. You say Myklaani people free but you give no choice."

"Not in this," she snapped, "since it is porrin which deprives the user of choice and life."

His glare glanced off her smooth veneer.

Matisse said, "We are getting tough with dealers. The last we caught was hanged."

"Myklaan only give that for murder."

Sighing, Jordayne indicated the prostitute on the floor. "Look at that girl. She's dying, Raj. Slowly, but before our eyes. And you don't think this is murder?"

"Her choice, her *choice*."

"Is that your best defence?"

Raj frowned. "You want porrin free? You take, you let me go."

"We want to know what you've been doing with the porrin you carry."

When Raj was silent, she flicked her eyes in the direction of Captain deq Lungo. The soldier brought his sword to Raj's neck.

"Myklaan don't execute prisoners," he said. "I be out of your prison in eight-day."

Matisse sat on the nearest divan and leant back. "Our prisons are overflowing. For foreigners, we might make an exception to the life sentence rule." He asked her, "Can an execution be artistry?"

"There is but one way to find out. I once consorted with an artist who was always looking for new mediums to express himself in. He might find permission to paint in blood rather titillating. Shall I ask Captain deq Lungo to fetch him?"

Raj strained his eyes towards the sword. "I was set up trade partners. I give them porrin so they start acquire clients."

Matisse shook his head. "Why? The Crown pays more than you'll ever make from illicit trade with commoners."

"Yes but we keep business with mages and do more with townsfolk. Porrin not scarce in Verdaan."

"We want to know the names of your suppliers and dealers," Jordayne said.

He was too startled by the request. "I work alone."

"Nevertheless, we will need those names," Matisse said.

"I don't know."

"Oh dear. Then I'm afraid you'll be left to rot in jail." Jordayne rose. "Captain."

Captain deq Lungo gestured. Two guards hefted Raj's feet off the floor and bore the struggling man out.

"You can't do this," Raj said over his shoulder. "I have permit. I have permit from Shah himself."

"What do you think?" Matisse asked.

"He is a hill dweller," she replied. "Lord Kamir treats them as lackeys. He is, by all accounts, worse in this regard than his brother, Hudassan. Raj will know something, but not much."

Madam Yinmae bowed. "Now I see to clients?" The majority of her clientele still engaged in modest explorations of the flesh. If there was a pair full conscious of what had taken place, they did not show it.

Jordayne took her arm and led her aside. "See if you can help that gentleman relax," she said, nodding in deq Lungo's direction. The dear captain was standing straight as a sword, trying to stare anywhere but at the female delights around him.

"My pleasure. Will see to it personally." Yinmae beckoned a girl with a tray of drinks, removed a tiny packet from the wide sleeve of her kameez, and deposited the white contents into a glass.

"Tell him that drink is courtesy of his lord. He will hardly be able to refuse it. I shall be ever so grateful I might even overlook the illicit trade."

Yinmae placed an uninhibited hand on Jordayne's bangles. "Come again, Lady. I get you black-skinned gladiator," she said with a wide smile.

Jordayne laughed. "I like you, Madam Yinmae." She patted the hand and went to collect Matisse from the reception room.

"Where is Captain deq Lungo," Matisse said, looking down his nose at her, like he well knew what mischief she had inspired.

"The Captain will shortly be enjoying himself." She gave him a shrewd look. "I am surprised you are not." His amused disapproval was rewarding. "Don't worry, it wasn't porrin," she said with a cursory thought to how twisted her reputation must have become if Matisse believed she was capable of drugging the captain with that particular illicit drug. "Something more along the lines of an aphrodisiac, I believe."

Chapter Ten

"YOU ARE UNUSUALLY QUIET," Arun noted as they walked through the stone arches of an out-of-the-way corridor on the ground floor of the palace.

Vinsant hummed agreement and resumed his daydreaming, more than a little peeved all the adventure was happening to his sister. She was a *girl. And* a grown up. He needed a way to save the day. A hazardous, heroic way, not this boring smuggling of books into her room. Something brazen enough to earn him pride of place in a tapestry fit to join those lining the walls.

"I expected you to have a thousand questions."

"Will I get any answers?"

"Perhaps if you are careful in your selection."

"Fine, then. Why are you calling me by name and not title?"

"While you are an apprentice, the Majoria and I outrank you. You will need to obey us and you certainly will not be giving us orders."

Vinsant skidded across the floor to a five-armed candelabrum. A backslash toppled a lavender-scented candle. A turn and a kick sent a second to clunk on the floor. He was about to bring both hands down on the third when Arun cleared his throat. Vinsant righted himself, and tugged his kurta straight. "You mean when I'm undertaking my lessons," he clarified.

"There is no part-time apprenticeship, not if you truly hope to master the crystals."

Vinsant hummed again. No doubt Father had agreed to this.

Levi might have taken the liberty, but Arun would not. Time for the next question.

His mentor stopped anything coming out of his mouth with a pointed look at the fallen candles.

"The ser–" Vinsant started to say.

Arun's expression grew sterner. Vinsant retrieved the candles, and jammed them into the holder. No one would be any the wiser about his candle-fighting skill if they lit the first. Too bad the second was broken through the middle. Since Arun had continued on, he left the top half flopping over the middle of the wick, and jogged on.

They stopped in front of a large tapestry depicting Shah Guntek making obeisance before a statue of Mahktos. It was supposed to hide the worn stone staircase to the mahktashaan lair. In truth, the lowliest scullion gossiped about the worst kept secret in the palace. Not that it mattered. Nobody except an initiated mahktashaan knew how to release the beeswaxed mahogany panel behind it. Vae'oeldin knew Vinsant had tried.

"Tell me how to access the stairs," he said, knowing he was pushing his luck.

"When the time is right," Arun said, a hand over the crystal at his chest. It pulsed once, a faint cerulean light seeping through the cracks between his fingers. The panel clicked open.

"You have to have magic, right?"

Arun did not answer, which Vinsant took to be an affirmative. He sucked on his cheek as they spiralled into a gloom penetrated only by the glow from Arun's crystal. Now the damp, dark stone shielded them from prying ears, the Minoria was about to regret his call for questions.

"Was it Levi's suggestion for Father to announce Lord Ahkdul's marriage proposal in front of Ambassador deq Ikher?" He would have asked Mariano but his brother was sounding condescending of late.

"You will hereupon need to address your master by his title, Vinsant. I do not know what conversation passed between the Majoria and the Shah, but your father is capable of reaching his own decisions."

"But Father…" Vinsant said, trailing off. Their feet tapped toward a faint light, and he detected traces of rosemary in the cool air. They had to be nearing the lair.

"Can you think of no reason for him to do so?"

Vinsant scratched his nose. "That's not fair. You are answering a question with a question and I asked first."

"You had better get used to it. The mahktashaan initiate only those who prove themselves worthy."

"You're supposed to be an instructor."

"A good teacher challenges his student to find answers for himself."

"It's not as though I haven't thought about it." He considered a few moments longer. "To embarrass Kordahla then, as part of her punishment."

"He was giving her a way out, Vinsant. When deq Ikher reports the conversation to Ahkdul and Lord Hudassan, they will have no recourse to offence if negotiations fall apart. Politics is a dangerous game. It would not do for Verdaan to believe Terlaan thinks itself so high above its neighbour it would refuse to marry a daughter to the heir."

Thoughtful, Vinsant chewed his cheek. "But that was before Levi discovered the meaning of the grappers."

"Indeed it was."

The dryness of the answer left Vinsant wondering. It seemed the only way out for Kordahla was to do as the djinn suggested. Unless – and now his thoughts seemed to fly of their own accord – a more suitable suitor could be found. Someone kind. Someone who would not mind having him around. Someone who would not *prefer* to have him around while he neglected Kordahla. Someone like–

"How long have you liked Kordahla?" he asked, swelling in the chest because the tiny pause was telling.

Arun turned his head a fraction. "About as long as I have liked you, Vinsant, which, since you are no doubt going to ask, was the first time we met."

"You can't blame my sister for acting the way she did with the porrin. She's usually quite responsible." He winced because he sounded obvious even to his immature ears.

Their boots scuffed onto cold stone. "I think your other questions will have to wait," Arun said.

Vinsant bent around him. Through an archway, the white glow of crystals threw the hexagonal antechamber into shadow. Djinn, did he want to explore! Too bad the next room was their destination. Inside, eight mahktashaan, robed, hooded and gloved in black, stood around a central stone altar lined with clear crystals and strewn with fragrant rosemary and thyme. Others waited around the periphery, each with a crystal which threw a unique colour into the room. He eyed a spot right in the middle of the action, but Arun tapped him on the shoulder and pointed to three boys dressed in white cotton churidar and kurta.

"What have I missed?" he asked, falling in beside them.

"Nothing," the tallest of the three hissed. "They've been waiting for the Minoria."

The opportunity for introductions was curtailed by a mahktashaan who held a finger to his lips before reaching for a crystal in a sconce. "*Allumin*", he said, and the crystal sparked to life. It was one awesome trick that looked easy enough. Vinsant jumped for the next crystal.

"*Allumin*," he said, brushing it with his fingers. How was he to know the word would echo around the chamber? He felt the hot, coloured eyes of every mahktashaan turn upon him and wondered how he could disown the incoherent gurgle coming from his throat. He tried to meld with the wall but risked a desperate glance up at the sconce. It dashed his hopes. Their stares most definitely did not signal the performance of an amazing feat.

"Are you djinn-touched?" the tall lad snarled when the mahktashaan had struck the crystal and moved on. "Shut up and keep still before you get us thrown out."

A commoner could not use such a tone with a prince and hope to remain unpunished. About to enlighten the vagrant as to whom he addressed, Vinsant caught the Majoria in his blacker than night cloak glowering at him, and clamped his jaw firmly shut. The rules had obviously changed in more ways than Arun had intimated. Lucky for him, the mahktashaan were keen to start the ceremony. He had a feeling Levi would be a hard master, even with an intelligent, talented and dashing prince. Problem was, he didn't understand a word of the rite. Ten minutes later, he was squirming. When Arun had said the Majoria was going to examine his fish, he had envisaged bolts of lightning flying, and the grapper coming to life to speak in Laanan. So far, the mahktashaan were merely forming ranks, chanting incomprehensible magic words, and stomping with military precision. There had to be something nearby worth investigating to relieve the tedium. He sidled to the next archway and looked in. The room was also hexagonal in shape, empty and boring. When he crept back, several of the soldier magicians were forming two rows in front of the boys. At an abrupt word from Levi, the entire contingent slapped hands upon their crystals, dimming the light in the room. The two closest mahktashaan stepped forward, took the plump boy's arms and escorted him down the row to the Majoria, where he knelt just like a prisoner about to face the block. Vinsant wriggled his way into a better position to see. It was nothing special. Levi held his crystal to the trembling boy's forehead, it glowed that peculiar black, and then the elated apprentice was instructed to move aside.

"Go for it," he said as the shortest boy trotted down the line. "Or not," he muttered as he was ignored. Then he suffered a pang of guilt. Levi's crystal failed to light. As if that wasn't humiliation enough, the mahktashaan stomped and turned their backs. Shorty swallowed and kept his head down as his guards led him out of the room in the direction of the stairs.

Beside him, Vinsant heard the last boy, the tall one who had spoken to him, take a deep breath. The ranks stomped and turned back, and the boy processed down the line in the firm grasp of his escort. As he knelt before Levi, Vinsant found himself crossing his fingers, and rocking onto his toes. The crystal barely sparked, but it seemed to be enough. The two boys were formally welcomed and urged to offer their thanks to Mahktos. A mahktashaan with a green crystal led them to the door beyond the altar. The tall one had the gall to smirk over his shoulder. Vinsant had a mind to strut right past him and demand obeisance. But this was not his father's throne room, and he was aware he had already been indulged.

Young as he was, he had honour. Father had seen to that. Quite apart from the lack of respect he would suffer from the other apprentices, he could not bear to think that one day Mariano would be accepting advice from an ill-equipped Majoria who had attained his position through political manoeuvring, and not because he had progressed through the ranks.

"Wait," he said, loud enough for all to hear as his own escort had him bustling after the apprentices. "I need to be tested."

All movement stopped. His escorts stepped away from him and looked to the Majoria for direction. Arun rescued them from embarrassment by guiding Vinsant into the hastily reforming rows.

"Vinsant, you have sealed your fate," Arun whispered. "Should you fail this, we cannot train you."

"And you could without this initiation?"

"Matters are complicated," Arun said, which was no answer at all.

Vinsant pushed his chin up, and kept what he hoped was eye contact with the Majoria all the way down the row. It was hard to tell with that hood drawn low. What he wanted to do was rib the guards with their burning grip. When they pushed him to his knees, he stared into Levi's hood, silently begging Vae'oeldin for the privilege to train as a mahktashaan.

The crystal, when it touched his forehead, was cool. He strained his eyes upward hoping to detect a glimmer of light. Felt his stomach drop when he realised the only illumination came from the periphery of the room. In the instant he sagged in defeat, the crystals on the altar sparked, and a blinding light burst from the Majoria's crystal. It seared the skin on his forehead, and a force unlike anything he had ever felt pummelled into him, sending him flying down the row of mahktashaan onto his back. Winded and shocked, he lay where he was, watching the shadows retreat across the ceiling as all the coloured crystals flared to life.

"Can you rise?" Arun's voice was urgent. He helped Vinsant into a sitting position.

"Do I get to train?" Vinsant asked, holding his throbbing head and wondering if the blow was a very public rejection.

Laying a hand on his head, Arun murmured a few words. Surprised to find his headache gone, Vinsant looked around. The mahktashaan stood rigid in their ranks.

"You most assuredly may train," Arun said, helping him to his knees to accept Levi's formal welcome. "Now come. I promised your sister I would take personal responsibility for you, and after that little display none will dare challenge your special tutelage."

Djinn, did he have questions. Too bad now didn't seem to be the time. He joined the other apprentices in the next room, and grinned when he realised their stares had turned from resentment to envy. Pretending to smugness, he looked straight ahead. And gawped. At the far wall, a huge crystal statue of Mahktos stretched from floor to ceiling, a core of gold visible inside. The three of them fell into a kowtow.

"Rise, lads, but keep your heads bowed before Mahktos," a mahktashaan with an amber crystal cautioned. He bowed before the image of the god, then beckoned the plump boy over and positioned him between the sitting god's mighty knees. "I, Branak, mahktashaan servant of Mahktos and Terlaan, beseech you, divine Mahktos, to bestow a quartz upon Gram deq Larren, Spark of the Crystal."

At Gram's name, chimes pealed through the chamber and the crystal god glowed, bathing Gram in its light. One of the god's nails flew off his pointed finger. Gram caught it with a joyous yelp. Given the force with which the stone flew, he must have been expecting it. Vinsant paid greater attention as Branak threaded a leather thong through a hole in the white quartz and strung it around his charge's neck.

"Naikil deq Versek, Spark of the Crystal," Branak said.

Proud shoulders back, the tall boy moved into position. The statue chimed again. Light flowed from the statue before a piece of quartz sprung off the god's nail to land neatly in Naikil's hand. Vinsant edged toward the statue. The finger was perfect all the way to the tip of the nail, no sign it had just lost two pieces of stone.

"Prince Vinsant deq Wilshem, Spark of the Crystal," Branak announced when the quartz was around Naikil's neck, drawing a gasp from Gram and a sharp movement from Naikil.

Vinsant stood in place. Beads of sweat formed on his brow as the light baked him, isolating him, cocooning him so that the chimes sounded like they were ringing beneath water. He watched the nail, waiting to catch the gift, struggling to breathe the humid, herb-scented light. Expanding his chest required so much effort that he collapsed to his knees. An eternity later, he keeled over, sure he was about to suffocate. He reached for the nail. The god's finger stabbed through his chest, into his heart bringing such excruciating pain that he wished he were dead. Maybe he was, or else how could he see the god with his eyelids squeezed tight. He begged Mahktos, Vae'oeldin, any god whose name he could remember for the pain to stop. His mind tripped back to all the minor hurts he had suffered as a child, to Kordahla kissing them better. Where was she? Where was she when he most needed her? A flicker of conscience reminded him that it was she who needed him. He grabbed at the raking finger and pushed back. Mahktos seemed not to expect that, hesitated in his torture. Vinsant cried out and struck at the God with a sword that miraculously appeared in his hand. Crystal shattered all around him, raining down from the idol, leaving only a core of gold.

He lay sweat-soaked and trembling, exhausted and gasping for air. "Wh-," Vinsant said, barely able to keep his eyes open. "Whe-ere's mm-yy quartz?" His fingers scratched around the floor but there was nothing there. As Arun lifted him into his arms like a baby, he reached down to keep searching.

"I can walk," he murmured, unwilling to bear the indignity of being carried like a swooning girl. Unfortunately, he passed out.

When Vinsant woke, he was lying in a rough bed in a hexagonal room dimly lit by a solitary crystal in a bracket above his head. A few black robes hung on a row of hooks on the adjoining wall. Six more beds lined the wall opposite, while tables and shelves with pots of salve in perfect, obscene order abutted the remaining three. An unfamiliar mahktashaan with a mint green crystal was sitting beside him, soft words on his lips, and a lean face shadowed under his hood. He broke off as soon as he saw Vinsant blinking awake.

"Can you stand?" he asked.

Vinsant meant to explain his muscles had turned to jelly but his voice only managed a croak. His hand travelled to his chest. There was no crystal hanging upon it. Groaning, he rolled so he could hang his head over the edge of the bed and be sick. Fortunately, someone had placed a bucket by the bed.

"You will follow me," the mahktashaan spat, striding out of the only door. Vinsant stared after him for several heartbeats before forcing himself to sit up, grip the edge of the bed and push himself onto shaky legs. He tottered from room to hexagonal room after his brisk guide, their passage confused by the varying numbers of doors each possessed. How anyone could wind his way through the maze, Vinsant could not fathom. Even the floor stones were hexagonal, which messed with his orientation big time. When he halted to catch his breath yet again, he notched it up as one more puzzle to crack. Not now, though. The impatient mahktashaan had returned to the far doorway where, arms folded, he waited until Vinsant forced himself to stumble on.

What little strength he possessed deserted him when they emerged into the temple through a side door. Mahktos towered above them, crystal shell intact and crimson eyes boring into Vinsant. An involuntary sound escaped him, strangled and weak. He leaned against the archway, rooted to the spot, because no way could he survive another magical battering. Shattered did not even begin to describe how he felt.

"Vinsant?" The Minoria placed a hand on his head, flattening errant spikes of his hair. Delicious warmth spread into his blood, easing the nauseating trembles. Too bad the hostility oozing from the dozens of mahktashaan filing into the room dulled whatever calming magic Arun had used. Vinsant pressed against the stone. Its cold support beat exposing his back.

"What's happening?" he asked.

The Minoria shook his head. "Do not speak unless Levi or I address you. You are in a precarious position, my prince."

His title was not what he had wanted to hear. The precise, echoing stomps of the troop, either. Approaching through the opposite arch, the Majoria's steps marked the rhythm. Glad to turn from the image of Mahktos, Vinsant peered under Levi's hood. Nothing but the line of his thin lips was visible and, judging by their press, Kordahla just might have been right about the man's evil intent. Too bad that there wasn't a graceful way to avoid Arun's guiding hand. Standing in the middle of the room, in front of the stomping troops, before the chanting Majoria made him feel the size of the flea the indigo djinn had named him.

"What vision did Mahktos grant you?" the Majoria asked after an unintelligible incantation.

Vinsant swallowed. "I don't remember." He was not about to tell a room full of mahktashaan he had attacked their god with a sword, even if it had been all in his mind.

The Majoria slapped a hand on his forehead, tilting his head back. A surge of pain blasted through his brain as his vision of the god resurfaced. An instant later, hand and pain were gone. Panting, Vinsant staggered back, clutched the archway and tried to remain standing.

"Mahktos has rejected him," Levi said flatly.

"Our laws are clear," the mahktashaan who had guided him here intoned. "He must be put to the sword."

"He must be put to the sword," the group chanted in perfect unison.

Vinsant's eyes went wide. "Arun?"

"I will stand in this boy's stead." Arun crossed to him and placed a hand on his shoulder. With Levi's midnight eyes locking onto Arun's cerulean ones, Vinsant hoped that hand would stay put.

"The boy is entitled to a Stead Plea," Levi said at length, "but your position precludes it. Choose another to represent you."

Arun turned to the ranks. "I promised this boy's family I would accept responsibility for him. We intended his visit today to be a courtesy. We planned instruction, and his initiation at a future date. He was not informed of the consequences of his choice, nor was he prepared for his ordeal. Let me stand in his stead, or let him go unharmed from here."

A single boot stomped. "He should have been tutored before he was tested," Branak of the amber crystal said. By a small mercy, the apprentices were nowhere in sight. "That fault is ours. There is no need to have one stand in his stead. Let him leave."

"It shall be by vote of the Inner Circle," Levi declared. He stomped. Eight mahktashaan stepped forward with precise military timing to form a circle around Vinsant as the others filed from the room.

"This boy never received instruction on the terms of his initiation," Levi said. "For that Minoria, you will atone."

Arun bowed his head. "It is as you decree, Majoria."

"The boy's lack of preparation is not in dispute," Levi stated. "I, Majoria, ask you of the Inner Circle of Mahktashaan, is Vinsant deq Wilshem free to leave with his life?"

The room darkened as the mahktashaan crystals died. Vinsant took a deep breath. For three heartbeats, nothing happened. Then, one by one, the crystals glowed at their owner's chests. Two, three, four, threw their light into the room. Vinsant looked to Arun to see if a majority was enough. Five of the eight now glowed.

"So it is decreed, Levi said.

"Come, my prince," Arun said.

Vinsant felt a flutter of panic. "I have to go?" He couldn't. Kordahla needed his help. She needed magic.

"Mahktos has rejected you. You may not train as a mahktashaan." Arun's hand was steady on his shoulder.

"What happens if someone stands in my stead?" Vinsant asked, staring straight at a mahktashaan whose apricot crystal was dark.

"That man will ask Mahktos to accept you in their name," Levi said.

"And I can train? If Mahktos recognises them, I can become a mahktashaan?"

"You can train," Levi conceded. "But heed you well, Mahktos chooses which apprentices to initiate into their full powers as mahktashaan. If you train and fail his final test, you will suffer the sword."

"And if...if Mahktos doesn't accept my champion?"

"There will not be a second reprieve. You will be put to death, Prince Vinsant."

"Not them? Not the one in my stead?"

"If the Inner Circle deem they have offended Mahktos by supporting your cause, they will share your fate."

Vinsant considered a moment. "I want someone to stand in my stead," he said, talking right over Arun's, *My Prince, no.* "Someone you don't think will offend Mahktos by doing this."

Low and urgent, Arun whispered in his ear. "You must retract that statement. Neither I nor your father can protect you if you fail."

"I want to be a mahktashaan." He crossed his arms and set his mouth in a line of grim determination.

"The child must learn deference," the mahktashaan with the dead apricot crystal stated. "Is that possible for one such as him?"

"I can learn anything," Vinsant said, not even bothering to glare at the stupid man.

"Enough," Levi said. "His aptitude for magic is indisputable. It is his loyalty to Mahktos which is in question." He pointed at Vinsant. "I urge you to think carefully before you answer, Prince. Do you recant your wish?"

"No," Vinsant said straight away. He let his hands fall to his side and stood soldier-straight. "I want to train." If loyalty were all it took, he would stop praying to Vae'oeldin, and switch his allegiance to Mahktos from his very next prayer.

The Majoria's shoulder's twitched. "Very well." In a quiet tone, he asked, "Is there one who will stand in his stead?"

Head bowed, Arun walked between the crystal knees of the statue. "I, Arun, humble mahktashaan servant of Mahktos and Terlaan, request you, Divine God of Old, accept Vinsant deq Wilshem, Prince of Terlaan and Spark of the Crystal, as apprentice."

Vinsant lifted his chin. Arun's calm, measured voice was awesome reassurance. It had to mean the Minoria thought Mahktos would accept him.

"I, Arun, Minoria of the mahktashaan, vouch for his loyal and dedicated service."

An unsettling murmur rippled through the mahktashaan when Arun stated his title. Vinsant couldn't help shifting from one foot to the other. So much for confidence. He had no clue what was really going on.

He was about to risk questioning the nearest mahktashaan when light surged from the statue. Arun's head jerked back, his hood fell off, and cerulean rays streamed from his eyes to those of the god. The beam disappeared and Arun's head fell forward as the god spat a chunk of quartz at the Minoria.

"All praise to Mahktos," the Inner Circle of mahktashaan chanted as one. The moment the last word was out, they exploded into argument.

"Silence!" Levi thundered.

The response was immediate, a stomp from each man in perfect unison, and hush as Levi and Arun again held each other's gaze. The intensity between them prickled over Vinsant's skin. He gasped as Arun nodded, bowed his head and replaced his hood. The mahktashaan were communicating without words! All his questions threatened to overflow, but a warning look from Arun as he placed the threaded crystal over Vinsant's head stemmed the tide.

"This crystal is a gift from our god, Mahktos. It is the core of your being as an apprentice. Keep it safe, for to lose it is to lose more than your right to become a mahktashaan. It is to lose your right to life," the Minoria said. He clasped Vinsant's shoulder. "Congratulations, apprentice," he said. Vinsant beamed. Then Arun stepped aside.

"Vinsant deq Wilshem," Levi said. "You are apprenticed to the mahktashaan."

Vinsant's elation dampened at the misgiving in the gravelly voice. The Majoria's stare lingered as the Inner Circle marched out.

Chapter Eleven

"AT LAST, DARLING," JORDAYNE said, pulling Drucilamere into her petal-strewn, candlelit chamber. She pushed the door and let it bang shut. "I thought I was going to have to send a forcible escort." She stopped short of kissing him, sobering when she saw his sombre face and empty hands. "You're not brooding, are you?" she asked, sliding a hand into his kurta and through the hair on his chest. She had made a mistake splashing her favourite oriental perfume around. Its woody notes mingled with the rose oils in the candles to overpower his masculine scent. "And how careless of you to forget the wine."

She had an inkling of what might be wrong; the brooding comment had nudged the thought awake. Drucilamere would only be fretting over one thing, one person, and Jordayne, who never, ever shirked the unpleasant, found herself inexplicably burying the thought deep beneath her cultivated passions. She drew him onto the floral carpet, kneading her painted toes into the pile and turning her face up as her fingers found a nipple. Taking her lead, Drucilamere grabbed her wrist, thrust his head at hers and kissed her with such force that it drove her back. As she collided with the bureau, she threw her arms up around his head and returned the favour. Their passions sent a silver handled brush crashing to the petals she had strewn over the floor.

"Enough," he said, pulling away, turning away.

She watched him with shrewd eyes, waiting for him to spill his troubles. The candles flickered in a draught.

"You were lovers," he said in the darkest moment. His voice choked on his emotion.

After this morning's performance, it was hardly necessary to name the other party. She crossed to an ornate, painted sideboard, poured herself a goblet of wine and took a generous but elegant sip. "Don't be a bore. No one is the slightest bit offended that Ordosteen beds a different lady every few months. Why should I be any different?" She twirled the long stem, guessing, not wanting to, there was more.

"How long?" he demanded. "How long were you lovers?"

She arched an eyebrow. He was in fine form now. "It is hardly your business Druce, since it happened well before I took you to my bed."

"Is that it? Am I no more than the man who best satisfies your desires? Someone to share your body but not your secrets." He was still by the bureau, appraising her with equal measures of lust and disgust.

"You know me," she said setting the goblet down on a blood red petal. "You know full well what a relationship with me holds."

"He was right you know. You're heartless."

"And you're not? To fling a past passion at me like this?" She sounded so very in control.

"Is it past? Or are we? Will you discard me if my body ceases to arouse you?"

"You know I will," she said, wanting to be cruel, to wound the way he was wounding her. And yet, what she feared most, in this land where women were all but equal to men, what she feared most after committing herself, was losing him.

A heavy silence hung between them. The hurt in his eyes brought no softness to hers. Jordayne had designs and no man, however profusely she ached for him, figured into them.

Drucilamere broke the tension. "He's dying," he said flatly.

"I gathered," she replied without any sarcasm. They were still feet apart, a first for them in this room after this length of time.

She might have sunk to the floor if Druce's shaky breath had not warned her to place a hand on the bureau. "I meant now," he said, giving her the explanation for their distance. "He never fully recovered from the second dose of porrin. I had to complete the divination."

Ah, she thought, pain creeping into her eyes. The porrin had left her mage jittery, not entirely himself. "Where is he?" she asked with a swallow. The grief was so very, very deep. Few who knew her would guess at the strength of her friendships, or her loves, those that mattered anyway. But her bonds were intimate, and life-long, and Trove most of all held a treasured place in her heart.

"The hospice."

Her *why* caught in her throat. Drucilamere read it, though, in the critical draw of her brows.

"The physicians there are well versed in treating porrin's daze."

The awkwardness lasted a moment longer. Then they were both striding towards each other, embracing, kissing, poignantly this time, as their tears flowed. Without another word, she donned a cloak over the emerald silks she had so seductively arranged an hour before, and tied sandals on her feet. Understanding, Druce opened the door. The two guards in the corridor fell in step behind her, their surprised looks making plain they had not expected Lady Jordayne to be abroad quite so soon after admitting a male guest. She hurried past the gilded mouldings of laden fruits trees and floral wreaths. Their glitter was obscene on this sombre night.

Outside the marble palace, the air was stifling. The servants carried baskets or carted armour at a languid pace, dallying at idle conversation beneath the cloudy twilight.

"Four years," she said in answer to his question, while waiting for the grooms to saddle their horses, and the horses of the retinue she must, of necessity, collect. She looked at him to see if he understood of what she spoke.

His thoughts had obviously not left their quarrel. "So long," he murmured, gazing straight ahead.

For her, indeed it was. Her lovers were so often random, picked sporadically over the years for the physical pleasures they could share, but there had been only two to truly touch her heart, and one was standing beside her while the other lay on his deathbed. What was it about the magi that moved her so?

They mounted, her on a white mare, him on a black gelding, and rode out of the gate wrought with the creatures of old: the tiny, flittering muid and the feather-throated schkaan, the thorny, tentacled bazwaeel and the scaled veli. Were it any other evening, she would have goaded the men sneaking glances of appreciation her way, flirted openly, laughing at their embarrassment and Druce's pout. This was Myklaan, after all. Tonight, though, she devoted her attention to the mage as they traversed the clean, wide streets, down the slope toward the centre of Kaijoor, under Daesoa's muted glow.

You have no need to be jealous," she said, uncharacteristic in her straightforwardness. The night's anguish demanded it.

"Was it so very long ago?"

Her sharp glance was lost on him. Porrin and circumstances were allowing this conversation, she decided, for against her nature she felt inclined to answer, if only to honour Trove, to remember what he was to her. She counted the clops on the cobbles, one, two, three.

"I was fourteen, and he was my first." Her lips twitched a smile as his expression turned to shock.

"Then it was..." His eyes flashed, his furious mind working.

"Under my father's roof, yes."

His hands tightened on the reins. His gelding quickened its pace. "By Vae'oenka, Jordayne, he had your father's trust."

"And mine. The seduction was mutual. I was ready for what he had to offer, and he never treated me as a child."

"You were a child."

Sensing her mood, her mare tossed her head. Silky mane fell to both sides of the elegant neck. "I don't think I was ever that. I wanted to marry him, you know. He refused, said Myklaan expected great things of me."

"So he used you, alluring as you were, and kept himself free."

"I rather think it was the other way around," she said, tiring of the conversation, of the seriousness of it. "He kept me unfettered. I do not think I would be so accomplished as someone's wife." She steeled herself against his look of disappointment. She had never encouraged him in that regard. She did not wish to encourage him now. Turning forward was the clearest indication she could give him that her candour was at an end.

They passed into narrower streets, their lanterns illuminating bright shop signs. Down the street, the strains of drunken discord spilled from a tavern. A pair of inebriated men sauntered out, gesturing wide and singing loud despite the early hour. One drunk tripped, cursed and turned back to boot the leg that had blocked his way. The owner of the leg, slumped in an unswept doorway, keeled into scraps of orange peel.

"Don't!" a shabby boy lingering across the street yelled as the drunk aimed a second kick.

"Do see what the problem is," she asked Sergeant Rokan.

"What you about, then?" he called, urging his horse ahead and tapping the hilt of his sword. Whether it was that or the maniacal smile he adopted at the first sign of trouble, the drunks took one look at his broad chest and skittered down the street. It was telling the boy let him close to within five paces before darting into shadow.

"Get you home, boy," Rokan growled, dismounting. He squatted to check the miscreant for signs of life.

"He's in porrin's bliss."

"Then bring him along," Jordayne said with a sigh. The day the populace adopted the term porrin's *curse* she would proclaim an annual day of celebration.

Her trusted sergeant hefted the unconscious man onto his horse. Wasted and sour smelling, the addict was too deep in the drug's grip to so much as groan at his rough treatment. A wave of her hand directed half her guards into the tavern to ferret out the dealer. The remainder escorted her into deepening night.

The two-storey hospice, purpose-built to her specifications, boasted a manicured garden with a canal that gleamed in the moonlight. The sick, Jordayne believed, required a peaceful setting to convalesce. What they did not need were spiked gates to restrict their access to the best physicians in the land. At least three major moons had passed since she had visited this project, choosing instead to summon physicians and builders to the palace. It seemed that timesaving measure had been a monumental mistake. She wondered what other developments would try her patience tonight. A quick word with her guards had them dismantling the barrier as soon as the yawning beanstalk of a watchman admitting her party.

"Hold," the sluggish man ordered as she started to the main door.

Jordayne turned in her saddle, ready with a cutting remark. Just as well the word had been directed at the grubby, dusty-haired boy from the tavern. Ignoring the command, he ducked through the gates and around the watchman, determined to follow her in.

"I'm with her," the boy said pointing at Jordayne, a cheeky confidence on his oval face.

"Then don't dawdle," she snapped. "And you," she addressed the dismayed watchman, who was rather entertaining in his aimless fumble with his sword now she had sanctioned the big, bad enemy, "have the honour of personally escorting every patient who arrives at this entrance to a physic."

Such was her ire, she trotted right up the white gravel path, unaffected by the rustle of the towering palms and ignoring the grinning boy with the protruding ears who ran alongside.

"Bin tryin' to get in for three days," he said as Rokan knocked on the bolted door.

"*I've* been trying," she corrected absently, dismounting.

"*I've* succeeded now," he said with a cocky thrust of his pointed chin.

"Indeed," she replied, appreciating his quickness. She spared him a look. Thin, but not gaunt, with brown eyes that remained suspicious of the people they alighted on, he seemed a hale twelve years.

"What business have you here at this hour?" Druce asked.

"Any hour's fine if I get in," the child replied, pulling up a sleeve. The crude bandage he had tied around his arm was bloodstained and dirty.

"You might not do that yet," Rokan growled. He pounded on the door.

At last, a harried, greying fellow opened up. "Lady Jordayne," he said, his worry wrinkles smoothing as he bowed. She recognised him as one of the senior physicians. Judging by the dark circles ringing his eyes and the waxen cast to his face, he might well have been in need of a colleague's attention.

"Why was the door locked?" she asked, motioning Druce to enter the bare stone passage. The boy trailed like a puppy, focussing on each of them as they spoke.

"I was not aware it was. The physicians are in some disagreement over the hours we might admit patients. I ask it be left open on nights I attend, but the watchmen are overcautious."

They passed into a treatment room rendered shadowless by the multitude of lanterns hanging from the walls. Various vials, pots and bandages cluttered three freestanding tables, while implements lay in neat order on a fourth that sat against the wall. An elderly physic was pulling a plump man's lower eyelids down and peering at the whites of his eyes. Another two men were sitting at the other tables, one sweating with fever, the other trying to stem the bleeding from a gash to his head.

"Do they have a need to be?" she asked, softening with the realisation the delay at the door had been because this man was busy.

"Of long hours? Perhaps," he replied, pleasing her with his honesty. Hamid deq Lamont, she recalled his name was. He ushered them through more rooms and down a hall to a dormitory. A number of pallets lined the sandstone walls, the mugs, damp cloths, bandages and bowls their occupants required cluttering the floor between them. She would need to send lavender to add to the bunches of sage and thyme hanging from the walls. The cloying odour of infection had to be nauseating patients and physics alike.

Jordayne wiped a tear when she saw Trove. He was lying on a pallet close by the door, his eyes closed, his face deathly pale. She did not need a physic to tell her he would not see the sun rise.

"The child has need of treatment, Physic deq Lamont," she said.

The boy loitered in the doorway, unable to mask his fear as he listened to the soft moans of the ill and injured. "He needs help more," he said, ducking out to make way for the two guards carrying the glazed-eyed addict.

Deq Lamont tutted. "There's nothing to be done but wait out the effects and see what lasting damage has been done. The beds are full. I'm afraid he'll have to spend the night on the floor."

"It's nothing less than he would have done had we not collected him," Jordayne said.

"Now, young man," the physic said to the boy, who had found the courage to peer around the doorway. The pair of them looked ready to fall asleep on their legs. "If you'll come with me, I'll take a look at that arm."

The child hesitated, but deq Lamont guided him out. "Will he be alright?" he asked, dragging his feet. He looked over his shoulder at the debilitated addict. The guards had laid him between two pallets on the opposite side of the room.

She did not hear the answer. In the privacy afforded by sleep, the only kind she would get in a room full of the sick and injured, Jordayne kissed Trove.

"You got one of those for me?" a hoarse voice enquired from deeper in the room.

She ignored it, took Trove's clammy hand and kissed it. His eyelids fluttered open, and he managed a weak smile.

"Thank you," he said, his chest rattling. His eyes moved to Druce. "I'm sorry." It was a whisper and Druce had to come forward, to stand next to her, to hear. "The porrin."

"I entered the trance," Druce murmured. "I followed Raj."

"We arrested him, thanks to you," Jordayne said.

Trove's hand tightened on hers. His lips moved. She reached for a mug of water. Barely a sip had passed his lips before he spluttered. The liquid dribbled down his chin and onto the thin blanket. Now there was no helping the moisture glistening in her eyes. She was grateful his attention remained on Druce.

"Not Raj," he said, and Druce had to lean closer still. "Terlaan. Terlaan brings chaos for the magi." The effort must have exhausted him, for he closed his eyes and did not respond to his name. Jordayne kept hold of his hand. For all the difference in their years, she had never regarded him as old. It was devastating to see him like this, so weak, so frail, when two months back he had led the magi with a wry tongue and vital example. Druce's arm around her shoulders was welcome comfort as Trove's breathing grew shallower. Who knew how long they remained together, she and Druce, as still and silent as Trove, before the physic re-entered the room. The wary boy shuffled behind him, his eyes on the comatose man filling the floor between the beds opposite Trove.

"Is there anything you need," the physic asked.

Druce shook his head. "How was your young patient?"

It was the physic's turn to shake his head. "He has a nasty infection in a cut that should have been stitched days ago, but he is young. He will heal if he gets the correct treatment." He lifted Trove's free hand and took his pulse.

"Is he suffering?" Jordayne asked.

"I would be lying if I said there was no pain. The ragroot no longer soothes him but the magus has refused porrin. I will administer it, if you so request." He looked enquiringly at them.

"No," Druce said. "Trove knew his mind. Let him die honourably, adhering to our oath."

Jordayne stiffened but bit her tongue.

Drucilamere would have guessed her thoughts. "It will not grant him rest. Rather it will carry him to the madness of the dream. It is the blessing and the curse of the magi."

She could do nothing other than blink the tears from her eyes.

"As you wish, Magus. Lady Jordayne." The physic bowed and took his leave.

"You." The boy launched himself at Drucilamere.

The boy pummelled into Druce, beating fists against the mage's chest. "You brought that filthy drug here." If anger scrunched his face any tighter, she might mistake him for a date.

Fit and broad-chested, Druce let the child spend his energy. In the bed, Trove stirred.

"Quiet him," she hissed as patients began to wake. This was not the dignified end Trove deserved.

The guards stepped forward to secure the boy. She could have slapped Drucilamere for warning them off. Just as well the boy shrugged away Drucilamere's comforting hand and sidled to the addict. Staring at them, he heaved a mighty sob.

"What's your name?" Jordayne asked.

"Ilyam," he said, defiant now.

"And who is that man to you?" Druce asked, far too mild in the wake of the tantrum.

"He's my father." The thrust of his chin challenged them to criticise his beloved, brainless sire.

Jordayne said, "Then I hope he recovers. But do not blame the magi for Verdaan's crime. Without porrin we would have long since succumbed to Terlaan. Here, take this to your mother. I imagine your father's habit has bled her dry." She opened her money pouch and held out a gold thulek.

The boy's eyes widened. He came and took the coin, backed to the addict and lay beside him, drawing an arm under his shoulder and around his body. The glaze-eyed man may as well have been dead for all he was conscious of the intimacy. She would have counted that numbness a blessing, here in this public house where she was close to breaking down. Where shuffling from the hall, too furtive to belong to a physic, threatened to unravel her emotions. A quiet word sent Rokan into investigate. Her mind hovered on the brink of recognising the wizened, oriental man backing out of sight, but a gasp from Trove drove the memory away. She caressed her dear mage's wrinkled cheek. His skin was icy but he was sweating, his eye movement erratic beneath his lids.

"The dreams come. Even without the porrin the dreams come. He is slipping between the worlds," Drucilamere said.

Time had no right to flow so short. She murmured a prayer to Vae'oenka, goddess of the earth. Perhaps the Nurturer heard her; Trove's eyes snapped open. How devastating that this time he lacked recognition. She took a deep breath and squeezed Drucilamere's hand. He bent to Trove's trembling lips.

"Crys-tal…des-troy." The warning cost the old mage dearly. His head slumped against the pillow. His chest failed to rise. Druce reached over and closed his eyes. Jordayne buried herself in his arms.

Chapter Twelve

THE TWO OF THEM sat at a round table in another hexagonal room with parchment, quills and ink stacked on shelves. It had only one entrance, the oak door to which Arun had closed. Vinsant eyed Arun as he spoke the magic to spark light in the clear crystals on the wall. The silence between them wore on. Vinsant waggled his lips. It had to mean something that Arun had refrained from igniting his crystal during the vote. He might have lost the one friend he could count on, and he didn't even know why. It crossed his mind that he should be afraid.

"You cast a glamour on me," he said, "so I'm not scared."

Arun lowered his hood. It was despicable, how his golden-brown hair emerged ultra neat. "I did. It was necessary or you may have expired before Mahktos, such was the extent of your fear."

"Take it back. Undo it. Whatever. Just get rid of it. Now."

"My magic is long gone, Vinsant. You retook control the moment Levi touched you."

Could he get any more pathetic, shrinking into his shoulders? "You and Levi, didn't vote for me," he accused. "You don't want me here."

"If that were true, I would not have brought you to our lair. To stand in your stead, I must be exempt from the poll. Levi was too, though in such instances he has a deciding vote. The rules of the Inner Circle are complex, Vinsant, and while you gained the approval of the majority, you have powerful opponents. Were it not for who you are, I suspect there would have been more. Even the mahktashaan are aware of the ramifications of killing a prince, though be extremely clear that would not have stopped them after you stood your ground."

"Tell me who they are." His eyes fell onto the cerulean crystal on Arun's neck. "One had a tangerine crystal, and another had a dark blue. I forgot the colour of the third."

"I do not know. In all but the most exceptional of circumstances, the Inner Circle vote by sparking a crystal, any coloured crystal, most likely one worn by another. It is our way of assuring anonymity."

"You can use each other's crystals?"

"Only the Inner Circle, Vinsant. The ability marks one for such a position, and there have never in our history been more than ten so talented at any one time. This has helped ensure order and obedience, since using another's crystal leaves the owner unprotected. For the Inner Circle, to call on another's power without permission is a serious offence." Arun rolled up a parchment on the table, nimble fingered even in his black gloves. "Do not fret; you will learn our ways in time." He tapped the end of the roll to his goatee. "There is a more pressing matter we need to discuss."

"Uh, like why everyone wanted me dead?"

"Yes, Vinsant. Mahktos rejected you. It is unusual but not unheard of for our god to deny an initiated apprentice full induction as a mahktashaan. Usually it is the power-hungry, defiant or overconfident ones, though at times the most promising candidate suffers beneath his gaze. The mahktashaan invariably put these apprentices to death. They hold too many of our secrets, of your family's secrets, to be allowed to re-enter the world. They suffer this fate because they assumed their apprenticeship willingly, with full knowledge of what I am now telling you."

"But I was only seeking to become an apprentice."

"There are only two other candidates in our history who sparked a majoria's crystal but incurred Mahktos's wrath. One had an uncle stand in his stead, and went on to be an unremarkable and limited member of the mahktashaan, until he killed another in a fit of jealousy and suffered our justice."

"And the other?" Vinsant prompted when Arun fell silent. He had a nasty feeling he was going to hate the answer.

Arun released the parchment. It rolled halfway open. "Was Wyn deq Kaelor."

Vinsant spluttered. "*The* Wyn deq Kaelor? The Wyn deq Kaelor who discovered how to access magic through porrin?"

"The one and the same, young friend."

"He was a *mahktashaan*?"

"No, Vinsant, he was not. After a friend of his family stood in his stead, he absconded mid-way through training, no doubt fearing to stand before Mahktos a second time. But he was privy to many secrets, and delivered a magic system, if a cursed one, into the hands of the Myklaani."

"But I didn't know this. No one knows this."

"Only the mahktashaan, Vinsant, and not even the Myklaani. It seems deq Kaelor was too proud to admit his failure. Mahktos is wise in his choices. I suggest you pray to our god with all your heart, and make regular offerings to appease his angst." Arun, Vinsant saw, was not jesting.

"What happened to the person who stood in Kaelor's stead?" Vinsant whispered.

"He was put to the sword."

"Will that happen to you if I fail?"

"Only if you disgrace your position. However, I shall lose my title of Minoria, since I stood in that name. I do not intend for that to happen."

Vinsant nodded. "I won't let you down."

Arun re-rolled the parchment, found a ribbon on a shelf and tied it up.

Vinsant turned in his chair. "I'll work hard to be a good mahktashaan."

Having slid the parchment into place, Arun faced him with the grandfather of all serious expressions and a disconcerting intensity in his cerulean eyes. "Vinsant, when I received your quartz, Mahktos spoke to me. He said we had sealed our fate by allowing you to live. The implication was it mattered not whether we allowed you to train. I know you have no inkling of why this is so…"

Well, actually, his promise to Kordahla might have had a great deal to do with it. Vinsant bit his lip. Oh, scums, was he ever having an attack of the guilts. Vae, how could such a simple thing as helping his sister almost get him killed?

"It is because of that," Arun continued, "we might hope the future which the god foresees is not ordained."

Vinsant shook his head.

"With that in mind," Arun continued. "I remind you that you are a prince no longer. You are under my direct tutelage, and if you ever disregard my advice again, I will order you whipped until the skin peels off your behind, and mete out the lashes myself. Is that understood?"

Even though Arun had to be exaggerating, Vinsant bowed his head. If today was anything to go by, his time as an apprentice mahktashaan was going to be one adventurous, rocky road. "Eh, yes, Minoria," he mumbled.

"Good," said Arun. He flicked his hood over his head. "Then let us see what the Majoria makes of your fish."

They twisted through the hexagonal maze, so Arun could make good his promise. Vinsant chewed his lip, ruminating over Arun's guess the ceremony was unlikely to have taken place with the bedlam his atypical initiation would be causing.

"Ar..." turned into a respectful "Minoria," when Vinsant caught himself in time.

"You may ask, Vinsant," Arun said with uncanny intuition.

"If I'm not a prince here, why did you treat me like one?" His near circumvention of the initiation rite had been bothering him more than the tension at the back of his neck.

He walked, and Arun glided, several steps. Sometimes Arun's thoughtful nature was frustrating to the point Vinsant wanted to grunt. Grown-ups placed far too much emphasis on gathering words. "We wanted to prepare you, to test you first, as we did with the other candidates. They had shown potential to a recruiting mahktashaan, who counselled them as to the potential consequences – all the consequences, including, if Mahktos rejected them, execution – before they agreed to participate."

They entered a bare hexagonal room with three arched exits, the tops doming larger than the bases. "But you would have trained me anyway. If I hadn't sparked anyone's recruiting crystal. I mean other than Lev– the Majoria's," Vinsant said. The right door took them deeper into the lair, into a room stacked with swords, shields, sharpening stones and polishing cloths. They veered left, through the only other doorway.

"There are certain treasures we could permit you to see, certain skills we could impart."

This room had a combat training square marked on the floor. "But it would have been an allowance. Because I'm a prince," Vinsant pressed.

"Yes."

Vinsant fell silent. Arun's promise to treat him as no more than an apprentice was proving to be as hollow as the ring of his boots on the stones. Vae'oeldin knew – no *Mahktos* knew – how strong the desire to serve his brother as Majoria burned. Didn't Arun see by treating him as special, Vinsant would never, ever earn the respect of his peers? If he didn't have that, he could never lead. He stopped paying attention to their route. It was not like he would ever be able to find his way back again. An intrepid explorer could wander around until he starved.

His broodiness finally wore on Arun, which, he thought, was well and good. The Minoria sighed and stopped in another training room. Vinsant refused to meet his eye.

"I tell you this in confidence, Vinsant. It was at my suggestion the Majoria did this, and it took some persuading. I feel there is magical talent in you that could blossom under our training. If I had any doubt, I would not have supported your request to join us, nor would I have jeopardised my position by standing in your stead. You are younger than our usual recruits. There was no urgency for you to begin a formal apprenticeship. But I would rest easier if there was someone close to Princess Kordahla who knew a little of our arts. So much easier I was prepared to go as far as I could to train you before you risked initiation. Do not question me on this. I will say no more for, at the moment, it is as much intuition as my belief in your suitability for the mahktashaan. I trust you are mature enough to keep this to yourself."

"Er…yes."

Arun stopped and fixed him with a lowered-chin, raised brow look that brooked no argument. "And to avoid associating my desire for the Princess's protection with your earlier assertion about my liking her."

Vinsant nodded, clear on the last. One was personal, the other professional. He understood that. What he wanted more than anything to ask, but could not, was whether Arun's professional loyalties lay with Kordahla or with Father.

"I want you to treat me like any other apprentice," he said instead.

"Like *an* apprentice Vinsant. You have already demonstrated you are not like the others. Which is just as well since it will raise no objections when the Majoria and I mentor you."

Vinsant opened his mouth, but was not sure what he wanted to say.

Arun gave a light-hearted tut. "Be thankful it is so, or you would not enjoy the privilege of seeing Levi examine that fish."

Vinsant chuckled, and followed through the confounding hexagonal rooms into the chamber that had hosted the initiation ceremony.

The members of the Inner Circle were standing around the altar, and there on the top was his smelly grapper, clear crystals arranged in a circle around it. Vinsant took a deep breath. There were crystals secured in sconces, and crystals hidden in the statue of Mahktos, crystals fast around the necks of mahktashaan, and crystals in the joints of djinn. If there was ever an opportunity to acquire one for Kordahla, it was here and now. Thinking hard, he edged closer to the table, watching Arun and Levi take their places on opposite sides of Errol's scaly head. He jumped when the mahktashaan began a staccato chant. It sure had the beat of a military march.

At the sudden cessation of voices, the crystals in the sconces went dull. The mahktashaan crystals flared, painting the room in awesome colours before the beams smashed into white over the grapper. One day soon, he was going to be able to do that. He wasn't keen on perfecting the boring chorus the mahktashaan had resumed, though, all except Levi, who lifted a crystal and pushed it into the grapper's mouth. He mimicked the mahktashaan when they clapped a hand over their crystals; knowing the gesture might give him an edge when he tried to work magic with his quartz. For the briefest of moments, the room plunged into silent dark. Then blinding light exploded from the grapper and the crystals around it. Vinsant winced at the pain in his eyes. The light had to be serious because Arun added his voice to Levi's hurried chant. As the room dimmed, several of the mahktashaan dispersed to the edges of the room and held their crystals up as others burst into garbled discussion.

"Djinn?" Vinsant asked nobody in particular when the conversation had petered out. The only point he had understood was that the mahktashaan were unsure what any of this meant.

"Indeed. The only possible reason for such an astounding reaction from the crystals is if a djinn has tainted the fish," a stout mahktashaan with a plum crystal and homely voice said.

"Our crystals are djinn-sourced," a taller man with a teal crystal explained. "That is how they are able to detect the creatures."

"Oh," Vinsant said, grateful someone understood he knew diddlysquat about mahktashaan lore.

"Thankfully, we don't seem to have any in our midst," the first mahktashaan added.

Around the room, the coloured crystals remained inert in mahktashaan hands.

"Majoria, a word," Arun said, his voice grave.

"Eh, Majoria?" Vinsant piped up before he lost his opportunity, "Can I have my fish now?"

The Majoria signalled to the stout mahktashaan, a dismissive gesture that implied he was not to be bothered with such trivialities.

"You may take it, my prince," the mahktashaan said while removing the crystal buried in the grapper's mouth.

"Vinsant. I'm just an apprentice here," he replied, eyeing the crystal. How stupid was he, to think the mahktashaan had forgotten it?

"Then you shall do well," the mahktashaan replied with a small bow. Vinsant gathered it was for his humility rather than his station. "I am Strauss, and this is Garzene," the stout man said, indicating the mahktashaan with the teal crystal.

"Pleased to meet you," Vinsant said, remembering his manners before he snatched the fish. He affected a careless retreat from the table, sweeping three of the crystals onto the floor in the process. He had to hope his body hid the falling number, that the mahktashaan still in the room were not the pedantic sort who would account for each crystal before allowing an apprentice to leave. Squatting, Vinsant stuffed a crystal back into Errol's mouth. He could always make up a story if he was caught, about wanting to practice magic or something. They couldn't punish Arun just because he was an over-enthusiastic apprentice, though Levi was bound to notice his sweaty palms and racing pulse. He palmed the remaining two crystals and set them on the altar. Levi and Arun had their backs to him, and were moving into the temple. The other mahktashaan were filing out of the opposite door. Vinsant tucked Errol under his arm, and tried to act natural. Garzene and Strauss kept chatting as he walked past.

"Majoria, a word," Arun said, his concern rising, but he had to wait while the forward young prince made his request. The palace servants were going to be extremely unhappy if Vinsant kept the fish in his rooms. Just as the Minoria was less than enthusiastic about what he needed to divulge. Princess Kordahla had little enough freedom and more than enough scrutiny as it was.

Inside the temple, Levi waved a hand. "*Selos*". The air within the arches shimmered, sealing the room from prying minds and ears. "I did not expect you to stand in the prince's name, else I would have forbidden it." He dampened the rebuke by removing his hood.

The deed was done. All was well, and Arun saw no need to comment.

Levi was not so content. "The djinn have mischief afoot, to drop grappers from the sky. Terlaan has need of you, Arun. As Minoria. The Inner Circle's talents, while considerable, fall short of your position. Do not relinquish your duties to the Shah for the whims of his immature son."

"It is no whim, Levi. Vinsant is keen. He has demonstrated talent, and Mahktos himself had an opinion about the child." Even after all these years, the intensity in Levi's expectant, black eyes disconcerted. How much more distressing must the breath-taking princess find his cerulean ones?

"What had Mahktos to say of our youngest apprentice, Minoria?"

Arun swallowed. As disturbing as it was, his duty to his order ranked above his loyalty to the prince. "Mahktos believes Apprentice Vinsant will betray our order." As Levi took a rasping breath, he hurried on. "Better our fate is sealed by one of our own than an outsider. By granting Vinsant a crystal Mahktos owns as much."

Levi's jaw clicked. His next words were little more than a breath. "It could well be."

"The god has decreed he may train."

"It is a gambit. One of our own can do much harm. In that regard, it is prudent to keep the child close." The Majoria pursed his thin lips. "So, we were wrong. The grappers fell on Vinsant, not the princess. But he is not of marriageable age. What jest do the djinn play?"

Arun forced his honesty between clenched teeth. "I believe the grappers are a separate matter. I believe the djinn attached to Princess Kordahla as we first thought." His guts twisted to think the shah would entertain the idea of wedding his vivacious daughter to Lord Ahkdul.

Levi frowned. "Explain this," he demanded.

"A still wind blew in her rooms when I collected the prince."

"But Vinsant was there. There is no way to determine which child was afflicted." Levi clipped his words with spite.

A long moment passed before Arun could bring himself to seal Kordahla's fate. "Her veil has disappeared."

It was Levi's turn to hesitate. No honourable mahktashaan would keep the garment, but still he asked the question with cutting sharpness. "Are there any who need discipline?"

"It was a djinn, Majoria," Arun said with finality. An embroidered corner had peeped between the scrabbling meatball sellers at the souk, to disappear in a tell-tale indigo shimmer when the mahktashaan hauled them to their feet.

"Double her guard," the Majoria ordered, spittle flying from his mouth. "She must remain in the palace."

Arun flinched. It was no secret that, under his powerful exterior, the Majoria harboured a conservativeness toward the womenfolk. This vehemence, though, bordered on cruel.

CHAPTER THIRTEEN

IN THE STILL OF the summer night, cicada legs whirring in the gardens below his rooms, Ordosteen gazed at the woman sleeping beside him and knew she had to leave. He lifted a lock of the pale, jasmine-scented hair fanning across her back and brought it to his lips, a private parting gesture that caused her to stir. Such a small movement to pique his desire. When Rochelle opened her blue eyes, and lifted an elegant hand to his face, he knew he would keep her one last night. He dropped her hair so she might roll over and display her plump breasts. "Too energetic for sleep, my lord?" she murmured.

The only possible response was to kiss her full on the lips, enjoy the feel of her hand in his white hair, her nails scratching the length of his spine. The delicious sensation made him shiver. He brushed a hand along her ample thigh, surprised to find it rough with goosebumps. He was rubbing them warm before the implication dawned. It near killed him to disentangle himself, to confirm her nipples were erect not with desire but cold. Groaning, he rolled off her. "You must go," he said, swinging his feet off the bed.

She bent her elbow to rest her head upon her hand, her long-lashed eyes more curious than offended. "And if I don't?"

He turned away. She ran a finger down his back.

"Just go, Rochelle." He would bring another to the vast emptiness of his golden bed tomorrow. There was no shortage of courtesans willing to accept what was on offer. Ordosteen was considerate in bed and out. If, in his hopeless situation, he had allowed a little flab to widen his girth, a little fat to wobble beneath his chin, he was still a shah.

She swished a languid finger along the sheet. "Perhaps I should meet this djinn of yours, and see what manner of beast he is to curse you to widowhood."

He stood and faced her, knowing before he spoke his voice would crack, with fury and desire. "Where did you learn of this?"

She sat up, gathering the sheet to her. "It is hardly a secret, Ordo. Five wives dead at their first birthing, no legitimate child surviving. Can Myklaan think other than that you are djinn-cursed?"

He grabbed fistfuls of sheet. "Djinn-cursed. I, the Shah? Who spouts this nonsense?"

"Don't play the ignoramus, Ordo. All five of your wives whispered of a still wind on the night they conceived, and their midwives of an unnatural chill on the eve of each birth. They were very young, very scared."

He tossed the sheet onto her lap. "Yet no mage sought my counsel. And despite months in my bed you speak of it only now?"

"Do you blame me? It is hardly a subject to raise in the throes of passion, my dear, foolish Shah. We are about to receive a visit for the first time in those rather delectable months, and still you deny it."

"Go. Get out of my bed. Return to your family's estates, and if you speak a word of this, I shall have you thrown into the dungeons."

She tossed her hair, giggling in her throat. "How easily you are defeated. I am hardly your wife. What danger is there for us to enjoy each other? You have bastards enough to prove it can be done." She allowed the sheet to slip from her hands, and reclined on the pillows, a temptress if ever there was one. His resolution dissolved as his arousal grew. Smiling, she held out a hand. "Come back to bed. My embrace will soothe you."

A moan escaped his lips, but he did as she asked, pulling a quilt over them to fend off the chill seizing the room on this clement night. The temptation to unburden his oppressed soul warred with his desire for her.

"Adessa was not my wife," he said, stilling her roaming hand.

For the first time, Rochelle looked uncertain. "Her too?" she asked.

"Her too." Selfish in his need for companionship, he had sealed Adessa's fate when he determined to name their firstborn heir. It had been pure conceit to think he could outwit that cursed djinn by refusing to marry. She had been little more than a child, sweet and attentive, and keen to ease the troubles of her Shah. For her devotion, he had condemned her to death. He had been a fool. Was a fool still.

Rochelle lay back and looked at the flower and vine arabesques on the ceiling. "It is love then, that is your undoing." Her insight lifted the burden of the years. She looked like a cream-fed cat as she said, "How touching it is to learn that you love me."

"And if I bed you once more, your fate will be sealed," he warned as she turned her head to look at him.

He did not expect her to kiss him, or her to be the one who pushed them apart. Sliding out of bed, she threw a robe around her shoulders, and began to dress, pulling her clothes off a gilded screen. "I do not imagine another man could fascinate me so thoroughly, in bed and out, but I am not willing to die for you, especially in so demeaning a manner as childbirth." She was almost past the age, but that was no hindrance to a vengeful djinn. Ordosteen would not risk it. His heart would break beyond repair if he lost another love, and so he could do naught but impress every beautiful detail upon his memory while she rolled a stocking up her shapely leg.

"Tell me, Ordo, what did the djinn promise for you to surrender love?"

It was because she held curiosity and no trace of judgement that he told her. "Myklaan has peace with its neighbours." Young, naive and by far too ambitious, he had almost begged the beast for a deal when it insinuated itself into his life.

She crossed the room and picked up a hand mirror from a table, dark oak with fancy gold mounts. Surrounded by the precious metal, he yet possessed not a thing of true worth. Rochelle turned her face, examining her pretty cheek bones from different angles. "Ah. The man is poor, but the Shah is great." She set the mirror down and turned, resting against the table. Myklaan has truly flourished under you, my love."

He sat up, panicked that she might misunderstand. "The wretched creature takes more than I agreed. I bargained with my loins not my heart. I agreed to remain heirless, not loveless. Yet he takes the heirs by killing the mother."

Once more she kissed him, quick and light this time. "It is the nature of the djinn, my lord. You know this as surely as you know our history. Have your meeting. I will send Katrine to you before the sun is up. Her interest has been none too delicate of late, and while her body is pleasing I do not fear you will fall for that fatuous one." Were it not for the tear in the corner of her eye, an interloper might have thought she were the lady and he the diversion. He let his eyes linger on the door after she left, certain she would be gone to Zulmei with the dawn.

An affected yawn drew his attention away. Ordosteen cursed aloud. Floating cross-legged at his right shoulder was the indigo djinn with the arrogant vermillion eyes. Four decades on, the creature was unchanged, right down to the repulsive taint of fish.

"An interesting choice of confidant," the djinn said. He linked and flexed his fingers, cracking his crystal knuckles. "Your candour surprises me after all these years." He dropped onto the quilt, lying on his side, head on hand in imitation of Rochelle.

Gagging, Ordosteen bounded out of bed. The search for a loincloth served as a pretext for moving away from the hideous creature. "What do you expect, djinn? In forty-one years, I've seen not a single hair on your head."

"I've been around," the creature said with a wry smile. "I should have thought that rather obvious."

"You make a mockery of our deal. I never agreed to remain loveless."

The djinn transformed into an indigo-skinned Rochelle. Despite their distance, the whiff of the sea assaulted Ordosteen as fully as her perfume lured. "Then love from afar and keep it chaste. I have kept my end of our bargain. There is seldom trouble within your borders, and never along them."

Ordosteen swallowed rising bile. "I dispute that when porrin decimates my population," he said after his stomach had settled. "You are selective in your enforcement. You have reneged, djinn. Give me back my life."

Returning to his true, hideous form, the djinn laughed. Ordosteen balked as the creature flew at his face, banking up just as the shah feared the creature would smash into his nose. The momentum carried the creature into a backflip. With a twist, he floated upside down, drifting closer and closer to force the shah against the wall.

"You remain ignorant of what mayhem your country has been spared, you self-centred insect. It is fortunate for you I have had my fun."

"Your mischief, you mean."

"Mischief, is it?" The djinn grew until his neck bent against the floor and his bloated body squashed into the corners of the room. Indigo flesh squashed against Ordosteen's lips, and his heart hammered his tightening chest. He pressed back, clipping the edge of the screen and toppling it against the wall. He closed his eyes as he gagged, opened them to find the djinn floating beside the bed, one arm lying along the top of the square, jewelled bedhead. An indigo finger brushed down over an emerald, knocking it from its setting to the dent in the pillow where Rochelle's head had lain. The creature sneered. "I release you from the deal. Does that not show you how magnanimous I am?"

As often as he called himself so, Ordosteen was not in truth an imprudent man. Years of regret had turned him wise to the duplicity of the djinn, and though his heart leapt, his intellect screamed. "What fun will this release accord you?" Eyes narrowed, he strode forward. Far from driving the djinn back, his movement set it rising. He walked right under the infuriating creature, and had to wheel to face it with a slaying glare.

One side of his mouth in a cruel curve, the djinn righted himself. "Take the offer or leave it. I care not either way, shah of insects, but there is a price. He clapped his hands, sparking the crystals in his joints. When his fingers parted, a green veil spread between them, its gold embroidery intricate and precise. A hand gesture sent it sailing onto the pillow. "If you return the owner of that veil to her rightful place, you will be free of our compact. If, and only then, insect Shah."

Ordosteen's brow furrowed as he looked from the veil to the djinn. The creature was fading fast. "Whose…?" he started to ask, trailing off as the djinn disappeared with a soft *whoomp* of air, and a laugh that chilled him to the bone.

CHAPTER FOURTEEN

THANKS TO HIS STUNNING reaction to Majoria Levi's crystal, Vinsant had it all worked out. Which was why Physic Nocrates's response stumped him.

"Look," he said, juggling the grapper so he could pull up his kurta and display the red area over the back of his ribs that was going to colour into a spectacular bruise. It hurt his pride to admit the minor yet hard won injury pained him. But he was faking it for Kordahla, so he affected a wince when Physic Nocrates's aging but gentle hands explored the area and hoped first that his manhood would not be called into question and, far more importantly, that the Majoria would never hear of this.

"I'll give you a salve to decrease the bruising," Physic Nocrates said in a voice that sounded like it needed that salve to smooth its creaks. He wended a stiff path around tables laden with dried herbs to a shelf stacked with pots where he selected one filled with a pungent greasy ointment. While he had the hunched posture of a doddering grandfather, he never faltered when it came to remedies.

"Er..." Vinsant scratched his head. The fair tuft of hair that always stood up tickled the side of his hand. "I really need to get a good night's sleep."

"If you lie on your stomach, you should have no problem at all. Would you care for me to apply the first dose of the ointment, Highness?"

As the cold salve went on, Vinsant articulated heartfelt groans he was sure would convince the physic of the seriousness of his condition.

He had, after all, had plenty of practice with the particular timbre during sword practice with Mariano. The ploy worked too well.

"An injury that distressing may mean cracked ribs, young man. I'm afraid you will have to suspend your training for a couple of major moons until they heal." The physic stopped his ministrations, claimed a padded seat, and leaned back. Vinsant dropped his kurta and turned in open-mouthed horror as the man thoughtfully rubbed the white stubble on his chin. An excellent physic, Nocrates often became so engrossed in his tasks he forgot to attend to his appearance, a characteristic the Shah tolerated from him and no other because of his reputation for miracles, a talent he vehemently denied.

"I don't think it's that bad," Vinsant said. "I'm sure I'll be fine with a good night's sleep."

"I'm inclined to agree."

Vinsant pushed the fish into a nook between some bowls on the table, wrinkled his nose because it really had begun to smell, and looked around the ordered clutter. Subtlety was not having the desired effect. "Perhaps a dose of porrin. Just to ensure I don't toss too much and accidentally crack my damaged ribs," he blurted. With luck, Nocrates would not notice he was unable to look him in the eye. His awkwardness provided good cover to spy out the plant in question. Too bad that nothing resembling it was in plain view.

Nocrates tapped a finger over his lips. "For cracked ribs, yes, porrin may be necessary." He slapped his hands on the arms of the chair. "Oh dear, I imagine the Majoria will be disappointed to learn of your infirmity."

"No!" Vinsant fairly jumped towards the physic.

Sighing, Physic Nocrates hoisted himself onto his feet. "Prince Vinsant, you do realise I am bound by the oath of my profession to keep my patient's medical history private?" When Vinsant looked at the ceiling in what he hoped was an angelic pose, the physic shuffled forward and placed the pot of salve into his hand. "Would you care to tell me why you visit my rooms rather than have me call at your chamber, then make great effort to secure porrin when you have sustained worse bruising at the end of your brother's practice sword?"

As he could think of nothing that, despite the physic's assurances, would stay within these walls, it was time to be gracious in defeat and exit before he landed himself and Kordahla into deeper scums than they had seen in his entire life. "It was a dare," he said, picking up the fish and backing away. "There's no need to tell the Majoria." One trait Levi would never possess was a sense of humour.

He lost the physic's reply turning to the door. In the corner behind it, a small gilded statue of Mahktos sat atop a pillar. The god couldn't be too pleased Vinsant had twisted the truth because His crimson eyes were glowing something stern. Vinsant squirmed aside to allow Nocrates full view of the statue. It figured that under the physic's gaze, the eyes would harden back into lifeless gems. His overactive, overtired imagination had to be playing tricks on him. He longed to fall into bed, a rather rare sensation for his boisterous self, and told Nocrates so as he moved to the door because it would help convince the physic how earnest he had been about his terrible injuries. Mahktos wasn't fooled. As soon as Vinsant obscured Nocrates's view, the stature's eyes tracked his path.

"Uh…Uh…Mahktos?" he managed, pointing weakly. He kept his disbelieving eyes firmly on Nocrates as the physic walked over and lifted the statue into his hands.

"A gift from the Majoria for tending the mahktashaan over the years."

"Huh?" That inarticulate mumble wasn't going to get him any answers.

Nocrates replaced the statue with the deference of a mahktashaan. Pressing his palms together, he touched his liver spotted forehead in obeisance. "I dare say you want to know what an old man could possibly do to incur a debt from the Majoria?"

"Yes, no, I mean, don't the mahktashaan cure themselves?"

"They have a gift for relieving particular hurts, but as far as open wounds, broken bones and certain diseases are concerned, there are few among them who have the talent to cure. Those that do usually need to study under a physic. Take Arun; he is one of the best I have ever trained but even he is no match for some of these herbs in cases of disease and…"

"Ehr, yes," Vinsant interrupted before the old man rambled him to sleep on his feet. He had somehow assumed the mahktashaan could cure all. Their limitation suddenly made his plan to get Kordahla out of the palace seem risky. "But why do you worship the mahktashaan god, anyway?" As hard as he peered, the eyes remained stubbornly inert.

"What. Such a question from you? I had heard that you were rather liberal in your thinking, Highness." Affronted, Nocrates wove his way back to his chair. "Forgive me. My spine is not what it used to be."

Vinsant dismissed the apology with a wave of his hand. To do otherwise would be to suffer a rebuke from father. Besides, the tending of an expertly set broken arm, a severe fever and a spate of childhood ills had earned this man the right to a little indulgence. "Isn't Mahktos the mahktashaan god?"

"Who's teaching you philosophy, boy? Pass me that jug, will you?"

Dutiful because he wanted answers, Vinsant put the fish down and poured Nocrates a mug of water. A furtive glance at the statue failed to catch anything unusual.

"Mahktos is a god. A god, you understand. Gods may be worshipped by any and all who choose."

"But..But.." What was philosophy anyway?

"It's a common misconception around here that the mahktashaan worship a secret god. That's only because most folks are keen on the Vae." Nocrates crumbled the leaves of a woody dried herb over the fish. Poor Errol still smelt. "You'll find temples to Mahktos scattered over the realm; small ones granted, but they're not there just to serve the mahktashaan on the rare occasions they turn up. His followers are everywhere."

"Ah," said Vinsant, with a glimmer of understanding.

"Well speak up, Highness. Your mouth looks about to burst with questions. And you don't think those mahktashaan are going to give you straight answers, do you? They'll have you believe they're the only ones with the right to His grace."

Vinsant wasn't sure where to start. Blurting the point usually seemed to work. Of course, in that regard it probably helped that he was a prince.

Considering bed was a more welcome option than a night of Nocrates garrulous tales, he decided to give it a go. "Why do his eyes glow at me?"

"What? What do you mean, Highness?" With a sigh, the physic rose, pulled Vinsant aside and squinted first at the statue, then into Vinsant's eyes.

"I mean its eyes were following me."

"Did you hit your head? Do you feel dizzy, or faint?"

"No."

Nocrates scratched at his whiskery chin. "Perhaps you should get to bed."

Vinsant grabbed Errol as Nocrates ushered him to the door.

"I'll check on you tomorrow. Of course, if the god is watching you, Mahktashaan Branak might explain it."

"Okay," Vinsant pulled the latch on the door, bit his lip and fell into thought. After today's initiation, he had as much intention of asking a mahktashaan as a scum dipper did of smelling sweet. He thought he knew well enough why the god might want to keep a close eye on him. It meant the stinking scums for both him and Kordahla.

Dragged from downy comfort of bed when Samille answered a knock at the door, Kordahla could only stare at the pillared, interlocking crystal in Vinsant's outstretched hand. She really had not expected it. Had thought deep down they were playing some childish game.

"You didn't," was all she could manage to say, aware her speechlessness was not entirely from the astonishment that her younger brother had managed to pilfer one of the most closely guarded secrets of the mahktashaan. The odour from the deteriorating fish had a trifle to do with it too.

"You have Errol to thank. It was the least he could do, seeing he got you into this mess in the first place." Vinsant beamed at her. Which was when she noticed the quartz around his neck.

She took his arm and led him to the daybed, over carpet so profound a dark red it appeared blooded. They huddled behind the curtains to avoid drawing the attention of the sleepy maids she had coaxed back to bed. As loyal as they were, she couldn't chance they would spill a secret this devastating. Devout, brown-haired Karie had a habit of gabbling when the mahktashaan guard she fancied came courting, and long-lashed, brunette Samille admitted to the least transgression under the mildest of enquiries. As it was, they probably suspected some wayward exploit; Vinsant had no business in her chambers at this hour.

She threw open the shutters on the bulbous arch above the bed, and set her dripping candle on the sill. Green moonlight bathed Vinsant's freckled face as he coddled the crystal in a depression he had thumped into a plump pillow. He whistled as the reflected beams cast a glow around them. His enthusiasm failed to infect. Kneeling, she flicked waves of her walnut hair back as she leaned in for a better look.

"Won't it be missed? Won't you be punished if they find out what you've done?" She could not let him take this risk for her. A risk which for anyone other than a prince might end on the point of a mahktashaan sword. Could not, if she were honest, take another step to commit herself to this foolhardy path. She peeped through the billowing curtains into the bedchamber as sheets rustled and female voices whispered.

Vinsant stroked his treasure. "They'll never know it was me. No, seriously, if the mahktashaan discover it here you can tell them a still wind blew just before you noticed it among the pillows. It was the djinn's idea. Blame him."

"Oh, Vinsant. I couldn't. Father would never, not when he meets Ahkdul." She slid off her heels, gazed out the window, and sighed. If only tonight, and not yesterday, had been the major moon, Levi might not have accorded such significance to the falling grappers.

"You want me to take it back?"

She heard the trepidation in his voice. Realised with a trill of shock how much he had risked simply to bring it to her, that he would double that risk by trying to return it undiscovered.

"How does it work?" she asked, too awestruck even to touch it. She hugged a pillow into the curve of her waist.

"No idea," he said with a shrug which failed to hide just how crestfallen he was. "Just find someplace safe for it."

Kordahla nodded.

"Do you think it will be enough?" Vinsant asked.

"I hope so. But Vinsant," – she hesitated on parted lips – "you know it can never happen. I mean, even if I managed to escape these walls, how would I get to Myklaan before the mahktashaan found me? If, by some miracle, I got to the hills, what interest would the hill tribes have in seeing me safe? They would as soon turn me over to Father for a reward."

He straightened one leg. "Then you'll just have to offer them a bribe they can't refuse."

"Gold would weigh me down."

"But porrin wouldn't."

"Porrin?" She blinked. "Whatever would they want with the drug? Their people are suffering its effects as much as ours."

"Exactly. So many of them are wandering into the towns looking for it. They can hardly afford to buy it, can they? I bet they're the ones responsible for all this crime."

She thought of the wharf, and the leg in the trousers with the brightly coloured braid. "Where are we going to get porrin?" she asked, regretting the words as soon as they left her mouth. She most certainly did not want Vinsant to be involved with the illicit drug, nor to encourage this crazy conspiracy. Vae'oenka knew it could never come to fruition.

"Not from Physic Nocrates," Vinsant answered.

Her lips tightened. "What aren't you telling me?"

He put on his angelic face.

Chapter Fifteen

THE GLITTERING, GOLDEN TEMPLE of the Vae was a travesty when one nursed deep sorrows. Unable to bear the bright exterior, Jordayne stepped through Vae'oeldin's entrance, which was in Vae'oenka's wall, and beheld the architectural marvel. Against protocol, she turned to her right, to Vae'omar's corner where a statue of the god's scaled body reflected in the pool from which it soared. Behind it, water babbled around the ferns studding the stone wall of the minaret, and melted into devastating calmness. The pool should have had the decency to churn for her loss. But the day was still, and the holes in the wall which channelled the spraying wind refused to whistle. The god's indifference did not leave her inclined to generosity. She slid one of the gold bangles Trove had gifted her off her arm, and let it slip from her hands into the pool. It had drifted past a goldfish and into the algae of the depths before she blinked herself back to the present.

She visited Vae'oeldin's busier corner next, taking the time to pray in the bright light streaming through the myriad windows that checkered His minaret. She had never cared for this particular depiction of Him, an austere warrior with feathered plumes streaming from His head down the length of His back. The mages travelled through His domain, however, and it was fitting she pay her respects. On rising, she tossed two of her bracelets, Trove's bracelets, into the air currents that spiralled around the god. With tears threatening, she did not wait to see where they would land, instead turning towards the dark corner of the triangular temple, the one dedicated to Vae'oenka, goddess of the earth.

"My condolences, my lady," a voice said.

Jordayne turned to find the haggard Physic Hamid deq Lamont behind her. He had suffered a busy night she deduced from his sunken eyes and stooped posture. The boy with the infected arm was beside him, contemplating her with a solemnity that exceeded his tender years. One had to grow up quickly living with an addict, she supposed.

"They are appreciated. And my sympathies to you, young man," she replied, for the boy was dressed in the white churidar kurta of mourning. For all the tears streaking his cheeks, he had to be better off without an addict in family.

"I have offered Ilyam a position at the hospice," Hamid continued.

She nodded, not truly caring, wanting to make her offerings and creep to the Mage Guild, where she could wallow among people who mourned Trove with sincerity. Only a pressing need to ascertain the intent of the shadowy visitor to the hospice detained her, for she had remembered who he was last night, as she lay awake after Druce's gentle lovemaking.

"Are you really Lady Jordayne?" the boy asked. He was clutching a grubby turban no self-respecting man would have contemplated wrapping over his head. Likely the only possession his father had left him, the paltry offering would, with luck, touch the heart of whichever god he chose to gift it to.

"People do address me as such," she said, too tired to converse but unable to abandon her habit of mockery. Her gaze had drifted to the mosaic of animals and plants on Vae'oenka's wall. Her usual empathy had deserted her, and she wanted to be about her day.

"Then you need to do something about the porrin. You need to tell the Shah to stop the trade."

She blinked, unable to recall if it was normal for a child to be so outspoken. Then she sighed. "I suppose I do," was all she could think to say.

"Forgive him," Hamid said. "He is as overcome by grief as you are."

"There is no need," she said. "He speaks the truth. Though perhaps he could consider how it might be done. The brightest minds in our land have yet to find a way." Her eyes drifted, to the statue of the goddess, and the kowtowing women before it.

"We will leave you to your obeisance," Hamid said, sensing her mood. He gave a small bow.

"A moment," she said, remembering the real reason she had forborne to accompany Drucilamere here this morning. Her mage had seen through the pretext of fatigue, but known better than to ask her business. "What affairs did the oriental man have at the hospice last night?"

The physic frowned. "There was no one of that description there."

"Are you certain?"

"My lady, you and the Master Magus were the last visitors of the night."

She nodded, and left him. Her mind roiling with anger, or anxiety, or both, she knelt before the goddess in the final corner of the triangular temple with its bowed walls and domed minarets. This night-clad niche was her favourite, though it offered no comfort today. The statue of the goddess seemed to rise from the very earth, its body garlanded with leaves and petals, its hair a braid of vines. She twisted three bangles off her arm and threw them into the surrounding pit. *Take him back to you*, she prayed, struggling to breathe through a stab of fear that Trove had not found rest. In a fit of desperation, she tore the remaining bracelets from her arms, an offering she flung into the bowels of the earth. *Don't let it be*, she pleaded. *You cannot let a heathen lay claim to Trove that way.* She cast a guilty look at the statue of Vae'oeldin, who bore the magi across his expanse, but she had never understood the warrior god, and so she renewed her pleas to the Mother, who welcomed Her children back to the womb when their time on this earth expired. Around her, monks garbed in sleeveless, wraparound, knee-length robes tended the corners, paying little heed to her tears. Watering eyes were common enough around the goddess. Collecting herself, she left through Vae'omar's exit, which was in Vae'oeldin's wall with its mosaic of winged creatures and clouds. Tears would accomplish nothing, and she had a task to complete before she could allow herself the luxury of collapse.

Her guards strove to keep pace as she exited the hectic triangle around the temple, misinterpreting her determined step as the need to stave off grief. Along the narrowing roads they wound, north to the crumbling stone dwellings and cracked cobbles of the old quarter, where the shadow of Faradil Forest tainted the twisting alleys. The narrow-fronted shop she sought hid between two vendors so nondescript she could not recall their wares, its crude, wooden sign helping to disguise the treasure house. After a brief moment to affect her sardonic persona, Jordayne pulled up the hood of her white mourning cloak, and gave a vigorous push to the door of Weng Wu's Eastern Emporium, ensuring the bell above it clanged.

"I have outgrown the need for nannies," she said to the guards, who had stepped too close. She had no tolerance for her sergeant's protests. "Go petition the Shah if you wish to override my command," she said, and shut the door in his face.

The interior was a chaotic shamble of eastern ornaments adrift in a heady haze of sweet-smelling incense. Flawless forgeries of ancient jade dragons vied for room on the splintering wooden shelves with painted porcelain vases and scrolls of parchment inked with artistic oriental script. Jordayne arched an eyebrow at the exorbitant price tags. A genuine artefact would have struggled to fetch the sum. Rummaging among the odds and ends, she waited for someone to attend her. When the inner door creaked open, she presented her back, pretending to scrutiny of baskets full of dried berries, hairy spider legs and fragmenting snakeskin.

"You want elixir to drown your sorrows? Or potion to stave off spirits?" a husky voice asked. "I give you good price."

Drawing down her hood, she turned. "Nothing so mundane," she said.

The little oriental man with white, shoulder-length hair, legs as bowed as the walls of the temple, and skin so thin his veins tinged him blue frowned. Together with his displeased tightening of his lips, it was a most satisfying expression. Then he cracked a smile and held up a finger. A long nail spiralled past his nose. "You want jade carving to match birthday present for Shah."

"Not this time," she said. "Certainly not without an expert in ancient eastern artefacts to verify your claims of authenticity."

"Lady, all genuine, all good," Weng Wu said. His bushy white brows drew together as he affected a hurt tone. The expression was comical on one so aged, so otherwise distinguished in features and manner.

"Then let's move inside and discuss the price. I can always have you arrested later for fraud. You might have heard the heir to the throne has adopted a tough stance with foreign crooks," she replied, picking up a jade dragon.

His shrewd eyes narrowed. Dropping all pretext of a slick salesman, he said, in a deeper, respectful voice, "Why you come here? Cannot oblige if don't know reason."

"I want to know what you were doing at the hospice last night."

"Legs bad," he said, tucking his hands into his wide sleeves and dropping his eyes. The painful curve of his thighs stretched the moon and stars embroidered all over his blue silk gown, but the momentary pursing of his lips gave him away.

"I do not appreciate being played for a fool."

"Why you think I lie?"

Jordayne dropped the dragon. It smashed into sharp, green shards.

The door burst open and Rokan tumbled through. "Are you hurt, my Lady?"

"I asked you to wait outside," she said, her eyes not leaving the unperturbed face of the merchant. If that was what he was.

The door clicked shut. "Your lack of reaction is why," she said, continuing as though there had been no interruption.

The old man shuffled to the door, opened it far enough to slip a neat sign with "closed" carved on it outside, then shut it again. The guards banged for entry as he slid the bolt home. Ignoring their vocal protests, Jordayne followed the ancient man into the interior.

"I deal in exotic," Weng Wu said with a slow wave of his arm across the windowless back room. Crates and life-size terracotta statues, granite carvings of mythical beasts, and chunky gold collars fit for empresses of old packed the vast space. Five times the size of the front shop, this room lay in as disordered an arrangement. It was in this musty, dusty space they had conducted business when last she came. The merchant had held the recommendation of the Satrap of San Tej, who harboured a fondness for all things Eastern, not least among them his retinue of petite women. On that occasion, Weng Wu had received prior warning of his noble visitor, favoured niece of the shah and second in line to the throne. He had not dared to insult her intelligence.

"Nothing more exotic than magus. I want see if he have souvenir to sell." Here at last was the dignity of the man she remembered, whose imperfect Laanan somehow befitted the wisdom of his years.

Jordayne strolled around the room, trailing a hand along the smooth bumps of the terracotta warriors' armour, draping a gem-studded necklace around her neck. The bright beauty of it was a stark contrast to the white mourning kameez she wore. Nothing in the room could have given rise to the rumours, those foul murmurings which had existed since the dawn of the Three Realms: a bobbing light in the night; the death of a detested relative days after the despiser had gone to his grave; even a glimpse of the unresponsive body of a dearly departed lumbering through the sleeping streets. Eastern magic. Black magic.

"There is nothing more exotic than a man's soul," she said as she placed the necklace around the neck of a statue, her words so soft and loving there was not the faintest hint of threat.

"You speak of Eastern mystery," Weng Wu said.

"I do. And I speak to one who holds its secret."

"It is dark thing of which you speak."

"Nevertheless, you will speak of it to me."

They regarded each other in a battle of wills. Under her intensifying stare, Weng Wu shook his head. "I know not of this."

She affected a sigh, and resumed her browsing, stepping back when a faded painting in a gilt frame caught her eye. The ancient oriental depicted bore a striking resemblance to Weng Wu. And how unusual to have a Myklaani artisan kneel before the eastern lord, hands outstretched to offer a crimson butterfly in supplication. She picked up the painting, careless despite her intrigue as she twisted it about. The edge caught a porcelain dog, scraping it across an alabaster table. When she heard the gasp she was listening for, she faced Wu.

"Now these, I believe, are genuine relics."

"Lady, I ask you take care."

With the utmost care, Jordayne set the painting down. "I am accustomed to handling the delicate. My guards, on the other hand, are somewhat less circumspect when carrying out their duty. I am afraid I will have to ask them to search the premises."

"You have no grounds."

"On suspicion of trafficking stolen goods."

"The Shah –" he started.

"Indeed," she interrupted, "the Shah values his taxes almost as much as his mages."

He bowed his head, shrewd enough to understand the balance of power. "Lady, do not judge what you do not comprehend."

"Then for your sake you had best ensure I do comprehend."

It was his turn to sigh, but he offered no more.

"Very well," she said, and admitted the guards with an order to search every speck of dust in the shop. "I absolve you of the need for caution. These *are* undeclared fakes," she told them as they squeezed between laden shelves. Weng Wu bridled as the confines of the front room saw dragons smash and parchment tear, but he maintained his stubborn silence so, when the guards had poked into every crevice, Jordayne took perverse pleasure in commanding them into the back. Here, the old man bustled from one artefact to the other, placing a steadying hand on a vase accidentally elbowed while reaching with the other for a jade carving of an emperor that threatened to topple off a crate as her sergeant trundled past. That left him indisposed when the newest recruit stood from his inspection of a canoe and bumped the terracotta warrior behind him. It tottered on its feet, overbalanced and smashed into large chunks before the startled guard-in-training had time to react. It really was careless of him, and the red-faced lad was staring at the carnage agape. Jordayne was inclined to offer him a bonus before booting him to Captain deq Lungo for further training. As for Weng Wu, his stricken face portended a seizure.

"Do continue," she said to the frozen guards. "I am eager to make my assignation before nightfall."

It was only a matter of seconds before the statue of the emperor fell and chipped his nose.

At which point Weng Wu quite sensibly swallowed and rasped, "Lady, you follow me."

"Well then. That was easy, wasn't it?" She dismissed the confused guards and waltzed after the merchant, through a narrow gap between stacks of oversized crates. Inside the concealed nook, he pulled aside a quilted wall-hanging of tigers stalking flat-topped trees, and opened a hidden door. Were it not for the spheres of coloured light, arranged on hanging shelves, the darkness would have smothered. It intrigued her, the way they ricocheted off the glass vials containing them. Jordayne studied the random movement, taking the opportunity to palm a vial when Weng Wu turned his back to light two candles.

"Two thousand year, the warrior survive, and you destroy in one day." The enormity of his loss was evident in the shadowed lines of his face. The wanton destruction had cut her too, but the loss of Trove was the greater pain.

"And what of souls and their right to rest? Is that not the greatest loss?"

He waved her into a simple chair as he sank into another on the opposite side of a table which stretched the width of the room. She held the vial below his sight, but the blue sparks in the apricot light kept drawing her inquisitive eye. Her curiosity got the better of her, or perhaps it was her fatigue. Easing the stopper out, she slipped her hand over the vial, allowing the sphere to surge against her palm. The contact sent a painful buzz along her arm. Her hand jerked away, and the light shot out.

A cautious Weng Wu rose from his chair, his eyes glued to the flitting sphere. "Lady, you go. You go now."

"Your hospitality is sadly lacking. I have just arrived." She glanced up and saw the light was resting above her head. She thanked the Vae she had had years of practice sounding nonchalant when her palms were sweating at the calamity behind her lie. "These lights are a nice trick. They would be a fitting touch at the funeral of a mage."

"Lights no trick. I tell you go."

Again, Jordayne looked up. The ball of light had descended. A quick study, she scuffed her chair back, unwilling to suffer its sting a second time. "If it is not a trick, then what is it?"

Weng Wu remained silent. She reached a tentative hand to it, intending to trap it in her fist. It would make an interesting keepsake, until Drucilamere could fathom its nature.

"No!" Weng Wu warned as she made a snatch. Her fingers closed on thin air as the light darted towards Weng Wu's heart. The elderly man sidestepped it with unnatural speed. With a crackle, the light changed direction.

Weng Wu's voice rang out. "*Ne dow san li kan soulous.*"

The light froze a hair's breadth from her chest, the lightning inside a riot of sparks.

"So this is a soulous," she said in a voice laden with indolence to mask her trepidation, for what else would cause the oriental magician such concern. "It is prettier than I expected." She reached a languid hand for it.

"Do not," Weng Wu said.

Too late. The earthbound soul of whichever poor unfortunate the magician had preyed upon zipped away and under the door. The magician stared at the dark crack.

"You do not know what you have done," he said.

"I hear that a great deal and it is almost invariably never true. So why don't you tell me, and then I can judge?" Lips pursed to keep her anger at bay, Jordayne selected another vial, this one with a turquoise light. The same blue lightning sparked inside. In truth, Weng Wu was right, but he would not have the satisfaction of hearing it from her. She glared until he sank into the chair, his expression a mix of fear and fury.

"That is better," Jordayne said, sitting. "Now what have I done? Or more to the point, what have *you* done that the simple act of opening a vial devastates so?"

He watched her toy with the vial in hand. "I say I create soulous, you arrest me for black magic. I say I don't, you destroy my treasures."

From whichever Eastern nation he hailed, she was certain he had acquired his treasures through dubious channels. She might have had a great deal to say about that, as patron of the arts, were it any other day. As it was, there was only one piece of information she wanted from him so, as another wave of grief assaulted her, she said, "If I was going to arrest you, I would have kept the guards present."

He acknowledged the truth with a bow of his head.

"I am here for one reason alone. Did you steal the soul of the mage?"

"Creating soulous is exacting task. Must have right potion, must be present at exact moment of death."

Leaning forward, Jordayne found herself needing a patent denial. This blatancy was so unlike her she wondered if, in all this despair, she could accomplish what she had set out to do. "I would still hear it from your lips," she said.

"I make no soulous last night. I have no chance with lady and Master Mage present."

"Your men? Apprentices, trainees?"

"This house source no soulai last night. On my honour."

"I trust you have a modicum," she said, rising. "Now, will you set these unfortunate souls free, or do I need to call the soldiers?" The number of victims staggered.

"Lady, you know not what you say."

"Then again I say you had better educate me."

He rose and pointed a very deliberate finger at the vial. "Trapped souls need magic to fly free. You just release trapped soul, it search for body. It search for eternity if need be."

With great purpose, Jordayne set the vial on the table. "Then you will work that magic." Myklaani citizens deserved the chance to travel to the Vae in death. This depraved servitude at the hands of a foreigner was insufferable.

Weng Wu folded his arms. His fingers with their grotesque nails perched upon his elbow.

"Release them, or I will have you arrested," she said, her ire so great subtlety eluded her.

"Too late for one you set free."

"Then the others," she insisted.

"Lady, dark force descend on world. It scare me more than your dungeon or your torture. You slay me, Lady, or I slay myself, but I will not face darkness without magic."

He had been too far away to hear Trove's dying words. Yet here he was, a magician versed in the mysteries of the East predicting a calamity akin to the one her magi glimpsed. To ignore the warning was tantamount to leaving Myklaan exposed to threat. "What force?" she asked, the sharp prickle of fear walking along her arms and down her spine.

He looked up and the ceiling dissolved, revealing a multitude of stars swirling in a night sky. "Mystery beyond my human grasp. Gods, djinn, spirits. I know not."

The illusion disappeared. Her mouth dry, she nodded and opened the door. "Very well, Weng Wu. You may work your magic for the protection of Myklaan." The words tasted foul, congealing into a rancid grief to add to her indigestible burden. It was a despicable act for which she had granted permission. She prayed it was not one on which she must call.

As she laid a hand on the entrance door, the magician forestalled her. "Lady, forgive me but I must ask. Why you were so sure I wield this power?"

She sighed. "There is a certain satrap who makes the occasional trip to Kaijoor to acquire artefacts for his collection. After one summer trip, word comes of his wife's untimely demise. His servants were rather loose with their tongues on his next visit, and gabbled to those at the palace of seeing their dead mistress walk beneath the moons. A rather…enthralling story, don't you think?"

He was quiet a moment. His words, when they came, were soft, and their truth was evident in his vacant stare. "I think not enthralling. I think story of dread."

She opened the door. "Beware, Master Weng Wu. If dark times

truly approach, Myklaan may have need of your talents. It would not serve me to have a population scared out of its wits by tales of dark sorcery. They would butcher you. And it is a butchery I will permit if I learn you use the souls of my citizens to serve your own foul ends."

The magician bowed his head. "Lady, look you to protecting the realm."

It was not the answer she had hoped for.

Outside, she found no warmth in the glare of the sun. The fidgeting guards did not even notice she had exited until she spoke. "A picture of disarray, aren't we?" she commented, walking off without waiting.

"My lady, there was an unnatural light," the normally solid Sergeant Rokan said. "It darted at each of us in turn. I have never seen the like. I swear it wanted to strike us down."

"A light, you say, Sergeant? And did this light injure your men?" she said, her voice dripping sarcasm. Weng Wu's mysteries would remain just that until she was ready to reveal them to the realm.

"No, my Lady," Rokan said, missing her tone in his agitation. "It darted to the north."

"So good to know my big, strong guards aren't afraid of the dark. But the light, now that is another matter. Entirely understandable, in my view."

His embarrassment made him step back, and so he missed the disquiet on her face. Faradil Forest lay to the north. Its malevolence ever lapped at the outskirts of the city, but today, today its brooding presence drained the life from Kaijoor. The folk they passed spoke in subdued tones, dawdling about their business; the hawkers forbore to call out; and the sun itself had paled.

Ill at ease, Jordayne hurried to solace in Drucilamere's arms.

Chapter Sixteen

CURLED IN A COIL of rope, Timak mumbled to Yazmine. He knew the hazy light over the dipping bow, the one due east despite the sweltering hour, was her. It stung that he had not heard a peep from her for almost an eight-day, but maybe she didn't understand him. He was muffling his words in the rope so *they* couldn't hear.

"I wish I could fly like the gulls." He moved his bare arm over his burning cheek.

"You should hush."

He gasped as he looked up, because he had thought he would never hear her again. She was above him now, high above. "Why?"

"They all stare at you when they come this way."

He rolled onto his back. His bruises pained him inside and out, and now someone was listening, it was hard to talk. "Why do you stay?"

"I like you." Her light dipped toward him. "What's your excuse?"

"You're the only one I can talk to."

"I meant why do you stay?"

He went quiet, although the hiccup kind of ruined it. She had to be simple to think he could run away from a boat. Or maybe she didn't understand men. Or else she meant he should plunge to his death beneath the nauseating swell. Drowning wouldn't be so bad, but he didn't want the sawtooths to eat him alive. In good weather, their triple fins kept circling the ship. Sometimes they even lifted their wide mouths filled with rows and rows of sword-sharp teeth out of the water to snap at surfacing turtles or diving gulls.

"You know what I am," she said, lowering her voice. He didn't know why. No one else heard her.

He peeked over the coil. Apart from the merciless sun, hers was the only light. He reached over for a discarded rag. It stank of raw fish and burned oil, but he draped it across the coils and nodded a solemn answer. Now she was speaking to him, he wanted to avoid notice. The tattered ends were difficult to tuck between the loops in the stinging hot wind, but he got the coil half-shady.

"And you know my name." She said it so soft he almost didn't catch it. He pretended for a time he had not, lying back down, letting his aimless fingers work at fraying the rope, and listening to the snap of the sail and splash of waves on the side of the boat. The temptation was sweeter than a honey cake. He had wrestled with it for hours after learning her nature. Had almost succumbed as Lord Ahkdul lingered over his pleasure.

"Do it," she said in an urgent whisper.

He curled right up, burying his face in his knees. He couldn't stop the tears this time, and soon he had to sniff. "Yaz-mine," he choked. He risked another peep but she was still the only djinn around. "Yaz-."

"Wait. Someone's coming."

He understood. The worst of Ahkdul's torture would not convince him to reveal her name to these wicked men. He held his breath as footsteps halted beside the coil of rope. A rough hand clamped on his arm and dragged him up.

"Your djinn about?" the hulking, leathery sailor who brought his dinner each night asked. Timak shook his head so fast the sea became a streak of blue. He was sure his wild eyes would not have fooled the adults he grew up around, but the sailor grunted a word that could have been *good*. "That why you crying, boy?"

Timak nodded.

The sailor scrunched up a grease-smeared cheek. "Accept it, lad. There's a peace to be found in realising things won't change." He set

Timak down and dragged him around. “Look you there.” To starboard, turbulent water foamed where the mouth of a wide river spilled into the sea. A city gleamed to its right, undulating in the afternoon heat. Far beyond in the east, tall mountains marched in a jagged, white-capped haze. “We’re in Terlaani waters, boy. That’s Dnea on the River Sheraz, though we’ll not be stopping. Lord Ahkdul’s keen to reach Tarana. That’s the capital of this realm.” The sailor turned him again, so he could look stern into Timak’s eye. “You’ll be seeing wonders the likes of which Verdaan will never know. A wondrous palace, refined princes and princesses, and fearsome mahktashaan. Don’t be getting any ideas about help. I ken enough ‘bout Lord Ahkdul to know yer life won’t be worth living if you try, and yer dear ma and pa’ll also pay the price. Serve him well, lad. Yer could probably learn to like what he does to yer, and it’ll only be a few more years or so ‘fore you outgrow his tastes.”

Timak sniffled at the ships skimming the wide, sandy harbour as he wiped the tears on his sunburned cheeks. All he wanted was to skittle down the streets of rundown Fayrhan with his friends, just for the treat of watching a galley dock. The thought of years of abuse curdled the sickness in the pit of his stomach. He almost cried out Yazmine’s name right in front of the sailor.

The muscled man nodded. “It’d be only the djinn who could change your fate, and we all knows they is almost impossible to trap.” He gave Timak, a long, hard look. “What d’yer call ‘im, your djinn?”

Timak clamped his hands on the side of the boat and bit his tongue. He stared at Dnea as the boat rose and fell, spraying salty sea on his cracking lips. What he wanted to do was run off in disgust, but he couldn’t raise suspicions he knew Yazmine’s secret. He fought the urge.

“I asked you a question, boy.”

“Genie,” he grudged. “I call her Genie.”

The sailor snorted and left him at the bow. Timak stepped back into the coil of rope and curled up under the flapping rag. Its small privacy was a blessing.

“Thank you, Timak,” Yazmine said. She sounded relieved. “Thank you for not telling.

"Never," he said, and fell quiet.

"There's no one about. You can say my name again."

He took a deep breath. "Yazmine." That was twice. One more time and she was bound to do his bidding, to remove him from this scumpit, to torture Lord Ahkdul if he asked. He squeezed his eyes tight and rocked.

"Timak?"

Her name caught in his throat. The guilt would devour him from the inside out if he enslaved her the way Ahkdul had him. It would be a death worse than sawtooths eating him alive, because it would take years and years. There had to be a word for it, a genie begging him to bind her when the world turned over every rock in search of the evasive creatures; his refusal to name her, when others gave up limbs, or loved ones, for the hope of a wish. On her intake of breath, he rolled away from her haze.

"Why don't you finish it?" she asked. "I want to help you." The offer squeaked with her doubt. He knew for sure then.

"The djinn will punish you."

"But it will be his fault. He spoke my name."

Somehow, Timak knew that would make it all the worse. For both of them. "Never," he said. "I could never do that to you."

Chapter Seventeen

ORDOSTEEN ENCLOSED JORDAYNE'S HANDS in his rough palms, and kissed her once on each rouged cheek.

"My dear, I am so sorry for your loss."

The words were small comfort: her darling uncle could not possibly understand how acute her loss truly was. But she accepted with good grace, and in her grief sat with uncharacteristic decorum on the sagging emerald couch in Ordosteen's comfortable study, arranging the sheer white mourning robe over her regular garments to alluring effect. The eight-day of bereavement she had spent withdrawn in the Mage Guild, while not alleviating her sorrow, had at least tempered it. Now affairs of state demanded her attention and it would do no one any good for her to remain ensconced in Drucilamere's passionate arms, least of all herself. Beside her, Matisse sat back, threw his arms along the top of the couch, and welcomed her home. She leaned in to let him know his characteristic lazy smile and tousled hair eased her despondency.

"Where do we stand?" Ordosteen asked when he had complimented the funeral ceremony and asked after the mages. Ordinarily, Jordayne enjoyed his attention, especially in this worn room. The simplicity of the square arabesques on the upper portion of the walls still tended to extravagance, but its mahogany desk, uncharacteristic in this bright palace, and the curios on the shelves opposite, had always reminded her of home. Today, she desired only the solitude of her rooms.

"In a rather precarious place," she answered, wondering how long she must remain. "The mages are convinced they are under threat, Uncle. In the mage dreams, they have disappeared from Myklaan's future. I would not say it is hard to believe. The porrin trader has been cheating them for months, and apprentices are becoming harder to come by. If I were them, I would take their latest recruit and pin him to a dart board. He is good for little else."

Matisse snorted. His eyes were red but he looked not in the least chagrined his pleasurable pursuits had robbed him of his rest. "Do not suggest it, sister, or I am sure you will inspire a new pastime." He sat forward. "We have established that even without porrin we can fend off any attack from Verdaan. More worrying is news of the north-east. There are rumours Verdaan seeks a marriage alliance with Terlaan. Myklaan cannot repel an attack on both fronts." He lifted an empty pitcher from the table beside him and tilted it.

"Forgive me. I have been remiss." Ordosteen went to the door, and beckoned a page. Having given instructions for refreshment, he resumed his place in the deep armchair opposite the couch. After years of use, its lumps and sags were a perfect match for his slackening body. "I take it Princess Kordahla is to seal the bargain. Shah Wilshem is not one to give his daughter away for a pittance. What possible advantage could he gain?"

Rubbing one eye, Matisse said, "Our spies deliver nothing but speculation."

"What talk do they hear?" she asked.

"A great deal."

Her thoughts drifted on the sweet perfume of the frangipane flowers arranged in the hearth as her brother detailed one report after another. It carried them through the vast keyhole window behind Uncle's imperial desk, into the blossoming gardens, where she had strolled through avenues of love on many an eve, with Trove, or Druce, or a suitor who took her fancy. She managed to blink herself to concentration as Matisse finished.

"We have to assume Shah Wilshem will receive aid for an invasion," he said. "Our strength lies in our ability to endure a prolonged campaign. A steady supply of food from Verdaan's lush hills will be all Terlaan needs to overcome our defences. Their mahktashaan are far more powerful than our magi. If the mages are constrained by a lack of porrin, it will be a slaughter."

"There is something about that too," Jordayne said. "Trove's dying words were 'Crystal. Destroy.'" She broke off as the page entered with wine and a platter of fruit, and set them on one of the side tables designed to complement the desk. Ordosteen gestured him out, and poured the prized white vintage into their pewter goblets himself. They did not resume their conversation until the door had shut.

"It is undisputed, then, that the threat comes from Terlaan," Matisse said.

On this little information Jordayne believed nothing undisputed, but she held her tongue. Where the military was concerned, Matisse possessed the greater knowledge. She contented herself with sampling the wine while he compared the forces of the two realms.

"Wilshem's daughter is reputed to have received her beauty from Tiarasae," Ordosteen said the moment Matisse paused for breath. Jordayne really could not blame him for drifting. The numbers Matisse spouted were decidedly boring. She put her goblet down. Uncle had his in hand. He contemplated the sapphires adorning it, but did not take a single sip. "Wilshem can be ruthless but would he trade his beloved daughter to Ahkdul for little more than the risk of war?"

This lovesick posturing was uncharacteristic. Jordayne hoped his growing feelings for Rochelle had not compelled him to cast her aside. That one had wit alongside her beauty, though if the rumours were true her looks paled in comparison to Princess Kordahla's. She had a vague recollection of a gorgeous, bubbly child dancing at Ordosteen's last wedding. She would not care to wager those qualities had bloomed. A woman in Terlaan, while accorded greater freedom than the slavery her sex endured in Verdaan, was far removed from the liberties of this golden realm. She felt a pang of pity for the girl, which was replaced at once by a sudden thought.

"Terlaan's shahs have always been conservative. Could Wilshem mean to attack in the name of the old ways?"

"It would be his best excuse," said Matisse, helping himself to a refill. "Though he may simply be growing power-hungry."

Ordosteen twirled the stem of the goblet in his fingers. "What else might account for the magi's prediction bar war?"

Jordayne and Matisse looked at each other.

"There is nothing, Uncle," Matisse said.

She placed a hand on her brother's knee. "The simple truth is lack of either porrin or apprentices will imperil the mages."

The Shah stared at his goblet like he did not know how it had come to be in his hand. His thumb worried at one of the sapphires decorating the cup. "How do we assure a continued supply?" he asked.

"Uncle, this ignores a great deal of what we know," Matisse cautioned.

"There has been peace in Myklaan for forty years. There is no reason to believe it will end." Ordosteen's thumb pressed. The sapphire fell out of its bed, dropped onto his lap, and slipped to the rug. My, he was touchy today. Jordayne could almost believe he was the one dealing with grief. And such conviction the magi's doom would come from another source.

"You cannot be serious, Uncle. We could not have clearer warning save for a demand for surrender from Wilshem himself," Matisse retorted. He had set his full goblet down.

"We must consider other possibilities." Ordosteen was up and pacing by the desk. "A forty-year truce is unlikely to come to an abrupt end without provocation." He stared at the drop of blood welling on one finger.

Jordayne took the goblet from his hand and put it down, spilling wine across the fruit. In her experience, rumours carried more than a shekel of credence. And in forty years, the rumours surrounding Ordosteen had changed little. She had done her share of wondering over Ordosteen's ill luck with wives. Until today, she had never guessed what a blessing his terrible burden had bestowed. She had thought the very personal price might have purchased a very private gain. In a prospering realm, he was certainly the wealthiest of shahs. With the realisation, her uncle assumed the aspect of a great man. Greater than the shahs who plunged wholeheartedly into war for the glory victory brought. Perhaps the greatest of them all. A nearby warbler thought so, singing his praises to the palace. She stood on tiptoe to plant a tender kiss on his forehead.

"You are both right," she said, "but the mages have declared Terlaan is a possible threat. We must prepare for every eventuality." The djinn were not to be trusted, after all.

"Let me prepare the armies and double the border patrols. We at least need to dispatch a good captain to Mykter Fort. That garrison has been left to its own command too long. There are disturbing reports of lapses in procedure which will need to be investigated regardless of whether trouble arrives from outside," Matisse said.

A honeyeater shrieked warning from its garden perch, a reaction to a slinking palace cat, no doubt. The warbler's song dissolved into a string of chirps.

Ordosteen nodded. "Prepare for war, but do it discreetly. I want no rumours to reach our northern neighbours, nor a populace unruly from fear."

"I will send Captain deq Lungo. He is the model of discretion. And under the guise of tightening discipline, not even the soldiers will suspect unrest."

"How is our dear Captain?" Jordayne asked.

Matisse leaned full back into the couch. "He left Madame Yinmae's with a red face, but I do believe he returned last night."

"In the interests of checking on his men, of course."

"Naturally."

"And you came by this information how?"

He looked at the ceiling. "I happened to be accompanying him at the time."

Their banter brought a smile to their uncle's face. "Matisse, perhaps you should take a lesson in discretion from the Captain."

"I am having far too much fun, Uncle."

"My heir must possess a certain amount of decorum. Lodge a girl you fancy at the palace. Lodge three if you will, but do not expose yourself so wantonly. The people must respect their future Shah."

The glint in Matisse's eye was the only sign of his humour. "The men do nothing short of worship me. As for the women, they fall over themselves to attract my attention, and those that can't, beg their partners to emulate me in bed."

"A wife, Matisse. You need a wife to settle you down and produce legitimate heirs."

"There is plenty of time for that. My age is not such an issue as hers. As long as she is pretty, fertile and a vixen, heirs will gush from her womb."

"I believe you," Ordosteen said in good humour. "But on this matter we shall talk further."

"When the threat of war is no longer upon us. A commander risking his life must find what solace he may," Matisse said with a wink. He rose. "If there is nothing more, Uncle, I will begin. This conversation is almost as amusing as a bedfellow, but I long for the savagery of war." He gave Jordayne a peck on the cheek and left.

Ordosteen turned to her. "What do you think? Will he make a good Shah?"

"Will you consider another?"

"I will not. So, I suppose the question is unfair." He took her hand. "Niece. You must believe I am a foolish old man with nothing to show for my age."

"Just the opposite, you old fool," she said, then gambled on his good humour, on the serenity of the perfect, blue sky, and the trill of one joyful warbler. "But how far do you trust your djinn?"

He pulled away from her. "I will not stand for innuendo, most especially not from you."

"It behoves you not to deny it any longer. And I am the only one from whom you could stand it, Uncle."

"You and Rochelle. Talk to her if you must."

"You have done a very selfless thing. But the djinn serve their own purpose. Are you so very sure the pact will endure? Is there anything which might nullify it?"

Ordosteen swallowed, so she had her answer before he said, "You always were the perceptive one."

She was not so naïve as to believe he would confide in her. He was too proud for that, had borne this secret alone too long. If he only thought through the consequences, Myklaan might weather whatever calamity the still winds dumped upon it.

"You have been, you *are*, an astounding Shah. Just look at how Myklaan has flourished." The eastern vases on the pedestals flanking the desk, the jade dragon and primitive ceremonial mask on the shelves were testament to that no less than the gorgeous gold-framed paintings and marble statue of Vae'oenka commissioned from the best artist and craftsman in the realm. "There are years of experience for you to draw on."

Ordosteen picked up her goblet and took a gulp of wine. "Ah, Jordayne, were you born a man."

It was enough. She had accomplished what she set out to do. An eyebrow twitched up as she smiled and brought them back to safer ground. "I would not be quite so accomplished, nor so happy without my feminine wiles. Dear Uncle, this is Myklaan. I do not need to be a man to rule."

"There is no precedent for a woman on the throne."

"Ah, but I shall find a way."

He raised his glass. The glint in his eye made it as much a toast as a caution. "Careful, Niece. If I did not understand the depth of your love for Matisse, I would be obliged to find you guilty of treason."

"Nonsense Uncle. I'm far too valuable. More valuable, in fact, than that brother of mine." A lesser woman might have thought it ominous the warbler stopped his song.

Ordosteen threw back his head and laughed. "That you are, Jordayne, that you are. I will remain forever indebted to Trove for teaching you more than how to use that body of yours to get what you want. His ingenuity will remain unsurpassed." When she felt her face blanch, he added, "You are not the only one with a measure of perception, my dear." He came and embraced her, his eyes brimming with sympathy. “I am truly, truly sorry for your loss.”

It seemed he of all people had the capacity to understand. Jordayne leaned into his hug. She had never felt closer to her uncle than just then.

Chapter Eighteen

SIAN HALTED AT THE gusty ridge above Meeting Field and sobbed. The other children skipped along the goat track, laughing and calling to each other beneath wispy cloud. She was not supposed to follow. She knew she was not. Looking down, she took a step onto the narrow ledge anyway. The alternatives were a lonely afternoon wandering the wooded hills of the Olono Range, or returning to the longhouse to help her grandmother shell a mountain of peas. At thirteen she was no longer a child, Grandmam Vila reminded two or three times a day. She had to make herself useful. Sian blew at the strands of her fair hair which had fallen across her brown eyes and slight chin. She had been making herself useful since she was old enough to clutch a vegetable. Just once, she wanted to play, to splash in the pond as she tried to catch a few wide-mouthed, gelatinous puffers to keep the gnats buzzing around the stilted longhouses at bay.

"Wait," she called.

Giggles drifted back on the afternoon breeze. Taking a deep breath, she placed a steadying hand on the wall of rock and shuffled one bare foot forward. Craggy and exposed, this hill sprouted tufts of scraggly grass and the occasional hardy thorn bush. The drop was dizzying, and her long legs, thin from lack of exercise, weakened. The trembly doubt inside her swelled into panic. She called out. As agile as the longhaired goats grazing the slope, the other children scampered on. Today, Sian decided, was going to be different. If she could just reach the pond and splash with the others, they might talk to her. They might even help her walk the ledge on the way back. Another deep breath helped her worm her right foot in front of her left. When she shifted her weight, her foot broke off a section of the ledge, sending a shower of pebbles clattering down the hill. She pressed against the rock, breathing hard.

The shadows had grown by a fingernail before she worked up the courage to slip her left foot through to the front. At a snail pace, clutching the ragged rock, she could get across. When she caught up, she would tell the others her too-tight trousers, a hand-me-down from her older brother, made running impossible. It didn't matter her feet and ankles bruised on jutting shards, but the path had too many loose rocks. Her ankle twisted on one. It tumbled, unbalancing her. She slid down the incline, the rock grazing her from arm to knee. Her cry stopped the laughter, but the others were out of sight. She kept falling. Her fingers blistered scraping at the grass, and she knocked the painful point of her elbow. She knew she was going to break her leg and need to be put out of her misery, like the goat they had eaten last month. Her legs crashed onto an outcrop, sending a jolt of pain up her spine and halting her decent. She sobbed through a clenched jaw, and clung on for her dear, miserable life. It was a long, steep way down. The track was a few body-lengths above her, and the safety of the wooded hill ten paces to her left, but she didn't have the strength to climb. Her breathing became as ragged as the rock. In her head, she heard Grandmam's voice tell her to stay calm, because she knew what would happen if she did not. Then her mam joined in with her biting rebukes, and Sian had to gasp for air. The slope fell into shadow before she heard footsteps close. Not the children but someone bigger, crunching through the forest. Between the poplars, she glimpsed a leather vest.

"Help!" she called.

A goat bleated. The crackle of leaves stopped. Footfalls came her way. Then chubby-faced, fair-haired Erok appeared at the edge of the trees, three dead rabbits slung over his broad shoulder. He scanned the ridge before his eyes dropped and alighted on her. She dipped her head, embarrassed. Why did it have to be him who found her? Now the whole tribe would find out how clumsy she was. She felt her whole body tense, and the hill begin to spin around her. *No*, she thought. *Not now.*

When she looked up again, Erok was striding down the hill, sure-footed even with his bulk, and not at all bothered by the incline. He reached her before she had drawn three more breaths, grabbed her wrist and pulled her onto the slope. As she looked up at him, her straight hair falling back, the land spun with greater speed.

"You're not supposed to be out this far," Erok said. He tugged her back up to the ridge. In his strong grip, she needed her legs for little more than balance. He bent to retrieve his rabbits as she stood there, too ashamed to speak to him, or look anywhere but her bleeding toe. Then her muscles tensed and the hill span faster. Blackness blotted the shadowed trees, and she collapsed.

When Sian woke, it was dusk, and apricot streaked the sky. Erok was sitting on a ledge of rock above her, chewing one end of a blade of grass. He had cleared the rocks from around her, and cushioned her head on his vest. Turning her face away, she brought a hand up and wiped at the spittle around her mouth. The children were clambering up and down the slope as though it was no more than an anthill. Spying her open eyes, squish-nosed Loyt stopped ordering the others about and stared. Then his friends noticed and did the same. Her whole head burning with shame, Sian rolled so she did not have to face them.

"Time to go," Erok called. The fit hunter hoisted her gangly body into his arms and set off down the leaf-strewn path. The children capered to his side without effort, chattering about their day and asking about his hunt. Sian wanted him to put her down, but then she would have to sit here, in the howling dark and all alone, until her legs found the strength for her to crawl over mossy roots and jutting stone. An ogre might find her before she reached home, and tear her limbs apart. She closed her eyes. It would have been better if she had tumbled to her death.

She hated her stupid self more when they reached the wooden long-houses. The stilted dwellings nestled in a cleared area, partially screened from each other by rustling beeches it had not been necessary to fell once upon a time when the Ho'akerin Tribe settled on this hill. She made Erok put her down before they were in full view of the door, but it was late and she was dirty and there was only one reason she would be hanging her head. She couldn't help it. Erok and the other children would tell anyway. She crept past the bright-skirted women seated on tree stump stools before the rock-ringed fires, trying not to sniff the herbs they were mixing into their sizzling pots because the heavy aroma was turning her stomach. The stairs creaked as she climbed up. That should have warned her she was in the wrong house, but Erok was coming up behind her and it was too late to do anything other than steal along the squeaky floorboards, past the men sitting on their woven mats, smoking their tookaweed pipes. When they moved their legs, the patterns their wives had embroidered on their trouser cuffs collided with the patterns on the mats. The combination made her so, so dizzy, and she stumbled into a foot.

"Watch out, you stupid girl," her pah snarled from somewhere down the row of the men.

All the way to the far corner of the smoky longhouse, Sian felt his eyes bore loathing into her. The bare meeting room offered nowhere to hide, and she couldn't shrink enough to escape his stare. Just to avoid giving an account of herself, she found a basket of pistachios to shell.

"It happened again," she heard Erok say to her pah, Vorn.

Her hands trembled as she glanced his way. A nut rolled out of the shell and along the floor. Pah's reaction was predictable. He stood and spat at her, then huffed out of the longhouse. She blinked back tears as she fumbled to split another shell, because years of suffering his loathing did not lessen the stab of pain right through her middle. It hurt all the more to see little Tara clamber all over her pah as Loyt recounted the day's adventures with grand gestures. Sian could not even look up when her wrinkled, sun-baked grandmam came in with a platter of steamed leafgreens.

"Your hands are dirty. Go wash before you touch the food," Vila said.

Without a word, Sian padded back the length of the house, sidling past the women carrying in bowls filled with steaming chunks of goat and baked tubers for the men. She wished Erok wasn't watching her, wasn't twirling a dried stalk of grass in the corner of his mouth. She averted her eyes because the circles he drew were making them hurt, and scuttled sideways as Loyt and Tara tore past, trying to beat each other out the door to the cooking fires. They nearly knocked a young woman down the steps in the process. Laughter lightened her scolding, as she ruffled Tara's hair with her free hand. Sian made sure she flattened herself against the wall to allow the woman plenty of room. Head still down, she didn't even see who it was.

Outside, insects were buzzing a welcome to the breezy night. A smear of Daesoa's yellow face was just visible through the lattice of leaves. Pah was standing in the patch of the smaller moon's light, dwarfing Mam, who squatted as she ladled his dinner into a bowl. Sian went dead still.

"No man will want to get children on a girl with half a brain," Pah said.

She took in a sharp breath.

"She can still work. Her hands are good," Mam said, passing him the bowl. "Draykan will let her stay if she does her share."

Far away, a wolf howled.

"Bah," Pah said. "The Leadsman's got a Tribe to feed and clothe. He's as sick of her as I am."

She tried to sneak a wide circle to the hollow-log trough they used for washing. They heard her feet crack twigs though, and watched as she broke into a scurry. She scrubbed her face and hands too quick in the dirty puddle at the bottom of the ant-ridden trough, but she wanted to find her bed.

"Bah," Pah said when she shook the drops from her hands. The word echoed so loud she jumped. She tried not to notice he spat into the dirt. "A snail's got more spine. And more use. At least we can eat them. She's a burden. You deal with her woman. I don't want to hear of her again. If you hadn't birthed Toko fit and healthy, I'd..."

The rest of Pah's oft-repeated sentence was lost as she sensed her muscles tense. "No," she pleaded as the trees spun into a dizzying blur of brown and green. But the world turned black at the hoot of an owl, and she had no time to form another thought.

Wakefulness was a struggle. The air itself pressed down on her, trapping Sian in a groggy haze. Rattles mingled with sweet smoke to drag her back to misery. A face, painted and feathered, swam over hers, pleading with the spirits to intercede on her behalf. Sian squinted and blinked until white-eyed Ishoa lost her blurry double. The soothsayer, clad in a ceremonial fox-fur stole, swayed her lithe body to the beat of maracas, rattled high and low. The dry rustle of her grass skirt reminded Sian of how thirsty she was. She rubbed the irritating smoke from her eyes, and swallowed. Her limp body lay on her own straw bedding, too weak to respond to her needs.

"*Masheraki eraka maran,*" Ishoa chanted, drawing the ritual to a close. Beyond her, a man coughed. Sian dared shift her gaze to her pah. He was leaning against the wall, the pale light of a candle hardening a look of blame on his long, weatherworn face. When their eyes met, he waggled his head, and strode from the long room in which the older girls slept. Not tonight, though. Tonight, no breaths and sighs surrounded her, straw didn't crackle, and hands didn't slap at the biting gnats darting through the cracks between the sweet-smelling logs in the walls. Sian guessed why and fought the lump in her throat. She did not want to deal with this. Ishoa had long ago declared she was not possessed, that the gods had merely seen fit to test her. To what end, nobody, not even the soothsayer, could say. Her pah believed they had seen fit to test *him.* And on bad days, when the fits took her again and again, Ishoa bent to the will of the Tribe and performed the Rite of Expulsion. It never did any good. The fits always returned. Sian gripped the sadness inside so it wouldn't consume her. She did not feel possessed, whatever possessed felt like. But she did feel damaged beyond repair. Perhaps one day she would not wake from the fit, would find herself in the Spirit Forest, whole and hearty, and loved by the trees, rocks, and animals.

"You must drink this," Ishoa said. Her hand brushed Sian's neck before it found her shoulder and eased her up. Sian took the cup the soothsayer held out, but Ishoa did not let go, tilting it until she had to lean forward so she could sip the bitter brew or risk it spilling over her blouse.

"Is she cleansed?" Grandmother Vila asked, stepping out of a dark corner. She was steady on her wrinkled feet despite the late hour. The sleeping hall, dark save for the flames of a stunted candle, was otherwise deserted.

Ishoa straightened. Her sightless eyes remained fixed on a square of the sleeping mat beside Sian's ear. "If you mean will there be more fits, there will. I'll leave a little of the drug. You may give her a quarter measure on days like today." Sip by sip, the soothsayer made her drain the porrin potion in the cup. Sian had grimaced it down enough times to recognise its peculiar tang.

"You've been fitting throughout the evening," Ishoa said when, unable to stomach any more, Sian turned her head. At least her stick insect sat over her moss pillow. His big eyes looked happy to see her. He would listen to her sorrows. She tried to tell him but the soothsayer's free hand tapped over her neck to her chin, and tilted it back. "You must drink enough to allow you to rest."

Sian took a final gulp and gagged.

The soothsayer brushed a lock of fair hair from her forehead across her cheek, one soft finger trailing across her eye. Sian settled back, clinging to the unfamiliar comfort of a kind touch. She could almost believe there was someone who cared.

Almost.

"See she is not upset. When the effects of the porrin wear off, send her to me."

The soothsayer's voice came faint through the haze of her lightheadedness. The dizziness felt safer than the aura of her fits. Sian surrendered to the blissful indifference it brought. That was better than brooding on the thought that her mam did not care enough to see how she fared.

Chapter Nineteen

THE FLUTES BLEW A fanfare to welcome the royal guest. The first notes drowned in the cheer of the crowd as Lord Ahkdul of Verdaan stepped onto the deck of the galley and waved to the Terlaani citizens who had crammed into every pocket of space behind the hastily erected barriers.

Arun stiffened. Whether coloured by innuendo or not, his dislike of the man was instantaneous. Over the past minor moon, he had found numerous occasions to converse with Baiyeed deq Ikher. Two eight-day, in which small Daesoa had returned to full, and not one of the ambassador's words had thrown his lord into a positive light, despite the man's fervent attempts to exalt Ahkdul's virtues. His praise dripped over sweet and fermented, like the buckets of the lemon and geranium scent he wore. The thought of Princess Kordahla in the man's grip appalled. Yes, Shah Wilshem had every right to wed her to political advantage, but to doom his spirited daughter to Ahkdul's cruelty was unforgivable.

Beside him, Mariano clasped his hands behind his back. The Crown Prince had dressed in royal burgundy over black shalvar. The gold embroidery on his turban and calf-length kurta was a bold declaration of his rank. While the Verdaani saffron Ahkdul wore stood out against the harsh azure, its cut was simplistic in comparison. Their foreign visitor had to comprehend how obvious the difference in their fortunes showed, for he clenched his jaw as he walked the gangplank to the scrubbed wharf. The mahktashaan lining it gave a single stamp of a booted foot, though their eyes never left the restless crowd.

"His appearance is as brutish as I recall. It is easy to credit the rumours that Nertese blood runs in the veins of the Verdaani lords, and not much harder to imagine the stuff of ogres has mixed with their human essence," the Crown Prince commented. The morning sun was already teasing beads of sweat from his brow.

Indeed, Ahkdul's bushy eyebrows, oversized nose and prominent forehead overpowered his narrow eyes in a manner reminiscent of the people from the western land. Worse, his stance, feet wide and elbows out, suggested the man was in a state of aggression.

"You do not reply," Mariano said.

"It is not my place, Highness," Arun replied, watching a small boy in a ridiculous frilled costume creep up behind Ahkdul.

"You are likely to be Majoria when I am Shah, Arun. I hope we can always be honest with each other."

"Then I will say that a man might be forgiven his appearance, but his nature is his and his parents to shape."

"So you believe the rumours." Mariano was staring straight ahead, at Ahkdul. If their visitor noted the conversation, he would have no inkling of the topic.

"I think the evidence is before you." Arun took a dutiful step back as Ahkdul, reaching them, bowed to Mariano. That was unprecedented, and most telling for a man who craved recognition as an equal. Mariano's fleeting smirk was not lost on him either.

A sudden foreboding compelled Arun to scan the crowd. The warm welcome aside, this man inspired loathing. Terlaani citizens aplenty would view his visit as an opportunity for revenge. Too many had lost loved ones to porrin's bliss, and the galley's brash pennant declared the drug's origin for all to see. Shah Wilshem had been wise to forbid Princess Kordahla to ride out in greeting. Her look of relief when her father ordered her confinement had been a surprise, but then every rumour about Lord Hudassan's son tended to repulse.

"Welcome to Terlaan, Lord Ahkdul," Mariano said, inviting Ahkdul to clasp his hand in the manner of equals.

"Your graciousness is noted, Crown Prince Mariano," Ahkdul

replied. His eyes flicked down the road as he gripped Mariano's arm. The sandalwood lotion he wore could not disguise the salt of sea and sweat. "I am looking forward to my discussions with Shah Wilshem." Stepping past the prince, he scanned the royal retinue.

"I believe he may be amenable to receiving you this morning," Mariano said, pretending Ahkdul had offered no slight. He took the reins of his stallion, black with a white blaze, and mounted, taking the upper hand in this verbal bout. It was a credit to the Shah that, at ten years younger than Ahkdul, his son possessed the greater poise. "Have your men leave their weapons with the customs officers so we may settle you into the palace."

"My men will wish to keep their swords." Ahkdul's jaw was tight now he must look up.

Mariano turned his horse away from the galley, returning Ahkdul's slight. "Only mahktashaan are permitted a blade inside the palace walls. I could, of course, arrange suitable accommodation nearby."

To suggest a guest lodge elsewhere was an insult to their rank, in however obliging a manner the words were couched. Arun felt a stirring of hope at the crook in Ahkdul's fingers. The Crown Prince was a perfect champion of Princess Kordahla's cause.

"If this is your custom, we will oblige." Ahkdul gave the signal and his men relinquished their weapons, the visible ones, at least. A groom led a horse forward, a solid bay mare of adequate pedigree, and the Verdaani Lord mounted. They had made no provision for his men. Judging by the darkness of the Verdaani lord's expression, this last snub did not go unnoticed.

"Lead my horse," Arun said, passing the reins of his black gelding to a groom.

Their disordered procession elicited rousing cheers and riotous jeers. Forgotten in their midst, the poor boy scuffled with stilted steps, as though he nursed some hurt. His head was down, but when he chanced a look up, Arun beckoned. The child froze. Arun dropped to one knee and raised his head so the edge of his hood slid back. The child regarded his shadowed face with solemn brown eyes which had lost the light of innocence. As the retinue marched, a scarred guard pushed the boy on. Arun took his arm as he limped past, ignoring his flinch and drawing him aside. Placing a hand on his brown hair, Arun held him fast. There was injury festering inside the boy. And something more. Had Ahkdul not twisted to observe his ministrations, he might have searched for latent magic. Such probing would have drawn unwanted attention, so he allowed warm healing to spread from his hand into the misery of a child. The glow in his cerulean crystal mesmerised, and the boy relaxed in his hold. Unable to do more, Arun mounted and fell in with the guard.

❖ ❖ ❖

Vinsant stifled a yawn. Up since dawn, he had wet down stray spikes of hair and dressed with pride in the plain royal blue churidar kurta of the mahktashaan apprentices before following Apprentice Master Branak to the bailey outside the armoury. His excitement at commencing training had overcome his reluctance to leave his bed before the sun had graced the sky. Just like it had every day of the minor moon since he had been initiated. Now, two hours past a blushing, cloudless daybreak, he was, as usual, wondering why he had bothered.

Rotund Gram was huffing and puffing as he slashed wild with the practice sword, tripping over his feet and overbalancing. It didn't help his brown hair, cut short and all the one length, fell into his eyes every time he bounced. Tall, lean Naikil, fitter and surer despite his big feet, couldn't even keep hold of his wooden blade. His long ears reddened every time it left his hand. So far, their tutor had required Vinsant to do no more than demonstrate a few basic thrusts and parries, manoeuvres he had perfected years ago under Mariano's remorseless instruction. His query as to whether he might train with the more experienced young men, who were executing some rather impressive attack moves across the dirt courtyard, met with an admonishment to hush and learn. So he began to dream of wielding a Myklaani sword. Everyone knew they were the best in the Three Realms. A weapon fit for a mahktashaan prince.

"Are we boring you, Apprentice Vinsant?" Branak asked, noticing his eyes had glided off Gram, whom he was supposed to be critiquing, to admire a mahktashaan disarm an older apprentice.

Vinsant grappled with the wisdom of admitting the truth. "Uh," was all he managed.

"I see," Branak said. "Then perhaps you had best show us your technique."

Vinsant needed no second invitation. He lifted his practice sword, and prepared to face Branak with glee. Swordmaster Mazronan had honed his skills over the years, after all, and while the mahktashaan swordfighting skill was rumoured to exceed that of the regular guards, nobody had yet bested Mazronan.

A lightning quick thrust from Mahktashaan Branak forced him to lean back. He lashed out, blinked at his empty hand, and heard his sword thump to the ground. Off balance, he toppled onto his behind. Across the yard, the older apprentice was laughing at him. Dumbfounded, he blinked. He was about to ask for another chance when Branak asked, "What did Vinsant do wrong?"

"He let his weight drop too far back," Naikil said.

"You see," Branak said to Vinsant extending a hand to help him rise. "These lads have learnt a great a deal today. It is more than I can say for you."

"Uh, maybe if I worked with someone of my own competence," Vinsant said, eyeing the older apprentice. The lad's good-natured grin seemed to suggest he had borne the brunt of such instruction in the past.

"Your impudent pupil questions the value of your lesson?" a distinctive voice rasped.

Trust Levi to choose this of all moments to materialise. Vinsant executed a dutiful bow and chimed "All praise to you, Majoria," with the others.

"He lacks the patience to learn," Branak said.

Frowning in indignation, Vinsant opened his mouth.

"As I understand it his balance was incorrect?" Levi said, holding up a hand to forestall any comment. At Branak's nod, he instructed Naikil to fetch a rope. "Now tie his left leg up," he said. Of Branak, he asked, "Who is the better of these two?"

"Naikil has the edge, Majoria."

"Then Vinsant shall fight Gram."

Too incredulous to protest, Vinsant gaped at Branak. He was still coming to terms with the instructions when Naikil handed him his sword, and Gram hit him in the chest, bowling him over and laughing despite their sobering company.

"Help him up," Branak said to Naikil, who had a stupid grin on his face.

Hauled to his feet, Vinsant faced Gram a second time. The plump boy sized him up before darting around and thrusting his sword at Vinsant's side.

"Ow! Not fair!" Vinsant cried.

"Again," Branak demanded.

For the next humiliating half hour, Vinsant added layer after layer of dust to the seat of his churidar. When the round teenager lunged under his trusts, he made wobbly hops away from the strike. When Gram attacked from behind, he fell onto hands and knees. He doubted Levi could demonstrate a suitable riposte on one leg but djinn curse him if he was going to grumble that thought aloud.

"Stop and think!" Levi roared, dark eyes blazing beneath his hood.

Taking a deep breath, Vinsant stood dead still. He blinked a bead of sweat out of one eye, licked his dry lips, and watched Gram thrust. Three unretaliated hits later, he realised that not only was his opponent's grip weakening with fatigue, but he was executing the same manoeuvres over again.

"Come at me again and I'll disarm you."

Gram smiled and quickly stepped to Vinsant's left side. Vinsant was ready for him. Hopping nimbly around, he chopped down onto Gram's shoulder before Gram had extended his arm.

"Again," Branak ordered.

This time, Vinsant dropped, swiped Gram's legs from under him, and put the tip of his sword to Gram's chest before the boy realised he was flat on his back and squinting at the sun. When he bested Gram twice more, he knew he had become a true master at one-legged swordplay.

"What did Gram do wrong, Vinsant?" Branak asked as the red-faced boy rubbed his wrist and grimaced at his sword, which now lay on the ground.

Vinsant gave a concise and humble explanation since it was probably the only way to regain use of his cramped leg. He let out a sigh of relief when Branak, nodding, instructed Naikil to untie him.

"You may come with me, Apprentice Vinsant," Levi said, the only recognition he received for his hard labour.

"Aren't you going to tell me I showed exceptional balance?" he asked, limping as blood gushed back into his tingling muscles. He slowed to observe the retinue passing through the gatehouse into the outer bailey. Levi neither answered him nor permitted him time to dally, so he caught a mere glimpse of the infamous Ahkdul before the man dismounted. The Verdaani lord looked like he had ogre blood in his veins, the more so for standing next to Mariano. The thought of Kordahla wed to the man made him snort. Father would never agree to it.

He hurried into the cool palace. Levi took him straight to the gloomy mahktashaan lair to stand before the massive statue of Mahktos. *Uh-oh*, thought Vinsant, not keen to face the god after his theft of the crystal.

"I expect my apprentices to follow their teachers' lessons. Without question," said Levi.

"Yes, Majoria," Vinsant answered with a sideways peep at the statue. The mahktashaan in charge of its care had sprinkled dried thyme around its base.

"Good. Then tell me what lesson Branak was teaching you before I arrived."

With a roll of his eyes Vinsant just couldn't help, he said, "Simple thrusts and parries."

"That was the lesson Gram and Naikil were learning. What was he teaching *you*, Vinsant?"

There was a deeper lesson in the basic swordsmanship? At a loss, Vinsant stared at the Majoria's pointed finger. "To recognise another's weakness?" he temporised. Under the black hood, Levi's moustache twitched. Vinsant started sweating as the seconds passed. He squirmed onto one foot, then shifted again. Levi remained steadfast in his demand for an answer, and Vinsant wished Arun was meting out this particular lesson. Still, he had to admit the Majoria was being uncharacteristic in his patience.

The answer burst into his mind. "Patience. He was teaching me patience," he said with a great deal more humility than he had shown thus far.

"A mahktashaan can neither serve Mahktos nor control the crystals without it. The god awaits your apology."

Vinsant shuffled around. He was smarter than to dare gaze through the crystal to the gold core. Dropping to his knees, he closed his eyes and composed a heartfelt prayer. *I'm sorry for having no patience and not attending my lesson.* With a wince, he added, *and for stealing the crystal.* Since the mahktashaan believed the gods knew all, he had no choice but to add, *and for what I'm going to take today?* Wondering if Mahktos was about to strike him down for the insincere admission, he cracked one eye open. When nothing happened, he opened the other and looked up. His breath caught in his throat, and he almost keeled over. The statue's crimson eyes were real, and they were boring right into him. Mahktos, or his statue, made a lazy blink, which couldn't have meant dire warning, right? Then the eyes turned to rubies again, which had to mean he was absolved, didn't it? Vinsant forced himself to suck in air. He did not dare look at the Majoria. In fact, he did not even dare to stand.

The silence was slaying. He should have known the Majoria would give him no instruction. He would have shown infinite patience in waiting for the man to leave before he got up, but the flagstones were imprinting their imperfections on his achy knees, so he had to stand or risk them wearing right through his bruised skin. He swallowed. The Majoria's hood had slid to his hairline. The man's moustache appeared thickened above his pursed lips, and his black eyes seared.

"Why does the god watch you?" Levi asked.

Vinsant bit his lip and looked down. He had as much as promised

Arun he would not lie to the Majoria, which discounted *I don't know* as an answer. "He didn't tell me," had to suffice.

Levi continued to regard him. "Perhaps," he said, walking around Vinsant, "Perhaps..." But he did not voice his thought. After a few more moments of consideration he said, "I had thought to teach you to navigate these rooms. The Minoria and I require a trustworthy errand runner. Mahktos cautions..." He broke off and bowed his head. The hairs on the back of Vinsant's neck prickled. "Yes, Divine One," the Majoria said. His eyes narrowed as he looked at Vinsant. "Come."

In the next room, Levi pointed to the glyphs above the door. Once explained, the system was straightforward to understand, if not to follow. The top symbol gave the number of the room they were in, not quite a simple progression from left to right given the hexagonal layout. The middle sign indicated the number of the adjacent room, and the bottom glyphs, the numbers of the rooms someone could access from that one. The glyphs themselves took longer than Vinsant anticipated to master, but soon Levi was supplying a room number and asking him to navigate. Within a couple of hours, he had become quite adept, the only annoyance his need to backtrack when he reached dead ends. He would, Levi assured him, learn his way in time.

"Which room did I recover in yesterday?" Vinsant asked.

Levi told him and he found his way there in record time, making a mental note to remember room fifty-two. A glance inside revealed the robes were still hanging on the wall.

"This lesson is finished. You will report to Branak in the library, room twenty-three. You will impart none of this knowledge to the other apprentices."

"Yes, Majoria," Vinsant said, curbing his questions.

"Apprentice Vinsant," Levi said as Vinsant turned to leave the room. The edge to his gravelly voice sent a chill crawling across Vinsant's skin. "It is a privilege for an apprentice to have the run of the lair. You will remember both Mahktos and I watch you. Do not disappoint."

"No, Majoria. All praise to you," Vinsant said, readying himself for a dull hour or two with books.

The walls of the apprentice's library were lined with shelves that extended from floor to ceiling, each filled with heavy books, leather covers faded and cracked, and pages worn and dog-eared from countless thumbs. At least Branak allowed him to study alone, Gram and Naikil having only rudimentary knowledge of lettering or the subjects Vinsant's tutors had spent years drilling. When, at long last, Branak dismissed them for luncheon, Vinsant dashed through the rooms and out of view before the others could follow.

In room fifty-two, he lifted three black robes off their hooks, folded them into neat squares, and made his way through three rooms before two mahktashaan glided into view. Vinsant held his breath and kept walking. He thought he was done for when they gave him a double glance. But they continued their conversation and exited.

The next few rooms were easy to navigate. He had to stop in a hexagon with six exits to check his bearings.

"Where are you going, apprentice?" a voice asked.

Vinsant jumped. "The laundry," he said, facing a mahktashaan with a yellowish crystal.

He received a quizzical look and a nod to send him on his way. Prince or apprentice, one robe was suspicious, but three could only mean a chore.

Exiting the lair was not the complicated affair entering was. When he pressed the hexagonal stone trigger at the top of the stairs, the door clicked open. Brushing the tapestry aside, he stepped into the corridor. No one was around to gawk at his new privilege, so he hurried towards the servant passages. Dutiful, he handed two of the robes to the first maid he saw, and then went to hide the last beneath his mattress.

Chapter Twenty

SIAN STEPPED OVER A comatose, unwashed body on the common room floor, and padded her way outside.

The longhouses stirred with activity during the day, though never as much as night. Able men were on the hunt, or scouring the wooded hills for timber to fashion new weapons, but those women not out gathering tended house, drying fruit or sweeping. The old and infirm basked in the web of sunshine spun through cracks in the canopy, and those young enough to need nursing toddled after wagtails through musty, rotting leaves. The fits had forced Sian to remain close to her grandmam's side for much of her life so she was used to all that. She was used to chattering monkeys swinging down from supple boughs to steal plums, blue-throated green bee eaters swooping for plump grubs, and one or two glazed-eyed hunters slouched on stumps. She was not used to seven or eight young tribesmen passed out beside the water trough and in front of longhouse stairs. In the last few turns of seasons, too many had turned vacant stares inward, allowing their bodies to wither in drug-induced bliss. It scared her cold. If they kept tipping the drug into her when she fitted, she too might shrivel to a husk. She might become an intolerable burden on her disappointed family, just like those young men.

"Lazy puffer. Get here and crack these nuts," her mam said as she crept down the steps.

Sian squinted through the leaves. The sun was at full height. She would have to work extra hard to make up for the time she had lost to exhaustion and the porrin daze. She picked up the rock her mam had been using and began to pound the nutshells, not even glancing up when Mam took herself to sit on a reed mat, wriggle her brown toes in a patch of sunlight, and chat with her friends.

She had cracked a handful of nuts and eaten half of them when her grandmother wandered past, a plaited reed bowl of whiteroots on her slender hip.

"The soothsayer wanted to see you, child. Go. Go. Where are your manners?" Vila said, depositing the basket next to Sian.

Unmarried nobodies did not keep Soothsayers of the Tribes waiting. Sian scampered from the village, and her grandmam's tirade at a mam who forgot to pass on such an important message. The thickening ashes and oaks along the winding trail soon dampened their shrill bickering. She twirled to bird whistles, danced with a purple butterfly and dodged the peach stones the monkeys tried to pelt her with. At the old hollow bole, she turned onto a ledge that led up the hill. The Soothsayer's cave, hidden by bushes and outcrops, had few visitors, except when the need to summon her arose. That need was seldom. Ishoa, Sacred Soothsayer of the Ho'akerin Tribe, Second Soothsayer of the Akerin, showed uncanny intuition in that regard.

The mouth of the dry cave yawned like the maw of a bear. It swallowed the relief she had felt when she ran from the village. One hand on the wall, Sian peered inside. A fire crackled in the centre, its column of lavender-scented smoke trailing up through a fissure in the roof. By some trick of the air, sounds carried up from the longhouses: a piercing voice, the wail of a child.

A twig cracked behind her and Sian spun. The soothsayer stood there, a bundle of reeds in one arm, her knobbly staff with the large pods dangling from the top in the other. No taller than Sian, and no wider though she had a woman's curves, she was an imposing figure with her painted face and feathered hair. With her milky eyes that held the wisdom of the ancient oaks. Sian wrapped her ungainly arms around herself and bowed her head.

"Is that you, Sian? Are you recovered?" Ishoa asked.

Her tongue tied itself in a knot. Sian could only nod. It was a stupid thing to do. She blushed as she started to stammer the formal greeting.

The soothsayer cut her off. "Come inside." The reeds prickled her skin as Ishoa nudged her around, taking her elbow for guidance. "It is not my intention to stress you into another fit."

They sat on stitched rabbit furs, the smoke of the fire curling between them. Ishoa cupped her chin and peered at her face as its woody smell drew her nerves from her fluttery stomach. When Ishoa passed her some reeds and bade her seed the heads, she was glad of a task to occupy her hands. The humdrum task, the burning herbs, Ishoa's gentle voice, speaking of their beloved woods as if they were alive, demanding nothing of her save a description here and there, of the season's blooms or a kid's frolics, eased her. By the time she had woven half the reeds into a bowl, Sian had never felt more comfortable next to another person in her life. She tied off the ends of the reeds as Ishoa gathered a mix of herbs from baskets lining the back of the cave.

"I want you to drink the tea of these leaves twice a day," the soothsayer said, passing her a mortar so she could crush the herbs with the seed. "It might be they help control your fits."

Sian stiffened. Ishoa reached out, felt only air, adjusted the direction of her hand and tucked Sian's wayward hair behind an ear. "The spirits burden us for a reason, and only in a measure we can endure." It was an oft-repeated proverb around the dwellings, one nobody ever said to her. Sian pounded that little bit harder.

"I dreamt of you," Ishoa said.

A soothsayer's dreaming was prophesy; Sian knew the lore. She put head down, let her hair fall over her face, kept grinding.

"You are important to this tribe."

The pestle clunked out of her hand. She mumbled an apology. Ishoa seemed not to hear.

"There is change ahead for our people, and you must be the one to lead."

The air thrummed with that telling. Sian managed to raise her dubious face. Not to say anything, though. She did not think the soothsayer would say this to make her feel better, but this dream could not be a true seeing. Ishoa was young to hold her power. All the tribes said so. It was true, too. Under the paint and feathers, her nut-brown face was smooth, her sap-brown hair glossy.

Sian shook her head. Her heart was pounding denial. "Not I."

Ishoa groped until her hand found Sian's. She squeezed tight. Her white eyes centred on some secret place. "Tell your grandmam I wish you here every morning. Tell her you are to have three afternoons an eight-day to wander the hills alone." Her hand relaxed. She fumbled it across, to the mortar, tipped the contents into a cloth bag, and handed it to Sian.

"I'm not allowed," Sian said. She turned her head as her cheeks flushed. There was shame in saying she could not be alone, in a fit striking her down, helpless-weak in the path of bear or ogre.

An owl *too-hooed*, early in its waking.

"I wish it," Ishoa said. It was reason enough for anyone in the Tribes. "Go now, child.

On the narrow path back to the valley floor, Sian passed Leadsman Draykan. Erok's father smiled at her, and she smiled back, a tentative thing but it reached her eyes.

"You had us worried," he said.

She bowed her head, the smile gone. "I'm sorry," she whispered.

His hand on her head felt like a blessing. "It is not, I think, your fault."

He was on his way before she could reply, up to the soothsayer's cave, a strong warrior even with the first lines of age on his broad face, and strands grey in his hair. She watched him disappear into the mouth before she dawdled on her way to peas and scoldings and belittling glances, stealing a few last shadow-lengths of freedom.

When she sat by Grandmam Vila and her pile of crunchy stalks, Mam glanced over from where she leaned on a twig broom. Seeing Sian had something to say and nothing to do, she squawked her way over. Sian clutched the bag of herbs as she waited for Mam to pause for breath. Then she fumbled her way through Ishoa's message.

Grandmam eyed her with wary suspicion. "If that's what the soothsayer said," she granted, shaking a beetle off a leafgreen. She tore off the stem and tossed the leaf into a clay pot.

"Today you work," Mam scolded, hands on hips and a frown longer than the broom on her brow. "You have done nothing but sleep and chat."

"Ah, put your own hands to work, Larpa," Grandmam said, and then, under her breath, "Lazy as a puffer."

A smile twitched at Sian's lips but she was careful to drop her head and let her hair hang to hide it. This was the best day of her life; she did not want a cuffing to spoil it.

"Stash those greens before you squash them," Grandmam said.

Sian was up the steps into the longhouse with a springier gait than she had shown in a while. A hop carried her over the sleeping tribesman. She even began to hum. At the doorway to the girl's sleeping room, she paused. Her stick insect was watching her pah rummage through her basket of possessions. It did not contain much: a comb; a wooden goshawk her grandpah had carved not long before he passed; a few coloured stones she had stumbled across. Pah stood all guilty-awkward and angry-tense as she shuffled to the door. The embroidered bag of porrin Ishoa had left was in his hands.

"This is too dangerous for you to leave about." He pushed past her.

The tears began welling when she saw him open the bag and inhale before one calloused foot had found a stair. By the time Daesoa shed her light, he would be as wasted as the other layabouts in the village.

Sian put the bag of herbs into her basket, sat on her bedding and hung her head. When her stick insect waved one spindly leg, she let the tears flow.

Ishoa took up her staff, rattled the dangling pods, and hailed Draykan.

"Let's stand at the entrance. I have need of a clear head," she told him.

Draykan, familiar but not quite at ease with her smokes and hazes, acquiesced with a grunt. They stood together in silence so he might watch Sian dawdle her way back to the longhouses. The tap of the girl's slowing footfalls saddened her. No child should suffer as she had.

"She smiled at me," Draykan said.

"That child has much need of smiles," Ishoa replied.

The leadsman sighed. "She is not well regarded in the tribe."

"Her affliction impedes neither her limbs nor her mind. It is the superstitions that erode her self-respect."

"The tribe fear what they do not understand."

"And you, Draykan? What think you of the daughter of Larpa and Vorn?"

"I think I would rather have a longhouse full of women like her than of hunters wasted on the drug of bliss."

"Ah."

A baby's wail reached them. "That infant has been screeching most of the morning," Ishoa observed.

"His mother is more concerned with her other younglings' next meal."

"Then Nak has not returned from the Wander?"

Draykan shook his head. "We are losing them," he said through clenched jaw. "We are losing them all."

Far away, thunder rumbled, thickening the air. The afternoon rains would fall heavy. Ishoa thrust her staff high in the air, tossed her head back and let forth an ululation that shook leaves off the surrounding trees. When she finished, utter silence reigned. A last leaf whispered through the air. She caught it and ran a practiced finger over its surface: caterpillar-eaten; veins bare. An ill omen that. "The babe will sleep," she said, thudding the butt of her staff on rock. That much, at least, she could do. "Come. I will cast the bones for you." She turned into the cave. She felt Draykan's humility. She was Soothsayer. She knew why they came to her. All these years and Draykan still could not fathom that.

His reason was dire. She had trailed it in the dance, had glimpsed it in the dream. From beside her sleeping furs, she fetched a sandalwood box. Her finger traced the sacred runes inlaid on its lid as Draykan laid her staff in front of her. He helped her kneel upon the furs, as solid in his strength as his son. It remained for her to open the box, and to remove the bones, an odd assortment that had once held the life of a mouse, an eagle, a monkey, a squirrel, a lizard, a bear. One bone for each manner of creature that crawled, walked or flew the forest, each carved with a sigil that drew on the mysteries of its kind. Ishoa set them in front of her, praying her thanks for their gift. When Draykan began to fidget, she offered him a fond smile, and threw a handful of stupor-inducing seeds atop the flames. They crackled and jumped from the hearth, red hot if she remembered right. Waving the fresh smoke that wafted up towards her, she inhaled deep. The only sound from Draykan as he lowered himself onto a fur was another grunt. She smiled, guessing he had tilted his nose to avoid the acrid fumes. Settling into the cross-legged position, she bade the Spirits of the Forest to mark her path, beseeched the Spirits of the Sky to bear her forth and the Spirits of the Earth to ground her soul, lest she fly too high, too far.

It came of a sudden, as always, the dizzying spin of the vision, the heightening of her senses. She gathered the bones in a single scoop and flung them across the fire, adding the last leaf downed by her wild call, the crucial element which trigged the tug of her soul. Season after season she had thrown the bones, and so she could time the moment she left her body to be borne on the Spirit Winds across the planes. Season after season she had entered the trance, but never could she foresee the disconcerting moment time jolted to a stop. The moment the bones hung suspended above the flames as the Spirit Winds whooshed through the cave, sweeping around the hearth, chilling her to the marrow. She hovered above them, over the fire, looking down with her inner sight at her immobile form; at Draykan huddled in on himself, too proud to retreat from the buffeting; at the ominous, black cast of the bones. They held at their centre the snake vertebra carved with the rune for the cursed drug. It was the newest acquisition to her set, placed there not eighteen moons ago when Nak had first returned from Tarana with his powdered prize. What amusement the young men had found in tossing the serpent a dead mouse sprinkled with porrin she would never know. Drug of bliss. Drug of curses. The Ho'akerin had once revered the land that succoured them. Now they tottered on the edge of sowing desolation as bleak as the lowlanders did. The spirits were fleeing, severing themselves from the Tribe, like the veins snapping from the midrib of the leaf she had tossed to the hungry flames. This it seemed was the fate of the Akerin. Not a rune emerged to temper the ill fortune, and the desolation cut to her soul. She released an ululating cry of despair, a cry as cold as she. The winds whirled faster, spinning the cave, the fire and time itself aside. Then there it was, clearer in the pattern, the smallest of her bones, the one she had cut from a fish out of water. It had flapped before her in the final throes of life, for some inexplicable reason reminding her of Sian. The spirits had whispered their blessing in the swish of the wind through the leaves that day, and so she had carved it with the girl's name. Now here it shone, leading the way through the mire, more important than she had intuited in her dreaming.

The return to her body was smooth, if sorrowful, the bones tumbling to the floor in front of her. Shivering, she groped for them. One by one, she replaced them in the box, thanking the spirit of each animal as she did.

"Was the reading good?" Draykan asked when the fire had warmed the shivers out of her blood. His voice was taut with the effort of his wait.

Neither the smooth surface of her box nor the rough pole of her staff gave her comfort. "It is not news to make you rejoice. A storm brews on the horizon, and it blows much hardship for the Tribes, much change."

"The Akerin have always weathered change."

"This time it is our traditions, our way of life," she bowed her head, "our home," she murmured, "which is at risk."

She heard him draw a bulky breath. "Why?" he asked. "What did we do to anger the spirits so?"

She stood, leaning heavily on her staff, gazing out of the cave into the heart of the cheeping, chattering, rustling Forest she loved like a child. A strange foulness seasoned the moisture clinging to leaf and frond. She had never tasted its like. "Need you ask?"

The fur rubbed Draykan's clothes as he too rose. "I must hear it from you, Soothsayer. I must have it from the spirits themselves."

"It began with the drug."

Curses ran rife among the women of the Tribe. They spat their disgust at the trees, condemning the spirits for bringing porrin into their midst, and then turned a blind eye while their men succumbed. Not a one admitted the weakness was the devilry of men. Not a one understood what disrespect the spirits felt. Stupors were for the shamans alone. They summoned evil magic down on the uninitiated. So haughty had the tribe become in blaming and demanding that Ishoa quaked to commune with the spirits on their behalf.

As if sensing her thoughts, Draykan padded to the mouth of the cave. When he made no rustles of leave, she shuffled her way over to join him. Were it not for her staff, she would have crawled so draining was her ordeal.

"I am thinking to banish those that imbibe the drug," the Leadsman said at length. "What say you?"

"It is a decision for our leader alone." Then, because she sensed his need for support, she said, "I believe that step is long overdue, but on this all five Hill Tribes of the Akerin must unite."

Draykan grunted. "I thank you, Soothsayer."

"There is one more thing," she said, listening to the whoops, and tweets, and roars. They reminded her of a time when these fertile valleys nurtured a proud people. "The child Sian is our hope."

"It will be a joyous day if the tribe returns to succouring its most dependent."

"The dream leads beyond that. Others must follow where she treads."

He shook his head. "That I cannot believe. And even if I did, it will never happen."

It was with her Spirit Voice that she answered, "At the Ho'akerin's peril, Draykan."

From the direction of the village, a babe began to scream.

CHAPTER TWENTY-ONE

TIMAK STOOD ON TIPTOE, reached into the fifth drawer of the tall oak chest, and organised the last of Ahkdul's things. If he could somehow climb under the fine kameez, he might hide for a time, perhaps an entire night. The mysterious man with the blue crystal had softened his aches, but the hooded soldier's magic hadn't packed the big hole in his middle. It felt like that was all he had ever known, that his parents' loving hugs and kisses were a figment of his longing, especially here, in this dim room. Heavy with dark tapestries, gigantic desk and poster bed, the room bore down like it wanted to bury him alive.

The monster, with his hunched bulk and menacing voice, turned the brooding room oppressive. His first instruction to the servant sent to pour his bath had been to close all the shutters on the light of day. Then, while soaking off the grime of the journey, he had murmured his appreciation of the horrible stitched battle scenes.

Timak shuddered. Headless men and gouged horses were scarier when lit by the flicker of candles. Making himself as inconspicuous as possible between the chest and the wall, he closed his eyes and hoped Yazmine could find him in this strange realm.

"Lord Ahkdul, it is good tidings," a toady, white-bearded man Ahkdul had addressed as Baiyeed deq Ikher was saying. He smelled flowery, like a girl. "The mahktashaan have scoured the histories and decreed flying fish herald a royal wedding."

Someone tittered at his ear. His eyes flew open. "Did you do that?" he whispered.

"I had no idea how excited everyone would get," Yazmine answered. One day she might let him see her. She would look real pretty, a match for the faint scent of roses wafting out of her muted glow.

"And what of the Terlaani princess? Is she as fair as they claim?" asked Ahkdul. He was dressing in a fresh saffron kurta the palace servants had laid out on the quilted bedding.

"My lord, with her in your possession, you could not fail to be the envy of every man on this earth," deq Ikher replied with a twitch of his cheek.

"Oh no, what have I done? I think I'm going to be in BIG trouble," Yazmine said.

Timak sucked in a deep breath. If the monster wed, it might save him from the attentions of this evil man.

"And what of the prince?" Ahkdul continued.

"Which one?" deq Ikher said, pinning his beard to his chest. He painted every word out of his mouth with the brightness of the gems in his rings.

"The elder, of course. The other is but a child," Ahkdul snapped. It hadn't been a stupid question. The monster's attention faded as he chewed on the last, and the colour rose in his cheeks. Timak pushed himself into the corner between chest and wall.

"Prince Mariano is shaping to be a strong leader, in body and mind. He will not be easy to depose."

"This scheme of my father's imperils us all. His greed for land–"

Deq Ikher's cheek twitched faster. Just then, Timak's foot slid against the chest. The soft tap drew Ahkdul's attention.

"And the younger prince?" the monster said, looking at Timak. His voice had grown husky.

"As you said, still a child. About thirteen, I believe, but small for his age."

Ahkdul licked his lips. Timak found it difficult to breathe. His chest stopped moving altogether when Ahkdul stepped towards him. With a leer that threatened of a lingering night, Ahkdul removed two packets of porrin from his pocket. Timak wondered if he could duck under those hairy arms and escape the room before deq Ikher grabbed him. A rap at the door dashed that plan. He tried not to notice the bulge in Ahkdul's shalvar as the monster, directing deq Ikher to respond, slid the packets of drug into the top drawer.

"Shah Wilshem awaits your master," his saviour, a hooded man with a green crystal said from outside the door.

Ahkdul channelled his frustration into a tighter grip on the arm of the padded chair. Shah Wilshem's polite queries after Lord Hudassan were tedious in the extreme. Engrossed in diversions of the flesh during the voyage, he had avoided mulling on the purpose of this visit. His father's purpose. Now, unprepared and tired, he wanted to be done with what must, and return home where he could idle at will and lord over all. He helped himself to another gulp of red wine, making a glib reply to yet another of Wilshem's questions while perusing the tapestries of immense mountains and barren plains that smothered the stone walls in the snug room. Wilshem claimed it was his favourite chamber. That was easy to believe. Ensconced in a well-proportioned chair before a gilded table laid with trays of venison pies and honey-glazed pastries, Ahkdul might well lull into a state of repose were it not for the shah's incessant and trivial queries. Wondering when they would get to the heart of the matter, he frowned at a tapestry of steam-veiled scums. It displayed nuances of colour missing from the weaves back home.

It was some seconds before Ahkdul realised Wilshem, a fist over his mouth, had fallen silent and intent. His pose was no doubt meant to impart an air of wisdom, his black kurta and shalvar, bordered in silver, to inspire the same dread as his mahktashaan. Well, Ahkdul saw straight through the neat trim of his dark beard.

"Your father trusts you to negotiate," the Shah said. He should not think his lack of inflection disguised his contempt. Wilshem might be a shah, but he had no right to judge. He deserved every scrap of loathing Ahkdul was wrestling to keep from oozing over his face.

"Would you not trust your son?" he asked, and downed the contents of his silver goblet. The generous chair well accommodated his bulk, but he was past bored. If deq Ikher were correct, this interview should be naught but a formality.

Wilshem allowed a pause, then picked up the wine pitcher and refilled the cup. "These are weighty matters. If our discussions must obtain Lord Hudassan's approval, it is best he and I meet on neutral ground."

"I carry my father's authority," Ahkdul said, staying his hand from the drink. Now they were on to matters of state, he needed a clear head. The thought called Wilshem's hospitality into question. He glanced at his goblet, twice filled when Wilshem's stood untouched, then at the elaborate embroidery on his saffron kurta and black shalvar. His acceptance of the fine Terlaani garb had proclaimed Verdaan the backwater it was; to refuse would have meant he appeared before the Shah in clothes this condescending realm deemed unfit for rank. His initial pleasure Wilshem had forborne a lavish reception gave way to suspicions this comfort was a shrewd design meant to lower his guard.

"Then let us see how well you can convince me to proffer my daughter's hand."

Seething, unable to help himself in the mire of that particular emotion, Ahkdul took another draught of wine, cursing his father as the drink seared his stomach. "Verdaan needs heirs." On this, he and his father had agreed, however insufferable a wife might be.

Curse Wilshem for mocking him with solemn eyes.

Ahkdul placed the goblet on the circular table beside his arm. He licked his lips as Wilshem rose just far enough to fill it once again, waiting until the shah was settled to speak. "Princess Kordahla's beauty is famed. If her company is as pleasurable, I should be happy to elevate her to queen. She would birth future kings."

"Do you do her a favour, Ahkdul, that you would be happy and not honoured?" The Shah was still, his voice taut in its softness.

Ahkdul's blood screamed for another drink but his sense – what little of it he was displaying, curse Wilshem – warned him off. "As my wife, she would be a queen in her own right."

"Kordahla is a princess. Do not pretend you and your father claim royal status. It is she who will bestow rank on you."

To the scums with deq Ikher and his tidings. Ahkdul leaned forward. He hated it when his face became tight. "We rule. Scour history and you will find as much bloodshed when your ancestors took the throne as when my grandfather did."

"Perhaps," Wilshem said, waving towards the goblet and lifting his own. Ahkdul was dismayed to find he was taking another sip. Had a mahktashaan been in the room, he would have suspected coercion of the magical kind. As it was, he had no one to blame except his own indulged self. "However, we live in a peaceable age, a very different time," Wilshem continued, "and your lineage is yet to prove its worth. This union you seek would lend substance to Hudassan's request for Shah Ordosteen to recognise him as an equal."

"Is that so very bad?"

"Then there is the matter of your reputation."

This conversation was treading on dangerous ground. Had Ahkdul guessed how direct Wilshem intended to be, he would have imbibed porrin to calm his nerves. This weak wine did not suffice. "Would you care to explain your remark?" he said, injecting a veiled threat into the words. A mere moment passed before he regretted the demand. In the privacy of his home, his guards outside the door, Wilshem very well might elucidate.

"I would not."

His relief was no doubt palpable.

"Nor am I so naïve as to believe a man's predilections might change," the shah continued. "But I ask you this, for my daughter will find her nature subdued in Verdaan, and life will be hard after the liberties I have allowed. She may be a mere woman, but she is a princess, and I will not have her humiliated. Are you a man of discretion?"

"I will do my duty as a husband. She will bear heirs, if that is what concerns you."

"It is not. My child might complain of the need for a veil, for sleeves that cover the wrists and long skirts that shield her ankles. None of this would I heed, for it is not long past that Terlaan demanded these not only in the street but also in the confines of the home. A husband who neglects his conjugal duties, who openly flaunts perverse desires, though, I would think has reneged on his marriage contract. A husband who cares not for the dignity of a royal Terlaani child, my child, within his court would not deserve her. Terlaan would bring her home. Whatever the cost. So I ask you again. Will you remain discreet?"

"A man may not help his predilections, but it is the soul which governs the flesh. Princess Kordahla will be the jewel in my palace." Ahkdul leant forward. "This union is right. There has been a clear sign from the gods."

"You, who in a matter of hours have become such an expert on Terlaani lore, stand advised. The fish denote a marriage, but from no one, and least of all me, has this union received sanction. Kordahla's marriage to a Myklaani lord would satisfy the Vae. Indeed, her marriage to a Terlaani of standing would do just as well."

"I ask you to consider the timing of the miracle. It came with the delivery of my proposal. The union can be intended with none other."

"You may test me on this, though it would be to your detriment to do so. Kordahla, though liberal by our reckoning, is a prize for any man whose loins lean in the right direction. For you, she is a trophy, and the means to a crown. So I ask you blunt, what has Terlaan to gain?"

Ahkdul smiled. Terlaan would appear to have a great deal to gain if he could but persuade Wilshem his words were sincere. He downed a long draught, for courage and a tongue loose enough to gild his words. "We come to the matter on which you have long desired action. Naturally–"

"This–," Wilshem interrupted, and Ahkdul's hand tightened on the goblet. He drained the remaining sips to help him endure another patronising caution. "–is not a pact glib words can broker. Terlaan has called for responsibility for some years. Not once has Lord Hudassan seen fit to address our concerns. And now he sends his son to barter on the most pressing political issue, the single one, perhaps, for which there is no solution since no measures can secure our borders against smugglers. Have a care what you propose, Ahkdul. A shah does not rule for thirty years without deducing other's wiles."

The empty goblet weighed heavy in Ahkdul's hand. Wishing it full, he set it down with more clatter than was elegant for a man of his standing. Such words were not appropriate for the next ruler of Verdaan. Words such as these brought doubt to his mind. Had Wilshem guessed their scheme? He could not think on it for fear a mahktashaan lurked close by, one talented in mindreading. Those soldier-magicians might voice vehement denials the skill existed, but a prudent man did not trust a hooded fiend. Ahkdul's fingers twitched as once again Wilshem poured wine, a good measure into Ahkdul's cup, a splash into his own.

The ruse was obvious but he licked his lips, craving the balm of the fiery drink. He stayed his hand. Too much lay at stake, his inheritance not least if he returned to his father in disgrace.

"Please," Wilshem said, picking up his goblet and taking a sip. "It is an especially smooth Myklaani vintage."

Ahkdul's nerves screamed for another draught. It took great effort to ball his hand and slap it to his thigh. There was porrin waiting, he comforted himself, and the boy. "I would engage in the negotiations, Majesty. You may decide for yourself what worth our offer holds."

The Shah reclined in his chair. His hand was back over his mouth, a finger tapping his lip as his eyes flicked between Ahkdul and his full goblet. Ahkdul smiled. He was far from inebriated, and he would show this Shah how much a master of his flesh he could be.

"Then speak," Wilshem said, when he refused to take a sip.

"Verdaan is prepared to direct its porrin trade to Myklaan. Lord Hudassan will order his brother, Lord Kamir, to send his merchants south. He will double the patrols along our border, and ensure customs searches any vessels headed for your shores." Ahkdul paused to gauge Wilshem's reaction. It was a mistake that saw him relinquish control of the conversation.

"These measures may slow the trade of porrin; they may even reduce it; but they will not eliminate it. What of smugglers that bypass your checkpoints, or enter through Myklaan?"

"We are not responsible for the actions of the Myklaani. You will have our assurances any traders through that route will not come from Verdaan."

"That is all I have. Your assurances, and those of your father if you are to be believed. But Hudassan does not have a reputation for keeping pledges. You will have to do better than your word."

"Verdaan will welcome Terlaani officers to serve alongside our own, in the watchtowers and in the ports. They will answer to their own command, of course, though they must adhere to our codes of conduct. In return, we ask that we might leave our ambassador with your court."

Wilshem's answer was a long time in coming. "I must admit, I had not considered this offer would come from Hudassan." The shah fell silent again. A contemplative mood, by the look on his face.

Ahkdul felt the time judicious for another sip of wine. "You obviously have an alternative in mind, or at least an adjunct," he said as the silence extended.

When Wilshem spoke, his quiet voice had divested itself of its superiority. "I ask you to burn the crop. Terlaan will provide recompense, and without doubt Myklaan will join us in supplying your farmers with wheat seed and corn. I ask you to grow what nourishes rather than what wastes."

"You ask us to surrender the most lucrative of our exports. Verdaan would perish without the income from porrin. No other crop will match its earnings." He picked up the goblet, and took a slow, considered sip. "And we must consider the balance of power."

Ahkdul had not known how Wilshem would react to that last. Grow angry, most like, he had thought. He had not expected the chuckle, for it was clear to them both, to all save the porrin-wasted addicts and right down to the barefooted youngsters at their mother's knee, that without porrin only one source of magic existed in The Three Realms.

"Rightly argued," Wilshem said, raising his goblet. "But why not allow Myklaan to grow their own seed?"

His father had expected this, had schooled him in the response and for all his growling at the time Ahkdul was now pleased for it. "The balance of power," he repeated. "Verdaan must have a place among the realms."

"It seems we are at an impasse," Wilshem said.

A bow of his head hid Ahkdul's smile. "It seems we are," he agreed, knowing the offer was everything Wilshem had hoped for.

The Shah's fingers laced on his lap, his thumbs tapping as he gave the proposal further thought. It surprised Ahkdul that he spoke next of something other than their agreement. "You must be anxious to view your father's ship. It is a pleasant trip to the boatyards. You will appreciate company, and Princess Kordahla will be grateful for the outing. It is not often I permit her to leave the palace." Ahkdul's surprise gave way to displeasure as the Shah rose, his words again bearing the weight of his authority. "My daughter, however much she is expecting an arranged marriage, will not be ecstatic about this union. I trust – no, I expect – you will be delicate in your handling of her. I shall hear from Prince Mariano of your conduct before I decide."

Ahkdul tugged the corners of his lips out of a smile. There was no question he had won.

CHAPTER TWENTY-TWO

JORDAYNE STRETCHED OUT ON the cushions a servant had arranged to her precise specifications on the bench in the drab little courtyard and appraised the behinds of the guards as they prepared to stage her entertainment. The burly executioner was knotting the noose as two soldiers escorted Raj the Verdaani porrin merchant out of the dungeons and into her presence. The amusing little man, puffed up with pride, gloated so much at the sight of her that he did not notice either the filth caking him or the gallows.

"Hah!" he said, his stench steaming off him. "I knew Shah would let me go."

"Indeed," Jordayne replied. "Shah Ordosteen believes a minor moon is long enough for a Verdaani thief to enjoy his hospitality."

Grinning, Raj executed a little bow.

Jordayne yawned, covering her mouth with spread fingers. In the languid stillness of the summer afternoon, she had little hope a breeze would sprinkle the fragrance of the frangipani over the man. "Well. I do appreciate your change in attitude. Has it extended as far as considering our request?"

He chuckled at that. "Lady, it is not reasonable request. Maybe next time we meet at certain inn we come to mutually acceptable arrangement." Could you believe he had the audacity to wink at her? Ignorant chauvinist that he was, Jordayne was beginning to like the man. If he had been even a smidgeon more attractive, she might have condescended to have one of her maids educate him in the finer points of the 'arrangement' he had in mind before casting him aside to mourn the divine mysteries he had but glimpsed. She rose into a lazy stretch, which set her bracelets jangling. Her lips could not help but pull into a smile. To him she must appear as elegant as the avocet flying overhead.

"We shall not be meeting again for a lifetime, I'm afraid. I have rather a great deal left to accomplish on this earth, not least of which is to initiate worthy males into Vae'oenka's feminine secrets. How many deserving males are there on this earth, Sul?"

The bald executioner, a happily married man nonetheless known for his lewd comments, tugged upon the noose. "Lady, I dare to hazard not a dozen fit to savour your charms."

She walked around the courtyard, sizing up the guards, to the feather-ruffling approval of a pair of multi-coloured parrots on the wall. "A mere dozen. How boring." Her slippered feet were silent on the cobbles. "Anyway, I should hardly think this specimen was one. Just consider the dashing physique of these guards, and only one of them sufficiently droll to relieve my tedium."

A splotch of embarrassment spread over Raj's neck. He could not have expected a woman to usurp control. As for the guards, they were casting curious glances at each other to discern of whom she spoke. It would amuse them for an eight-day or two, to try to trap each other into an admission, until they realised her jest. It would amuse her more to note the heightened colour in their cheeks when she next addressed them. They made a quick adjustment of their posture when Matisse sauntered through the ivy-covered arch separating the high-walled courtyard from the palace gardens. His dishevelled hair and rumpled clothing suggested he had enjoyed an interesting night. He wore his crumpled appearance like a badge of honour, and nobody, she least of all, could deny it increased his appeal.

"Has the prisoner decided to cooperate?" her brother asked as though it bore little import.

"He says he believes our request unreasonable," she replied, sinking back onto the bench and drawing her feet up.

"He looks discomfited, but not afraid. Is his neck not under discussion?"

"Our conversation has not quite reached that point," Jordayne said, refusing to make room for her brother to sit. If he wanted to pretend he was passing through on his way to his chambers, she would foster the charade.

"He is not a very observant fellow," Matisse smirked.

The funny little man broke into an agitated shuffle. One of the guards wagged a finger in Sul's direction. The executioner gave the noose a yank, returning an exaggerated wink Raj's way. Raj had the good sense to start to panic.

"Ah. You see? There is no arrangement to be made," she said. "Would you like to reconsider abasing yourself at my feet?"

Raj's legs were too shaky for him to succeed in holding himself proud. "Myklaan do not execute prisoners."

"Times change, and Myklaan has a stellar reputation for keeping with them."

"What times? There is no change." He was looking about now, searching for an elusive escape. A few more words and she would have him in the palm of her hand.

"The sad truth is they have changed," she said.

Discarding his nonchalant air, Matisse said, "Verdaan creates suspicion of war. The rules during times of conflict differ from those in peace, as I am sure you are aware." Every bit the ruler-in-waiting now, he paused, his eyes hard and still. "As," he finished, enunciating each of his last words so there was no mistaking their import, "the Verdaani are wont to remind us."

Dear Vae'oeldin, she had not considered her brother so bloodthirsty. What was it about royal men that they measured their worth by the blood they spilled? If they could not forget the past, they should at least lay it aside.

"I do not work with others," Raj said.

"No?" Matisse raised a hand. The guards flanked the prisoner and dragged him to the noose.

"Up you go," Sul said, gesturing to the crate. Raj's slippery struggles would have drawn the crowd at a pantomime. "May I expect that artist, Lady? Blood curdles quickly in the dead."

Raj's eyes went wide in perfect time with her covert signal. The guards relaxed their grip, and the cheat of a porrin merchant tugged free. With utter predictability, he dropped to the ground, and kowtowed.

Jordayne affected a yawn. "I grow bored. Give me information or give me an execution."

"Lady, spare me."

She sighed as the guards seized his arms and dragged him up. The world had seen the last of the truly brave aeons ago. She nodded at Sul, who drew a hand across his thick neck.

"I deal with taverner in Zulmei," Raj blurted. "Korwin of Crooked Bow."

"Who else?" Matisse demanded.

"One or two youth in village on road from Mykver Fort." They waited. "That is all. I swear."

"What are Lords Hudassan and Kamir deq Ramil planning?" The ruler and the drug lord were notorious for their ruthless pursuit of power.

Content to let her brother garner the brutal information, Jordayne searched Raj's face for signs of deceit.

Raj shook his head. "No war. I swear, no war. Lord Kamir want gold and wealth. He has much porrin to sell. He is rich man. Richer than brother Lord Hudassan, some say."

"And you do their bidding."

"I am humble merchant. Lord Kamir pay me for sell porrin to fools with desire for bliss."

"Your contract is with the Crown, and permits you to sell only to the mages or the palace."

"You can't blame man for seeking to expand fortune."

"You were right, sister. He has cooperated," Matisse said. At his nod, the guards dragged him back through the portcullis leading to the dungeons.

"Wait. Wait. I cooperate. You release me." Raj called.

"As soon as we corroborate your testimony, Raj. We can't just take the word of a thief and a cheat, can we?" Jordayne said, rising.

The poor merchant looked positively dumbstruck.

"Do you believe him?" Matisse asked when the prisoner was out of earshot.

"About our neighbouring lords? It is plausible, I suppose, though the real threat lurks in Terlaan. Their populace is ravaged by the drug. If the rumours of a marital alliance are true, Wilshem is astute enough to demand limits to the quantities that reach his shores."

"It is a strange bargain," Matisse observed, ruffling the hair at the back of his head.

"There is little else for him to gain by bartering his daughter to the savages."

"Perhaps, then, the threat of war is unfounded."

"Whatever Wilshem's intent, more drugs will trickle past our borders. Lord Kamir is a merchant and, as Raj has demonstrated, that breed will go to great lengths to secure a profit."

"And so we had best be about the business of securing our borders, sister."

"Well then. There is a visit to Zulmei to organise."

Matisse grinned. "I have no business here that cannot be tied up within a day. This matter is of such import, I think I might deal with it myself."

"I thought you might," she said, giving his arm a squeeze. "Do give my regards to Lady Rochelle. And try to remember the real reason you are there."

Chapter Twenty-Three

KORDAHLA PLEADED A HEADACHE. She had to hope the flickering candles in the stuffy, inner parlour cast her dread into a mask half as ghastly as that on her maids. Since it did not deter the mahktashaan guard marching straight from her father, she could not, despite her Samille's earlier assurances, be sitting to worst advantage.

"Permit me to cure it," the mahktashaan said, igniting a tiny spark deep inside his carrot-coloured crystal.

She set her needlework aside, rose, and took her sheer, sky blue shawl from Karie. Vae'oenka strike her if she was going to allow a mahktashaan to lay a finger on her again, particularly one she did not know and most especially when she was lying. It was ill fate the little used room, a few chairs around a hearth really, had not concealed her past the luncheon hour.

"Where are we to meet?" she asked.

"Your veil, Highness," the mahktashaan reminded, no doubt at Father's prompting.

"You forget your place." She held his stare, if one could call the shadows beneath the hood that, and thanked the Vae he averted his face first.

"I'll fetch it," Karie offered, her hands clasped in front of her.

"There is no need," Kordahla said, allowing Samille to fuss the shawl over her shoulders. "Will the shah be joining us?"

"His Majesty has matters of state to attend," the mahktashaan answered. “His Highness, Crown Prince Mariano has the duty of escorting you.”

Her lips parted at the perturbing implication. She had entertained no doubt Father would instruct her to accompany the men, but for him to instruct Mariano to chaperone her! It could only mean he was considering Ahkdul’s distasteful proposal in earnest. She could forget the affected headache; she really was beginning to feel sick.

“You don’t look well,” Samille said. She turned to the mahktashaan with a blink which highlighted the length of her lashes. “You must send her guest her apologies.”

“Yes,” Karie added. “She has been suffering all morning. You can see how little needlepoint she has worked.”

“The shah insists.”

Kordahla swallowed. It seemed there was no escaping the detestable task. “Then our guest will have to excuse my reticence.”

Her nerves carried her through the tapestry-lined halls and down the stairs to the ground floor. They passed the wall hanging depicting Mahktos without so much as a twitch from her escort, and descended the five steps at the end of the hall to the bare foyer outside the flooded boat room. Her older brother was waiting, garbed in the rich Terlaani burgundy in which he had ridden from the palace earlier that morning. He parted from the knot of mahktashaan guards assigned to escort them, and kissed her fondly. Holding her at arm’s length, he looked her up and down.

“Tell me what Father said,” she demanded when he forbore to comment on how her slate-grey kameez ill-suited her complexion. He was astute enough to guess it had been a deliberate choice.

He shook his head. “I was not privy to that conversation, but I gather Ahkdul looked smug at its conclusion.”

Kordahla frowned. “Then prepare me for what I face.”

“Kordahla, Father would not request you marry Lord Ahkdul for a trifle, but as Princess you have an obligation. Try to consider Terlaan. The porrin is destroying us.”

Then why not just go to war! It was easy for him to be so cavalier about marriage. As Crown Prince in a time of peace, he had his pick of the ladies, here and in Myklaan. Nobody even thought to suggest he marry a Verdaani woman. "You are not Father. Do not talk to me like you are."

"A fair comment, sister," he conceded.

She could not help herself. She had to ask. "The gossip, do you think it's true?"

Mariano gave her a reluctant nod. "He brought a page with him. I gather Arun healed the boy of some hurts."

So, this burning was what pure rage felt like. She was shaking with it. That Ahkdul would flout his predilections so openly in their home. And in the face of his marriage proposal! To think how close Vinsant had come to falling prey to this monster. She turned and paced the length of the stairs and back. "We cannot leave the child to such an appalling fate."

"Then what would you do?" he asked. Turning from her, he instructed one of the mahktashaan to check if the boat was prepared.

She glimpsed the vessel floating at the bottom of the boatroom steps when he opened the door. She watched the black-robed figure descend, waiting until he had begun his enquiry of the boatmaster. Then she pulled her shoulders back and lifted her chin. "I shall instruct the Treasurer to purchase the child."

That forced him to take her seriously. "Don't be so naïve. If not this child, then another. I cannot imagine the pervert making the return trip without some form of entertainment. Better he destroy one child's life than two. Better that horror belong to a Verdaani child than a Terlaani one."

"He wouldn't dare," she said. She blushed to recall Vinsant's identical outburst. Deep down she had to admit that if the rumours were true he would, and Terlaan would be powerless against a parent willing to sell his child.

"Hush now, Ahkdul comes," Mariano said. "I expect you will conduct yourself with decorum. The last thing we need is open hostilities if Father is to broker an agreement."

An agreement with her life. Her nose twitched in disgust to think of how he used the poor little boy. Well, she would do what she could. She whispered an instruction of her own to another of the mahktashaan guards. As he left, Ahkdul arrived, his saffron kurta an insult to the sun. He dipped his shoulders in a gesture that could hardly pass as a bow.

"Lord Ahkdul, may I present my sister, Princess Kordahla."

"It is an honour," Ahkdul said, taking her hand and raising it to his lips. "Your beauty is celebrated, and yet that fame is no match for the vision of you before me."

No human could call the ill-proportioned man attractive, and worse still, his rehearsed words drifted to her on the stench of drink. Kordahla regretted not donning the veil. Why had she thought his perverted preference would preclude him from appreciating feminine beauty? If he sought a token wife, she would be a prize. Disagreeableness was her only recourse, so she stared him in the face and said nothing.

"Shyness is an admirable virtue in a woman, though I hope the three of us will have the chance to become better acquainted this afternoon," Ahkdul said, drawing together his bushy brows.

He understood nothing, though Mariano's arched eyebrow told her that her brother did.

She turned and entered the cavernous boat room. The waters of Lake Sheraz lapped at the shed on the western side. Inside, the young boathands labouring over repairs stole glances her way. She descended to the berth, where the friendly head boatman assisted her to board the first of two barges. Mariano was no longer smiling at her silence, and frowned at the heavy way she sank onto the burgundy cushion, before the men were even aboard.

"Please wait," she said as the boatman went to untie the rope. "I have asked Lord Ahkdul's page to join us."

"That is a presumption," Ahkdul said. "My page has duties to attend."

"You will have to forgive this shy woman, I'm sure," Kordahla said, managing to keep her voice meek. "But all I presumed was that the child has never set foot outside Verdaan. It will surely be a treat for him to experience our lake. And I do enjoy the company of children. Don't you, Lord Ahkdul? Don't you desire a brood to continue your line? I can think of no other reason you might propose."

She glanced at Mariano, but had to look away. Her brother looked like he did not know whether to laugh or berate her. They sat in awkward silence until the dark-haired boy arrived. He hesitated when he saw Ahkdul, and she bit her lip, suddenly, guiltily wondering if he might have preferred to remain in the palace, free of Ahkdul for a few hours. Thank providence Arun appeared behind him. The child did not relax, but she felt safer in the Minoria's presence.

"Come, I would like you to sit by me," she said to the child. He was dressed in simple black shalvar and green kurta, as bright as he was bleak. When Ahkdul remained silent, he came down, setting both feet on each step.

"What's your name?" she asked.

He looked straight through her without answering.

"It is Timak," Ahkdul said as though it were of no consequence.

She gestured the child into the seat opposite Mariano.

"Which part of Verdaan are you from?" she asked as the boatman ordered the crew to row the boat to the portcullis that separated the room from the walled section of the lake.

"Answer!" Ahkdul commanded.

"Teqrin, my Lady," the child whispered, keeping his eyes down.

"You will address the Princess as Highness," Ahkdul interjected.

"That is not necessary," she said right over him with a wink at Timak. "While we're in this boat, you can call me Kordahla."

"I'm afraid protocol is necessary," Mariano said as the portcullis winched up, and the boat glided into the private semicircle of lake.

She ignored him, too. "You remind me of my little brother." A more dissimilar child there could not have been, but how else could she connect with the broken soul next to her? "Vinsant takes a keen interest in far off lands. Perhaps you could spend the evening with him. He craves company his own age. The chamberlain will provide you with a servant, Lord Ahkdul, one who knows the palace and could better serve your needs." Having delivered the last words in an icy manner, she resumed a light-hearted chatter about swimming in this private, shadowed pool, pretending not to notice Ahkdul's clear contempt.

As they reached the outer gate, the boatman whistled a signal. A guard on the rampart whistled back, and a metal door ground up into the wall, allowing the boats to pass into the lake proper. Together with the Arezou River, the vast waters of the lake cradled Tarana, providing its water and commerce. Kordahla loved the lush lands around its gentle shores, the sweeping view to the eastern peaks and the distant hustle of the city on the western shore. The rhythmic swoosh of the oars rippled the calm surface. She fell into a lull, the better to soak up the freedom of gliding upon the sun-warmed waters.

Unfortunately, Ahkdul was of a dissimilar mind. After a cursory glance at the scenery, his eyes alighted on her, and he began a barrage of mundane questions designed to draw her attention to him.

"Mariano is more knowledgeable than I," she said, and turned to gaze at the snow-capped mountains.

"My sister is modest," Mariano said. "Come, Timak. The view from the bow is not to be missed."

Kordahla threw her brother a withering look as the compliant child went forward, leaving her with no choice but to answer Ahkdul.

"Your modesty does not extend to covering your hair," Ahkdul said, bolder now they were out of Mariano's hearing.

"I am not wont to follow outdated customs," she replied.

"The citizens of your city do not regard it as such. My men spied not a single woman uncovered as we traversed your river and lake."

"You exaggerate, surely."

"I do not. I hope the inconvenience of covering yourself will not deter you from outings when you visit Verdaan."

"Veils are not a nuisance, merely unnecessary to prove a woman chaste. Regardless, I am not inclined to visit your intriguing country at present."

"You speak directly for a woman, a trait you garnered from your father, I am sure. Women in Verdaan are not outspoken. They defer to their husband, and they perform their duties willingly or face his discipline."

"I am sorry I disappoint," she said with no hint of an apology, "but Terlaan is moving forward. You will find our women more forthright than your own. I hope your stay here will reveal the merits of equality among the sexes."

Ahkdul's face clouded. "I am given to understand equality does not yet exist. Indeed, Shah Wilshem seemed cautious of Myklaani ideals when we spoke. I will wager your happiness that you capitulate on this when you accompany me to Pengari."

"I am afraid I must decline your generous offer, most especially since my happiness is at stake."

"Most women would express joy at what I offer."

"I am not most women. I am a princess of Terlaan. Speak as you would in the company of my brother, or speak to me not at all."

"I will do better. I will speak my intentions in the presence of your father. In fact, I have done so. It is a pity you lack the influence of a mother. A demure nature is as tantalising as beauty in a woman. Without one the other is not complete."

"Then my beauty cannot be as celebrated as you claim."

For Kordahla, the journey to the dry docks passed in an agony of Ahkdul hinting at their betrothal. The one comfort was Arun, standing back and watching for any sign of impropriety on the part of her despicable companion, his black robe a stark contrast to the horse tails drifting across the sky. Strange how she valued the Minoria's presence more than her brother's in this. Arun's gravity matched her mood more closely than Mariano's inclination to jest at her expense. It was a match as perfect as his cerulean crystal to the heavens.

On her feet before the boatman had secured the boat, she disembarked after the first mahktashaan ashore had nodded his permission. The area was a hive of carpentry and rigging, shipwrights shouting and banging upon the magnificent, masted vessel Lord Hudassan had commissioned. The workers downed tools as they noticed the royal party. Many flocked to the gunwale to cheer. How typical of the brute that

Ahkdul basked in the attention. Taking Timak's limp hand, Kordahla signalled to one of the mahktashaan. A walk along the lake would get them both out of range of Ahkdul's tongue. It was a pity the docks had marred the wildflower beauty of this stretch of bank. The men would need to take their time inspecting the ship for her to move far enough from the bustle to appreciate the wooded surrounds. If only a lewd wolf whistle weren't cutting through the air. She stiffened as she turned, tossing her walnut locks behind her shoulder with a shake of her head and determined to lash out with her tongue. Every man in sight was staring at her, tools loose in hand. Cheeks colouring, she wished again, very much in spite of herself, she had donned a veil.

Of a sudden, she shivered. High on deck, indigo flashed behind the shipwrights. Her intended rebuke caught in her throat. Her feet refused to budge. Dream-distant, she heard Mariano order the mahktashaan to seek out the culprit. He was pointing at a red-headed man who straddled the gunwale. Staring at her like he was granted a vision, the carpenter did not notice two mahktashaan gliding up the gangplank towards him. Swords glinting at their sides, their intentions were clear. She ran to her brother, not caring she acted like a child, like an uneducated girl from the farms instead of one versed in palace etiquette.

"Stop them," she said, taking his arm and refusing to acknowledge his look of disapproval. "It wasn't him."

"Enough Kordahla. He looks at you like he dreams of defiling your body. That alone is enough for me to demand justice."

A cold anger took hold of her. She let go Mariano's arm and faced him like an equal, which, if she was truthful, as a woman she was not. "It wasn't him, I tell you," she said, not recognising her steady voice. "And he acts like one who would serve, which is more than I can say for some you would have me associate with." It took all her will to avoid throwing a look of contempt Ahkdul's way.

Mariano swept his eyes over every man on the ship. When he looked back at her, she saw nothing but resolution on his face. No dishonour could come to the Princess of Terlaan, not while her brother held blood oath for her. "Is this another of your ploys to avoid our justice? This is your land, sister, your birthright. It is your laws we mete out to preserve your honour so that you might honour us in turn."

The mahktashaan had drawn their swords, were standing back, awaiting orders. The poor soul astride the gunwale stared at her, unaware of his precarious situation.

"Will you stand like a powerless git while the princess is insulted?" Ahkdul asked. He was red in the face, as full of rage as if his honour had been sullied. "Or is Terlaan so loose with its womenfolk any may voice their crude desires?"

When Mariano clenched his jaw, she closed her eyes. It was impossible to ignore Ahkdul's disdain. Mariano could not leave the slight unpunished if he, if she, if the whole chauvinistic kingdom was to retain its esteem in the eyes of Verdaan. She had no sway in the matter, could only protest again that Terlaan should see justice, not vengeance, done.

Help came from an unexpected quarter. "Princess Kordahla is right, Your Highness," Arun said. His cerulean crystal was glowing softly at his chest. "A still wind blows. I saw your sister shudder as the culprit whistled. There is a deed unnatural afoot."

Mariano studied the gawking men. "The innocent will not be punished," he said.

Some trick of the air and the ill-timed hush of aggrieved murmurs carried his words. Misfortune had them misconstrued. Shouts sounded as men protested their innocence, heckling those they did not trust as they sought to bully others into an admission of guilt which would spare them royal justice.

"Let the guilty one admit to his offence," Mariano called loud and clear.

Mouths clamped shut. Aboard the vessel, the mahktashaan swung their swords through air thick with apprehension. The blameless carpenter must have heard the whistle of the blades. Turning, he caught fright. A hand flew to his chest as his mouth contorted in agony. A few seconds later, he thudded from the rail to the ground below, a leg bent in an unnatural way beneath him. Kordahla flew to his side, dodging the slower mahktashaan. Her knee sank into a puddle as she took his calloused hand. The mahktashaan approached, and anxiety joined pain in the poor man's eyes. She used her own to plead with Arun.

"No," the carpenter groaned at her hooded guard. He tightened his grip on her hand as sunlight glinted along the length of a sword.

"He will ease your pain," she said, fidgeting with nerves.

Oblivious to the dirt, the Minoria knelt beside her, laid gentle hands on the man's leg, and whispered archaic words. The glow from his crystal bathed the tension out of the carpenter's face. The strapping hand clutching hers relaxed.

"He will need a physic to set that leg. And porrin for the pain," Arun said.

Ahkdul looked down at her with disgust. "You will get up," he said.

She did so, aware her hem was mud-stained, her hands dirty, her face ashen.

"Is this how you conduct yourself in public?" Ahkdul asked, sneering.

"That I show compassion for the people who serve my realm? It is indeed." She prided herself on being stubborn, but this man was wearing her down. Whatever the cost, she could not let him fashion her into the ornament he sought to wear at his side. "Would you have Physic Nocrates attend him?" she asked Arun.

"The workers will remember the princess for her generosity," the Minoria replied.

"I shall take a walk while you conduct your business," she said to Ahkdul, noticing Timak, deathly still, was staring at the ship.

"I had hoped for a woman's opinion on furnishings for the cabin," Ahkdul said.

There was no easy way to decline the request of a guest, however loathsome. As she opened her mouth to frame a reply, she wondered how rude the refusal would emerge.

"With a djinn about, I ask you to stay close, Princess," Arun said, breaking off his instruction to the two nearest mahktashaan in order to settle the matter.

She walked the sagging gangplank onto the ship with misgivings, but the labourers bowed respectfully and averted their eyes. The overseer directed those who could to continue their work. Hammers echoed on nails and saws scratched at wood, but with mahktashaan surrounding her, there was little chance of harm from either man or djinn. She entered a cabin, spacious but bare, careful to remain by the door. Deflecting Ahkdul's attempts to seek her advice, she walked back on the deck. The industry around her was fascinating in its unfamiliarity. High above, a rope and pulley was lowering a crate. The breeze, while fresh on her skin, seemed too faint to cause it to swing as it did. Rubbing her arms, she watched its precarious descent.

"The air chills." Arun had followed her out, had noticed her draw her arms close.

"It is simply the open air after the closeness of the cabin," she replied, wrinkling her nose against the stench of rotting fish.

In mockery of her words, one of the ropes around the crate snapped. She stepped back from the precarious tilt of the box.

"Highness, take care," a voice called from the shore. Kordahla looked down to see a bearded worker wave a warning.

"Princess, he is right. We should leave," Arun said.

The Minoria's crystal flashed. In a crack of thunder, the indigo djinn appeared atop the crate. For a split second, he transformed into a shimmering, indigo image of her, lying on her back, legs splayed, bodice ripped from her heaving bosom. Her cry caught in her throat as her chest tightened. She couldn't breathe. Then, moulding into his disgusting, vermillion-eyed self once more, the djinn clapped his hands high over his head and laughed, a spine-chilling sound of derision which knocked the wispy clouds into a rumble. The next instant he was gone.

The crate was plummeting to the deck. Throwing an arm around her, Arun dived towards the bulwark. They hit hard, Kordahla springing back against the Minoria. The crate banged to the deck. Timbers cracked beneath it, and it continued its fall into the hold. Wrapped in the surprising softness of Arun's cloak, ensconced in his strong arms, she sobbed for breath. She felt giddy, from shock, and from his scent, cedar and spice, mingling with the sweetness of the new-sawn timbers. He helped her rise, his hand firm on her elbow even through the fabric of her kameez. He said something, she could not understand what, but when he entrusted her to the distant care of a strange mahktashaan so he might approach the jagged hole, it left her bereft.

"Sister, are you hurt?" Mariano had come running from the cabin and took her by the arms.

The concern in his eyes undid her. Tears welled even as she shook her head. Her cheeks burned, but she risked a look at Ahkdul. He was standing on the other side of the hole, enthralled. The swine did not even glance her way. Sick with shame, she crept after Mariano to stand at the edge of the hole. The crate had landed on its end. As if possessed, it rocked and banged over. When the puff of sawdust settled, her gasp was the only sound that rose above the echo. There in the wood, a message smouldered.

PRINCESS BEWARE THE SWINE.

A shaking hand over her mouth, she returned to the bulwark. On the muddy bank, Timak stood muttering to himself, unmindful of the commotion. His ignorance would be bliss. What right did the djinn have to toy with her like this? Her life was miserable enough without his interference.

"Princess, do you know what it might mean?" Arun asked.

"How would I know," she snapped, allowing Mariano to draw her close and comfort her. Truly, he looked as troubled as she felt.

"These men must be punished. This goes beyond jest," Ahkdul said.

"This is the work of djinn. You cannot have missed how bright my crystal flared."

"Its blaze brought us out, even before the crash," Mariano replied, holding her close.

She tipped her head against his shoulder and breathed a sigh of relief. If Ahkdul had witnessed her humiliation, she would have died.

The odious man looked at her through narrowed eyes. "What significance has the swine in Terlaani lore?"

"The swine is but a farm animal. It is the boar which has some import as a harbinger of strife. Under the circumstances, we might ask the same of Verdaan," Mariano said.

"It figures in no tale," Ahkdul said, so quick Arun made a slight turn of his hooded head. She pressed closer to Mariano. When they returned to the palace, she would ask Vinsant to ferret out the veracity of that claim.

"Don't go," Timak's thin voice carried up on the breeze.

"If there is a djinn about, that brat is involved." Ahkdul strode down the plank, grabbed the child by the arm and dealt him a backhand swipe. The boy yelped. Ahkdul hit again and again. Kordahla rushed to the ground, heedless of the bend of the plank beneath her beaded shoes. She had to lean back to avoid his fist as he raised his arm for another slap. A step behind her, Arun seized the child, spinning him out of harm's way. Ahkdul's fist swept through the air, right past Arun, who stood tall and still, waiting for Ahkdul to face him. The Verdaani lord had a murderous look, and she could not help but step back.

"The child is innocent," Arun said.

Timak was sitting in the dirt, rocking, his face buried in his knees. Kordahla went to him. Kneeling, she placed an arm around his shoulders. Ahkdul would have to get past her before he laid another hand on the boy, and to do that he would have Arun and Mariano to contend with.

"That *innocent* speaks to djinn," Ahkdul said. "If he was party to this havoc, he has dishonoured the Princess."

Thoughtful, Arun turned to where he held Timak.

"Then it is our laws that will deal with him," Mariano said. He positioned himself so close he must have felt Timak tremble. "Is this true boy? Did you consort with the djinn involved?"

Disgusted, Kordahla lifted the boy to his feet. Only men would expect a child this abused to speak under threat. "He was looking away. If he was not muttering to himself, he was talking to someone in the other direction."

"Permit me." Arun squatted before the child. Holding his crystal to Timak's bruised cheek, he chanted his mahktashaan magic. The boy continued to stare into the distance, a single blink the only indication he was aware.

"What say you?" Mariano asked, a grim frown on his face. She knew him well enough to know as distasteful as the act may be, he would not hesitate to put an afflicted child to the sword. Her honour-bound brother made no distinction where the law was concerned.

"I sense no evil in this child. If he consorts with djinn then we have a duty to see he does not fall prey to their schemes," Arun answered.

"Your discipline will suffice," Mariano said to Ahkdul. He walked along the side of the ship to the bow. It was a fine vessel of good proportions, every care taken to demonstrate how skilled the Terlaani were, not just in craftsmanship, but also in aesthetics. She hoped the repairs would delay its maiden voyage long enough to convince Ahkdul to leave.

"Have you thought about a name for this beauty?" Mariano asked Ahkdul, examining the hull. "*Djinn's havoc* or *Djinn's warning* perhaps?"

"Such liberties would court trouble. No, this ship will be called *Kordahla*."

"That is a high honour," Mariano said, looking at her. Until she caught the quick lift of his eyebrow, she thought him oblivious to the irony. "I shall leave you alone to thank our guest. You have had precious little time together, and he has yet to learn how effusively you accept gifts."

And with that she knew she had Mariano's permission to behave with less than the decorum expected of a princess. This commoner who pretended to a throne would learn the respect he claimed their citizens lacked.

"You do me no honour," she said before Mariano was out of earshot.

Ahkdul flashed a vicious smile. "Flatter yourself not, Princess. None is intended. I would have you remember when this ship sails with you on it what havoc your immodesty caused. You will recall this incident if ever you deign to appear in public without your veil."

"This ship will be out of my sight before long. A name is all you will have of me."

"Where is that consideration you claim you show your people? Will you not aid them by becoming my wife? There are certain concessions Verdaan will make to ease the heartache porrin brings."

"I do not wish to be a slave to your conceptions of morality, nor to your whims. I am a Terlaani princess, not a Verdaani commoner."

"Whose duty is to the Crown. And will soon be to me."

CHAPTER TWENTY-FOUR

SHAH WILSHEM REQUESTED KORDAHLA attend his private chambers not long after they had returned from the docks. That alone boded ill. More worrying was Ahkdul's smug expression as he emerged from his second audience of the day. She halted at the end of the hall, holding her breath and willing him to the turn the other way. He did not, so she picked up the full cherry red skirt of her kameez, and hastened on, giving him no opportunity to speak as she passed. After a polite knock, she entered Father's chambers without invitation, just to evade the uncouth stare the swine threw over his shoulder as he made his loathsome way. Even worse, was Father's dismissal of the two servants polishing the oak dining table in the large reception room. Together, the signs sent her into a state of defensiveness that on previous occasions had seen her tongue fly loose enough to land her in considerable trouble.

Her answers to Father's queries about the outing were brief. Neither of them mentioned their uncouth guest, and she wondered when he would get to the point. When Father bade her sit on one of the cushioned, highbacked armchairs arranged around the unlit hearth, she perched on the edge. Father took the chair opposite her, rested his elbows on the armrests and pressed the tips of his fingers together, his index fingers tapping away as he contemplated her. Neither one of them touched the pot of steaming cardamom tea on the low, round table between them. Kordahla smoothed her kameez over her knees. When she was small, the mythical creatures carved on the table skirting had made her jittery. Today, it was Father's eyes.

"I understand your choice to go bareheaded has for the second time borne unfortunate consequences," he said at last.

"My choice was not the culprit. There was a djinn."

He studied her before he spoke. The bulbous windows were unshuttered, and the doors to the two balconies behind her stood wide, so she had the sun's last light to study him back. His features held an elusive emotion she had difficulty pinning down. Reluctant disappointment, perhaps? "The Minoria tells me it is not the first time. He thinks that djinn has attached itself to you. Tell me child, have you brokered a deal with the creature?" His voice, while stern, was not unkind.

"Do you think me so foolish?" she asked.

"No, Kordahla, but I would have it from your own lips."

A breeze fluttered the drapes at the doors. Warm though it was, she shuddered. "I have not made compact with one of their kind," she said carefully. "Nor do I understand why the Minoria would think one haunts me."

"Has one appeared to you?"

Her cheeks burning, she swallowed. "I caught a glimpse, today at the shipyard." Vinsant's passion for secrets would protect her, but she could not vouch for the misery that must be visible on her face. Her aptitude for deception was a near match to Samille's.

"Relax child, I believe you, but the mahktashaan are trained in these matters. If they suppose a djinn trails you, then it is only a matter of time before he manifests. The capricious creatures turn guile into an art. Their offers are difficult to resist."

She had nothing to say to that, except breathe a sigh of relief Father could not yet be privy to the humiliating vision of her defiled body, thank Vae'oenka for that. It made pretending to concentrate on his long caution against djinnkind that much easier. The indigo creature's devious manipulations were fast convincing her how dire her future would be in Verdaan. He had to be waiting for the Shah's sickening decision before offering her a pact she could not possibly refuse.

"I think you are aware Ahkdul has asked for your hand?"

She started. Her mouth had turned dry, although if she were honest, she had known from the moment he summoned her this was where the conversation would lead. She poured a measure of tea into both their cups, took a sip, and set the cup back down. Father knew she was aware, and yet he framed a question. This gentleness was uncharacteristic.

She nodded. "The more I learn of him, the more odious I find him."

Father stood, and paced the length of the dining table and back. She was forced to look over her shoulder to follow him. Outside, pink streaked the airy clouds in the western sky. "Mariano said much the same thing, but–" he stopped and faced her, hands behind his back. She rose, in order to see him. "Royalty brings privilege, Kordahla, but also responsibility. The man is neither a charmer nor blessed with fair looks. He would expect unquestioning obedience, I think, but this is no more than a husband should expect of a wife. And he does not seem unduly cruel."

Except where little boys are concerned, she wanted to shout, clutching the back of the chair. She chose to bite her tongue.

"Lord Hudassan is prepared to make remarkable concessions to border security if this union comes about. Today alone the patrols apprehended two smugglers attempting to sell porrin to children younger than Vinsant. The guilds claim productivity is falling, and women are reduced to begging when their husbands succumb to addiction. I cannot neglect the benefit to Terlaan if we can stem the flow of the drug into our land."

Her heart quavered now, certain where this was going. "There are goods to trade with," she said.

"None that would not compromise our security."

And so she learnt she meant less to her father than a handful of magical crystals. And that beneath skies of deepening red, hearts could not just break but shatter. She swallowed back tears.

"And then there is your behaviour of late, and the threat of this djinn. I begin to think you would be safer far away from here."

This was too personal. "That's not true and you know it. The Majoria warned you I was not to leave the palace. I did not even wish to go. It is your fault the creature accosted me. You want to feel better about selling me into a life of misery. I shall not agree, I tell you. I shan't." She wavered on blurting out Ahkdul was the swine the message on the crate had warned against. But how could she? To admit a djinn had referred to the Verdaani lord as such would be to admit she had just lied. And that she was in the very danger Father sought to protect her from. The Shah did not trust the djinn, and neither did the mahktashaan. They were as likely to force her into marriage because the djinn counselled against it as to offer her a reprieve.

He opened his arms to her. The blood rushed out of her face. Her outburst had not provoked him to anger. When calm, Shah Wilshem was steadfast and resolute. She did not, could not, move. He came and took her into his embrace, holding her against his chest like a much younger child. She lost herself in the rich spicy scent he favoured, a mix of leather, wood, nutmeg and cinnamon.

"Kordahla, you are your mother's child. The love I bear you is boundless. But there are strange happenings. The Majoria can shed little light on the falling fish. Now I learn one of the djinn tags you." She tensed, and he released a small grunt of justification. "You may believe I try only to placate, but the reasons I have for granting Ahkdul's request are not solely related to matters of state."

Pulling away, she dropped her eyes and took care to speak soft. "Marry me to a Terlaani, if you believe there must be a wedding. I will even accept old Satrap Danosh, rheumy and impotent though he may be. But I will not wed Ahkdul gracefully."

"The omens suggest it is with him you must join. Do not look so glum. The marriage will not be for months yet. In the meantime, he has requested you accompany him to Verdaan. It will be a good opportunity for you to acquaint yourself with his family and their customs. It will smooth your ultimate transition to Verdaani wife."

"When will this be? The ship will not be fit to sail by eight-day's end."

"Ahkdul is keen to return home rather than tarry. Under the circumstances, I think it best." He put his fingers under her chin and lifted her eyes to his. "You will leave with your maids tomorrow, for two major moon's sojourn."

A large lump caught midway down her throat. She could barely articulate her words. "It is decided then. There is nothing I can say or do to change your mind?"

As the skies bruised to indigo, Father gave her a single nod. "Yes, Kordahla. You will marry Ahkdul."

◆ ◆ ◆

The evening passed in restlessness, in sitting, standing and pacing, in pecking at the meal Kordahla had requested served in her room, and in picking up and putting down her jewelled brush, her silver horse, her wooden dolls. The books Vinsant had smuggled failed to hold her attention, much to the exasperation of her handmaids, who pleaded for the tale of the Periwinkle Djinn as they folded kameez into trunks in preparation for a hasty departure. She could not, she would not, marry Ahkdul. No sane person would believe her brother's feeble plan to trade crystals for her freedom could work. Yet here she was, seeking the rifts in its fabric not to convince herself of its stupidity but to contrive ways to darn them. More than three hours after she had left Father, the glimmer of a foolhardy idea began to take hold. Ignoring her maids' disappointment, she sent Samille to the kitchen for a basket of fruit and Karie to Physic Nocrates with a message.

Alone at last to brood and scheme, she pulled out parchment and ink from her drawing desk and flipped past the sketches that served as a cover should any man question her right to own such implements. Then she began to pen the most difficult letter of her life. Bereft of practice, she scratched out the strokes until she had formed a plea from the heart. Taking a deep breath, she folded and sealed the parchment and tucked it into her bosom with shaking hands and a prayer to Vae'oenka that the recipient would offer assistance, not betrayal.

Her maids returned together, Samille with a page lugging an oversized basket of oranges imported from luscious Verdaan. Kordahla asked little Banesh to set the fruit on the table, then busied herself rearranging it, asking the girls to fetch her this pair of slippers and that veil (*the green one with the gold embroidery; turn the bedchamber upside down if need be, but they must find it; it was her mother's).* Under guise of rearranging the fruit, she slipped the letter to the bottom of the basket, turning with guilty sharpness as Karie emerged with the ruby red veil draped across her arms, proclaiming it better suited to her complexion. Kordahla turned back and placed an orange inside the basket. The parchment crackled as it settled. She thanked the Vae Karie thought nothing of it. Minutes later, Nocrates arrived, the heavy bag he refused to entrust to a page under one arm. Smooth as a man half his age, he took her hand and kissed it.

"I would say it is a pleasure, Princess, but I am ill inclined to enjoy the distress of others." Her eyebrows twitched in surprise as she wondered how he could possibly have heard her fate so soon. "I hope it is nothing serious. You shouldn't be standing, you know. Not if you aren't feeling well," Nocrates continued, ushering her to the daybed. A few stars were visible through the open window above it, and a nightingale sang in admiration of the jasmine in the garden.

"I'm well, I thank you," she said in a taut voice, glad his earlier comment was nothing but professional concern for a patient.

"Well you could have fooled me," he said, peering at her face.

Kordahla gave a weak smile. "It has been an arduous day."

Nocrates gave a harrumph. "So I gathered."

"It's nothing a good night's sleep won't cure," she said, grateful for the comfort of her fussing maids.

"But you're not likely to have one of those tonight, are you Princess?" He grew thoughtful, and she knew he was studying the dark circles under her eyes, the strain in her jaw. Nobody ever hid the slightest bodily dysfunction from Nocrates, least of all someone whom he had nursed through every ailment since birth.

Her door opened. "Hello." Vinsant stuck his head inside. Seeing Nocrates, he came right in. "I knew you wouldn't be feeling well. Mariano told me what Father said."

"Oh? What was that?" Nocrates asked.

She looked her request for reserve at Vinsant as Karie and Samille brought the physic a chair. Her boisterous, little brother stood straight and still. She could only imagine the royal blue kurta of the mahktashaan apprentices had instilled a sense of responsibility in him. "I have a favour to ask," she said to Nocrates when Vinsant remained quiet. She forced her wringing hands still. "I was hoping you might deliver a basket of fruit to the carpenter whose leg was broken when you next call." The evening breeze swept in, bringing a sudden unnatural chill. One of the cushions rolled off the bed and onto the rug. Kordahla shuddered.

Vinsant came over to the day bed and jumped on. "Brrr. He reached up and pulled the shutters closed, then gathered one of the curtains around himself.

Nocrates' hazel eyes watched her in that astute way of his. "You wouldn't be suffering from an attack of guilt now, would you?" he asked. A peep caught in her throat, giving her away. "From what I hear it was an accident."

Karie picked up the cushion, holding it to her midriff as she listened for any detail Kordahla might have omitted when she confided the whole, distressing incident to her dear friends.

"It was. But all the same, I'd feel better knowing he rests easy." She held her breath, hoping his fondness for her would prevail.

Nocrates gave a ponderous nod. "His leg is set – though a real problem that was, getting the bone together – and he has porrin for the night."

"Kordahla needs porrin," Vinsant said, twisting the curtain into a veil over his head and mouth. "So she can rest."

"Still, I'd rather not leave it to some inexperienced twit to assess the splint," Nocrates said right over him. "I might just take myself over there before I dine."

"You should take Karie and Samille."

"Kordahla!" The pair of them ran to her, Karie dropping the cushion.

"They can represent me in this."

"We need to help you pack," Karie said.

The girls could protest all they liked. This night belonged to

Vinsant, to family bonds, and, if her trembling heart dared, to their plan for escape.

She held their hands. "Do this for me, and then the night is yours. You should bid your families goodbye before we leave."

"Are you sure you are well? Your hands look clammy, and there are goosebumps on your arms," Nocrates observed.

She pretended the curtains weren't fluttering, a tiny movement the others might have attributed to Vinsant's fidgeting. "Quite well, save for my concern for the man."

"I shall leave a valerian potion to aid your slumber."

Kordahla rose from the daybed and gave Nocrates a peck on the cheek. These few steps from the window, the heat was oppressive.

"All right, all right," the old physic said, flustered, though there was a smile on his face. "But after this I'd have you remember I'm too old to go gallivanting all over the town for the sake of a commoner. Next time, do not be so quick to volunteer my services. I don't want to die on the job, you know."

As panicky as she was, Kordahla laughed. In Nocrates's mind there was no better way to go, she was sure.

❖ ❖ ❖

Arlem was not a stupid man.

When the court physic was done with his attentions, and had departed with a bow – to him of all people – his wife returned to his side with a plate of exotic orange segments, a parchment sealed with wax, and a look that after twenty-two years of marriage was unfathomable. A little ribbing later, Arlem was protesting fatigue to the gaggle of mates who had insisted on hanging around to hear the physic's verdict. They left him with his leg splayed over the pillows on his pallet after just one more round of laughter at his expense.

"What's this, woman?" he asked, indicating the letter. He frowned when she shook her head, gesturing to her veil with annoyance. While Sareta had lost the blushing beauty of her youth, he yet found her fair to look upon. Granted, she had covered head in deference to the visitor from the palace, but the trying day had left him ill inclined to patience. If he could not look upon the auburn hair of his wife, the day would have no saving grace at all. Grumpy with pain, he fumbled with the seal.

Letters were an oddity to Arlem, a mystery to decipher when he was in the mood for a headache. He was inclined to put the message down until morning when his woman told him where it had lain. He was not a stupid man. A poorly uneducated labourer, yes, but stupid no.

Several squints later, he thought he understood the gist of the daring request. He looked at his wife with no small apprehension and stuttered the message aloud. Her face became pinched by degrees. That was rich, since she was not the one in agony. Wincing, he sank further down on the mattress, clasped the letter to his broad chest and stared at the ceiling. A monumental decision was begging his attention. At least his pain imparted a certain clarity of thought.

"Take the porrin," the physic had said.

"Send me a mahktashaan if you grieve for my pain, for I'll not," Arlem had replied. On his deathbed, he might condescend to imbibe the cursed plant that had whittled his cousin away to a shell, but not before.

It was just as well. This secret missive demanded a sharp mind. What he had seen atop the mast, as he lay in the boat while they rowed him to the city, was a scene so ghastly he had wondered if in his pain he had hallucinated. Except there had been no pain. The mahktashaan had seen to that. Because the Princess had requested it.

Djinn, magic and gods were not in the ken of an ordinary, hard-working man like himself. He wondered why Vae'omar had seen fit to burden him so. The answer came to him with such clarity he had to wonder if Vae'oeldin himself had planted it there. Had his daughter been so disgracefully exposed, he would have done everything in his power, everything beyond it even, to spare her the outcome. He would even have risked beheading to approach the palace and demand an audience with the Majoria himself. Another man in this barren country at this crossroads in time might have denounced the girl, said she brought the humiliation on herself. Arlem had never understood how the aggression of men was the fault of a woman. At least not those as were suitably attired.

Arlem looked at his wife. Her expression had turned guarded as she awaited his decision. It would have to be her, he realised, who took the risk. With his leg as it was, he could barely stand.

"There is something you should know," he said, "before we decide."

She listened without interruption to the story of the docks. He added the rumour his mates had delivered, of an impending royal marriage to that pig of a Verdaani man. The swine would have left him suffering in the mud, and after Arlem had laboured for eight-days on his father's ship. Lord Hudassan's son, was it? That scumdweller was likely responsible for smuggling porrin into this Vae-abiding land.

When he had finished, Arlem gestured at the hearth. Without a word, his woman dropped the letter in and stoked the cooking fire. He watched until the last scrap had turned to cinders. Arlem was not a stupid man.

Chapter Twenty-five

"WAKE UP."

Timak buried his face in the lavender-scented pillow, and fought to stay asleep.

"Wake up!"

He kept his eyes closed. Wakefulness had a particular meaning in his lord's bed. The longer the stinky monster kept snoring, the longer Timak moaned with bad dreams, the safer he was.

"WAKE UP."

He jolted full awake. The hazy light by the chest of drawers stabbed at his eyes, and he winced. Beside him, Lord Ahkdul's snores choked to a stop. Timak held his breath. The luck of the djinn turned the monster away, toward the velvet curtains, and the yellow moonbeam which shot through the gap and over the bear-shaped foot of the poster bed.

"Can you get out without waking the beast?" Yazmine asked. "Don't speak. Just do what I say."

A *very* small sliver of curiosity wanted to ask her why. The greater part of him, the part Ahkdul had thrashed into meekness, told him to lie dead still.

"There's a chance for you to escape with the beautiful princess," Yazmine persisted.

It took a couple of breaths before the words sank into his sleepy brain. Then they sounded like a bad idea. He didn't want to be hacked to pieces and fed to jabberweis. So he lay there stiff and sore, wondering if he ought to close his eyes and go back to sleep. That would be better than listening to hope. He didn't want hope. Hope ended up slashed into pain. Besides, the monster was slumbering through drunken dreams. If Timak lay dead still, he might escape torture tonight.

The hazy light drifted closer. "If you don't get up, I shall leave and never talk to you again."

He blinked a tear out of his eye, and let it dribble down his cheek.

Yazmine's voice grew quiet. "You have to help her. She doesn't want to wed him and she can't escape without you."

A wife would spare him Ahkdul's naked attentions night after night. He didn't need to run and risk losing all his fingers and toes.

"Your father will never find you if you stay with the beast. He wanted you to escape."

He turned his head, but that put his nose near the monster's sweaty shoulder. The stink of it made his hot tears worse. He wasn't ever going to polish his father's sword or help bait a hook for sandfish again. Yazmine should have left his scabs alone. Now they were picked, he couldn't keep the sob bottled up. The noise made Ahkdul roll. His large hand flopped onto Timak's ribs. Timak held his breath, waiting for the wobble of the slack lips as Ahkdul breathed out. Then he slid himself from under the naked body and damp sheets, and crawled out of bed.

"Move your pillow beside him," Yazmine said.

The feather stuffing was not as lumpy as a body, but it filled the dented space where he had lain.

"The chest," Yazmine said as he threw on his shalvar and kurta and tiptoed away. "You need to bring them porrin."

He was too sleepy to question her. Too scared to speak, too. He grappled with a chair, lifting its bulk against his hips so it wouldn't drag and wake Ahkdul. The tap of the legs on the floor sounded loud in the night. He stared at his tormentor. Even his breath sounded harsh.

"Hurry!" Yazmine said.

Standing on the chair, he managed to scrape the top drawer open. He paused, but if the piggish snores didn't cover his rummaging, nothing would. Rising onto tiptoes, he reached up and felt inside. His fingertips just managed to sift through the silks to the bottom of the drawer. He felt crisp parchment buried among them, worked it to the edge and up the side. Yazmine needed to stop pleading for him to hurry. It made him nervous, and he needed to slide the drawer shut, climb down, and pick up the chair nice and slow. He needed to put it back by the table so when monster woke, he wouldn't think Timak had taken his porrin; he wouldn't think Timak was trying to escape. At least not right away.

The monster groaned. Like he was waking up drunk. Timak froze. The chair sagged heavy in his arms. He dropped one side, and almost toppled after it. The clunk stopped the snores. Timak's eyes went wide as Ahkdul woke and patted the pillow.

"Run!" Yazmine yelled.

He dashed for the door, the chair falling behind him. It flung open, and he was out in a flash, darting past a startled mahktashaan and one of Ahkdul's own men, following Yazmine down a corridor lined with the marble heads of kings and queens. Behind him, he heard Kahlmed curse and give chase, his heavy boots thundering on the stones. A fragment of conversation between Ahkdul and the guard boomed over it.

"My lord, you must dress before you may roam the halls." The mahktashaan was firm. And so he gained a minute on Ahkdul. Swinging around a corner, he followed Yazmine's light.

"Keep going," she said, before zipping over his head.

A mighty crash followed, then a yelp. He chanced a look back. Kahlmed was hopping through the fragments of a broken statue. Then Yazmine was back in front of him, leading him down some stairs and along more corridors, dark and deserted, the arms of the unlit candelabras threatening to snag him, until he turned one final time into a torch-lit hall where two black-robed mahktashaan stood guard outside a door. His abrupt skid drew their attention.

"Don't hesitate," Yazmine said, gliding past the guards. "Just get inside."

He sprinted for the gap between the guards. At the other end of the hall, Yazmine's light curled into rose-scented smoke. The guards shivered as the temperature dropped. They lifted their crystals, forest green and peach. Coloured light burst forth, but it couldn't have held powerful magic, because it didn't scare Yazmine away. She was solid now, a shimmering rose-pink genie, flying teasing loops down the hall. One mahktashaan ran in pursuit. The other turned to bar his way. Timak slowed to a walk. The soldier-magician had to be glaring something fierce beneath that shadowing hood. He pretended not to care, and stared after his friend, pretending the chase was the sole reason he was out of bed at night.

"Genie," he whispered.

A giggle drifted down the corridor. Yazmine's giggle. Raising a cautionary finger, the mahktashaan hurried after his partner. It was the worst luck of the night that, as Timak gripped the handle to the princess's door he looked back. Timak shoved the door open just enough to squeeze inside. The beautiful princess was deep in conversation with her younger brother. They looked up at the interruption, their faces guilty, then surprised.

"Take me with you," Timak said, the first words he had spoken to a human in days.

They stared at him. Then the prince yanked him into the room and slammed the door.

Nobody spoke for several heartbeats.

Yazmine appeared, an indistinct floating light nobody else could see. Having her there gave him the courage he needed. He held out the packet of porrin, held his breath and dared to hope.

Someone banged on the door, and they all jumped.

"He's given us away," the princess said.

The banging became louder. Vinsant pushed Timak into Kordahla's sleeping chamber and growled at him to hide. There was nothing for it. With a deep breath and regal toss of her head, Kordahla opened the door. Outside, Lord Ahkdul, tousle-haired and hastily dressed in a flimsy, white open-necked kurta and black shalvar, glared at her.

"They told me this was your room," he said. The backlight from the torches in the hall did nothing to romanticise his large nose.

"Father might be considering your proposal but this is improper. You will kindly leave."

"You flatter yourself, princess. My page has run amok, damaging palace property and waking an entire wing in a foolish chase after what he claims is a djinn. It is him I have a desire to find."

A malicious, perverted desire. She crossed her arms, and stepped into the harsh light of the moons. Their blessing washed through the arches of the windows and doors Vinsant had thrown open to the night. "Nevertheless, to appear before your betrothed in such scant attire with Daesoa and Dindarin risen is unseemly."

Ahkdul thrust his hand flat onto the door, swinging it wide. "I demand my property."

Somewhere in the gardens, an owl hooted. He stepped forward; she stepped back; her hands fell limp at her side. "I have nothing of yours."

"You will give me the boy."

"What makes you think he is here?

"The guard saw him enter."

The man seemed strung on the verge of aggression, and for once, she was grateful for the mahktashaan outside. Weak in the knees, she stepped aside. "As you can see, he is not. My brother, however, is. It was he the guard saw enter."

Vinsant was sitting on her daybed, watching the exchange like it were a fascinating piece of mummery. If Timak did not possess the wits to bury himself out of sight, her little brother had better come up with an ingenious excuse for his presence.

Ahkdul sneered. "Then you will not mind if I have my man search these rooms. The boy is expert at hiding and I would not have him compromise your considerable modesty by revealing himself at an inopportune time." He walked past her, onto the rug. She flinched as a brawny man followed and leered. He was a common mercenary, his face creased by jagged scars. Would the balcony arch not curve so elegant and the stars not shine so pretty as they framed the beasts.

"I do mind. I mind very much," she said as Vinsant stood, wary now. Were the breeze billowing the curtains not hot and stale, she might never have addressed the mahktashaan standing hesitant in her doorway after their noisy chase. "Please escort Lord Ahkdul and his man back to their rooms."

Her hooded guards flanked her unwanted guests. Her stomach lurched at the curl of Ahkdul's lip, the fisting of his hands. Her indrawn breath convinced one mahktashaan to lift a handspan of his sword from its scabbard. Providence saw Dindarin's thin green beam polish its edge to a sheen. Thank Vae'oeldin the precariousness of his situation dawned when Ahkdul rested narrowing eyes on the weapon. He dipped his shoulders, a mockery of a bow if ever there was one. He was a fool to take no heed of the way the darkening pile of the rug muted his brute strength, and a swine to stop before her and drop his mouth to her ear.

"Your visit to Verdaan will be a pleasure to savour. There, a woman never outranks a man."

This hideous man, the neckline of his kurta wet with sweat, the hairs on his chest dusty with the day's distress, would *not* mar her dignity. She thrust up her chin and spoke so all could hear. "I would have you remember my older brother holds blood honour for me. The Shah will enforce it, no matter who brings disgrace." Then she dropped her voice to pay him back in kind. "And these are his guards, not mine. He will hear of this come the morrow, if not this very night." A most unfortunate truth. She needed to think on it, to consider how to return the child so he suffered no harm from the swine. Ahkdul would most like prowl the corridors in wait. As if evading the guards was not hard enough! And when the entire palace was abroad, roused from slumber on this of all nights, by the very man she wished to elude!

"Princess, I must check the rooms for djinn," the mahktashaan with the green crystal said.

She forced a smile. "It is not necessary. There has been no still wind."

"Nonetheless, your safety is my concern." He lifted the crystal from his chest and swept the room. If the hand she placed on her bosom betrayed her nerves, he gave no sign.

"Your Highness," he said when he had poked into every nook, "could you request your maids to don suitable attire."

"Karie and Samille are farewelling their families tonight."

The mahktashaan entered her bedchamber. Vinsant followed, mimicking his actions with his own piece of quartz. Kordahla closed her eyes and felt herself sway. Could it be the mahktashaan would not discover a taint of the indigo djinn, the stolen crystal, or the runaway child?

"Highness, do you ail?"

She snapped her eyes open and took a fumbling step back lest he attempt to lay a hand on her. "No!" Her heel caught on a corner of the rug. Taking a deep breath, she forced herself to a calmer voice. "It has been a trying day. I wish only to salvage what I may by sharing news with my brother."

"Highness, your rooms are free of djinn. I bid you and all other occupants a safe night."

Vae'oenka help her, but her face must have revealed her guilt. To her intense relief, he bowed and exited. With the door safely shut, she wandered into the bedroom. "Timak. Timak? He's gone. You can come out now."

The poor child remained hidden. Chuckling, Vinsant checked under her canopied bed, then plunged between the elaborate gowns in her wardrobe before starting a more frantic search in hidey-holes which could only have hidden a mouse.

"Maybe the djinn…"

"Nonsense," she said, throwing the pillows from her bed. Djinn did not steal children.

"But the tales…"

"The tales speak of foolish wish-seekers making barter with their infants. They do not tell of the creatures kidnapping an innocent." She patted the empty bed.

"He might have made a deal," Vinsant said, returning to the wardrobe and climbing inside.

"Perhaps," she whispered, though she hoped it was not so. Vae help her but her impending marriage might tempt her into a ruinous pact.

She picked up a candle from the sill. With care, she could light the recesses behind her most voluminous skirts. As she turned, she spied five little bumps along the edge of the shutter. She leaned out, and found the terrified child on the ledge, pressing back against the wall, his fingers gripping the frame, his toes wriggling over air. She grabbed his arm, and pulled him onto the sill. He tumbled off, landing in a heap at her feet.

"What now?" Vinsant asked.

She wanted to weep. Ahkdul's beating had left Timak's face an angry, red mess. She shook her head. "The entire palace is awake."

Her little brother's jaw dropped. "You can't just give up. Mariano said Ahkdul behaved like a pig this afternoon.

"It's over Vinsant."

"So you're just going to send this page back to him?"

She sighed. Vae'oenka help her, but there was no way she could. "We need help."

Her relief was another of the day's mysteries, but relief it was when Arun arrived, hooded and cloaked and with the cerulean crystal of his office around his neck.

"How may I assist you, Princess?" he asked. She might have imagined the warmth.

"I hoped…" The nightingale was trilling again. She took a deep breath. Wondered at how Vinsant and silent Timak had convinced her to salvage their plan. The nerves were setting her heart racing – by Vae'oenka she was scarcely able to credit what she was about to do – but they were less for Arun's presence. He had asked for her trust, and trust him she did, though why was beyond fathoming. Perhaps that was the strangest of all the day's occurrences. It saddened her that she must sorely test that trust but, of all the mahktashaan, Arun might understand. Just might, if their plan failed, show leniency.

"Please do not be afraid to ask," he said, misinterpreting her hesitation.

She saw Vinsant smirk, and pushed the why of that to the back of her mind. "I hoped you might heal Timak," she said, beckoning the boy from inside her sleeping chamber. He stopped in the doorway, his eyes devoid of that fleeting spark of hope.

Arun removed his hood, a kindness really. "*Allumnos.*" The whispered word created a ball of light above their heads. The carpet beneath his boots sweetened to the colour of a red rose. "It was done at the docks, Princess. I would not leave a child to suffer under Ahkdul's hand if I can offer ease."

"His face…" she protested to the man who, through his disrobing, had made it clear she might speak to him as a friend.

"Ahkdul will be inclined to punish the child if there is no trace of his earlier beating. The bruises will colour and fade." He turned to the child. Timak's eyes widened to see Arun's startling cerulean ones. Mahktashaan eyes never failed to disconcert. Perhaps that was why they chose to wear the hood. "Do you hurt, Timak?" Arun asked.

The boy managed a barely perceptible shake of his head.

"That is true of your face, at least," Arun said.

A gust banged the shutter above the daybed, and toppled the pillows propped against the wall. Kordahla jumped, a hand flying to her throat. The nightingale broke off his serenade. Not even Vinsant's whistle could entice it to resume. Looking down, she took a deep breath. She had chosen her outfit with care, a calf-length, full skirted kameez, shalvar and veil that would make travel easy. She had given no thought to the colour that was almost a match for Arun's eyes. Karie would have called it fate. Vinsant branded it perfect planning. Kordahla could only resent it. Black, a colour unsuitable for an unwed princess, would have better assisted her to hide on a moonlit night.

The moment of decision had arrived. One request and she would be committed to her folly. For five heartbeats, she struggled with the words. In the end, Arun beat her to speech.

"You seem troubled, Princess." He was close enough she could feel his warmth, inhale the cedar scent he wore.

The shame of the afternoon was still fresh in her mind. She had trouble lifting her eyes to his. "May we take a walk outside?" she said, and by doing so chose her path.

They walked the dim, arched halls of the palace without speaking. The soft night-time sounds fell muted on the stone: the mahktashaan guard changing; servants walking to and fro; a courtier on one knee begging admission to a lady's chamber, a minor disagreement between maids. The bickering echoed, and made her palms clammy. In a household this large, was there ever a quiet moment to steal for illicit acts?

On the ground floor, Vinsant pulled Timak away with an excuse about visiting the kitchen. He was young enough that the cook tolerated his midnight raids, indulged them even, but it was not where he headed tonight. She let her gaze linger on his back.

"He is growing up," Arun said.

"He is," she admitted, allowing the Minoria to escort her down the main steps.

The blooming garden was refreshing, the heat of day having dissipated into the starry sky. As Arun turned towards the path that led to the greater part of the enclosed lake she hesitated. "Let us go this way first. I yearn for a long stroll," she said, indicating the southern walk. Her heart was hammering, and she had no appetite for words as they wandered the line of pink oleander framing the palace and the neat squares of herbs across the main path until, as they approached the lake, Arun led her into conversation.

"Princess, I am forever honoured to serve, but many mahktashaan and certainly your guards are skilled in basic healing."

"I..." She faltered. The truth required trust of a depth she did not have for any mahktashaan. And this one, who had a measure of hers, was about to find his betrayed. "I have need of a friend," she said. It was not an untruth.

"And something more, I think." His gentleness held an invitation to confide.

The breeze gusted, and the rippling water warned of a current beneath the calm. "Can you always sense djinn?"

A wisp of cloud drifted across Daesoa, dimming the night.

"It is part of who the mahktashaan are."

"And so you knew Timak's djinn and the indigo were different?"

"I didn't." The answer was unexpected, and she turned to him. "I meant it when I said I am not prepared to condemn a child on mere speculation. From what your guards tell, I was right. The genie Ahkdul claims troubles Timak is a mischievous entity, though I doubt she is an evil menace."

"And what of the indigo djinn? Could he cause serious harm?" She felt queasy, thinking of it. How foolish she was, to think she could run.

"I rather think he already has."

She couldn't control the sob. Her hands flew over her face as her humiliation surged. That horrendous image at the docks would forever drip poison into her mind.

"Hush," Arun said. Without thought, she leaned into him. He raised his arms around her, but he hesitated and lowered them before he could complete an inappropriate touch. "The shame is mine, for I did not protect you from his evil."

This proximity alone would see him flogged, and her locked up in full veil, but she could not deny how sweet it reassured when it the nightingale bestowed his whistle.

"There were so many men."

He stepped back, separating himself from her. She swallowed, and attempted to gain what poise she might, standing tall even as she felt insecure, beneath the green moon, Dindarin, a warrior in his own right.

"Neither Mariano nor Ahkdul saw," Arun said. "As for the dock workers, I think fewer than you believe witnessed the djinn's foolery, and of those who did, there is more honour among them than Ahkdul would have you think, and more fear of Mariano's sword than you are aware. None will utter a word of what they saw."

He was telling her what she needed to hear. She accepted it because, to face the sun in the company of men, to hold her head high, she must. "Do you truly believe so?"

"I do."

Daesoa chose that moment to lift her veil. She could take that as a sign. Closing her eyes, she said, "I want to ask you to keep it a secret, though I know you cannot. But Vinsant. There is no need for him to know. You will keep him safe?" That last sounded so odd, so removed from what they discussed, but it was near the time to attempt her escape, and her little brother was her one regret.

Arun offered his arm, a permissible contact for the Minoria to make. She took it and they walked down a path lined with crown imperials, their red lantern flowers topped by a mop of strappy leaves.

"No one need know, Princess. Not Levi, nor your father."

She stopped, not understanding. "You are sworn…"

He indicated they should walk on. "I have told the Majoria and the Shah of all else. To divulge of what we speak will shed no light on why the djinn haunt our halls. Princess Kordahla, I do not wish to complicate life for you. Both the Shah and the Majoria are inflexible where matters of honour are concerned. Save for keeping you from distress, I have discharged my duty as Minoria. I repeat. They need not know."

The gratitude she felt at that moment was unbounded. Almost, she confessed to the djinn's previous visit, but to do so would be to reveal all the lies, and dash her chance to escape her cruel fate.

"Hey, you snails." Vinsant came tearing towards them.

"The mahktashaan look after their own. My oath to mentor Vinsant is unbreakable, but you have always kept him safe."

Vinsant passed them at a run, heading for the southern steps to the rampart. Timak followed him at a more sedate pace, a hem tumbling from a tangle of gown in his arms and sweeping the ground in his wake. Kordahla's heart caught in her throat. After tonight, she might never see her brothers again.

She had not meant to stop, nor to speak her fear. "A major moon in Verdaan followed by a hasty wedding. I shall not have the chance to see him grow."

Arun, who never faltered, did so then. Vinsant's laughter drifted down from the steps, filling the void in their conversation until the Minoria could say, a strange catch to his voice, "It is arranged then?"

"You did not know." It was neither a question, nor a statement, but something in between.

He hesitated. Daesoa again donned her veil. "No doubt Shah Wilshem will make public announcement tomorrow."

She took the moment then, in the hope he might later remember the explanation for what she was about to do, forgive her the lies and, above all, absolve her for involving him, the one person who had tried to alleviate her burden. "I will not marry Ahkdul willingly."

"No," he murmured, and looked at the boys on the steps. Timak stood motionless with his bundle while Vinsant bounded up and down in a mock sword fight, pretending to jab him in the chest with an imaginary sword. Raising a hand in victory, he ran up onto the wall. His antics drew the attention of the patrol, good-natured men who were happy to oblige his request for a bout. Step by step, the traumatised boy followed, making no attempt to engage in play.

She turned and led Arun away. The Minoria was likely to have keen eyes for mischief.

"If the Shah knew of the djinn's cruelty, he might delay–"

She stopped him with a gesture, beneath an almond tree laden with nuts. "Since Father is convinced of both Ahkdul's suitability as an ally and the duplicity of the djinn, he is as likely to marry me off tonight."

"None can know the mind of the djinn. The mind of the Shah is another matter. Will he send Mariano as an escort?" She nodded. "Then you have no cause to fear. Until you are properly wed, the Crown Prince will permit no man to touch you, betrothed or otherwise."

But even then it will be dishonour, she thought, *every time that hideous man touches me.* An infrequent torture it might be, if he procured enough boys, but a single night in Ahkdul's bed was a horror capable of smothering her last vestige of self-respect. *If only Ahkdul were like Arun. I would happily relinquish family and home.* She stopped, and bit her lip, for it could never be. Mahktashaan claimed rank by training not birth. Such an alliance could offer no advantage to the realm, and so even the ranked among those magicians were an unsuitable match for the only daughter of a shah. Besides, beyond the formality of his office, she did not know the man. She frowned at herself, and her hand stiffened on his arm. Such daydreaming would accomplish nothing.

"Are you well, Princess?"

"May we walk?"

They continued in silence, a stroll past the palace to the pretty park that abutted the pool. Under crescent moons, the carving of Shah Gustav and the meddlesome grapper was too dark to study, but the perfume of the frangipani and chrysanthemums blossoming beneath made visiting this section of the gardens in moonlight a treat. Above, on the rampart, Vinsant continued to engage in mock swordplay, his silhouette a magical piece of imagery against crescent Dindarin. She shook her head at his energy, for he must have raced along the parapet to beat them here. It surprised her that Timak was already descending to the garden. The timid boy did not look like he had the wits to run. He stopped an arm-length away and held out the unadorned black cloak he carried. From the fineness of cloth, she guessed it was Mariano's. If Vinsant had not been born a prince, he could have made a decent living as a thief. She draped the cloak over herself even as her sneaky little brother's call carried through the night.

"See what I learned today."

Her little brother had wedged himself into a crenel. Balancing on one foot, he continued to wave the imaginary sword. His antics reduced her to laughter. Spurred on, he shimmied up the sides to the top of a merlon, where he attempted to repeat his one-footed stunt, an impossible feat given the slope of its pyramidal cap. Their plan suddenly seemed foolhardy not just for her, but for Vinsant too.

"It's not safe," she said, taking a few steps towards him, and meaning it. Then, unable to stop herself, she called out, "Vinsant, no!"

Too late. Arms waving back, Vinsant overbalanced and tumbled backward to the lake below.

"Vinsant!" she screamed, as a huge splash brought the full complement of the patrol on this side of the wall running.

Arun was already taking the steps two at a time. The lake was deep. Mariano and other young courtiers had jumped into its waters in displays of bravado on days of scorching heat. Vinsant had too, but not into the lake proper, where he could land atop a rock, or fall prey to any thug who might seek to hold him to ransom. It did not deter Arun. He was removing his outer robe in preparation to dive.

Beside her, Timak gave a small tug on her cloak. She looked down and saw the ghost of a plea in his eyes. They ran for the side gate. The distance stretched unbearably and, unaccustomed to the exertion, she began to puff. In the commotion, the guards did not question her exit through the wicket. They surrounded her as they ran to Vinsant's aid, for the Minoria himself was outside, his plunge marked by a smaller splash and the shouts of guards. If the diversion worked it would be a miracle, for the whole palace must be awake by now. She hesitated, every maternal instinct in her body beseeching her to check if Vinsant was hurt.

"You won't get another chance, you foolish flea," a familiar voice drawled in her ear. The whiff of fish was gagging strong, and she held her wrist to her mouth.

"Djinn!" the call went up.

All around her, crystals were ablaze, a rainbow of colours flaring into the darkness. Kordahla pressed herself against the wall. She expected the wicked indigo djinn to materialise, though whether to help or hinder her escape was moot. Instead, a giggling, pink, rose-scented child plucked Kordahla's veil from her head as she swooped in the direction of the lake, her skin shimmering in Daesoa's light, the crystals at her joints aglow.

"I can splash too," she called.

"See to Prince Vinsant. The genie is headed his way," Kordahla said when a mahktashaan approached. She pulled Timak under the arch of the gate. "I shall return to my rooms until I hear from the Prince. My mahktashaan guards are still there," she added as he protested the need to protect her.

Another splash inserted itself into the chaos, followed by more giggling, and another flare of crystal light. The mahktashaan ran for the lake, telling her to get inside the walls. By what miracle he left her alone, she would never know. Setting foot outside the walls without an escort was unheard of for her. She took a tiny step towards the lake and felt Timak take her hand.

"The genie won't hurt the prince," he said, so low she almost lost the words.

If the boy had not been there, she might have turned inside the gate. The pleading in his eyes undid her, and the swollen, black eye that, though Arun assured did not hurt, was a reminder of what lay in store for them both in Ahkdul's house. She squeezed his hand and they ran the other way, turning along the front of the palace. She slowed to a frustrating walk, drawing up the hood, and pulling the black cloak tight around herself as they approached the main gate, a cluster of guards patrolling the ramparts above it. She had never expected them to abandon the post, and so she guided Timak down the footpath of Royal Way, hoping it would appear as though they sought no business within the palace walls. The shadows and the palms were scant shelter for a plan so bold, but when clouds covered the moons, night swallowed them. They ran again, across the street and around the side of the palace, down steps to the rocky bank, where only three feet of ground separated the wall from the fast-flowing tributary of the Arezou River as it swirled into Lake Sheraz.

Timak had aimed well. The black mahktashaan robe lay in a crumpled heap at the foot of the wall, a small bag of food and the crystal tucked well within its folds. Vinsant's quartz pendant was there too. He had not told her he would relinquish it, and she felt a surge of love so painful it crippled her. There was no question Levi would discipline him for losing it. She looked up, at the high wall she dared to leave forever. Only Timak's gentle touch reminded her of the need for haste. She removed Mariano's cloak and wrapped him in it, then donned the robe, hiding the crystal in its folds. A presumption it was, but she picked the quartz up and passed the leather strap over her head. Vae'oenka help her! The stone flared as brushed her chest. She tugged it off, and dangled it deep inside her gown, letting it drop into a pocket. With a surreptitious glance around, she searched for any sign mahktashaan or guards had spied the light.

CHAPTER TWENTY-SIX

HITTING THE WATER BACK first hurt a *lot* more than Vinsant anticipated. Worse, it was shocking cold. He hadn't meant to blow out, but the smack of the water just crushed his chest flat. So now he was struggling for the surface, and weak and gaspy when he broke into air. He tilted his head back so he could suck in long breaths. He had landed close to the wall, in a beam of Dindarin's green light. As luck would have it, a guard spotted him and called out. One more breath would have to do. Full of air, Vinsant dove and kicked hard for the dark horizon of the opposite shore. Not that he had any hope of making the crossing, but then he wasn't trying to reach the far bank; just move distant enough from this one to delay his needless rescue. How hilarious was that! The guards, mahktashaan and otherwise, would all be panicking over his safety, and here he was, doing his best to thwart their efforts. 'Course, he lost his breath in a chuckle, which meant he had to surface. He didn't plan on dallying long enough to be spotted a second time, but he hadn't planned on getting caught within a blue sphere of light, either. Cerulean blue to be exact. Scums. The game was over. If he kept swimming, it would draw suspicion, so he thrashed about feigning confusion and a spluttery cough until Arun called his name and he had to pretend to spy the Minoria for the first time. Arun released his crystal, casting them back into the semi-blackness of a starry, moonlit night, and struck towards him. Vinsant looked up at waning Dindarin chasing waxing

Daesoa across the sky, and made the smallest kick back. He sure hoped it was not Kordahla's fate to be pursued and caught.

"Are you all right?" Arun asked. His eyes were so bright they reflected on the surface, two full moons.

Threading water to buy more time, Vinsant nodded. "That was kind of fun, actually."

"Your fun has your sister worried sick. How did you come to be this far out from the palace walls?"

"Uh…" said Vinsant, thinking hard. Up on the rampart, the guards were holding lanterns over the water. "I got confused. I thought I saw a light in this direction."

"Have a care, there are djinn about," Arun said. It was too cool the Minoria bought his story. No way was he going to get in trouble for any of this. "Can you swim?"

"Of course I can swim." He kicked off and got a whole five strokes on Arun. At this pace, he was going to beat the Minoria to shore. Except that was exactly what he didn't want. He treaded water to buy Kordahla more time. "Just a bit puffed. I need to go slow," he said, when Arun caught up. The Minoria's golden-brown hair was darker wet, but that wasn't an advantage with those mahktashaan eyes.

They waded out onto a shore swarming with mahktashaan. Forget lanterns, these guys had awesome balls of light floating over their heads, each one as bright as a full moon. He walked under them, and didn't notice the sopping blue veil lying crumpled in the mud before his scuffed step wrapped one corner around his toes. He shook his foot free of it, and Arun picked it up. He didn't seem to care his feet were all muddy. Vinsant shook his head. A mahktashaan should not be without boots.

"I'm perfectly fine," he insisted when a guard draped an oversized cloak over his shoulders. All the fuss was stinging his boyish pride. He would never live it down if Naikil got wind of it. "It's not as though this is the longest I've ever spent in the water." Then he coughed to good effect. Except that set off a whole string of coughs which the mahktashaan nearest him assumed meant he needed a slap on the back.

"Eh, yep, I think I'm okay now." He straightened up, ready to start a conversation about his bravery, or his stupidity, whichever was going to keep all these guards right here, out of the palace.

"Where is your quartz, Vinsant?" Arun asked.

Vinsant's hand moved to his chest. "I don't know," he said, the plain truth. The stone was with Kordahla, and he had no idea where she was. Well not exactly, anyway. So he didn't feel guilty, which meant he wouldn't look guilty. Too bad the Minoria looked like he was standing over someone's grave. Vinsant had a real bad feeling it was his. He squelched back to the water's edge as Arun lifted his crystal over the lake and spoke one of those hard to catch magic words. Nothing happened.

"I'm sorry," he said, returning to the Minoria.

"It is not me to whom you need to apologise. Mahktos entrusted that quartz to you."

Vinsant went a little unsteady on his feet. He had thrown the stone over the palace wall with the mahktashaan robe Timak had carried. Too late now to think that had been a tad impulsive. Getting a replacement was bound to be complicated. He coughed.

"You need to see Physic Nocrates."

"I'm fine, really." He swished through the grass, head hanging as his hands fretted in and out of fists while he pretended to search for his stone. When he turned, he bumped right into Arun.

"Um, sorry." He started to go around, but Arun placed a firm hand on his shoulder.

"Your quartz is not in the lake."

Vinsant looked out over the water. A distant twinkle marked the shipyard. He shivered.

"Physic Nocrates," Arun insisted.

"I really don't need–"

"You really do," Arun insisted.

It was only when they were approaching the physic's door that Vinsant recalled the statue of Mahktos in the corner. Given his history with the god, there was every chance of a curious incident. Kordahla needed the time a suspicious glow in the statue's eyes would curtail. At least it would be curtailed if Arun were present. Which was a far more noble reason for a mahktashaan apprentice to enter alone than his desire to delay repercussions from his little stunt. He stopped by the door. A small puddle pooled at his feet.

"I do not need a nursemaid while I'm examined," he said, every bit the prince. "You will wait here for me."

Arun, as dripping wet in the plain black shalvar kurta of the mahktashaan, made a solemn dip of his head. Vinsant couldn't recall the last time he had seen the man without his outer robe. The mahktashaan seemed to live in the garment. "I will indeed. Do not forget I hold responsibility for you. Else, why would I be here when there are djinn to hunt?"

There had to be more to those words than, well, their plain meaning. Only, Vinsant could not figure what. Grumbling about everyone treating him like an infant, he turned to the door. Arun knocked and opened it for him, like he wasn't capable of doing it himself. He had no choice but to step through.

Nocrates was shuffling from an inner room, a candle in one hand, the cord of a night robe in the other, his white hair looking thinner in its disarray. "What's this? There's enough noise to wake the dead tonight."

Vinsant's back burned, but no way was he going to turn and confront the statue. "I went for a swim and swallowed a bit of water. Now the mahktashaan are fretting that I might drown in my sleep."

"Yes, well that's obvious, isn't it, Your Highness," Nocrates said with a pointed look at the damp floor beneath Vinsant's feet. "Are you short of breath?"

Vinsant shook his head, looking around the room. The servants had brought pots of fresh herbs onto one of the tables, and thin bundles of dried valerian covered another. The smell was sweet for a chamber so cluttered.

"And you no doubt wish me to prescribe a dose of porrin," Nocrates said, putting the candle down next to a coil of fine binding and prying Vinsant's eyelids wide.

"I only want you to tell the Minoria that I'm fine. He's waiting outside."

Nocrates placed an ear to Vinsant's chest, then struck him on the back. "Breath in. The Minoria, you say? And does he have a reason for bringing you to me?" he asked in his high, creaky voice.

"I told you." Vinsant said, and was about to repeat himself when he realised just what Nocrates meant. Holding his breath, he turned to the idol. In the shadow behind the door, Mahktos sat atop the pillar, a gold statue with crimson eyes too far to catch the glint of light from the wavering candle. "Did you mention my last visit?" asked Vinsant.

"Young man, did I not advise you physics keep their patients' ills confidential? Tell the Minoria you are fit as a cheeky djinn, and he should let an old man get some sleep."

Vinsant rubbed a foot against the back of a calf, wrinkling his wet shalvar. If Arun wanted him here, it was for a reason. No doubt, the best place to discover it was the place he wanted to avoid. He crabstepped to the statue and risked a sideways glance. He could have sworn the brow ridges had formed a frown.

"Does Mahktos often frown?"

"It's a statue, boy. What are you talking about?" said Physic Nocrates, yawning.

"Does it look any different to you?"

"In this gloom?" The physic blinked as he peered. "My eyes are not what they were, you know."

A long sidle and an expert snatch of the candle ensured Vinsant turned his back on the statue for a mere second. He should have known that would be enough for any god, because when he held the light to the statue the frown had disappeared. Scratching his head, he said, "Eh... One more thing. What do people offer when they want to appease Mahktos?"

"I take it you haven't had that conversation with Branak?"

"He's rather busy at the moment."

"With you and your fellow apprentices' questions, no doubt, given his job is to teach you these things. One day, Highness, you will be old enough to realise both what grief you cause your elders and how obvious the young are when they seek to be cunning. I suppose you are not going to tell me what this is all about?"

Vinsant turned to face him but kept his mouth firmly closed.

Nocrates said, "I see. Well then, to answer your question, Highness, Mahktos is a wild god, a pure element who is said to have walked the Spirit Winds of this land before the Vae were even born, if gods can be birthed into existence. He thrives on passions, emotions, instincts and none of the finely crafted trinkets the rich place before the Vae when they seek their intercession. When you understand Mahktos ruled supreme before humans became civilised enough to fashion these items, it's not hard to see."

"Okay." Vinsant slid the candle onto a table crammed with half-scooped pots of beeswax, mud and some sort of green goo.

Nocrates lowered himself into his padded chair. "His followers offer something of themselves for his favour. I for example, as a healer, burn leaves of the eidlewort."

"But isn't that hard to come by?" If only he had paid better attention to the Physic's lessons, he might have remembered what the herb that grew near the Crystal Falls was supposed to cure.

"That, young man, is precisely the point of an offering. Now if you wish to learn more, keep an old man company tomorrow, and put your hands to good use with this fiddly binding. But not too early. A man my age needs his rest."

"Good night, Physic." A dismissal didn't count when exhaustion was making his eyelids droop. If he pretended to sleep walk out of here, Arun might even spare him the lecture until morning.

Arun watched Kordahla's soaked veil drip water onto the floor. The princess had been right. His station had obliged him to inform Levi and the Shah of the mischief at the docks, but sorting personal feelings from duty in the intricate web being spun was becoming harder by the minute. He had his suspicions. Vinsant's tumble seemed nothing like an accident, and Kordahla's absence from the scene signified a great deal.

As the mahktashaan last in her company, duty demanded he check on her. That much he could not avoid. It was what he would be obliged to do if he found her absent that sent his heart into turmoil. He had failed her miserably. She would never know that when the djinn had cast that devastating image of her for all the realm to see he had wanted, with a fierce protectiveness he had never thought to experience, to hunt it down and trap it in a magic lamp for an eternity of eternities. He would relinquish his magic to erase the humiliation from her memory, and the memory of every man who had witnessed it, for just as he had told her, the shame was his.

"I'm fine," Vinsant said, emerging from the physic's room. Arun hoped he had gleaned an inkling or two of his predicament from Nocrates. The physic was an ardent follower of Mahktos and would have realised in an instant the Minoria had no need of his advice.

"Good. Then we can both change into some dry clothes. See you visit the princess before you retire. You caused her quite a shock." It was the one caution he could give without betraying them both. Vinsant nodded, and Arun went to the lair to change.

Dry, robed and hooded, he plodded the stairs to Kordahla's chambers, buying time, though for whom he was not sure. It was better he meditate on Vinsant's loss of the quartz. The ramifications of that were no less serious, and doing so refused to permit the other thought – the one about Kordahla and her whereabouts – purchase. If he allowed that, he would be duty bound indeed.

Lord Ahkdul was pacing outside the Princess's rooms, a complication Arun did not need. Their guest was in a shabby state of dress, his night kurta half tucked into crumpled shalvar and unlaced at the neckline. His eyes fell to Arun's crystal as he scratched at the hair on his chest. "These men tell the Princess is in your company." The man spoke like he would to a servant.

"She was," Arun admitted, "until Prince Vinsant suffered a minor accident. I have come to assure her he is well."

"She is not in her apartment," Ahkdul said, leaning close. The man was a bully, trying to use his height to domineer. "And my page is nowhere to be found."

Arun looked to the mahktashaan guards, good, trusted men both. They had flooded the hall with light to dispel the aggression bred in the shadows of night.

"She has not returned, Minoria," Mahmed of the cadmium crystal said.

"Your attentions at this time of night are inappropriate," Arun said to Ahkdul. "You must return to your room."

"Where is she?" Ahkdul demanded.

"It is none of your concern."

Vinsant would choose that moment to stride around the corner at the end of the corridor. The prince halted as soon as he saw them, and looked from Arun to Ahkdul twice before he dawdled forward. The novelty of apprenticeship had not yet worn off; he had chosen to change into a dry pair of royal blue churidar kurta.

"Your sister is not in her rooms," Arun said. Smart as he was, Vinsant just might understand what Arun's duty entailed. If he was right. About the thought as to Kordahla's whereabouts he was trying not to have. And he wanted it to be right, with an intensity which almost dropped him to his knees. Princess Kordahla deserved better than this Verdaani brute.

Vinsant shuffled so he faced Ahkdul. "I heard that Lord Ahkdul was hanging around outside her rooms. I came to tell him that Kordahla was in my chambers."

"Was?" Ahkdul said.

Vinsant nodded. Unruly strands of his damp hair bobbed at awkward angles. "She isn't used to male visitors at this hour. She's really very modest, you know."

"Where is she now? If she has my page I have a right to know." Ahkdul persisted.

Vinsant shook his head, his confusion a touch exaggerated. "Your page wasn't with us."

Arun kept silent. He was not the one who had been asked about the boy.

"Where is Kordahla?" Ahkdul asked again.

"She said she was going to retire in one of the guest rooms. For her honour's sake. I forget which one."

It was intelligently done. The boy had not lied to his master. Still, with all Vinsant's scheming, Arun had a disquieting feeling his days as Minoria were numbered. He waited until Ahkdul deigned to leave, and Vinsant, befuddled as to why he had not yet received a scolding, said goodnight. Then he sent a mental message to Levi. If he was going to say what he thought he was going to say about Vinsant's quartz pendant – the only thing he could say which might save the boy the sword – it could not wait until morning.

Sareta peered through the night. The wall of the palace was a formidable barrier on the opposite side of the fast-flowing Arezou River. There had been movement on the battlements, but none below. Had someone not thrown a bundle to the ground, she might have returned to her husband and pleaded a lack of nerve on the part of the Princess. The deficiency was all hers, but a woman had a right to protect her family when Her Royal Privileged Highness wanted to use Arlem for her own ends. That raised more than misgivings, it did.

Bringing the boat had seemed the right thing to do at the time, when her husband had explained the circumstances and asked if she would help. Arlem was like that. Progressive. She needn't wear her veil in public, or fear to disagree. He gave her few decrees, valued her opinion and insisted their daughter attain a degree of learning beyond his own, all a rarity among Terlaani men.

But now, alone in the dead of a moonlit night, waiting to help a privileged woman who had no good reason to defy her men, she had to be daft. Forget the poverty that came with unemployment. If she were caught, it would be her head. Sareta sighed. There was no question she loved her man. When her father had declared his plain daughter was of marriageable age, she had hoped only for a husband who would treat her with respect. He had engaged her to a man who held her in esteem. She hadn't counted on her man worshiping the Princess almost as much as he worshipped the Vae. She supposed it was lucky for their daughter he commended Her Privileged Highness's modern ways, and brought them into her home. She had never dreamed there would be a day when the Princess held his hand while he lay in the mud, or when Her Highness argued with the Verdaani lord about the welfare of the common folk. It had sealed Arlem's adoration. And earned Sareta's grudging respect. So here she was, standing by their boat, nervous breaths competing with the whoosh of the water as she waited to assist with an exploit the high-born woman had no business undertaking. Sareta was devout enough to know when she needed to bow her head to pray, to both Mahktos and the Vae.

It was a pity the prayers wouldn't count for much, seeing as how a faint commotion distracted her from the words. She supposed that meant she ought to return her attention to the walls. Or better yet, since coloured lights were blazing at the front of the palace and shadowy figures running toward the lake, she should slink home. It was her misfortune she would never be able to face Arlem if she did, so she lay in the boat, muttering about the scum-tainted plan, because how was she supposed to smuggle the girl out with a troop of mahktashaan swarming the banks. *Merciful Vae! Was that a genie!* Watching the giggling child flitting this way and that, she almost missed the two figures who slipped around the corner and donned the dark cloaks in the bundle below the wall. On a final, heartfelt prayer, Sareta poled the barge from the bank, angling the bow so the current would carry her across.

"Catch," she hissed, throwing a rope to the taller of the figures. The end slapped the ground and snaked toward the water. The hooded silhouette lurched forward and, falling to her knees, snared the rope just as it splashed off a rock. "Pull, curse you," Sareta said, forgetting to whom she spoke. The current was strong at the mouth of the river. She poled against it, grunting with the effort it took to steer the boat.

The useless figure had no strength in her tug. Sareta strained, and managed to bump the boat against the bank. There was too much slack in the rope and the stern swung out. Stern rope in hand, she jumped from the boat, and grabbed the rope attached to the bow. She heard a deep breath from the figure but princess or not, now was not the time to speak.

"Get in if you're coming," she said, more gruffly than she had spoken to anyone in a long time. She wasn't about to dally so the mahktashaan could discover their escape.

"Thank you," a woman said, dispelling her doubts this was a trap.

"Get in before I lose my grip." She strained against the chaffing ropes as the cloaked woman assisted the child down onto the rock. Their ginger footing made slow progress, but Sareta bit her tongue. There wasn't any rescuing if one of them got washed into eddies. Not by her at least. "Not on the edge!" she hissed as the young one placed a foot on the gunwale. The boat rocked, the boy wobbled, and the woman pulled him back onto the rocks. Sareta, swinging as far as she could in the opposite direction, just managed to avert both a capsizing and a drowning. "Get in," she hissed. The woman crouched and threw a bag. Lady Luck had veiled her face, allowing the current to twist the rocking boat. The bag hit the side and splashed into the roaring water.

"Leave it," Sareta said, as the fool of a woman leaned to fish it out. She struggled to bring the stern back round. "Get in," she hissed again. The woman half fell inside, then opened her arms and caught the boy as he jumped. He landed off centre, which rocked the boat some more. Sareta pulled back on the rope and peered into the night while she waited for the movement to settle. Two moons and a whole heap of lighted mahktashaan crystals. It was a wonder no one had spotted them. Her practiced leap got her safe aboard. She had the pole in her hand and was pushing off the rock before her passengers thought to hang onto the sides.

"Get down and cover yourselves with those cloaks. Don't let a scrap of flesh show."

The river eddied with a rage she had not expected, dragging the pole to the side. She struggled to plant it and point the bow to the front. She needed to succeed before they entered the lake. If a guard chanced to look this way, he would challenge the swirling boat. The confluence of the Arezou River and Lake Sheraz offered abundant fishing, but only the most experienced braved its hazards. Another push just managed to point the bow forward as they swept beneath a pair of guards. Bringing the pole aboard, Sareta gathered a net and cast it out.

"Stay down, and keep still," she said as the princess began to rise. A few minutes later, she retrieved the net. A number of fish thrashed within its holes. She worked to free them, letting some flap upon her guests until she could bucket them. It would be the least of the indignities a runaway princess suffered. Then she cast the net again, and once again, before she took the oars and rowed past the palace into the lake. If she had taken advantage of the fine fishing spot a little earlier than the regular folk, it was not unusual enough to bear comment in this time of peace. Not when the boat was so artfully controlled, and not unless the guards spotted two figures crouched and covered. Such figures might be smuggling the illicit drug. Or escaping from within the palace walls.

◆ ◆ ◆

The Majoria was leaning on the parapet, gazing out across Lake Sheraz. Arun paused at the top of the stairs before moving to his side. The water was a perfect sheet of black glass, reflecting Dindarin and Daesoa in solemn state. Majoria and Minoria stood together a moment. Then Levi, yet looking across the lake, murmured a prayer to Mahktos before casting a sound shield around them. Its energy thrummed black-green, warning any who approached.

"They have gone," Levi said, turning to his second. He had adjusted his hood so it did not obscure his face. The stubble of a trying day darkened his chin.

"There was more than one?" Long years in the company of his superior had eliminated Arun's need for clarification. The djinn were foremost in both their minds.

"By all accounts. Most saw one young in body and spirit. She was taking few pains to hide herself and appeared to be toying with the guards. But Mahktashaan Strauss and Garzene sensed another, one enraged in his power and far more ancient."

"The genie was in the palace," Arun said. He told Levi what

Kordahla's guards had seen. "As for the other, I fear he is the same that has been haunting Princess Kordahla of late."

"Apprentice Vinsant was present, was he not? In fact, the entire upset is of his doing."

Arun had to admit it was. However grim the circumstance, he had never broken a vow. Even now, with all that had happened, he would keep secret the extent of Kordahla's humiliation on the boat. Gathering his thoughts, he gazed across the lake. At its centre, a huddled figure rose in a barge. The boat was heading to the opposite bank, an incongruity at this time of night, for the eastern side housed the dry docks and was reputed, with its noise, to hold slim pickings for fishermen.

"There is too much of the preternatural in this one place of late," Levi said. "I would seek a resolution before it tears our realm apart."

Arun had feared just this. Many a long year had he worked with this Majoria, a man not given to discussion, a man hungry for recognition, but a man blessed by their god. "What is your decision, Majoria?"

"I would uncover the Eye of Mahktos."

Arun's heartbeat quickened. This most sacred, most powerful artefact lay buried deep in the mines for good reason. "It is not a relic to bring into the light of day without dire need."

"Do you dispute the need?

"If Mahktos has guided your judgement, I do not, all praise to Mahktos, all honour to you, Majoria."

Arun wondered at Levi's deep breath. Indecision was not one of the man's traits.

"Mahktos warns of an evil descending upon us. I cannot but think the mischief centres on the royal children."

Slow and deliberate, Arun turned from the lake. He needed to face Levi to reveal this news. If he had no opportunity to ponder that incongruous vessel, it was for the best. "You may be right," he said. "Apprentice Vinsant has lost his quartz."

Two harsh breaths escaped Levi's lips before he said, low and hard, "The boy is too irresponsible. This is why the mahktashaan do not take apprentices until three years past the prescribed bond age."

"I fear there is more to it than that," Arun said. "He was wearing the quartz this evening in the gardens, but not when he emerged from the water." He hesitated. "It is neither within the lake nor the palace grounds."

Levi took a moment to absorb that. "You do not need me to tell you what the true loss of his quartz means."

"I fear it is the work of djinn."

"Can you prove that?"

"I cannot."

"Regardless, there is only one way he might remain with us," Levi said, "And only one way for him to remain alive."

Arun looked across the lake, his knuckles white with his grip on the edge of the parapet. He closed his eyes as he remembered Mahktos's harsh rejection of the young prince, and the god's uncaring stance when he had stood in Vinsant's stead. "It is certain death," he said.

"Stay down!" the woman hissed as Kordahla started to rise.

Kordahla flattened herself on the bottom of the skiff. Next to her, Timak lay in utter stillness, the tickle of his warm breath on her hand the only indication he was alive. The gentle swoosh of water as the skiff glided further onto the lake helped soothe her nerves, if not her body. She was cramped and damp from the flapping fish. Their smell reminded her of the grappers that had fallen from the sky. Was there no end to the discomfort fish were to cause her, she wondered with wry humour.

The bottom of the boat scraped against ground, silencing croaks and chirps.

"Stay here and don't move a muscle, for I won't vouch for Simeon's secrecy."

The boat rocked as woman splashed onto muddy land. There were voices, the snort of a horse, the clink of coins. Beside her, the boy did not even blink. Lady Luck or Lord Time might find a way to cure him if they made it to Myklaan. Until then…she contemplated whether a boy who did exactly what he was told, no more, no less, would aid or hinder their escape. When footsteps sloshed close, she eased the cloak over his arm.

"You do Arlem's bidding you say, woman. But no god-fearing man would have his woman out alone at night," a harsh voice said.

"You heard what happened to him?"

The responding "Aye," was cautious.

"We've a need to survive. I'll take my chances scum dipping if I must. Arlem's been a good friend to you, Simeon. All he asks is that you keep your peace about this. Speak your mind to him, if you will, if you're not convinced he knows it."

"That I will," Simeon said. "Just 'coz this ain't right. I judged Arlem to have better character than to let his wife scour the scums."

Footsteps veered to the right. Water splashed as a boat pushed into the lake. Even after the lapping waves faded into stillness, the woman did not return.

What now? Kordahla wondered. *How can I possibly escape on foot, with a damaged child and mahktashaan swarming the countryside come morning?* She was about to take her chances and sit up when the woman spoke.

"Come ashore. No sudden movements mind." She offered Kordahla and then Timak a rough hand and led them quickly behind Ahkdul's ship. "The palace should not be suspicious of my boat because of the fish I hauled there, and Simeon's boat has disappeared from view. His sight is short, and he'll not have spied you rise. There's a horse for you. Only one. We didn't know there'd be two of you. Head south for a day and you'll reach the scums. There's a ford just before the land turns to mud but it's sees heavy traffic from the scum dippers. If you intend to take your chances across those mires, then you may as well ride as fast as the poor beast will carry you. Work him to his grave, if you must, for he'll be no good to you in those wretched swamps."

"Thank you," Kordahla said, pressing three gold thulek into the woman's hand.

"I won't pretend to understand what drives you from the privilege of those walls, but you were kind to my husband when that Verdaani scum-bag would have left him to rot." The woman looked in the direction of the palace with its twinkling lights. Over the lap of water, Kordahla heard her swallow. "It's our heads if the Shah finds out."

"There's no reason he should," Kordahla said. "Even if we're caught."

The woman made a wistful sound. "My life's been good because of you. Arlem admires your ways, and our daughter is almost as educated as our son."

Kordahla started. She was pampered indeed not to have grasped the woman before her wore full veil as a precaution, and not in deference to the old fashion. Not a minor moon past, Sareta would have witnessed the sickening sight of the meatball vendors' heads stuck on the pikes on the palace walls. The threat of a beheading was real.

"Thank you," was all Kordahla could think to say, only this time there was a great deal more emotion in the simple words.

Chapter Twenty-seven

ITS ABSENCE WAS NOTICED at once. Vinsant, who had spent a near sleepless night wondering both how Kordahla was faring and how he could appease Mahktos, wore his best sheepish smile.

"Scour the palace from top to bottom if need be, but find that piece of quartz!" Branak ordered. He removed his hood to fix Vinsant with the full weight of his slaying glare. Gram and Naikil fidgeted their way apart from Vinsant, Naikil's joke about the Gram's fondness for bean stew causing the putrid smell in the courtyard forgotten the instant Branak unhooded. It figured. Until now, Vinsant had never imagined brown-haired, long-faced and patient Branak could look furious. The amber eyes had to have something to do with that.

"Well?" Branak demanded as Vinsant tried to sidle toward his fellow apprentices. Safety lay in numbers even if numbers wanted to distance themselves from trouble.

Nobody had forbidden Vinsant to lie to the teacher, at least not in those direct words, but having an older brother had taught him wiles enough to understand Branak would talk to Arun. The last thing Vinsant felt confident enough to do was backtrack his way out of an accusation by the Minoria. "I don't think it will do any good," he said.

Branak closed his eyes, swaying as though overcome by fatigue. It could have been the solid heat that did it, or the stink weighing over the crowded courtyard, but the way his nerves were knocking, Vinsant didn't think so. He looked at the scuff marks in the dirt, and muttered about the Minoria knowing.

Branak waved him in the direction of the palace with an order to have every page search every nook and cranny of every room he had so much as passed since he last remembered wearing the stone. Vinsant snuck to the stinky bag he had deposited in the corner of the courtyard, the one he had been up at dawn to prepare, holding his breath until he could turn his nose away from the ghastly smell. Then he sauntered off for a nap. A morning relieved of toddler-level swordplay was a bonus. If he could spend it with his eyes closed, it was a double treat. Although he had to admit that, between his fretting over Kordahla and his lack of sleep, even Naikil might have bested him today.

It seemed only minutes before Arun came to his room to fetch him. He jumped off his bed, grabbed his bag, and scampered after the Minoria's back. Catching up made him feel worse. One look at the bleak face inside the hood and the questions that had been about to overflow disappeared. He began to feel as weak as Branak had looked. The stench wafting from his bag was not helping. At least Arun did nothing more than give it a disapproving look. Vinsant opened his mouth and closed it again. He would have felt a mite better if the Minoria had said something before he pushed aside the tapestry and opened the entrance to the lair.

"You have been called to account for yourself, Vinsant. Without your quartz, there is no way to train, no way for you to initiate as a mahktashaan. I'm afraid your hours as an apprentice are numbered."

The palace seemed to spin around him. He felt the blood rush from his face. He tried to convince himself it was worth it if Kordahla was safe far away, but it was not supposed to be this way. His plan to protect her hinged on him wielding magic none would dare oppose. Arun was several steps into the damp gloom before he found the will to follow.

"Can't I get another?" he asked, his voice thin with uncertainty. Since Arun maintained his silence the entire plod down the stairs, the answer had to be no.

Eight mahktashaan were gathered in knots around the altar in the

Room of Ceremony, the Inner Circle at a guess. They were speaking among themselves, Levi the only one apart, but every last one turned their hooded head Vinsant's way when he stepped into the room. The full intimidating presence of the robed men hit him in a way it had not since he was just a dumb kid. He hung back as Arun went to stand by Levi, thankful the crystals in the sconces emitted a faint glow. Standing between the looming shadows was less spooky than fumbling over the uneven, hexagonal flagstones in the dark.

"Summoned to attend another gathering of the Inner Circle. What trouble are you in now, Apprentice Vinsant?" a genial mahktashaan asked.

The warm voice was familiar, but Vinsant had to check the mahktashaan's crystal was plum coloured to be sure. Not sure what Arun had told these men, he glanced at the Majoria. "I've lost my quartz, Mahktashaan Strauss," he said.

"Lost, not just mislaid?"

"Um…lost?"

The few seconds of silence from Strauss made it feel like the world was ending. "I thought you might have been somehow involved with this rampant djinn, but this I did not expect. You understand the gravity of the offence?"

Vinsant took a deep breath. The earthy smell of the herbs sprinkled over altar and floor was reassuring in a primitive sort of way. "I think so."

The mahktashaan had tipped his hood back far enough to reveal a deep furrow on his brow. "No, I don't think you do." The man's jowls quivered. "You are who you are, regardless of what you have been told of your status as an apprentice. I cannot see Levi condoning your execution, but pray with all the fervour you can muster this will go well for Arun."

Vinsant's knees wobbled. He fought hard not to choke on the large lump that had formed in his throat. "Er…Er…Um…"

"The Inner Circle is convened," Levi said.

There went his chance to find out what deep mine he had fallen in. He stepped back as the mahktashaan formed a circle around Majoria and Minoria, placing himself well outside their ranks. They could ostracise him all they liked until they reached a decision. He wanted to be in a position to run if one of them so much as twitched a hand toward a sword.

"All praise to Mahktos. All honour to you, Majoria," they intoned with a stamp of their left foot.

"This gathering involves our youngest apprentice," Levi said. "He has lost his quartz." A murmur rippled around the room. When it died, Levi continued. "Our laws are clear. Is there one who might offer evidence in mitigation?"

"I do," Arun said.

"That's hardly a surprise. You pledged your title for him," a mahktashaan with a sea green crystal said.

"I did and I will bear the consequences," Arun replied, unruffled.

"And yet you seek absolution for him."

Garzene of the teal crystal said, "Do not judge out of lust for power, Cromwell. It ill becomes one of the Inner Circle."

"Are you accusing me of treason, Garzene?"

"It is common knowledge you have coveted the position of Minoria since the day you were admitted to the Circle."

Levi stamped his foot and the men immediately fell silent. "Minoria, you stood in this apprentice's stead. Our laws are clear. Your fate rests with his."

Cromwell said, "As you say, Majoria, our laws are clear. This offence is punishable by death. He should never–" The mahktashaan broke off, his eyes bulging, as Levi's crystal slowly glowed.

"The Inner Circle is convened," Levi said over Cromwell's gurgling sounds. "You will observe protocol and you will pay the Minoria the respect he deserves while he yet holds that title. Be warned. There is chaos afoot and I will tolerate no deviation from custom."

Cromwell coughed, as though released from a stranglehold. The entire cohort stomped their left foot and stood at attention. "All praise to Mahktos. All honour to you, Majoria," they intoned.

Vinsant drew a shaky breath. While the military precision of the mahktashaan was awesome to watch during their guarding duties, it was gut-rumbling terrifying when they were discussing his life. Again.

"With regard to the culpability of Apprentice Vinsant deq Wilshem, what evidence have you, Mahktashaan Garzene?" the Majoria asked.

"I have no evidence to bear," Garzene replied, making his teal crystal flare.

Levi turned to the next member of the Inner Circle and repeated the question. Vinsant wasn't sure it was good that he too forbore to comment. One by one, Levi questioned the mahktashaan. None offered evidence until at last, when Levi came to Arun, Vinsant found himself biting his lip.

"I saw the young apprentice with his crystal moments before a djinn appeared. All present are aware two such creatures haunted these walls last night. While the boy was being foolhardy upon the merlon, we cannot divine what mischief the djinn intended with him."

As one, the cohort stomped their left foot.

"With regard to opinion on the matter of Apprentice Vinsant deq Wilshem, what say you, Mahktashaan Strauss?" Levi asked.

"There are limits to how many concessions we can make. I think it clear Prince Vinsant is not meant for our ranks. However, he has not yet been inducted into our secrets. Let him return to his father's side."

Vinsant's heart sank. With a mahktashaan he had thought an ally advocating the order throw him out, what hope did he have?

When Levi put same question to Cromwell, the mahktashaan stared at Vinsant, his sea green eyes the one nightmarish feature distinguishable under his hood. "Already we have conceded much to have this young apprentice train. Without the crystal, he can never become a full initiate. That much is not in dispute. But he was warned of the consequences when he chose to have the Minoria stand in his stead. You say with djinn flying wild, we must observe custom, Majoria. Well let us observe it here and now. This boy is under a death sentence by our law and were it any other, there would be no debate."

The next mahktashaan, Leyland by name, a crystal of rust, spoke. "His father sent him with full knowledge of our laws. You yourself said you informed him, Majoria."

"The Minoria offers evidence of djinn, but never has a crystal come loose from its bearer for a reason other than carelessness. I presume the Lake was searched?" another mahktashaan asked when Levi turned to him.

He was sinking into deeper scums by the minute. Hanging around for the final vote seemed like a bad idea. Trailing his hands along the wall, Vinsant edged around the group, deeper into the lair. The rough stone gave way to a void, and he stumbled into the temple. Swallowing hard, he dared to look at the crystal and gold statue of the god.

From inside the Room of Ceremony, another mahktashaan voiced his dreaded opinion. "For the reasons stated, Apprentice Vinsant deq Wilshem should be put to the sword."

Arun and Levi did not argue, allowing each member of the Inner Circle their voice. That was five against him and two in support, if he had counted right, and three that called for his head. Knee-knocking stuff, but nowhere near as terrifying as Mahktos's crimson eyes firing into life. Suddenly, Vinsant knew. The god he had wronged, and the god he must appease. He had nothing to lose when his life was forfeit. He stepped up to the statue, his eyes glued to the god's, and fell to his knees.

The Minoria's voice rang out. "Vinsant! No!"

Too late. Vinsant prostrated himself before his god. Around him light blazed with a blinding fury. "All praise to Mahktos," he said, meaning it even though every muscle in his body trembled.

From the gold core, a robust voice boomed, a sudden crack of thunder during a storm. "Who dares to place himself in my presence?"

The words juddered through every fibre of Vinsant's being. He gulped, kept his head down and prayed the god understood he had perpetrated his deceit so that he could better serve in the future, because wasn't it a mahktashaan's duty to protect the royal family, and didn't saving Kordahla from the swine count as protecting her, and if he couldn't see himself as a grown up with loads shouldered and curiosity curbed, it didn't mean he wanted to be a mahktashaan any less.

A velvety chuckle startled him out of his thoughts. "Rise, little one."

Vinsant managed to lift his head. The statue had disappeared, leaving only a rich glow that obliterated all save the warmth bathing him. When he was not struck down for presumption, he dragged himself to his feet. His knees hadn't got any of their strength back, and he wished the god had ordered him to remain upon the ground, where he would be safe from embarrassing collapse. He thought of apologies while the light faded, or rather deepened into vibrant colours and sharp shapes until Vinsant found himself in a glade of incredible beauty. Strange trees soared to the heavens, their foliage singing in a refreshing breeze. Sunlight streamed from above, stroking leaves of every hue with gold. The grass was a cushion beneath his feet, the sky a blanket above his head. At the edge of the clearing, the forest teemed with life, insects clicking, deer frolicking, lions shaking shaggy manes. Vinsant wanted to bound over and run with them, his heart was bursting so full of a joy he feared he would never again touch once he left this place. Unable to help himself, he whirled and whirled and whirled, whooping and calling until dizziness dropped him to the ground.

"You have not yet answered my question." The silky voice rebounded from every tree, surrounding him so that though he followed the echo he could not locate the source. "Who dares to place himself in my presence?"

"Your apprentice," he said, throwing his chin to the heavens. The sun was a fiery ball but there was no sign of the god.

"Your desire to serve burns stronger than in many twice your age. Your path is laid before you. And yet you choose to betray me. What manner of apprentice are you?"

Vinsant bit his lip. If he clung to the merriment in the voice, he could almost convince himself he was suffering Father's teasing. "One who wishes to atone." He grabbed his bag and hugged it like might save his life.

There was a great rustling, as of a bear swaggering through deep grass. The canopy swayed and a giant figure stood at the edge of the glade, thighs deep in the trees, head blotting out the sun. Golden light obscured its face but the hairy, bowed legs and the clawed nails were unmistakable. Mahktos was not the creepy image of His statues but a divine being of such beauty that the human form seemed ill-proportioned next to it. Vinsant dug inside his bag and removed a sprig of frangipani.

"For my sister. It's her favourite flower," he said, shuffling to lay it closer to the god's feet, then backing away. Miraculously, the sprig took instant root, its stem growing and branching, its flowers multiplying until a mature tree thrived. When Mahktos stooped and plucked a red flower, Vinsant blinked back into awareness. "For me," he said, bringing forth the grapper. The stink of decay had vanished. He laid the fish at the foot of the bush where it flapped as though quite unaware it been dead these past days. Where it hit the ground, water seeped, pooling until a pond had sprung and the fish leapt happily from the water. Vinsant raised his beaming face to the god and found himself forced to close his eyes against the blinding light.

"You may not look full on me, child." Humour tinged the rumble. "Not yet, though I might permit it when you are Majoria."

Vinsant opened one eye and said, "Am I definitely going to make it to Majoria, then?"

A chuckle brushed his skin as the god diminished in size and brilliance, yet remained so much more than any mortal man. "Perhaps. If you train well, young apprentice."

Vinsant opened his other eye. "So I'm not kicked out of the mahktashaan?"

"There are those who after a lifetime of service would not gift me the riches you have laid at my feet. There are others whose ambitions lack the noble purpose you seek. You, little apprentice, have pleased me, and so you may serve."

For three breaths, Vinsant contemplated how frank he could be with a god without giving offence. Whether it was worth pushing his luck when Mahktos had granted him his request. For an instant, he wished Arun were here. Then, a wicked grin spread across his face because this mind-blowing experience was his alone. "You're not mad I gave my sister the crystal and the quartz?" he asked.

The god bowed until his obscured face rested in front of Vinsant's. "Oh, I'm mad, all right," He murmured, "And you will pay for that treason, little boy."

Vinsant felt like a little boy, all right, for all it dented his pride. He had stuffed up bad. He wasn't sure how bad, but the price would sure be taxing. "What do I do to atone?" he asked.

"The mahktashaan stand warned that admitting you to their ranks will spell havoc for their order. There is much at play here beyond their ken. Deliver that message to them and tell them too that I give you no sanction for your service. Your secrets, and your sister's you may keep, for they are part of what transpires beyond the realm of men. Go now. I will not tell you more. You must carve your own destiny, for I will not interfere." Mahktos grew in stature, glowing brighter and brighter, blurring and fading the glades until Vinsant grew disoriented, then dizzy, and stumbled into what seemed to be a void of chords and shimmering lights.

When his senses returned, he was first aware of the ground below him, hard and unforgiving. Then a solemn ache asserted itself in his heart, as though it were bereft of some need. As though he grieved. It welled up until a sob escaped him. Then he felt an arm at his elbow, and Arun's voice urged him to stand. He forced his leaden legs to work, and turned to face his judgement. With his apprenticeship sanctioned by Mahktos, the Inner Circle could hardly turn him out. That swordstroke that had threatened would never end his life. He expected a rebuke. A furious argument as to how his freedoms would be curtailed. What he did not anticipate, could never have guessed, was the stunned, open-mouthed silence that greeted him. That washed away the faintest traces of ire on every single mahktashaan in the room.

"Er…" he said, looking at Arun.

The Minoria released his elbow but beneath the hood, the shock was plain upon his face.

Vinsant turned his head to look at Mahktos. The statue was a hard lump of crystal.

"It's all right," Vinsant said, turning back to the Inner Circle. "Mahktos has said I can train."

A metallic rasp drew his attention. Strauss had drawn his sword. Vinsant backed away. He would have stumbled over the statue's foot if Arun had not caught his arm. It was his turn to gape when Strauss knelt and rested his sword across raised knee. One by one, the mahktashaan of the Inner Circle mimicked him, wide-eyed, open-mouthed or pouting.

Except for Cromwell, who was spitting and snorting in his fury. None of it made sense since the statues eyes were rubies.

"Er...Arun...I mean Minoria?"

Arun stood before him and went down on one knee. Vinsant reminded himself to breathe.

"Majoria?" he asked the silent man, the only other person standing. The hood of his cloak was drawn so far over his face Vinsant had no clue as to how he felt.

Not yet, apprentice, Levi's tense, gravelly voice sounded clear in his head.

Vinsant dropped to one knee. "All praise to Mahktos. All honour to you, Majoria," he said. Mahktos, did he need this, whatever this was, to be over. "I meant it when I said I don't want to be treated like a prince."

"All praise to Mahktos," the mahktashaan intoned.

When they remained kneeling, Vinsant looked around in panic.

"Stand, Vinsant. They will not rise before you do," Arun said, rising.

Vinsant stumbled over his own foot. "Mahktos said I might be a mahktashaan," he repeated, as the Inner Circle got to their feet. His hand went to his chest. It was a reflex, really, because in the short time he had worn the piece of quartz that marked him as a mahktashaan apprentice, he had been unable to keep his hands off it. He truly, truly, *truly* had not expected to find another piece in its place. Not yet. Not until he had stood under the great statue with Branak to give a ritual greeting. But there it was, a replacement stone around his neck. At his touch, a crimson light flared into the room.

Chapter Twenty-eight

THEY ASSEMBLED BEFORE HIM on Meeting Field, every man, woman and child of the Ho'akerin. They came in traditional dress: shirts, black trousers or skirts, hems embroidered with the spiralling circles and squares which marked the tribe. Draykan grunted his approval. His talk with Ishoa had decided him. He had charged runners with ferreting out wandering huntsmen and gatherers to urge them home. The summons had gone well until Erok's party intercepted an emaciated tribesman returned from Verdaan, his bare feet blistered from the long trek, his torn pockets stuffed with porrin he tried to barter to the tribe. Draykan had entrusted the drug to Ishoa. She had scattered most of it to the wind.

"There is more porrin in this village than a soothsayer can safely store," she had said.

Draykan had clucked his agreement. His soothsayer was a wise woman. Posting guards on the approach to her cave would have placed an additional strain on their scarce hunters.

The Leadsman ran a practiced eye over his tribe. When the drug did not leech hunger from the starved, he had four hands of able men to feed four times that many. For certain, the spirits had noticed the dereliction of the tribe. The hills no longer teemed with prey, and few goats had kidded this season. But perhaps there was hope. Today, barely a glassy eye stared out from the crowd. Vorn was the exception of course. And Lutham, who looked up to Vorn. Vila had sought Draykan out to make sure he knew those layabouts had stolen Sian's porrin. His ear still hurt from her scolding. Draykan shook his head at the pity. The elder man had been a fierce hunter in his day. The younger, wasted on the drug, would never lift a spear to prove himself. Him and too many others of Erok's generation. Draykan gave thanks to the spirits every day that his son had not fallen to the false bliss. Still, he bled for his tribe. Stamping out the drug was a near impossible task when the addicts stored their supply in secret caches among the rocks.

The sun rose full over the hill, flooding the valley with light. It was time. Gold-tipped ceremonial spear in hand, Draykan hefted his stocky body onto the flat speaking rock behind the blazing hearth. He had ordered the fire lit for ceremony. At the end of this meeting, it would serve another purpose. He raised his hand high, and the tribe fell quiet. His extended family sat on the dry stubble between the protruding rocks on the small stretch of flat, open land, waiting on his word. The gurgle of a babe mixed well with the rustle of leaves, the cry of the hawk circling overhead, the bleat of the goats on the steep, rocky hill behind him. Sounds of life, all of them. At this moment, he was proud.

Perhaps he was not entirely pleased. Sian sat at the back, away from her parents, apart from the youngsters. Behind her, Erok caught his look. It would bring trouble, what he had asked Erok and his friends to do. It would bring worse strife to follow tradition. He raised the ceremonial spear. On cue, Ishoa stepped forward, twisting her body and rattling her staff in the spirit dance, praising Forest, Sky, Earth and Water. The extra feathers she wore in her hair, around her arms and wrists, the bright paint on her face, befitted the solemn occasion.

They hear her, Draykan thought when the boughs sighed. He breathed the deepening scent of moist earth and sweet hay, drew courage from the darkening hue of the sky. The Ho'akerin were blessed in their soothsayer.

Ishoa swept her staff across the curve of the crowd and thudded the end into the ground. She remained below the speaking rock, and for that Draykan was grateful. He could speak with conviction knowing she chose to ratify his decree.

"Tribesmen and women, my brothers and sisters, my children, I am here to make a law," Draykan began. He was a skilful hunter with no rival despite his advancing years. He ruled with a deep understanding of his people, not a bone fist. He led by wits, not words. It had always been enough. Today, faced with a tribe that depended on the vile drug to get through the day, he was not so sure. Vorn was lying down, staring at the sky. The babe that screamed day and night was silent in his mam's arms.

"Our people are falling to the bliss." The people started fidgeting. They had not expected this. Draykan blinked. How could they not have? No other threat could have forced him to declare a meeting of the tribe. "Our men shirk their duty. Our boys do not learn the skills they need to sustain the tribe. Our women scrounge for food to nourish their babes." It was blunt, but true. He saw the consternation on the faces of the women. Their men were falling to the drug. They lamented it every day, but they could guess where his speech was going. A woman with a useless man was a married tribeswoman with status. A girl who never married, who never produced young hunters and gatherers to ease the existence of the aged…His eyes alighted on Sian. She was looking down. She always looked down. Spirits forbid she met the eye of a tribesman. Draykan shook his head. A longhouse full of ones like her. It would be a blessing compared to the leeches they fed. It was time the tribe returned to taking care of its own. It was time the tribe stopped sapping strength from the weakest.

Murmurs had broken out in the seconds he had fallen into reverie. The fire crackled before him, leaching heat into the hot morning. Sweat beaded on his brow. Draykan had always believed one led by example. He hated this need for words, but they had to understand. He frowned as he gauged each face, suspicious, resentful, cautious. He was ready to lay his spear down over this.

Perhaps it would not come to that. It was a measure of respect that when he spoke again his tribe quietened straight away.

"We no longer cherish the Earth and the Forest and the Sky and the Water. We no longer pay homage to the spirits for their gifts. Instead, we worship the false bliss that porrin brings. It takes from us but it does not give. We have become like that drug. It teaches us the habits of the lowlanders. More and more of us take from the spirits that nourish us but do not give. The Ho'akerin will no longer succour these leeches." He stopped to gather his thoughts, gave an imperceptible shake of his head. He was a man meant to have a spear in his hand, not words in his mouth that tumbled over each other and ran back inside to repeat themselves. A small marvel the tribe were still looking at him, expectant. He took a deep breath. From here they would unite, or divide until the Ho'akerin were no more.

"No more," he said. "We must renounce the drug before the spirits renounce us. We must deny any who use it the shelter of the tribe. We must seek the cooperation of the Five Tribes of the Akerin, and ask each of them to do the same."

Draykan looked around. Every sober body was strained forward, their mistrust clear on their weathered faces. Waiting for the decree that would deprive them of loved ones. He lifted the spear of his leadership high. By luck or by divine intervention, the sun struck the golden tip. Rays reflected onto his tribe, gilding them with light. "I am Leadsman and I do say porrin is outlawed from our midst save by direction of a soothsayer. I am Leadsman and so do I say."

Stunned silence erupted into angry shouts as Erok and his friends entered the Meeting Field, sacks slung over their shoulders. Draykan nodded his response to the guarded query in his son's eye. The hunters approached the fire and tossed their sacks in. The cotton smoked and smouldered. Sweet-smelling smoke rose in a thin, black line. The murmurs became shouts. One derelict excuse for a tribesman charged through the field, and attempted to snatch the booty from the flames. He must have been high on the drug to be so heedless of the injury the roaring fire could cause. It took both Erok and wiry, dark-haired Brax to restrain him. Delirious, he fought with the strength of an ogre. It was Harz, Draykan saw, a hefty hunter whose prowess had been diminishing, and not because of age. He climbed off the rock and waited for his son to subdue the addict.

The rest of the tribe was up standing now, watching the flames eat what caches of the drug Erok had uncovered while the tribe had gathered for the decree. There would be other stores, but this was a sore test for those consumed by the false bliss.

With a rustle of her grass skirts, Ishoa jumped in front of Harz, posed in a crouch and waved her hand before his face. He quietened, but glared at soothsayer and fire. His wife, Lelola, stepped forward.

"We have not been asked our thoughts. We have not voiced our consent to this decree. It is void, Draykan."

Ishoa waved her staff at Lelola. The pods rattled as the feathers flew about. "Who speaks?" she asked, planting the staff in the ground. "Lelola of the Ho'akerin, born to the Ta'akerin, or the drug of the false bliss?"

Lelola had the restless, furtive look of the addict, Draykan saw with a start. He had not realised it. Had not thought the women infected.

"The tribe has not ratified this," another voice agreed. Then a third spoke up, and a fourth.

"The tribe does not have to," Erok reminded them, jumping upon the speaking rock. His voice, strong with the conviction of youth, cut across the dissent. "A leadsman may make a decree in the best interest of the tribe."

"I need it," Harz said, breaking free of Brax and raising an angry fist to Erok. "And so do Vorn and Lutham."

"Why should the soothsayer be the only one to commune with the spirits?" Lelola said. "Why do you deny us that right?"

Ishoa moved around the group, her hands dancing before her to feel the energy of the group, to *see* them. She clapped her hands. Daylight flickered and the staff she had abandoned was once again in them. Pointing it unerringly at Lelola, she said, "What honour do you bring them by destroying the bounty they gift you? What communion do you make when you surrender to the drug?"

Vorn wandered over. "This decree is not good. We do not want it." He lay by the fire and continued his contemplation of the flames.

Vila pulled Sian over by the hand. "Erok is right. Leadsman Draykan does not need your consent. You have no memory of a decision the tribe opposed, so you think a voice is yours. The Leadsman is our leader. He decides when the tribe cannot."

"We can decide," Lelola said. "And we do."

"No," Draykan said. "The drug does."

"We want it," a new voice said.

"We want our husbands," Larpa added, hands on hips, to a chorus of assent.

"I challenge the leadership," Harz called.

Draykan snorted. "I'll not fight the ill."

Harz rushed headlong at Draykan. A simple sidestep and extended foot tripped the addict.

"You see how weak the drug leaves our finest," Draykan said.

He was losing judgement. In not bothering to check Hartz, he had made a mistake. Harz leapt on him from behind. The ceremonial spear flew from his hand as they tumbled to the ground. Far from wasted, Harz pummelled his fists into Draykan with a furious strength. Draykan lay trapped beneath the crazed man, unable to hit back. Tradition maintained they fight to the death. For a brief, heart-stopping moment, Draykan feared that Harz's delirious state might mean his own demise. Then a hard elbow to the chest tipped Harz's balance enough for Draykan to roll over and force Harz beneath him. Twisting so that they lay face to face, Draykan released a punch that Harz blocked with his arm. They wrestled and grunted, until Draykan managed to slip an arm across Harz's neck. Bringing a knee up, he dropped his weight down, choking the man with whom he had once hunted side by side. Harz's face turned deeper shades of purple as he rasped for air. When he was on the brink of passing out, Draykan released him, picked up the spear and stood.

"Leave," Draykan ordered.

"No." Lelola grabbed Harz's arm, and half helped, half pulled him up.

"I challenge the leadership," Vorn said from the ground.

"I challenge too," Lutham said.

"And I," another voice added.

"There are too many of us," Harz said. "The Ho'akerin keep the drug."

Draykan looked at the hostile faces surrounding him. How devastating was his failure. This was no challenge. It was a revolt. In the face of such opposition, he could not prevail. Weary, he climbed upon the rock and threw the spear as far as he could. The tip buried itself in dirt, beyond the furthest lingering tribesman.

"Choose your new leader," he said, his heart breaking as he stepped down from the role he had assumed as a not-so-young man. He would not, could not stay here in this tribe he no longer recognised, which no longer offered respect. If need be, he would travel far to the north where the drug might not yet have a hold. There were others who might care to come.

"You have no authority," Vila said to Harz. "You lost the challenge."

"I have the weight of numbers behind me."

Vila sat upon the rock, her limbs too stiff to climb. "You do not honour the tradition of the tribe. If you flout our laws, it is you who must leave, and all who seek to adopt your new ways. This is the home of the Ho'akerin. It will shelter the people who follow its ways."

"Bah," Vorn said. "You have no say. You are an old woman."

"Oh doesn't she?" ancient Farina croaked.

One by one, the elderly women came forth, voicing their support for Vila. As if not to be outdone, the elderly men raised fists high in the air, their hunter's salute directed to Draykan. Erok and Brax and their friends came forth, and the whole tribe took a stance. At the last, Draykan noted with a tear in his eye, there were equal numbers on each side of the speaking rock. He shook his head. That it had come to this.

Ishoa stepped between the two factions, raising her staff high. The soothsayer stalked through the crowd, crouched steps and stealthy turns locking her sightless white eyes upon the ringleaders. The wind began to screech. The distant wolves howled. The grass grew and tangled about the feet of the dissenters. The sky darkened to grey. Emitting a frightful keen, Ishoa jabbed her staff into the ground. It trembled beneath them, and the young and the frail fell.

"Begone, you who would defile the spirits. Begone, they say." Her words rang with the authority of Forest, Sky, Earth and Water. Under the curse, the dissenters fled in every direction, into the forest, down the valley, up the rocks. It was a long drop of the sun before anyone found the courage to speak. Ishoa was yet standing, staff pointed after the outcasts when Erok brought Draykan his spear. His son dropped to one knee, the spear laid across both hands.

"Leader of my tribe," Erok said, the formal bestowing of a leadsman's title.

"You must find the Five Tribes of the Akerin," Draykan told his son, one eye on the frightful figure of the soothsayer. "Go immediately. Tell them what has come to pass and bid their leaders come. If we are to survive this, the Akerin must be of one accord."

Ishoa turned and fixed him with an unerring gaze. "It will not be enough." Slowly, so slowly, like a blind woman three times her age, she shambled from the Meeting Field.

Draykan could only watch with a growing sense of doom.

CHAPTER TWENTY-NINE

A MAHKTASHAAN GUARD WITH a nut-brown crystal hurried into the Room of Ceremony, halted, and stomped his right foot. "All praise to Mahktos. All honour to you, Majoria. The Shah requests the immediate presence of Majoria, Minoria and Prince Vinsant in Princess Kordahla's chambers."

"Uh oh," Vinsant muttered under mask of the guard's second stomp and sharp salute. There was no question what the matter was. Tempers were likely to fray in the next few minutes, and that meant a very inconvenient delay in answers, for days, for eight-days even. He sidled into the archway after the mahktashaan in the hope of slowing Levi's exit long enough to force an answer. The guard paused in mid step and turned back, the curious creases at his eyes smoothing to wonder. Vinsant removed his hand from his crystal. The crimson illumination died. A pity the crystals in the sconces gave enough light for him to see the guard drop to one knee and, as the Inner Circle before him had done, intone, "All praise to Mahktos."

"Oh, turd of a scumhopper," Vinsant said, making frantic gestures for the man to rise. "Will someone please tell me what's going on?" A moment of astonished and rather uncomfortable silence ensued, during which Vinsant found his annoyance rising in equal measure with his alarm. Then Strauss laughed out loud.

"It seems our young friend still has much to learn," the jovial mahktashaan said.

Vinsant looked around to find merriment on the faces around him. His brows knitted together. "I know, and Mahktos said I must train well. But I intend to do better. Really I do." He hoped he was not the slap of a joke he would never understand.

"We know, Vinsant," Arun said before addressing the newcomer. "Perhaps you could humbly request the Shah's indulgence."

"With respect, Minoria," Nut-brown Crystal said. "The Shah has made it explicit your attendance was required yesterday. He is calling for mahktashaan blood."

"Robe him," Levi ordered, pointing at Vinsant. Vinsant blinked but the shortest mahktashaan was already disrobing. He helped Vinsant don the ridiculously large gown. Even rolling up the sleeves and tucking the hem of the garment into his churidar did little to prevent him stumbling after Levi and Arun. The way his bottom was padded out, Naikil was sure to make some jibe about him being in swaddling clothes.

"You will keep that hood up," Levi said.

"Am I in more trouble?" Vinsant asked Arun.

The Minoria looked over his shoulder without missing a step. "That depends," he said. "Do you have any idea what has the Shah so upset?"

The Shah was upset indeed. Vinsant had never seen him in so foul a mood. Karie and Samille were huddled on the quilted spread on the poster bed, gazing in fear at their ruler, whose nostrils were flaring wide across his purple face. The girls weren't even sparing a glance for Mariano, and Vinsant knew from Kordahla they normally could not keep their eyes off the hotshot heir to the throne, even Karie who made google eyes at one of the mahktashaan. His arrogant, handsome brother was staring at Ahkdul, who was leaning forward, his fists clenched and his red face tense enough to split open if he tried to speak a single word. In front of them all, on a shadowed area of the cold, stone floor, two mahktashaan knelt, heads dipped so low their chins touched their chest.

Levi and Arun halted at the edge of the rug. "Majesty," Levi said, as he and Arun bowed low. Vinsant decided it was a good time to show the utmost respect, and followed suit.

"Princess Kordahla is missing," the Shah said. "From what I can gather from this group of incompetent imbeciles, she was last in your company, Minoria."

Arun bowed his hooded head in acknowledgement. "She was, Majesty, until late last night."

"And what, pray tell, was the betrothed Princess of Terlaan doing in your company at such an hour?" Vinsant winced at the uncharacteristic bite in the Shah's tone. Karie and Samille drew their legs onto the bed and huddled tighter together.

"The Princess was disturbed by the earlier events of the day. She was seeking both counsel and reassurance about the djinn."

The Shah's eyes narrowed. "And you decided to check on her state of mind? After sundown?" Vinsant felt his stomach churn. How could Father put his sister's honour at stake like that? The Majoria and Minoria were sworn to protect the royal family. Tradition held them, of all men, above reproach when mingling with the women of the household.

One of the kneeling guards shuffled. "Majesty, I fetched the Minoria at the Princess's request," he said.

"Did you return her to this room, Minoria?"

"I did not. The matter of Prince Vinsant's safety drew my attention. I left the Princess at the northern walls as I dived into the lake after the prince took a fall."

Vinsant would not have believed Father's anger could grow, but his eyes almost bulged from their sockets as he looked at his youngest child. "What foolery is this?" he snarled when Arun was done relating the night's events. He strode towards Vinsant and grabbed at his arm but caught only the wide fabric of the sleeve.

"The boy will remain robed," Levi said with all the authority of his position.

"His sister is missing and he is the last to claim to see her. I will look upon his face when I question him," the Shah said, yanking the hood down.

Vinsant gurgled as the Shah stumbled back. Mahktos had to have turned him into a toad or a puffer, the way Father was spluttering. He didn't think he could live with himself if that was the price he had to pay.

"What is the meaning of this?" the Shah demanded at last.

Vinsant wanted to add his voice to that demand but, with Father in his current mood, leaping into the conversation uninvited was a spectacularly bad idea. Father was clutching the carved bedpost so tight, he wouldn't have been surprised if it snapped in two.

"It is a mahktashaan matter," Levi responded.

"Djinn roam my halls, my daughter goes missing and my younger son appears robed before me to hide his face, and you dare tell me it is not my concern."

Vinsant made an exaggerated openhanded shrug while mouthing a screamed *What?* Any other day he would have been glad his brother started. Today, he was relieved Mariano recovered super quick and pointed at Kordahla's dresser. He shuffled across the room with no grace whatsoever, the doubled hem of the overlong gown catching beneath his feet. Hitching up the sleeves, he picked up Kordahla's looking glass and surveyed his completely normal looking hands. He was pleased to note the robe was so voluminous that his fear of looking like a swaddled child was groundless. He would have to parade past the other apprentices before Levi made him take it off. Then he caught sight of his quartz. Opaque quartz it was, but instead of the creamy pink stone he and the other apprentices had received at their initiation, this one was crimson. Like Mahktos eyes crimson. Naikil and Gram were going to be mega jealous! He tilted the looking glass to practice his smirk. And in his shock promptly dropped it.

"Stinking scumhopper droppings!" His heart beating wild, he picked up the cracked glass and studied the segments which reflected his eyes. Whichever way he turned it, his irises, all praise to Mahktos, were a crimson that matched the stone. He dropped the glass on the inlaid dresser and spun to face Levi and Arun.

"What's going on?" he asked, wilting as the two kneeling mahktashaan sang the god's praises.

"I think I know who my Majoria will be," Mariano said, glancing at Levi.

Father had turned white. It didn't suit him any better than purple. "How is this possible? It takes years to train as a mahktashaan. You said so yourself."

"Mahktos has marked Mahktashaan Apprentice Prince Vinsant for his own." Levi's voice was strained, like this was a bad thing. He stepped onto the rug, turning to face Vinsant. "Twice, this young apprentice has stood in the presence of the god and lived to tell the tale." Now he sounded almost jealous. Looked it too, from what Vinsant could glimpse of the glint in those black eyes under the hanging hood. Vinsant took a step back. He was beginning to think his apprenticeship would be simpler with a plain piece of quartz around his neck. "Mahktos's favour is bound to be of import," Levi continued in his breathy, gravelly voice, "but I gauge the matter of Princess Kordahla more pressing."

Speechless, but drained of anger, thank the Vae, Father ogled Vinsant. "Was Kordahla in your room last night?"

Vinsant shook his head. "I lied," he said, deciding the truth was best in the presence of parent and master. "*He* was hanging about," he said, folding his arms and thrusting his chin towards Ahkdul. The swine looked like an ogre even in neat, decent dress. "She doesn't like him. She doesn't want to marry him."

"That is a declaration I would hear from her own lips, in front of this entire company," Ahkdul said.

"She's already said so," Vinsant said, snorting the words. "Not that any of you care what she thinks."

"Enough!" the Shah roared. "You are not too old for a thrashing."

If Vinsant had learned anything about Father over the years, it was that he made no idle threats. He glowered at them both because no way was he willing to submit to the humiliation in front of the pervert.

Levi tapped one of the kneeling mahktashaan on the shoulder and whispered in his ear. The man rose and left the room.

Vinsant didn't understand why Father couldn't see right through Ahkdul's calculating calm. "If you wish to withdraw from our agreement, I would know now," the swine said. "Otherwise, I demand she be punished for this dereliction. And know, for all your understanding of my nature, Shah Wilshem, I will not wed a dishonoured woman."

The Shah, pacing from one of the bedroom rugs to the other, did not spare Ahkdul a glance. "There is blood honour to uphold. If she has disgraced her title and family, I will mete out justice myself."

Vinsant sidled to Mariano. His brother would have chosen to stand in a patch of light. "What's going to happen?" he asked while Father yelled for one page after another, and sent them off to unlikely destinations, from the stables to the dungeons.

Mariano looked at him as though he were a problem child. Under the circumstances, with his crimson eyes and mahktashaan robe, Vinsant thought that rather inappropriate. "We're going to look for her. Do you know anything about this?" Vinsant shook his head. One could not trust a brother who wanted to serve up one's prize grapper for dinner. When Mariano said, "This time, she has gone too far," he was glad he had chosen not to confide.

The mahktashaan Levi had dispatched returned with another and resumed his place next to his kneeling comrade.

"You were stationed at the gate, last night," the Shah said. It was not a question.

"Majesty, Princess Kordahla came to the gate to check on Prince Vinsant. When a genie appeared and seized the Princess's veil, I gave chase."

"You left your post unguarded. You left the Princess alone. Outside the gate." The Shah's voice was dangerously low and his face had coloured again. "Majoria, these men are in dereliction of their duty."

"Mahktos is exacting. Mahktos is just," the Majoria said. Vinsant began to panic.

Sure enough, the three mahktashaan, despondent resignation in their voices, answered with "All praise to Mahktos." The Majoria held out his hand. One by one, they removed their crystals from around their neck and looped the thong over Levi's hand. Then they rose and followed the Majoria from the room.

"What's going to happen to those Mahktashaan?" Vinsant asked Arun as Father stormed from the room and everyone else, except Karie and Samille, began to disperse. The dumb girls were weeping, like that was going to help anyone.

"They are to be put to death."

"Because I lied?" Vinsant asked, his eyes wide. He thought he might cry too.

"No. Because they failed in their duty to protect the Princess. Regardless of what you claimed, they should have checked after her safety. As should have I."

"Father doesn't blame you, does he?"

"I'm sure he does. But your little prank absolved my leaving her. I am lucky that was inside the gates. Had it been outside, I would share their fate. You are well aware a mahktashaan's first task is to protect the royal family. Now report to Branak. You are to keep the hood up and to avoid discussing anything that befell you before Mahktos. If he's busy, tell him I said to give you Guntek's tome on the crystals."

"What are you going to do?"

"I'm going to join the search for Princess Kordahla."

Chapter Thirty

DAWN BROKE WITH AMAZING speed, an explosion of red that, were Kordahla to believe the tales, portended an ill-fated day. The horse was dragging its dusty hooves after hours of travel on the straight, southbound road. In front of her, Timak dozed, his fragile body sagging against her. Yawning, she glanced over her shoulder as she had done with constant fear throughout the night. They were in plain view of farmers beginning their daily toil in burgeoning fields of wheat. Catching sight of her black robe, the peasants downed their tools and dropped to one knee. Kordahla lowered her hooded head, drew the cloak across her shoulders and forced herself to ride a dirt road towards a ramshackle cottage. The arrogant mahktashaan would have done no less. She clenched her jaw as a worn woman emerged, her young ones clinging to her skirt while she deposited a small loaf of bread and hunk of cheese in their path. With a wary nod, she backed into the house.

Kordahla reined in the horse and nudged Timak awake. "Go get it," she said.

The boy slid off, collected the meal, and allowed her to lift him back up. Unwilling to tarry, she kicked the horse on, careful to allow the sleeve of her robe to cover her delicate hands. If this was how the populace revered the mahktashaan, starvation would be the least of their problems. The poor might suffer a pang of hunger for their generosity–she could bear the twinge of guilt when she was in direr straights than they. Out of sight of the cottage, Kordahla turned the horse into grass long enough to obscure them if they lay. The horse needed to rest and graze, and sleep pulled at her heavy eyes. They tucked into the crude breakfast on horseback, guarding it from the fat crows strutting to peck the falling crumbs. Timak slid off as soon as he had licked his fingers, and she followed. One hand yet on the roan horse's withers, she looked up and down the road. The hard ground was no bed for a princess, and a traveller would investigate a bridled mount. There were brigands, too; she had heard Father rant of the horrors they perpetrated on the unwary. Beside her, Timak folded to the ground and curled up unconcerned. Despite the burning heat on the back of her hand, Kordahla rubbed her arms. On a sharp intake of breath, she shuddered.

"You can rest," Timak murmured. "Genie will keep watch." He was asleep within seconds.

After a final, fleeting scan of the bare horizon, Kordahla braved the coarse grass. She ran a dry blade through her fingers. A day ago, she would never have sat on earth without a servant spreading a thick rug for her. Had she really dared to run away? To take her life into her own hands, she corrected. One thing was sure: she could never go back. Honour would see her imprisoned in the tower under constant guard. If Father allowed her to live. Defying his wishes was unthinkable, but to bring shame on his head in front of Verdaan. . . his anger would raze the thoughts from her head. She shuddered again as she clutched the quartz pendant at her chest. It was her one link to Vinsant. She hoped he was not suffering on her account.

It seemed a mere moment later that the urgent voice sounded in her ear. In truth, it must have been hours, for the sun beat high overhead.

"Wake up." Timak was standing between her and the road, his head just visible above the grass. "Wake up." He was a picture of misery as he twisted his neck to check the danger. He rustled back as she eased up with a grimace for her sore muscles, silent and still now he had her attention. Vinsant would have been all rough and tumble over her. Vinsant would have devised some mischievous scheme to avert whatever danger threatened. This rigid child faced the road, waiting for her to assume control when she had no idea what she might do other than to stand in the hope the figure of a mahktashaan might scare off whoever approached.

Lady Luck had veiled her face; it was a mahktashaan who lurked by the road. She grabbed Timak and pushed him toward the horse. The child had the presence of mind to grab the horse's withers and hoist himself on. She mounted after him and kicked the horse into a sedate walk, hoping a wave might discourage an approach.

"Halt!" the mahktashaan called.

The smallest scrutiny would be her undoing. Kordahla urged the horse into a trot.

"I said halt!" the mahktashaan called.

She chanced a look over her shoulder. His cream crystal held a soft glow. She spurred the horse into a gallop, pushing Timak down so she might lean low over its neck. Dear Vae, but she hoped that Levi stationed the less adept in this unpopulated, minor satrapy. Her hope died as on either side of the horse, grass sizzled to cinders: a warning, given the precision of the blasts. She sat up and reigned in the horse, knowing too well the form mahktashaan justice took. In front of her Timak sniffed.

"Now would be a very good time for that genie friend of yours to do something."

Timak shook his head. He had to be scared out of his wits. Her heart went out to him. At Ahkdul's hand, she would live in misery borne of freedom lost, but for this child, already little more than a shell, perverse torture awaited, if not a lingering death.

"I mean it, Timak."

The mahktashaan glided towards them. He pointed a hand at her heart. "Dismount and disrobe."

A princess after all, she remained where she was, shifting her shoulders back and lifting her head high despite her thundering heart.

"I will not ask you again." The crystal pulsed with threatening light.

Her hand touched the soft hood, tentative, unwilling. His surprise might, just might, purchase an escape before the thought-link that would seal their fate. The surprise was hers. A whirlwind erupted between them, a dizzying, indigo blur which gained form as it twirled into the sky until the devious djinn loomed above. Arms and ankles crossed, he flashed a black-toothed grin and bellowed out an evil laugh.

"Puny soldier." Bending his head, the djinn blew a gust that knocked the mahktashaan off his feet. "This little trinket is mine."

The mahktashaan regained his feet fast. His crystal was aglow with light that blasted right through the breadth of day. It remained steadfast against his chest even as his cloak and hood whipped back to reveal an age-spotted face and greying hair. His squinting eyes and dripping nose left no doubt the wind raged strong, yet his feet stood firmly on the ground as his lips moved in incantation. Untouched by the storm, the nervous horse fidgeted under her. The hairs on her arms prickling, she backed him up, wanting to be far from the creature that made sport of her humiliation. The pit of her stomach growled at the memory of the wanton image of her atop the ship. *The Kordahla*, she remembered with a start. Suddenly, whatever justice the mahktashaan might mete out seemed inconsequential next to the degradation the djinn had bestowed. She forced the shying horse into the raking wind.

"Imbecile!" the djinn roared. The indigo crystals in his joints flared so bright they overwhelmed the shimmer of his skin. "Do you crave the humiliations of that swine of a Verdaani?"

She stretched her fingers in silent plea to the mahktashaan. He was standing his ground, his lips working at some spell she could not hear. His crystal burst bright with ineffectual light, but the wind gusted, forcing him back step by step. The shimmering djinn laughed. A muted glow sparked in the crystals in his joints as he lunged at her. Her horse reared. She struggled for control, found herself facing the other way.

"Shall I show you again what lies in store for the Princess of Terlaan, display it high for all who pass to see?"

A snap of the djinn's fingers quelled the wind. With a terror she was unable to control, Kordahla urged the horse into a gallop.

❖ ❖ ❖

The three robed executioners pulled the hoods off the heads of the kneeling condemned. Levi's right hand came down. They swung their blades, precise and clean. He allowed the three coloured crystals to topple from his other hand. They dissolved before they hit the blooded cloaks. Mahktashaan justice was swift.

He caught movement at the library window high above as he strode the width of the secluded courtyard. A startled face was peering down. It was just. The spoilt brat needed to learn of consequences. This dereliction in duty reflected on them all. To have men dead on account of an apprentice and a *woman* was unconscionable. The apprentice would bow to him before this was done. Thrice over he, Levi, Majoria, had earned the favour Mahktos so cavalierly bestowed on a *boy*. As for the princess, she would pay for the liberty when he found her. Oh, yes, she would pay for the death of his men.

A gentle nudge intruded on his thoughts. *All praise to Mahktos. All honour to you, Majoria.*

Well? he demanded, granting the Minoria permission to thought-link.

Mahktashaan are dispersing in every possible direction. The Inner Circle is contacting those in the nearest villages and towns.

Whether the overindulged princess travelled the Arezou River, crossed Lake Sheraz or headed inland, she would be found. And then… Levi swallowed. He would consider it his duty to re-educate her on the role of women in this realm. She was much too headstrong for one of the fair sex, flaunting her lascivious body as though unaware of the passions it roused. Blood honour or not, Wilshem *would* entrust her to him. He would ensure it. Would ensure the shah understood the mistake he made. Had the fish not fallen upon him before it hit the perverted Verdaani lord? Had Shah Guntek, founder of their order, not sanctified the marriage of mahktashaan and royal?

Another mind bumped him out of his thoughts. *All praise to Mahktos. All honour to you, Majoria.*

Report, Levi snapped.

The piddling presence identified itself as Zermane of the cream crystal. His flustering if not his talent demanded note. *An impostor has just passed through the region. She wore the garb of a mahktashaan but with an apprentice's opaque quartz around her neck.* The stream of thought hesitated. *It is only an impression you understand, but I think I am correct to say her. I think it was a woman and not a man.*

Explain, Levi demanded. He wanted to take every detail to the Shah.

Her hands. It was all I saw of her, but they were delicate. There was a boy, too. I was about to apprehend them when an indigo djinn appeared.

Levi's hands curled into fists, his nails digging harder and harder into his palms. The foolish girl would stand cursed to the end of her life if she had dealt. All the more reason for the shah to entrust her to him. Most powerful of the mahktashaan, he alone might salvage her soul. *It is the Princess Kordahla*, he said. *You will pursue her. Risk every breath of your life to return her to the palace unharmed.* He snapped off the link.

Arun's voice immediately intruded into his mind. *I will see if Vinsant knows anything of this.*

Levi cursed himself for not severing their link when Zermane had initiated contact. It was an indulgent thought. The Minoria had as much right to the information. For now. It seemed his second had gained a measure of the girl's trust. The princess would never have accompanied *him* through the gardens unless ordered. His breaths sounded harsh to his own ears. *I will be there*, he snarled. It would not do for the royal children to have one to whom they could turn before him.

Yes, Majoria. All honour to you, came the respectful reply.

Vinsant stopped shuffling down the hall, and turned to look at the two mahktashaan flanking him.

"I suppose you're here to make sure I get to Mahktashaan Branak?"

"If you wish, Highness."

The title took a moment to register. "Highness? Oh, you're guarding me," he said, perking up. He had assumed this pair were either accompanying a wayward apprentice, studying a mahktashaan freak or, worst of all, shadowing an accessory to Kordahla's flight.

"Orders of His Majesty and the Majoria."

"We're taking a detour to the library." With all the fuss, nobody was likely to notice if he played hooky for a while. Hitching up the robe, he doubled his pace, letting fly one or two childish sounds as he tripped over the hem and ordering a loitering page to bring enough food for an army. Talking to a god had left him with a hunger mightier than his curiosity.

"Wait here," he ordered at the doors, scrutinising the men for any sign of protest. Getting none, he closeted himself inside and considered the rather impossible task of finding a detailed map of Terlaan among the musty tomes on the oversized shelves. He located a somewhat faded one rolled on an upper shelf next to a window after climbing on the huge desk and pulling off an assortment of scrolls. He jumped down, pushed the oversized, leather chair to the side and swept the ink vials, quills, paperweights and books to the back of the desk so he could unroll it. As he was smoothing the crackles out, the page entered with a silver tray of snacks. Vinsant was halfway through a gooey apple pie when he chanced to look out of the window, down onto the courtyard below. Letting the pie drop from his hand onto the map, he cursed as three unhooded heads rolled in the execution yard. He jerked back as Levi looked up. The Majoria would blame him, and it *was* his fault. He swept the pie from the map. It was difficult to concentrate on anything but the greasy smudge it left right across the Olono Range when he was choking up. Those mahktashaan had been good men. Ranesh had a hunting hawk he had once allowed Vinsant to fly, and Sagtir had mentioned a young family a few times. He didn't know the third but he could imagine a whole life.

A rap sounded at the door. Vinsant ignored it in favour of deciphering the apple-stained name of a village. "I don't want to be disturbed," he said, springing to his feet and glowering at Lord Ahkdul when the doors opened to admit the intruder.

"The Shah has given me access to the entire palace."

"Well she's obviously not in here." He picked up the pie, bit off a large mouthful he really didn't feel like and sat on the cracking seat, chewing noisily. It was a mistake. Swallowing made him feel quite queasy. The apple tumbled out of the pastry onto his lap as the swine crossed the floor to stand behind him. The whiff of stale, unwashed skin oozing through the oceans of man's sandalwood perfume didn't help settle Vinsant's tummy any.

"My page is missing," Ahkdul said, looking over his shoulder at the map.

"He's not in here either." Vinsant dumped the remaining crust on the tray.

"I suspect he's with Kordahla, which gives me twice the motive to find her." The swine lowered his voice and placed a tight hand on Vinsant's shoulder. "And twice the reason to discipline her."

"Then go look for her," he said, pretending to study the contours of the land when all he could concentrate on was that brutish hand.

"As soon as you tell me where she is."

"How should I know?" He felt a thrill of nerves that had nothing to do with his secret and everything to do with the swine's proximity.

"From that map," Ahkdul said, sliding his hand onto Vinsant's chest.

A corner of the map rustled into a curl as Vinsant twisted up and out of Ahkdul's clasp. He tried to sidestep, but he was pinned between the desk and the large body. Kicking the chair out of the way, the disgusting swine pressed close, forcing him to lean back over the desk. His hood fell back and Ahkdul, looking straight into his eyes, flinched. In that moment, Vinsant squirmed sideways. He was blocked by a thrust of Ahkdul's leg.

"Get away from me." Bile was burning his gullet. He pushed at the man's chest. "Get away before I call the guards and have them throw you in the dungeon."

"Hush," Ahkdul said, putting a squat finger on Vinsant's lips. "You are in a compromising position. Do you really want the mahktashaan to find you like this, their revered protégé just a little boy unable to defend himself?" He planted a moist kiss on Vinsant's forehead and stepped away.

For a shocking second, Vinsant lost all thought. Then a white-hot embarrassment exploded in him.

"Go on. Call the guards. The moment for accusations is past, Vinsant," Ahkdul jibed as he took a breath to do just that. "Do you think they will believe you after your outburst earlier?"

"You pig!" Vinsant flew at Ahkdul, pummelling him with every limb. The swine had the audacity to laugh, to catch his hands, pull him into his sickening odour, use the assault as an excuse to grope. Too late Vinsant realised his mistake. He went limp. Without the excuse for contact, Ahkdul was forced to drop his hands.

"You will never find her!" Vinsant said, his voice so low it was barely audible. He would never let this pig have Kordahla. Not if he had to kill him.

"Don't be so sure. Dozens of mahktashaan are combing every inch of the land as we speak."

"Not even they can go everywhere." The hate was talking now. He wanted Ahkdul to stew.

Ahkdul stepped forward. "Where is she?"

Vinsant stepped back. "Where you can't get to her!" He regretted the words the instant they were out, but in this poisonous mood he had no control.

"Ah," said Ahkdul, his eyes dropping to the map. "Then she's not in Terlaan."

Vinsant glowered and bit his tongue till he tasted blood.

"So where is she?" Ahkdul said, coming towards him. "Not Verdaan, if the mahktashaan are barred." Vinsant moved back. Ahkdul kept coming. "Myklaan then."

"Guards!" Vinsant bellowed, feeling smaller than a gnat for his indiscretion. The blood drained from his face when the Majoria entered behind them.

Levi took in his dishevelled state, pointed at Ahkdul and said, "Leave." Flecks of dried blood dotted his hand. Ranesh's blood. It was more than Vinsant could cope with. Clutching his stomach, he doubled over and emptied its contents onto the floor. As Ahkdul strode out, Levi extended a hand to his forehead.

"Don't touch me," Vinsant barked, swiping at Levi's arm. His cheeks flamed brighter when he saw Arun had entered the room, but he would die if someone's flesh touched his body.

"Prince Vinsant has confided that Kordahla is headed for Myklaan,"

Ahkdul said from the door. "I expect her to be found before she crosses the border."

"I asked you to leave," Levi said. His threatening glide hurried the Verdaani lord out of the room.

The Minoria asked a servant in to clean the vomit. "What happened, Vinsant?" he asked, closing the door.

Vinsant sank to the floor and rested against a bookcase. He was shaking and his breathing was ragged. And he wanted to vomit again. Arun sat down beside him, mimicking his pose with arms around bent knees, waiting until the servant left.

"What happened?" Arun asked again. "Did Ahkdul touch you?"

"He tried," Vinsant replied. "Though I don't suppose you'll believe me."

Arun gave him a strange look, stood and went to have a word with the mahktashaan guards. "You are never to be alone in his presence. Those mahktashaan have been charged with seeing that is so. Do not evade them, Vinsant, or they will suffer the same fate as Kordahla's guards."

It was not what he wanted to hear, and he retched.

"Stand up," Levi said. "You are not a babe. You should have called for those guards as soon as he entered the room." Vinsant stiffened. "You deceived us, Apprentice. Do you wish to confess?"

Pouting at Arun, he murmured, "I knew you wouldn't believe me."

"Enough!" Levi said, in much the same tone Father used when he was at the end of his patience. "I speak of your conduct among us. Your quartz was not lost. You gave the symbol of your office to a lay person, a *woman*, then organised a diversion that allowed the very person you are training to protect to roam into danger. Your liberties with your training and your superiors are unforgivable."

"Mahktos knows," Vinsant said through clenched teeth.

They were exactly the wrong words. Levi loomed over him, almost as close as Ahkdul had been. Beneath his hood, his black eyes glared something fierce. "But I did not! Your deception is inexcusable. Not only have you violated our trust but you have also placed a member of the royal family at risk. Your behaviour warrants punishment. By my authority as Majoria, you are sentenced to the Crystalite Mines for a period of one eight-day." The Majoria turned to face Arun. The two mahktashaan engaged in silent, intense concentration that set his heart thumping and teeth chattering. Then Levi strode from the room.

Vinsant slid back down to the floor. He wished he could slow his nervous breaths. "He's s-sending me a-away?" he asked as Arun joined him. "How can he do that when Mahktos sanctioned my actions? Ahkdul should be the one to leave."

"Do not question me on this. The Majoria has forbidden me to talk on it. Suffice it to say, this is not what it seems. He is right in this, Vinsant. The mahktashaan are founded on loyalty and rank. You must respect that if you are to succeed in this office."

Vinsant shook his head, then tilted it back, dislodging some books. Too much was happening at once. It was impossible to know where to start making sense of it all.

Arun settled that for him. "We need to talk about Kordahla."

"Ahkdul thinks she is riding for Myklaan."

"Riding. She has a horse then?" Arun asked.

Really too much was happening. It was unlike him to make slips like this. "I just assumed. She would already be caught if she was on foot, wouldn't she?"

"Nice try, Vinsant, but I think you know. Now are you going to talk to me?"

Vinsant stared straight ahead, arms folded on his knees.

Arun sighed. He stood, removed his robe and hung it over the leather chair. Taking a deep breath, he clutched the crystal at his chest, lifted it over his neck, and placed it atop the robe. Then he sat back down, his arm against Vinsant's shoulder.

"You can't do that," Vinsant said. "The mahktashaan are always mahktashaan, even when they're not working." The remarkable blue in the Minoria's eyes was already fading.

"Vinsant," Arun said gently. "The mahktashaan are here to protect you. And right now, I think the best chance I have of protecting both you and Princess Kordahla is by getting you to confide in me. Tell me as one man to another and I promise whatever you say will remain a confidence. A mahktashaan has already sighted the Princess. It is only a matter of time before she is found. Both Ahkdul and the Shah are in foul moods over her flight. If one of them invokes blood honour, she will need someone to champion her cause."

The kindness was his undoing. The pent-up mix of fear and guilt ruptured in a single sob. He wiped the traitorous dampness in his eyes with the back of his hand, stiffening as Arun gave him a quick hug.

"There is no shame in tears. A grown man may cry if the occasion calls for it."

"Yeah." Without thinking, he was pouring out his guilty heart. It felt so good to have someone else know, he had to catch himself before he admitted to stealing the crystal. Somehow, he did not think that act would be in any way forgivable.

"Are you sure she made no pact with the djinn?" Arun asked. "Perhaps his assistance in her escape for some curse on her life?"

Vinsant shook his head. "She said no boon was worth the price."

"Let us beseech Mahktos she remains of that mind."

"Father can't make her marry that man."

"There is more to politics than looking after those you love," said Arun.

"So you're just going to hand her over to him?" It came out as a growl.

"I am going to do what I can to see her happy, Vinsant. But surely you understand, if she reaches Myklaan, it could mean war."

CHAPTER THIRTY-ONE

A SQUELCH WARNED KORDAHLA to pull up. They had been riding hard along the Arezou River for hours, and the horse was lagging. The grassed verge had ceded to damp earth, which was becoming more sodden with each step. If that was not warning enough the scums drew near, the reek of decay pervaded the hot, still air. Neither man nor horse could traverse those stinking marshes without an experienced guide. They would have to follow the river along its turn to the west from here. Walking to land firm enough to bear them back south would eat precious time, and they would first have to find the ford. Wide and fast flowing, white water churning over rocks, the Arezou River offered no inkling of where it might be safe to cross. She looked behind them. Down the road, a black speck was raising dust as it raced to catch up.

"Can you swim?" she asked Timak without hope of making it to the other bank alive. He gave a small nod. He had retreated into himself and she, too tired and dazed and disbelieving of what she had got them into, did not have the strength to draw him out. At least he was more alert now, startled by what had occurred in the field and curious about the land.

The horse was refusing to walk on, so she dismounted and led it. Surely if they kept close to the bank, they would succeed in reaching the hills. These waters reached Lake Arezou untainted. Boulders or solid earth had to keep them separate from scum. She started to climb the rocky bank. The horse could not pass, but if they were lucky, they might find some nook in which to hide. Shooting another look around, she let out a cry; the speck had assumed the form of a mahktashaan.

"The ford's yonder," a creaky voice said in the antiquated dialect of the scum dippers. A man covered in filth from head to toe climbed over a rock and walked towards them. "Though ye'll not be a swimming it in that garb." Kordahla spun, slipped off a rock and almost twisted her ankle as he hopped past, bringing the stench of rot with him. Under the layer of muck, he was naked save for a loincloth and a knobbly bag over one shoulder. Though he moved with the agility of a mountain goat upon his spindly legs, his lean ribs and gaunt face suggested the thinning of age. Without pause, he jumped into the river and began scrubbing. The agitated water whipped sticks right past.

"What lies on the other side?" she asked.

The scum dipper closed one eye and looked at her. "Nothing but fields and farms and the scum dipper town. Ye interested in derral, lady?"

Rare and expensive, derral was a princess's dream. In the palace, she had exclaimed over the prized rainbow lining of the coychan shells found nestling deep in the scums. As for Pashderral, the scum dipper town was a wonder. Its large dwellings, their facades inlaid with derral, were said to rival even Myklaani villas in beauty, and no wonder because the scum dippers were among the richest citizens of Terlaan. Never mind the stink that oozed from every pore of their body after years of diving the foetid scums. It took a special man – or woman – to ply this trade, and they received ample rewarded. The scum dippers were the Shah's people to the last, for few others could afford the derral that sustained the scum dippers' lavish lifestyle. She would be god-blessed to avoid capture in that town.

She made her decision in a heartbeat. "We're interested in a guide, to take us across the scums. This instant." The mahktashaan had drawn so close she could pick out his crystal in the glint of the sun.

The dipper closed one eye and looked at the rider. "Trouble ye be in, then."

"You can have the horse, and I'll pay a purse of gold."

She had not expected him to chuckle. "You can't take the horse across. He was already mine, if he doesn't die under the boy." He wagged his head and sucked on his cheek, considering at his leisure. "Aye," he said. "I'll take ye."

"Right now," she said, when he insisted on scrubbing his hair with his webbed hands. She wrinkled her nose because she could smell him from here. She shuddered to think the vapours in the scums would overpower even his reek.

With an exaggerated sigh, he climbed out of the river. "Well it's not scum dipping we be going," he said, and leapt back to the sodden ground, then onward, not waiting for them nor offering to help with the bundle she pulled from the horse. They scampered after him as best they could, Kordahla sparing only a passing thought for the mud that sullied her hem. Mud, she thought with a wry inward smile, was what had got her here in the first place.

A slimy green blob of an animal sprung up in front of her and she started. When it landed with a plonk, she almost tripped in an attempt to avoid stepping on it.

The old man laughed. "Ye not be scared of scumhoppers now, be ye?" he called back.

Walking became more of an effort. Their boots sank deeper with every step, the mud sucking them loose from their feet. The barefoot dipper was walking easy, but Kordahla was determined to hold her boots to the last. The terrain in the hills would be rough. If they made it that far.

The mud gave way to ooze. She gagged on the noxious vapours rising off the slate coloured water and batted at aggressive dragonflies as they passed gnarled and stunted trees groping their way out of the scums. Puffers broke the surface just long enough to snare the buzzing insects with a sticky tongue, and scumhoppers skimmed the top, their bulbous webbed feet able to hold them on the surface until they sprang to withered lily leaves, the only green vegetation in the water.

"Mind ye be walking behind me," the scum dipper said.

Kordahla took extreme care to match his footsteps heel to the toe. Whether by some uncanny sense or long years of experience, the old man led them a wending path that had them slush no more than ankle deep in muck. The foul liquid splashed cold upon her calves. Scumhopper excrement mixed with mineral leach was what the scholars proclaimed the scums. The rich cared not while derral came in abundance. She cared less with a mahktashaan hounding her. She chanced a look back. He sat astride his horse, a midnight figure on a midnight mount, watching them wind their way through the bleak barrens. She took a step without turning her head, splashed knee deep into the scum, and cried out as her stomach lurched from the stumble.

The old man shook his head. "Be more of this if ye continue. 'Tis when ye be in to yer chest or over yer head ye have to worry. Them's where the bazwaeels live."

At mention of the razor-toothed beast, she scrabbled back onto the path. Behind them, the mahktashaan had entered the scums. Every few steps, he paused and turned, continuing when his crystal glowed. Kordahla could only hope his was the slower path. Then, in front of her, Timak stopped and squealed.

"What's wrong?" she asked.

He pleaded with his wide, frightened eyes. She tried to take his hand and pull but his body lurched forward, one leg trapped in whatever lay beneath the muck.

Their guide clucked his tongue. "Told ye be careful, didn't I?" He rubbed one foot against the other calf and closed one eye as Kordahla tugged harder.

Three bubbles burst the surface in succession. "Now yer just lucky, ain't ye?" the dipper said, and launched himself into the ooze at Timak's feet. Kordahla held her breath, willing him to reappear. The seconds passed, and then Timak lurched forward, a bootless foot lifted from the mire. She caught him as he toppled. The dipper broke the surface, a large knobbly shell in hand, and winked at the boy. "Ye wanna be rich, ye just apprentice to old Ali," he said. He grinned as Timak retched, and added, "You'll get a-used to the stench."

"Hurry," Kordahla said through the segment of cloak she had lifted over her nose. The mahktashaan was a mere hundred paces behind. The grinning dipper led them deeper into the scums. The wretched wastes stretched to the hilly haze on the horizon. They would not traverse these mires in a day. Eventually, they would need to rest. If the mahktashaan conjured a light after dark, they would have no hope of evading him.

"Here now," Ali said, alighting on a mound of earth. At its centre, a barren tree's twisted branches bent to the water at awkward angles.

It was a relief to set foot on the spongy, moss-covered islet. "Wait," she called as the scum dipper hopped back the way they had come. Ten paces out, he tossed the shell to Timak. "Just ye stay put if ye value yer lives," he said with a wag of his head.

Her dismay as Ali traced a nimble path towards the mahktashaan was lost on Timak. Her young companion was turning the shell over, oblivious to all else.

About halfway to the mahktashaan, Ali made a bow. "Be it these fugitives, ye seek?" he asked. "I can lead ye to them or lead them away. 'Tis all the same to me."

The mahktashaan moved on at a steady pace. "You'll be rewarded to keep them there."

"Ah me. Me poor, old body ain't as strong as it once was, and scum dipping be physical work, ye see. I've a need to supplement me income in me age, and the beauty's offered a full purse of gold." Ali sprang back towards her, finding his path with unerring precision. Not once did he look around as he zigzagged to the mound. His webbed feet might be aiding his balance, but Kordahla had to wonder if the scums were as treacherous as the tales would have them believe. They were scum dipper tales, after all, crafted to protect the folks' lucrative interest. A leap back, a step sideways, a shuffle along. Would Ali be so confident in his footing over treacherous ground?

"You will receive ample reward from the Shah himself," the mahktashaan said.

That decided her. "I'm going," she said to Timak, placing a tentative foot off the mound. The boy could make his own choice since he responded to her not at all. Like as not, he would be as scared of moving as he was of staying. If he even had the capacity to feel anymore. The Vae should curse Ahkdul thrice over for that. As for her fear, it was overcome by the anger she felt at Ali's betrayal. When the sole of her boot merely sloshed through a puddle before contacting firm ground, she strode out. Behind her, Timak's splashes marked his pursuit. There was nothing to finding this firm footing. She broke into a run.

"Halt! Halt! Ye dain't know where ye be going," the dipper called.

A glance over her shoulder caught him dancing towards her.

"It will be your head if any ill befalls them, dipper," the mahktashaan said.

No danger could menace so dark as the one closing in on them. Abandoning all care, Kordahla flew forward, straining in vain to detect solid land beneath the steam that wafted off the foul waters. A footing was there beneath her each step of the way.

And then it was not. Her foot slid through the muck and she was toppling into the stinking filth. It slithered warm into her nostrils, eyes and ears and mouth, dragging her down, binding her with its weight. It would be so easy to drift below. So easy had she not felt a searing stab at her breast. By some will of its own, the quartz around her neck drifted upwards. The pain subsided, but not her alarm. Her lungs began to burn even as she willed her sluggish hand to follow. It seemed an age before it heaved through the muck. Then her fingertips broke into humid air. She pushed and her hand came free. Ali seized it and yanked hard, the webbing between his fingers sticking fast to her skin. Her head popped into air. Ali adjusted his grip and hauled her onto a wet ledge. There was more strength in his sinewy limbs than she would have guessed. On hands and knees, she gasped for air, spat drops of the foul scum from her mouth. Her legs trembling, she watched the mahktashaan release his crystal from his hand. The quartz thudded against her chest, heavy as her mud soaked garb. She struggled out of the mahktashaan cloak and robe, taking the crystal and tucking it deep into her kameez.

Tremulous fingers touched her shoulder. She looked up at Timak, his eyes meeting her own for the first time. She closed her filthy hand over his, then stood on legs as gelatinous as a puffer. A tirade of abuse was streaming from Ali's mouth. She was not listening. The mahktashaan had taken another step. Holding Timak's hand, Kordahla placed a tentative foot forward and checked the ground. When she was sure it was solid, she placed her weight on it.

"No ye don't," Ali said, catching her above the elbow.

She spun and pushed him at the same time Timak kicked. The startled dipper fell into the muck. It sucked him under until there was no sign of him, save for the dented impression of a body on the surface. She touched her fingers to her clammy lips as the vapours wafted over the pool and clouded even that. Dear Vae, she hoped they had not just murdered a man. Then his fingers wriggled free, and she lost any trace of guilt.

"I can see the way," an urgent voice said. "It's a step to the right of the boy, and then three forward."

Kordahla snapped her head up. There in the misty sky a rose genie hung upside down, arms folded, legs crossed like she sat on an inverted cushion of vapour, her unbound hair falling up to her waist. Beaded chiffon covered her arms and legs, and pearls sequined her bodice. Kordahla made the warding sign but bit her lip when the genie's eyes clouded in hurt. Beside her, Timak was smiling, beaming even. He reached a hand up and wriggled his fingers. Kordahla shook her head. The boy had a genie after all. The trouble they could have saved if he had commanded her powers from the start.

"Come on." She grabbed Timak and followed the instructions. The genie righted herself, and floated along.

"I'm not talking to anyone," the rose genie said, looking at the hills, at a deep pool, at the mahktashaan. Looking everywhere but at them. "I'm just exploring this maze. There's a ridge two steps to the left of those humans and it runs ahead thirty paces or so."

This genie was as mad as the boy, but it was trust her advice or suffer the justice of blood honour. As she counted the last step, she looked back. They had gained a good few paces on the mahktashaan. As for Ali, he was dragging himself from the water. Covered in scum, he looked like a primal beast of the swamp. With a start, she realised she must look the same. The stench had thickened into a cloud, and the churning in the pit of her stomach suggested she was about to lose what little breakfast remained inside. Worse, the caking muck was not only hindering her joints but weighing her down. The pool to her left seemed liquid, if just as foul. She squatted and eased herself in, convinced it could be no worse than the mud. They would move faster and lose the weight of the caked mud swimming across.

"Get out! Get out!" Ali called, his arms waving wild. He was taking great strides towards her.

"Quick. Left. Two steps left then right," the rose genie said, sinking to their level but staying just out of reach.

Timak hesitated, torn between her and the genie.

"How dare you!" a voice Kordahla would never forget boomed. She froze as the indigo djinn popped into being. He sent the genie reeling head over heels with a vicious kick. The girl shrieked, and disappeared in a puff of rose smoke.

Scum streaming down her face, Kordahla paddled through the pool. The thick water tired her arms and legs. She angled for the side and grabbed a submerged crag. Ali was almost upon her, the mahktashaan not far behind. Given she had travelled a mere five feet, swimming was proving a poor choice. She wriggled her chest free of the pool to find her face level with a vermillion slipper. Her eyes travelled from the curled toe, up the leg, body and shimmering neck to the furious snarl of the indigo djinn.

"Djinn do not aid mortals without recompense," he said.

"We didn't ask for help," she said, unable to pull herself out with him in the way.

"But you got it," he said. His toe nudged her shoulder, pushing her back into the pool.

"Not by request."

"The genie will pay the price of her generosity."

"No," Timak said.

"Be gone, cockroach," the indigo djinn said. He blew Timak onto his bottom with a single puff. "And you, traitorous scum, this is no concern of yours." He flicked thumb against forefinger in Ali's direction.

The scum dipper flung back as though he were a piece of dirt scraped from a nail.

Kordahla edged along the submerged ridge. She tried to pull herself up but the djinn blocked her way. Under the water, a slimy creature slithered against her leg. She jerked her knee up, scraping it against the jagged reef. "Let me up," she said, scrambling onto his foot. He kicked her in. She flailed her arms. Her chin dipped into the water. She tilted her head to keep her mouth free of the disgusting brew. Blunt teeth nibbled her calf through the fabric of her shalvar and she cried out.

"Do you wish for help, little gnat?" the djinn asked.

"No," she said, stretching to grip a crag.

The djinn stepped on her fingers. "The mahktashaan approaches." He pressed down with his foot. Sharp rock cut through her fingers.

She pulled her hand free, opening wounds. "He will not imperil my soul," she said, and struck out across the pool. A band twined around her ankle. She yanked her foot away, calming herself by watching slender brown weeds wave in a clear patch of scum. The next stroke brought her up against something hard. She grappled for purchase but her fingers slid against indigo muscle.

"I can take you out of here. I will not ask for your soul," the djinn said. He stood in the water, his arms crossed. She kicked back.

"What then?" She meant her question as a distraction, so she could concentrate on what Cream Crystal was doing. The mahktashaan's stone was aglow, but her attention snapped to the water as a slimy tentacle wrapped around her wrist. She cried out and jerked her arm into the air. The action drew up a puffer, eyes bulging in astonishment. It retracted its tentacles into its swollen, whiskered face and dropped back into the water on its tadpole-like tail. Kordahla sobbed in relief. The amphibian was harmless to everything except the bloated insects it ate. Not so the mahktashaan. He had stepped to the edge of the pool. From his utter stillness, she guessed he was thought-linking. It would not take the djinn to keep her in this stinking cesspool until the Shah sent his army.

"You are running out of time. I wish only to claim an unwanted gift," the djinn persisted.

"You may take whatever possession of mine I have left at the palace," she said, trying to swim around him to no avail. His body appeared in whichever direction she struck. If there was an item of whose value she was ignorant, he was welcome to it.

"This is nothing you have yet," he said floating out of the water.

She kicked forward. Her foot contacted an object soft and spongy. She felt it slide between her legs. Something sharp cut her thigh. Her scream startled Timak into a sympathetic yelp. She struggled away, losing coordination in her panic. She must have turned around because the mahktashaan was in front of her.

"Think about it," the djinn said, turning upside down in the infuriating way of his kind.

"I can't give you what I don't have," she said, casting about. Her heart leapt into her mouth as a thorny black head emerged between her and the mahktashaan. It rolled, revealing a shiny black eye that looked right at her. Then it submerged. Kordahla gulped and back-paddled.

"Bazwaeel!" Ali called in warning. "Get out. Get out of the water."

"Pledge me what you will get," the djinn persisted.

"I must know what it is."

"And spoil the surprise? I will tell you only this: you will not want it."

She really could not evade him. He was everywhere she turned. "I have only your word for that."

"And why is that not enough, you piddly, conceited gnat?"

"You are djinn." Duplicity and deception. Treachery and treason. The uncomplimentary list went on.

He said something more. She could not fathom what because a row of knobbly dorsal fins was undulating around her, rippling all sense from her brain. The creature spiralled inward. It lifted its horny head from the water, opening fanged jaws to reveal a pocked, fungal-encrusted maw.

It surged towards her. Kordahla screamed. Cream light streamed around her. The bazwaeel roared and breeched. Its splash created waves that rocked her back towards the mahktashaan. She struggled towards him, the enemy now her salvation.

"I will brook no interference," the djinn said, pushing his palm forward. The mahktashaan's crystal died as he flew back and landed in another pool with a splash to match the bazwaeel's.

"Let me out," Kordahla screamed at the djinn.

"You are free to go," he said, floating up. "But can you make it to the shore?"

She cast about. A cankerous fin broke the surface. She swam in the opposite direction only to see another rise in front of her. Again she changed direction, to be faced with a glimpse of the bazwaeel's head.

"What do you want? Tell me exactly what you want," she said.

The djinn drifted towards her, his body horizontal. "It shall bear the name Xander, despised and despiser."

She was floundering, her panic draining her strength. "It has a name? A pet?"

"Enough. Your life for a gift you will not want. Make your decision." He whirled into the sky, an indigo tornado. The water churned. The bazwaeel's gruesome head rose up in front of her. Behind it, the mahktashaan dragged himself out of the water while Ali scampered toward solid ground.

Her horse had a name, and her dolls from childhood. Vinsant's dead fish had a name. Vae, even Father's sword had a name.

"Take us. I agree if you take us," she shouted, tilting her head up to him. He was no more than a blur in the sky.

"You. I will take you," his voice boomed down.

The bazwaeel opened its putrid mouth. Fangs flashed. "No. You must help the boy."

"The cockroach is not part of our agreement."

Snarling, the monster bent towards her. She closed her eyes tight. "It's part of mine." She kicked back, knowing she could not avoid the snap of its jaws. She prayed the end would be quick and painless, and that the boy would not know more suffering.

"*Ahk ta domas te*," the mahktashaan intoned, his voice weary and weak. She opened her eyes, but no magical light flashed. "*Ahk ta domas te.*" He sagged to the ground. "*Ahk ta domas te.*" A cream glow hit the monster. Roaring, it thrashed it tail, raising a splash which drenched the mahktashaan. Still the monster's jaws bore down. The mahktashaan hunched over. "*Ahk ta domas te.*" The whisper sent a spark flying at the bazwaeel. The bazwaeel barely flinched. What chance he would work his magic before those fangs pierced her spine? The monster's head fell. Its decaying breath burned her face.

"Bring Timak and I deal!"

Indigo light obliterated all as the djinn's callous laugh echoed through the land. Kordahla whirled into utter, frigid nothing.

Chapter Thirty-two

VINSANT SPED AROUND THE corner, ducked under the mahktashaan guards' ceremonial spears and thrust open the doors to Father's reception chamber before they had time to respond. He skidded to a halt beside Ahkdul, realised his mistake and bounded away to stand near the semicircle of padded chairs, next to Levi. It was not a position he felt entirely comfortable with, but since the alternatives were either to stand next to Father or be excluded, he opted to stay put. Obviously, running here had been a mistake. The silence was stony, even after Mariano came in and stood at Father's right, where the afternoon sun streaming through the stucco lattice across the arched windows gilded him, the show-off. Vinsant wished he had not dashed ahead of Arun, who had been about to comment on the subject of his eyes when the page interrupted and demanded the Minoria's immediate presence in regard to Princess Kordahla's escape.

"What's going on?" he asked during the interminable wait. He rolled his eyes at Mariano, who was ignoring him just like everybody else, and set about trying to arrange his oversized robe. Ahkdul was the only other person who moved, filling a silver goblet from a silver jug set on a cabinet to the right of the door. He checked out the carvings of mythical creatures on the wood. Kordahla might have caught a glimpse of a secretive schkaan if she was lucky, or a bazwaeel. If there was a way to get Ahkdul to the scums, the stonemasons might end up carving the monster devouring the swine. Now that was a relief he would love to view but, since the swine had the good sense not to take one of the padded chairs around the hearth, Vinsant doubted Father would order him to travel unaccompanied and unprotected through the scums. Father was the only one seated. He was rigid in a carved chair he had turned from the dining table, the exaggerated rise and fall of his chest the only evidence he was flesh and blood. A gold jug of wine and a goblet sat on the table behind him. Red liquid pooled on the tray beneath them. Father had drunk more than one glass. It was a wonder the songbirds in the garden hadn't sensed his ire and gone mute. When Arun finally entered, hooded but with face visible, Vinsant tucked his shoulders into an exaggerated droop, trying to break the sombre mood. Nobody paid him the least heed. Arun adopted the same stiff stance as the Majoria. He bet they were in thoughtlink, and wouldn't he like to know what they were saying because he was jumping-out-of-his-skin desperate to discover what they knew about Kordahla. So he said the one thing guaranteed to get a reaction.

"Has Kordahla escaped?"

Sure enough, Father rounded on him. "You sound pleased about it."

'Course he was, and he could not keep the smile off his face. Did not even try. The hood had some use, after all. It didn't fool Father, who in two steps came close enough to deliver a forceful slap across the face. The layer of fabric between their flesh did not stop it stinging, inside and out. For all his escapades, it had been a long time since he had suffered beneath Father's hand. He stared his stunned hurt at Father, who looked like he was exerting every last drop of his self-control not to thrash Vinsant to pieces.

"How?" Mariano asked.

"Yes, how, Majoria?" Father repeated in an icy voice. He was standing yet.

Levi turned to the Shah, the first sign he was out of the trance. "Mahktashaan Zermane reports she was kept from his reach by an indigo djinn which later removed her from the clutches of a bazwaeel."

Father's fists clenched so tight they flexed at the wrist. Vinsant bit his lip. The only time Father was that silent was when he did not trust himself. When the shah finally spoke, his voice cut through the rays of sun. "She bargained for her escape with a djinn."

"So it appears."

"And my page? Was he with her?" Ahkdul asked. His face looked like stone, and his hand was way too tight around the goblet.

"He was, and included in the pact. He, too, has disappeared," Levi replied, the traitor.

"I demand compensation," Ahkdul said. "The boy cost a great deal, and your daughter makes a fool of Verdaan and of me."

Father said, "You will be reimbursed double what you paid for the boy."

Ahkdul nodded once. The two men locked eyes.

"We had a formal contract," Ahkdul said.

"Do you wish it annulled?" the Shah asked.

"Father, this is hardly the time," Mariano said.

"Silence," the Shah snapped, and Ahkdul's raised brow relaxed. "This is exactly the time. Kordahla has brought dishonour to this family, to Terlaan and to Verdaan. Lord Ahkdul is entitled not only to release from the contract but also to a say in his betrothed's fate."

Vinsant's jaw dropped. He tried to catch Arun's eye, but the Minoria was studying Ahkdul. The pig looked vindicated. Nobody seemed to understand he would punish Kordahla for the rest of her life. "But he can't. He's the reason she's gone in the first place," he blurted.

"One more word out of you, and I'll have you thrown in the dungeon." Father said, not even looking his way.

"But…" Vinsant said, then clamped his mouth, bowed his head and backed away. He could not risk it now, but scumhoppers would Father hear exactly what he thought later. Too bad he was standing in a patch of sunlight which, laced with the shadows of the stuccowork, looked like a cell.

"I am satisfied you understand my stake in this," Ahkdul said, refilling his goblet and taking a gulp. He walked in front of Levi, set the cup on the low, round table between the chairs and faced the shah with the bearing of an equal, the despicable swine. Father had to see this delay was a power play. Vinsant didn't understand why Father stood for it. "Both of us had a great deal to gain from this union," Ahkdul said. "I will not beg Myklaan for her return. Nor can Verdaan wage war against them. But neither will I stand by to let a woman decide the fate of my realm."

"You cannot wage war of the military kind, but Verdaan is not without influence, even in Myklaan," Wilshem replied.

It had to be porrin. It was all that Vae-forsaken realm had. Vinsant shook his head. All this politicking was beyond him. He would have to seek out Mariano and pester him into explaining after he had dealt with Father.

"I doubt she is yet in Myklaan." All eyes set on Levi. His black crystal glowed as Ahkdul reached for his goblet. The swine's fingers wrapped around air as it slid across the table. The shah's lip curled in a sneer. The Majoria glided to the table and picked up the goblet. It disappeared from his hand. "The djinn would not have bargained on saving the boy. The Princess would have argued for it. For that concession, he will take her no further than out of harm's way. It is in their nature to dissemble. He has more opportunity to coerce her into another pact if she must travel far."

"You could be wrong about this," Wilshem said.

"Majesty." Levi bowed his hooded head in acknowledgement.

"Even so," Mariano said. "Even if she is only on the other side of the scums, we cannot race to intercept her in time. It is an eighteen-day ride to the Termyk pass, and another three days to cross."

Arun stepped forward with a glance at Ahkdul. The swine was keeping his back to them as he stared at where his goblet had sat, not even pretending to pay attention. "We do not know where she is. She might wander the hills for eight-days or traverse Kaijoor in a royal carriage in one. Prudence dictates the Myklaani know the gist of the matter."

"The matter is still to be decided," Wilshem said. "If it is blood honour, our interests are not served by informing them."

Vinsant gasped as Ahkdul turned. Father could not be serious. Kordahla's shame was not great enough to warrant putting her to the sword. He opened his mouth, but Arun's warning tilt of his hand made him bite his tongue.

"Father," Mariano said. He was silenced with a raised finger.

A dove landed on the balcony wall, and cooed. That had to be a sign from Vae'oenka. Vinsant willed Father to understand.

A moment of excruciating quiet was followed by Wilshem's "Well?"

Ahkdul and the Shah stared at each other. Ahkdul said, "I will not demand blood honour if she is untouched, though I claim the right to deal with her as I see fit. I will not take a disobedient wife, and she must learn how to obey if I grant her this reprieve. But she is also your daughter, Majesty. The final say on blood honour is yours."

"It is only on account of our contract that I do not declare it in every village and town in the land. You are generous, Lord Ahkdul, and, if she is unsullied, you may deal with your future wife as you see fit."

The dove flew off. Vinsant bit his lip. Hard. It had to come back. Father had left unsaid what would happen if Kordahla took herself into the arms of a man. He didn't think she would do that, but he had a sinking feeling that to her death might be preferable to a lesson at Ahkdul's hands.

Hands behind his back, eyes narrow, the Shah addressed Levi. "Send as many mahktashaan as you can spare to the hills. They may use any means within their power to locate the princess. Consider anybody who aids her a traitor to this land." He turned to Mariano. "You will lead a delegation to Myklaan. Take the Minoria with you. If Kordahla is there, convince the Myklaani it is not in their best interests to harbour a Terlaani princess. If she is not, advise them she has become separated from a hunting party and solicit their aid in recovering her. I care not what you say as long as it does not sully our honour."

"The charge to re-acquire the princess is mine," Ahkdul said, "since she is my betrothed. And I must determine she remains undamaged before I accept her hand. I will accompany this party. It is my due."

"Very well."

They were talking about Kordahla like she was a possession! "I want to go too," Vinsant said. "She's my sister too." If he was there, Mahktos might protect her. He had offered the frangipani for her.

"Prudence dictates one heir remain in the realm," Levi noted, but there was calculation in the delivery. The Crystalite Mines loomed large, but Vinsant did not have time to consider what Levi had in store. Three strides brought the Shah to him, which was impressive given how far he had backed away. Father's iron grip as he pulled Vinsant close so their faces almost met was downright menacing.

"The Majoria is right, else I would send you to mete out justice under the supervision of your master before he has you whipped to an inch of your life for your part in this. And if she is besmirched, I will beg Ahkdul that you be the one to wield the sword that restores honour to our name. You will not forget this as long as you live, and if you ever pull a stunt like this again, I will invoke blood honour upon you!" The Shah shoved him against the wall.

"Mahktos said…" Vinsant squeaked. No sooner were the words out of his mouth than his body became unresponsive to his command. *My eyes. Someone needs to tell me about my cursed eyes* was all he had time to think before Levi's voice boomed in his head.

You will not take our god's name in vain, nor will you lie in his name.

One leg slid forward as Vinsant sagged. A pounding headache akin to the one after his initiation ceremony dropped him to the stone floor. He vomited what little of the apple pie remained in his stomach.

Father threw him a disgusted look. With Ahkdul reaching for the shah's goblet, that just wasn't fair. Vinsant wiped the revolting spittle from his mouth. He was right. Kordahla was right. Mahktos help her! Father and Levi and Mariano had to see how wrong they were. He had to convince them. "Ahkdul doesn't even want Kordahla as a wife," he said from the floor. "He takes children to his bed."

The swine's face reddened. Spluttering, he slammed the gold goblet onto the dining table and stepped back, right into one of the chairs. "Is this how you treat a guest? Is this slander what I and my offspring can expect of you?"

Father yanked Vinsant up and dealt him a backhanded blow, not even caring the pig was a drunk. "You will apologise."

Blood trickled over his lip and into his mouth. He sulked up at Father, defiant. The scums would turn to drinking water before he apologised to that ogre.

"Guards!" Father roared before turning to Arun. "You leave in one hour. I will hold you personally responsible for both Prince Mariano's safety and the return of the princess."

"Let the Minoria stay. I will accompany Prince Mariano," Levi said as the doors opened. There was a quick eagerness in his voice Vinsant found disturbing, like the Majoria relished the chance to oversee his sister's punishment.

The Shah emptied the bottle of wine into his goblet and took a long swig, holding Ahkdul's eye. "This may yet come to war. I cannot permit my Majoria to fall into enemy hands. No. The Minoria will go. It is only fitting since he fell for the deception of children."

"You seem willing enough to send your heir, and for no other reason than revenge," Vinsant muttered.

Just his luck Father had the ears of a hound. "What did you say?" His voice was dangerously low.

Vinsant glared but kept his mouth firmly closed. It did not appease the Shah. Realising the guards were awaiting his bidding, Father made an offhanded gesture at Vinsant. "Throw him in the dungeon for the night. It is time he learned duty and respect."

"There is the matter of dereliction as an apprentice," Levi said, his parched voice cracking with frustration. Vinsant eyed the Majoria as the guards hauled him to his feet. He wouldn't put it past Levi to think inflicting pain on a spirited prince was an appropriate outlet for his resentment. The dungeon would be a holiday compared to whatever punishment that zealous man dreamed up. If he could manage to stop thinking of his comfortable bed.

The Shah had turned away. "Tonight he faces my wrath. Tomorrow, do what you will with him. I do not want to see him again until this is over." Father waved his hand and the guards dragged Vinsant out.

After two hours, the continual plink of water dripping off the walls was beginning to wear on Vinsant's nerves. The green slime that clung to the stone made leaning back disgusting, and the musty straw let the dampness leach through his tight churidar if he sat. The guards, not mahktashaan, were rather wary of him in his cloak. After they had secured him in the cell, he had managed to coerce a rather stilted conversation. That was until he had removed his hood and revealed his startling eyes. At that point, they had promptly remembered urgent tasks and left him all alone. The joke was wearing thin. He was bored, starving, and nearly out of his mind wondering what was going on. When the door at the end of the passage clanged, and steps drew near, Vinsant leapt to the bars, ready to offer Father an effusive if insincere apology. He did not expect a hooded mahktashaan.

"Am I glad to see you," he said when he saw the cerulean crystal.

"Have you had enough time to cool off?" Arun asked, in a tone that suggested he quite supported Vinsant's incarceration.

Vinsant let go the bars and stepped back. "Why don't you let me out of here and find out?"

Arun turned to leave.

"Wait," Vinsant said. "I'm sorry."

"I thoroughly doubt that. *Latchtos.*" The lock clicked open. Arun stepped inside, drawing the barred door closed after him. Vinsant heard the lock latch back into place. Arun waved his hand and murmured, and the straw dried out, losing much of its stale odour. At another gesture, a stool appeared, and a final *selos* had the air thrum.

"I have created a sound shield. We may talk in private," the Minoria said, seating himself.

Vinsant sat cross-legged on the straw, leaned forward, and sucked the ulcer on his bottom lip. He eyed the stool, wondered if the same magic could produce a bed, and asked, "Do you think you'll find Kordahla?"

"I have no doubt we will."

"Will she…I mean Ahkdul and Father…will they…"

"They are both in a rage, and your father's at least is unprecedented. Either one may invoke blood honour. I think a lot will depend on her attitude when she returns. It is why I am relieved to part of the search party. She might listen to my counsel if I can speak with her alone."

"Then Father won't recant his offer."

"The shame is his, Vinsant. It is up to Ahkdul whether to honour the terms agreed, and the Verdaani have too much invested in this marriage to back out if she remains pure. Though I have no doubt he will make her pay for the rest of her life. If she returns, you must bid her humble herself. It may mean her life."

Vinsant did not think she could bear to live with Ahkdul's constant punishment. He bit his tongue – literally since it had got him into so much trouble of late – but gave Arun a look he knew would communicate the sentiment.

"I did not come here to discuss Kordahla," Arun said.

"Uh, my eyes," Vinsant said with relief. He felt his brow relax and his headache ease.

"Your vision of Mahktos, yes, if you will not mind later on recounting what you tell me to the Majoria, and perhaps listening to a repetition of all I say."

"Where is he?" Vinsant asked, craning his neck to check the dark corridor and half expecting Levi to be lurking in the shadows.

"Busy. It is only because Kordahla is involved in this that I seek to learn anything which may temper her predicament."

"Not because you want to put me out of my misery?" He caught Arun suppressing a smile.

"A little of that. It is important we know exactly what Mahktos said."

The entire experience was etched into Vinsant's memory. He was sure he would never forget a single detail as long as he lived. "I thought if the mahktashaan were going to kill me, I might as well see whether Mahktos forgave me and die at his hand if he didn't. It is the more noble end, don't you think?"

"You disobeyed me yet again."

"It worked out, didn't it?"

"Vinsant, I am close to washing my hands of you."

"Just so you know, just for a moment, I wished you were there with me."

"I feel privileged," Arun said dryly.

Vinsant cleared his throat and squirmed on the rustling straw, then saw the warmth in Arun's eyes. "Mahktos accepted my offering but said He was mad I gave my sister the quartz. He said I would pay for that treason. Then He said the mahktashaan were warned admitting me to their ranks would spell havoc for their order. And he also said there is much at play here beyond their ken."

"That is interesting indeed," Arun remarked. "Anything else?"

Vinsant ran his tongue over his sore lip, and frowned as though trying to recall. What he was really doing was trying to decide how much to tell Arun. He met the Minoria's eyes and knew this man though years his senior was perhaps the truest friend he had. And Kordahla's only hope. "He said He gave me no sanction for my service. What does that mean?"

Now Arun's smile widened as he chuckled. "It means we are yet to treat you as an apprentice for all the god has marked you as special. He wants you to rise through the ranks by proving yourself."

He tore a piece of straw into strands. "Well how else would I do it? I mean I've been saying I want to be treated like a normal apprentice all along."

"If you were that, Vinsant, you would be long dead. At least thrice over."

Vinsant looked down to hide the flush in his cheeks. "There was one more thing he said." There was nothing to be gained from holding back. His secret, and Kordahla's, were exposed. "He said I might keep our secrets, Kordahla's and mine. He said He would not tell me more because I must carve my own destiny. He said He would not interfere."

"That is most intriguing of all."

Vinsant waited, but Arun was thoughtful. "The gods can influence us then?" he asked.

"We have free will. They will not interfere with that. But Mahktos has implied events are being shaped in the higher realms, events that will impact on this earth. Such events rarely deliver a peaceful end."

"But if he was so mad at my actions, why did He give me permission to keep them a secret?"

Arun sighed. "I do not claim to know the mind of a god, Vinsant."

"But you can guess. I mean, you know about all this stuff."

"I am hardly an expert, but I have to think that you will somehow be involved, for better, in whatever events Mahktos hinted at, but that your actions may imperil the mahktashaan."

Vinsant slid his eyes to a glob of slime oozing down the wall. It looked ready to splat to the floor. It didn't make sense that the theft of a single crystal could place the mahktashaan in such peril.

Astute as he was, Arun noticed his thoughts had drifted. "What are you not telling me?" the Minoria asked.

"I need to know about my eyes," Vinsant said, with a fleeting crooked smile as the slime stretched.

"Not before I have all the details."

"I don't think it matters."

"Let me be the judge of that," Arun said.

"You said I could trust you."

"You could hardly be in more trouble than you are in now."

"So tell me about my eyes first. I'm obviously still an apprentice. Why do I have the eyes of a mahktashaan?"

The glob plunked. Arun stood and paced the width of the cell. "What I am about to tell you is our most closely guarded secret. It is made known to mahktashaan only on the day of their induction. I told you there are those who fail that test, and of the fate they suffer." He paused and Vinsant nodded. "Of the promising apprentices, it is generally those who cannot accept what they learn that day that fail." It had to be one massive secret, because he sucked in a deep breath before he was ready to reveal it. He put on a real earnest expression, too. "The mahktashaan draw their power from a very specific source."

"The crystals."

"The crystals are a conduit for the power, but not its source."

Vinsant sucked on his cheek. "The power comes from Mahktos."

"Indirectly." Arun moved his hand. The air thrummed with a higher frequency. "Our true power is sourced through the djinn."

Vinsant felt his jaw slacken. "You mean," he said, and had to stop to suck his cheek because the idea was almost beyond comprehension. "You mean the djinn do your bidding?"

"I mean we tap into their power. We draw on them as a power source, but we certainly do not control them."

"But aren't they evil?"

"They are djinn. Quite simply, their nature is not our own. We perceive them as treacherous, but that is applying our standards to beings beyond our ken."

"And they just let the mahktashaan use them?"

"It is not them we use, but their power. And there is a price to pay. As we bind to them, so they bind to us. We presume our magic allows them to interfere in the world to a far greater degree than would otherwise be possible."

"So if there was no magic, they wouldn't be looking to trick us into making pacts."

"They will always do that. It is their nature. But I think the nature of the pacts, and their impact might be different, less personal. We have no real way of knowing for sure."

Except by forsaking magic, Vinsant thought. *But nobody is going to do that.* It was a lot to take in. He shook his head and found his brows were knitted so tight his headache was worsening again. "I don't get it."

"I'm not surprised. You will probably need to undergo the induction ceremony before you comprehend."

"What does this have to do with my eyes?"

"A mahktashaan's eyes reflect his power."

Vinsant bobbed his head about. He had always known mahktashaan eyes were the same colour as their crystal. It wasn't as though the hoods concealed their eyes. "Yeah?"

Arun sat on the stool. "Our crystals are the colour of the djinn whose power we channel. Our talents are limited by the abilities of those djinn."

Vinsant pulled several different faces, to no effect since he had no idea what he was feeling. "So some are more powerful than others?"

"Yes. Some are created that way but they may grow and learn as we do. If the stories of the same djinn appearing to subsequent generations are true, they have thousands of years in which to do so."

Vinsant shook his head. "That means a mahktashaan is only as strong as the djinn whose power he channels. That's not fair. You could work incredibly hard and never amount to much in the mahktashaan."

"Do you really want to apply the word fair to the djinn? For some inexplicable reason, a mahktashaan seems perfectly matched to the crystal he bears. Mahktos's hand is in that, which is not surprising since the djinn are his creation."

"Huh?"

"I will leave that for now. We have your eyes to discuss."

"Mahktos has already decided I'm to be bound to a crimson djinn?" He scooped up a handful of chaff and let it sieve through his fingers.

"Oh no. This is an honour more profound. That particular shade of red is the preserve of Mahktos himself. You, Vinsant, will be calling on the mightiest power of all. You will channel the power of the god."

Vinsant could only blink. After a very long time he opened his mouth. Only a croak came out.

Arun said, "Do not get too ahead of yourself, my young friend. From what I understand, Mahktos has decreed you are to complete your apprenticeship, and you have still to pass your induction." He broke into a sardonic smile. "From the way you attend to your training, your acceptance might not be a given. What I don't understand is why, when he warned us to abandon you, when he hinted you would be our undoing, he bestowed this unprecedented honour."

Much to his chagrin, Vinsant could only shake his head again.

Arun rose, once more the Minoria asserting his rank. "I am a mahktashaan, Vinsant. I must protect our order even as I protect the royal family. What is it you are holding back?"

In the face of these revelations, Vinsant took a deep breath, stood up and faced Arun. "You said I could trust you. You said you would listen man to man."

"If it helps Kordahla."

"I gave Kordahla a crystal to take to Myklaan. I took it after the Majoria examined Errol, my grapper. We thought it would help convince Myklaan to grant her asylum."

The Minoria lips were tight. "I see." He faced Vinsant some seconds more, then picked up the stool, went to the door of the cell and let himself out. Vinsant followed, but Arun swung the bars in his face. "This is not something I will tell the Majoria, and I suggest for the moment you hold your tongue. Your violation of our trust is enough to have you put to the sword. Do not try to invoke Mahktos's name, it won't save you, not when he decreed he has not sanctioned your service. A ghost may channel Mahktos's power as well as a living soul, and the Majoria will not hesitate to create ghosts if the mahktashaan are threatened."

Vinsant gripped the bars. "I didn't mean to do any harm. I did it before Mahk…before I atoned."

"It is for that reason I will take no action on this. Vinsant, if that crystal gets to Myklaan, it could do us irreparable damage. I hope the night will see you reflect on the path you wish to take. And your true allegiance."

"You're not really going to leave me in here, are you?"

"You did the right thing by telling me. It is information I should have if I reach Myklaan. But I'm afraid I am in accordance with the Shah on this. It is high time you learned some respect."

Vinsant stared as Arun walked away. When he turned back into the cell, the rotting straw was dampening again.

Hours later, after a frugal meal of stale flatbread and dry cheese, it became obvious he really was to spend the entire night in the musty dungeon. After sitting and standing alternately for hours, depending on how tired or wet he was, Vinsant craved a blanket. And he was bored. Ballads of heroes languishing in dungeons did not do justice to his suffering. He tried to rattle the bars of the door but they held fast. Since the guards were not about to bring him any comforts, he needed to come up with a plan. In a locked dungeon, with soldiers who would not be cajoled for fear of what their Shah might do to their heads, magic seemed the only option. He was a mahktashaan apprentice, after all. Was it that far a stretch to assume he had some talent for it?

Vinsant closed his eyes, concentrated really hard and tried to repeat

Arun's gesture. Ten minutes later, he rubbed his forehead. The truth was he had no idea what performing magic was supposed to feel like. The mahktashaan he had seen at work had appeared unperturbed, but Arun had told him the power came from the djinn, the last creatures he was likely to relax around. No, not the djinn, the same source as the djinn, and that was tied to Mahktos. Well, if his power came direct from Mahktos, perhaps he had to recreate the radiance he had felt in the god's presence. It made a twisted kind of sense. After all, porrin also allowed magic and he had seen how well a small dose annihilated stress.

There was just one problem. In the midst of mouldy straw, between the plink of water, splat of slime and worrying about Kordahla, Vinsant wondered if he could relax. He smoothed his features, closed his eyes, took a deep breath and immersed himself in the memory of the awesome glade. He said a quick prayer before repeating Arun's gesture and spell. It was *sumbek*, wasn't it? Inside him, a thrumming akin to the one Arun had created arose. A piece of wood clattered to the floor. Vinsant looked at the leg of a stool and scratched his head. It was a start, he supposed. He tried again. And again. A second and third leg clanked into the cell, bringing with them a smoky stink. He took a closer look and kicked a smouldering leg into the wettest corner. With nothing better to do, he tried again. Four, five unattached legs. Another prayer, an adjustment of his posture, which heightened the thrum in his veins, and a stool appeared before him. Upside down, uneven in the legs and scorched, but a stool nonetheless. Vinsant danced right around it. Then he conjured a score more. He was arranging the stools into a bench when an idea sprang into his mind. Hands on the bars, he closed his eyes and pictured what he wanted.

"*Lachos*," he said, the energy buzzing through his body. "*Lachtos. Latchtos.*"

There was a click. Hands around the bars, Vinsant pushed the door ajar. From down the corridor came the rattles of a dicing game. He listened a moment, tempted to try and sneak past. Quite apart from a night in his own bed, he wanted *someone* to know what he could do. But nobody seemed to condone his actions. Not even Arun who liked his sister. He pulled the door shut again. Father, Levi and Arun, adults though they were, just might be right.

"*Latchtos*," he said, but the incantation did not seem to work in reverse. He hoped whoever collected him from this stinking scumpit would not assume he had escaped for the night only to return before dawn. He curled up on the stools, snuggled into his robe and tried to stop thinking of what might happen to Kordahla.

Chapter Thirty-three

FLAT ON HER BACK, Kordahla spluttered, trying to dislodge foul scum from her nose and mouth. She rolled over and wiped her face but found a hand covered in muck, and had to be content with mopping what filth she could onto the grass. Her wretchedness was no excuse to delay. She stood up, staggering sideways under an assault of disorientation and fatigue. Where foetid vapour had blanketed a sodden expanse, forested hills now cradled a narrow valley. Wildflowers bobbed in the breeze and wisps of cloud rippled across sweet sky. She collapsed to her knees, closed her eyes tight and rocked back and forth. What had she done? A djinn-cursed existence was no trade for life under Ahkdul's thumb.

A small, filthy hand touched her shoulder. She steadied herself with a deep breath and opened her eyes. A spark had appeared in Timak's eyes, and the hint of a smile played about his lips. She wondered, sadly, cruelly, how long it would last.

"We're a long way from Myklaan," she said.

Removing his hand, he sobered. "You made a pact with a djinn."

"I don't think you can talk," she answered, standing and moving off because the reminder stung. Besides, there were more immediate concerns. The sun was almost behind the highest of the hills, there was nothing remotely edible in sight, and she stank. She had, she realised with a pang of dread, no idea what to do.

Timak moved up behind her, careful not to come too close.

"Is your genie about?" she asked, staring at the beech and ash.

He looked around, then shook his head, standing lopsided because he had only one shoe.

"Call her, and tell her to get us out of here."

He shook his head again.

With an exasperated release of breath, Kordahla began to scramble up the hill. Timak was certain to mimic the swinging monkeys and follow. The steep slope was slippery. Wet grass yielded the land to fern, rock and decaying leaves. The exertion cut through her fatigue with an almost meditative effect. Her feet slipped, her kameez tore and mud seeped through her clothes, though it was hardly an inconvenience when scum sealed every pore in her flesh. By the time she reached the summit, her frustration had dissipated. In its place, exhausted despair stretched as far as the northward horizon, where Lake Sheraz glistened. The scums marred the land between, whiffs of noxious vapour tainting their breaths on isolated gusts. Myklaan was a long way away, somewhere to the southwest, beyond leagues and leagues of giant hills. Were the boy not with her, she might have burst into tears. Instead, she placed a hand over her rumbling stomach, seeking comfort in the feel of her own body.

"We need to find water," she said.

They trudged for hours, down, then some way up the next hill. Their footsteps disturbed crickets into giant leaps and lizards into waggly darts. She gave no thought to their safety until a beast growled its presence deep in the thickening forest. Until monkeys feasting on fallen apricots screeched their warning and leapt from a careless weave of knotted roots into vine-tangled branches. Until birds of bright plumage shrieked in exotic tones before taking flight from the laced canopy. She stopped, and Timak bumped into her back. The tree trunks were becoming indistinct, and the patches of visible sky had turned grey. They needed refuge for the night. She slowed, searching for a crevice, a bush, anything that might protect them from whatever lurked in these foreign parts.

The mosquitoes started buzzing and tickling with their bites. Timak limped behind her, his bare foot slowing his progress. She batted at a fly crawling across her face. A feather-light touch brushed the back of her hand. She flicked it away as she whirled. Timak flinched, his eyes betraying his hurt. Then he pointed at a hollow trunk. Whether haven or trap she did not know, but there was nowhere else to hide. Lifting a fallen branch, she approached, wrinkling her nose in distaste and on the verge of tears. This nightmare was not what a princess deserved. She thrust the branch into the entrance, keeping it at arm's length, and then jumped back. No bear or fox sprang out. She stepped up again, more confident as she prodded deeper, raking the stick through the dried-out leaves. Satisfied the hollow was unoccupied, she looked at Timak. He trotted over and crawled inside. With a shudder at the thought of the bugs that would creep through their nest, she followed, careful to maintain a hold on the branch that was their only weapon.

Now she was sitting down, her back against rough bark, her parched throat began to burn, the hunger in her stomach gnaw. She looked at the boy. Chin on knees he was looking at her as though she would provide. He had to be as dry and ravenous as she, but he would not dream of uttering a peep of complaint. She sighed. Vinsant would have proclaimed his discomfort for every wild beast to hear, then come up with a foolhardy plan to procure dinner using no more than the stick she held and his bare hands. She missed him already.

A yowl startled her. Low and plaintive, it sounded hungry to her ears. She moved the branch to the dip between her knees.

"The djinn won't abandon us after saving us from the bazwaeel," Kordahla whispered, for both their sakes. She was surprised when Timak answered.

"He would. He can make another pact if we're in danger. That's what they want us to do, make lots of pacts."

The deepening gloom shadowed his face but his voice was a comfort. She shifted the stick to a stronger position through cracking leaves, and strove to keep him talking. "What was your pact, with the genie?"

"We don't have a pact." His voice rasped from thirst.

"Then why does she always hover about you?"

"We're friends," he said simply.

"She isn't bound to you?"

She heard a soft scraping that could have been the shake of his head against his shalvar. "If you discover her name, we could get some help." He didn't reply. She tried again, more to keep the loneliness at bay than because she expected an answer. "How did you meet her?"

This time she heard a gulp. When the silence oppressed, she knew she had lost him. She sighed. At least she now understood why he had not asked the genie to interfere. Quiet persistence might win him over to the idea of discovering her name. Without assistance, they would not get far, and indebting herself further to the manipulative indigo djinn was unconscionable. The thought of owing that creature brought tears to her eyes. She felt Timak sag against her shoulder, heard him yawn and kept still to avoid disturbing him. Before long, his head had fallen into her lap. She shifted into a more comfortable position and wrapped an arm around him, grateful for the warmth of his body beside her. In sleep, he did not seem to mind her touch.

With night came the eerie scratching, clicking and rustling of the forest. The drone lulled her into a drowse. As she nodded off, prickles of warning erupted all over her skin. She snapped awake, listening. Something was sniffing outside. Something large was grunting as it rooted around the bole. A shadow passed across the entrance, and a sour, musty smell rolled in. Kordahla tightened her grip on the branch and shook Timak awake. For once, his silence was a blessing. The scums might have masked their smells but their shuffles and ragged breathing were discordant in the night's symphony.

The beast yowled. A hairy arm thrust inside their hole, brushing against her before clamping on Timak's leg. He latched onto her, choking on a cry. Kordahla swung the branch and beat the arm, but the branch was too long to manoeuvre well. The beast growled and tugged Timak the harder. As the boy slid off her lap, she grabbed his arms. Luck saw one leg catch against the bole.

"Need help, little gnat?" a hated voice drawled. The bark above the hole deformed as the shimmering face of the indigo djinn extruded from it.

"Fight, Timak," she said, ignoring him. She gasped. The muted indigo shimmer of the djinn's skin lit a shaggy, brown, muscular arm. Save for its length and sinew, it might have been human.

"An ogre," the djinn proclaimed with feigned interest. "Never known a plump city dweller to survive an encounter with one."

"Help him," Kordahla said, her heart pounding. With his leg braced against the trunk, Timak was sobbing and screaming like he was being torn apart.

"I think it is winning," the djinn said with a yawn.

Kordahla threw herself over Timak so she could grab his legs. The ogre must have felt her movement, because his other arm latched onto hers. She screamed as he dragged her out of the hole. Unable to do anything else, she let go of Timak and fumbled for the branch. It batted against the sides of the trunk, stuck in a crevice, and jerked free as the ogre pulled them both out and dragged them over roots and rocks.

The hated djinn flew from the tree and floated in front of them. "An easy victory."

The ogre let them go and raked an arm towards him. The djinn winked out and reappeared just out of reach. The ogre leapt after him, but he vanished in a puff of smoke.

Kordahla struggled to her feet, pulling Timak after her. "Run," she said, not sure how far they could get with only shafts of moonlight to light their way. Snapping twigs and swishing fronds hindered their passage and revealed their path. Her foot twisted on a root. She yelped as a sharp stab of pain lanced through her ankle. Beside her, Timak puffed as he stumbled over stones. They had to slow to feel their way past trees. Not so, the ogre. In a few bounds, it was close enough to seize them. There was no opposing its brute strength as it pulled them into a pool of moonlight and sniffed them up and down. Spittle drooled from his open mouth as his barbed tongue lolled over his fat, black lips.

"Agree to a pact and I'll see you both safe and sound," the indigo djinn said, appearing at her side. Indigo light poured from the crystals in his joints.

The dumb ogre let go to hurl a backhanded slap at the djinn.

Tumbling upside down, the djinn avoided it. He presented both arms toward her as she backed away.

"Be my guest," the djinn said to the ogre. "These uncooperative mortals are not to my liking."

The ogre's expression turned eager. Kordahla sprang into ferns. Her foot landed on a rotting log. It cracked, and split. Her foot twisted as it went down, and she fell. The ogre grabbed Timak around the waist and threw him down next to her. The boy groaned as he thumped to the ground, and curled into a ball. Legs straddling them, the ogre beat its shaggy chest. The djinn held one edge of his vermillion vest as he reclined above, out of its scrawny reach, out of its puny mind.

"If you don't help us, I won't be around to deliver on my first promise," Kordahla said. She grasped at a section of the log and pulled a sharp segment free.

"An interesting prospect, since if you aren't, your soul shall be mine. Pacts bind until the end of time, flea."

"No," she murmured, letting her head drop back.

"Yes!" the djinn sneered, his disembodied vermillion eyes appearing before her.

She gagged on the fishy smell clouding her, whimpered as the ogre dropped to his knees and ran rough hands over her thigh, searching for the juiciest morsels.

"What? What do you want?" she screamed. Her muscles were bruising, her bones bending.

An indigo hand joined the eyes, its index finger poking into the hollow of her neck. "Oh, nothing much. Just your second born child."

She closed her eyes and shook her head, sobbing.

"Agree," the djinn said.

"No. Not to that."

"It's your *second* born."

The djinn popped. She opened her eyes and turned her head to look at him, floating above the ogre, arms and ankles crossed. If she died, he would have it on his conscience. If the djinn had such a thing. "So I keep my first born? And that makes it all right?" She would never have thought the stench of decay pouring from the ogre's mouth could overpower the fish smell. She thought she might retch.

The djinn's smile was a malicious, cruel twist of his mouth. "Who knows what the future will bring?" He yawned, and flicked a piece of dirt from beneath his fingernail. "But will you have one?"

The ogre lifted a rock and pulled a straight arm back as he prepared to strike the killing blow. She sobbed. What choice was this, to die or relinquish a child? She reached over to take Timak's hand. She couldn't help a desolate cry when he rolled away from her. She sobbed again, this time in relief when he kicked the ogre between the legs. The ogre froze, his arm raised, his wide nose, thick lips and hairy face contorted in pain. Kordahla wriggled back. Before the ogre could recover, Timak kicked him twice more. He scooted to Kordahla, and they ran for the bole. Behind them, the ogre yowled in fury. His big feet thumped on the chase.

"Make the pact," the djinn said. The note of desperation in his voice gave her hope.

She kept running. Timak overtook her and scrambled up a tree. She followed, hoping the ogre could not climb. Two branches up, Timak stood on tiptoe and wriggled his fingers shy of the next branch. She lifted him until he could wrap his arms around it and swing his legs up. She needed to jump to hang from it. Pulling herself up cost her dear effort. She hung over it, panting, trying to balance so she might bring her legs up. The ogre leapt onto the first branch and swiped, just missing her foot. She crawled to the trunk and worked her way higher, the climb getting easier as the limbs grew in closer proximity but more precarious as the thinner branches bent beneath her. Below them, the ogre groped his clumsy way up. A branch snapped under his bulk and he toppled, landing on his back across the lowest limb.

Kordahla held her breath. The indestructible ogre righted himself and climbed. To her relief, Timak managed to wedge himself in a fork higher up. She made it to the next bough, and scratched for purchase on the trunk as it creaked a warning.

"Ogres never give up," the indigo djinn said.

"You could have taken us to Myklaan."

"I honoured our pact, which was to remove you and the boy from the jaws of the bazwaeel."

"You know I travel to Myklaan."

"Then in future, take more care with the terms of your contract. Just remember that next time you might not be so lucky on your own." The djinn disappeared with a whoomp of air.

Another branch cracked, sending the ogre toppling. Twice more they heard him climb and fall. Letting out a hoot, he shook the trunk. The branches wobbled. The bough she stood on peeled away from the trunk. She sat, gripped it tight, and eased onto a lower branch. Her feet kept slipping off the smooth bark. The bough she held jerked lower. She dropped, straddling the branch and holding it tight as it bounced. When the shaking stopped, the utter silence of the forest sent prickles of fear down her spine. The ogre's clogged snores brought her little relief. She did not dare nap lest she fall at his feet. Her head nodded, her mind drifted, drifted, and latched onto a fragment of some tale about ogres and the day.

The first grey strokes of dawn seeped through the leaves, outlining him slumped against a tree. As birds chirped a welcome to morning, he snorted, woke, and sprung to his feet. Throwing his head back, he howled and beat at the tree. Weak from hunger, thirst and exertion, they had little chance of waiting him out. Kordahla peered through the leaves. The sky was paler in the east. She wormed along the shaking branch, snapping off twigs as she went.

"Timak. Timak." She could neither see nor hear him, but that meant little with this child. "Clear leaves to the east." She pulled a handful of foliage off a branch and let it drift to the ground. When sticks tumbled past her, she sighed her relief. A single ray of sunshine seeped through, and lit a weedy tuft. The ogre roared, and bolted. She reached over, took hold of a thin branch with a bush of leaves at its end, and jumped. The branch cracked into a stomach-lurching sag. Light chose that moment to burst through the canopy. It speared through the hole they had cleared and sprayed the ogre. He froze. His hair and skin paled. As the sun pierced more holes, it illuminated a pile of rocks where the ogre had stood. When screeching monkeys clambered over it, she worked a cautious way down past the snapped branches. The monkeys scattered at her step, allowing the prominences in the rock to assume a form: a bulbous nose, jagged teeth, fingers on a hand.

Timak clambered down and crept very close to her side. He picked up a rock and tossed it at the statue. Nothing happened. It was all the reassurance he required. His head nodded, his eyelids drooped. She ushered him back to the hollow bole. They crawled inside and, wrapped in each other's arms, fell asleep.

❖ ❖ ❖

Sian carried the last bundle of sage to the mouth of Ishoa's cave, and hung it to dry from one of the ropes which ran the length of the rock. She couldn't remember so happy a morning, talking to an even-voiced, reassuring companion. Ishoa was just like the other women when she did not wear her feathers and paint, only smarter, and much, much nicer. The sun-shadows needed to draw out, and out, and never end. She lingered a moment, breathing in the summer scents of the shrubby hills, naming them as patient Ishoa had taught her.

The soothsayer was tucking parrot feathers into her sap-brown hair when Sian went inside. "Did you take the herb tea this morning?" Ishoa asked as she threw a handful of seeds into the fire.

"Yes," she answered, breathing shallow to avoid the thick smoke waving up to the ceiling.

"Then you will go to the pond this afternoon."

Sian hung her head, blinking the tears from her stinging eyes. Ishoa was the one person who might care about her last attempt to cross the ledge above Meeting Field. She had to be the one person Loyt had not blabbed to.

"Bring back what you find there," Ishoa said.

Sian waited. If she waited long enough, Ishoa might understand something was wrong. The cricket chirps dragged on. The embers crackled. Her wary breath grew sharper. It didn't do any good. The soothsayer stared through the flames with her sightless eyes, not blinking, not moving a muscle.

The trance was scary, but Ishoa would soon come back from the Spirit Realm. Disappointing her would raise a terrible guilt after all the soothsayer was doing for her, but Ishoa would forgive her.

The trance was sacred. The Spirits would punish her with fits if they were the ones who decreed she must go. Sian hated she had no choice but to leave the one safe place in the village. Perhaps Erok would come if she said Ishoa bid her go. She paused at the entrance to the cave, looking down over the narrow path with its loose rocks and prickly bushes. She could hear murmurs from the village. Esa's baby was crying again.

"You will go by yourself," Ishoa said.

Sian jumped, and peered into the dim cave. Ishoa had not moved. "What should I bring?" she asked.

What you find, Ishoa's voice sounded in her mind.

Sian dawdled on the track back to the village, trying to ignore all the butterflies in her empty chest. She zigzagged through the longhouses without meeting anyone's eye, out to the broad trail along the west side of Meeting Field which led up into the forest. When she had to step from the trees onto the narrow ledge, her legs cramped. The other children scampered on and off the ledge and up and down the slope like the grazing goats, but no matter how hard she blinked, the drop off the ledge stayed dizzying steep.

She took a deep breath. Ishoa wanted this. Ishoa would not wish her harm. The others, maybe, but not Ishoa. She took one step out, and then another. Step by step, she crept along the path. It was hard work, making sure she balanced, and she wasn't used to long walks. She was a few paces along and her legs were too tired to keep going.

"Hoi! Where are you going?" a voice called.

As she whipped her head around, one foot slipped over the edge. She grabbed at the rock in panic as her body pitched back. Loyt was watching from the tree line, his face a mixture of horror and indignation.

"You're not allowed, Sian. Come back, you're not allowed."

She flattened herself against the rock, squirming until her feet were secure. Loyt ran off, to tell Grandmam Vila or Mam, so she would get in trouble. Sian stared at the spot where he had stood. If she went back, she could pretend she had never tried to cross.

Bring back what you find.

She gasped at how clear Ishoa sounded in her mind.

She turned her head to the other side. She was halfway there. She had never crossed before. Mam and Grandmam did not want her to do this. Ishoa did. Taking a deep breath, she slid her feet over loose pebbles until they met the opposite hill. The climb through the pear trees was steep. She scrambled on all fours up over the grassy summit to the little pond the children splashed in.

The water was clear in its stillness. She could see the gelatinous puffers, all mouth, head and tail. One floated to the surface and sucked in air before hurling its tongue at the unsuspecting dragonfly that skimmed past her nose. As she leaned over to get a clearer look, the movement of her reflection caught her eye. She didn't think she looked like that. Her hair was fair and combed, not dark and mussed up. She leaned closer. It was a boy she saw in the water, younger than her, and so sad. His eyes moved, and it was like he saw her.

She jerked back. But now the world was spinning, the ground was rushing up to meet her and the day was blackening to oblivion.

She was lying face up on the ground, dirt embedded in her hair and nails, too weak to move. She sobbed, because it wasn't fair she had fitted again, not after she had drunk the herb tea every day, just like Ishoa said. It wasn't fair she could not tell Ishoa the tea didn't work, because the soothsayer would ask her about the fit, and this time it had been different. Oblivion had not come. Instead, she had dreamt of the little boy. She could remember every detail of his sorrowful face. Could have cried for him, for them both, had she any tears in her. She had sunk too low for that. So she wished the image would fade away, because he reminded her of her horrid self.

Looking into the sky's dizzying heights while the wind cooled her skin and ruffled her hair didn't help to bring back her strength, but finding animal shapes in the clouds meant she could stop thinking about the boy. The big cloud was moving fast, shaping into a bird, a parrot, no an eagle. She drew a sharp breath. No cloud animal had ever formed into a perfect image with speckled feathers and a dark, rolling eye. It was diving, diving, diving into the pond. She yelped and blinked. The shapeless cloud was tall and white, tinged underneath with grey. She rolled over, pushed herself onto hands and knees, and crawled to the water's edge, daring herself to look. Dried leaves danced across the crest of the hill, but a stilling of the ripples sent her rocking back onto her heels. She couldn't help being a coward, but she needed to see even if it meant she shook to her bones. She leaned forward. Only her own hated face greeted her in the water. She averted her eyes.

At the bottom of the pool, a white object gleamed among the stones. She dipped a hand in to retrieve it because here might be another prize for her basket. The bone fit snug in her palm. Sian tucked it into the fur pouch around her neck, and rose to return. On an impulse, she stepped into the pool to wash the dirt from her face and hands, and discovered it was fun to splash about. For the first time in a long while, she laughed. The strangeness of it stopped her. She gave in to it, laughing as she gave thanks to the water spirits. They showered her as she climbed out of the pool, ran over the ridge down the slope.

It was good the rain had stopped and the ledge was dry or she might have stayed right where she was. This time her slow feet were more confident as they picked their way across. She kept her hand on the rock. At an excited shout, she looked across. Loyt was pointing, jumping up and down. Beside him, Erok was sucking on a blade of grass. The hunter's wide-eyed surprise changed to thoughtfulness. When she stepped to safety, dripping water at his feet, she hung her head, expecting a rebuke.

"You have the feet of a mountain goat," was all Erok said.

Loyt settled as his mouth turned down. She could guess he wanted Erok to scold her, and was glad he ran ahead. The hunter gestured to the comforting shelter of the forest path. Sian's legs were so shaky, she had to walk slow. Erok walked right behind her until they passed Meeting Field. He left her there, to go hunt in the east.

Sian ran past the longhouses. The women tsked at her wet clothes and tangled hair.

"Ishoa wants me," she called when Mam summoned her to a pile of grubby roots. She broke into a run for the cave, using a hand to swing around the hollow bole before she climbed the cliff path.

The soothsayer was sitting cross-legged on a rabbit fur by the fire. The shyness gnawed out Sian's insides, and she hung back.

"What did you find?" Ishoa asked.

Sian tiptoed in, and gave her the bone. Ishoa fingered it, and smiled. "It is a precious gift. Did you give thanks to the spirits?"

"Yes, to the water spirits. I found it in the pond." She bit her lip, guilty her thanks had been for her fun and not her find.

"It is from the neck of an eagle. The sky spirits deserve praise too." Ishoa grabbed a handful of tiny, black seeds. "Sit."

As Sian sat on a rabbit fur, Ishoa sprinkled the seeds into the flames. She thrilled a few notes that spun Sian out of the cave and into the heavens, where constellations twirled through the black void. The note ended. Sian slumped back into her body, only just remembering to give her thanks. She rubbed her sweaty palms on the edges of her fur. She didn't know why her breathing was so heavy. The spinning had been like her fits. Like them, but not the same.

"Bring my box of bones and the little implement you find next to it," Ishoa instructed.

The treasures were at the back of the cave, next to the pile of furs Ishoa used as bedding. The small box was inlaid with a pretty shell in rainbow colours. Carrying it was an honour, and Sian used two reverent hands to set it down in front of Ishoa. Ishoa opened it, ran her fingertips over the contents, and selected a bone that was similar to Sian's.

"Do you see this rune?"

Sian nodded, bit her lip, and whispered, "Yes."

"Carve the same rune onto your bone." Ishoa's free hand closed over Sian's. "Take care. You will only have one chance."

The firelight grew dim, and mysterious. The scent of seed and herb swirled out of its smoke. This was a soothsayer's charge. Sian studied the rune. The spirits needed to help a damaged girl carve well. They did. Her fingers were deft. When she had finished, Ishoa traced the rune.

"It is a great work," the soothsayer declared, feeling over Sian's knee to her hand, turning it, and placing the bone on her palm.

Sian felt an unfamiliar stirring in her chest. Gentle as a ladybird, she returned Ishoa's bone to the box. She started to put the one she had carved by its side. Ishoa's unerring hand stayed her own.

"You must keep this close about you."

Sian slipped it into her pouch. If she was lucky, it would protect her from fits. She looked outside and blinked. Night had fallen thick. She rose to leave.

"Sleep here, child," Ishoa said, stoking the fire. "I could use the company, and you have need to learn more soothsayer lore."

Alarm warred with her desire to linger. The spirit land was forbidden to all save the chosen and she, with her fits and cowardice, would never, ever dare to presume.

A rustle of wings brought a golden eagle to the mouth of the cave. It hovered, barring the way before it winged south. Sian sat back down.

"Tell me what you saw," Ishoa said.

◆ ◆ ◆

When Kordahla woke, her skin was prickling. She held her breath, ignoring the stick poking into her back so she could listen to dry leaves crack beneath feet. Timak lay fast asleep beneath a cobweb, his face serene. She reached over and roused him, putting her finger to her mouth. He huddled as far back as he could, a pointless move in the confines of the bole. Leaves rustled beneath her as she propped herself up, no louder than the rummaging of a rat. The footsteps stopped at the entrance hole. She pulled her legs in and tried to shallow her breath, tilting from the branch which poked through the entrance. It swung, clipping Timak's knee before striking her bruised thigh.

"Ow!" She winced. They were revealed. The branch retreated. Voices spoke in a simple tongue. Human voices, she sighed to hear, though the narrow face appearing at the hole did not inspire trust. Its owner reached in and caught her ankle. Both she and Timak kicked out. The intruder barked, and had the sense to withdraw his hand. The broad, friendly face which took its place may have intended to mislead. She bit her lip, and looked at Timak. Her throat was parched, and they were weak from hunger. This stranger's words sounded reassuring, and he kept his large hands to himself. They had no choice. She crawled out of the hollow, blinking in the full light of day. The two Hill Tribe men were waiting, spears clutched in hand, fragments of leaves sticking to their crude trousers and shirts. Their hems were embroidered with the bright geometric designs on the bags and reed bowls sold at the souk. The same design on the cuffs of the man the mahktashaan had slaughtered at the docks. She shuddered. For all she knew, the victim may have been kin to these men.

The short man, lean and dark of expression, advanced, his spear held out though not aimed. Timak's arms circled her waist. She put her arm around him, and stood firm. A woman and a child – they would be unable to avoid any hurt these men intended to inflict. Unable, too, to fend for themselves among the growls, hisses and roars of the savage morning hunt. She thanked the Vae that the broad, fair-haired man, was no fool. Seeing where her gaze alighted, he stood the butt of his spear on the earth. When his companion responded with a shake of his head, and a raising of the lethal tip, she sidled closer.

"Please, water." She pointed at the bladder draped over the broad man's shoulder. He passed it to her. She gulped a mouthful, and gave it to Timak.

Waiting for him to swallow his fill was torture. Drinking deep rivalled porrin's bliss.

The men's noses wrinkled as she returned the bladder. What they must have thought of her and Timak, foul scum-tainted mud caking on their faces, tattered clothes and bruised legs!

The men gestured at the stone ogre, and started talking over each other, petering out when they realised they had no hope of understanding what had passed. A raindrop plopped on her head. The broad, fair-haired man looked up through thin canopy, and sucked one cheek. He could not have divined a scrap of worth of the grey sky but he ushered them past the leaf-littered ogre statue, down through the maze of scrub oak and pistachio trees. The pair of them pulled faces of impatience each time thorncushion snagged her hem or she lagged to catch her breath. Smirked each time she twitched, started or jumped at a bizarre click, a menacing grunt or derisive hoot.

"No further," she protested, leaning on a rough trunk. Folding his legs beneath him, Timak sat against her, and hung his head.

A sudden patter of rain muddied a rivulet of scum on her cheek. It seeped into her mouth, and she spat.

The fair-haired hunter pointed through the trees. She shook her head. He was as heartless as his companion, to shrug and walk away. She eyed the darker man. His mouth wiggled in mistrust. Of *them*! His shrug mimicked his companion's as he turned away.

She leaned forward, her heart quickening. Those men needed to come back. "Stop!" A twist in the track took them out of sight.

She jumped up and peered through the trees. A glimpse of bright thread was all that remained of them. "Stop!"

A lone wolf howled in despair.

She took Timak's hand and ran. A sudden downpour greyed the air. She stopped, panicked, because she had no sight of them. It might have been foolish to assume the puddles forming along the faint track were footprints, but it was all they had to follow.

The rain stopped as abruptly as it had started. A flash of purple hem showed her the way.

"Wait!" The hunters at least turned when she trudged up and bent over to recover her breath. "Wait," she pleaded as they walked on, forcing her and Timak to stumble along or brave the unknown dangers of the hidden twig-snappers alone.

Thank the Vae it was but a single *chebel* before the hunters stopped by a rocky stream in a damp, shady valley. She fingered one of the berry-laden cotoneasters which prettied the area, and moved to slip into the water. A spear dropped to bar her way. It startled her into stepping back. The broad man gestured for her to sit. She remained standing on her aching feet. No princess of Terlaan would be a meek prisoner to Hill Tribe men.

This princess imagined threat where there was none. The spears thrust into the water and impaled a wriggling fish. A moment later, they had skewered another. When ten fish flapped on the bank, the broad man grinned as he gestured toward the stream. She offered a shy smile before stepping in the cool water, glad to soothe the blisters on her feet and rub the stinking scum from her skin. The peaks blocked the worst heat of the sun, but the water was pleasant and she lingered.

She climbed out, relishing the stream of water out of her hair and clothes. Timak, scrubbed and standing straight in shoes one of the hunters had fashioned out of bark and vine, was gobbling a peach. The tall man looked over and drew out two words. His tone in a handsome courtier would have left her laughing, good-natured, and smiling to sweet effect. In a Hill Tribe hunter, it alluded to a threat. She hesitated, but he beckoned her to the fire they had lit, and held out a peach. She tried to eat with decorum, but her hunger drove her to devour the fruit. Her lack of manners might have marked her as common, but she licked every last drop of juice from her fingers while the fish smoked on waxy leaves. The hunter's interest in her did not diminish, but his clucks were more amused than disapproving. She eyed him back as she ate.

"Erok," he said, pointing at himself after she had placed her stones in a neat line five paces from where they sat. He pointed at her.

"Kordahla," she said, and then pointed at the boy. "Timak."

"Brax," Erok said, pointing at his friend, who was filling their water bladders from the stream. The smaller man sniffed, and nodded. Erok poked a stick into a fish on the embers and handed it to her. It was the most delectable meal she had ever eaten. She didn't even care Erok and Brax raised voices in disagreement – over what to do with Timak and her, she was sure.

"Myklaan," she said when they fell quiet. If they recognised the name, they might understand she was asking for a guide.

"Myklaan?" Erok said in surprise. He plucked a blade of grass, popped one end into his mouth and closed one eye.

"Myklaan," she repeated, firm.

The way he wriggled his arms may have meant a rough journey, over high hills. She knew it was a long one.

Timak crept over while Erok and Brax conferred. In his silent way, he dug a packet out of an inner pocket in his kurta, and held it to her.

"You still have that?" She wasn't able to imagine how.

Timak just kept holding it out.

She took the packet, laying light fingers on his shoulder before she remembered his aversion to touch. At least the child no longer flinched. That kindled a warmth that transcended the pity she had felt until now.

"We can pay our way," Kordahla said, standing. She held out the packet. Erok's offhanded acceptance offended her. She was used to obsequious courtiers bowing repeatedly for the most trivial of her gestures, and here she was bestowing with her own hand a prize for which the Hill Tribe travelled leagues.

"It's porrin," she said with a haughtiness Father would have thought unbecoming. Erok seemed to recognise the word. He opened the packet and shook the unmistakeable red powder inside. "Will it pay for a guide to Myklaan?"

A jab in her back pushed her to her knees. Brax exploded into a flurry of angry words as his foot sent her sprawling into the dirt. She rolled over to see his spear poised above her heart. Only Erok's quick hand averted the stab she had no doubt was meant to kill. A furious exchange ended with Brax spitting close to where she lay. There was no mistaking Erok's dark countenance as she dragged herself up, or Brax's fury as he manhandled Timak to her side and shouted at his friend.

Erok shook the contents of the packet to the ground. The powder dusted the earth red. Erok was, she noticed, intent on her reaction. If the drug did not secure safe passage through the hills, it meant nothing to her. She lifted her chin, gathered what dignity she could, and looked him in the eye.

"You have made it quite clear how you feel about the cursed bliss." She took Timak's hand and walked along the stream. The water, shallow as it ran, should not have roared. Nor should the trees have shuddered, knitting their branches into a roof to blot the light of day. This place was cursed, these people fearsome. She hurried to be free of this haunted valley, where yellow eyes shone from dark hollows. Somehow, they would make it to the plain on their own.

The Hill Tribe men had other ideas. Brax shouted. The next thing she knew, he had bounded in front of them, his spear levelled at her midriff. She turned to see that Erok had assumed a similar pose. He gestured them to the right. They walked on, blistered feet, weak knees, tight chests and all. The points of the hunter's spears remained raised.

Chapter Thirty-four

THE CLANG OF IRON alerted Vinsant to the presence of a visitor. Hopping off the stools, which had made a tolerable bed if he did say so himself, he waited at attention.

"Good morning, Majoria," he greeted when Levi came into view. He had done his best to sound completely respectful and not at all smug. If he stood slightly straighter than normal, his chest thrust out and his shoulders back, Levi might presume it was because of the respectful soldier's pose he adopted rather than pride in the feat of working magic with absolutely no instruction at all. Even Levi would have to admit he made an impeccable soldier, unflinching as drops splattered to the mucky floor around him, or hit him on the head.

The slight movement of the Majoria's head as he took in the stools betrayed his surprise. His gloved hand paused on the door of the dungeon when the latch clicked free. Vinsant took a deep, expectant breath as the Majoria swung the door open and entered the damp cell. It didn't look like he had lost any sleep over locking his star pupil in the dungeon. Beneath his hood, his moustache was impeccable, and his black eyes bright with rest.

"Why is your robe not on?" The Majoria asked.

Vinsant's face fell. The oversized garment had made a better blanket than sleeping robe. The slime-stained hem had draped so far over the last stool, he hadn't even noticed it was wet. He cursed himself for not remembering to don it. Snatching the robe from across the stools, he fumbled to work his arms into it.

"Leave it," the Majoria said, and beckoned a mahktashaan who had been waiting in the shadows. The mahktashaan offered Vinsant a blue robe of perfect size.

"Eh, blue?" Vinsant asked when he pulled it over his head.

"You are not yet a mahktashaan, nor will you ever be if you do not lose your pride. Pull up your hood, and see that it stays there."

In a robe, not the churidar kurta of the apprentices, he was having considerable difficulty being anything but proud. "Shall I report to Branak for training?" Just let Naikil and Gram see him today. He would conjure a stool to sit on while they flung their practice swords about.

Levi pointed at the stools. "You will return each one to the Inn of the Shadow Hound, where the owner is currently complaining about mischievous djinn."

"Huh?"

"Objects cannot be conjured from thin air. I expect better of my apprentices than to steal from those working hard to make a living."

Vinsant, muttering about how nobody gave him credit for remaining in a stinking hole when he could have walked free, found himself tying stools to a horse as Naikil and Gram snorted at him while trying to land ineffectual blows on each other. Even leading a pack animal, it took him two trips, since Levi had forbidden his mahktashaan escort to help in any way.

The sunny inn boasted an ordered arrangement of tables. A veiled barmaid kept her eyes off them as she brushed the crumbs off the smooth tops and picked up fallen mugs. The turbaned innkeeper, not aware to whom he really spoke but made quite aware of Vinsant's apprentice status by the guards, let him have a piece of his mind. "If you could let me know I'll be losing my furniture before it happens in future, my patrons would appreciate not finding themselves on their backsides in puddles of ale."

Vinsant was glad the trepidation the mahktashaan inspired prevented him from saying more. "That won't be a problem," he replied, noticing how dry his mouth had become from the morning's work. "Eh, could we have an ale before we're on our way?"

The spoilsport mahktashaan turned him around and herded him out before the keeper could reply.

"Impudent imp," he heard the barmaid say behind him.

Respect, it seemed, was an elusive lesson. Too elusive to contemplate on the ride back to the palace when children were clambering the walls of twisting streets to watch the mysterious mahktashaan ride past.

No sooner had he walked his horse into the outer courtyard and dismounted than Levi bade him follow into the palace and down the post and lintel halls to the boat room.

"Where are we going now?"

"Do you forget your sentence?"

The Crystalite Mines? Right now? "Don't I get to say goodbye to Father and Arun? And I haven't had breakfast yet." That was the last time he was going to take Levi at his literal word when he insisted righting a wrong was the first order of the day. Just to prove how deeply he was suffering, Vinsant's stomach rumbled with all the rebellion of an unbroken stallion.

They walked down the steps to the water.

"The Minoria left early this morning, and the Shah was not idle in yesterday's words. You will return when matters are set to right."

That could, in his estimation, be moons, years even if Kordahla was lucky. "Um, wasn't the punishment for an eight-day?"

"This is a pilgrimage as much as a punishment, Apprentice Vinsant. There are mysteries for you to contemplate. If you are to progress in your studies, you will carry out my every last instruction to the letter. The first is for you to remain silent unless you are addressed."

"Yes, Majoria," he said, stepping into a boat, and wondering how he was ever going to learn anything. He was beginning to think he would have to tell Kordahla she had been right about Levi, if he ever saw her again.

The gatekeeper winched up the outer portcullis and they glided onto Lake Sheraz where fishing boats skedaddled out of their way. Though the air hung limp, the boat propelled itself forward with unnatural speed. Vinsant sat back and enjoyed the cruise through the long stretch of silence, his thoughts drifting to the feats of magic he would use to astound the realm. All for the good of Terlaan, of course.

His excitement when Levi made him recount his experiences with Mahktos was barely containable. It fizzled to disappointment when Levi permitted him no questions. At least he had the benefit of Arun's insight. When they both returned, he would make sure he cornered the Minoria and tricked, begged or commanded him into divulging more mahktashaan secrets.

In the middle of the lake, where the palace was so far it could only be discerned as a speck, the quartz around his neck began to throb. It was awesome, the way it glowed from within, but not so much the way it grew hotter and hotter. He held the leather strap to lift it off his chest.

"Majoria? Why is my quartz glowing?"

Levi, who had been facing forward, turned and stared.

"Do you seek to work magic? Without permission?"

"No. I wasn't doing anything," Vinsant said, juggling the swinging quartz. "Nothing like last night, anyway."

"Clear your mind," Levi snapped.

Vinsant pretended to sit in calm while his mind churned. Nothing changed. Levi had to be mega powerful because he enclosed the quartz in his hand without a sizzle of singed flesh. Not all-powerful, though, because when he let the quartz go, its inner light was brighter. The Majoria closed his eyes and hummed. The quartz drifted up and pulled towards the lake. Deep below the water, reddish light throbbed in unison with the quartz. It was so far down, it was a tinge in the depths, but it called to his quartz, pulling it from his neck.

"Majoria? Uh, Majoria."

The quartz was dragging him to the side. "No," said Vinsant, wrestling as best he could with the hot stone. He was not going to lose this piece of quartz. He was not going to go back to Mahktos and admit his incompetence.

"Majoria!"

They were right on top of the light now. The quartz jerked and Vinsant tumbled over the side of the boat. Water splashed onto Levi. Droplets sizzled into steam as they fell on his quartz. The lake closed over his head. Below him the light pulsed, white with a heart of red. It beckoned to his quartz, tugging, tugging hard. He would not lose it, not if it meant he had to drag whatever was emitting the light from the bottom of the lake. He swam down. Down so far. His lungs burning. His heart thumping. His chest wanted to flatten. His mouth fought to open. He was never going to reach it, let alone resurface. He strained against the quartz, managed to halt his descent, and kicked back up. The red light tugged so hard, his steady strokes brought him no closer to daylight.

Mahktos, no, please no. This wasn't fair. His survival couldn't depend on wriggling free of the quartz. Taking hold of the stone, he bowed his head out of it and kicked for the surface. The strap started slipping through his fingers. He was going to lose all his dreams. *Mahktos!* The lake parted over his head. He gasped and gasped as he rose between the walls of water. They crashed together below him as he cleared the surface and lay suspended in the air. Levi was standing at the stern with perfect balance, a hand raised towards him. The Majoria beckoned, and Vinsant's body swung over the boat, hung for a moment, then thudded to the planks. Heaving in air, he flipped the quartz back over his neck. It was all he could do to put a hand on the gunwale and drag himself up far enough to see over the edge. The waters were smooth. They were past the cursed spot, and the pull was weakening. So too was the heat and light.

"D-d-did you s-see that?" he asked Levi, his teeth chattering. The afternoon sun scorched, but he was chilled to the bone.

The Majoria picked up his quartz. The stone was inert.

"There was a light. It tugged at my quartz," Vinsant said, feeling a need to explain, though Levi ought to be explaining things to him.

"Silence!" Erect once more, the Majoria raised his hand over the lake. "*Crystallumin*", he said, the word ringing with a power which set his black crystal and Vinsant's quartz blazing. Out on the lake, the waters remained calm and dark.

"There is nothing there," Levi snarled.

The Majoria sat back down, this time facing Vinsant. The boat sailed on.

By the time the sun had begun its descent, Vinsant was dying of hunger. And bored out of his mind. There were only so many animals he could imagine in the clouds while lying cramped in the bottom of a boat before his unanswered questions began to drive him crazy. He was tempted to try and work some magic. Just so he could see what he could do. The problem was, Levi had remained intent on him since the episode in the water, if the direction of his hood was anything to go by. Vinsant couldn't really tell. The Majoria had not said another word. His punishment had obviously started, and an attempt to work magic, the consideration of an attempt even, if Levi's humour this morning was anything to go by, was bound to land him in deeper scums.

They sailed past rickety fishing villages, children paddling, and women washing baskets of clothes, the boat gliding on without sail or oar. Levi's magic was awesome, allowing them to cover the leagues to the northern shore in under half the normal time. Still, Vinsant's sore behind was glad when the boat bumped the pebbly beach. At its edge, a path led across a grassy flat to a cluster of neat stone cabins on the lower slopes of a hill. The Crystalite Range provided a stunning backdrop of steep, purple ridges and snowy caps, the more spectacular because sunset had turned the wispy clouds pink.

His stomach rumbling in anticipation, Vinsant jumped out. The Majoria drew his sword and crunched over the pebbles to a dry strip.

"Uh…isn't our best chance of dinner that way?" He pointed at the path.

"Imagine your practice sword. Use this gesture to summon it to your hand. You already know the magic word."

"You want me to do magic," Vinsant said, grinning. "*Sumbek.*" He made the gesture to no effect. Tried again and failed. Thought about what he had done in the dungeon, set his quartz aglow, and found a stool in his hand. He snorted as he thought about a drunken sailor suddenly on his behind in the Inn of the Shadow Hound. It was his sincere hope Levi was not about to make him trudge all the way back to Tarana to return the seat before they continued on.

"Concentrate," Levi said. He waved his hand, and Vinsant found himself ogling the empty space the stool had occupied a moment before.

Vinsant screwed his eyes shut and thought about the sword. A headache began to threaten at his temples.

"Relax. Find your focus," Levi said, walking around him.

Relax, concentrate. Trust a grown up to give conflicting instructions. He took a deep breath and, just like he had done in the dungeon, recalled his awe of the god. Other thoughts fled from his mind. He imagined the sword. Pictured his quartz aglow. Said the word and made the gesture. Toppled forward from the unexpected weight of the weapon in his hand.

"I did it," he said.

"*Dispumos,*" Levi said, waving his hand. His black crystal sparked, and the sword disappeared. "Now do it again."

Easy. Vinsant summoned his sword.

"Again," said Levi, making the sword disappear.

The third time he succeeded, he readied himself to make the sword disappear. Levi caught his wrist before he could gesture.

"You will confine yourself to what you are instructed to do, apprentice. Magic is not to be wielded lightly. There are dangers for the uninitiated."

Vinsant sighed as Levi returned the sword to the palace armoury. Less enthusiastic, he summoned it again, and again and *again.* He supposed there was something to be said for practice since he ended up summoning with only the barest spark of his quartz.

"That will do," Levi said.

Coming from the Majoria that was high praise. Vinsant grinned as his stomach grumbled with an intensity that surely could be heard over in the village. He was looking forward to a hearty meal. Levi had to have noticed he made no complaints about suffering a whole day without sustenance.

"Raise your sword," Levi said.

Vinsant blinked. He needed a second telling before the instruction registered. He did not expect the Majoria to swing and disarm him before he was fully prepared. Nursing his aching wrist, he picked up the sword. For over an hour, the Majoria led him through simple drills that, on an uneven, shifting surface required more concentration than he had used in his one-legged bouts with Gram. Just when he thought he was doing okay, a quick swipe knocked the sword out of his hand. Vinsant bent to retrieve it and found himself unarmed before he had righted himself. He stared at the Majoria. His wrist was stinging, and he was sure a nasty bruise was going to colour it come morning.

"Pick up the sword," Levi said.

Vinsant placed his hand on the hilt knowing the instant he was up it would be out of his hand. Humiliation was not what he had envisaged when he dreamed of training with the mahktashaan. He wondered if the repeated battering was meant to teach him a lesson. Meant to make him discover a way to beat his opponent, perhaps. He let go the sword and visualised Levi's, made the magical gesture and prepared to find the Majoria's sword in his hand.

He found himself lying face down on the pebbles instead.

"Your presumption will be the end of you. Now get up, and pick up the sword."

One wary eye on Levi, Vinsant did as he asked. When, instead of disarming him yet again, Levi showed him the manoeuvre, a clever trick that was nonetheless difficult to master on an empty stomach, he sighed in relief. The hour Levi forced him to spend perfecting the technique was the longest in his life. When Levi pronounced it was enough, Vinsant could not help another sigh. Bone weary, he sank to the ground.

"Bring the sword," was all Levi said as he started up the narrow track to the small village of Winpril. His feet dragging, his wrist smarting and his stomach in knots, Vinsant had no choice but to follow.

"You may request a loaf and some fowl for your master," Levi said, indicating a house.

Vinsant's knock was answered by a middle-aged man. "My master,

Majoria Levi, requests a meal," he said, hastily naming the requested foodstuffs. This was bound to be another of Levi's embarrassing lessons. The man looked over him to the silent but imposing mahktashaan Majoria.

"Wait here," he said, closing the door. A few minutes later, he returned with rice and grilled eggplant.

They ate in the boat. In silence. The crude meal did wonders to restore Vinsant's humour. He stretched. "Where are we going to sleep?" he asked Levi. Daesoa had risen one day past full.

In answer, the Majoria levitated himself onto a bed of air.

"How did you do that?" Vinsant asked.

His only reply was a soft snore. He tried to repeat the Majoria's gesture, forcing himself to find that inner rapt attention that allowed him to spark the quartz and perform magic. No surprise it didn't work. He tried again. And again. Was *levitos* the word the Majoria had used? And there he was in a flash of crimson, off the ground, his legs and arms dangling, his body swinging backwards and forwards. He pitched himself back and found himself upside down. In any other circumstances, this could be a lot of fun. After a day's travel and a near drowning, all he wanted was to get to sleep. He reached for the bench in the boat. His fingers did not even brush the gunwale. So, pulling himself down was not going to work. He rocked back and forth until he managed to spin himself upright. Only he ended up turning a somersault, and now his legs were drooping, as though he were suspended through the middle. However tired he might be, there was no chance he would drop off in this position.

"Majoria," he said, cringing.

The snores stopped instantly. The Majoria waved a hand his way, and he fell into the boat. Curling up, Vinsant contented himself with the hard deck.

CHAPTER THIRTY-FIVE

SIAN WOKE SCREAMING. PAIN seared along her arm. Her entire body throbbed with it. Around her, a hundred senseless shouts broke the night, shattering her fragile dream. Grandmam dragged her from the fire. Erok threw water on her arm. Screaming, she lashed out through the blinding white light of pain and struggled up. Her arm brushed against a leg. The touch was torture. She keeled over and vomited, again and again. They brought a pail of water and made her dunk her arm. It soothed enough for her blurred vision to settle. She looked in the pail. Saw a red and black mess. Pink fingers at the end. Hers. Her arm. She screamed again. Retched.

They carried her to Ishoa. Screaming. Laid her on the pallet at the back of the cave. Screaming. The soothsayer's painted face loomed above Sian's. Flashes of light seared her eyes, paining her as badly as the fire which had ravaged her arm. She tried to move. They held her down. Ishoa forced bitter liquid between her lips. Porrin. She gulped. She screamed. She trashed. The soothsayer hummed, danced, and twirled. It was wild energy. It was raw emotion. It grappled with her soul, tugged her from her body. It released her from the pain. She floated above it. Sian was down there, her useless left arm propped off the ground, her drugged eyes wide, her breathing slow. The pain cut through the bliss, but it was tolerable because she was above it all.

"The vision," the soothsayer commanded, standing tall, a hand on her feathered staff. The pods at its head were floating as though lifted by a gust.

"The sad boy comes," Sian heard herself say from high above.

The words brought it back: the encompassing oblivion as she succumbed to her affliction; the twisted visions that had plagued her since she first dreamed by the pool. They slashed through the blackness as the pain subsided beneath porrin's bliss. The same child. The sad child. He was coming to her.

❖ ❖ ❖

Levi had Vinsant up and practicing swordplay on the pebble beach at first light. It was all right for the Majoria – he had slept on a cushion of air – but Vinsant's pampered young body was unaccustomed to feeling so stiff. Unfortunately, he had a feeling Levi would keep him at training until he demonstrated a measure of skill in reposting. That alone drove him to summon enough energy to counter almost every attack. The remainder left him with much the same bruising Mariano did when his brother condescended to practice with him.

"You would do better if you concentrated with the same energy you use for magic," Levi said, sheathing his sword.

"All honour to you, Majoria," Vinsant said, stamping his right foot as Branak had taught him to do. He hoped it sounded sincere. Quite apart from the fact that a rattle of pebbles lacked the respectful authority of ringing stomp, it was taking a phenomenal effort not to curse the man in his thoughts. Only the sneaking suspicion Levi would somehow know it and make him atone by skipping breakfast kept him from imagining he was squishing a puffer with Levi's face beneath his foot. As it was, the image of Levi as a puffer nearly made him choke with laughter.

Breakfast, it so happened, came with a mahktashaan who led two black horses to the end of the grassy path. The man bowed and, after a glance at Vinsant and a quick word with Levi, retreated, unable to resist one more look at the blue-robed oddity of an apprentice. Vinsant maintained a dignified pose until he was sure the mahktashaan had done with looking over his shoulder. Then he pounced on the salty loaf and smoked ham.

"All praise to Mahktos for his bounty," Levi said with the air of the truly devout.

Feeling a smidgeon of guilt, Vinsant echoed him between a swallow and a bite. The phrase had to have been as much a reprimand as a prayer, and Levi would no doubt expect him to exercise more decorum at future meals. Well, if the man didn't near starve him, he might remember his manners!

They were on the horses before the sun had risen over the mountains, following the rapid Crystalite River toward the distant snow-capped Crystalite Range. Levi engaged in instruction the entire day, citing Mahktashaan lore with an uncanny knack for detail. Vinsant took it all in with relish. This was what becoming a mahktashaan was all about. In the open air, in the lush riverside country, life could not be better. That was until Levi began a quiz, making him recite verse after intricate verse until he was word perfect. Vinsant shook his head. His tutors had never demanded this much.

They dismounted in the evening outside a small farming community, in the flowery meadow beside the dirt road. Vinsant could only groan when Levi pulled out his sword. He groaned again when his perfect demonstration of yesterday's disarming move made Levi drive him harder in the execution of a new thrusting manoeuvre designed to penetrate beneath the defences of a heavier opponent. Mastering it would have been easier if he didn't have to wade through knee high grass to engage his opponent.

"You may request a meal," Levi said when the first star emerged, looking toward a farmer who was ambling home with a sack hoisted over one shoulder. When the sullen peasant saw their interest, he halted in his tracks.

Vinsant sauntered over with little enthusiasm for what might be in the sack. "The Majoria requests a donation for our dinner."

"Tell your master food is scarce with the little rain we've had. I've a family to feed and none to spare for the Shah's men." The farmer spoke over his head, refusing to take his eyes off the Majoria.

"You have a duty to your Shah," Vinsant said, unsure how to handle overt refusal. Until he had joined the mahktashaan, obsequious pandering had been the norm for a prince of Terlaan.

"Men around here earn their keep, boy," the farmer said. He trudged away.

Vinsant slunk back to Levi.

"Summon his sack," the Majoria instructed.

Vinsant blinked. He had permission to use magic. Real magic for a real purpose. He frowned. "What about the man's family?" Starving toddlers would prey on his conscience for an eight-day.

Levi released a nasal breath and curled his fingers. Vinsant had no desire to test his patience further. He poured his concentration into his quartz, and summoned the lumpy sack into his hand. Too bad it wasn't small enough to hide behind his back. The farmer turned and spat at him. At him, holding the bag, not Levi. He lowered his head until the man moved on. Hunger warred with shame for about three breaths. Hunger won out. His hand dove into the sack. The apples inside were disappointing. Small and bruised, they would hardly take the edge off his appetite before threatening a bellyache. Levi allowed them two each before tying the sack closed. Vinsant stared, ready to revolt if Levi insisted the snack comprised dinner. His rumbling stomach had to be good indication an apple was not enough sustenance for a hardworking, fast-growing boy.

"Summon your practice sword," Levi directed, refusing to acknowledge his challenge.

Quartz aglow, Vinsant brought the sword into his hand, wondering what form his mutiny could take so that he did not end up face down eating mud with Daesoa, two days on the wane, illuminating his humiliation. Before he could form any sort of plan, Levi dispelled the sword. Between summoning this grey stone, that brown stone, and then the black stone Levi placed behind his back, he didn't have a thought to spare.

"Again," Levi said, surprise laced with displeasure in his voice. He showed Vinsant two unremarkable stones before ordering Vinsant to turn his back and summon the smooth black stone he placed between them. The rock that appeared in Vinsant's hand was moss covered.

"Uh, that wasn't it, was it?" Vinsant asked.

"Conjuring an unfamiliar, unseen object is not beginner magic," Levi replied, his voice thoughtful. He walked around Vinsant, looking him up and down.

Vinsant smiled. Not that Levi would know it beneath the blue hood he was bound to wear. "Why did the farmer think us so awful?" he asked. An apprentice had to take the opportunity to ask a question while his master appeared pleased with his progress.

"You may not speak until spoken to, Apprentice. You will remember you swore to obey without question," Levi reminded.

"All honour to you, Majoria," Vinsant said without enthusiasm. The respect the Majoria was so fond of seemed to flow in one direction.

"You have one more magical act to perform tonight."

That act came at the end of a moonlit hike down a track through the stubble of a dry field to a drystone cabin. By the end of it, Dindarin, a waxing sliver, had shown his face. Vinsant thought he might fall asleep on his feet.

"Knock. Note the room and what meal the farmer eats, and return," Levi instructed.

"Yes, Majoria."

Four pink-faced children sat spoons in hand around a rustic timber table from which the mouth-watering aroma of chickpea stew arose. It was all Vinsant had time to note before the farmer slammed the door in his face. Vinsant did not blame him one bit. With a shrug, he returned to Levi.

"Now summon the farmer's meal," his honoured master said, as he broke from the daze of the thoughtlink.

Vinsant squirmed.

"You will do it, Apprentice," Levi said when his hands remained empty.

Vinsant sighed. He imagined the room, said the magic word, and waved his hand. Crimson light flashed out of his crystal, and an empty bowl clattered to the ground at his feet.

Levi mumbled and two bowls of stew topped with flat bread appeared. "We will eat here," he said, summoning a fringed carpet patterned with the Tree of the Vae. He played the revered master, sitting right in the middle.

Vinsant kicked sticks and stones off a dirt patch, and sat with his back to the cabin. He did not want to think about the figure looking out of the window. There was no chance he faded into the night with Daesoa shining overhead. He shovelled a spoonful of the spicy stew into his mouth. The portion he could swallow past the lump in his throat was hearty, but the wails from the house made him drop his spoon. Kordahla's voice rang in his ear, admonishing him for allowing multitudes to starve while he made a glutton of himself. Levi had to be heartless, because he took Vinsant's bowl and ate the remaining portion. When he had scraped the bowl clean, he passed it back to Vinsant.

"*Sumbek.*" In a burst of blackness, six succulent kebabs presented themselves to Levi's hand. They looked like one of the palace delicacies. Vinsant's mouth watered. He reached for the juicy meat.

"You will take these to the farmer and offer thanks," Levi said.

Vinsant waited until he was out of earshot before he grumbled. He wondered if he might nibble on the outermost morsels without discovery. Somehow, he didn't think so.

The farmer grabbed the sack of apples and the kebabs from his hand, and slammed the door in his face. It was hardly less than Vinsant expected, but at least he got to lick the fatty juices from his hand.

"Summoning an item you cannot see is challenging," Levi said when he had returned and unrolled a sleeping mat the Majoria had summoned. "When a mahktashaan has to rely on memory it takes immense skill and depends on the object lying where the mahktashaan believes it to be." He proceeded with a lecture that Vinsant had to admit answered all the questions he had been bottling.

◆ ◆ ◆

Alerted by an advance rider, the aged Satrap of Zulmei, clad in formal silks and coat despite the late hour, clambered to the gurgling, bear-based fountain in his colonnaded entrance courtyard. He waved his attentive footman away, determined to greet his royal guest in person. When the doddering old man lost himself for the third time during his welcome speech, Matisse stopped listening. The silent but suggestive exchange he struck up with pale-haired Rochelle, who waited a demure five steps behind her father in Daesoa's near-full light, was far more engrossing.

"Where are your sons?" Matisse asked when the formalities were done. He slowed his pace to match bent Satrap Elan's. The old man's joints creaked as they climbed the marble steps to the waterfront mansion.

Elan scratched the thin white hair on his head as they passed through the glazed-tile *pistaq*, thinking about the question. "Eh, Denkan is in Point Rai, wants to set up a merchant business, you know, and Rubrin is sailing for the Eastern Kingdoms. Always been one for adventure, that one," Elan cackled.

"How long has he been away?"

"Rubrin?" This time the satrap had to stop. "Let me see, must be a few months."

"Two years, father," Rochelle said, with a telling, close-lipped smile for Matisse.

"That long? No girl, surely not."

"Tell Denkan to present himself at the palace on his return from Point Rai," Matisse said. "Better yet, send a rider for him."

"Yes, yes," Elan said as though it were of no import. He looked about the mosaic walls and lapis honeycombed vault of the *iwan*. "Ah now, where were we to? Ah yes, your chambers."

"Allow me, father," Rochelle said, with a teasing look Matisse's way.

"No, no." Elan waved her away. He resumed his shuffle to the interior. "His Highness might have matters of the province to discuss."

"They can wait," Matisse said. His confidence in Satrap Elan's faculties was waning by the minute. The ride through the town had revealed the once celebrated city was falling into ruin. Collapsed street roofs, chipped mosaics, and scratched calligraphy marred the beauty of its elegant streets. If that wasn't concerning enough, figures engaged in furtive exchanges had disappeared down holes in backless corners as his party's horses clopped past. Bodies slumped in doorways and doors slammed shut as soon as frantic runners, glancing over their shoulder, squeezed through. Raj would have required little effort to start a lucrative business. Right under the withering Satrap's nose. It was past time Denkan assumed responsibility for the running of Zulmei, in practice if not in name.

"We bid you good night, Rochelle," Elan said, at the top of a tiled landing. The cracked stucco-work across the arched windows patterned Daesoa's light across the floor.

"Sweet dreams, my Lord. Goodnight, Father," she replied, her lingering gaze travelling down Matisse's body.

Matisse smirked. Two nights camped by the road had left him with a desire for more than a bed and a bath. Elan, his back already turned, was waddling in the opposite direction. The room he assigned Matisse was right at the end of the left wing. The old man was perhaps not quite the fool he appeared.

A hot meal and a wash later, Matisse wandered down the passage. This most ancient of Myklaan's palaces was becoming as rundown as the town. The plaster scrollwork on the walls was crumbling, and ingrained dirt had dulled the colours of the floor tiles. He nodded to Elan's white-haired footman, a demure lady-in-waiting, a bubbly maid. The heir to the throne had the benefit of outranking every member of the household. No one dared to question his errand. Until he bumped into Satrap Elan. The satrap stood at a window, contemplating the myrtle bushes lining the canal in one of the inner courtyards.

"Eh, everything is to your satisfaction, I presume," the satrap said, attempting to turn him around.

"Indeed. I wish to discuss a lightening of your tithe to the Crown to enable some restoration of this city. May I accompany you to your chambers as we talk?"

So the bewildered satrap, who was surely beyond rational if he remained ignorant of how Rochelle employed her talents, found himself installed behind his own doors as Matisse traversed the final cubits to his rendezvous.

The room was easy to locate. It was bound to be the one furthest from his own. A door left ajar, a wedge of light shining through, was clear invitation. Matisse stepped inside, closed the door and beheld his uncle's fair mistress as she reclined on a bed made with silk sheets and strewn with jasmine flowers. Her nightgown was arranged with seductive allure to reveal every contour of her feminine shape. Superb though they were, the gilded corbels and filigree walls paled in comparison.

"I hoped you would come," Rochelle said. "Nights have been so dreary since I returned home."

Matisse removed his housecoat. "Does my uncle mean so little to you?"

"On the contrary. I hold him in great regard. You may recall it was he who discarded me."

"You put up little resistance."

"I am not willing to die for him. At least, not in a fruitless cause."

He unwrapped his kamarband, went to the bed and looked down at her. Her moonlight-pale hair fanned out over the pillow. "You move readily to another."

She sat up, took a fistful of his kurta and pulled him to her. "Do you object?" she asked when their lips parted.

His answer was to slip his kurta over his head and climb onto the bed. Their lips met again as their hands tugged at each other's clothing, diving inside to release their secret pleasures.

"And what of you, my Lord," Rochelle said when he moved his lips down her neck and onto her breasts. "Do you not find my beauty faded compared to the young courtiers you usually pluck from their sleep?

"You yet glow, Rochelle. And I'll wager your talents are unsurpassed."

"What?" she asked, her teasing brushes turning to firm gropes, "What will you wager?"

Matisse had no spare breath to answer her as he discovered one of the reasons Rochelle had shared Ordosteen's bed for so long. After, they lay on the sheets side by side, spent, sated, silent.

"Come back to Kaijoor with me, Rochelle," Matisse said at last. He shivered. The night had, despite the season, grown cold. He rubbed a tickle on his shoulder, smearing blood where she had scratched him. Rochelle's exaggerated sympathy as she dabbed with her kerchief made him laugh.

She dropped the kerchief onto the floor and turned onto her side. "I do not wish to cause Ordosteen pain."

"He has suggested I keep a mistress or three at the palace. I do not think he will be displeased if it is you." He turned his head to look at her. This remarkable, talented woman would do more than keep him at the palace nights. She would have him running to it. Ordosteen could not object to that.

"So I must pass from the Shah to his heir."

"The heir will be Shah in his turn."

The way she twirled the hair on his chest was pleasing. The way she ran a finger over his lips, and whispered at his cheek, stirred his blood. "And will this shah be wise? What will he barter with? What will he barter *for*, I wonder?"

He kissed her, rolled to face her, and stroked her breast. "I will make no deals with a djinn."

"No? Does every man not have his price?" Her hands were exploring him again. His own moved down to the small of her back. The goose-bumps erupting over him promised an exquisite night.

"The cursed djinn are likely to demand my night-time pleasures. It would not become a shah to relinquish these."

She chuckled. "Nor would it be seemly for the future shah to remain cold." Her hands moved to all the tender places with expert grace, her lips were at his again, and he was regaining his desire faster than he ever had before. He rolled on top of her, working his lips over her.

"Come back to the palace with me."

"How else will you experience everything I have to offer?" she said, making sure he could talk no more.

◆ ◆ ◆

The next, sweaty day unfolded in a predictable ride along the babbling river, learning and reciting mahktashaan lore. Come evening, Vinsant had his sword out before Levi could order him to do so. An hour's sword-play on the uneven, rocky bank, and Vinsant was ready to wolf down his meal. This time reverent, mud-hut dwelling villagers pressed them with trout, fruit and bread, beating a respectful withdrawal as soon as they laid the victuals at Levi's feet. Vinsant relished every bite, speculating on what magic Levi might teach him when the moons rose. An extension of yesterday's failure, no doubt.

Instead, Levi bid him summon an onyx-handled dagger from his hand. Now this, Vinsant thought, slapping at a biting mosquito, was super useful. Mega difficult too. Empty-handed, he picked up a stone and skipped it across the river. It bounced five times before plopping down.

"A lay person who wishes to keep hold of their object will not relinquish it easily, even to magic. Other magicians will not let you steal their possessions without a fight. Now concentrate. I am barely keeping a grip on my dagger."

Vinsant sighed, and dragged himself around. The mosquitoes buzzing around his neck in the still, hot dusk did not make concentrating easy, but if it took him all night, he would get that dagger, if only to show Levi he could. All he needed was a memory of Mahktos to kindle the soft glow in his quartz.

"I did it. I did it," he cried raising the blade into the air. It was back in the Majoria's hand before he could gloat further.

"Do it again," came the expected reply.

And again and again, of course. He yawned. The trick was becoming easy-as, despite Levi's firmer grip. One day, he would be a great hero, plucking swords from the hands of any who dared to challenge him. He would wield a golden-hilted Myklaani sword of the finest workmanship, the Terlaani royal emblem emblazoned above the mahktashaan Majoria one. He pictured the smith etching the symbols of his office in place of the Myklaani royal crest. A prowling leopard in front of a sun instead of two facing bears beneath a great oak. He waved his hand to summon Levi's weapon. Lifted it in triumph. Gawked. Levi was still grasping his dagger.

Vinsant looked at the blade in his hand. It was a sword. A heavy Myklaani sword with a golden hilt. With the Myklaani royal crest etched on it. With fresh blood dripping from the blade.

Vinsant dropped the sword and backed away.

"What have you done?" Levi asked. The Majoria's hands had curled into fists.

"I…I was trying…" he said and stopped because he had no idea what he had been trying.

Levi strode forward, driving him back. "Your distraction may have cost the wielder his life."

Vinsant gulped as he tottered on a boulder at the edge of the water. He could not take his eyes off the bloody blade. "Can you return it?"

"From where did you summon it?"

Vinsant shook his head. He had no idea.

"Then the owner must fend for himself."

Without another word, Levi levitated himself in preparation for sleep. Vinsant sat on the boulder. It was a long time before he found the courage to pick up the sword and clean it. For the time being, it was in his care. After all, stolen objects had to be returned to their rightful owners. He was a model apprentice, and had learned that lesson well. So not even Levi could deny he now had a legitimate excuse to travel to Myklaan.

The Crooked Bow looked every bit as unreliable as its namesake. The tavern's lopsided sign swung on a single chain, its wooden planks had warped and, despite the din raised inside, little light spilled from the interior into the narrow alley. It was not hard to conclude they had reached the right place.

Matisse sent four of his men to cover the back door of what was undoubtedly Zulmei's seediest establishment. Swinging open the door, he stepped inside to the reek of sour ale and unwashed bodies, and was greeted by immediate hush. Uniformed guards tended to have that effect on the unsavoury, most especially when half bore the palace crest upon their emerald green cloaks and tabards.

"Hai!" a burly man with a great ale gut protruding out of a soiled kurta greeted. "Our quality ain't for the likes of you. The Sour Leaf is where you lot'd best go."

The men, his and the satrap's, spread around the walls, blotting the weak light of the dribbling candles. The iron sconces the melting stumps squashed into sat at intervals guaranteed to preserve shadowy corners. Matisse ambled past tables cobbled together with rough-cut, ill-fitting planks, straight to the grimy bar separating the drinking room from the kitchen. Resting against the counter he beckoned the burly taverner with his index finger. The fat man wiped his hands on his soiled kurta and leaned across. His flabby arms had once been muscle, and were tattooed with the feather-throated schkaan.

"A tankard of your finest," Matisse said, depositing two lek on the counter.

A wary eye on him, the taverner poured a cloudy brew into a mug smudged with fingerprints and slid it over. Matisse took a gulp and spat it out. Horse piss could taste no worse.

"Who is trying to poison me?" he asked.

Wobbly chairs scraped across the floor as three patrons decided an exit was in order. His soldiers had swords drawn and the entrance barred before they had left their table.

"Who is the owner of this establishment?" Matisse upended the tankard so the ale sloshed on the floor. The silence turned ominous. Matisse set the vessel on the counter, and drew his sword. "I asked a question. Two in fact."

Chairs flew back as patrons drew knives and swords while others bolted for the door. The street fighters lacked skill but they greatly outnumbered the soldiers. As chairs cracked onto heads and tankards flew at faces, his men found themselves dodging blows more than parrying, fending off missiles rather than thrusting their swords. One of his men cried out as a knife lodged in his arm. Two more soldiers grabbed the culprit and threw him to the ground. The injured guard placed a foot on the riffraff's chest and pointed his sword at his neck. The three of them ducked as a chair sailed their way. It flew over their heads and crashed into the counter.

A robust sailor grabbed a stool and rushed at Matisse, cussing palace scum. Matisse jabbed the sword into his belly, sidestepping the blow the sailor intended to deliver on his head. The stool instead smashed upon the counter. The man's eyes opened wide in surprise as he sank down to the floor, his hands clutching his bloodied stomach. Matisse withdrew his sword and wheeled. Three of the man's mates were running at him, knives poised. Trapped between the counter and the dying man, he raised his sword. The scrawniest fellow threw his knife. Matisse struck up with his sword, deflecting the knife from his heart. Following the swing around, he changed grip in mid-air and cleaved the second fellow's hand off. The third he kicked as the maddened man lunged for him. Twisting, Matisse only just managed to avoid being sliced. As the man overbalanced and toppled against the counter, a soldier rammed a sword into the attacker's back. He too collapsed.

These mercenaries had to be insane. By now, any rational fighter would have realised the quality of the competition and withdrawn. But two more men were rushing their way. Side by side, grinning, Matisse and his lieutenant prepared to face them. Swords raised, they put their head together and sang the last line of a victory song. At which point something beyond Matisse's experience as a man, soldier and royal personage occurred. Something so unbelievable it stopped the four men dead in their tracks. His sword disappeared out of his hand. Just like that.

Two blinks and the mercenaries resumed their dash. Matisse cursed as his companion prepared to defend his lord. As the soldier engaged one man, Matisse leapt onto the counter to avoid the oncoming blade of the second.

"Teryl," he called to his closest man, who was fencing with a chair.

The man worked his opponent round, saw the heir unprotected

and threw his sword. That moment of pause gave Teryl's opponent opportunity to smash the chair over his head. Dazed, Teryl collapsed. Unfortunately, his sword fell well short of Matisse. Seeing the leader undefended, Teryl's assailant lost interest in the unconscious man and made straight for Matisse. Cursing every inch of the anatomy of the djinn, Matisse jumped over a slash at his ankles, then dropped behind the bar. By some savage twist of fate, his companion appeared evenly matched for his attacker. No help would be forthcoming for critical moments. With two swordsmen now aiming for him, luck seemed to have fled. Matisse crawled the length of the bar as his first attacker rolled over the counter. With a precision borne of years of sparring with friends, Matisse reached up, grabbed a half-full tankard of ale, threw it at him, and hoisted himself onto the counter as the man landed. Skipping over another slash, Matisse leapt onto his shoulders, toppling him over and avoiding a stab from Teryl's assailant, who had appeared at the end of the bar sporting a nasty smirk. He jumped onto the fallen man's sword arm, pinning it beneath him. Matisse punched the man, stomped on his hand, and plucked the sword from his grasp. As the man tried to rise, Matisse delivered a fatal blow between the ribs. He whirled to face the other man, whose astonishment Matisse had managed to arm himself settled to a determined frown. Sword held in challenge, the mercenary strode forward.

"I grow tired of this sport. Lay down your weapon," Matisse said.

"Submit to a tired dandy? I can't think of easier prey," the man replied.

"Not quite what I meant," Matisse replied, parrying a crude slash without effort. He allowed the man a few more strikes before taking the sword into a series of lightning-quick thrusts that forced his assailant back. As the man moved past the end of the bar, Matisse leapt onto it, hopped over the inevitable low slash and struck down onto the man's neck.

"I meant the lack of adequate competition was rather beginning to bore," he said as the mercenary crumpled to the floor.

From his vantage point, Matisse looked around. The action seemed to be dying. The rabble were cowering in the centre of the room, ringed by restless soldiers who were either tossing the final stubborn dissenters into their midst or threatening prisoners who so much as eyed the exits.

"That," said Matisse, wiping blood from his face and throwing the poorly balanced sword into the fray, "was a cursed expensive sword. Who is responsible for taking it from me?"

Nobody answered. He jumped down. Striding around the room, he picked up and discarded every common sword in sight. The riff-raff followed his every move but, Vae'oeldin strike the culprit down, there was not a single smug expression in sight.

"By the hairy butt of a stinking djinn," Matisse cursed. "I'll have something to say to Drucilamere about this." He stomped along the counter and grabbed the taverner, who was sidling towards the back door. For a moment, the hulking man looked set to fling himself on Matisse. The blade at his neck convinced him otherwise.

"Kneel," Matisse said. Cussing, the man obeyed. "How many?" Matisse asked his lieutenant as the satrap's men pushed those still standing to their knees. Around them, the room was a wreck of splintered chairs and overturned tables, injured men and angry soldiers.

"Six of the lowlifes dead and that howler whose hand you cut off soon to be if he doesn't shut his trap. Grumps has a knife in his shoulder, Foz and Teryl have slashed arms. Nothing that won't heal."

"Then I thank you for the diversion. There is nothing like a spot of sport before bed," Matisse said to the taverner, gesturing to the man whose hand he had sliced off. The unfortunate lad was screaming while attempting to stem the flow of blood. Two soldiers restrained him while another bound the stump before dragging him out.

"Now we can hear ourselves think, I am waiting for my answers. Who owns this establishment?"

"I do, you stinking palace dog," the taverner said.

"That," said Matisse as a soldier bound the man's arms behind his back, "is no way to talk to the heir to the throne."

The taverner's eyes narrowed as he scrutinized Matisse. Recognition turned to a flash of fear before his face settled into a resentful pout. "I tried to warn yer," he said.

"Yes, I suppose you did. But there is still the matter of my second question. To be fair, I shall change it. What name do you go by?"

"I'm known as Korwin the Stout."

"Then it is you my business is with. You could have saved yourself the trouble and expense of this shambles had you only cooperated from the outset."

"And deprived you and these lads of some fun, Highness. I wouldn't dream of it."

Matisse laughed. "Quite right. And for providing that free entertainment, things might not go so ill for you. Tell me. What business have you conducted with a Verdaani called Raj?"

"Don't know 'im," Korwin said with a shake of his head.

Matisse sighed. "I am not above a little further sport." He nodded and the soldier behind Korwin twisted up his arm. The taverner winced. "I would rather not take you back to Kaijoor. The Crown would have to confiscate this valuable piece of property."

"Don't know 'im, I tell you."

Matisse shrugged. "Then you can enjoy the hospitality of Zulmei's dungeons before we head to Kaijoor."

Chapter Thirty-six

FOOTSORE AND WEARY AFTER two days traversing the hills at the point of Erok's spear, Kordahla limped into the Hill Tribe settlement. Heads turned from weapons, knives and cooking pots to stare. In truth, she had seen so few tribespeople in Tarana that their feather talismans and bone tools intrigued her. Refusing to succumb to ill-breeding, she forced her gaze forward. Timak had no qualms looking around, and she was glad for his curiosity. Out of Ahkdul's clutches, he might heal, though she doubted he would ever be the same boy he had once been.

"They don't look like they use porrin," he whispered to her.

With a start, she took more notice. The child was right. These people, weather-beaten and tanned, had gleaming eyes and toned bodies. She looked at him looking at them, uncertain what startled her more, that the Hill Tribe were clean, or that the child had begun to think for himself.

In the centre of the village, a stocky, middle-aged man climbed off a roof he was patching with mud and straw. He wore similar clothes to the hunters, leather trousers and vest, and a loose, rough-spun shirt embroidered with the spiralling squares and circles which marked this tribe. His expression when he intercepted them, alert and considerate, lacked the kind of shrewd, judgemental intelligence that would have seen her risk an escape. His frown deepened as he spoke with Erok through the distressed wail of a babe she wished the mother would comfort. They waited while he washed his hands in a trough, and drank a cup of water pulled from another in one long draught. When Erok prodded them past the disordered collection of wooden longhouses, into stands of ash and beech, it almost brought tears to her eyes, so dashed was she to forgo a bath and meal. The rough track they took out of the settlement with the two displeased men set off a flutter of nerves.

"Can you call your genie?" she asked Timak.

His eyes widened and he shook his head.

"Please, Timak. I'm not asking you to bind her, just to invite your friend here."

He looked straight ahead, returning to that insular state so he could pretend he had not heard. She sighed. The indigo djinn was bound to turn up at the first sign of trouble. It was just she was not sure exactly how deep was the pit she had already dealt herself into.

At a huge hollow trunk, they turned up a hill. The older man strode on ahead, his feet finding effortless purchase on the precarious pebbly ledge. She crept after him, thanking Vae'oenka Erok was not an impatient man. She was under no illusion about their status, but the hunter had, until now, treated them with crude respect. The gaping, black hole which became visible when they passed behind a pink-flowering bush changed matters. He said something that was clearly an order to move on. She was almost ready to risk his spear when the older man ducked inside. With him out of the way, a woman became visible. Dressed in nothing more than reeds and leaves, she clutched a staff decorated with a frightful array of pods and feathers. She stood gazing out over the valley with an air of ownership. When she turned her head, Kordahla started. Her milky eyes were sightless, and yet she planted them with unerring accuracy, as though she *saw*, dear Vae, not just tangled, walnut hair and torn, muddy clothes, but deep into the soul. The air became heavy. Kordahla fought for breath.

"I have been waiting," the woman said. Ochre stripes lined her face, and her bound hair was dressed with feathers.

The weird searching sensation lifted. "You speak our tongue?" Kordahla asked, easing the tension in her forehead. Their misunderstanding could be cleared up. They might even leave with a guide.

"I speak what you need to hear, Princess," she said.

A ripple of fear chilled her. "Father!" She peered into the cave but no mahktashaan lay in wait. There was only a girl sitting on a rock on the far side of the entrance, beneath bundles of herbs strung from vine. A few years older than Timak, her straight, fair hair screened her bowed head as she cradled one horribly burned arm in the other.

"You are far from those you love," the woman said, and turned into the cave.

Erok nudged her to follow. It was dry inside, with furs arranged around a hearth over which a pot simmered. Sunbeams speared to the back, gilding dancing dust motes. A faint smell of ash imbued the place with an unsettling timelessness.

"How do you know me?" she asked.

This time, the woman looked past her. "I am Ishoa, Soothsayer of the Ho'akerin. You should not have offered us poison."

"I…I thought only to make a gift. I am sorry if you are offended."

"Were your family not outraged when you were presented with such a gift? How is it you think our tribe would delight in porrin's curse?"

Kordahla flushed. To know these details this woman had to be in league with the djinn. "Your people wander our towns, searching for any means to acquire it."

"Had you thought about it, you might have wondered why they were not with their families. The drug is outlawed, as are all who use it. It is only because Erok thought you might know something of our missing people that you live. He tells me Brax wanted to slaughter you. It would have been justice of your people's kind."

Her cheeks were aflame. She could think of nothing to say. If this were some sort of trial, she was doomed from the outset.

"Sit. There is much we need to discuss," the soothsayer said, using her staff for support as she lowered herself onto one of the rabbit furs.

"If you know so much about me, then you are not going to help." These people would want her returned to Ahkdul, to an agreement that dwindled the supply of porrin.

"And leave the surplus to pervade the hills of the Akerin?"

The woman was a mind reader. This talent she displayed was of a calibre that surpassed the mahktashaan. Staring, stunned, Kordahla could only sit as she was bid. Timak settled between her and the mouth of the cave as the soothsayer bid the girl fetch some wooden bowls. The child's face was tearstained, her left arm blistered and raw. There would be heavy scarring if infection did not set in.

"There are people who could heal that," Kordahla said to the soothsayer.

"Your mahktashaan would as soon put her to the sword."

Kordahla swallowed. The tiny woman had stolen her confidence.

"Do you think us ignorant of the world?"

"I can give you the name of one to seek. He would help." The soothsayer made no reply. Kordahla dropped her eyes. Arun *would* help.

The girl set the bowls by the fire. Erok ladled stew from the pot, placing the first bowl into Ishoa's hands and handing the second to the older man. When she and Timak were catered for, he bid the girl sit, and settled a bowl on her lap.

"What do you want of us, Princess?" They had scraped the bowls clean and been introduced to Draykan, Leadsman of the Ho'akerin, and Sian, daughter of the tribe. The girl still refused to lift her head. Kordahla winced to think what dishonour one her age could have.

"Can you provide a guide to Myklaan?" she asked, more assured for her full stomach.

"You ask much of us at this time. Our numbers are depleted, our hunters are scarce and we require the best of our guides for the Gathering."

"I can give you gold." She had intended it to pay her way to Kaijoor once they reached Myklaan, but it was worthless if they wandered the hills lost.

"I care little for the riches of your world, and in the wrong hands your coin will purchase porrin. Do not reveal what you carry in the village, or the spirits shall demand retribution."

She had nothing more to offer. "Will you at least indicate the direction?"

At her side Timak must have recalled some trifling possession for he was rummaging in his shalvar. She hoped he had more wit than to produce another packet of porrin. The coychan shell he withdrew brought a murmur from the men. The heedless boy wriggled forward to present it two-handed to the soothsayer. Sensing a gift was being made, Ishoa patted the air before her until her palm alighted on the shell. Her start, as she rotated her painted hand, was noticeable. She fixed her sightless eyes right on Timak with an intensity that made Kordahla shudder.

"I thank you," the soothsayer said, "but this belongs to Sian." Her hand remained outstretched until Timak crawled forward, took the gift and extended it to the girl. Ishoa spoke to her in the language of the tribe. At last and by degrees, Sian lifted her anxious face. She stared at Timak like she had seen a ghost. She blurted a few words, waiting for the soothsayer's gentle reassurance before she took the shell. Her worried eyes never left Timak's face.

"What did she say?" Kordahla asked.

"She has dreamt of this boy."

Kordahla swallowed. Too much was happening that she did not understand.

Beside her, Timak rocked off his knees onto his feet. "I don't know," he said, his face tilted to the roof of the cave.

The girl sprang up. The bowl on her lap clattered to the floor. She backed to the wall of the cave and pressed against the rock. The child was a mouse but her face was frozen in fear of the same high point Timak watched.

"Sian?" Draykan queried.

The girl did not respond. Kordahla shivered.

"I think she knows you're here," Timak said.

Of all the moments for the genie to turn up, this had to be the least opportune. She should not have been surprised. Meddle was what those infernal creatures did. Kordahla looked at the soothsayer. The wise woman had to have some advice.

Ishoa gazed into the flames, her back to the spot the children believed the genie to be. "Come, genie," the soothsayer said. "There are none who would hurt you here."

Sian ran to the soothsayer and buried her face in Ishoa's lap.

"Hush, child," Ishoa comforted, then spoke in the tongue of the tribe.

After some seconds of silence Timak said, "You mean like I can?" Again he listened before turning to Sian. "What is she doing?" he asked the girl. There was a pause during which he smiled. "I want someone else to say."

Unnerved, Kordahla looked at the hunters. Erok was scratching his head. Ishoa spoke to Sian, stroking her back. Keeping her face buried, the child shook her head until Ishoa tapped a single sharp finger on her head. With a strangled sound, Sian raised her face, first to Ishoa and then the point smiling Timak watched with the rapt glow of innocence. She whispered an answer to her tribeswoman.

"She says the genie has a face that is eager to smile. She is kneeling with her hands on her legs," Ishoa said.

"Sian can see her?" asked Kordahla.

"These two, they are like Dindarin and Daesoa. Our sky is not complete without either."

"Or the sun," Kordahla said offhandedly. She wanted answers, not rhetoric.

"Yes, or the sun. And so there must be another." Ishoa warbled a note.

"You're scaring her." Timak cried.

Ishoa broke off. "Her heart is pure. She has nothing to fear from me. It is we who must fear the djinn. Princess, there is a shadow from the spirit world about you. Your future holds much suffering for the pact you have made."

Her response was a frustrated release of breath. "Tell me what the djinn will take."

Ishoa stood and shuffled to the mouth of the cave, her staff tapping the rock to guide each step. "I do not know," she said, her back to them. The feathers in her hair stood out at awkward angles. "But it is a thing of great import." She turned. Her white eyes locked onto Kordahla's, and her voice took on an ethereal cadence as sunbeams flared around her and the wind moaned through the trees. "The spirits believe you must endure, Princess. Through your heartache, you must prevail, else the world will change around mortals, and our lives will fade away. Remember that when you suffer."

Kordahla stood. Her hands were trembling. She had hoped to forget the terrible thing she had done until the djinn came to claim his due. Now here it was, confronting her. "What do you foresee?"

Ishoa's gaze drifted. Her voice dropped to a murmur. "That the fates of our peoples are entwined.

"Then you will help me?"

Ishoa lifted her chin. Her bearing made her seem tall. "You shall have your escort to Myklaan."

Kordahla woke sore and unrested on the hard pallet she had been allocated in the communal sleeping hall. In the depths of night, a baby had woken and screamed. She had been surprised how quickly its distress had passed. Timak had fretted for longer when Erok had tried to separate him from her. The hunter had eventually wearied of his mute struggles, and allowed him into the girls' hut. He was curled on a pallet beside her, oblivious to the squawks and bleats that heralded dawn. She lay there, listening to the regular breathing of the children they had been placed with, all much younger than her, until the patter of feet and clatter of cooking implements told her the village had begun to rise. She found a comb among a wooden goshawk and polished stones in a basket beside her bed, and attended to her wayward hair. Then she tiptoed across the creaking floor of the common room and entered the sultry dawn, scratching at insect bites until her skin turned red. In a trough at the back of one of the longhouses, she found water for washing. When she returned, a lean, wrinkled woman beckoned her over to a fire and handed her a bowl of fragrant porridge sweetened with honey and a score of different birdsongs. The woman broke into a gap-toothed smile as she scraped the bowl clean.

A gaunt woman emerged from another longhouse. She must have been new to motherhood to drape her baby precariously over her thin arms, to swaddle it so tight, and in black, a colour most unfitting for a child. It was strange that the infant made no protest, no gurgle or burp, and stranger yet the lean old woman beside her clucked in anger as she forced the other to surrender the child. This grandmother may have raised a brood, but to push a grubby finger into the babe's mouth was to invite an illness more severe than the malaise afflicting it. How could this mother have dawdled unconcerned when the babe did not suck, did not cry, did not even twitch? The old woman was already shouting to a boy who was watching Erok sharpen a spear tip at the edge of the houses. He ran in the direction of the soothsayer's cave, leaving Erok with a frown as he downed his work to investigate.

When Ishoa arrived, a hand on Sian's good arm, they gave her the child. She held it in tender arms though her head swayed back and forth as she keened a sound so choked with mourning it brought tears to Kordahla's eyes. It summoned the tribe from longhouse and forest into a drizzly morn. Hunters peered from the trees, silent amid the pat, pat, pat of raindrops on leaves. Women broke off their gossiping to rise by the crackling fires, and children crowded on the steps, jostling each other for a better view. When the note ended, not a bird chirped, not a fly buzzed, not a monkey chittered. The forest itself was bereft.

In this silence, Draykan trudged up the steps of a longhouse, and turned to face his tribe. Oblivious to the strike of raindrops on his face, he weighed his words with such import, some calamity must have struck. Kordahla edged toward Ishoa. The soothsayer had the gift of sight, but this was a people in dire need of a physic. Sian's teeth were clenched, her eyes glazed. Her burned arm had to be agonising.

"See what sorrow porrin's bliss brings our people," Ishoa said. She had not lifted her eyes. Without paint on her face or feathers in her long braid, she looked young to bear her power. "This baby's mind is gone. He was addicted to porrin before he ever breathed the air. With care, he might have stood a chance, but Esa cannot bear his screams. Each day she feeds him a little more of the cursed drug."

The baby's wide eyes stared unseeing, its little body immobile, not a finger nor a toe wiggling, the slow, shallow rise and fall of its chest the only sign of life. Kordahla lowered her eyes. Was this what the Terlaani faced? Was she selfish to avoid a marriage that could ease the burden of the drug?

"I'm sorry," was all she could think to say. She truly was, for all she had not supplied the drug.

Esa was wailing now, screaming even, her hands entreating, grabbing at Draykan. The leadsman had to be heartless to stand firm in the quickening rain. How could he think a mother would have anything other than the best interests of her children at heart? The three untidy youngsters who ran and clung to her skirts were bawling in sympathy. They didn't just need her, they wanted her. Surely the old women picking up the toddler and pulling the children away saw that. What manner of tribe was this, that Erok would aim his spear at a mother as soon as her children were out of harm's way?

Monkeys gathered in the trees, bouncing their backsides. Esa backed up.

"What will happen to her?" Kordahla asked as several men herded the woman past the longhouses. Timak squeezed his way out of the longhouse, past the children, and came to stand close, his young body tense.

"She is exiled from the Ho'akerin."

The monkeys bounced and hooted.

"And her children?"

"They will be cared for by the tribe."

Monkey hands rained plum stones on the woman.

A shout from one of the men turned their attention. A figure staggered towards the longhouses. The man reached the wash trough, mumbled then collapsed. Warm rain fell. Esa's guard halted. Every member of the tribe began talking at once. A rosy-cheeked young woman fetched a cup of water and held it to the injured man's lips. As hunters helped prop him up, the sight of his bloody, mangled leg drew a gasp from the tribe.

"O-GRES," he cried, batting the cup from the woman's hand. "O-GRES." He was delirious, from fear or from pain.

Kordahla's blood ran cold.

Esa screamed and hurled a tirade of words.

Erok looked to Draykan, who gestured with his chin at the babe and shook his head. It was wrong of Erok to force Esa back with the point of his spear. She would never survive more than a night alone. Kordahla took a step forward. Ishoa's hand clamped on her arm.

"Do not meddle in our affairs, lowlander."

Kordahla stiffened. She would have thought the tribe callous, were it not for the vacant child who sucked on air, oblivious to the commotion about it. Who, if Ishoa was right, was deprived a meaningful life.

"He is gone, Farina," Ishoa said as a hunched old woman took the babe from her arms. "May he find his way to the spirits." Tears glistened in both their eyes, though the boy yet breathed. "Take me to Lutham, child," she said to Sian. Never looking up, the serious girl guided the soothsayer step by step, and helped her kneel by the mangled leg. The soothsayer's hands hovered as she trilled a discordant prayer. Her instructions for cleaning and binding the wound were followed with alacrity.

"Another exile," Ishoa said, as Kordahla helped her to her feet, and hunters carried the injured man into a longhouse. "Lutham repents and has asked for re-admittance to the tribe."

"Will Draykan accept him?" she asked.

The soothsayer seemed to shrivel. Her eyes held the suffering of the tribe. "His addiction corrupts the young. Once he is well, he must leave."

The group that left the longhouses was silent. Erok led the way into deep, shaded forest, his grim expression clear indication he was unimpressed with his task. She followed with Timak, both of them in clean but worn Ho'akerin garb, a sleeping mat and blanket strapped to their back. Sian trailed with her grandmother, Vila, the lean, wrinkled woman who had cooked breakfast. Her few rusty words of Laanan were music to Kordahla.

Progress was slow. Both Vila and Erok foraged as they went, pulling up white bulbs and green stems and plucking peaches, nuts and early date plums from trees. It made for tasty meals, supplemented with any rabbit, fish or partridge Erok caught. At times he disappeared off trail, returning hours later with his catch. It was then Kordahla understood the steep terrain, the endless climbs and descents that turned her legs to puffer jelly, that left her stiff and miserable was no hindrance to the hunter.

The first night they camped in a valley, wrapping thin blankets tight around themselves as stars winked through gaps in the canopy. So tired was she, the hard ground did little to stop her drifting into restless sleep.

She woke with a start. Disoriented by the blackness, she turned. The fire had died to embers. Spooked by the rustles and whirrs, she listened for a sound out of place in the dark. Her eyelids were drooping when a yowl send shudders down her spine. She disentangled herself from the blanket and went to the children. Timak and Sian were sitting up, and Vila was clucking about them like a mother hen. Erok was standing alert, holding up a wet finger to gauge the wind. A second yowl startled the children into gasps. It sounded no nearer, small comfort that it was. She hesitated as Erok waved them back to sleep.

"Ogre too far. No reach us before morning," Vila said, and hushed the children down.

Kordahla watched both Erok and Vila tuck themselves in before she was game to return to her blanket. She barely dozed the rest of the night.

Come dawn they were up again. Her feet, blistering in the sturdy pair of moss-stuffed, bark shoes the village had provided, were agony to walk on. Her skin was raw from scratching at insect bites and her mind foggy from lack of sleep. She would have welcomed someone to talk to, but Laanan was a strain for Vila and she limited herself to the bare necessities of communication. As for Timak, he fled into his own world. He and Sian had found their own way to have a one-sided conversation through the tireless genie. She watched Timak reply through gesture to some comment Sian had made. It was more than he had done with her. Kordahla's isolation began to suffocate. She longed for Karie and Samille's frivolous banter.

That afternoon, their way was barred by a wall of rock. Kordahla bit her lip. It didn't matter how many crevices pocked the rock, or how agile the hunter climbed, it was an impossible ask. She had worn slippers all her life, had carpets laid under her feet and gallant hands to escort her up steps.

"I can't," she said, when Erok came back down.

Without attempting to understand, he ushered them around the cliff with an urgency that left her not just relieved, but wondering, until a peculiar, musty stink drifted to her. The intensity of it left her in no doubt that more than one ogre inhabited the nooks above. She was not the only one to cast wary looks over her shoulder as the day progressed. Erok urged them to hurry, pushing them on until dusk, dishing out a cold meal before forcing them into tall trees, up and up until they could climb no more without risk of a bough breaking beneath them.

As Dindarin set and crescent Daesoa rose, the yowls drew close. Erok's snores did little to reassure her. When the snap of branches announced a predator was scaling their haven, she began to panic. One night of evasion was the province of Lady Luck, but two? She clung tight as bough after bough broke, praying to the Vae, listening to the children sob and Vila murmur.

They made it to morning, when the only sign of their ordeal were branches scattered over the ground and foul spoor. Forced to sleep for a few hours at sunrise and a few more before dusk, they covered little ground each day. Every night Erok made them scale a tree. His knack for picking a refuge was uncanny, as was his ability to wend his way through forest and select the faintest of twisting paths. Night after night an ogre attempted to snatch them from their perch, howling at its failure to reach their heights.

"No same," Vila had said when Kordahla voiced the opinion one ogre might be tracking them. "Male, female, big, small. Is bad. Many, many ogres. Never before."

Which made Kordahla feel decidedly worse. She scratched at a bite on her face and drew blood. Predictably, Vila clucked.

That night the old woman waded through a nearby stream. She returned with a pair of puffers she deposited in a piece of wood Erok had hollowed, and lugged it up the tree and into a fork near Kordahla, emptying half her water bladder into it. The puffers zapped the buzzing insects, content to fill their podgy faces. Kordahla could not thank her enough. In the morning, she released the critters and suffered the extra burden of the bowl in her sack. Erok laughed when he saw her pack it. She laughed back. It felt so good. There was a time she might have laughed every day, at something Vinsant said or did. That time seemed so distant now.

On the sixth morning, the stench of rotten eggs wove its way onto the ridge they traversed. Uneasy, Kordahla approached Vila.

"Spirit Lake," Vila said, pointing west, through trees and hills. She called something to Erok. He watched Sian, who was walking on, head down and shook his head. The soothsayer's name was the only word of his response she caught.

In the afternoon, they reached a flatter valley covered with red and yellow-flowering imperial crowns. Travelling was easier. Silent Sian pointed out objects, naming them for Timak. Glad of the distraction, Kordahla joined in, laughing when Sian giggled at her pronunciation.

"*Weegarita*?" she tried.

Sian shook her head. "*Weege–*" An odd look twisted her face, cutting short her repetition. The girl stiffened.

"Sian?"

Sian fell to the ground. Her eyes rolled back and her muscles twitched and convulsed.

"Sian!" The thrashing girl risked knocking her head on a rock.

Kordahla could do nothing but cradle her head. One of the palaces pages suffered such an affliction. Nocrates yelled at anyone who even intimated a djinn possessed him, but how could the physic know the djinn were not making a jest? The froth coming from Sian's mouth was unnatural, and the shade of the slope was still-wind chill. She thanked the Vae Erok and Vila were close, thought they did naught but hold Sian down and clear the largest of the bruising rocks from the grass beneath her.

A terrifying eternity passed before the fit stopped. It was a blessing Sian fell straight into a deep sleep. Kordahla stepped back as Vila brewed some of the pungent herb tea she gave the girl each morning, and forced it between her lips. When Sian woke, her eyes were clouded. She blinked in confusion as Erok helped her sit, then hung her head. No matter who spoke, she refused to meet their eye. It was an hour before she could stand. It was two before she could walk. Before three hours had elapsed, it happened again.

Helpless, Kordahla pleaded with Vae'oenka to help the child. The goddess took no heed. Perhaps Kordahla had chosen to abandon Her ordained path when she fled Ahkdul. Perhaps this child worshipped her own gods. Either way, Sian was unconscious for a long while, and it was obvious as the sun began to set she would not have the strength to climb a tree, let alone remain in one.

"Wood," Vila said.

They gathered as much as they could, working well into the hours they should have spent sleeping. The piles grew, and still Erok did not seem content. At last, they set about fashioning a ring of hearths. Vila shook her head, clucking her disapproval.

"What is it?" Kordahla asked.

"Ogre no like fire but ogre know people near fire."

"They come anyway," Kordahla said.

"Downwind they smell. But upwind, downwind, left, right of wind, they see fire."

Her heart sinking, Kordahla looked south, to Myklaan. Safety lay a long, treacherous way away. What had she been thinking, to abandon the safety and love of her home? What had she been thinking? She started as Timak came to stand so close, and look up at her with all his hurt in his eyes. *Ahkdul.* She swallowed down a surge of bile. That was what she had been thinking.

After dinner, Vila approached. "You sleep first, you watch last."

And so she understood the incredible danger. Sian had stirred but was not strong enough to sit, let alone stand. Faithful Timak lay near the girl, watching intently until he was unable to keep his eyes open any longer. She unrolled her sleeping mat near him, grateful for his company.

When Erok woke her, green Dindarin was shining above the canopy. The fires were low and few branches remained. She moved the puffers she had caught earlier between the children. Incessant insect bites might help keep her awake.

The last log was on the fire when she heard it. A snuffling like a pig rooting for truffles. She grabbed a branch. Its end was no more than glowing embers. Holding it out, she turned a circle. Vae help them! Flames struggled for life in two of their hearths. The other fires were dead.

The snuffling drew closer. A soft hoot answered it from behind.

"Erok!" she shouted.

The tribesman was up in an instant, the spear he slept with balanced in his hand.

"There's two of them," she said, hoping he could see the fingers she held up.

A shadowy form came out from behind a bush.

"*Telta*," Erok said, holding up three fingers.

Grass swished to her left. Beyond Erok, something large and heavy smacked the ground. They were surrounded. Five or six ogres yowled. Vila and Timak scrambled for burning logs, waving them at the gaps between the dying fires. Sian remained oblivious. Overhead, the sky showed no sign of lightening.

The largest ogre charged at her, leaping right over the glowing cinders. Erok's spear flew into it. It stopped only to pull the weapon from its shoulder and snap it in two. She ducked and rolled under its legs and back onto her feet as its club crashed to the ground. Turning she jammed the hot end of the branch between the ogre's shoulder blades. It arched its back with a roar of pain. Erok attacked from in front. She scooted around, scooping up the broken spear and flinging it at an ogre that was advancing on Vila. The arrow tip caught it in the thigh. As Erok landed a blow on the first creature, she waved the blackening log to ward the others off. Their steady creep was bringing each to the boundary of the fire. The burned ogre fumbled back, stepped onto a hearth, and yowled in pain. Enraged, he loped back into the centre of the circle, slashing wildly at all of them. Then he noticed Sian.

With two ogres in the circle and four more looking for a way in, danger confronted her every way she turned. Erok was jabbing, ducking and turning like a seasoned warrior, managing to keep the other beasts at the boundary while landing more blows on the pained ogre. It kept advancing, batting at Erok's branch like it were an annoying insect. She came from behind, adding her blows to Erok's until Vila was not faring so well. The second ogre loomed over her. Cinders fell off the end of her blackened branch, forcing her to back away. Sensing an easy kill, a third ogre approached from behind. Trapped, Vila swung the branch in circles. Both creatures swiped at her. At the last moment, the canny old woman dropped to the ground, leaving the ogres to claw each other. They broke into a vicious fight, their feet booting Vila around. She cowered on the floor between them, hands over head, unable to escape.

As Kordahla broke to help Vila, the first ogre hit Erok, sending him flying into the leg of a fourth beast. He slashed at the ankle tendon with his hunting knife and rolled away.

"No," she yelled as Timak dived under her arms, toward the first ogre reaching down to snatch Sian. Timak dragged his torch under its legs and rammed it into the creature's loin. It howled, paralysed with pain. In that moment, Erok got to a knee and threw his hunting knife. It landed in the ogre's eye. The beast staggered. An immense foot pounded dangerously close to Sian. Kordahla lunged, and pulled the unconscious girl from its path. The ogre managed a few more steps before falling face down.

There was a sickening crunch. Villa screamed. She rocked on the ground, an arm crushed as the two ogres continued their bloody fight above her.

Erok retrieved his knife, and dashed to her aid. One of the pair, ragged wounds over chest and thigh, limped away, its chilling whimpers echoing off the trunks. The other snarled at Erok and grabbed Villa by the middle. Again, Erok slashed for the tendon. The ogre sidestepped him and he managed to inflict no more than a superficial graze. The hunter would need to fend for himself; the fifth ogre, emboldened by the others, was bounding at Sian and Timak. Her branch cold, the fires dead, all she could do was say a desperate prayer to Vae'oeldin and charge. Dindarin, in his first quarter, had long set, leaving the stars to shine bright; daybreak travelled from too far away. The wounded ogre was dragging itself away, the ground trembling as it hopped on its good leg, and the last one, a child by the look of it, fled without setting foot in their circle. Two remained, devilish in their persistence. One grabbed Timak and dragged him away. He cried out as he bounced over rock and root, dropping his branch. For all the boy had rammed ogres with it, the end still burned.

"You can't have him," she yelled, picking it up and dropping her own charred branch on the chase. The cumbersome creature was faster than she. She fell to the ground, fumbled for rocks and pelted it in the back. It hung onto the boy as it thumped its way through the forest.

If only the sun would rise.

She looked up. A mahktashaan might have conjured a blaze of yellow. The flame she carried was all they had. It needed to burn high. She clambered into a tree, resting the torch over branches so she could use both hands to climb, setting it as high as she could so it burned between two sprigs.

"Sun," she yelled, the only thing left to her to do. "Sun."

The ogre tripped, releasing Timak. It recovered its footing and doubled its pace, glancing at the torch. Kordahla almost fell from branch to branch. She ran to Timak, flat on his back, groaning, and patted him down.

"Are you hurt?" she asked. "Are you hurt?"

He was bruised and shivery, but seemed intact. She gathered him into a hug. To her surprise he burst into sobs and hugged her back. She rocked him for a time, then set him on his feet, and wiped away his tears with her sleeves.

"We must get back to the others," she said, taking his hand.

In camp, the ogre that had attacked Vila lay with a knife between its ribs. Kordahla walked a wide circle around the hairy, sinewy corpse. Vila was lying with a hand on Sian's arm. Under the silhouette of leaves, beneath indigo patches of sky, she knelt beside the old woman.

"Clever girl," Vila said, two words which exhausted her.

"Is there anything, I can do?" Kordahla asked. It was not like Vila to lay still, to moan, to leave Sian tossing and turning.

Behind nearby bushes, an ogre hooted. Kordahla stood, trembling.

It was impossible to tell if a shadow lurched or her tired eyes played tricks. She turned a slow circle, peering into the predatory forest, Timak stuck to her hip. A sure-footed figure emerged from darkness. She screamed before she realised it was Erok, carrying a bundle of branches. He selected a few, and kindle a flame in one of the hearths. Kordahla relit the others while he checked on Sian, brushing a lock of hair off her forehead. The girl murmured, and opened her eyes. Erok spoke to her as he picked up Vila's hand. The Vae grant all they needed was rest. Kordahla sat with them, dozing, and then waking, to find the sky had lightened to violet, to see the full, horrific extent of Vila's injuries. She fought to keep tears from her eyes.

"Sian?"

The girl had risen and was walking toward the fallen ogre, oblivious to Erok's call. She knelt by the beast and, taking its hairy hand, stared at the knuckles. Her look Erok's way was quizzical. She said something, a question, and Kordahla caught Ishoa's name. Erok pulled his knife from the ogre and went to sit next to her, responding with some gentle words. When Sian nodded, she looked confused. With deft hands, Erok skinned the hand and dug out a knuckle bone. Sian cupped it in her hands, like a delicate prize.

"Sian," Vila called.

The girl crept over. When the old woman could finally part her from the bone, she insisted on crawling to a fire and boiling it clean. Bent double and bleeding, she refused any assistance as she fished the clean bone out and gave it to Sian. The girl tucked it into a leather pouch she wore around her neck.

"Why does she want the bone?" Kordahla asked. Both Vila and Erok were looking at the child with an expression akin to awe.

Vila shook her head but did not answer.

Timak came and slipped his hand into hers. He too had a queer expression on his face as he listened to the air. "She's going to be a soothsayer," he whispered, "but she doesn't know it yet."

A groan escaped Vila's lips. Closing her eyes, she lay down. Kordahla looked a plea at Erok, but he shook his head. Sian's face set into glum stubbornness as, making a demand of the hunter, she took her grandmother's hand. Erok hugged the girl. Tears trickled down her face and onto her grandmother's hand, pooling between the wrinkles. The sun reached its zenith, and still Sian refused to move. Vila's eyes flickered open. Kordahla had learned enough of the language of the Akerin to understand her say, "Listen to Ishoa."

The old woman's brow was smooth, her mouth content, when she passed to the spirits.

Chapter Thirty-seven

JORDAYNE STIFLED A YAWN. The sunbeams streaming through the huge keyhole windows behind the elegant arches and tiered balconies of the Court made concentrating on misery a bore, especially since the petitioners in front of her looked like a dose of sunshine might cure at least a third of their ills. Their solemn gawking did not do justice to the splendid mosaic on the dome. The detail with which the craftsmen of old had fashioned the shiny images of the Vae gave the impression the gods presided over Shah and Court. The honest took comfort in that. As for the deceitful, she'd seen one or two squirm their way out before they ever opened their glib mouths. She waved a peasant with an imagined grievance against his neighbour away, and called for the next petitioner. The picture of misery who shambled before her caused her to sit up straight on the minor throne. The unfortunate man had ruptured pustules over every inch of exposed skin. He was supported by a wife whose clothes were little more than rags.

"Why aren't you with a physic?" she asked before he could speak of his injustice.

"We tried, my Lady. The hospice turned him away," the woman said. Her ugly face was prematurely aged with deep lines, and she sounded as grisly as the carved oak bears rising from the two minor thrones.

"Why?" Jordayne asked, guessing what the answer would be. They were the fourth claimants this morning who had been refused treatment.

"We've no coin left. The ointment the physic gave us cost us the last of it. We've not even the lek for a loaf of bread."

"Am I to understand you paid the physic for an ointment which did not work?"

"My lady, please, my Lady, we did all he said, dawn, noon and dusk. It weren't for the lack of trying. If he'd just see us again."

"Who did you see?"

"Physic Chas deq Arios."

"I see." She turned to Ordosteen, solid as the carving of the massive oak tree springing from the back of his golden throne. "What are we to do about this?"

Her dear uncle blinked and looked at her with a harried expression. "Hmm? Yes. Your judgement is acceptable," he temporised yet again.

Jordayne sighed. The poor, lovesick man had not heard a single complaint. It was just as well she enjoyed wielding power or she would have left this tedious open court hours ago. "Take him back to the hospice and ask for Physic Hamid deq Lamont. Tell him I sent you. You may collect a dozen lek from the Treasurer on your way out."

"Me Lady," came a reedy voice.

Allowing herself another sigh, though for an entirely different reason, Jordayne slumped back in the uncomfortable chair and spun one of her gold bracelets. After an eight-day suffering the begging masses, the reason for Matisse's poor posture was becoming obvious. It was time she was back to dealing with the larger matters at hand, not this petty grovelling.

"Forgive the intrusion, my lady, but I believe my lord has returned," Sergeant Rokan interrupted.

She was off the throne in an instant. The timing of her brother's return was irregular enough for her to want to ferret out the cause.

"But Court is not yet over," Farsil the fastidiously groomed chamberlain protested.

The faces before her were a sea of dismay. "Who among you seeks the attention of a physic?" she asked. The sudden chorus was telling. This refusal of the healers to work for the common good was a vice she was going to have to deal with, and soon. "Go to the hospice and tell them I sent you." Half the crowd backed out of the doors into the *iwan*. "Go with them Rokan, there's a good fellow. You can act as an official sanction. And don't trust anyone other than deq Lamont to see they are given the attention they need." She turned to Farsil. "You see. We have just cleared the quota for today. You men should learn to be half as efficient."

"My lady, one healer could not possibly deal with this number of ailing citizens." The man's face was pinched in disapproval. It contrasted beautifully with the immaculate cut of his purple kurta.

"Then you will just have to see that he gets help. Recruit every physic in the city if you have to. I'm sure there's enough gold in the coffers to cover the expense."

"My lady, the taxes are not acquired to be returned to the poor, or to make the rich richer."

"Farsil, you must learn not to scowl so. It encourages wrinkles. As for the gold, I'm sure there will be enough left over to buy me a new bracelet or six." Leaving the irate chamberlain to herd the remaining peasants out, she skipped down the marble dais steps, and along the aisle hastily cleared for her exalted passage.

"You may tally coin sufficient to treat all these citizens at the hospice," she said to the treasurer in the *iwan*. He sat with quill and ink behind a table, undaunted by stunning mosaic of the oak and bears on the dome above him. She left him stammering a protest, and passed through the *pistaq*, its coloured tiles perfect complement to the mosaic, emerging with a flick of her skirt into the gorgeous day. She hurried along the cypress-lined canal, one of the three leading out from the palace. The alternating bear and oak fountains enchanted both wagtails and the healthier of the petitioners into dawdling in the gardens. Indulgence bred a grateful population and an irritated Lady. Ignoring her direction, Rokan was providing close escort along a perpendicular canal bordered by flower beds. The hospice, she knew, would have to wait until she was safe in the company of her brother and his men.

The sun was not yet halfway through its arc, which meant Matisse had timed his journey to avoid camping close to Faradil Forest's edge. For someone who bragged about dicing with death, he had chosen a prudent course. She slowed when she spied the reason slipping off her horse into Matisse's arms. The woman was aging well, granted, and she displayed a rare intelligence, but was there a shred of decency in her, that she would return to flaunt her newest liaison in front of her Shah?

"Did you quite enjoy your visit, brother dear?" Jordayne asked.

"What do you think?" he answered with a grin at Rochelle, and no thought for the men his lieutenant was organising.

Jordayne rolled her eyes as the older woman adopted a coquettish stance. "I think our dear Uncle does not deserve this. Not after everything he has done for you. Or you," she added to the shah's former mistress, frost in her voice.

"His idea, Jordayne. Besides, I don't think he wants to see Rochelle pine away from lack of attention in Zulmei. He might even find he enjoys her company. I am not the jealous sort."

"But I'll wager he is, and that chaste companionship is not what he seeks."

Footsteps behind her made her turn. Ordosteen was looking ashen. A fool would not have missed the teasing glances between the pair before him. The two parrots flirting on the wall certainly didn't. Fresh from an early dip in Lake Tej, they didn't even have the decency to look travel-stained and weary.

"Zulmei is a shambles, Uncle. I have asked Elan to recall Denkan from Point Rai," Matisse said, unabashed. He put an arm around Rochelle's waist and pulled her closer.

"Does the satrap not require your assistance then?" Ordosteen said to Rochelle. She had worn a rather demure, pale pink kameez with a skirt which hugged her hips before flaring, and sleeves which did the same to her arms.

"Majesty, my father is old-fashioned where women are concerned. If Denkan heeds the call, it will not be long before he assumes responsibility for the province." She was relaxed in Matisse's hold, though she had the grace to seek Ordosteen's approval with her eyes.

"So I take it you have returned to enjoy yourself."

"I have decided to take your advice, Uncle," Matisse said. He looked at Rochelle, their bodies, their lips close. "You can expect me at the palace more often."

"I am sure you will be happy together." Ordosteen never could deny his brother's children anything and that, Jordayne thought as she watched him shuffle back to the palace, was the cause of the problem with her hedonistic brother who would one day rule a prospering realm but could never elevate it to greatness. One needed a degree of self-restraint for that. A modicum of concern for someone other than yourself, even if, no *especially* if, you were slated to be the next Shah. She would have to find Ordosteen a lover more intellectual than Katrine. Nobody too astute, of course. It would not do to have him fall in love again. Just a courtier nubile enough to smooth the stiffness of a broken heart out of his gait.

"Well I trust you at least accomplished what you set out to do," she said to Matisse.

"There's a disagreeable prisoner trussed up for our amusement this afternoon. I've had my men take him to the dungeon."

"To the interrogation courtyard it is then. You do intend to come along?" She raised an eyebrow as Matisse and Rochelle kissed.

"Now?" Matisse said, refusing to tear his eyes from Rochelle.

"Do I get one of those?" Drucilamere, escorted by a guard despite his regular attendance at the palace, was heading straight for her with long purposeful strides, his pathetic excuse for a red-headed, freckle-faced apprentice trailing in his wake.

"Will this do?" she asked, standing on tiptoe and pulling his head to her for a long kiss.

"Not bad, but I might have to try again to be sure."

She tucked a hand into his green kamarband, and allowed him a briefer union. "Be careful what you say," she warned.

"It does very well," he answered, his lips broadening beneath his wide but neat moustache. "Though we could do better later."

"Not above it, are you sis?" Matisse said.

"I am not flaunting my lover in my Shah's face," she replied, glaring at the sour apprentice. He was ogling her and Rochelle, and not once did his eyes rise to their faces. "Did you need to bring your pet toad with you?" she asked Drucilamere. She noted his emerald green kurta and black shalvar. "And since you did, I take it this is not a social call."

"He does need minding, and with Shom ready to practice magic, I thought it best to have this one out of the guild. His only interest centres on when he can imbibe porrin." Drucilamere turned to Matisse. "My lord, your message suggested your need for a mage was urgent."

"How urgent I cannot say, but I thought it best to get your opinion. A cursed strange thing happened in Zulmei." Matisse indicated they should walk. They took the path by the wide central canal. The fountains of mythical creatures babbled. "I was in the midst of a swordfight–"

"Tavern brawl, more like," Jordayne interjected. He ignored her.

"When my sword disappeared right out of my hand."

That stopped them all in their tracks. Right at the midpoint of the canal, where an intricate fountain fashioned as an oak tree dripped water from its leaves while the six stone bears it sheltered spouted water.

Drucilamere blinked. "Where did it go?"

"I was hoping you could tell me."

"My lord was in a precarious position at the time," his faithful lieutenant said.

"Dear Vae, were you hurt?" she asked.

Matisse ran a hand through his blonde hair. "Would I be standing here if I were? You are supposed to be the intelligent one, Jordayne."

For all his faults, she did harbour an uncommon affection for her brother. "Don't you ever do anything so foolhardy again," she said, giving him a hug.

"I did not exactly have a choice in the matter," he said, plainly amused. "Why don't you settle back in," he said to Rochelle. She turned away with a flick of her hips and an inviting raise of her eyebrow that brought a grin to Matisse's face.

"Who were you fighting?" Drucilamere asked as they continued down the canal. The magus glanced at Brailen, whose ears had pricked up even if his eyes had not.

"A contact of that swindler of a merchant you deal with."

They walked to the private back gardens, through the ivy-covered arch into the drab courtyard adjacent the dungeons.

"I need to take porrin," Druce said, and sent the sullen boy to fetch a mug of water.

While they waited for the prisoner to be dragged up, Jordayne inspected the prayer she had ordered carved into the walls. The stonemason had done an expert job on the calligraphy. The political prisoners interred here were unlikely to repent, but the Vae might accord her credit for trying.

"Master Magus, can I try too?" Brailen asked when he returned.

"Considering the number of unexpected things that happen when you take porrin, and your decided lack of both training and focus, I do not think this an appropriate time," Druce answered dryly. "But you should know how to mix the powder. Here, make sure it is all dissolved. Then you can brag to your friends about how you helped."

Drucilamere kept the eyes of a hawk on Brailen as the boy stirred the red powder into the water. When Drucilamere handed the imperfect solution back for another mix, the lazy git rolled his eyes. Jordayne wanted to string him up, Drucilamere too, if the mage persisted with the folly of trying to train the lackwit. She should have guessed he would shake the last specks of powder in the packet onto his tongue while Drucilamere drank the potion.

"You have an addict for an apprentice," she said as Druce's eyes took on the tell-tale glazed look.

"If you left enough in the packet to wreak any sort of havoc, there'll be a reckoning the like of which would send Vae'oeldin cowering, boy," Druce said. His voice had already acquired the mistiness of the magical daze.

The boy's pupils had dilated but he seemed alert. She was about to dismiss him when the empty mug flung itself across the courtyard. Matisse only narrowly avoided it before it clanged into the wall. That magic was not the controlled act of a Master Magus. Jordayne had reached the limit of her tolerance. She put her fists on her hips and said, "I'll have him hanged if there's so much as a peep out of him."

The boy snorted. "Don't doubt she'll do it," Druce growled, and Brailen shut up, though he did have the gall to creep within touching distance of her. At a gesture, the lieutenant dragged him off to the side with a pointed glance to the gallows that had remained erect since she interviewed Raj.

Unfortunately, the scruffy, cussing, pot-bellied taverner two guards dragged before her would most like need the threat of a hanging to spill information. "Korwin the Stout, I presume. He's all yours," she said to Druce when the guards had pushed him to his knees.

"Don't you touch me, you oversized piece of god dropping," Korwin bellowed, struggling hard.

"Here I was thinking the schkaan were shy," Jordayne said, observing the tattoo covering his left arm.

Drucilamere stepped forward as the guards flattened the taverner. "I'm afraid that's exactly what I need to do."

"Wait. Wait. I'll confess."

"Dear me, that was altogether too easy," Jordayne said. "And schkaan being secretive creatures, too."

"You get this abomination of a man away from me," Korwin said as the guards hauled him off his paunch and back to his knees.

"What is this realm coming too? Everyone is a coward at heart," said Matisse, sprawling along the bench opposite the gallows.

"I'm afraid the magus stays. Now what were you going to confess?" Jordayne said.

"Whatever you want. You ask and I tell you what you want to know."

"For starters, how long have you been doing business with the Verdaani smuggler Raj?

Korwin eyed the birds landing on the walls to and from their way to the fountains like he wanted to wring their necks for chirping. "A few moons," he admitted, most like because he knew she was aware of that titbit.

"What exactly is your arrangement?" Her bangles clinked as she crossed her arms. They were not making quite the chime she had hoped for since she had bequeathed so many to the Vae. A shopping trip was in order. She had a reputation to uphold, after all.

"He brings in porrin and I dole it out to them as want it," Korwin said.

"And make a tidy profit on the side."

"No harm in that."

"But there is," Matisse said, completely relaxed, "when people who can't afford to pay work up a huge debt. How do you collect?"

"They give me what they have and work off the rest. In the tavern."

"You mean to say intoxicated drug abusers pour the ale? No wonder it tastes like horse piss." Matisse's eyes narrowed and he leaned forward. "The satrap's guards told rumours of people disappearing off the streets. Down-and-out types whose relatives report they were addicted to the drug. What has that to do with you?"

"Nothing."

"I don't suppose you might surrender the culprit?" Jordayne said.

"Don't rightly know who that is."

Drucilamere stepped forward, hands on hips.

"It's nothing to do with me, you piece of –"

"Yes, god dropping. I've heard it all before," Drucilamere said mildly, though Brailen's amused snort drew a glance of annoyance. She sympathised to the point she nearly asked if he wanted the sorry excuse for an apprentice dragged over here beside Korwin.

"Well," Jordayne said. "Let's see what Raj has to say about it." Guards jumped to her gesture, pulling Korwin, still bellowing about his innocence, toward the gallows. Chirps changed to alarm calls as the birds on the wall flew off.

"What! You can't do this. You can't," he said, as he realised the gallows it actually was.

Sul had appeared, black hood in hand, bless him. The holes for his eyes were a nice touch. It had to inspire fear if the prisoner believed the hood was for *her* benefit. The bald executioner's chubby hands slid it over Korwin's head. The man kicked and screamed as they dragged him to the block. What perfect timing Raj appeared just as Sul dropped the noose around Korwin's neck. So satisfying to see the little man balk. It did increase the chance of a confession.

"I cooperate, I cooperate," Raj said. He had lost weight he could ill-afford to lose.

"So you did. A pity co-conspirators must share the same fate. I do believe the pardoning question is what happens to the unfortunates who can't honour the debt for the drug you supply?"

The poor man looked like he might have a heart attack. She could have kissed Korwin, well blown him one anyway, for peeing his pants as Sul tightened the noose.

"Whoever organised this forgot a bowl of roast nuts to go with the show," Brailen said.

She flung her arm sideways and pointed at the miserable lump of creation without taking her eyes off Raj. "One more peep out of you and you'll hang next.

"My, we're in a mood today, sis," Matisse said. He had flopped back onto the bench and appeared to be enjoying the proceedings as much as Brailen.

"Try sitting through tedious hours of Court," she said.

"I believe I do. On a regular basis."

"Well?" She demanded of Raj.

The whites of his eyes flaring, Raj shook his head.

"These vagrants aren't going to tell us anything. Hang them both. If this one confesses after that one dies, hang him anyway." She stormed towards the arch that led out to the gardens.

"Wait. Wait. They go to Verdaan."

The beastly smuggler had left his confession until she was standing near Brailen. He deserved to pay for that alone. Her cleavage was not for the admiration of snotty-nosed children.

"What do you mean they go to Verdaan?" Matisse said, a dangerous edge to his voice. He was up, sword in hand.

"We take to Verdaan. They work for drug lord until debt paid off."

"You mean Kamir deq Ramil?"

"Yes."

"Who sates their craving for the drug."

"Yes."

"So their debt will never be worked off."

He did not deny it. She pursed her lips to keep her anger in check as she marched back to him, her bangles clanging. "How do you persuade them to go?"

Raj looked past her, his face blank. "Same methods you use."

Not quite the same, she guessed. She did not dispose of too many bodies, and certainly did not threaten innocent members of a family.

"Do your little games ever go awry?" Druce whispered into her ear. She was grateful for his proximity. It anchored her enough to subdue her unproductive ire. For the moment, at least.

"I've never had to execute anyone I didn't want to yet," she replied, patting his chest, though her eyes were not on him. Her nonchalant veneer had worn parchment thin in the face of Raj's shocking admission. In an attempt to regain control of herself, she leaned into his ear. "I would not be making an exception if I hanged your apprentice. Just say the word, my dear."

"Not today, though he might wish you had if I send him back to his mother. Now, I believe my services are called for."

Drucilamere walked to Korwin, tugged off his hood and, as the guards restrained the dealer, placed his hands at the man's temples. The man screamed his head off. Anyone would think he was under torture.

"Cowards all," said Matisse with a smirk. An accurate assessment. She wondered if he had had occasion to feel the gentle nudge of a mind probe. Its paltry gain hardly seemed worth the risk of imbibing porrin. Sometimes she thought the magi a limited lot.

"Oh do keep quiet," she said as Drucilamere rejoined them. The screaming prisoner was beginning to give her a headache.

Sul punched him in the face. She started. It was not the technique she had had in mind. Then Korwin spat out a bloody tooth, in her direction mind. She tossed her head as Sul gave him another cuff. In her present mood, effective was just that, however it was achieved.

"He is not magically oriented in the least," Drucilamere proclaimed. "Anyone in the tavern at the time could have had latent talent, but I would have expected the sword to fly past their hand."

"I can guarantee that did not happen. Anyway, there wasn't a man among them worth half as much as that miscreant over there," Matisse said, indicating Brailen, who was slumped against the ivy-covered wall, his chin on his chest.

"Unfortunately, that miscreant does have a gift."

"So what are we left with?" Jordayne asked. "Djinn?"

"It begins to look that way," Drucilamere conceded, "though I cannot say for sure without examining the sword.

"What's that?" Brailen asked, dragging himself up.

"Lieutenant," Jordayne said.

"Aye, I'll string him up. Be right glad to."

"What is it?" the lad asked again, paying them no heed.

The urgency in his voice made her flick her eyes his way. She paled. An apricot ball of light, blue sparks crackling at its centre was flitting around the lad. "Drucilamere," she said, gripping his arm with the same sense of urgency. The Magus walked towards it. "Wait," she said, troubled by Weng Wu's warning.

"I never," Druce murmured, frowning. He lifted a hand towards it.

"Don't," she said, imitating the eastern magician's caution.

The light sensed the movement. It darted at Brailen's heart. The boy jerked as it entered him. His body stiffened and his eyes turned vacant. For a heartbeat, he glowed apricot from within.

Drucilamere placed a hand on the boy's head. Sweat beaded on his brow as tendons formed a prominent fan across his hand. His low chant sounded forced. Just as his voice broke, the light catapulted out of Brailen and over the walls. The lad crumbled into an unconscious heap at her mage's feet.

"What was that?" Matisse said.

Her eyes flicked from heir to mage. This was not a secret to which she wanted to admit.

"If I didn't know better, I would say it was a soulous," Drucilamere answered, gazing in the direction the light had taken. He crabstepped and grabbed at the wall.

"Magus?" Matisse enquired as Jordayne went to support him up.

"A soulous is the captured soul of someone who has died. It's dark magic that binds the will and prevents it joining the Vae."

Her mouth dry, Jordayne said, "How do you know better?"

The mage let go the wall and blinked. "I don't," he said. "In fact, I don't."

Brailen stirred and groaned. His hand rubbed his forehead.

"How do you feel?" she asked. Her guilt compelled her to offer the dazed lad a hand up. If the pervert had not taken the opportunity to look down her cleavage, she might have continued to feel sorry for him. As it was, he deserved the hard slap that sent his other hand to his face. She turned back to the prisoners. Their fate was the perfect excuse to avoid further discussion of the soulous. Her dutiful Master Magus would investigate, and it was only a matter of time before he discovered Weng Wu. There were only so many diversions she could throw his way to forestall the inevitable. Then there would be a reckoning. But whether he accepted it or not, dark times called for dark measures.

The swarthy Verdaani smuggler had settled. He looked at her, calm, expectant, and her anger rose. "You are going to go back to Verdaan. You are going to continue trading with us as though nothing happened, and you are going to bring extra porrin to compensate for the quantity you cheated us out of. What's more, you will report to Lord Matisse here on the whereabouts and welfare of any Myklaani citizens you abducted."

"My lord Kamir will suspect. I been away too long."

"I imagine a fellow who values his life will discover the intelligence to manufacture a cover story."

Raj shook his head. "Lord Kamir not forgiving man. Those betray him, they wish they never born."

"We can always save you his wrath by executing you right here," Jordayne said.

Matisse placed the blade of his sword against Raj's throat, slicing the skin on the left with precision. To his credit, the little man did no more than wince. A pity the lip tremble as Matisse mirrored the cut on his right side gave him away. Otherwise, he might have disproved Matisse's theory about brave men.

"We will get our citizens back. If it takes us a year, we will. The only question is will you give us cause to deal with you in an excruciating manner when next we meet. And make no mistake, we will meet again," Matisse said.

"You will inform Lord Matisse of every detail of the scam," she said watching blood from the smuggler's wounds dribbled down to form a red noose. The courtyard was beginning to depress her. In fact, she was feeling decidedly ill. She strode for the arch and the fragrant gardens. A good jasmine scented bath was what she needed to scrub the stench of this appalling conspiracy off her.

"What about this one?" Sul called.

"Hang him," she said flatly without looking back. Anyone who made a living out of selling his own countrymen deserved far worse.

CHAPTER THIRTY-EIGHT

AT THE TOP OF the last hill they gazed down onto a withering plain. Far to the west, a broad river carved a laborious journey but no settlements hunkered along its life-giving waters. Sian hung back. Without canopy or underbrush to conceal, she stood exposed. The plain's vast reach sharpened the emptiness inside her. It was as sharp as the talons of the golden eagle which circled overhead. She had cried, and cried, and cried after grandmam passed to the spirits, wiping tears away with her good hand. The other arm dangled by her side, useless like she was, because if she hadn't had the fits, they would have climbed the trees, and Grandmam would be safe to lash out with her tongue.

"Don't be such a baby," Grandmam had said, when she cleaned the burns each night. Sian had gritted her teeth, unable to prevent tears welling in her eyes even knowing once the wound was clean the salve Ishoa had supplied would help dull the pain. After, she had curled up in her blanket, high up in a tree, and listened to Grandmam and Erok speak.

"She must be possessed. The evil vapours have not swollen the dirty arm," Grandmam had said.

Those words had brought slaying pain of a different kind.

"The Soothsayer says not," Erok had answered. At that moment, Sian had wondered if she loved him more than Grandmam.

The numbness had crept in as she watched Erok erect a cairn. They had left Grandmam in the forest, away from the tribe, and trekked on, silent and glum. Erok got short with the Terlaani woman when she struggled to reach a muddy summit, when she fumbled with the skinning or the roasting, when she tried to keep the tears of homesickness from her eyes, but he had not once lost his temper with her. Every night he helped her scale an oak or an ironwood, pulling her up to the highest branches. He was looking out for them, even though it was only because Ishoa had entrusted them into his care. She knew he would rather be free to hunt, or to call the Akerin to gathering. She understood. She wanted to return to the tribe too, even if the children refused to let her join in the games and the adults shooed her from their fires. It had been a fretful day the morning the soothsayer had woken her, bidding her prepare to leave.

"You must travel with the woman and child," Ishoa had said, preparing a pack of herb tea and salves. A golden eagle had perched on a rock at the cave entrance, watching with a sentient eye.

"But they're going to Myklaan." A flat country with few trees, far from their safe village.

"They are going where they go."

This was Ishoa. Her word was law. "When can I come home?" she had asked, panicked butterflies surging out of her stomach and swarming right up her throat.

"The spirits will guide you."

Then Loyt had come charging into the cave calling for the soothsayer and blabbering about Esa's unsettled babe.

Sian swallowed. The journey should end here, on the border hill, above the plain.

"Myklaan," said Erok, indicating the flat land before them with the new spear he had crafted.

"Thank you," the Terlaani woman said to Erok, her raw, anxious face softening.

The hunter pointed back at the hills. "Ho'akerin. Ogres."

Kordahla nodded her understanding. Taking Timak's hand, she started down the grassy knoll. Timak looked back and whispered a farewell as he scampered to keep up. Ignoring Erok's impatient shuffle, Sian watched them go. Overhead, the eagle stopped circling and swooped down the hill. Of their own will, her feet swished through the dry grass.

Leaving home was not so bad, she tried to tell herself. Timak had become her friend, and the spirit creature Ishoa had named genie too. Friends. That word felt like the sun. Friends. They helped her smile.

"Sian. We're going home," Erok called.

She broke into a run, tears flowing, because if she halted, if she looked back, if she saw that Erok did not follow, she might lose the will to go on. The journey had built her strength, but her hunter was fitter. He jogged up beside her. Ahead, Kordahla looked around, and waited for them to catch her up. Sian stood beside her, and folded her arms. Erok spoke her name. She dared not turn. One glimpse of the summit and she would lose her resolve.

Erok squatted, plucked a blade of grass and placed it in his mouth. Sucking on it, he waited. She could not look at him. "What's the matter? You don't want to go home?"

Her lower lip trembled. "Ishoa said I must go on."

Erok spat out the blade. "The soothsayer asks much."

Sian whirled and flung her arms around Erok. Without hesitation, he hugged her back.

Sighing in resignation, Erok pointed forward. "Myklaan."

Vinsant was on the verge of getting out of the boat and walking all the way to the snow-topped mountains and then on to Cascade with his arms crossed if need be, just so Levi would recognise how fed up he was. And if Levi refused to exercise his legs, he could propel the boat himself. Vinsant would just meet him there. They had picked up the boat in a remote village on the second day of their trek at the base of the mountains. After a full eight-day of sitting in the cramped vessel going absolutely nowhere against the raging, icy current it was a wonder the Majoria had not taught him to magick his legs off. But that would preclude their intense twilight swordplay on the rocky shore, now wouldn't it?

"Concentrate," Levi said for the twenty-seventh time. Vinsant was counting today. It was just about all he could do if he wanted to avoid the evil son of a malicious djinn taking them further back towards Lake

Sheraz. The Majoria was taking this no question, no answering back business way too far. Apprentice or not, he was still a prince.

"You weak-minded excuse for an apprentice. Decide you want to do it and concentrate!"

"Scum of a hopper, I'm trying!" By the Vae, he had barely noticed how wild the flower-dotted fields had become, or how chill settled the moment a cloud covered the sun.

"Today's outburst has earned you an extra hour of sword practice."

"Vae strike it. I said I'm trying," he said, then closed his eyes and hit his forehead with both fists as Levi let the boat drift back with the current. At this stage Vinsant would have preferred a sound beating to further loss of ground. Days in this boat learning to steer with magic as the current bore them back the way they had come was enough to drive even the patient Minoria crazy. Towards day's end, the Majoria usually returned them to their starting position upstream. Well and good. They had not made any progress, but neither had they lost ground. That was until Levi had instructed him to *propel* the boat upstream. The only concession the Majoria had been willing to make was to hold the boat steady in the middle of the fast-flowing river as Vinsant attempted to drive it forward. The man had to love watching Vinsant fail because, for three days in a row now, he had steadfastly refused to help move it. When the sun sank, the Majoria moored the boat where they found themselves, invariably further away from Cascade than they had started. The breakthrough had come two days ago, when Vinsant had managed to keep the boat steady. He had thought it a monumental effort. Levi had called it less than satisfactory.

"Concentrate," Levi said. That was twenty-nine times now.

Ignoring his headache was a feat in itself, but Vinsant squeezed his eyes closed and poured all his energy into beseeching Mahktos.

"You are trying too hard. Remember what working magic feels like."

That was the best piece of advice Levi had given so far. Vinsant relaxed, kept begging Mahktos and found the boat was nudging forward. Filled with glee, he discovered the enthusiasm he thought Levi had murdered. The bow wobbled, the speed was slower than a walk, but by Mahktos they were moving in the right direction.

Vinsant stood up threw his arms wide to the mountains, and shouted for all the world to hear. "Thank you, Mahktos." He thumped back onto the seat as the boat began to twirl, and set himself to concentrating again.

"The correct phrase is 'All praise to Mahktos'," Levi said, as they picked up speed. He was just wondering if Levi might permit a break for lunch, when the Majoria issued a new instruction. "Keep the boat going and magick my dagger to you."

Inwardly, Vinsant groaned. Keeping the boat pointed forward demanded all his effort. He huddled over and tried to spare a magical thought to procure the dagger. It jumped into his hand. About to cry out his triumph, he noticed the bow had drifted around.

"I'll concentrate," he blurted, as Levi reclaimed the weapon and forced the bow upstream again.

An hour later, they were miraculously still on course but he had not managed to budge the dagger. Deep in concentration, he was barely aware of Levi. A new awareness was beginning to assert itself in him. Power trickled from his mind. *This time*, he thought, and smiled when cold metal rested in his hand. And the boat was sailing on. In the right direction. Levi, facing forward, had not even blinked. Vinsant stepped over to the bow, returned the dagger and repeated the trick. How had he ever thought it difficult? While the Majoria obviously felt it was not, a little praise would not go amiss. This total disregard was worse than a rebuke. Just to annoy the man into speech, Vinsant allowed the bow to drift. It would have been suspicious in itself that the Majoria did not stir, but the altered heading allowed him a glimpse of a rippling image. It startled him into losing control of the boat. That was his sister reflected in the water, dirty and scratched but walking away from the hills. She had made it to Myklaan! He fought to turn the bow back upstream. Slow and steady, he sat next to the Majoria. Kordahla was his sister. If Levi was tracking her, he had a right to know how she fared. Especially since Levi was clenching and unclenching his fists with an intensity that set the hairs on the back of Vinsant's neck prickling. He was about to risk a request for an explanation when the image changed. A scruffy man was holding a knife to Kordahla's face.

"No," Vinsant said, toppling back.

The boat rocked. The Majoria flinched. He snatched Vinsant's shoulder and yanked his hood off, glaring deep into his eyes. In its hood, the Majoria's shadowed face was hard. "What did you see?"

"You looked like you were working magic," Vinsant said, which was not a lie. His darting eyes had to be giving him away, but the water was churning blue. Kordahla was left to face her fate alone.

"What magic?" Levi persisted. "What magic did you see?"

"See?" Vinsant improvised, for now one thing was sure: Levi did not want him know he could scry Kordahla. Unfortunately, discovering why was going to be near impossible when he was not allowed to speak. He held out the dagger. "Were you helping me steer the boat? Shall I do the lesson again?"

"Not today."

Vinsant's mouth opened in dismay as the shore sped by, the current bearing the boat back to their starting position.

"Your punishment for this morning's disrespect," Levi said, bringing the boat to the bank in sight of Lake Sheraz. "Now don your hood and draw your sword."

This time Vinsant cussed under his breath. Forget the eight-day his punishment was supposed to span. At this rate, it was going to take a year Just to reach the Crystalite Mines.

They veered west under hot, clear skies, Erok saying they needed to cross the river.

"After that?" Sian asked.

He shrugged.

They slept in the open the next two nights, nestled in the tall grass after Erok assured them ogres did not venture onto the plain. It was just as well; there was no shelter in sight. Little food either. The hare Erok managed to snare left them hungry. It was funny how tasty the stale grain cakes they had carried from the village became.

On the third evening, they sighted the broad river. The sound of a strange animal carried across the plain. Sian jumped. A whinny, Erok named it, and told her of the large, gentle beast men called the horse. Kordahla wanted to go to it, but Erok made them bed down in the tall grass well away from the stone bridge. He left them to stalk across it and scout the land. When he returned, he unrolled his blanket but remained sitting a long time.

"What's wrong?" Sian asked, raising herself onto her forearm.

"The Myklaani send frequent border patrols."

"Are they dangerous?"

"Don't worry. They're no match for a hunter who can fend off six ogres." He winked at her and she fell asleep with a warm feeling inside.

Dindarin and Daesoa were sailing high when she woke, he waxing towards full and she at her first quarter. Not sure why, she stood. The others tossed in fitful sleep. Erok's grunts clashed with the click of insects and rush of water, drowning Timak's whimpers. Their faces were shadowed by the grass, but a yellow moonbeam danced by the river. It drifted west, lighting the bridge. Gingerly, she slid Erok's bone knife from beneath his arm. It was a cruel thing that felt wrong in her hand, but she could not cut fur without it. She walked towards the light, drawn by the same call that had brought her to all the bones. There were five now sitting in her pouch, each carved with a symbol she had dreamt. They would make a fine gift for Ishoa when she got home.

The river was wider than any she had seen, the stone bridge sturdy, unlike the fallen logs and stepping stones the Akerin used to cross their narrow streams. The moonbeam drew her to the other side. The plain was threatening in its openness, the moons so large above it. From somewhere to the west came the nicker of a strange animal. Perhaps predators were prowling. She needed to be hunter brave, because Daesoa called her on.

She found it in a camp, two tents and the horses Erok had told of, tethered a little distant to iron stakes. A magnificent wolf in his prime, his thick fur a tribute to his kind, strung over poles, lifeless, forgotten. Daesoa's gentle beam caressed his face. Dindarin's green light shone a halo around him. Nobody had mourned for him. Nobody had thanked the spirits for his life. A useless death, she sensed. His meat would not nourish his killer's bellies, his furs not warm their skin. Shedding a tear, she crept towards him, buried her face in his fur.

Take him, she pleaded with the spirits. *Let him roam free once more.*

The moonbeams drifted to his paw. Begging forgiveness, singing praise beneath her breath, she knelt by him and cut his flesh to take the bone that glowed brighter than the rest.

There was a snort and a whinny. Unnerved by the strange sounds, she twisted to check where the horses were, overbalanced and toppled against the poles. They clanked as they tumbled one on the other and she was unable to stifle the cry of pain as her raw arm rubbed wood.

The tent flapped opened. Jumping to her feet she tried to run, but he was on her, tackling her before she had passed the other tent. She landed hard, face down, pinned beneath his weight. He bashed her hand against the earth and she let go the knife. He grabbed it, sat atop her, held the blade to her neck.

She did not understand his words. Did not need to in order to know she need lie still. The man rolled her over, his blade still pressed to her skin. She was shaking with fear, barely able to breathe. Other figures were moving in the shadows. The man called out and one brought a lantern. They looked her over, then the one on top of her broke into a leer all the nastier for the skew of a jagged scar at his lip. The others offered a murmur of reservation, a mocking laugh, a lewd comment, then gestures that dripped with vulgarity. Sian struggled. The blade nicked her skin and she screamed. The man tossed the knife away. She fell quiet. His leer returned. Then he pressed his mouth against hers, hard. She squirmed but he pinned her down. Tore her blouse open and slid his hand onto her small breast. Pinched hard. One heavy hand flattened her to the ground as the other yanked her trousers down. She tried to gouge his eyes, but he grabbed her arms and forced them down. She screamed again as his hand constricted around her scalded flesh. She struggled as he swelled against her. Screamed and screamed as he lowered himself onto her, into her, his thrusts searing as deeply as the burn.

❖ ❖ ❖

Kordahla woke with a start. Timak was shaking her, though darkness yet shrouded the plain.

"Sian, Sian, Sian, Sian."

The girl's blanket was empty.

"Quick, quick, quick."

She lunged to the hunter. "Erok," she said, shaking him, "Erok."

The hunter grabbed her wrist. She jolted back. He registered it was her and let go.

"Sian. Quick."

He picked up on her urgency. His right hand leapt to his spear. His left fumbled for the knife he always slept with. It closed empty.

"Hurry," Timak said, backing away. When he saw they were up and following, he broke into a run, heading straight for the moonlit bridge. He looked up as he stepped upon it, and pointed, so sure of the direction that the genie had to be leading him on.

On the other side of the river, they heard the screams. Erok charged toward the two tents looming on the grassy plain. A sob curdled and died. Figures moved around a prostrate body. Rough voices barked.

"Vae'oeldin's rot. The whore's possessed." A bearded man with a lip-twisting scar rose from the ground. Sweet Sian lay sprawled beneath him, her clothes ripped to shreds. "What stinking curse's that bitch given me?"

Erok threw his spear. It punctured the man through the chest. His wide eyes looked down in disbelief before he dropped his knife and crumpled to the ground. He landed atop Sian. Spittle frothed at her mouth, but she did not stir.

"Attack!"

A horse neighed. Three more of the brutes surrounded Erok. Half-dressed and aroused, they were still trained fighters. He snatched up the knife, adopted a fighting stance, turning about, slashing while they laughed and closed in. A knife was no match for one sword, let alone three. Kordahla had no weapon but the rocks. She picked one up and hurled it with all her might. It struck the closest of their assailants, a hefty red-headed brute, in the head.

"Ow!" he yelled, staggering. His hand went to his temple as he dropped to one knee.

"Sian!" The girl, pinned beneath the dead thug, did not rouse. Kordahla reached for another rock, but the man she had assaulted was up, striding towards her. Her hasty throw clipped him in the shoulder. He growled as his body tensed with a rage that looked set to explode in unchecked violence. She backed off. The man kept coming. She ran.

An indigo face protruded from the ground. "Cowardly flight? I had expected a little more entertainment than that."

She twisted – a reflex to avoid landing on the djinn – and tripped. She spurred herself on, straight into the indigo body rising from the ground in front of her. The djinn grabbed her, pulled her up and kissed her. His fishy breath nauseated her. She retched as he released her.

"Looking forward to it?" he said, and disappeared.

Her shock cost her the lead. The bearded man grabbed her from behind and tugged. Her feet went out from under her. Uncaring, he dragged her back to camp. Her captor dumped her near the tent, pinning her with his booted foot as he untied his kamarband. "Don't kill him yet. Make him watch."

A clean-shaven man was pulling Erok's knife from his shoulder, leaving the hunter to face the last man unarmed. The hunter had a nasty gash on his arm. At the edge of the camp, Timak stood immobile. His face was a frozen mask of shock.

"No," she said. "Stop."

"The hill rat speaks Laanan."

"I'm Terlaani. We are here as guests of Shah Ordosteen."

He laughed as he came down on top of her. Blood was caking around his temple where she had hit him with the rock. "And I'm carrying out the Shah's orders protecting our border. Whose story's got the ring of truth?" He turned to see what his comrades were up to.

They had Erok on his knees at sword point, blood flowing from his wound. A quiet rage simmered in the hunter's eyes.

"I'll kill him real slow, for this," the one with the shoulder injury said, checking his wound.

"Bind him. I don't want any surprises from behind," her assailant said, his hand worming inside her blouse. Her struggles only seemed to excite him further. "And check those horses," he added. They were trotting back and forth along the length of their tethers, as undisciplined as the men.

She caught a whiff of a fish. An icy breath tickled her cheek. The indigo djinn's shimmery face poked out from the dirt, locks of his black hair crossing his forehead like blades. "Too proud to admit you need help?"

"Leave," she sobbed, when what she wanted to do was beg him to get them out of this.

"And miss all the fun?" He drifted to his full height.

"Djinn!" the man on top of her called, scampering back.

All three thugs cursed as they made the warding sign.

Kordahla wriggled to the back of a tent, toward the closest horse a few paces away.

"Dung beetles. Pox-ridden imbeciles. You're letting that hill rat escape."

It took two heartbeats for the brute to comprehend, two heartbeats in which she kicked one tethering stake from the ground and bolted. Of course the horse would shy, skittish creatures that they were. She slowed and held out her hand, speaking gentle reassurance she had no time to give. It let her approach. Another step, and she might get close enough to mount.

"Not so fast," the thug said, grabbing her hair and slapping her on the face before shoving her back to the tents. He turned to the djinn who, arms folded and ankles crossed, regarded them through narrowed vermillion eyes. "Do you want to deal for the girl?"

A chill, deathly still, banished the mildness from the night, bringing an unnatural mist to dim the light of the moons. Their captors shuddered.

"You don't go dealing with djinn," said the one who had bested Erok.

"They've got to pay for Hilm's life," the injured one said.

Her bearded captor smiled. "She'll pay all right if the djinn takes her. And with the riches he grants us, we'll buy us a virgin every night for the rest of our lives." He let go and stepped aside as the djinn floated prone above her body.

"The only one I want to deal with is her," the foul beast said. He lowered his foul-smelling mouth to her ear. "Do you think any Myklaani will take a dishonoured woman for his wife? Do you think them so liberal?" he whispered.

She shivered, with the cold and her fear. "My child," she said. "You want my flesh and blood. Nothing you can spare me is worth that price."

"Not even to help your friends?"

She looked at Erok, arms tied behind his back, a sword at his neck. There was no incrimination as he looked back. It gave her the strength to refuse to answer.

With a roar of frustration, the djinn twirled high above the camp. "The wretch refuses my aid. Enjoy her. And be sure to taste her sweet lips." The light in his crystal joints pulsed. The thinning mist dissolved.

Laughing, the bearded man stood over her. Stark moonlight illuminated an ugly cruelty. "You're going to wish you had taken whatever perverted bargain the djinn offered."

He broke off as Timak rushed at him, ineffectual fists beating. "Stop it. Stop it. Don't hurt her," he yelled.

The man shoved him away. "I'll deal with you later, brat. You'll make a nice diversion when the wenches are too bloodied to entertain. Now let's see how satisfying this piece of flesh is." He dropped his shalvar as the third man, dark shaggy hair falling over his hunched shoulders, advanced on Timak.

"Boy!" the djinn said, holding out a hand. The crystals in his knuckles had dulled to a seductive glow. "Boy, come with me."

"No. Timak, no." Kordahla said, struggling against her captor. He groped her and she screamed.

The third man leered. "Boy, you will do while I wait."

Eyes wide, Timak shook his head, took a step towards the djinn. "Make them stop."

"Timak, don't," she said.

The man's rough hands were all over her. His beard prickled at her face. Humiliation exploded in every inch of her body. She would die from shame if he dishonoured her, and she was doubly shamed at that. They had shown poor Sian no mercy. She saw the horror on Timak's face, the memory of Ahkdul's torment. The boy would bargain, as much for her as for his own lost innocence. When had she come to feel so responsible for him? Oh Vae'oenka, she could not permit him to enter a pact that would annihilate any glimmer of hope in the ruins of his life. Not when she was the one the djinn desired.

"I'll deal," she whispered.

The djinn appeared next to her. "Your second and third born child," he said.

She gritted her teeth, turned her head. The brute's hand slid across her thigh. Self-loathing drowned the vestiges of her resistance. Agreement sprang to her tip of her lips, a single short word.

The thud of galloping hooves forestalled her. The men looked up at the sound. A small group of riders wheeled around the camp, swords drawn. The leader, a thin man with a straight back, dismounted and kicked the man from on top of her, ordering him up at swordpoint.

Kordahla gathered her torn shirt about her and crawled to Sian. Shoving the dead man off, she tried to arrange the tattered remnants of the girl's clothing. The rags did not cover much. Blood trickled down Sian's thighs, and red welts covered her face and limbs. Kordahla wiped away blood and spittle. The girl managed a tiny movement of her head, and moaned. Timak came over and stood looking down, an expression of such guilt on his face he must have believed he could have prevented this. She did not have the strength in her to comfort him.

Within minutes, the three renegades were disarmed and on their knees next to Erok. The leader, a lean, dark-haired man, walked her way. Roaring, Erok jumped to his feet. He was knocked down by a soldier, who kicked him in the back.

"Hold," the leader said, and another man helped haul him back to his knees.

Kordahla planted herself in front of Sian. Timak kicked the man in the shin.

"You're an honourable little fighter," the man said, pushing Timak to arm's length. His eyes were kind. "Did they hurt you?"

"The girl. They violated the girl." She pulled the torn edges of her blouse tighter.

Surprise flitted across his face before his jaw set in anger. He took off his light cloak and covered Sian. "You're not Hill Tribe."

"The girl is, and the hunter. I'm Terlaani. The boy's from Verdaan."

His eyes betrayed his curiosity. He stood straight for one of his tall, slender build, and regarded the dead man. "Your work?"

She did not bother to answer. Another soldier brought over his cloak and gave it to her. She wrapped it tight around herself.

"I'm Captain Edard deq Lungo. You're now in the custody of the Myklaani border patrol."

He went to inspect the prisoners.

The brute who had attacked her spoke up. "We were protecting ourselves. The girl came at us with a knife, and that hill tribe scum killed Hilm."

"Was that before or after you attacked the women?" deq Lungo said.

"The hill rat meant to murder us in our sleep, I tell you. She had a knife in her hand when I found her."

"Tell it to the court. You'll stand trial in Kaijoor. Until then, you are relieved from duty."

These were soldiers who had attacked? Kordahla felt sick to the pit of her stomach. If this was what the liberty of Myklaan produced, her hopes were misplaced. Were they in Terlaan, their heads would be rolling. The mahktashaan she despised would have risked their lives to prevent this from happening to her. A sudden, overwhelming sense of homesickness made her sob.

Deq Lungo glanced her way. "Bind these worthless miscreants up, and let the Hill Tribe man free." He turned back to Kordahla. "Tell your friend if he gives any hint of non-compliance, I'll tie him so tight his hands and feet will fall off."

She pushed her way to Erok and, gripping his arm, looked him in the eye. He held her gaze a moment, then pulled his arm free, pushed past and went to Sian. Gathering her into his arms, he started walking towards the bridge. Three soldiers used their swords to block his way. Erok barked at them but stood firm.

"He wants to go home," Kordahla said, hugging Timak close to her. The boy was limp, staring after Sian. "Just let him take the girl home."

"I can't do that. He's killed a soldier," deq Lungo said. "And I need to know why a Terlaani woman has made an illegal crossing into Myklaan with a Verdaani boy and two of the Hill Tribe people."

She needed to remember she was a princess. By Vae'oenka, she needed to act like one to have any chance of pulling this off. "We have business with Shah Ordosteen."

"The Shah is a busy man."

"He will want to see me."

"That I doubt. Tell your friend to come back to camp."

She called to Erok and shook her head. He gave a reply. She thought she knew what it might be, but what could she say?

"You don't speak their tongue?" deq Lungo asked. She could sense his curiosity brimming.

"No."

His frown deepened as he gestured two of his men to fetch Erok. "How is it you come to wear their clothes and travel in their company?"

"That is for the Shah's ears alone."

Her answer displeased. She recognised the set of his jaw; determination to serve honour and duty. "It will never get that far if you do not account for yourselves," the captain said. Alienating him would be a mistake, but how far could she trust this man, whose soldiers ran riot?

In Erok's arms, Sian stirred. The girl's whimpers tore through Kordahla's heart. The hunter glowered at anyone who ventured too close, and she thanked Vae'oenka the soldiers were sensitive enough to give them space. A little distant from the tents, Erok laid Sian down and knelt by her. She rolled over and curled up. Kordahla sat beside her, and brushed the hair from her face. It was not enough. She had nothing more to offer. After a time, Sian tilted her head back. Her hand went up and out to Daesoa. The small moon was sinking to the hills. Kordahla did not expect her to rise, or totter away from Erok.

"She wants a knife," Timak said.

"And what, pray tell, does she intend with it?" the captain asked.

"She wants a bone from the wolf."

"Give it to her," Kordahla said. "What can a battered little girl do with a knife when she is surrounded by soldiers? You owe her this and more. Or is everything I hear about Myklaan a lie?"

Captain deq Lungo raised an eyebrow. "Would you have me risk injury, either to my men or the child?"

"She won't. That's not what she wants," Kordahla said.

"And you know this how?" the captain asked.

"The genie said so," said Timak. "The genie said she has to have that bone."

Kordahla put a hand on Timak's shoulder. "It is a tradition among the hill tribe. Grant her this. There is little else that will be of comfort."

The captain stared at the boy. He nodded and spoke his permission to a curly-haired man taking inventory by one of the tents.

Timak ran to get the knife and took it to Sian. The girl accepted it without acknowledgement. Her steps were slow and awkward. Kordahla could only imagine the pain she was suffering. Erok trailed her to the wolf, his scowl warning them all to back off. Kordahla felt compelled to follow and place a steadying hand on him. Devastated and furious, there was no telling what he might try. He bristled under her touch but kept his attention on Sian.

The girl pressed the wolf's paw to her lips. Throwing her head to the setting moons, she trilled a sound that sent shivers down Kordahla's spine. In the sky, Daesoa and Dindarin flared. A moonbeam dropped from each, alighting on the wolf. Kordahla made the sign of the Vae. A couple of soldiers rubbed their eyes. Then the illusion was gone, the moons no longer full. Using careful, reverent strokes, Sian cut the paw and extracted a bone. When she was done, she dropped the knife and turned to Erok. He dived for the knife, was up and around before the soldiers could react. Sian dropped to her knees and spoke to him. Her eyes were unfocussed, her hand extended to Daesoa. The soldiers advanced. Erok hesitated. Sian spoke again and he dropped the knife. Then she keeled over and fell into a deep sleep. Kordahla gasped in wonder as the moonbeams travelled over her face in a tender caress. Once more the moons flared, yellow and green, before the beams retracted into the sky.

It was some moments before the camp stirred to the soldiers' murmurings. Unable to do more, sensing how truly inadequate the gesture was in the face of what one little girl had suffered, Kordahla took the bone from Sian's hand. Erok only watched with cautious eyes.

"Please," she said to the captain, "May we have some water to boil this?"

"What is this? What is it we have just seen?" he asked.

"We believe she is a soothsayer," Kordahla said.

The captain watched the girl, her face troubled even in repose. "You need to speak to the Shah, you say." He picked up a lantern. Casting a look at his men, he gestured her to follow him into the privacy of a tent. Two untidy bedrolls reeked of stale sweat and sour liquor, and tilted saddlepacks spilled tangled clothes onto the canvas. The captain hung the lantern from a hook in the centre of the roof. His back to her, he adopted a soldier's pose, head erect, feet apart, hands clasped behind his back. She heard him take a deep breath before he turned to face her.

"You present me with something of a problem. I have duties to perform, yet now I must return to Kaijoor."

"What occurred here is clear. We broke no laws when we defended ourselves, and if your soldiers turn renegade, you deserve the discipline of your superiors."

"It is precisely those renegades my superiors have commissioned me to weed out."

"Then we have assisted you. We are headed to Kaijoor. You owe us an escort since it is your men we have to fear."

"That you chose not to arrive via the Mykter Pass is reason enough to hold you, even had your party not displayed intriguing talents."

"We came by the most direct route. As for the talents of the children, it is the wish of the Vae."

"Your appearance is as rough as any Tribesman, yet your words are cultured. Your bearing has the air of the nobility about it, though you are still shaken. The girl is a soothsayer, the boy talks to a genie and the hunter is here to protect and guide. Where in all this do you fit, mistress?"

Kordahla straightened. There were two secrets she could trust him with. The one about her neck was her only bargaining tool. And so she revealed the other. "I am Princess Kordahla, daughter of Shah Wilshem of Terlaan. I am in Myklaan to seek an audience with Shah Ordosteen."

His jaw dropped, though to his credit he snapped it back straight away. The redness that burned his cheeks, though, he could not hide. No doubt the implication of her predicament, the embarrassment that might have resulted had events played differently were running through his mind. At last he said, "How is it a princess of Terlaan comes to be in Myklaan unannounced and without a royal escort?"

She held his gaze. It was not a difficult conclusion, even for a soldier. She could see his mind working over the facts, could tell he reached understanding long before he spoke.

"Can you offer proof of what you claim?" he asked at length.

"To Shah Ordosteen, yes. But only to him."

"If what you say is true, your actions will drag us into war."

"It is not for you to decide. This matter is for the Shah, and for him alone."

He nodded once. "I will escort you to Kaijoor. What will happen to you when we get there is for others to decide. Get some rest. We leave in a few hours."

She turned as he stepped past her and pulled the flap of the tent aside. "I will not travel with those ogres you call soldiers.

"They come with us only as far as Mykter Fort. They will travel under a separate guard to Kaijoor." He stepped through, then turned again. "You are lucky we were riding to San Sidris for provisions, and that I chose to reconnoitre the area myself. There may well have been no one on the plain to hear your screams. Your corpse may have been picked clean by buzzards long before your skeleton was found."

When the flapped closed, Kordahla collapsed onto the stained bedroll. Captain deq Lungo had not addressed her by title. Neither had he indicated he believed her. But she was going to Kaijoor under escort. For a little longer, she was out of Ahkdul's grasp.

CHAPTER THIRTY-NINE

TONIGHT, GIBBOUS DINDARIN LOOMED large and low, casting a ghostly green glow over the wooded banks of the upper Crystalite River. Vinsant was having trouble sleeping, and it had nothing to do with the light from the moons, the Majoria's soft snores or the roar of the squat waterfall. The image of Kordahla, knife to her face, haunted him to distraction. Levi, insisting on the no-speaking-unless-spoken-to rule, was his usual font of no wisdom. Vinsant had wondered if he piped up enough whether they would go further than retrace their steps, and travel all the way back past Tarana and into Myklaan. One look at Levi and he abandoned the thought. Amazing how it was possible to tell the man's mood even beneath the engulfing hood and robe.

Tossing and turning was no use. Vinsant got up from the hard ground he was gradually becoming accustomed to and padded to the river. If only he knew the magic word Levi had uttered to conjure the image of his sister. With it, he was sure he could duplicate the feat.

Above him, the water churned over boulders, crashing down into the rock-strewn river, splashing up spray and barring the way to the boat. Without a still pool, there was no hope of steadying an image. Up on the fall, large rocks sequestered bodies of water that trickled over the edge when they filled to overflowing. Groping at shadowed knobs and crevices, Vinsant hauled himself up. Scraped knees and scratched arms added to the adventure. Calling yourself brave was not an option without them and, Vinsant had decided, if there was one quality a mahktashaan needed more than obedience it was bravery. When he next saw Kordahla, in Myklaan if the Vae possessed any mercy, he needed to sport a few scars to embellish his tale.

At the top of the falls, he edged along the mossy boulders. The water sluiced between the largest of them, leaving a damp and slippery path. As luck would have it, the far side held the gentler current. Reaching the middle of the wide river entailed no more than getting his feet wet. From there a wide chasm between the rocks acted as a funnel for the water. Vinsant eyed the eddies that clouded the pool below. They might have been the safer option. He stepped away from the edge, testing the depth with his toe. From the look of the water, the most passable route lay further back. He leapt for a crag. His foot twisted as he landed. He slipped and went splashing into the water. The current pummelled him under and up and under, driving him towards the edge, toward the craggy, spine-breaking rocks at the bottom of the fall. Panic and instinct took control. He needed magic, but the only trick that came to mind was the force to drive the boat.

"*Impellimos*," he yelled above the din of the falls, picturing himself rather than the boat. "*Impellimos*," he repeated, closing his eyes and remembering the glade. By the unbelievable grace of Mahktos, he held steady. He risked a quick glance to check his position, and almost lost his concentration. Suspended just at the drop, he had missed plummeting to his death by a mere second. Only Levi's voice repeating his command thirty-nine times had saved him. He fought to keep the god-awe in him, to clear his mind, to straighten his limbs. "*Impellimos*," he repeated and repeated and repeated, and concentrated, really concentrated, on beating the current. Forward and up he edged, straining to sustain movement. The effort to sling a hand over a rock was almost too much. He dragged himself up over the lichen covered surface, and turned onto his side to fill himself with air, too exhausted to do more than collapse. He rolled onto his back. His arm flailed. The movement carried him over the other side of the rock, and he fell through the air beside the falls.

His leg smashed into a branch lying across a pit. The jarring impact halted his fall. Vinsant breathed a sigh of relief. He lifted a leg to step across, onto rock. His movement snapped the branch, and he toppled. He landed heavily on one leg, and cried out. Standing was agony, but he forced himself to clench his jaw and explore the pit. The sides of the boulders were worn smooth and devoid of grappling roots. Without a handhold, he was never going to get out by himself. Was Levi ever going to make him pay for this. There was nothing for it but to shout for the Majoria. Typical of his cursed luck, the sound was drowned by the roar of the falls.

Five minutes later, his leg shooting pain up his spine and into his jaw – terrible, dreadful pain beyond what a brave mahktashaan should have to endure – Vinsant sat on the damp leaf litter, resigned to wait until his presence was missed. He brushed aside decaying clumps and, wouldn't you know it, a murky puddle emerged. Since he was hardly able to land in deeper trouble, he concentrated on the memory of that ride in the boat, trying to hear the magic word he had missed in his concentration. Daesoa's yellow beam stroked his face, prompting the Levi in his memory to whisper his spell. *Impature.* His agony and fatigue would have to wait until after he had exhausted the last vestige of concentration. *Impature.* The surface of the murky puddle rippled and stilled. Reflected in it was not his own freckled face, but Kordahla, a knife at her throat. He had to still the shakes. He had to push time forward, so he could discover what followed. He could concentrate, he knew he could. He *was* concentrating, but the image didn't change. The water was supposed to show him what happened, not to sizzle and evaporate in a column of steam. He swept the debris aside. Nothing but mud lay beneath it. He slumped against a rock. He was too tired to try again right now.

When he woke, dawn was nowhere in sight, his throbbing leg had swollen to twice its normal size, and his throat was parched into soreness. Adventure time was long over. He yelled for the Majoria. No surprise his only answer was an echo. Squeezing his eyes shut, he beseeched Mahktos, felt a shift in his mind and sensed the presence of his strict mentor nudge through his thoughts.

Ten minutes later Levi's silhouette appeared at the pit. Vinsant scrambled up, careful to keep his weight off his bad leg.

"All honour to you, Majoria," he greeted in the meekest voice he had ever used. He waited for the tirade.

"*Levitos*," the Majoria said, the rasp of his breath all that betrayed his ire.

The cool command levitated Vinsant right off the floor. "Thank–" he started. Scum of a hopper, the evil son of *two* malicious djinn dropped him back in the hole. He landed on his bad leg, and cried out.

"Get up and concentrate," Levi said, his voice dripping with spite.

Long after his callous master should have summoned him lunch, Vinsant floated himself out of the hole. Remaining just off the ground to ease the throb in his leg, he bowed his head. At a gesture from Levi, he fell, collapsing under the agony of his own weight.

"Bring the boat and come," Levi commanded. The Majoria levitated to the top of the falls. Vinsant struggled up, levitated himself, and then reached for the boat. He felt it wobble into the air, smiled, then crashed onto the rocks, the double task beyond his skill.

"You will walk," Levi hissed from the top of the boulders.

No doubt a day of physical torture was his penance. Vinsant hobbled up the cliff, taking as much of his weight as he could on his arms. He waited until his agonising leg was on dry, firm, root-bound land before he tried to bring up the boat. It was just as well Levi added his guidance. In his exhausted state Vinsant would have dropped the boat right into the splintering fall.

"Draw your sword," Levi said, when the boat was moored.

Stifling an inward groan, Vinsant adopted a defensive stance. He knew very well how to do that one-legged, but in his opinion he deserved a medal for suffering a multitude of bruises without a single complaint as Levi knocked him down again and again.

After magic practice, they ate a portion of the dried meat ration they carried. Vinsant fell asleep before he had taken the last bite.

"You may choose one act of magic to learn," Levi said when he woke.

The offer was so unlike the Majoria, Vinsant stared into the black hood, stunned. In his muddled sleepiness, he nearly blurted his desire to scry. He caught himself just in time. This generosity could be a trap. He needed a different way to help Kordahla.

"Thoughtspeak," he said.

"Why do you wish to learn thoughtspeak?"

"In case I need to call you when you can't hear me."

"You presume too far, apprentice."

An invisible kick in the back pushed Vinsant onto his hands and knees. He hadn't meant he intended to be reckless.

Levi stood. "And you have pledged not to lie."

Vinsant knelt and wiped the gravel embedded in his palms. "I want to talk to the Minoria," he said.

"Why?" Levi demanded.

"So that I can find out what happens to Kordahla." *And because I'm sick of having nobody to talk to*, he added silently.

To his surprise, the Majoria acquiesced, forcing him to practice the technique over and over until he had perfected it, of course.

"You are not to use thoughtspeak without permission," Levi said, calling a rest.

"May I contact Arun?" Vinsant asked.

For three breaths the Majoria considered, then gave a slow nod. "This once."

Yippee! He hadn't been so happy in days! Vinsant reached for the Minoria. A remote connection when the other person remained ignorant of the attempt proved a lot more difficult than he had anticipated. Under considerable guidance from Levi he felt the familiar calmness of the Minoria.

Vinsant, a pleasantly surprised Arun greeted him, followed a moment later by *All honour to you, Majoria.*

Vinsant's spirits sank. This was to be no private conversation. *Have you found Kordahla?* he asked, opting to be direct because he was not sure how long he could sustain the link.

Our journey has been plagued by unexpected interruptions. We've had to take the indirect route because of unseasonable flooding. We are not yet at the Termyk pass.

I'm worried. I think something terrible has happened to her, Vinsant said, judging that much safe enough.

Is there any foundation to your worry? Arun asked.

Just a feeling. Like you had when...before.

You are in pain.

My fault, Vinsant sent, and it sounded like he had said it through gritted teeth.

Our young apprentice has not yet learned to obey, Levi said.

He will.

I'm learning a lot, Vinsant said.

I will advise you of our progress, Majoria, Arun said, in a detached tone.

Levi broke the link.

For the rest of the day Vinsant propelled them upriver. Evening saw him struggle under the burden of his regimented training on a bad leg.

"*Levitos*," Vinsant murmured as the Majoria levitated in preparation for sleep. This time, he found he could stretch out on a cushion of air. It was a welcome change from the ground. His droopy lids were about to close when the Minoria's voice sounded in his mind.

You have about ten seconds before the Majoria is alerted to this conversation.

Vinsant lost two of them before he thought to send Arun the images of Kordahla with the knife to her throat and Levi's secretive reaction in the boat.

You are growing strong, Vinsant. Trust Levi to train you well, even when his motives are not apparent. The Minoria severed the link.

Beside Vinsant, the Majoria stirred. Vinsant took a deep breath. Just in case, he kept his mind off Kordahla. It was a long while before he drifted back to sleep.

Chapter Forty

CAPTAIN DEQ LUNGO WAS true to his word. Leaving three of his men to reach San Sidris on foot, he led them to Mykter Fort. The renegades were interred in a dungeon, and Kordahla and Sian were treated to a hot bath followed by a hearty meal and a real bed. Despite the open curiosity of the men, they were addressed with respect, even if the barred doors and armed guards were a constant reminder of their status. By Kordahla's calculations, the mahktashaan could only be an eight-day behind. She was eager to proceed, and the day they lost at the Fort while deq Lungo organised the command saw her pace the ramparts and gaze down the pass for any sign of riders. If the men were uncertain as to her identity, her actions added fuel to their rumours.

Sian and Timak were little more than husks, jumpy if the men approached, unwilling to be drawn into conversation or play. They sat side by side, staring out of the narrow windows or following well-meaning soldiers to the bare yard then sitting in the furthest corner they could find and staring at nothing. At the genie, Kordahla presumed. The men grew uneasy around them: Timak talked to the air and Erok brooded close by, refusing to let Sian out of his sight. When Kordahla opened their door in the morning, she found him sleeping across the threshold.

When they mounted fresh horses and set out for the capital, Kordahla breathed a first sigh of relief. The second came when it became clear deq Lungo was willing to forgo a sedate pace. Five days after they left Mykter Fort they rounded the edge of a brooding forest.

"Faradil Forest," deq Lungo said, an edge to his voice. "Tell your friends to keep well clear. The best trained soldier won't set foot inside if he is ordered."

Kordahla glanced at him. His terse, dour conversations had moderated her loneliness but the effort of drawing him out was too great for her travel-weary mind. "I never imagined brigands and robbers to plague Myklaan."

"There's no such thing in Faradil, for there's none with anything worth stealing who would enter it. That forest is possessed." He rode to the head of the group before she could question him further.

There was no village with an inn that night, nor any farmhouse with a stable for deq Lungo to requisition. They camped on the hard earth and withered grass, the dark shadow of Faradil looming. The men grumbled about skirting so close to the edge but Captain deq Lungo remained adamant they make good time. As the soldiers organised tents, Erok and the children wandered to collect deadfall. For want of companionship, Kordahla accompanied them. Several times she paused at the task, a mysterious force tugging her eyes to the dense trunks and twining canopy.

"Drop that!" deq Lungo yelled, when he chanced to look in their direction.

Startled by his uncharacteristic harshness, Kordahla and the children let their bundles of twigs fall. Erok frowned. The captain strode their way, his fury unchecked. Grabbing Timak, he brushed specks of bark from his midriff. Timak stood and stared at the forest, enduring the rough attention. Her heart weeping for the little boy, Kordahla kept her words soothing as she advised deq Lungo she would finish the task. She plucked the remaining particles off his clothing, but the boy remained as unresponsive as she had ever seen him. When deq Lungo tried to check Sian, Erok stepped in front.

"Get back to camp, and don't bring that," the captain ordered, pointing at the bundle still in Erok's arms.

Kordahla blinked. They were barely fifty paces from camp and had roamed further on previous nights. With a resentful admonishment for his sharp words, she herded the children between the tents. Behind her, she heard Erok mutter and slam the sticks to the ground.

Talk during their frugal meal of cold travel rations was subdued.

"It's the forest," one of the soldiers, Dario deq Pitran, said. The locks of his brown hair sat at slightly different lengths, as though his girl had taken a knife to it with more good intention than skill. "You can feel it pull, luring anyone who's out here."

"What is it?" she asked. "This feeling is queer. I feel a longing, but no nefarious intent."

The cheery soldier sobered, his round face growing long. "Don't be fooled. It's evil, all right. Those who go in almost never come back, and that includes the ones as go looking for them."

"And the ones that do return?" she asked, noticing Timak and Sian were listening. She should worry about that.

"Depends. Some are maimed so bad they'll never work again. Some don't have a mind, end up worse than a babe. Some head to the wilds and live by themselves." Dario shrugged. "None of them that return can remember what happened, but most just disappear."

"Is that why we don't have a fire?"

"The wise will not risk Faradil's ire," deq Lungo said. He sat as straight-backed as always, his lean jaw tight. "It's her wood we'd be using. Even in the dead of winter, the sane will not light a fire this close to her border, not even if they carted their own wood with them."

In the eerie presence of the forest, with that tale on her mind, she was a long time in falling asleep. Though the air hung hot and stagnant, the leaves rustled their disquiet. A restlessness brewed across the entire camp. She tossed and turned in the tent she shared with Sian, and heard those around her do the same. The owls had stopped hooting by the time fatigue won out.

She groaned when she woke in oppressive dark, prickling cold at a stalking threat. She reached towards Sian's bedroll. It was empty. Dragging herself up, she padded outside. Habit dictated Erok should have been sleeping outside their tent. It took a moment to locate him, a hastening shadow under Dindarin's waning form. Beyond, two small figures walked towards Faradil, following the bob of an apricot ball of light. No one else stirred. Soldiers lay in disarray around the camp. The watch were asleep at their posts.

"Help, please," she said, giving one a nudge with her bare foot. She did not wait, but ran towards Timak. The dry grass prickled her ankles, and stones bruised her soles, but the boy was almost at the forest's edge.

"Timak!"

He paused as he entered its silent, brooding shadow, paused at his name.

"I can't," he pleaded.

For a wild, hopeful moment, she thought he would return.

"Timak."

"Let me go." He lifted his pitiful face, not to her, but up to the moon. "It hurts too much."

The words cut her. She lunged and pulled him back with more force than he deserved, but whatever malign entity lurked between the tangling branches could not claim him. His eyes went wide; he gasped and stiffened. She knelt, put her hand to his cheek, tinged with Dindarin's sheen.

"Don't do this," she said. "You brave, generous boy. Listen to your genie." She hugged him to her, held him altogether too hard. "Listen to your genie. She's never told you wrong before."

He sobbed, once, twice, then wrapped his arms around her, rested his head on her shoulder, and cried. The air around them slackened. A cricket chirped. The moon glossed the waxy leaves.

"It will be alright," she said, not knowing if it were true, not even knowing how Ahkdul had procured him, what manner of life he had lived before.

Further along the tree line, Erok grabbed Sian. The silent girl was struggling against him, reaching for an oak rattling with all her frustration.

Timak pulled away and wiped his eyes. "It's different for her," he said.

"How? How is it different?" She searched his face, wanting to understand, knowing, as close as she had come to being violated, she could not.

His eyes were so large, so serious. "The forest warns me away, but it calls to her."

She glanced at Captain deq Lungo and the soldier she had roused. The cricket fell quiet as they approached, swords drawn. She regretted waking them.

"What does the genie say?" she asked.

Timak sniffed. "The forest won't hurt her. Erok should let her go."

"Lady, I warned you," deq Lungo said, stopping short of the trees.

Kordahla stood and took Timak's hand. "You have noted these children have talents. Sian is making use of hers now." Dear Vae'oenka, she wished someone were here to make sense of all this. Why was she thinking of Arun? The Minoria would never have permitted her to leave Terlaan. She approached the hunter. "Erok. Erok. Let her go." She shook her head.

The hunter ignored her, circled Sian around the waist, hoisted her over his shoulder and stomped back to camp, ignoring the blood that trickled from his reopened wound and Sian's incoherent protests. She followed with Timak, deq Lungo at the rear.

Around the camp, soldiers were stirring. Erok barged into their tent and dropped Sian on her bedroll. She was quiet again, dazed almost, as she looked around and said something in a small voice.

Captain deq Lungo stood at the entrance. "That child is prone to wandering into trouble. You will tie her up if need be, but she will not be the death of my men."

Erok seemed to understand the sentiment and for once he seemed to agree. He held the door flap open as Sian curled up and showed no intention of moving for the rest of the night.

Kordahla tucked Timak in her blankets and slid past Erok to face the captain. "These children are hurting, in no small part because of what your men did to them. Now your watchmen fall asleep," Kordahla said. "Why do you not discipline them?"

"Lady, you forget your position," deq Lungo said, and strode off.

"It's always this way," Dario said, handing her a cup of water, "this close to Faradil. No watch can stay awake." He looked to the trees. "If we camp this close to her edge again, it'll be a wonder if we don't lose a man." He shook his head and left her to bed down.

She remained standing, her arms tight around her, watching the forest, sensing it watch them.

"You'd best get some rest," Dario said from inside his bedroll. "If I know the captain, he'll push us hard tomorrow, so we don't have to sleep in her shadow again."

The captain indeed spurred them on. They camped the next night on the lush grasses around Lake Tejolin. Faradil Forest was no further distant, but the serene water, perfect in it reflection of the moons, tempered its pull.

"Are there legends around this lake?" Kordahla asked Dario.

"Aye, a fair few. Vae'omar has taken his fair share of sailors, and there's those who swear water sprites frolic in its depths. But it's nothing to rival Faradil." The soldier's affable nature made her wish she had struck up a conversation with him earlier in their journey. She might have discovered more about the realm she hoped to call home.

They approached the city just before sunset on the next day. Kordahla's childhood memories had faded too thin to prepare her for the sight of the towering walls. Intricate carvings adorned the entire structure, an area several thousand times the walls of Tarana palace.

"Impressive, isn't it?" Dario said.

"Indeed." Impressive enough to overwhelm Erok and Sian into silence. Timak was at least looking around him with a scrap of child-like wonder. As for her own fatigue, it evaporated in the ambience of a city which flaunted a culture refined enough to rival the Vae's. Dazzling white houses lined wide, ordered streets, their intersections surrounding tended squares in which statues of legendary beasts stood proud. She caught herself smiling as she spied a man lead a woman to a tiered fountain of fawns. How romantic a courtship would blossom under its spray! But Vae'oenka spare her; the couple were kissing in public. She turned her hot cheeks away, only to see men and women walk hand in hand, fingers entwined, the bustle of the day melding into the languid pleasures of night. The brightly woven silks and chiffons of their garments turned twilight into a festival fit to rival sunset. The men wore kurtas of the style Mariano preferred. And the women! So many bared midriffs. And not a veil in sight! Was it any wonder men took unspeakable liberties in the face of this wantonness?

She might have choked on her thoughts had Captain deq Lungo not led them into a walled garden of tall palms and fragrant shrubs. The neighbourhood had to be safe, for the property lacked a gate. The Captain bid them dismount, and led them down a pebbled walk to a wide, two-storey house. The door was locked. He knocked. And pounded. And pounded again.

His call was at last answered by a young gentleman with a button nose that emphasised his boyish appearance. The oversize cut of his silk coat, the fraying threads of the embroidery hemming it, betrayed a lack of true wealth.

"I have important visitors to entrust to your care," deq Lungo said. "Until you hear otherwise, they are to be given the quality of attention you might lavish on the Shah himself."

"What is this place?" Kordahla asked, as deq Lungo gestured her into a bare hall.

"It is a hospice. The children at least are in need of care, and both you and Erok would benefit from the physic's ministrations."

"I thank you for your consideration but I assure you, I am fine. I wish you to escort me to the palace. It is Shah Ordosteen to whom I must present myself. All else can wait."

"Lady, the Shah will decide to see you or not. I strongly urge you to accept the generosity of the physics. You will find this house far more hospitable than the dungeon."

She flushed, ashamed of her naiveté, but managed to look the captain in the eye. "Your thoughtfulness is appreciated," she said in a more grateful tone.

The young physic huffed. "Hurry up. It's late and we're about to lock the doors."

Ushered by soldiers, they entered the hall.

"As I understand it, Lady Jordayne requested these doors remain open at all hours," deq Lungo said, remaining outside.

"If you supply me with soldiers, it is done. Otherwise, I will not place either myself or my patients at risk from addicts or brigands," the physic replied with a scowl. His nose wrinkled in distaste as he looked over Erok and Timak in their Hill Tribe garb, and then Sian, whose heritage was unmistakable.

"Tonight you have soldiers, and the doors shall remain locked besides," deq Lungo said with a lingering look at her. "And I repeat, you will lavish your best care on these guests." He nodded at her, and disappeared into the night, his boots crunching pebbles on the path.

Dario stationed himself by the door while the other soldiers fanned through the building.

The physic sighed. "In there."

The treatment room, neat, ordered and brightly lit by lanterns hanging all around the walls, smelled of the same herbs as Nocrates's muddled chamber. A ginger-haired boy in ill-fitting, worn clothing was sweeping the floor between two tables. He glanced up at them, then resumed his task. The physic selected a salve from a table laid with frightful instruments at one end and small pots at the other, and passed it to her. "It will help with the insect bites. Are there any injuries that need immediate attention?"

His brusque manner left her wary. "The girl has bad burns to her arm," she said.

The boy dropped the broom, ignored the physic's glare as it clapped the edge of a table and clattered to the floor, and scooted from the room. His hasty footsteps pattered upstairs.

"Come here," the physic said to Sian, pointing to a chair at one of the three treatment tables in the centre of the crowded room. Sian stared at the seat. The physic frowned as he stomped towards her. It was no surprise she scuttled back, or that Erok planted himself in front of her. "I cannot examine her if she will not cooperate. You will tell her to sit here."

"She has been through a great deal, and is not about to let a man she does not trust examine her," Kordahla said, moving to stand beside Erok. This brusque man had no business with their intimate secrets. Their eyes locked in silent battle as the stairs creaked.

A harried, greying man, stooped from fatigue, entered the room, the boy trailing behind. "We have patients, I see," the elder physic said.

"They are prisoners, I think, and not truly in need of emergency aid. I was about to send Ilyam to find them a pallet."

Dario deq Pitran followed the physic in, frowning as he saw them standing. "Captain deq Lungo made it plain these guests are to get all the care they need."

"The girl will not allow me near her.

The older physic swept his eyes over each of them, Sian last. "With good reason, I think," he said, his voice soft and kind. "Why don't you finish the rounds upstairs, Chas. I believe I can finish in here."

Chas swept from the room without further encouragement.

"Excuse me," the older physic said, and followed him out. Dario turned and went too. Their voices in the hall, though low, were clear.

"I expect more of you, despite the hour," the older physic said.

"The Hill Tribe people are not citizens. They are not entitled to our care," the young physic replied.

"Your profession demands a more compassionate nature to every fellow human being."

"The state does not."

"It does in this case." Deq Pitran's voice. "You were assigned by a captain in the Royal Army to tend to them."

"They have little need for a physic," Chas said, his voice querulous.

"That I cannot agree with," the other physic said. "Please attend to the patients upstairs."

"Addicts who brought their misfortune upon themselves."

Footsteps thumped up the stairs.

The elder physic came back into the room. "Ilyam, run to the kitchens and tell Cook we have four guests in need of a nourishing meal. You may get your own dinner while you're about it." The boy, who was swishing the broom over a spotless flagstone, stole one final glance at them, set the broom against the wall, and ran to do his master's bidding. The physic turned to her. "I'm Physic Hamid deq Lamont. Who do I have the honour of treating?"

"This is Erok, Sian and Timak," Kordahla said.

"And you?" he asked when she paused.

"You may call me Samille," she said.

"Am I right in assuming you have yet to eat?"

Kordahla nodded, and deq Lamont, soft spoken and measured in his movements, led them to a dining room adjacent the steamy kitchen. Ilyam bounded out of the steam amid the clang of spoons and bang of lids, onto one of the long benches, and picked up his knife before the cook had served hunks of tender venison. Hamid joined them as they ate, describing the hospice and city with meticulous detail, happy to answer Ilyam's disbelieving queries, but demanding nothing of them. By the time the plump, pink-cheeked cook presented them with a platter of fruit, Timak was listening and Sian had almost met his eye as he handed her a choice plum. Digging into a pocket, deq Lamont extracted a coin and gave it to Ilyam, saying it was a little extra for the long day.

"Does he not have a family to return to?" she asked when the boy went to ready the treatment room.

"He has a mother and siblings, but the lodging here is better than she can provide for him. His father succumbed to porrin addiction, and the allowance of an apprentice is too low for them all to survive on."

"Then the drug is a problem here?"

"Porrin is the bane of the continent, dare I say the world."

Why she had imagined otherwise of this utopia, she could not say. It was after all, despite its strangeness, not so very different from home.

"Now," Hamid said as they returned to the treatment room. "I hope I may examine you." He started with Erok in full view of them all, cleaning and dressing the wound on the hunter's arm. Ilyam buzzed about, fetching what his master needed, anticipating his requests so when Hamid seemed about to speak, he only hummed and picked up the salve or bandage Ilyam had placed to hand. When the physic turned to Sian, she flinched. Opening his hand, Hamid gave her a soft smile, and waited for her to place her arm in it.

"How old is this injury?" he asked, examining the scarred muscle and blistering skin.

"About three eight-days," Kordahla said.

"And it has not become infected?"

Sian had gritted her teeth and turned away.

"It pains her. She has only just started using it," Kordahla said.

"It is a miracle it has healed at all. You have travelled across hills and plain, I take it? You should offer thanks to Vae'oenka. I would expect a person with a burn of this severity to lose their arm if not their life, and quickly at that, but she is on the mend."

Hamid went to the shelves above the implement table, selected a salve and handed it to Sian. Erok took it. "Rub this on. It will help numb the pain. With long sleeves, no one will notice the disfigurement." He indicated what he wanted with actions. Erok nodded. Satisfied, Hamid dismissed yawning Ilyam, and then sat back and looked at the child. She bowed her head. "There is more, I think, than this injury." His tone had not changed, and although the question was directed at Kordahla, he still faced Sian.

"She is afflicted by seizures." Kordahla clamped her mouth shut. She had to force herself to say it all. "And she was violated." Sian might guess what they said, but it would not be from a change of tone.

"I see," the gentle doctor said in a manner that very much suggested he did. "And the boy? He too has the look of one traumatised about him."

Timak was curled up under the implement table, his back against the wall. He was talking to himself again. Or the genie.

"Him too. Repeatedly," she whispered.

Drawing a deep breath in through his nose, Hamid rose and faced her. Looking at her through eyes raised in a lowered head, the most non-threatening person she had ever encountered, he asked the same of her.

She found she had to look away. The filthy, despicable memory burned too strong. "He was not able to carry his intent to completion." And it was her turn to look at the floor.

"My dear, the shame is not yours."

She swallowed and had to concentrate to keep the tears from her eyes. "Where I come from, it is."

The physic patted his hips and became more animated. "If you choose to stay in Myklaan a while, you might find your perceptions change. I hope you will. I would like to become better acquainted with all of you. It is not so often I find myself among such diverse company." He handed her an ointment. "This will ease the itch of those insect bites, and help reduce scarring."

She stepped aside as an emaciated man wandered into the room, his unseeing eyes glazed. Ilyam ran in after him. Tucking his small body alongside the man, he used his hip to turn the addict around and herd him out.

"That is all for tonight, Ilyam," deq Lamont said. "You will let Chas finish with the patients."

Kordahla stared after them. This meaningless waste of life held an unparalleled sadness.

"They are harmless enough," Hamid said, misunderstanding.

"Will he recover?"

"His body is wasted beyond repair. There are others who might find the will to fight the curse with the right support. Too many fall victim again once they leave. But this is not something you need concern yourself about. Is there anything else I can do for you tonight?" The physic looked at each of them in turn.

Erok stepped forward and held out the pouch that contained the last of the herbs Sian took. Hamid shook the contents and sniffed. "Ah yes. For the seizures, I take it. If this mix doesn't work, we may need to try other combinations." He bustled about collecting dried herbs to fill the pouch and handed it to Sian. The girl lifted her eyes to his as she took it.

CHAPTER FORTY-ONE

ORDOSTEEN EXHALED A LENGTHY breath. Across the bedchamber, Katrine's incessant prattling as she lifted one jewelled ring after the other was wearing on his nerves. While his latest young mistress delighted between the sheets, her penchant for inane gossip left him empty. The girl, as he thought of the sensual slip before him, though she was four years past her majority, had the body of a goddess but the brains of a spoiled child. The night was young, but they would need to retire soon if his sanity was to be preserved. He went to her and pulled her into a kiss. As her supple flesh responded, his irritation began to die.

She pushed him away. "Aren't you going to answer my question?" she said, petulant lips pouting as she turned her back on him. She picked up a sapphire and set it in her belly button.

Not aware she had asked one, Ordosteen put his hands on her shoulders and buried his face in her neck. The scent of her, roses and a hint of exotic spice, stirred his desire.

"I asked you a question," she said, stiffening.

"Enthral me now and ask me later." An argument about whether or not he had been listening would dampen his mood.

"I would think you are only interested in me for the pleasures of the flesh," she said with a toss of her golden hair.

Ordosteen let her go. Did the girl really think she was anything more to him? He had to remind himself how young she was, how naïve. His sense of honour did not allow him to deny it. Nor was he callow enough to confirm it. She set the sapphire back in the silver filigree jewel box on his oak dressing table. Its clawed feet moved, ruffling the delicate fabric of the green veil he had left to trail over the golden acorn mounts.

"Come to bed," he said, avoiding the delicate issue as best he could.

Her back still to him, she lifted her chin, as though considering, as though he had made a request.

Thank Vae'oenka three sharp knocks at the door interrupted.

"Enter," Ordosteen called.

Katrine spun, eyes wide. He caught the fleeting worry she had lost his interest before he turned to the presumptuous intruder.

"Your Majesty," Farsil said with apologetic deference. It was testament to the late hour that the sash on his comfortable house coat was crooked. "Captain deq Lungo insists on seeing you."

"Your Majesty." Captain deq Lungo barged straight past the chamberlain and bowed.

Ordosteen swept his eyes over the travel-stained soldier. The man had not even bothered to wash his face. "Were you aware I had retired?" he asked. For Katrine's sake, really. For this man to have returned from his northern post, for him to disregard protocol, there had to be excellent reason, at least in his estimation.

"Chamberlain Farsil did advise me, Majesty, but I have news I believe you should hear."

"And it cannot wait until morning?"

"That is not a decision I can presume to make. But I believe it best I deliver my report in private," deq Lungo said with a meaningful glance at Katrine. He must have ridden hard, to be leaning from the waist.

"Yes, my dear," Ordosteen said, taking her hands to guide her to the door. "You had best go. I would not think to bore you with matters of state."

She slipped her hands out of his, picked up the green veil and flipped it over her hair. Ordosteen had lingered an hour over the embroidered fabric before summoning her to his room to drown his loneliness in the pleasures of the flesh. He had determined to weigh the djinn's offer against the exquisite if temporary sating his mistress provided as she slept in his arms. He clenched his teeth. To see her treat the object of his salvation in so cavalier a manner was to rouse a modicum of resentment in his heart.

She came to stand beside him. It was presumptuous of her to assume the position of a queen. "I shall stay. You might have need of some feminine advice."

"You will go," he said, his tone brooking no argument. The court gossip was the last person he wanted around when there was serious news.

"Then I shall take this, as a token of your affection," she said turning this way and that to show off the veil.

"Leave it. That does not belong to you," he said, the Vae forgive him for sounding harsher than he had intended.

She let it drop to the floor and ran from the room. Ordosteen sighed. There would be tears in her eyes when she returned. He must have a word with Jordayne. His niece must sort the girl out or find him a more suitable mistress.

"Well?" Ordosteen said to deq Lungo when the guards outside had closed the doors.

"Majesty, I brought four prisoners with me from the border. A Terlaani woman, a Verdaani boy, and two of the Hill Tribe. The boy communicates with a djinn. The Hill Tribe girl the others believe is a soothsayer and the woman–" Deq Lungo took a deep breath. "The Terlaani woman claims to be Princess Kordahla, daughter to Shah Wilshem of Terlaan. She requests an audience."

For a long moment, Ordosteen took the captain's measure. "Do you believe she is who she says?"

"Her words are cultured, her manner refined. She claims to have proof but refuses to offer it to anyone other than Your Majesty. Beyond that, it is not my place to presume."

"Yes, yes," Ordosteen said, brushing aside the man's humility. He frowned. The implications were staggering. "Is there more?"

"Yes, Majesty."

Ordosteen found his ire mounting as he listened to a report on the conduct of his soldiers. There would be a price to pay, if this girl was who she said she was.

"Bring the woman to the Throne Room. And find Jordayne and Matisse. I want them both there."

"Tonight, Majesty?"

"Yes, tonight," Ordosteen snapped. International relations rested on a precarious ledge if the Terlaani Princess had absconded from her protectors.

Long after the captain had left, Ordosteen was still standing. His eyes drifted to the veil. "I wonder," he murmured, not sure exactly what. Nothing as yet made sense.

◆ ◆ ◆

Even were she not clothed in the oversized kurta and churidar of a soldier, Kordahla would have felt presumptuous imagining she belonged in Kaijoor Palace. The vaulted ceilings, covered in detailed arabesques and supported by columns with elaborate corbels, the huge arched windows, and the marble floors of white, green, pink and black made the dusky decadence of Father's palace seem almost provincial. She made a point to lift her chin as Captain deq Lungo opened the side doors to a great hall and announced her presence.

The Terlaani Lady we intercepted at the border was less than she had hoped for. Still, elegance did not depend on fancy clothes. She paced her walk past the tiered balconies, and imbued her curtsy to Shah Ordosteen with the regal air of one bred to the ways of the court.

"Your Majesty," she said to the man on the golden throne. He sat solid as the carving of the massive oak tree springing from its back. "My Lord. My Lady," she continued to Matisse, who slouched in his chair, and Lady Jordayne, who reclined with sophistication. Shah Ordosteen might have accorded them the supporting standing-bear thrones, but they were her equals. To them, she would not dip her knee.

Behind her, the doors clanged closed.

Moments passed as Ordosteen regarded her. White-haired and with dark circles under his eyes, he was not aging well, but he had the air of one used to peaceful times; one who had never needed to struggle for authority; one who had indulged rather than one who had let himself go.

"Captain deq Lungo has advised me of your claim. Are you certain you wish to repeat it in this court?" he said at last.

She was aware of the sword at Matisse's side, and his hand on the pommel. Of his rumpled appearance, as though he had been dragged from bed despite the early hour. His lazy gaze fixed upon her. It held the regard of a well-fed cat that might stretch a clawed paw to bat at a mouse that dared to approach. And behind all that she was aware of a rugged appeal. She had heard he was a lady's man. Seeing him here, blonde and blue-eyed, she could believe it. Could believe also he would smite her down in an instant as Father had the meatball sellers.

She swallowed down the ghoulish image, willed her erratic heart to slow.

"I am Princess Kordahla, daughter to Shah Wilshem of Terlaan. I have come to Myklaan to request asylum." She fixed her eyes on Shah Ordosteen. Considering Lady Jordayne's sharp gaze, it seemed the safest place. The woman was slight of figure, with dull ash-blonde hair, but her presence matched the devastating image of the Vae gazing down from the dome. For all the immodesty of her flesh-baring dress, no one would ever dare dismiss her.

"You make a monumental claim." Ordosteen rose and descended the dais until he was level with her. "It is many seasons since I saw Princess Kordahla. She was but a child then." For all the caution in his slate-blue eyes, for all the kindness beneath it, his scrutiny set her heart racing. "How can I be sure you are she?" he asked, walking around her.

"I am she."

"I am afraid I will need more than your say so, child. You can hardly expect me to take the word of the bedraggled woman before me."

"I have proof. And something more. A gift if you will grant me refuge." Her hands were trembling, she realised, as she retrieved the crystal from a pocket and the quartz from around her neck. The nerves tickling her stomach weakened her. She had to steel herself to speak. "I offer you the crystal of a mahktashaan in return for your protection."

The silence was total. Ordosteen reached a hand to her gift, retracted it, reached again, but did not touch. Both Lord Matisse and Lady Jordayne sat up straight on their wooden thrones.

"They are harmless, I can assure you. I have carried them with me from home. I cannot attest to how they might work, but perhaps your mages can unlock the secret." She stopped, aware she was prattling.

Ordosteen took the crystal and quartz and held them up.

It was Lady Jordayne who, rising, broke the royal silence. "I rather think we need the mages, Uncle." She glided to the double doors amid the tinkle of bangles and anklets, opened them just wide enough to issue the summons, then closed them again, not in the least embarrassed pages and guards could ogle her bare midriff.

Ordosteen dropped his hand and focused his bewildered curiosity upon her. "Your presence here cannot remain a secret. Shah Wilshem is almost certain to wage war to avenge his honour, and if the rumour you are betrothed to Ahkdul deq Hudassan is true, Verdaan may join the fight. You place Myklaan in a precarious position. I am not sure this realm is prepared to go to war over you, no matter how renowned your beauty.

"The question, Uncle," Jordayne said from the back of the room, "is whether you are prepared to go to war over those crystals."

"Ah," Ordosteen said, scrutinising the crystal in his palm. "I suppose it is." He looked at her again. "It is not a question I am inclined to answer on the spur of the moment. Wilshem or his emissary are likely to come calling. I do not know how I shall respond. You have risked a great deal to come here, and not all of it yours to gamble. If I am to jeopardise my realm by extending you the hospitality of this court, I must know why."

In this expansive room, with these level rulers, she could hardly speak of a djinn. Her reasons seemed petty at best. "The rumours you heard are true, Majesty. My father betrothed me to Ahkdul, and he has already intimated he will make my life a misery. I am tired of being chattel."

"What does Wilshem hope to gain from this union?"

"Lord Hudassan has agreed to stem the flow of porrin into Terlaan."

Matisse rose, his hand still on the pommel of his sword. It was a plain weapon, well crafted but lacking the beauty for which Myklaan was famed. "And how long does he expect that arrangement to last? If your population is addicted, they will go to great lengths to seek it out."

"They will recover if the drug cannot be had."

"That, my dear," said Jordayne, re-joining them, "is a very naïve outlook." She had the determined look of someone who had hatched a scheme in the minutes she stood apart.

"More important," Matisse continued, "it confirms our suspicions. There are reasons beyond those crystals to entertain our guest." He was standing very close, a smile just visible on his lips. His proximity was distracting, confusing, as were his words. Kordahla turned away, seeking to regain her balance. And caught Jordayne's pursed lips.

Shah Ordosteen said, "What did you hope I would do, child, so that Ahkdul cannot stake his claim? Or did you think I would simply embrace you into my fold?"

"Will you marry me to a satrap or his son? He can lay no claim upon a legal union."

His Majesty smiled. "So you would have me treat my subjects like the very chattel you so despise?"

Tears of frustration threatened to well. She had come so far for this. Everything considered, she had to remind herself, the conversation was progressing well. They had not yet thrown her into a dungeon.

"You might find there are those willing enough," she said.

"But are you, my dear?" Jordayne asked, placing a hand on her arm. "It hardly makes sense to flee one marriage only to enter another loveless union. As for you, Uncle, do remember where we are. The day Myklaani women require a bond with a man for protection is the day this land shall cease to be Myklaan. And I rather thought you would welcome the opportunity to educate our less refined neighbours to that effect. Now, it will be some time before the mages arrive. Until then, I believe we would be remiss not to offer Princess Kordahla a bath and a gown."

"I came with companions," Kordahla said.

"For now, they will be fine at the hospice," Ordosteen replied.

"They will indeed," Jordayne assured, squeezing her arm. "You can reunite with them tomorrow. Now come along."

"You believe me," Kordahla said as they walked through airy halls decorated with mouldings of vines and wreaths, and climbed stairs with lessons of old painted on their tiles.

"Men are blind. They cannot see past those scratches and bites, or the image of the child they retain from Ordo's last wedding. Anyway, those crystals did the trick."

They entered a chamber with cream and gold tiles on the walls, and green marble floors. Kordahla sighed. It was luxury to see a maid filling a tub, and another dressing a bed with an embroidered cover.

"I trust you will be comfortable here," Lady Jordayne said.

The chamber, lavish in its femininity, was fit for a queen. As the maids helped her undress, Kordahla couldn't help looking at the scenes of noble life painted on the cedar bedhead, dresser and wardrobe. She sighed as she stepped into the hot water. Its luxury made Jordayne's insistence she recount every detail of her flight tolerable.

"That poor child," the lady said of Timak. "I shall see he is brought to you in the morning."

"Erok and Sian will wish to return home."

"I think that can be arranged. Now," Lady Jordayne said, when Kordahla was dry and her hair had been combed, we must attire you in the splendour befitting your station." She lifted a sky-blue choli beaded with pearls from the bed. A tongue of lace narrowed to a large gold-set diamond that sat in the navel. Kordahla gasped and tried not to squirm as Lady Jordayne helped her into the tight top and the matching skirt that but for the sheer volume of layers would have revealed far more than was decent. As it was, she knew she was blushing. Half her hips were bare, and her arms.

"Shouldn't the maids do this?" Kordahla asked.

"If you stay here, I intend to take a personal interest in your education," Jordayne replied, fastening a golden necklace around her neck. The five bangles that followed really were too much.

"I can't," Kordahla said.

"Nonsense. I have plenty to spare and suitors aplenty who will fall over themselves to buy me more." She handed Kordahla a chiffon scarf. Kordahla wrapped the garment tight around her, certain it concealed nothing.

Jordayne stepped back to admire her. "You are a vision, but try to relax."

"Is there perhaps a cloak I could wear?"

"Nonsense," Jordayne said pulling the scarf away and leaving her revealed. "There. That is better. It never hurts a woman to bring all her powers of persuasion to bear."

A knock prevented Kordahla protesting further. Father and Levi would smite her down for these clothes alone, and they would not need to see her in them. Hearing of it would be horror enough. She froze in shock as the maid opened the door to Matisse. She would die from the impropriety of a man seeing her so naked. He had to think her crude; he was staring at her.

"Princess, you look ravishing."

Her blush deepened at his choice of words. The hint of an eyebrow lifting convinced her they had been intentional.

Jordayne tossed the scarf onto the bed. "Brother, did you come with a particular purpose?"

"The mages have arrived. Uncle Ordosteen awaits your presence. I have come to escort you back to the court," he said, gazing at *her* all the while. Her heart was thumping. Until now she would have said it was impossible for a man to be more handsome than Mariano.

Jordayne beckoned one of the maids to tie an anklet around her foot. Squeezing Kordahla's arm, she leaned in close. "My dear, this is Myklaan. There is no dishonour to man or woman if they enjoy each other outside of wedlock. The men you meet will behave as such. All the men," she warned quietly. "Bar your door tonight if you do not wish uninvited visitors."

Gazing at Matisse, Kordahla had to wonder whether she might. It was impossible not to keep glancing at him as they made their way back to the court, Vae help her.

All heads turned to her as they entered the domed room. The murmurs of appreciation made her stop before she had gone fully through the doors. The strange men unsettled her and she intended to leave the minute Lady Jordayne did, though from what she had heard of her hostess's reputation that might not be soon enough.

"My dear, what you have is power. If you wield it well, it is stronger than those swords men are so fond of," Jordayne whispered to her. "Now come along."

Her suspicions were confirmed when Jordayne stood on tiptoe to kiss the tallest man full on the lips, right there in plain view of all. They only broke apart when the Shah, seated on his throne, cleared his throat.

"This is Master Magus Drucilamere," Ordosteen said, introducing the completely unabashed mage, whose build allowed him to carry his height, and his moustache, well. He was dressed in an identical manner to the other two mages, a green kurta, tucked in at the waist with a wide kamarband and black shalvar. She recalled green was the colour of the House of Giordano. "And Mages Kaztyne and Santesh."

The mages bowed. Dark-haired Santesh was perhaps two or three years older than she, and pleasant of face, but would not meet her eye, while brown-haired Kaztyne gave her a friendly smile.

"Do you understand what you bring to us?" Drucilamere asked.

"Yes and no," she replied, recovering from the embarrassment. "I cannot attest to how they work."

"There is another matter we might put to rest first. Will you allow me to confirm your identity?"

"Will you not take my word?" she said, turning to Ordosteen.

"My dear, seeing you here I have no doubt, but there are protocols to follow, especially if we end up at war," the Shah replied. Unaccustomed to such attention from men, she had to make conscious effort not to hunch her shoulders.

"It is duplicity of which we are concerned," Drucilamere explained. He was not unkind, and there was a smile around his eyes.

"You wish to read my mind?"

"In the vaguest sense. I will gain impressions and emotions, but I cannot read your thoughts." He took her hands. The contact was inappropriate. The Majoria would condemn her to eternal fire if he ever discovered a man had touched her in this state of undress. She pulled back, her eyes growing wary. He released her with an apology. "The mages are bound by a code of honour. I will cause you no distress, I promise."

"It won't hurt a bit," Matisse said. He was polishing the pommel of his sword with the end of his kurta. She did not dare keep her eyes on him. "You may even find it...stimulating."

"Mind search may jog memories," Ordosteen hastened to explain as Lady Jordayne rolled her eyes.

Kordahla looked to Ordosteen, sitting straight, silent and inflexible.

"Best to get it over with," Jordayne said.

Kordahla lifted her chin as she took a deep breath, bracing herself for the touch, suppressing a shiver. The Vae knew she had no choice in this. "Very well." If the sensation was as unpleasant as Levi's hand had been on her forehead, she would take Lord Matisse to task, however much such words might bring a flame to her cheek.

Santesh brought a goblet from a table behind the thrones, swirled the contents, and handed it to Drucilamere. The mage drank deep, and passed the goblet back. When his eyes glazed over, she stepped away.

"It is nothing to fear," Magus Kaztyne said.

She nodded, once, sharp and clear, and allowed Master Magus Drucilamere to brush his thumbs across her forehead. The nudge in her mind was intrusive. She closed her eyes, trying neither to resist nor to allow the strange consciousness full access to her own. A variety of emotions washed over her, excitement, fear, distress, despair and hope, each fleeting before it mingled into the next. In a few seconds it was over, his mind no longer there.

"Princess Kordahla makes the gift in good faith," Drucilamere said. Her lips parted at the clarity of his speech. Had she not known, she would never have guessed he was under the influence of the cursed drug. "Now, let us see about the crystal. The quartz is for apprentices, I believe."

Kaztyne placed the crystal in Drucilamere's hand. The three mages chanted, soft but firm, repeating the rhythm, loud and louder. A light flickered in the interior. Gasps and murmurs welcomed it a second before it died. Kordahla bit her lip as the mages chanted again, but Vae'oeldin did not see fit to kindle its light. She held her breath as Kaztyne and Santesh drank their share of porrin before cupping crystal and quartz in their hands. It was the will of the gods the crystal stayed clear. They stood in judgement of her, contemplating her fate from the heavens as They observed events from the dome of this room.

"There was a light." Ordosteen was leaning forward on his throne.

She bowed her head. After all she had endured, she would yet perish if the Shah declared her gift useless, at his hand, or Levi's or her own.

"Indeed there was," Drucilamere said.

She blinked, and a tear rolled down her cheek.

"Your Majesty, I request this crystal and quartz be entrusted to the Mage Guild."

Gripping the arms of the throne, Ordosteen stared at her. "It is fitting," he said. Turning his attention to the mages, he stood. "You have no need of me to tell you what they are worth to Myklaan."

Brailen waved the buxom barmaid over to their cramped corner. Three tankards had done nothing to slake his thirst. He hiccupped and slammed the mug on the dry, cracked wood of the table. It banged good and loud, right through the busy evening buzz.

"She wanted to kiss me, you know," he said, and belched.

Slack-jawed Ulmy looked suitably impressed. Brailen had always known he was a true friend.

Stoopy-shouldered Orhan blew bubbles into his drink. When he finally got his mouth out of the tankard, he shook his head. "You're full of it."

"You won't be saying that when I'm Master Magus," Brailen said. "Ay, wench, you gonna top this up?"

The barmaid poured brew into his tankard, avoiding his groping hands, the tease. At least she was displaying meaty cleavage.

"You wan' me to show ya some love tonight? You can boast t' yer friends what it's like to lie with a mage," Brailen said, reaching up to catch strands of her frizzy, blonde hair.

"Perhaps when you grow up a little, honey," she said, not paying attention to her job because she allowed some ale to slosh onto his lap. "There's real men that need me tonight."

That sent both Ulmy and Orhan into hysterics.

"You can't even get a whore to lie with you. You really think we're going to believe Lady Jordayne's got a thing for you?" Orhan said, nudging Ulmy in the ribs.

Loud conversations squeezed around every rough table. Brailen didn't think anyone had noticed the dills, which was lucky since greasy hair, shifty eyes and unshaven chins marked the patrons as an unsavoury lot. They'd probably have beat him up just for enjoying royal favour, they would, just because that proved he was better than them. "They're pleased with me, you know," he said, sniffing up the steam of the soup the barmaids were serving. The cook had to be boiling leather to get it to smell so bad. "Even trust me with the porrin."

Ulmy's blue eyes went wide, but Orhan snorted snot right out of his narrow nose.

"When you have any then?" Orhan asked. "Can you even perform magic yet?"

"Takes years of dedication and study," said Brailen, leaning back. The bench rocked and he near fell off. It was only the wall which caught him. Took some doing to get his behind out of the gap between it and the bench.

"Can you do *anything*?" Ulmy asked.

"'Course I can," Brailen said, "But it's not doing that's the real test of a mage."

Orhan jumped up on the nicked surface of the table. "Dear Magus, I'm going to run you through," he said, pointing an imaginary sword at Ulmy.

Ulmy clasped his hands over his heart and shook his limp, shoulder-length hair. Made him look like an ugly girl, that did. "Alas, fine warrior, in order to prove my worth as a mage I may do nothing." They both collapsed in a fit of giggles, Orhan stamping and slapping the table.

It wasn't respectful, this derision. Brailen dropped his head to his tankard and slurped up the ale. Nothing was going the way he'd planned. Orhan and Ulmy picked up their mugs and downed their ale in a race to the end. Brailen thought about joining in but his stomach was churning from that foul gruel, and throwing up in front of his friends would destroy any cred he had left. Curse those mages for doing nothing except insist he put his nose in a book.

"You gonna get a woman tonight?" Ulmy asked Orhan as the older boy hopped off the table onto the wobbly bench.

Orhan wiped his mouth with the back of his hand. "No coin."

"We gonna get porrin then?"

Orhan jabbed the point of the knife into the table top. "No money for that neither."

"We get it on credit," Brailen said. "Like usual."

"Dindarin, have you been gone a long time in that uppity guild. The dealer ain't doing that no more," Orhan said, twisting the knife to add his own nick to the ones covering the table. "'Sides, I still owe him seventy lek. I ain't about to show my face 'round there without it."

"Apprenticeship's the deep mines," Ulmy lamented. "Do this, clean that, work twice as hard as your Master and you never have any coin."

"Your Master's a dream," said Orhan, and didn't Brailen know it. Ulmy was always telling how the smith tossed him a coin and a free afternoon once an eight-day. It was because he wanted a romantic liaison with the milkmaid, Ulmy had discovered by spying on him on one of those afternoons. Like that was a good enough reason to slack off work. Drucilamere spent heaps more time in the company of Miss Poshy Laydee-da Jordayne. Brailen didn't get an afternoon off. On the flea-ridden contrary, he got lumped with extra chores.

The younger boy slumped across the table. "Ain't no fun anymore since you changed apprenticeships, Brailen."

Brailen buried his face in his ale. A true friend wouldn't have reminded him of the day Physic Hamid deq Lamont had caught them in his porrin stores, his medicines and tools in disarray around Brailen. Tripping to the moons for free, and not for the first time, had made his sacking worth it, till his mother moped around the house in tears for three days, then embarrassed him by dragging him to the hospice, dropping to her knees right in front of all the addicts, and begging for his reinstatement.

"The boy has no aptitude for this," the Physic had said. Brailen had let out a sigh of relief. Mopping up vomit and emptying reeking bedpans was a scummy career. A good thing it was the old man had taken pity and told her to see the magi. His mother had dragged him back out to the physic's stern caution not to blow the opportunity.

Drucilamere had listened, had him imbibe porrin, though the stingy man had not given him enough for a proper trip, and observed for himself the objects that went flying whenever Brailen was under the influence. There had followed such a lecture on responsibility and the abstinence of apprentices, that Brailen had wondered if the porrin and prestige that went with being a mage was worth the training. His mother had blown her nose on her headscarf, clasped her hands and blessed the mage, bowing her way out of the fancy guild, and leaving Brailen with no choice in the matter.

Determined to make the best of the situation, Brailen had looked at the moustachioed mage and said, "How often do I get to take porrin?"

The mage had arched a thick eyebrow. "Not at all if you don't prove your worth."

When Brailen had bragged of his fortune, Ulmy and Orhan had revered him like a god. *A mage, golly, what fun would that be* and *oh, did this mean a steady supply of porrin?* they had gushed over the ales they had paid for. Brailen had pretended to virtuousness to cover the fact he had never had so much as a taste after that first day and – djinn curse those hoity-toity, condescending mages – did not even know where it was stored.

Well now he did.

"The crazy thing is, the mages probably have cartloads and wouldn't even miss the speck we'd need for a trip," Orhan lamented.

Ulmy shook his head, reached across for Brailen's ale and took a gulp. "You sure have forgotten your friends."

"They've heard about him, see. Got the porrin under lock and key. He's just blustering when he says he uses it."

Brailen snatched his tankard back, downed the contents, belched long and loud, and stood up. "They trust me, I tell you. Come and see." Orhan was right. The lackwits – wasn't that what Lady Jordayne had called the mages? – did not even notice when they were cheated right under their noses.

Ulmy's giggle made him self-conscious enough to lose his next words.

"Looks like he's wet himself," Orhan said.

Curse the clumsy barmaid. He would come back and teach her a thing or two. Right after he proved to his friends he was as worthy of their admiration as the day he became a mage.

"Laddies, I'm about to treat you to a night on the moons," he said.

They staggered out of The Wild Wind arm in arm, singing a rousing if out of tune ditty about loving a girl to death. Their belches added the final touch, Brailen thought, as they reached the cove and leapt over the precarious rocks to the guild by the light of a single lantern, the annoying lap of the lake, and the sting of the salty wind.

The guild was dark, thank the moons. Whatever business the snooty mages had at the palace, it was keeping them late. Brailen produced a key with a flourish and they stumbled their way along the hall to the back room, and down to the lower floor. Crescent Daesoa and gibbous Dindarin could glare through the vast windows all they wanted. Like painting the faces of the people on the frescoes in their ghastly light was going to scare an apprentice mage.

"Over there," Brailen said, pointing to the wall with the trapdoor. He teetered past the desks to the other side and fumbled around for the trigger.

"What's the delay?" Orhan asked, bumping the neat stack of books on Kaztyne's desk over with his hip so he could park his behind there.

"Vae'omar's cursed my eyes with all that liquid," Brailen said. The frieze of porrin leaves blurred in and out of focus. He pounded here and there. The cursed trigger had to be somewhere.

"Hey Brailen," Orhan said.

"Almost got it."

"Brailen."

"Just wait."

"It's open you lackwit."

"Oh." Brailen cleared his throat. "Told you."

They crowded into the storeroom.

"Tidy little bundle here," Orhan said, setting the lantern on the shelf.

"Save some for me," Ulmy said as he waddled down the cellar stairs.

"Did I tell you they trust me, or what?" Brailen pulled open a packet of crushed leaves and took a long sniff.

"Or what, when they get back," Orhan said, rummaging through the shelves. He stuffed dried leaves and packets of ground seed into his shalvar.

Ulmy returned with a jug of wine in each hand and the hem of his shalvar soaked. "This'll be the trip of all trips." He tucked the jugs into the crook of an arm and joined Orhan and Brailen in plundering the stores.

"Got to be seventy lek worth in just one of these," Orhan said, snatching the open packet from Brailen.

"Let's go," Brailen said inching toward the door. The toads were taking too much. The magi were going to notice stock missing for sure.

"Why not stay here? It looks comfy enough," Ulmy said, squeezing out and plonking himself into an armchair.

"And be caught red-handed?" said Brailen.

"He's right," said Orhan. The older boy headed up the stairs.

"Come on," Brailen grabbed Ulmy's kurta and one of the jugs, and tugged him up. The front door was further than he remembered, but maybe that was because he had to drag Ulmy the whole way. If Brailen had to wait until they got out to trip, Ulmy could just lower his arm and stop trying to get powder onto his big tongue while running.

Brailen pulled the front door so it slammed closed. He fumbled with the key but the cursed lock would not snick. By the time he decided to leave it, the others had picked their way over the uneven rocks and were halfway to the short pier.

"Ay! Wait for me!" Brailen called. He clambered over the rocks, taking care not to slosh too much wine over the lip of the jug. "Wait or I'll put a spell on you."

Ulmy giggled, but he stopped, 'coz he was a true friend. Orhan just snorted and kept striding. When Brailen reached his side, Ulmy raised his pitcher. "Here's to old times. And the best friends in the world." He clapped Brailen on the back.

Brailen took a swig from his own jug. "Let's get onto the good stuff." On a belly full of cheap ale, the wine was no treat.

"We've enough here to trip for days," said Ulmy.

"I'm taking some of this to our dealer. It'll square me debt," Orhan called.

"Sell it, lackwit," said Ulmy. "Then we'll have enough money for whores as well."

Orhan brought out a packet and tipped some of the red powder onto his tongue.

"Give it here." Ulmy scrambled over, took the packet and shook a good dose in.

Brailen, not to be outdone, swallowed two shakes. On second thoughts, perhaps three shakes was the norm for performing magic. That emptied the packet, and he dropped it. No way was it going to incriminate them with the wind cartwheeling it over the rocks.

"Someone's coming," said Ulmy, pointing to a bobbing light. He already had another packet of the drug in his hand.

"Ho," Brailen shouted. "You're on perilous ground. Declare yourself or face the wrath of a mage."

"It's Daesoa," Ulmy said. "She's come to us." He started hopping towards the light.

Brailen tilted his head. The two moons spun around the heavens, a whirl of green and yellow. "No, she's still up there." He flung up his arms and whirled around too. Wine slopped out of the jug and slapped the rock. The cursed thing threw him off balance. He stumbled over a rock and landed on his knees. Someone was painting them red. Nice colour. He would put them up there with Dindarin and Daesoa. He lay on his back and lifted a leg into the sky. Lady Luck had seen fit not to break the jug. He tilted more wine into his mouth. Criminal how so much washed onto the rocks.

"What are you doing?" someone asked.

Brailen laughed. "Tripping to the moon."

"The moons, the moons," Ulmy said. He staggered and fell face first.

"You're intoxicated," the someone said.

"So what?" Orhan said. He had laid himself out and was watching the heavens. "It's a fine trip."

"Porrin and Ale," said Brailen. His body had stopped spinning but his mind, wow, that was way up there. Higher than Dindarin. Higher than his knee. "You ought to try it."

"Get a grip on yourself. This is unseemly behaviour for an apprentice mage."

Brailen swayed. Shom blinked into focus. "Oh, it's you," he said. "You're a real bore, you know."

Shom plucked the packet from Ulmy's hand. "This has the Mage Guild seal on it."

Brailen lurched up and towards him. "For your information," he burped, "I am a member of the Mage Guild." He belched. And farted.

Shom held the light high. "How many of you are here?"

"He's going to tell," Orhan said. "You're going to get booted out the door. Again, again."

"For your information, they won't throw a mage out of the mage guild." Brailen belched some more. It was pure music.

"Master Magus Drucilamere is not going to like this."

"Ma-gas Drew-kill-me-ear is not going to find out," Brailen said, giggling at his wit.

"Get inside and sleep it off."

"You think you're better than me?" Brailen said staggering into Shom.

Shom pushed him off and turned for the guild hall.

"You think you're better than me? Do you? Do you?" He did. Brailen swung the jug. It connected with Shom's head. The toff toppled to the ground. "Do you, do you, do you?" He was so high, so dizzy. He threw his arms wide, flinging the jug into Lake Tejolin. It fell short and shattered on the rocks. "Fly, fly, fly."

And the rocks did. They whirled around and around, pummelling into Shom again and again. Brailen threw his head back and screamed, "Do you see? Do you see? It's magic." Only now he felt drained and the rocks smashed down and the world was silent except for the whoosh of a breaking wave.

Orhan clambered to the half-buried body. "Mercy, Brailen, I think you've killed him. How much porrin did you have?"

"Did you see, Ulmy?" His friend was still slumped over a rock. "I did magic. Yippee. Whippee. I'm a mage. Go on, say it, I'm a mage."

"You're going to get banned from the guild," said Orhan.

Brailen slumped onto the rocks that covered Shom and let his mind twirl with the stars. "Yeah, but it was worth it. 'Coz I'm a fearsome mage."

He laughed. Then he passed out.

CHAPTER FORTY-TWO

AS SOON AS THE Court cleared, Jordayne flung herself at Drucilamere.

"Are you sufficiently recovered from the porrin to engage in some fun?" she asked, tilting her lips up.

He stubbornly kept his hands on his hips. "I'm a mage. I master porrin not succumb to it."

"That did seem rather a novel idea for our guest." She pressed closer.

"Do you think she will be safe under your brother's escort?"

She traced the line of his moustache with her finger. "As long as she heeds my advice and locks her door."

"With a body like that, she will have trouble hanging onto her honour in this court."

She moved her hand into his hair, gripping hard. "Never fear, I'll educate her."

"Like this?" he asked, moving his hands beneath her bust, and kissing her at last.

"And this," she replied several moments later, pressing his face between her hands and kissing him.

"I thought so," Drucilamere said. "Unfortunately, it's precisely your sort of education I fear, Jordayne. She is young."

"Never even kissed a man, I expect."

"Unlike you," he said, planting hot kisses down the side of her face, and neck, and on her shoulder.

"So what was it that gave you pause when you read her?" she asked, sliding her hands around his waist.

"Do you miss anything?" His lips met hers again.

They parted enough to look into each other's eyes. "Would I be me if I did? Now tell me, there's a good boy. I have a kingdom to run."

His look held amused caution, as one might bestow on a mischievous child. She doubted even Druce knew how seriously she meant what she said.

"There was an aura about her. It may be a djinn figures in all this." He caught her guarded look and hurried on. "She herself is innocent. More innocent than *you* could possibly imagine."

"A Terlaani Princess? I think I can imagine. Only Lord Kamir's daughter, Pettina, is likely to be more closeted than she. It is just as well I was born in Myklaan. The Verdaani would have stoned me long before now."

"Were you born Verdaani, you would have been raised so prim the mere idea of you would have made you swoon," Druce said.

She shimmied to the table at the back of the dais, with a seductive wiggle of her behind of course, and poured them some of the San Xalid wine a page had served before their lengthy audience. "So why did you not inform Ordosteen of the djinn?" she asked, handing him a plain gold goblet. She took a sip of the divine red. The inspired mosaic of the Vae over the dome provided the perfect setting to savour its rich notes.

"Is it your aim to have me too intoxicated to please?" His free hand was back on his hip.

"No. Only intoxicated enough to answer my questions."

Druce raised an eyebrow. "Our princess was fearful of the djinn, but I sense it was on a personal level. Until I can ascertain it is a threat to our realm, I think this information more the province of the magi."

"Perhaps you are right, but keep me informed."

He took a long sip, and his face relaxed. "Your estate has outdone itself with this vintage."

"It has indeed."

"If you deign, you could grace the guild with your presence for regular updates."

She turned from him with a jingle of bracelets, looking back over her shoulder with a tip of her hips. "At night, I presume."

His hands found her shoulders and brushed her straight hair from her nape. "There would be added benefits." His thumb stroked the back of her neck.

She closed her eyes and let him hear her pleasure. He stopped too soon. She took the goblets, set them on the tiled floor, and took his hand. "I wish to claim them now."

His fingers locked around hers. "Lead the way," he said, just looking at her, the dear man. She had to pat his hand to get him to move.

He pulled her into his arms when he discovered they were turning out of the palace. "This is hardly the way to your chamber."

"I thought we might set the mood by watching the sun rise over Mage Cove." With Kaztyne and Santesh spending the night at the palace, and the apprentices likely to be drinking themselves senseless on an evening off, they could afford a leisurely morning of it. Besides, the Terlaani crystals required investigation, and for that her mage would need both the knowledge and the porrin stored in the guild. She kissed him, and led him on.

"It's a good half hour's walk past the city boundary to the promontory."

"Don't grow old on me, Druce."

He stroked one side of his moustache with his forefinger. "I wouldn't dream of it. For one thing, I would hate to be replaced by some young lackwit you only wanted for his body."

Dawn was seeping into the world when they strode across the rocks to the edge of the rippling lake. Jordayne leaned back against Drucilamere, luxuriating in the kisses he brushed down her neck. The pink wisps of cloud were lightening to grey, and the lap of the water was soothing her into contentment. She really ought to take more time to savour the simple pleasures of life. Too often in her political interfering she forgot to enjoy *herself* rather than her scheming.

"It is a fetching sunrise," she said with uncharacteristic wistfulness.

"I believe I have the superior view," he replied, looking down her cleavage.

For once her reason for making him wait had nothing to do with their relationship and everything with a sunrise far too beautiful to miss. Day had soaked the vista when she asked him if he intended to make good on his promise and perfect the morning. He responded by kissing her again. Their hands groped and searched as they stood and approached the guild step by passionately interrupted step.

He had no right to stop his caresses so abruptly. After all, she was supposed to be the tease. Jordayne adjusted her touch. A light brush up his side would crumple his will to resist her. Then she saw it: a limp hand protruding from a pile of rocks, the ghostly white palm turned up. They ran to it, hefted rock after rock off the body, flinging them away until they uncovered the prostrate apprentice. He lay on his stomach, his lifeless eyes staring out across the water. Clotted blood formed a jagged scar from the corner of his lips to his chin and purple blotches covered his broken body.

"Dear Vae'oenka," she murmured as Druce felt for the pulse of life. As the sun burst full from behind a cloud.

"He's alive," the mage said, his voice a harsh whisper.

"I'll go for a physic."

"There's no time. I'll try to summon one." He lifted Shom into his arms.

Jordayne's glance was sharp. In all the time she had known the mages, never had a one of them intimated they could thoughtspeak with ordinary folk. She made a mental note to query them on this as she guided Drucilamere across the treacherous rocks. Encumbered as he was, she saw the open door first.

"Druce," she said, laying a hand on his arm.

His alarm was obvious as they went inside. Nothing appeared disturbed but they did not linger to check.

"I'm going to need porrin," Druce said, heading for the back stairs. His absorption with the lad prevented him from seeing what was right before their eyes as he settled the apprentice into one of the armchairs before the vast glass window looking over the serene lake. This time she was too shocked to speak. When Drucilamere turned towards the trail of ground porrin leading from the hidden room, he blanched white with rage.

"Brailen," he growled through clenched teeth, before storming into the open store. In a daze, Jordayne followed. It was bare save for a scattering of crumbled leaves and a fine dusting of red powder on the floor. Drucilamere gripped the shelf and stared at the wall. There was nothing he could use.

"Are you sure it was Brailen?" she asked.

"No one else knew this stash was here."

She had to squeeze his arm to draw him out of his devastation.

"The rocks that buried Shom," she started as they returned to the unconscious lad. Drucilamere held his hand the way a father might. There were no open wounds upon the broken body, nothing to indicate he had been buried after he was attacked.

"Can you see an ordinary man flinging them?"

She needed no more evidence to incriminate him. Brailen had made powerful enemies. The magi were left without a single apprentice, and neither they nor she would rest until he had been made to atone with every last fibre of his body.

"Has he no chance?" she said of Shom.

Drucilamere shook his head. "He never did. No physic could fix this amount of internal damage. He will be dead by the time one gets here." His body tensed with rage. "A few trips on the drug are worth more to that miserable miscreant than a man's life."

Shom had been promising, she knew that much. Jordayne slipped her arms around Drucilamere and leaned against his back. She had always found immense comfort in the proximity of another body. At her touch, Druce collapsed into sobs of despair.

"This is meaningless. This is Trove's vision come to pass. He deserved more."

Those called premature to the Vae so often did. And in times of peace, rarely could one so young die a meaningful death.

Or could they?

"Will he survive until we can get him to the temple?" she asked, once more the schemer. She disengaged herself from Drucilamere and ran an astute eye over the lad. The ducks paddling on the lake could quack her folly, but her lover's favourite apprentice might yet serve his realm.

"Moving him will only hasten his death."

"But his death will not be in vain." The command in her voice was unmistakeable.

Drucilamere took her measure. He would have no idea what she planned, and for the time being, he would stay in the dark. A risk-taker her mage might be, but of this he would never approve.

"Do it," she said, before he could object.

Her only concern, as Drucilamere lifted Shom into his arms, was to detect the shallow rise and fall of the lad's chest. Drucilamere never faltered as they retraced their steps along the path out of the cove. The sun sparkled on the water, the last of the wildflowers bobbed in the breeze, but the grass had the decency to shoot brown. At the city gate, a sergeant, aghast she was abroad without an armed escort and horse, summoned unwanted guards and a stretcher. They walked the streets in silence, ignoring the respectful greetings of the populace. In the cobbled triangle outside the domed Temple of the Vae, Drucilamere lowered an ear to the lad's lips. "It will not be long," he said, moving towards Vae'oeldin's entrance.

"Not here," she said, drawing a quizzical look. To ease his suspicions, she added, "We are not petitioning the Vae."

She led him past the queries of the well-meaning monks flocking from the abbies bordering the square. They entered the older twisting alleys, trampling shoots struggling for life between cobbles, and kicking broken chunks of masonry with their ceaseless stride. An arched passage provided cool relief from the cheers and entreaties of the poorer citizens, and brought them to the non-descript lane with its non-descript shops.

"In here," she said, opening the door to Weng Wu's Eastern Emporium. The bell above the door tinkled as it admitted them into the dusty clutter of the front room. The scent of ginger and ylang-ylang tickled a guard into sneezing. Sweeping lacquerware from the bench into an empty basket, Drucilamere directed the stretcher bearers to lay Shom down as the bow-legged old man shuffled into the front shop. The moon and stars must have held mystic symbolism in the East, for he was wearing the same silks she had last seen him in.

"He is near death," she said without preamble.

Weng Wu passed a hand over Shom's body. The blue veins pushing up his thin skin matched the colour of his gown. "I cannot save him."

"It is not why I brought him here."

The magician's lips settled into a thin line. "You would do this?" the old man asked.

"Those things of which we spoke are coming to pass."

"Then bring him."

She sidled past the tables of imitation jade and cheap porcelain. At the inner door, she turned back. Druce was staring after them, one hand over Shom's heart.

"The taint of magic clings to this place, and it not a clean smell," he said.

"Let the apprentice serve his realm," she replied, returning to him.

He narrowed his eyes as he took Weng Wu's measure, noting the ancient knowledge in the watery eyes, the pattern on his gown. She sensed the prickles of fear as understanding dawned. "You bypass the temple in favour of an oriental magician. Tell me you do not wish to take his soul."

A djinn had possessed her, to think she could hide her intention from a mage until it was too late. Magic was his art, whether porrin induced, Eastern myth or mahktashaan lore. The passages in those thick volumes the apprentices grumbled about served a telling purpose.

"We must," she said.

"You cannot."

"We can." She turned into his arm, barring him the body. She had expected resistance, but not the rough shove, nor his complete disregard for any injury he might cause.

"You will leave him," she said, pulling rank as he slipped his arms under the lad's shoulders and knees.

"I'm taking him."

"Guards."

The draw of swords was awkward when elbows could not pull back. She would see Weng Wu was compensated for the vase the knobbliest of the joints knocked to the floor. Not to the quantity specified on its tag. The fake was worth a few lek at best. Nothing to take the guards to task about since their ungainly stances among the crooked tables and splintering shelves were clear threat to her mage.

Drucilamere straightened, dropping his arms to his sides. "You would truly strike me down over this." It was not a question.

"No. I would have you detained, unless you give me cause to do otherwise." She stepped closer, reaching for his face.

He grabbed her wrist, his face a cloud of anger. "You cannot sway me with a kiss, Jordayne."

"I want you to understand."

"I understand, better than you. This is magic of the darkest kind. It is everything I have foresworn as a mage of Myklaan. It is a travesty of the Vae." His fingers pressed tight, bruising her skin.

"Your porrin is gone, and there is little hope of securing a supply before the Terlaani are upon us. We need a defence."

"Not with my apprentice's soul," he said through clenched teeth.

"With whatever it takes."

"You heartless bitch." He flung her arm down. His face was a picture of hate.

That stung enough to bring a tear to her eye. She would snitch it was the incense if he ever brought it up. She had made her choice. Myklaan had become her lover long before the mage. It would lie with her long after he was out of her life. "I will be what I must for Myklaan."

"You will be what you will be for your own twisted ambitions, Jordayne." With that he swung around. He should have walked out the door. Instead, he batted a fist into a guard's wrist, jabbing a knee into his stomach at the same time. Wrenching the sword out the guard's hand – the same young fool who had broken the terracotta warrior, she saw – he whirled and swung at his comatose apprentice. Two guards reacted by ramming into him. Drucilamere was a big man, but the momentum unbalanced him. The tip of the sword slashed across Shom's middle. He struggled to force it in but the guards set upon him, wresting the weapon from him and tackling him until they had pinned him against the door. One final look of regret at the second of the only two men she had ever loved did little to appease her conscience. His eyes threatened to neither forget nor rest until he had set this to his vision of rights. The Vae forgive her blackened soul, it lasted the entire duration of his escort out.

"Is it too late?" she asked Weng Wu, tearing herself around. Blood was welling from Shom's wound.

"Must hurry," he replied.

She beckoned two guards who carried Shom into the back room with its relics on chaotic display to the few wealthy enough to afford the treasures: figurines and paintings, carpets and plates. Weng Wu folded his arms and dropped his chin as they set Shom down so they could drag empty crates together to form a bed. They laid Shom on it, and stepped back.

"Go," she ordered the jittery pair, anxious to start the ritual. They crept back, insubordinate no-good do-gooders. Weng Wu made a noise deep in his throat. "Go," she needed to say a second time.

When the door thumped shut, the old magician shuffled between stacks of crates. She heard the flap of a wall hanging pulled aside, the off-beat patter of his bent feet, the clink of glass. The vials he brought out were full of glistening liquids, thin earthy red, thick honey, and rust. He bid her douse all but one of the candles as he poured a noxious concoction into a crucible. Setting it over the candle, he heated the liquid until a slip of steam rose. It curled across sinister shadows looming tall on the walls. She stepped closer. The responsibility was hers. She would not dissociate herself from his actions.

"You touch poison, you die." Weng Wu said.

It was all the warning she needed to step back.

A door she had not noticed, across the wide room, opened. At Weng Wu's sharp bark, a young man retreated and banged it closed.

"You say *ne dow san li kaan*," Weng Wu instructed. Those words tasted filthy in her mouth, and yet he drilled her until they rolled off her tongue, in tones that swung from high to low. "You speak. You don't stop or magic no work." He was at his task again, unflustered, as soon as she had it right. This task was of consequence to her alone. Its failure would not aggrieve him. Dear Vae, its success would tear her apart. A dark rage boiled through her with the utterance. Drucilamere had been right to brand this practice unclean. There would be a price to pay for cheating death, and the atonement would be hers.

The magician dipped the tip of his overlong nail into the brew and pushed it into the wound. He coated the bloodied nail with more poison and forced it into the mouth, breaking the contaminated portion between the teeth. The corpse was deathly white. A corpse it was, though in the wan light she could not gauge if it breathed, for, Vae bear witness, had not two blessed with magic declared it beyond saving? Into air hanging close with the aura of death, Weng Wu chanted words that chilled her marrow. Evil gripped her heart, squeezing the breath from her chest. Almost, she faltered over the words, remembered the warning and recovered. The hiss of air cut through their mantra. A thread of emerald light curled out of Shom's mouth. It twined into a crackling ball high over his heart.

"*Kra tow li kan*," Weng Wu chimed, holding an empty vial high. Blue lightning struck from Shom's heart into the light. The ground shook beneath them. The dark corners of the room slunk inward, gobbling up the feeble flame on the candlewick. Jordayne struck out a hand to grab a crate. The magician scooped the emerald ball of light into the vial, and plugged the neck. The dark crept back to the corners of the room. The flame righted itself and flared.

"This is soulous," he said when she was standing straight.

Jordayne stared at the emerald eddy within the glass bottle. It bounded off the sides. It was not alive. It could not be seeking an escape. "I will keep this safe," she said at last.

"As you wish, Lady," Weng Wu replied with a bow.

He held out the prize. It was some moments before she worked up the courage to accept it. It was warm in her hand, warm as living flesh. She tucked it into her bosom, a weightless vial of swirling green that nevertheless pressed heavy on her heart.

Chapter Forty-three

WHEN VINSANT KNELT TO make his morning obeisance to Mahktos, Dindarin had not yet faded from view.

"Not today," Levi said, beckoning him onto a track that snaked further up the side of the snow dusted mountain. "Bring what you need."

"All honour to you, Majoria," Vinsant said by way of greeting as he limped after his master with as much speed as he could muster while levitating the Myklaani sword.

They had crossed the confluence of the two rivers that joined to form the Crystalite, entering a crisper province where morning dew glistened on fresh grass and wildflowers burst open at the first kiss of the sun. Vinsant appreciated its beauty all the more for a good night's sleep on a cushion of air. Waking early and sleeping late had, if anything, improved his spirits. The short, secret communications he had established with Arun were fun if, by virtue of their brevity, not very informative. He had ascertained Arun could not heal his leg across the leagues, Kordahla was still nowhere in sight and that it was normal for the mahktashaan to monitor an apprentice across the links (it apparently avoided misuse of the talent and allowed the magicians to curtail any mischievous scheming, mistrusting grownups that they were) but he had not learned much else. The Minoria insisted Levi would detect longer links, so Vinsant had to content himself with a single question each dusk and dawn while Levi slept. Since the Minoria would not have gone against the explicit instructions of the Majoria if he had full faith in his leader, Vinsant had to conclude Levi was just being a pig of a mentor, the more so for leaving him with an injured leg.

His next request of Arun would definitely be for a healing word. Swollen and bruised, his leg pained him beyond enduring the deeper he dragged himself into the rugged Crystalite range. In the lower reaches, birds, rabbits and insects teemed among the stones and brush. Higher up, the barren slopes were more reminiscent of Terlaan's arid interior, although a climb that high would tax a fit individual. Vinsant paused to ponder the caps of white that set the majestic mountains apart from all else in the Three Realms. By Mahktos, he hoped Levi did not intend to scale those heights. Perhaps the Majoria needed reminding mines were supposed to be underground. After a moment regarding Levi's robed back, he decided to be sensible and keep his mouth shut.

A half day's hobble later – about twenty drops of the heavy sword – they reached the boundary of bush and scree. And the path still wound up. Around yet another bend, a rickety village came into view. The handful of stick huts seemed deserted save for a nursing mother who curtsied, a barefooted child who danced around them and a grandfather too stooped with age to do more than shuffle a few steps at a time. He nonetheless hauled himself to his feet and bowed, the respectful man. After Levi signed a blessing, he led Vinsant on, to a rough track that climbed to a stone temple overlooking the huts. It was little more than a hunk of granite inside a depression gouged in the rock. The squat features and bowed legs were the only recognisable features, but the crude carving was laden with wreaths of scraggly, narrow-leaved branches.

"Mahktos is a wild god and still worshipped in the wild places. This close to His mines, He eclipses the Vae," Levi said with his uncanny knack for predicting Vinsant's forbidden questions. "This temple predates our founder, Shah Guntek himself. It is said he made pilgrimage here when Mahktos granted him the secret of the crystals."

The power in this place thrummed so ancient that it eclipsed the power of the statue in the lair. Vinsant dropped to his knees. He kept the sword floating behind him. Mahktos had to be proud of him for managing that. "I feel Him. I feel Mahktos," he said. This awe was just what he had felt when he stood in the presence of the god. The other sensation, the chill in his bones that had nothing to do with the altitude, he didn't like so much. He turned his head to Levi but caught himself in time. No questions, no speaking. And pray his earlier comment had not fouled the Majoria's mood. He had no wish for a repeat of today's trek on his injured leg tomorrow.

"You may speak," Levi said. Wouldn't you know his voice was reverent in the face of his god.

"I," said Vinsant. He stopped with his mouth open as the little blonde girl who had followed them up danced around him. Mahktos was bound to love the stunted flowers she threw at the statue's feet, but the funny tune she hummed was mega distracting. And the ragged shift that left her arms bare and barely touched her knees was making his teeth chatter. She was weird to appear so comfortable in this cold.

"I can sense the djinn. It's like there's a constant still wind," Vinsant said with a shudder.

"This temple is built on a rift between the worlds of gods and men. Here, the djinn make easy passage between the two."

The girl stopped before the Majoria and looked up, expectant.

"Can't they do that anyway?" Vinsant asked. He intended to take full advantage of Levi's uncharacteristic openness.

"Did the Minoria not explain mahktashaan and djinn draw on the same font of power? Accessing that font is straightforward at the points it bridges the planes. The djinn come to feast upon it." He looked down at the child. Smiling, she presented him with a blue daisy. "You serve us well, little one," he said, placing a hand on her forehead and murmuring a blessing.

A young woman appeared at the head of the path. Her plain shalvar kameez was worn to a dull brown, and her wavy hair was tangled by the wind, but her poverty had not made her destitute because her hands and face were clean. "They…send me to you," she said in faltering Laanan, peeping up under her pretty lashes.

Vinsant heard Levi's breath quicken. The word the Majoria spoke had to be as ancient as the site. The lass lifted her eyes, and nodded.

"Stay here," Levi said to him, his voice husky. He walked – *walked*, not glided, and clumsily, too – towards the young woman. "If you move, I shall make you climb to the peak thrice in a day."

She was *so* misguided to think Levi would like her holding his hand as she led him down to the village. Vinsant shuffled around on his knees and tracked their path. Some time soon he would have to close his mouth. He had no doubt Levi meant what he said. But the pair of them were entering a hut. Surely the *Majoria* could not intend *that* with a girl.

He shook his head.

The little girl rested her arms on his shoulder.

"What do *you* want?" Vinsant asked.

Stone scraped against stone. She pointed towards the statue. The hollows scraped into the rock to serve as eyes were glowing crimson. And they were fixed right on him. The little girl stepped back, curtsied, and said something in whatever ancient tongue these people spoke before running off.

Vinsant presumed he echoed her sentiments when he said, "All praise to Mahktos." Why the god insisted on watching him he didn't have a clue. He had been a model of an apprentice. Well, almost. *I'm trying to serve you well*, Vinsant prayed, his eyes meeting the god's expectant orbs. There was no response. So perhaps the eyes were looking past him, down to the hut Levi had entered. Vinsant glanced at the ramshackle village. Levi had to be well and truly occupied by now. The woman had been very young, a girl really. She had seemed willing, but she couldn't have understood the blood honour.

Arun. Oops, er, Minoria, Vinsant called over the mind link.

Vinsant. Are you in trouble? came the immediate reply.

His indignant *No* brought the sensation of a raised eyebrow. *I don't* always *get into trouble.*

You are flirting with punishment the like of which will see you a grown man before you set foot in Tarana again.

Tell me about it! But the Majoria is occupied. Actually, I think he's dishonouring a girl and Mahktos is watching me like I should do something.

Where are you?

A temple in the Crystalite Range.

The Temple of the Rift. Vinsant, she belongs to the old religion. She follows Mahktos, not the Vae, and for her there will be no greater honour than serving the Majoria in this way.

But, but... Mahktashaan are sworn to protect the people. And Kordahla. Levi makes such a fuss about her showing an elbow to someone outside the family. How can he do that when he brings shame on women? Just because she's a poor mountain dweller doesn't mean –

Vinsant, Arun interrupted, *we do not vow to be celibate. Leave your judgement until you know more of our ways. And from all I've seen and heard, Mahktos is likely to be watching you. Now sever the link before Levi notices you're up to mischief. We've already been connected too long.*

Well I doubt he's going to notice anything for a while, Vinsant grumbled. On the verge of severing the link, he felt the temperature plummet. *Djinn!* he yelled as indigo smoke curled and thickened into a corporeal form. There was no question Levi had heard the panicked call.

"What a perfect mahktashaan apprentice. Obedient before Mahktos while he flouts his master's rules," the indigo djinn said. His muscled arms and legs were crossed as he floated at the far side of the shallow cave. Behind him, more djinn materialised, taupe and mauve, and a saffron genie with a long ponytail, all with the glowing crystal joints and shimmery skin that marked their kind.

"What do *you* want?" Vinsant said backing away. One djinn he might be able to outsmart, but three?

From below, a clamour arose as the few people who had drifted into the village gathered at its stony heart. Levi dashed from the hut, pulling his hood over his head. Behind him, the young woman stood in the doorway, the straps of her slip off her shoulders, the neckline low on her breasts.

"From you, flea? What could a lowly apprentice have to offer me?"

"Then why are you here?"

"It is what I can offer you. Go on, ask."

Vinsant chanced a look down. Levi was only just starting up the path. "Kordahla, is she safe?"

"And sound in Myklaan. But for how long? Your brother is on his way, and the blood honour runs strong in his veins."

"You want to make a deal. To keep her there."

The djinn zipped across the cubits. He was a typical show off to recline on air while he whispered in Vinsant's ear. Hideous too, with his greasy black hair, big nose and fishy smell. "It's not what I want, now is it?"

Vinsant levitated himself into a cross-legged position. "So you don't want anything? You'll help her without obligation?" The cheeky djinn had better watch out because he had learnt a thing or two and he had just possibly outwitted the creature too.

"Insect," the djinn said, flicking a finger off his thumb. Vinsant crashed to the rock amid the laughter of the other djinn.

"Hey!" Vinsant said, looking up at Indigo. The big, bad bully was floating over him.

"Excrement of a parasite on the butt a scumhopper. Do you presume to think your puny power can match mine?"

"Eh, no," said Vinsant. Okay, he had been hoping just that, but he was wiser now, or would be if the other three djinn would stop flitting around him in a dizzying haze of colour. They moved so fast they whipped the flowers the little girl had thrown to the edges of the cave.

"Then make the pact. That trinket you wear around your neck for your sister's honour."

Vinsant blew a petal off his nose, propped himself up on his arms, and looked up at the statue. Its eyes were welcome to life as long as the darkness of djinn was hanging around. It had to mean Mahktos was looking out for him. "No."

The djinn whirled on the statue. The eyes were grainy, black hollows. Which meant Mahktos was watching him and not the djinn. Which couldn't be an entirely good thing.

"You are going to a mine, flea. There are plenty of other crystals to be had."

"Then I'll get you one of those. But Mahktos gave me this one." He shut his mouth as Levi appeared at the top of the path.

"Begone, filthy creature." The peculiar black light spread from the Majoria's crystal.

"Your Princess is safe in Myklaan. Does that goad you to unleash your fury on the disrespectful renegade? I can see she is delivered into the just arms of your second."

"Hey! You just offered to keep her in Myklaan."

The djinn shrugged. "Terlaan, Verdaan, Myklaan. It's all the same to me. It's you plague-riddled grubs that places matter to."

Levi rounded on Vinsant. "Do you suffer no regret?"

"I didn't deal!" Vinsant protested. "I didn't even suggest a pact." He scrambled to his feet.

"Begone, you wretched creature. Take your duplicity elsewhere," Levi commanded.

The djinn yawned. "I don't think I shall." His vermillion eyes flashed pure malice.

"Begone, I say." Levi stepped forward.

"Um," Vinsant started.

"You will not move from that spot, or I will flog you until the skin peels from your back." Step by step, Levi approached the djinn, a pointed finger outstretched, a chant on his lips. The man was brave, considering Indigo towered above them. He was floating just above the ground, arms and ankles crossed. Mahktos help them, but his joints were starting to glow.

"Begone, I tell you," Levi said.

The djinn lowered his face into Levi's. "Make me."

The Majoria resumed his chant. The mauve djinn glanced about and popped out of sight.

The genie tossed her long pony tail. Her sharp features were kind of handsome, but she smelled a bit like boiled rice. "A single mahktashaan against a djinn?"

The taupe djinn laughed. His face was flat, his cheeks were slack, and he smelled of horse sweat. "Against three."

Levi's chanting grew louder. The two strange djinn whirled around the Majoria, their crystal joints aglow. Levi's voiced cracked.

"Ooh," Vinsant said. Just his luck the genie changed direction to twirl around him.

"Well little boy, do you want to deal? Do you want to save your sister?" Saffron's face transformed into Kordahla's, and the taupe djinn became a gigantic knife.

Mahktos, help us, Vinsant pleaded. He turned his head but the statue was solid rock. At least he could recognise a pattern to the chant. He added his voice to Levi's. The quartz at his chest grew warm. Pink rays burst from it, hitting the genie. She cried out and disappeared in a fizzle of smoke.

"I got her!" Vinsant said.

Levi's voice grew strong. Vinsant picked up the chant. He had to be helping because the taupe djinn regained his true form.

"Will you deal, you selfish boy? Does that trinket mean more to you than your sister?" Indigo asked.

Vinsant stumbled over the words.

"Hah!" the taupe djinn cried in glee. "It's easy. Hand it over."

He couldn't give his quartz away again. Mahktos would never forgive him. Levi would skin him alive. "Not the quartz," he said. He had to become a mahktashaan. It was the only way he would gain enough power to protect Kordahla.

Maybe the Majoria thought he was wavering because he rounded on the djinn. The impossible blackness that issued from his crystal brushed Taupe's arms. With a throaty yell, the creature vanished, all honour to the Majoria!

Indigo smirked. "You will have to do better than that, leader of nobodies. Your inconsequential magic cannot touch me."

Levi raised his voice to a song. The blackness surged out of his crystal. Vinsant stood so straight, paying full attention. Indigo was in trouble now. Except the blackness bounced right off the creature. The djinn threw his head back and laughed, which kind of made Vinsant feel as big as a flea. About as strong, too, since Indigo sent him flying into the wall of the cave with a puff that flipped the wreaths off the statue. He twisted to avoid them, because the battering had left him too winded to get up.

"Majoria?"

The Majoria was bracing himself against the buffeting. His robe whipped against his body. His hood flew down. His foot slipped back. "You will not plague this boy," Levi said. With a grunt, he lunged far enough forward to place a hand on the djinn's chest. The djinn pinned it there with his own.

On his backside, Vinsant summoned the Myklaani sword. It was heavy in his hand, but maybe with the help of a little magic he could wield it well. He started the chant again.

"That flea? What would I want with *him*? His sister is the more useful bug by far. Don't pretend you don't covet her flesh, filthy dog of a mahktashaan. You purport to protect her when what you want is to break her. As. I. Will. Break. You."

Indigo's hand erupted into flame. Levi screamed as, under it, his own hand caught fire. The djinn pushed the Majoria away. Levi dropped to the ground, his face screwed up in agony. He rolled on the dirt, but the magical blaze wouldn't douse.

"Do not seek to challenge me, you speck of dirt on the sole of my shoe. When I am done with you, I will snuff out your life with the flick of my finger. Until then, live in the fear I will call on your puny powers to serve my own ends."

"No," Vinsant yelled, charging towards the djinn. His pointed sword had to be a threat. "Stop it. Leave him alone."

Levi's hand was turning to a charred skeleton. The djinn needed to put the fire out right now.

"Turd of a scumhopper. Have you no sense?" The djinn jerked his chin and the sword went flying out of Vinsant's hand.

An uncanny knack for finding himself in the scums did not preclude common sense. Vinsant pulled up before he pummelled into the djinn. On his chest, his quartz was burning. Random rays of light burst in every direction. As hard as he concentrated, he couldn't form the spreading halo the mahktashaan crystals emitted when they worked their magic. One of the rays hit Levi. The Majoria sighed and his face relaxed. Vinsant edged closer to his mentor. He had to get more rays to fall on the burning hand. They seemed to be going everywhere but where he hoped they would. Levi was groaning again, his hand shrivelling. A hunk of flesh sloughed off his fingers. It was time to panic because it sure looked like the Majoria was going to die. What chance would he have against the djinn then?

"I'll deal. What do you want?"

"Oh you'll deal, will you, flea?" the djinn said, poking Vinsant in the chest. The force drove him back. "Give me that pretty trinket you're so fond of."

"I order you to silence," Levi groaned.

Vinsant clapped his mouth shut and shook his head. The quartz was his whole future. Kordahla's too. He needed magic if he was going to save her.

Indigo sneered right into his face. "Would you see your precious Majoria burned? Would you face the mahktashaan and admit the Majoria perished because you refused to relinquish a piece of stone?"

"You-will-keep-that-quartz," Levi said. He exploded into a series of gasps. The djinn wagged a finger at Vinsant and the flames that danced on Levi's hand crept past his wrist and onto his arm. The Majoria screamed.

"Stop it!" Vinsant said. More rays of reddish light burst from his stone. He rushed at the djinn, concentrating beyond thought. The random rays bounced off the djinn. He concentrated harder, willing them to strike the djinn. And one did. Right on the foot. The djinn flicked his vermillion slipper, as though stung. One side of his mouth curled into a snarl. Vinsant backed up. This was probably going to turn out to be one more example of his reckless behaviour.

"You dare!" the djinn roared, grabbing his robe between thumb and forefinger, and picking him up as though he were a dirty rag. His feet were way off the ground. He tensed as the djinn released him. A fishy puff hurtled him past the statue and into the rock. Again. He landed among the wreaths, cracking the twisting sticks, bruised but not broken. He didn't think. He picked himself up to make sure.

"When I'm a mahktashaan–" he started.

"What is this?" the djinn demanded, floating back. "What trick do you dare play with those eyes?"

"Mahktos gave me these eyes," Vinsant said. He stomped forward. "When he gave me this quartz. Which you can't have."

The djinn pointed a finger at Vinsant. "I could burn you to a crisp."

Rock ground against rock. Mahktos reopened his crimson eyes.

"You'll have to do it, then," Vinsant said. He sure hoped his faith in Mahktos was warranted. His knees were knocking together, but under his robe the djinn might not notice.

A wonderful perfume mix, drifted through the cave: exotic jasmine, sweet frangipani, heady lavender and fragrant rose.

"Indigo djinn," said a melodious female voice. Her golden form was taking shape behind the indigo djinn, and was she ever beautiful with her heart-shaped face. The sparkling diamond tiara on her head paled in comparison to the radiance of her skin. The djinn and genies appearing behind her – a whole darkness of them, ten darknesses even – looked dull despite their shimmer.

"Graaaah!" The djinn whirled. His mouth twitched up in a snarl but he bowed to her. It was about as deep as Lord Swine had bowed to Father, but it was an actual bow.

"You should not presume with a vassal of the god."

"My Queen, I would never," he said and disappeared with a *whoomp* of air and a hint of indigo smoke. Several of the djinn winked out with him, while the others faded from sight, thank Mahktos. That left the Queen. Vinsant could not help bowing. Nice and deep.

"Mahktos plays with our lives," Tiarasae, Queen of the Genies, said. Her fame was well deserved, for even with the crystals in her joints, a more wondrous being could never exist. She bore a resemblance to Kordahla, as though his sister's beauty were indeed the gift deq Ikher had proclaimed it to be, but Kordahla would not pull a second glance if she curtsied before this genie. "My court will abide by my rules," she said, her voice sweet as a harp, "but will you abide by those of your order, young apprentice?"

Vinsant opened his mouth but found himself unable to speak.

And then she was gone. No smoke, no *wup*, just the lingering scent of flowers, and the thud of his heart. Vinsant stared at the spot she had occupied. Levi's moan brought him back to his senses. He skidded to his knees beside the Majoria.

"I didn't move, I swear, Majoria, all honour to you, all praise to Mahktos, all honour to you," Vinsant said biting a fingernail. The flames had gone, but Levi's hand was a blackened mess of bone and sinew, and his fingers were curled into a claw.

Vinsant stood and looked at the villagers down below. "We need a physic. A healer," he shouted but they were on their knees, staring up at the cave like the djinn were coming to wreak vengeance on them. He turned back to Levi. "Teach me the healing word. I'll concentrate until I get it right."

Levi exhaled through clenched teeth and got to one knee. Grasping Vinsant with his good hand, he pulled himself up. "Healing is not in my power."

Arun, Vinsant called across the leagues.

"Do not trouble the Minoria. There is no salve for the sting of the djinn. Sever the link and draw your hood. You will speak to no one of what occurred here."

Bent double with pain, Levi staggered toward the path.

Chapter Forty-four

KORDAHLA TOOK A DEEP breath and smoothed the front of her impeccable skirt as the guards admitted her to Shah Ordosteen's study. Her walnut hair hung loose, the ends curling over the puffed sleeves of her dusky-pink kameez. The garment covered her midriff and legs, but left her arms bare, not quite the epitome of demure she had requested from the bubbly lady-in-waiting Jordayne has assigned her. It put her at a disadvantage before the conversation had begun.

"Princess Kordahla," Ordosteen said, rising from behind his plain but stately mahogany desk. It had been positioned with care. The window behind it framed a view of the traditional cultured gardens, of the flowering frangipane for which the palace was famed, while the eastern vases on the flanking pedestals reminded the visitor of this realm's reach. She curtsied. He came around the desk and kissed her lightly on both cheeks. "Please, take a seat," he said with a warm smile. The strain she had noticed yesterday had dissipated, and his white hair suited him well. "Your friends will be here shortly. Captain deq Lungo is bringing them, so they should not be alarmed. From what I hear they are a unique group. The mages will want to talk to them."

"Timak is reticent with strangers, and the Ho'akerin do not speak our language," she said, too quick, as she sat on a well-used couch. The emerald brocade was in good repair, but the stuffing had dipped into comfort. She clasped her hands in her lap.

His smile turned indulgent. She bowed her head to hide her blush. Of course the mages required no words.

"I was wondering if your accommodation pleases you," he went on, polite to overlook her ignorant comment, standing yet.

"It is more than I could wish for, Your Majesty," she replied, looking up.

"I trust Jordayne is not persuading you to do anything you are uncomfortable with." The smile and raised eyebrow suggested he was intimate with the foibles of his niece."

"Lady Jordayne has been very kind."

"I realise you may find our ways somewhat strange, and our garb a little daring," he said, opening a drawer behind the desk and pulling a length of fabric out. "I wondered if this might make you feel a little more at home?"

Kordahla gasped as she took the green veil he offered her. Impossible that this was the one she had lost at the Tarana souk. Yet every stitch down to the pulled thread in the fraying corner was identical.

"Is something wrong, my dear?" the Shah asked.

In disbelief, not denial, she shook her head. "It is a perfect match to one I had in Terlaan." She looked up at him. His smile had been replaced with shrewd appraisal. "How did you come by it?" she blurted.

"It belonged to my first wife." His words rang hollow.

She took a deep breath. "I thank you, but I could not possibly borrow such a sentimental item. Besides," she forced a smile, "it was my choice to forsake the veil that sparked my desire to come here. It would be hypocritical of me to don one now."

"Your bravery is commendable," Ordosteen said, as he replaced the garment in the drawer. He locked it, she noticed. It was hers; she was sure of it. Days had passed since she had thought of the wicked djinn; of what he had truly exacted from her; what he might have to gain by delivering her veil to Shah Ordosteen of Myklaan, for it could have arrived in his hands by no other means. And now she had confirmed it was hers before she understood the consequences of doing so.

Ordosteen was saying something. She managed a wan smile to cover her lapse. Vae'oenka was kind to see a knock at the door alleviated the need for an answer.

"Enter," Ordosteen said.

In the same garb as yesterday, his body tense with rage, the Master Magus entered and bowed.

"Drucilamere? What has happened?" Ordosteen asked.

Kordahla rose. Raised at court, she was well aware protocol dictated she take her leave.

"Forgive my lack of control, Your Majesty. This could not wait," the tall mage said. In his mood, he dominated the room. "One of our apprentices has murdered the other, and fled with our entire stock of porrin." He trailed off as he caught sight of her, his lips tightening under his wide moustache.

Kordahla curtsied and hurried for the door. The Master Magus permitted her passage by stepping in front of one of the shelves on either side of the hearth. She could not help notice, as she approached, the title on one of the books in cosy disarray among artefacts so diverse they must have been gathered from across the known world: *Tales of the Djinn: Duplicity and Deception*. Her step faltered.

"A moment, Princess," Ordosteen said before she had reached the mage. She turned. The Shah, though furrows perturbed his brow, remained thoughtful. "This concerns you, however indirectly."

"Your Majesty, there are matters best discussed in private."

"Then leave them for now. What of the crystals Princess Kordahla brought? Are they safe?"

"They are still in my possession," the mage said. He lifted the quartz out through his green v-necked kurta and retrieved the crystal from a pocket.

"What magic can the mages work at present?"

The door opened again and Matisse sauntered in, followed by the proper Captain deq Lungo, looking leaner than she remembered now he was clean and dressed in the emerald tabard and black cloak of his office.

Drucilamere, with a glance at her, answered, "Absolutely none."

All eyes turned to the heir to the throne. His unruffable demeanour quickened both Kordahla's pulse and breath. Matisse ignored everyone else to cross the room and kiss her hand. The token gesture stole any words of greeting she may have had.

"I have just heard of the misfortune of the mages. My condolences," Matisse said to the mage, turning his back on her. She swallowed, unsure if his disregard, so close on the heels of his intimacy, hurt or calmed.

"Where is Jordayne?" Ordosteen asked.

"In private," Drucilamere said through gritted teeth.

"Your disapproval is hardly call to hide the truth," the lady in question said as the door opened yet again. Her gaze swept over the occupants. Unconcerned by Kordahla's presence she continued. "Our Master Magus condemns my efforts to secure magical protection for our realm."

The mage rounded on her, grief now defined beneath his rage. "You barter with that which belongs to the Vae."

Tales of the Djinn fell over. Its thump cut off Jordayne's reply.

"What have you done this time?" Ordosteen asked with a wary weariness. His hands came to rest on the back of an armchair which, judging from the depression in its padding, was clearly his seat of choice.

Magus and Lady faced each other, the one looking down with stern condemnation, the other with her arms crossed stubbornly under her bust. After three heartbeats, it was the mage who answered. "She has trapped the soul of my apprentice. She has created a soulous."

A long way into the shocked silence that ensued, Kordahla said, "Perhaps I should await my friends in my room." She pulled up her skirts, determined to leave before everyone had lost their wits entirely. This chaos was not what she had envisioned ruled Myklaan. The presumption much of it was her fault, however irrational, was beginning to niggle.

Matisse caught her by the shoulders. Her eyes betrayed her, widening at his proximity. Vae'oenka help her but she could only gaze into his, so blue, so *tantalising*. "They are still at the Hospice, Kordahla." His minty breath was warm on her face.

Amid this confusion, the touch of another was comforting. As immoral as it was, she did not want him to let her go. Nor was he in a hurry to release her. His hands remained on her as Jordayne and Drucilamere continued their argument.

"This thing can truly be done?" Ordosteen asked. His hands were very tight on the back of the chair.

"It is dark magic. It draws on the souls of the vulnerable, preventing them from reaching the Vae in death," Drucilamere said, glaring at Jordayne.

"In present circumstances, it is the only recourse left to us," Jordayne said, rearranging the outermost layer of her sheer skirts. The bangles on her arms slid down and tinkled against each other as she did.

"It is another of your power plays."

Her head snapped up. "Do not presume to tell me how to run this realm."

Shah Ordosteen removed his hands from the chair and straightened. "The last I checked, I was the one running this realm, so you will both kindly shut up and listen to me," he said without raising his voice. With a final glare at each other, Jordayne and Drucilamere turned to hear their Shah. Matisse rubbed her arm, and then dropped his hands so she too could face Ordosteen. She was acutely aware of how warm her skin was where his hands had lain. How close behind her he was standing. How bare her elbows were in the presence of a man.

"Everyone in this room is aware Myklaan is under very real threat. For now, we will all do whatever is in our power to secure its borders. Lady Jordayne is more than capable of assessing the risks of certain… endeavours. Whether those risks prove acceptable is something the Crown will decide later. Until then, it seems the mages require more porrin, not least so that the more distasteful elements of their profession need not be brought into play. I am willing to hear suggestions as to how the drug might be secured."

"Uncle, porrin is in abundance among the artists and artisans of our city, not to mention the increasing supply to those who can ill afford it," Matisse pointed out.

"Are you suggesting we confiscate it? From the homes of our well-to-do?"

Matisse shrugged. "Have you a better idea?"

"Certainly not one which will provide you with as much fun," Jordayne said.

"We will have a riot on our hands," Ordosteen said.

"Either that or a massacre because our mages cannot counter the mahktashaan in a war," Matisse said.

"Very well," said Ordosteen, though he appeared less than pleased with the decision. "I will draft a decree, effective immediately. But see that the influential among our citizens are aware of the need for this action. And Matisse, try to keep things civil."

"Of course, Uncle," Matisse said, one hand on the pommel of his sword and grinning from ear to ear.

"The hospice has need of porrin," Jordayne said. "You cannot seize its supply. And if the addicted are denied their dose, it will overflow with those in withdrawal."

"Then see the hospice has an adequate amount, and have all available physics take turns at duty there. Tell them they will be rewarded for their service, of course. Now, is that all?"

"There is one more matter," Captain deq Lungo said.

Without making a sound, the Shah's body appeared to sigh. "Yes, Captain?"

"I'm afraid the Akerin girl went missing from the hospice early this morning. Dario deq Pitran gave chase. He sighted her at the edge of Faradil Forest, but was unable to prevent her entering."

Kordahla's hand flew to her mouth.

"I take it this is the girl who is marked for a soothsayer?" Drucilamere said. He might have taken the information from either her mind or Lady Jordayne's mouth.

"It is," deq Lungo said, with a sidelong look at her.

"Is there a soldier who will volunteer to enter Faradil?" Ordosteen asked with an emotion akin to regret.

The hardened soldier's straight back went a little crooked. "If it please Your Majesty, I will go."

"It does not please me. I need you at the border."

Edard deq Lungo squirmed. Recalling the strange pull of the forest, Kordahla sympathised. "I cannot ask a man to do what I would not."

"I cannot spare you, Captain. You must oversee a change of the guard at the Mykter Pass. Nobody who has heard the ghost of a rumour about our guests is to remain on duty there."

"Yes, Your Majesty," deq Lungo said with a bow.

"Sian needs help," Kordahla said. After all they had been through, she could not abandon the girl.

"I will go after her," the mage said.

"Without porrin?" Jordayne asked. "Are you mad?"

"I am still a trained mage, whether I am under the bliss or not."

"We cannot risk you, not with a war threatening."

"Now who presumes to tell whom his business."

"Leave your lover's quarrel for the bedroom. The girl is a guest of this realm and not an unimportant personage among her people, I gather," Ordosteen said. Kordahla did not disillusion him. "Even so, Drucilamere, Jordayne is right. If we cannot spare the Captain, we can spare you less. You do not have permission to seek her out. Is there another you could send?"

"Perhaps, but let me scry her at the forest's edge, so I may set him on the right path."

"That is acceptable. But do not put yourself at undue risk," Ordosteen said.

"Let me come with you," Kordahla said, unsure why she was offering.

"It is best you don't," the mage replied.

"I feel responsible for her."

"You will be a hindrance to me at best, and a danger to the girl at worst," he explained, though his voice was nowhere near harsh. She was, in truth, glad of it.

"Leave the magical to the mage. If you wish to take your mind off matters, you may accompany me," Matisse offered, holding out his hand.

"On a raid?" she asked, confused. Witnessing the beheading of addicts was not the distraction she craved.

He winked at her. "Of sorts."

Seeking reassurance, she looked to Jordayne. "It will be fun," the lady said. "A chance for you to see something of our fair city. And perhaps with you there, my brother might keep his sword in its sheath."

"You never know. In the right house, I might have found the perfect reason to unsheathe it," Matisse said with a wicked grin.

Jordayne answered with an enigmatic smile of her own.

Kordahla felt compelled to take Matisse's hand. She could not help feeling she was missing something.

"By the djinn, it is Tiarasae, Queen of the Genies, herself," the svelte artist proclaimed, palette and brush in hand as Kordahla followed Matisse into a bright, open studio on the ground floor of a mansion. It took a moment to register he was talking about her. When she did, the blush came unbidden. Tongue-tied, she could only stare as he made an effusive bow.

"You may worship from afar, Naldo," Matisse said.

"Will you not introduce me?" the artist asked. His face was narrow and angular, with sharp features which hinted at intelligence behind his ebullient manner. Much to her alarm, he dropped the palette onto the plain tiles, clasped his hands over his heart and fell to his knees before her. His strange turban, floppy-topped and cropped so the ends of his hair were visible, slid lower on his head. The cut of the head garment precluded modesty and could only have been a statement to southern fashion.

"As this is not a social call, Tiarasae will do just fine. Now get up before I am forced to defend the Lady's honour."

"A kiss, a single chaste kiss," the artist begged. He removed his turban from his russet hair, clasping it tight in his hands.

Ready to flee outside, she gave Matisse a beseeching look. He laughed.

"Oblige him, Kordahla. Then he will be yours to command. He might even hand over his porrin without a fight."

"What!" Naldo cried, leaping to his feet.

Kordahla let out a sigh of relief, and moved closer to the impassive Captain deq Lungo.

"By decree of the Shah," Matisse said, flipping through a stack of half-finished canvases. "There's trouble along the border and the mages need a steady supply."

"You cannot be serious. My work, my art," – Naldo waved a hand at the canvases – "they will suffer without the caress of the bliss."

"Then find your inspiration in suffering."

The short, slender artiste threw his hands into the air. "It is an affront. It is an outrage." He indicated the splatters of paint over the tiles. "Do you not see how hard I toil?" You cannot demand this of an artiste."

"I will fight you if I must," Matisse said drawing his sword.

"Huh. Well you must," Naldo declared. He extended his arm, realised all he held was a flimsy paintbrush, and threw it and his turban past the columns, out of the open side of the room and into the untamed garden which formed the inspiration for a number of pieces of his work. "A sword. Fetch me a sword," he called. As soon as a servant delivered one, the pair began sparring across the room. Matisse forced Naldo against a table with pots of unmixed paint. Naldo twisted away and pressed Matisse to the columns. "'Will dissent's heated sway, our summer friendship wither in the height of bloom,'" the artist read from the lines of classic poems carved on the section of wall between the corbels and low vault.

Biting her lip, Kordahla retreated to a corner. "Will you not do something?" she asked deq Lungo. He had come to stand by her, polite enquiry in his eyes.

"Do not fret. They are the best of friends. This is their idea of a bit of fun."

"Then," she said, "no one will get hurt? Matisse won't behead him for defiance?"

It was deq Lungo's turn to smile at her, though it contained measured reassurance and not the unsettling amusement Matisse seemed to find at her expense. "I doubt either of them wants to die today. The only place we are likely to encounter real resistance is on the streets of the slums, and my lord is not about to take you there."

Their blades clashed above their heads, swung around and met at the level of their knees.

"Matisse has a sword plainer than Naldo's. Is he so very modest?" The idea sat at odds with everything she had seen of the heir to the Myklaani throne.

Deq Lungo deepened his smile. "Far from it. His sword disappeared during a fight. There was magic at play, probably a djinn, though no one can fathom the why of it. The smith is still forging another worthy of the heir."

The tale was intriguing but further inquiry was forestalled.

"A trick. It was a trick," Naldo declared as the sword went flying out of his hand. It clattered on the tiles and spun to a disproportioned self-portrait set against a column, knocking it face down.

"Do you admit defeat?"

The artist hung his head. "Alas, I have no choice."

"Then fetch your porrin. All of it," Matisse said, returning his sword to his belt.

The artist turned to her. "Will the fair Tiarasae not bestow upon the conquered the consolation of a kiss?"

"I rather think that the prerogative of the victor," Matisse said, striding forward. He picked up her hand and pressed it to his lips, looking at her all the while. Her cheeks had become hot again, as hot as his breath on her fingers. Too flustered to speak, she realised she had offered no resistance. She made a tiny movement, and Matisse dropped her hand.

"Despite his vagrancies, Naldo is a passable artist. Would you care to view more of his work?"

Unable to do anything else, Kordahla nodded. Matisse offered her his arm and she took it.

"Who are you calling passable, you ignoramus?" Naldo called from the next room. "I am pure genius."

Matisse laughed as they entered an internal room. Naldo's work was lined along the frescoed wall, the female form his most common subject. The half-naked female form, she noted with growing alarm. She tried to look away, only to find her eyes had alighted on a couple engaged in an illicit embrace.

"Well," said Matisse. "He has outdone himself this time."

Not knowing where else to look, she deciphered the pattern of the tiles on the floor. Strange emotions were stirring in her. Vae'oenka denounce her for a harlot, but she wanted another peak. She stole a glance and wished she had not, because now she was wondering what it would be like if someone touched her that way. If Matisse held her so close. And, dear goddess, he was looking at her like he craved to do just that.

"Your beauty would put them all to shame," Naldo said, returning with packets of the drug. "I beg you to honour me with a sitting."

"Not even you would do my Tiarasae justice," Matisse said, taking her arm and leading her from the room. "Where's the rest?"

"That is all there is, my dear Matisse."

"Would you trade a kiss from Tiarasae for it?"

Naldo sighed and beckoned a servant in. The lad counted packet after packet into a sack a palace guard held.

"I thank you," the artist said, as deq Lungo issued him with a receipt. He made an elaborate bow as he reached for her hand. Stricken, Kordahla pulled it back.

"I am devastated you do not consider me worthy, divine Highness." Naldo turned to Matisse. "Our queen values her chastity more than the porrin. Give the extra back."

"We did promise. And it is for the good of your adopted realm," Matisse said to her. When she hesitated, he added, "Surely, it is the custom even in Terlaan."

She could not deny that it was, but these two men turned a gesture of respect into a dangerous play of seduction.

"For your service to the Crown," she conceded, allowing Naldo to kiss her hand. His lingering liberty was disconcerting, turning the swell of her chaste heartbeat into a wild gallop, but she could not say the attention was unpleasant.

"Our next port of call awaits," Matisse said, presenting his arm. He took her free hand in his, easing her close to his side, keeping her there as they walked past the lilies clogging the garden canal while Naldo trailed, reciting poetic lines of love. Vae'oenka knew she did not encourage this shamelessness, that she tried to edge away. But he was strong, and insistent, and held her fate in his hands; and his thumb was rubbing the back of her hand, and he was smiling at her with those teasing eyes even as the groomsman brought their horses and Naldo offered one final bow.

Her eyes betrayed her, to keep glancing at him as they rode to the gate. He knew, he must have, though he looked ahead the whole way. It was her doing he reached over and halted her horse as a guard ordered the gate open. Reached over and stroked her cheek with the back of his fingers. "You must learn to have a little fun, Kordahla. A woman as gorgeous as you has the power to steal the hearts of men." Then he leaned over and kissed her on the lips. She closed her eyes and revelled in his lingering touch, in the heat tingling through her whole body. If this bliss was the sin of a disgraced woman, Vae'oenka could condemn her all she liked.

❖ ❖ ❖

Daesoa had been showing her the way. The yellow moonbeams glided over the knoll on which the terrible city stood, across the sunburned meadow, to the edge of the fretting trees. Through a daze filled with the rustle of leaves and a cold prickling on her warm skin, Sian heard the soldier's distant call. Faradil Forest lured her on. The air grew heavy; the shadows fell thick. Boughs bent towards her; litter swirled at her feet. An ancient presence whispered through the foliage, welcoming, warning. This was not a place where mortals could hope to tread and return untouched. That scared her, but pretty Daesoa led her on, the dense canopy no barrier to the moon's bright beam. It swept across the moist floor, and came to rest in the middle of a babbling brook, where crystal water tumbled over mossy stones. Sian knelt and gave thanks to the water spirits before scooping a handful of the icy liquid into her dry mouth.

"You are welcome," a girl's voice tinkled.

Sian jumped up. A blue spirit was sitting on a boulder in the middle of the brook, pretty patterns of clear ice interlocking to form her body, white water cascading off her head. As she stood, she melted into the stream, her filmy shift of droplets disintegrating into a spray which sprinkled into Sian's hair. Sian stared at the boulder, at Daesoa's beam sliding over it and plunging to the shallow bed. Stared because it was safer to do that than face the life of the forest. Stared because a bone lay at its heart, glistening, smooth, and unfamiliar. Taking a deep breath, she set a wobbly foot into the brook and waded to the light. She dipped her hand into the water to pick up the bone, thanking the spirits for the offering as Ishoa had taught her.

"You were brought here for that." On the far bank, a girl with a bundle of moss for hair leaned against the trunk of a white poplar. Her fingers and toes were seeds, her ears wingnuts, her eyes the knots of an aged trunk. In her hand sat a creature that looked like a stick with huge eyes. As solemn as the other was gay, the forest-spirit girl picked a dried leaf, crumbled it and blew the fragments into Sian's face. Sian coughed. When she opened them again, the girl was melding with the tree, her leaf-brown tunic crumbling to mulch.

A wind stirred. Leaves rustled. Sian went cold with a sudden gnawing prickle something was watching. She ran. Back home she could judge the mood of the trees and the humour of the hilltops, but this wood was as foreign in its whims as the city.

"Never to you," a voice said. "You are home."

She ran harder.

A boy swooped out of the canopy and around a flowering myrtle. His body was a cloud as translucent as the air, his eyes small suns too bright to meet. "Bring them back to us," he said, floating before her in a swarm of tiny creatures with buzzing iridescent wings. A cry of fear caught in her throat as he faded, his rippling robe sparking into a rainbow.

Sian turned about. She was lost. Worse, she was an intruder in a sacred place, too frightened to steady her rapid breath. She closed her eyes, praying to the Spirits of the Forest to open her path, the Spirits of the Earth to guide her step, the Spirits of the Air to light her way. The silent forest woke into whirrs and chirps, and she with it. Damp earth soaked her feet, and a breeze played through her hair. They woke her to memories too brutal to bear, an agony so intense she fell, and cried out, and tore at her hair. Her tears flowed until her head was spinning, and the world was shrinking, and she was clawing and fighting her way out of the consuming darkness.

"Don't fight it," said the dark-skinned girl.

"Give in to the dream," the boy said.

"Let us help you," the others added.

"Surrender to the forest."

It was oblivion, at least for a time. A refuge from a past she didn't have the courage to face. She dove into the dark maw of her fit so that she might be spared. Spared the future, too.

It was different this time. They were with her, no longer children but beings of pure light. Their voices soared and echoed, singing of mysteries lost, and forgotten ways. They bore her through Faradil, to the dewdrops on the mossy rocks, the bugs under the rotten logs, the veins of the budding leaves, and the hairs on the knobbly root. The forest twined around her soul, its vines winding through her until they were one. It embraced her pain, drawing it into the essence of the ancient place. The streams wept for her. The sturdy trunks groaned. The boughs soughed, and the earth shook for her ordeal. And when they did, she knew the Forest was damaged too. She bled for it, for the trees that had been ravaged, the animals slain, the waters polluted.

And when she woke, she understood. She was not lying down but upon her knees. The strange bone was in her hand. Like a four-pointed star, it glowed from within.

"Sian."

This voice was adult, human. She glanced up and saw a tall man, a dark moustache over his lip.

"You should not have come here," she said, returning to her contemplation of the gift. It was a mystery deserving of Ishoa.

The man went down on a knee. The crickets quietened, disturbed. "Your friends are worried."

"They don't need to be." She kept her head low, so her straight hair draped across her face. Washed and combed, it was the colour of Daesoa's light.

"You are a very brave young lady."

The ironwoods around them rattled their leaves. The man was straining in his effort not to stare. He didn't understand the Forest. He didn't understand her. She shook her head, refusing to look at him, a stranger, a man. The forest bore the worst of her pain, but the memory of those others burned raw. "You need to go."

"Some bad men did some very bad things to you," this man went on.

She could see the concern on his face in green Dindarin's light. The moon had sent a thousand of His beams through the gaps in the leaves. She wished He hadn't. If the canopy had twined tight, if the moon had left her in darkness, she might have blotted out the man's words. She kept looking at the bone. It was safest to do that.

"Look at me when I speak to you. Look at me, Sian."

His insistence wore through the mist surrounding her. Her eyes slid sideways onto his. Finding nothing of evil there, she eased her head around until her eyes were once again centred, on him.

"I think you are the bravest person I know."

The owl hooted as it flew over her head. A mouse darted into a burrow between the roots of an oak. She wanted to do that: run, cower, hide.

"I'm not brave at all. I'm scared of everything."

He said, "But still you go on. That is courage of the best kind."

"Why did you come?" Men feared this place for good reason. Faradil had succoured her and she understood.

"They say you can see the djinn. Is this true?"

The forest had fallen serene in its stirrings, the flitter of a leaf beneath the flutter of a moth, the whir of a wing in the sigh of the breeze. It did not mind this man. That was reason enough to trust him.

"Two of them. There's only ever two."

"Are they here now?"

"No."

"But you see them as plain as you see me."

She nodded.

"You are going to make a formidable soothsayer, Sian."

"I'm not a soothsayer." The words were out as quick as Dindarin flared. Her breath was fast, nervous for him. The forest might punish him for such presumption.

"And that?" he asked, indicating the bone in her hand.

"The Forest wanted me to have this." Ishoa might even love her for its beauty.

"It is extraordinary. Do you know what it is?"

She traced its outline, and shook her head. It was like no bone she had ever seen. "Ishoa will know, when I give it to her."

"I do not think she will take what is intended for you."

"Spirit bones are for soothsayers."

"And how is it you understand me?"

She looked up sharply. Her straight hair swung back, exposing her face, exposing her. "You are speaking Akerin."

"I am speaking Laanan, the tongue of the Three Realms."

Again she shook her head, this time to dispel her doubt. She was despised among her people. Even the outcast addicts would laugh to think the afflicted girl, the girl with half a brain, could command the spirits. Soothsayers were revered. Soothsayers were feared.

The stranger leaned forward, one arm across his knee. "Did your soothsayer not give you her lore?"

Sian turned her face away. The teaching, the tasks, the bone casting – they were favours the soothsayer had bestowed on a friendless outcast. They were that, if she did not delve deeper into her trembling. This was not a truth she could reveal in the wake of her suffering, and so she reverted to the other truth, the protective one. "You should not have come. Faradil is angry."

"I came for you. And you, I think, Faradil wants to protect. For that reason alone, it will do me no harm."

She sensed the truth of his words. This man commanded power, though his force paled in comparison to the ancient mysteries in the heart of the trees. If ever there was one to confide in, it was him. The forest had admitted him, leading him to her when it could so easily have lured him to madness or death. Around her, leaves rustled along the ground. Tiny pairs of bark-skinned hands lifted the decaying foliage so strange round eyes could peek out.

"A new mystery approaches," she said. "A presence as ancient as Faradil."

"Something that threatens the forest?"

"Something that threatens us all."

"And the forest seeks our help?"

"No. But you may need the help of the Forest."

An apricot ball of light flitted between them. The nearby trees cried out in indignation. The stick creatures shrieked with cracking-twig voices, and hid beneath the leaves. The light was wrong and wrongness. She frowned.

The man stood up. "Do we follow the light?" he asked, as it flitted up and over their heads.

"It is not part of the forest," she answered twisting her neck to follow its zigzagging path. The trees around them sighed their relief as it left. Its presence remained an ache at the back of her mind, but the larger threat bore back down. Her deep breath caused the man to look at her once more.

She was human. The forest could not change that. "Faradil has not chosen her side."

"Will it come to that?" he asked, deep worry in his eyes.

She gave him a single nod.

"Can you tell me more?"

She shook her head.

"I understand," he said, gentle still.

Biting her lip, she studied his grave face. Perhaps he did understand. She was too tired to help it, now. Her pain was too deep. Tears trickled down her face.

"Sian, are you all right?"

She was an abandoned child in a strange land. "I want to go home."

He held out his hand. "I think that can be arranged."

She placed her small hand in his. "I'm scared of that too."

"I know." He stood. As she rose, he plucked a dirty leaf from her hair. "Just promise me this. When the time comes to face who you are, do not run."

He was a stranger. He seemed to know her better than anyone except Ishoa. She knew she ought to make the promise; Faradil desired it. She opened her mouth but the words would not come. That was fine. Daesoa was telling her so by sending a yellow moonbeam to caress her face. It swept across root and frond, asking her to follow, leading them past ironwood, oak, and beech, out of the ancient heart of the land, onto the withered plain. Under the stars, she searched the sky. Dindarin showed but half his face. The small moon was gone. She faltered.

The mage had a gentle query on his face.

"Where is Daesoa?" she asked. She needed to thank the moon.

He shook his head. "She is new this night."

Levi's increasing groans and bent stance as they wound along the steep mountain paths worried Vinsant until his stomach hurt. He bit his lip while staring at the floating Majoria and waited until Levi was finally asleep.

Arun, Vinsant called, levitating himself into the air.

I'm here.

I need a healing spell.

Levi said you might ask.

Huh? You mean you talked to the Majoria without me?

Do you have a problem with that, apprentice?

Eh, no, Minoria. So are you going to teach me?

I believe the Majoria said your injury was result of your disobedience.

Well, not exactly. But–. Vinsant sent a mental picture of Levi's hand. And to emphasise his own dire need, he let Arun feel *his* pain too.

What is this? Arun asked quickly, focusing on Levi's burn.

The indigo djinn, Vinsant said, confused because hadn't Arun just said he had spoken to Levi. A second later he found himself flat on his back on the damp ground.

"How dare you, apprentice," Levi floated towards him, finger pointed at the end of an outstretched arm.

Vinsant wriggled back, not that he was going to avoid the Majoria's blasting. Thank the Vae Levi only raised his head in the silence of thoughtspeak. Well he should be a part of that too. It was his conversation after all. He concentrated on reforging the link with Arun. It was downright unfair, unjust and unmerited he found himself excluded, and not for lack of trying.

Levi bids me tell you myself that an accident with a healing spell may leave the patient worse off, Arun's voice intruded into his concern. The Minoria's tone became more sympathetic. *You have faced more in a month than many mahktashaan do in a lifetime. Be patient Vinsant, and trust your elders.*

"What punishment do you believe your presumption deserves?" Levi asked, when Vinsant had bid Arun a good night.

Vinsant sighed. "A trek back to the shrine?"

"I think not. Come here." Levi placed a hand on Vinsant's forehead. Warmth spread through his body and Vinsant found his pain was gone. "You will sleep upon the ground tonight."

"Yes, Majoria," Vinsant said, trying to levitate just enough to assert a covert defiance. He should have known he would find himself magickless.

"And Vinsant," Levi said as he reclined on air. "Your concern for your leader becomes a mahktashaan."

"All honour to you, Majoria," Vinsant said, moving the stones that poked into his back.

Chapter Forty-five

NOT READY FOR BED, Kordahla doused the candles and threw open the double doors to the balcony outside her room. Would that her feverish yearnings drifted as effortlessly as the scent of the frangipani on the breeze. Its caress was both soothing and welcome after the humidity of the last few days. Down in the candlelit gardens, another strolled beneath the quarter moon. The lady moved with a grace that belied her chosen role in life. She stopped beneath a blossom-covered bush to pluck a bloom, and with it, dear Vae'oenka, plucked the echo of Matisse's words.

"You are as beautiful as this flower," he had said, snapping the pink frangipane flower off the shrub. "But I cannot believe, delicate as you are, you bruise as easily." He pressed the tip between thumb and forefinger. She could find no words when he showed her the petal, crushed to translucence.

She had been wandering the canal beneath the hanging gardens when Matisse had approached, Timak quiet at her side, relentless guards behind. She wrapped her pink sheer shawl tight around her, covering her bare arms, her midriff. Between the bouts of fearful shame at exposing her skin, trills ran up and down her belly. Jordayne had seen fit to ignore her requests for a modest dress. In the privacy of her room, she twirled the beaded skirt, delighting in the allure of the revealing garments, their sheer femininity. In the presence of the flirtatious heir to throne, they struck her mute. Her feeble protests when he sent the boy on a trivial errand and dismissed her escort had not swayed him.

"But we are not alone," he had said, amusement dancing in his blue eyes and along the slight upturn of his lips. "We are together." They had meandered to a bench beneath a shady arch draped with the canes of a clematis. He had held her hand as they talked of Terlaan. She was not so naïve she did not guess he was probing for weaknesses, or figure the warm pressure of his hand aimed to disarm. Better this than the barrage Ordosteen would beset her with if Father dragged an army to the border to reclaim his honour. She had little to offer, but it had never been her intention to betray her home. Vae, but it was difficult to look at him, that teasing smile on his face. At least he did not begrudge her uselessness.

"Have you walked among the avenues of frangipane for which the palace is famed?" he asked when she had shuddered her distaste of the secretive mahktashaan, and told him what little she could.

"I have not as yet," she said, her heart fluttering.

"They are a delight not to be missed." Turning their talk to Myklaan, Matisse led her into the arcade, up steps to the first terrace, where pink blooming frangipanis lined the hot, stone wall, and aqueducts trickled cooling water from the terrace above. He stopped beneath a statue of a water-bearer, her robe parted to reveal a perfect, plump breast.

"Do you have such art in Terlaan?" he asked.

It had to be deliberate, this vagueness in his words, this allusion as much to nakedness as splendour. It had to deliberate, this setting of her cheeks on fire. If she faced him to answer, she need not see bare stone flesh. "Our artists are not as refined," she said. "The shipwrights are the pride of the realm."

"The exalted artist has more statues within the gardens. Would you care to see them?"

She could hardly refuse, either the offer or his proffered arm. And it was deliberate, that last, for when she took his arm, his free hand came around and divested her of the shawl.

"This garden was intended to reveal the beauty the Vae bestowed on this earth," he said, guiding her down the row, past the magnificent marble statues which stood between the trees. Vae'oenka protect her, but each was in an increasing state of undress. The artistry of it, the tactful placement of the leaves, was undeniable, but in these scant clothes, with a man who took every opportunity to touch her flesh, she was in danger of losing her honour. His hands found her bare waist to turn her towards an intricate detail. His nail brushed away a strand of hair that had flown into the corner of her mouth. If only she knew what bothered her more, his liberty or her secret longing for him to go on because, dear goddess, an attractive man's attention was a perfume as potent as the fragrance of her favourite flower.

"Would you not agree?" he asked.

She had to take three breaths before she could recall his comment. "Indeed," she whispered, her cheeks flaming under the sun.

"I am sorry. My attention discomforts you," Matisse said. He leaned against a statue, resting his head between the woman's bare thighs.

He had to think her a naïve child, but better that than a harlot. She managed a false smile. "It is only that such immodesty is condemned in my land."

His eyes, unusually serious, searched her face. "Is Myklaan not your land now?" he asked.

"I hope very much it will be."

"Then my uncle has not given you a formal decision?" Straightening, he put one hand where his head had been, and held the other out to her. She placed her fingers over his, his grip forcing her to come to him. "You must not worry so." Turning, he made the words ambiguous by adding, "It is only stone, Kordahla." He placed their hands on the statue's knee, guided hers up along the smooth contour of the leg, pressing close. Too close for decency. A man who presumed so much against her person in Terlaan would have his head loped off without trail. If this was how lovers courted in this decadent land, her honour was lost for sure.

Then he plucked the bloom. Uttered those disenchanted words. "You are as beautiful as this flower. But I cannot believe, delicate as you are, you bruise as easily."

Her breath quickened as he slid the frangipani into her hair and moved his hands to her bare elbows. An image of the Majoria's accusing finger flashed before her. She tensed. If Matisse noticed, he did not relent. Leaning closer by degrees, he brushed her lips with his own. Preparing for the hunger of his kiss, she closed her eyes. It never came. Instead, he pulled back and stroked the bend of her indecent joint.

"You see. There is not a single blemish upon your perfect skin." His kiss at her elbow surprised her. She gasped as his lips travelled up her arm. Vae'oenka forgive her, she meant to pull away, but suddenly his lips were pressed to hers and there was nothing in her mind save the breezy, masculine taste of him.

After, he had bowed with mocking formality and parted from her. She had lost the dazed afternoon dawdling through the hanging gardens, discovering terraces of frangipani apricot, yellow and red while wondering if the heir to the throne might take her for a bride. It was a union of which Father would have to approve. If only she could be sure that was his intention. Never could she be like Lady Jordayne, content to enjoy the pleasures of the flesh with every man who caught her fancy.

As the evening shadows lengthened, a glimpse of him had sent her hurrying to her rooms. Two encounters in the one day was more than her confused emotions could take.

Now, on the breezy balcony, Dindarin risen, Kordahla wished there was someone she could watch to discover how a Myklaani lady should behave when confronted with the seductive attentions of a man. But there was only Jordayne and the pale-haired lady below, whom she had gathered from her young handmaid, Nina, was a mistress at the court. Her insecurities mounting, she wrapped her arms around herself. Her modest silk nightgown was luxury, as sensuous as his touch.

"Rochelle." The voice drifted up to her on the cool night air.

The lady turned and smiled at Shah Ordosteen. White-haired, sombre, he stood a discreet distance away. Behind him, at the limits of the garden, the plants draping over the tiers swayed in harmony.

"Do you desire my company, your Majesty?"

"I wish your honesty."

"That you may have," Rochelle said, drawing close.

They stood together, her face turned up to his for the space of several breaths, a pose both intimate and wary.

"Do you love him?" Ordosteen asked. Quiet-spoken, but the wind and the silence of the night carried the words to her.

Kordahla pressed into the shadows against the wall, an intruder too mesmerised to leave.

"He has my affection."

"But your love?"

"You would ask me this? Of a man not inclined to give himself to any one woman?"

"And I? What do you harbour for me?"

Rochelle raised a hand to Ordosteen's face. "You have my deepest affection."

"But not your love?"

Dropping her hand, she turned away, out of shadow and into the green cast of Dindarin's light. "It is not a luxury I have allowed myself."

"If things were different…" Ordosteen asked, his voice rasped with emotion.

"But they are not. If it pains you to have me here, I will leave. Denkan is not yet returned home, and my father ails by the day."

"You may do as you wish, Rochelle."

The voice was harsh and made her turn back. There was pride in her bearing as she said, "It was not my intention to make you miserable when I returned."

"Then why did you?"

"He asked me to." She took Ordosteen's hand, kissed each of his fingers, pressed his palm against her lips. Then, shockingly, out here in the open for all to see, she slid it inside the low neckline of her kameez, pressed it against her bosom. The Shah groaned. Kordahla's hands tightened on the wall. Engrossed in their private discussion, she had crept too close. She pressed back, conscious of every prickling point of contact between her body and the rough wall. Below, the breathy conversation continued.

"I am a kept woman. I have been for a long time. I would rather it were here, where I may enjoy my talents and reap the benefits of generous lovers, than cooped up in my father's house where I would be treated like an old maid."

"I would never treat you like that," the Shah said, taking her hand, kissing it fast and urgent, pressing her curled fingers to his face. "If I can guarantee your safety, will you marry me, Rochelle?"

"You cannot outsmart the djinn, Ordosteen. What is done is done. Leave it be. If Katrine does not please you, find another."

He ceased his amorous attentions, grasped her arms, and pulled her to him with strength enough to make her gasp. "Your honest answer. If I can arrange a way for us to unite, will you accept?"

Immobile, she stared at him. At length, she tucked an arm between them and pushed him away. "You would make me Shahbanu?" Her head held high, she looked the queen, for all she had offered her body to the goddess knew how many men.

"Yes," Ordosteen replied, his voice all but cracked. Whether it was desire or a more visceral longing Kordahla could not say. She found herself holding her breath.

"You would not wish to take a woman of a more suitable childbearing age as wife?"

"Vae'oenka may yet grant us a child."

"What would you ask of me in return?" Rochelle asked.

"Your fidelity."

The lady tilted her head. "Only that?" A moment of silence was broken by the rustle of her skirts as she gathered him to her, pulling him onto a bench so he might rest his head at her breast, and she might stroke his thinning hair. "My dear, sweet Shah, I will be yours for eternity if that cursed djinn relents."

Kordahla stared out at the starlit heavens. What manner of nation would elevate a mistress to Shahbanu? And what manner of shah would allow his passion to mount in full view of the palace. Their hands were groping at places too indecent to name. She slipped through the doors, pulling them after her. They were about to click closed when a voice drifted to her.

Through the crack, she saw the lady had risen. "Enough, my Lord. You must ask Katrine to sate your hunger tonight."

"Will you lie with him till then?"

"If he comes to me." Rochelle was standing behind him now. Placing her hands on Ordosteen's shoulders, she kissed the base of his neck. "Do not despair, my love. His sights are already set on another, and a conquest she would be. I can guess what this new bargain of yours might involve, Ordosteen. You might yearn for me, my darling shah, but are you willing to sacrifice decency?"

"You would. Do not deny you would, Rochelle."

"But I am not Shah."

As a cloud darkened Dindarin's face, Kordahla clicked the doors shut. Her stomach was a roiling bundle of nerves. *If he comes to me*. In the dark it was all too clear to whom Rochelle had referred. The teasing look she had seen Matisse exchange with this woman alluded to secrets Kordahla was only beginning to grasp. After a day of his amorous attentions in the vineyards, she had suffered an isolation so keen not even Timak had been able to draw a word from her.

The day – was it only yesterday? – had promised delight when Matisse suggested an outing. Ever shy around him, she commented how well the fresh air would agree with Timak. At which Matisse had declared a vineyard an unsuitable place for a child. Her ineloquent stutters had revealed her alarm. She did not trust him. Did not trust herself, if truth be told, to be alone with him that far from the palace. The bumbling language which was all she seemed capable of around this self-confident man had put a smile on his face until Jordayne had exclaimed what a grand idea it was and hauled her off to her bedroom on the pretext on donning suitable attire.

"What is the problem? Do you not enjoy his attentions?" Jordayne asked, spraying her with enough perfume to last an eight-day. Since she did, Kordahla could think of nothing to say. "Ah, but I see that you do."

Meeting her eye had been hard. "I cannot…" was as far as she got.

Jordayne patted her arm. "Nor do you need to. Enjoy it, but let him know when you've had enough. The goddess knows you could do with a kiss or two after all you've been through. You can hardly say there is shame in that."

"Perhaps not here."

Jordayne sighed. "But you are here, my dear. And whatever the outcome, no one is going to berate you for a kiss. Or even find out for that matter. If my brother can soothe away some of the trials of the last few eight-days, then let him. If your modesty is so precious to you, you need only bolt your door at night."

Lock her door she did, and with good reason. The handle had twisted three nights past, and she, alone in her room, as was the custom in this ardent land, had huddled beneath the cover both fearful and thrilled.

"Now do let's enjoy the day," Jordayne said rising from the stool at her dresser.

Safe in Jordayne's company, Kordahla relaxed as they rode to the lake and, sun sparkling on the water, sailed to Mage Cove to pick up Drucilamere.

"What do you want?" was the mage's ungracious query of the lady. He had walked out to the dock to meet them, the only cloud on this bright, blue day.

"Get in the boat, Drucilamere. We need to talk."

"I have nothing to say to you."

Jordayne disembarked amid the jingle of her jewellery. "I have a great deal to say to you."

"Then have the decency to say it before all the mages."

The journeymen mages were dark figures looking through the window on the lower floor of the mage guild, watching, waiting for the break of a storm. It seemed this outing was not to be the restful occasion Kordahla had thought.

Jordayne turned to the barge. "It seems, my dears, I shall not be accompanying you after all."

Kordahla leaned forward, ready to make an excuse to get out.

"You see, you are spoiling our guest's fun," Jordayne said. "She is much too well brought up to consider an outing without a chaperone."

"I'm not sure how that reflects on me," Matisse said, reclining among the cushions that cluttered the deck, too relaxed among all the awkwardness. "Or if in her mistrust she should reconsider her desire to lodge at Kaijoor palace. It *is* my principal place of abode."

Kordahla felt her cheeks burn. She swallowed and looked at the water lap against the rocks. Vae'oenka only knew if she had made the right choice in coming here, but the mere thought of Ahkdul turned the world grey.

"He is teasing, Kordahla. You have every reason to mistrust him. He is more mischievous than the djinn in the presence of beautiful women. But I'm sure he'll be a model of decorum today." Jordayne touched her fingers to her lips and blew a kiss to the boat. "Enjoy the outing, and have a kiss or three for your own sake."

"You are not going to allow them to go off alone?" Drucilamere said through clenched teeth. His moustache twitched his anger.

"Well we do rather need to talk," Jordayne replied. "And there are the servants."

The tall mage gripped her arm and pulled her onto the boat. "You are worse than the conniving djinn, Jordayne."

"In my estimation, that is a high compliment," she said, as the boatmen cast off. She lifted a hand to his face and kissed him.

He pulled her hand down. Her bangles clanged at her wrist. "I am not so easily swayed."

"As you wish," she said with a sigh, leading him to the relative privacy of the bow. Their dispute did not prevent her from reclining against him, shameless in her contact.

"Have you made any progress with the crystals?" Kordahla heard her ask.

"We have not."

"Well, that gives all the more validation to what I have done."

"Nothing could justify your actions." His voice was heated.

Jordayne pulled away from him. The barge glided past a low cliff, toward meadows grazed by long-haired goats which chewed their cud as they ruminated over what the tension in the boat might mean. "What do you want me to say? You acknowledge Terlaan poses a threat. Both Trove and the soothsayer girl intimate there are stirrings in the spirit world that may affect every person in the Three Realms, and you don't want to prepare every resource available to counter it."

"I want you to admit what you have done is wrong."

Jordayne sighed and softened her voice. "I have never said it was otherwise."

"Let his soul go."

"Not yet."

"You really are heartless."

"I promise I will not use it save at direst need."

"Whose need will that be?"

"One you accede to."

"And if that need does not arrive?"

"I will let him go to the Vae."

"I will make you do it, Jordayne. By the Vae, I will make you do it."

Her answer was to kiss him, and this time he dragged her close to him, hungry in his response. Kordahla looked away to find Matisse watching her.

"My sister is passionate about everything she does."

Kordahla nodded, and made shy replies to his conversation until the boat docked.

They stepped onto land more verdant than any around Lake Sheraz, to be met by a bowing vineyard owner who had been alerted to their visit by an advance sailor. He led them across a pretty grassed area to tilled earth bearing rows of intertwined vines sagging under their oversized crop. Drucilamere picked a bunch of grapes and pushed the most succulent between Jordayne's lips.

"It is tradition. A blessing for a fertile crop," Matisse said with the amused smile he reserved for whenever she felt discomfited by the men around her.

Her eyes wide, Kordahla allowed him to push a grape into her mouth. His fingers lingered at her lips as he leaned to whisper in her ear.

"You must take it from me."

And she was forced to burst the fruit with her tongue, brush his fingers with its tip so the sweetness could explode in her mouth.

"That," he said, loud enough for everyone to hear, "is a start." And he kissed her there, in front of them all.

Her legs wobbling, she could do no more than stare at him. There was nowhere to escape, nowhere to hide.

"You see," Jordayne said, trailing a hand along her back as she swept onto a path between the vineyard and a myrtle hedge. "It is not that difficult to have some fun. Keep this up and I shan't need to educate you at all."

Which left her with a flurry of emotions she couldn't identify. Her livelihood depended on the goodwill of these people, and yet here she was, avoiding Matisse's touch for the rest of the tour, a difficult feat with Jordayne alternately engrossed in Drucilamere's attentions and Drucilamere's ire. By degrees, Matisse's amused indulgence turned determined. At lunch, she found herself forced to sit by his side on the kilim the servants had laid out. Jordayne and Drucilamere reclined on another in a tangle of limbs, more interested in each other than the sloping vineyards and crystal lake before them, their argument raging between their kisses.

"It is Myklaan's finest," Matisse said, handing her a goblet of undiluted wine.

The first sip suffused her body, richer, sweeter, more potent than anything she had tasted in Terlaan. The food was a long time coming, and she found Matisse was refilling her goblet before Gahdri, the vineyard owner, had served the first succulent morsels of fish. She continued sipping the wine Matisse kept pouring. It was a way to divert her gaze from the intense blue of his eyes.

"I think you have had enough," he said, pulling the goblet from her hand. "I do not wish to pass a dull afternoon because you have fallen asleep."

"I think I could quite happily fall asleep," she said, stretching out the drowsiness from wine and sun.

"I have a much better idea." He leaned forward.

She anticipated the kiss, but not his gentle push, or him to lie beside her and brush a lock from her forehead. Then his lips were on hers again, gentle and undemanding, their touch diluting both the bickering of the other two and the strains of a rowdy ballad drifting from somewhere behind the hedges.

She heard the tinkle of Jordayne's bracelets as she rose, pulling Drucilamere with her.

"This we need to settle once and for all," the lady said, leading the mage to the vines.

In the sudden silence, Kordahla's heart thudded in her ears. The servants, she noted, had retreated up the path. They were alone, and she was lying very close to a man who was not hesitating to make his feelings known. Who sat up and turned when she tensed so that his hands were placed one on either side of her. She lay at a disadvantage beneath him, tipsy from overindulgence and the tickle of the finger he ran up and down her arm. She wondered if she ought to sit up too.

"What are you afraid of? I shall not dishonour you," Matisse said. Then that smile returned. "At least not until you ask me to."

His hand slipped around her bare waist, to the small of her back. The touch of his skin on hers kindled the fire he had already awakened. Without thought, she raised her head ever so slightly, her lips apart. The invitation brought him down on her, his hungry mouth moving over hers, pressing again and again and she was returning his passion, surrendering herself to a fierce burning as his kisses rained over her face and down her neck to the small hollow at its base.

Abruptly, he stopped. Their breaths came heavy between them. She opened her eyes, not aware she had closed them. Aware, though, whatever his assurances, she was travelling a dangerous road. And yet, one small part of her had to swallow disappointment as he stood.

"Come on," he said, his voice wound tight. He helped her up only to leave her far behind with his quick, heavy strides.

Unsure of herself, she followed. She caught up in a clearing crammed with peasants stomping on grapes in huge oak barrels as they lifted mugs of cheap wine to toast the minstrels among them. Before she could react, Matisse and Gahdri were lifting her into a barrel as someone else pulled the sandals from her feet. She squealed as grapes swished beneath her soles, lost her balance and toppled against the side. Laughing, Matisse jumped in after her. Juice oozing between her toes, she tried to walk to him, tripped over her long skirt and fell onto hands and knees. Juice splashed onto her face as she sank to her elbows, mouth open in shock.

"You are a delectable sight," Matisse said, pulling her to her feet against his body. He wiped fruit off her face and licked his finger. "And if you mention how our clothes are ruined, I will rip them off you right here."

Surprising herself, she laughed. The music, the wine, the sweet passion had combined into an intoxicating potion. "Just you try," she said, and pushed him. He was too strong for her to topple but he returned in kind, sending her onto her behind with a splash. She grinned at him, extended a hand, and when he offered his, brought him down with a pull and a kick to the ankle. The peasants succumbed to a riot of laughter.

"I suppose you think this is funny," he said, turning to face her. Whether by accident or design one hand had landed on her thigh, its press firm through the soaked fabric of her skirt. She gazed into his eyes, hardly able to complain since she had pulled him down. Not sure she wanted to anyway.

"Very," she replied, for the first time relaxed in his presence despite the inappropriacy.

He clambered to his feet, hauling her up so her breasts pressed against his chest. It was no liberty if it was merely so that he could steady her.

"I am glad." he said and whirled her around the barrel before lifting her out and taking her back to Lake Tejolin to bathe as best they could.

Soaking and stained, they boarded the barge. Clothes dishevelled, faces flushed, Jordayne and Drucilamere reappeared from behind the myrtle hedge. They sat quiet and apart in the boat as it headed north to Kaijoor, but their sombre mood failed to infect. Happier than she had been in a long while, Kordahla leaned against Matisse, enjoying the feel of his hands around her, the light strokes of his fingers on her arm, the occasional kiss on her neck, the rarer one on her lips.

He left her in the palace with a brief kiss. Still damp, she waltzed down the vaulted hall in the daze of a daydream where Matisse proposed to her and Father bestowed a blessing. Why she turned into the wrong hall, she would never be able to say. But she had, and she had seen them. Rochelle, framed in a doorway, her nipples erect under a sheer top, her pale hair fanning over her shoulders. And Matisse, who, an incredible hunger in his eyes, had gone to her, his arousal evident. The lady invited him in with a twist of her shoulders, and Matisse, that infuriating smile on his lips, pushed open her door with the flat of his hand. Crushed, Kordahla had fled to her lavish, empty room, refusing to join Ordosteen for dinner and ignoring Timak's tentative hand on her own as she sat facing the arched windows, allowing the perfumed night to gather its shadows around her.

"Why are you sad?" Timak had asked. He was acting as a page, running messages around the palace.

"I miss my little brother," she had replied.

"Will you go home?"

"I hope not." She had looked at him then, aware she hadn't given him a second thought since arriving in Kaijoor. Colour had returned to his cheeks but he was far from robust. "Do you want to go home?"

"I want to be with my mother and father."

"Matisse could arrange an escort for you to the Mykver Pass."

Even as she wondered why she named Matisse, the boy had backed away. Even in the twilight she saw he was trembling.

"He will find me," Timak had said.

That day – yesterday – she had stared at nothing, sitting in much the same way she was standing now among the ghosted shadows the flickering candle was throwing across the cream tiles of the walls. "Then I suppose we are both stuck here for the same reason," she had said. She had not even noticed when he crept away.

She steadied herself with a hand on the bedpost. She was deluding herself if she believed Matisse was interested in courting her. The idyllic scenes painted on bedhead and dresser were a romantic's dream. *A conquest.* That was how Rochelle had described her. All Lord Matisse's attention had been designed to entice her into his arms, with no regard for what it might cost her if Shah Ordosteen reneged on his promise.

Chapter Forty-six

A COMMOTION OF RAISED voices. A sudden chill in the air. Then, a panicked cry of *djinn*.

In a daze, Kordahla turned toward the balcony. The doors burst open and the indigo djinn whizzed inside. He flew around and around her, his legs blurring into smoke, until she was so dizzy that, crying out, she fell to the marble floor.

"Fool," the djinn roared. "Imbecile. Do I have to do everything for you?"

"I don't have it," Kordahla said. She was shivering uncontrollably. "I don't have anything called Xander." She wrapped her arms around her chest. Her silk robe slid against her skin, slippery as the djinn.

He loomed above her, shimmering in Dindarin's light, his slippered feet just off the floor. "You do nothing to earn that gift."

"Why are you here?" Was there no end to the demands placed on her?

"I overexert myself to deliver you a chance at happiness and all you do is wallow in self-pity. Why? Because the second most important person in the realm is paying you both too much and not enough attention."

"I am who I am."

"Get up, you ungrateful wretch. The floor ill becomes a princess, even one of fleas."

She swayed, too fearful, too miserable to do as he asked. "Please go." This supernatural haunting was more than she could bear. "Just go."

His large hands gripped her and hauled her up so she was forced to look into his ugly face, at his cruel, vermillion eyes and jagged black hair. Only it was not his face. It was Matisse's, indigo and larger than life, and exuding that stomach-churning, fish-tainted smell. With a wicked sneer, he kissed her full on the lips. She struggled, but he kept her pinned, dragging his sickening, sloppy touch on and on. She wanted to die from the humiliation as his lips worked down her neck, reminding her of how horrid a man's uninvited touch could be, how close she had come to being violated. The moon was witness to this travesty. Dindarin was but a crescent, half hidden by the lintel, but He could see.

"Stop."

He pushed her back, hard enough that she stumbled into the door. She huddled over, trying to rub the goosebumps of cold disgust from her arms. The djinn floated towards her, his shimmering, leering face his own.

"Don't touch me," she warned, working to free the bolt. Her breath puffed into the icy room, speckled by the glint of the gold tiles.

"You like it when that womanising layabout kisses you. Admit it, you grovelling speck."

"What if I do?" she said, self-loathing rising.

Lips puckered, he advanced on her. She was forced to back toward the bed or suffer another of his violations.

"You entice him with your beauty, allow him to fondle your ripe body, then bar him from your room."

"You've been spying on me."

"What if I have? You owe me your life." He smacked his lips, blew her a fishy kiss.

She circled. "Xander. Something called Xander. That's all I owe you, and I don't have it."

He pointed, all the joints in his arm aglow. "You play games. He kisses you, you kiss him back. He touches you, you touch him back."

"No! I never."

There was a pounding at the door. Alarmed voices called her name. She edged toward them but the indigo djinn, his face flickering between that of Matisse and his own, floated right past her and barred her way.

"Keep away from me."

"You are mine till you repay me, foolish girl. And repay me you will."

The djinn turned up his palm and blew. Sparkling motes showered her, encasing her in a shimmering haze. She shuddered as they faded, only this time it was not with cold. That deep yearning in her blood was piquing, that memory of Matisse's lips on her own. Its tingle was as pleasant as the djinn's kiss was foul.

"Keep away," she whispered under the continued pounding at the door.

The djinn whipped around her. She huddled into herself, dreading his touch. His hot breath tickled her ear, and sent shudders of revulsion down her spine. She hated herself for whimpering, but Vae'oenka spare her this rapid shift between elation and disgust.

"You insect. The heir to the throne takes an interest in you and you send him into the arms of another.

"I cannot give him what he seeks."

"After all he has done for you. You ingrate. You cruel temptress."

The candle on the dresser flickered and went out. Dindarin ascended beyond the top of the doors. The room darkened. Her breath caught in her throat. "Go."

"As you wish, Princess."

He blew on her, a warm fishy puff that fired passion into her blood.

Wood cracked. She jumped. The door flung open. Malicious laughter echoed off the walls as people stormed into the room.

"Enjoy him while you can," the djinn sneered, and disappeared in a puff of smoke.

Teeth chattering, she stood in the centre of the room as they crowded her, queried her, sympathised until tears welled in her eyes. By Vae'oenka, she wished they would all go. Alone she might weather these fiery feelings, regain a modicum of the dignity she had abandoned the night she fled Tarana. She clutched her arms tighter to her, unable to look at them, saved from needing to under the cloak of darkness.

"Kordahla." Matisse's arms encircled her. "By the Vae, you are shivering like a leaf in a gale." His hand tilted her chin so she was forced to look at his shadowed face. "Did the djinn harm you?" he asked.

The concern in his eyes was her undoing. She sobbed as she shook her head. Was grateful for the cloak Rochelle had found to drape around her shoulders, though she forgot to utter her thanks.

Ordosteen took one of her hands. "He was indigo. With vermillion eyes," the Shah said, in what was neither question nor statement.

She nodded.

"The mage saw the taint of his kind about you. Has the creature tricked you into a pact?" he asked, a deep, gentle understanding in his eyes.

There was a collective hush as they waited on her answer. She saw no point in denying it. A haunting was bound to make them suspicious, make them question the wisdom of harbouring her.

"He saved me from a bazwaeel in the scums."

"What did he demand in return?" The gentleness was still there, though there was an edge to Ordosteen's voice. The Shah needed to know his people, his family was safe. She understood, and was glad she could ease his mind.

"He lays claim to a gift I will not want."

"Did he tell you what that was?"

"No, he did not. I am sorry. I'm so sorry," she said, a tear trickling down her cheek.

"My dear, I think there was nothing else you could have done," the Shah said, rubbing her hand. "But the djinn rarely collect on a pact the way we imagine they will. Whatever the creature intimated, you will pay a dear price for his help." He was staring beyond her, just as she had gazed through the walls, a haunted look in his eyes. Rochelle's words drifted back to her, the ones she had, in a fever of jealousy, ignored. *You cannot outsmart the djinn.* The recognition came, then, how deeply this shah was indebted to one, most probably this one, indigo with vermillion eyes. She felt a fleeting rush of compassion give way to fear. In Shah Ordosteen's eyes she might be little more than a pawn to barter for his happiness. Had she fled Father's schemes only to fall prey to those of a foreign ruler? Her trembling grew worse. She put a hand over her mouth as bile rose in her throat.

"Enough, Uncle. You are scaring her witless," Matisse said. His arms were still around her. These men, these strangers, were standing so close. Inside her, the fire was rising again.

"She needs rest," Rochelle said, drawing Ordosteen away. "We will have the servants bring in a cot. Your handmaid can keep you company tonight, Princess Kordahla. You should not be alone."

"I'm sorry," she said again, looking Matisse in the eye. They were alone, and he was holding her, and she was not speaking about the pact.

"Hush, Kordahla. From what I have heard of the bazwaeel, you would be dead if you had not acquiesced to the djinn's demands." He stroked her hair from her face. There was an emotion she could not read on his but it was as if he was at war with his feelings. "I'll send your page to you." When he released her, disappointment cut through her like a knife.

"Don't go." She was breathing way too fast.

Matisse looked her up and down. "I don't think the djinn will bother you again tonight."

"He kissed me," she whispered, and shuddered at the foul memory.

"That could not have been pleasant." He made no attempt to come closer, but neither did he have a trace of that mocking smile about him.

She took the initiative. Stepped right up to him so she had to look up to see his face. "Don't leave me with the taste of him on my lips."

"If I ever learn his name, he will pay for that liberty."

His arms slipped around her waist. She shuddered again. By Vae'oenka, this burning was like an insatiable hunger. He was standing there, making no move. Goddess, could he want to be with Rochelle? Rising onto tiptoe, she kissed him on the mouth. He responded at once, and her hands were in his hair, and his were moving up and down her back. His scent, spicy and masculine, mixed with the frangipani wafting up through the open balcony doors. Together, they drove away the taint of the djinn, and her mouth moved harder, faster, erasing all memory of the revolting creature's touch.

Too soon he was breaking them apart. She stood panting, eyes wide in disbelief at what she had done.

"Is the taint of him gone?" She heard the smile in his words, and knew the corners of his lips had curved.

"Almost," she breathed, scarcely believing what she was inviting.

Smile growing, Matisse crossed to the door, had a word with the guards now stationed outside, and closed it. She swallowed, unable to move, unable to speak.

This time he came to her. His hands travelled inside the wide sleeves of her nightgown as he bent to kiss her, and his touch sent shivers of delight down her body.

"Let me help you forget," he murmured.

Then his mouth was travelling over her face. Closing her eyes, she revelled in the warmth of his kisses. When his hand tugged at the laces of her gown, and slid down to her breast, it felt so right. She reached for him, her own hand moving inside his kurta, over his shoulders, up to his head. Then her gown was at her ankles and his own clothes were on the floor and somehow he had moved her to the bed. His teasing hands and mouth roused her to unbearable ecstasy so that she thought she would explode until he joined with her in a climax she had never dreamed was possible. And at the height of it all, her name was on his lips, and it had never sounded so sweet.

And another name, also, drifted to her on an icy breeze. *Xander. Xander*, came the glacial whisper as their passion peaked. Under the still wind, Kordahla shuddered.

Basking in the daze of their lovemaking, Matisse did not notice. "Tiarasae," he murmured as the temperature climbed. He was lying on his back, his hands behind his head. "You truly are Tiarasae."

She rolled so she could put her arms around him, lay her head on his chest, hoping he would embrace her and tell her everything would be fine. He did not. But there was comfort in the feel of him against her, and she knew he had meant what he had said about making the djinn pay.

Happiness eluded her, but secure, at least, she fell asleep.

Chapter Forty-seven

LEVI HEAVED HIMSELF UP from the rock.

"How's your leg?"

"Getting better," Vinsant lied. The swelling was as painful as ever. Levi's soothing magic had lasted till the next morning but Vinsant's resentment that the Majoria would leave him crippled had abated when Levi taught him to borrow light from the sun. It was a nifty trick, once he had mastered the knack of it. The interim stolen candles and campfires, while useful, did not fit with the image of a dignified mahktashaan. Thank Mahktos his failures had only coaxed an amused snort from the Majoria. "How about your hand?"

"Can you go on?" the Majoria asked looking, of all directions, up. Through the gap between the ridges, the sun shone wincing-bright on the patches of snow dotting the scree. To their right, an icy peak jutted into the clear sky.

Vinsant struggled up from his own rough seat, careful to keep his weight on his good leg. Without further chat, they continued their clamber, their feet sinking into ankle-deep snow. As moisture seeped through his boots, Vinsant began to shiver. The woollen kurta, shalvar and gloves the temple village had given him were inadequate protection against the numbing cold. He spelled warmth into his clothes, the last magic he had learned, earning an approving nod from Levi when he managed to keep the Myklaani sword levitating in the crisp air at the same time. Excused neither swordplay nor magic lessons, he had been relieved at the slackening of their gruelling pace over the days since they had left the shrine. The Majoria was turning out to be all right after all. At least, he was since that one last punishment for just talking to the indigo djinn.

Too bad he was not learning magic today. Just tedious, repetitive lore.

"A mahktashaan swears absolute fealty to Mahktos, Terlaan, the majoria and the minoria, and the shah in that order," Levi continued with the lesson he had begun before their rest.

"So if the majoria and shah disagree, the mahktashaan must serve their majoria?" Levi had been uncharacteristically chatty since Vinsant had sought Arun's help, for him anyway. The do-not-speak-unless-spoken-to rule had thankfully fallen by the wayside even if Levi did not deign to answer all his questions.

"Unless the majoria's actions threaten to compromise Terlaan."

He had to risk it. "But who determines that? I mean if the Majoria disagrees with the Shah, he could claim–"

Levi actually halted, took Vinsant's hood and yanked it down. His gloved hand seized Vinsant's chin and tilted it up, squeezing his jaw so tight it hurt. "Do you think to presume Mahktos would not know? Do you think to presume our god would invest power in a corrupt leader?" he said, bending over Vinsant. Beneath his hood, his eyes glowered that peculiar abysmal black.

Unable to speak, Vinsant shook his head. Levi let him go and strode on, ignoring the hovering buzzard. Pulling his hood back up, Vinsant scrambled up the ridge after his master. His worn boots dislodged chunks of shale. The clatter was the only sound in the brittle air. At the crest, Vinsant stopped and gaped. The land here formed a natural bowl, rising on the other side to a gaping cave. He would have sworn the mound above it had never been touched by human hands, but it had the features of a primitive face. Mahktos's face. The eye sockets were filled with red moss, a skinny boulder formed a squat nose-like bump, and pointed rocks rising from the floor looked like fangs.

Forgetting his pain, Vinsant hobbled after Levi. "Are we going to go in?" he asked, stumbling forward as the Myklaani sword floated into his backside.

His face masked by his hood, the Majoria remained a silent mystery.

"I'm sorry I questioned you, Majoria," Vinsant said. He should have saved himself the effort; his apology failed to draw a response. Taking a deep breath, he shuffled to the mouth. He was about to step inside when a warning prickle ran along his spine. His skin tingled as power vibrated through the air. He looked up and for a brief moment sky, shale and peak spun into a blur.

"All praise to you, Mahktos," Vinsant said when the world had steadied.

Levi knelt. "All praise to you Mahktos," he said, dislodging a blackened scrap of flesh from his burned hand and holding it for the strengthening wind to gather. Vinsant fought to keep his meagre breakfast down.

"You must make an offering," Levi said, rising.

He had nothing to give. Something of himself, Nocrates had suggested. Although it was not exactly hard to come by, he plucked a hair from beneath his hood and laid it across his open palm. A gust tugged it from his hand.

"Come," Levi said. "You will keep your hood up at all times."

They entered the mouth. Vinsant breathed a sigh of relief. That test was over. Levi could have warned him! He sure hoped the Majoria's neglect had nothing to do with his punishment. He had forgotten that small detail about this trip. It was nerve-wracking, considering what it might entail. His stumbled on the uneven ground. Not that Levi showed the slightest bit of concern. Silent, the Majoria led him to a twisting, rough-walled passage at the back of the cave. Vinsant created a ball of light to guide the way. Whichever mahktashaan worked the mines, they would be left in no doubt about his amazing apprentice skills.

"Majoria, is this cave natural?"

"It was present when Mahktos led Guntek to it but pictograms show it was inhabited long before then. Whether those inhabitants found or created it, we do not know."

They went on and down. The dank air turned stale. At last, the passage opened into wide chamber. Vinsant caught his breath. Stalactites in all the colours of the rainbow formed *muqarnas* on the ceiling while tall stalagmites ringed the chamber. Lit from within, they glowed and ebbed with a magical rhythm. He couldn't take his eyes off them as he followed Levi into the chamber. At his chest, his quartz responded by radiating a soft light.

"It's awesome."

Of course Levi didn't answer.

A mahktashaan with a crystal of an intense violet walked between the stalagmites, and knelt before Levi. "All honour to you, Majoria." Around the wall, several other mahktashaan stamped a foot and spoke in echo.

"You may rise, Mahktashaan Fenz," Levi said. "Are the preparations in order?"

Getting up, Fenz nodded to a mahktashaan waiting at the side of the cave. "As you requested, Majoria."

The mahktashaan came forward. He held a crystal-studded chain in his hand. A sudden bad feeling about all this made Vinsant step back.

"The prisoner will approach," Fenz said.

Vinsant stared. So this was to be a formal reprimand after all. His cheeks burned. His heart thudded loudly into the silence. He fought a strong desire to proclaim his identity and announce the sanction he had received from Mahktos. With these dour mahktashaan surrounding him, he didn't really have that choice. Chin up, just like a man, he stood before Fenz, arms out. Chains and hard labour he could bear for seven days because afterwards was he ever going to get a heap of sympathy from Kordahla! Of course he would neglect to tell her that he could spell light and heat to improve his lot in the most dismal of dungeons. Just to ensure his gaolers knew they were dealing with an extraordinary apprentice, he brightened the ball of light. The murmurs of surprise were gratifying. He could not help sticking out his chest as the mahktashaan clapped the shackles onto his wrists and ankles. With the final clang of the locking rivet, his light disappeared, and the Myklaani sword clattered to the ground.

Huh? He struggled to magic the light back into existence. The harder he tried, the stronger the clear crystals in the irons glowed. And the weaker he felt. He looked at Levi in dismay.

"How long is the prisoner to serve?" Fenz asked.

"Seven days," Vinsant said, shoulders drooping because the eight-day was going to be the scums after all.

Levi shoved him to his knees. "He is detained at my pleasure."

CHAPTER FORTY-EIGHT

AN APPLE FELL OUT of Timak's pocket and rolled against the wall.

"So you're thieving." The sniggering older page flicked a pebble into the middle of his back.

Timak kept walking down the long corridor, past the ceremonial swords and shields hung on the plain walls. A pinkish light trailed through the air beside him. He didn't think the nasty page could see his silent genie. The bully wouldn't have picked up the apple or crunched into it if he could. He wouldn't have tried to follow, or waited until a sword floated off the wall and barred his way to let the apple thud to the floor and patter away.

Yazmine shouldn't have thought that made anything all right. Timak turned into a musty room and shut the door on her fuzzy light. When he turned, she was there anyway, bobbing in the centre.

"You don't visit," he accused.

"I'm sorry. They won't always let me come."

"Who are 'they'?" Motes floated in the sunbeams spearing through the broken shutters, but there wasn't any other bobbing light.

"The other djinn."

He loitered among the cupboards lined up against the walls, opening and closing doors carved with the oak and bear Myklaani crest. A thick layer of dust had dulled the cluttered ornaments inside. They clinked as he tried to push them back but they didn't slide far. He sneezed. "Why are they so mean?"

"I don't think they are."

"You don't think?" he asked, spying a chest to one side of the keyhole window.

"I don't remember much when I'm here. There are the rules. And the indigo djinn I must obey. I know I will remember when I go back to Court."

He went and knelt by the chest, undid the rusting iron clasps and hefted the lid open. It was full of mildewed clothing. "That doesn't make sense."

She sighed. "I know. I have a vague feeling I must prove myself. I remember before though."

"Before what?" He pulled out a bundle of clothing.

"Before I was a genie."

Sitting back on his heels, he looked at her light. "You mean you weren't born a genie?"

"No, silly. I used to be human. Well, almost."

He blinked. Now he really was confused. "Human?"

He heard her sharp breath. "I don't think I was supposed to tell you that."

"I won't tell. What happened to your parents?"

"I miss them so much."

Timak looked down. "Me too. Genie, will you sing to me?"

She hummed a familiar tune. He couldn't remember the words either, but her voice helped drive the loneliness away. After a verse, he got up, stuffed the clothes into a cupboard on top of a set of dusty crockery, then climbed into the chest. It smelt horrible but the woollens at the bottom made both a soft bed and a good place to stuff the portions of dried meat and fruit he pulled from inside his clothes. The cooks and scullery maids were kind to him even if the other pages were not.

"What are you doing?" Yazmine asked.

"I'm getting ready. Just in case."

"The indigo djinn said they will be here tomorrow."

Timak climbed out, pushed open one creaky, split shutter, and peered through the window. It was a six storey drop to the oak and bear fountains in the canal. "I won't go back to him."

◆ ◆ ◆

Three nights in a row Matisse came to her, bestowing his passionate attentions and, on that third, longed for visit, a green gem with a crimson heart.

"A symbol of how our Realms intertwine," he had said, holding its gold chain so it twirled in the cleft between her breasts. Kordahla had ignored the tease in his voice as he wrapped his body around hers. Crimson for Terlaan, green for Myklaan. Dare she hope it carried meaning? Dare she believe it a pledge when the mocking glint remained in his blue eyes?

On the fourth day, she was denied even a glimpse of his fair head. On the fifth, dressed, an embroidery in hand, Kordahla opened the doors to the balcony, inhaled the rich perfume of the frangipani, and gazed at the twinkling stars. Daesoa shone full, Dindarin new, and so the two were yet a minor moon removed from brushing their lips in their lover's kiss, as *he* had brushed hers. The memory of his touch evoked a tremor of desire. Her hand strayed to the watermelon gem around her neck.

Behind her the unlocked door clicked ajar. She turned, far too eager when not a quarter moon past she had checked, and checked again, the bolt was home. She suppressed her disappointment as Timak squeezed through the crack between door and jamb. He halted before he was full inside the chamber, too sensitive to her mood by far.

She stepped into the room she had left bright with lanterns. It was flecked with the wink of gold tiles, and the gilded ornamentation on dresser and drawer. She held out her hand. "It is late for you to be up."

He walked across the marble to her, and placed his fingers across her palm. "They are coming for us."

She had always known they would, though that did not soften the blow. She squeezed his hand. He was looking at her, expectant and sure. "Can the genie tell you who?"

He looked up and listened. "The Crown Prince of Terlaan, *him,* and a hooded man."

Kordahla closed her eyes and swayed. "What colour is the mahktashaan's crystal?" *Dear Vae'oenka*, she prayed, *let it not be Levi.*

"Bright blue," Timak answered.

She exhaled relief, opened her eyes and took a breath of false cheer. "How many hiding places have you found?"

"A few."

"Then you'd best stock them with supplies." He looked at her with those serious round eyes. She led him to the padded seat at her dresser, and patted the emerald and gold brocade. He perched beside her, not quite sitting. "Whatever happens, there's no reason for you to return to him."

"Are you going to hide too?"

"I'm afraid they would tear the castle apart looking for me. Then we would both be found."

"You could marry the heir."

A breeze gusted in. A lantern flickered and went out.

"Matisse? Perhaps," she said. The longing sent a painful twist through her heart. She fingered the gem, traced the circle of gold which enclosed it. He had never held her in comfort; never once said *I love you.* She forced a smile. "I don't think it will happen before they arrive. Now, run and do as I say." The task would help keep him from fretting.

The boy stayed where he was. She rose and went to close the balcony doors, to hide the nervous wring of her hands.

"We could go."

The yearning was unbearable. She whirled to face him, the layers of her skirt rippling in the draught. "Oh, Timak. There is nowhere left to go. You are safe. That will comfort me if I must leave, but we do not know it will come to that."

He threw himself at her, threw his arms around her. She held him back. "Hush. It is not so bad. He won't touch you again, I promise."

"I wished he would marry you," he said, rubbing tears from his eyes. "On the ship. I wanted him to stop so I wished he had someone else to torture."

She stroked his dark hair. "It's not your fault. None of this is your fault." She held him until his hiccups subsided. "Will you tell me who your parents are? If I must go, I will see they have a message you are safe. Then perhaps, I will have two friends."

"My father is a soldier under Captain Subhi at the third watchtower." The boy was proud of his father's position, that much was plain.

She drew a breath. A soldier would not be an easy man to reach in confidence. "Is your genie still here?" He nodded. "She'll steer you away from Ahkdul." With the help of the Vae, it might be true. The rose genie had always looked out for Timak before.

"If she's here, the djinn must be too." He pulled away. The unspoken suggestion in his eyes startled her.

"You think I should make a pact?"

"It won't be worse than living with *him*."

"I still don't know what I bargained with last time."

An icy prickle travelled along her arms. A tendril of smoke curled beneath the balcony doors. "Find some food to stockpile," she said, ushering him out. "I need to talk to Lady Jordayne." This child had suffered too much to sacrifice himself to the djinn.

"The boy is right."

Kordahla started. Legs and arms crossed, the indigo djinn was hanging upside down by the balcony doors.

"Or rather my rosy charge was. I am here," the djinn drawled. Golden streaks of lanternlight reflected in his skin.

A finger to her lips, Kordahla closed the door on Timak's glare.

"Want to deal?"

"Ask me again when my brother and Ahkdul get here," she said, picking up a sheer shawl to drape over her shoulders and midriff. The costumes Jordayne insisted on plying her with got briefer by the day.

The djinn slid onto his side and yawned, sending a whiff of fishy breath her way. She wrinkled her nose.

"Why draw out the inevitable?" the creature said, picking his.

"Why are you so sure I need your help?" She went to the dresser, took a mirror, and smoothed her hair. With luck the creature would not see how her hands shook.

"Are you certain you will not? The price will increase, you know. A single kiss now and your second born, and I shall ensure the heir is besotted. Later, who knows what I might ask for."

"I am not so free with my kisses." She sprayed her neck with a floral perfume.

"I am well aware of it, chaste Princess that you are in his company. Three nights, was it?"

The bottle slipped from her hand onto the dresser, spilling the contents. "You watched?" She could have died from mortification.

"I am djinn. I see all. Now, what do you think that liberty will cost when your brother and fiancé claim you? In comparison, do I demand that high a price?"

The freedom granted her in this land was a bliss porrin could not rival. Her capture was a thought she could not entertain. She bolted from the room, wondering if she had misjudged Rochelle. She would beg Matisse to permit her to stay. She would let him kiss her in public, lie with him every day if he turned Mariano and Ahkdul away.

She found Jordayne in a parlour, tending to lists of provisions.

"My dear, how nice to see you. But you have a purpose, I see." Jordayne said, raising an eyebrow. She dismissed the maids to a worktable in a corner of the room, and drew Kordahla to a settee, curling her legs up beside her. "Don't be shy. Tell me how I can help."

"If I want to attract someone's attention, how might I do it?"

"A male someone, I take it? And you have competition?"

Kordahla nodded, surprised by how perceptive this woman was.

"Then get rid of this for a start," Jordayne said pulling the shawl off her and tossing it over the back of the settee." She called a maid over to divest Kordahla of three of the underskirts. Kordahla looked down. The shadow of her legs was visible beneath the diminished layers of skirt. Days in the skimpy garments could not stop the blush rising in her cheeks.

"You really must learn to make use of those glorious curves of yours," Jordayne said, sliding most of her bracelets over her slender hand and piling them onto Kordahla's arm. Kordahla's fading blush deepened.

Jordayne stepped back to survey her handiwork. "I don't think any man will be able to resist you. But you don't want any man, do you?"

They settled back on the settee. "How do I make him take me seriously?" Kordahla asked.

Jordayne took her hand. "Have you thought about being the one to start the kissing? He might simply think he's honouring your wishes by keeping his distance."

Given the nights he had taken pleasure in her, Kordahla doubted it, but she held her tongue. "If I want to please him, I mean intimately."

That gave Jordayne pause. The older woman blinked. "Are you asking how?"

Kordahla shook her head. "What," she breathed.

"I see." Jordayne leaned over and whispered in her ear.

Kordahla's eyes grew wide. Her cheeks were aflame before Jordayne was finished. In the shock of the secret, she could think of no response. After a few seconds of silence, Jordayne brought her other hand onto Kordahla's. "My dear. Do be careful. Intimacies here do not bind so deep as they do in Terlaan."

"They are coming for me," she said.

Jordayne kissed her on the forehead. "Then go to him."

Heads turned as Kordahla glided the internal palace halls in a mist of sweet perfume. Had the lanterns not muted the calligraphy on the walls, had dusk not rendered the lines from histories extolling fair Myklaan illegible, she might have lost her nerve. Their truths, of the liberties women usurped in this land, and the atrocities realm had perpetrated on realm, were at worst confronting by day. By night, they condemned her wanton choice.

"Timak you must go," she said, stopping at a corner. The boy had followed her to Jordayne and back. His touching loyalty was a hindrance at this private moment. Her emotions were awhirl, akin to the spirals in the motifs framing the quotes. Her heart beat with irregular strength, like the heart of the pigeons which flew into the windows in Tarana. This giving of herself was not an easy thing. And yet, when he came to her, she was like a lump of clay, moulded under his desire into precious derral. Into, if she were not to discard her upbringing, dishonour.

Timak slipped his hand into hers. "You need me to draw the guards away.

Looking down at him, she squeezed his hand. In truth, the guards standing at distant intervals along the halls had been worrying her, and not because they might choose to bar her from their Lord's room. Rumours were flying around the palace of a Princess oft in the Lord's company, and a djinn that had invaded her room at night. *Enjoy them*, Jordayne had said. *There is nothing so delicious as a scandal.*

"I want to help you," Timak said. "I want you to stay here with me."

She felt a rush of affection as she touched his cheek. "I adore little brothers."

His shy smile was a blessing. It brought a sad, sweet smile to her own lips.

"I can help." He stepped away.

She let him turn the corner.

"She has to." She heard him murmur. "There's no other way for her to stay."

The genie, it seemed, did not approve. She heard the soft tap of his feet, then the quiet urgency of his voice. "The djinn is scaring the princess. She's crying."

She slipped behind a pillar, waiting until the guard's quick steps had retreated beyond detection. Taking a deep breath, she went to Matisse's door and gave a timid knock. His voice did not ring out to bid her enter. Such a welcome would have played too easy. Trembling inside, she lifted a hand to try the door. It was bolted.

"Al-low me," the echo of a hated voice drawled.

The lanterns dimmed. The door swung open. Reason begged her to walk away. *Duplicity and deception*: aid from the djinn was a curse under any guise.

They were coming for her. He had come to her. And so she walked inside. The outer chamber was furnished with oak furniture, fashioned in a style that evoked his masculine strength. She coasted to the door on the right. Low voices drifted out. A giggle. The sounds of rustling sheets.

Blood whooshed in her ears. *Just walk away.*

Her feet did not obey.

They were coming for her.

A light touch was all it took for the inner door to creak wide, to leak the sweaty musk and jasmine from inside.

He had exploited her.

They were naked atop the sheets. Rochelle sat astride him, her shameless caresses enticing his arousal. His eager gropes sent shivers of delight down his mistress's spine. Their wicked conversation continued, as though their intimacy were nothing more than diverting play. The whoosh in her ears became a roar. The few paces it had taken to cross the outer room had revealed the catastrophic depth of her folly. She was filthy, degraded, dishonoured. *A conquest*, that was all she had been. His eyes drifted, alighted on her. The amusement in them snuffed out.

Kordahla fled the room, tears streaming down her cheeks. Matisse called her name. Rochelle giggled a few words. He laughed out loud.

Chapter Forty-nine

THE GUARDS CAME FOR her before the luncheon hour, a formal escort into the throne room through a side door. Shah Ordosteen sat upon his gilded throne, crooked under the burden of his gravity and his crown. He blinked when he saw her, as though she were some apparition. How peculiar she felt like one; both leaden and light, as though she must glide right through these walls before she might wake from this devastating betrayal. Her eyes swept over the airy room, over the tiered balconies garlanded with intricate stone carvings rising over the grand arches. Was *he* observing from among them, amused by how easily she had capitulated to his desires? Bored by her company now she had?

Ordosteen straightened. “Your brother and fiancé have arrived.”

Fiancé. That single word bespoke her fate. She turned her stone face fully toward him. He cleared his throat, could not meet her eye.

“They are demanding to see you. Demanding Myklaan turn you over or declare war.”

She nodded slowly, absently. There was no place for a runaway princess here. “You have chosen to meet their demands,” she said, making it easy for him. She harboured no recrimination. Her shame was too great to look the man who had taken the most precious gift she had to give in the eye. Whatever Shah Ordosteen decided, she could not stay here.

“Our realm is not in a position to shelter you. I am sorry, my dear.”

“I hope you will be happy together,” she said, and meant it. No one deserved to feel this filthy despair, this emptiness that was keener for having thought she loved.

Embarrassed, Ordosteen cleared his throat. His age had never been more apparent in the lines on his brow. He held out her veil, her mother's veil, the green one with the golden threads. "I believe this is yours. Take it. It may offer a morsel of comfort."

She glided to him, too light to walk, too heavy to fly. The veil looked odd, draped over her hand, a relic from another age. "Was he indigo?" she asked. He owed her that much.

His answer was strained. "Yes. And you will never speak of it."

A spark of surprise took hold in her, not for the admission but for the burden he shouldered. After the numbness of the night, the emotion was a jolt, and she reacted around the eyes.

Sleep had been a long time coming. When it had finally carried her away, it was deep and dreamless. She had woken unrested, her sense of betrayal unmitigated. In her nightgown, she had shifted about the room, restless, sullen, and sick, refusing to allow doors or shutters to be thrown open to the day. She had stared at the visage of the gambolling figures painted on bedhead, wardrobe and dresser, counted the small gold tiles between the cream ones, and found patterns in the green marble on the floor. It was hours before she had found the wits to request a demure dress, a servants' full length shalvar kameez if need be.

"I will receive no visitors," she had told her handmaid, Nina, as the girl laid the garment on the bed. "No one at all. Leave me now."

"Yes, Your Highness," the girl had said with a graceful curtsey, yet allowing Timak to slip beneath her arm as she opened the door.

The sensitive child had hidden under the bed, remaining silent and still until she, seated at her dresser and lost in contemplation of her folly, forgot he was there. A hundred times she must have relived Matisse's every contrived touch, heard Rochelle's voice. *I can guess what this new bargain of yours might involve.* So, when the commotion from the gardens announced her brother's arrival, Ordosteen's decision was clear to her, perhaps even before it was clear to him. Without thinking, she dressed herself, tucked the watermelon gem between her breasts, and awaited her fate.

It was not until she laid a hand on the door to admit the guards that Timak emerged, clinging to the bedpost, so fragile and hurt.

"You must hide. Don't come out until you are sure he has gone," she had said. His silent tears had almost been her undoing, but she had closed the door before he could run to her.

Walking to meet the Shah, down the halls scribed with profound poems of love, and of loss, her armed escort marching before her and behind, she had wondered what cruel game the djinn played. Two pacts made, two lives intertwined, only one which could discover joy. The folly was hers. The djinn had their own agenda. She had known that from the start.

"You will never speak of it," Shah Ordosteen said.

Soon, so soon, her lips would seal forever.

Kordahla draped her mother's veil over her hair, careful to cover every strand, and wound the ends along her bare arms. Nina, a city satrap's younger daughter at ease with the fashion of this land, had not heeded her wishes. The short-sleeved choli, though it covered her midriff, was less than modest. Even with the veil wrapped around her body, it was obvious the bodice did not meet the skirt. Another transgression for Ahkdul to punish.

"I am ready. But you will refrain from calling Ahkdul my fiancé. I do not regard him as such."

"Kordahla..."

Her eyes were away from him again, her head high. She had felt a spark of surprise but that fledgling emotion had been unable to take flight. There was refuge in feeling nothing because feeling something would tear her apart from the inside out.

"My dear," he tried again. "Both Jordayne and Matisse speak highly of you. Under different circumstances, Myklaan might have welcomed you with open arms. If there is anything I can do to make this easier for you..."

Her eyes slid to his of their own volition. How could she blame him when she had suffered the cruel manipulation of the indigo djinn herself? "You have been generous beyond expectation, but I dare to request a favour. Do with me as you will, but look after the boy."

Ordosteen's eyes softened. "I am not a barbarian. Lord Ahkdul has no claim to him save the value of the coin he paid. The boy will be safe. On that I give you my word."

It was a comfort, if not a hope, the Vae see that it be done. Their images sparkled on the dome, observing all, but not presiding. Never that.

"I would see my brother now."

"Yes, of course." The shah of Myklaan gestured to the guards, who marched down the length of the hall. She turned as they opened the tall arched doors dividing the throne room from the *iwan*. Mariano and Ahkdul stood framed for a moment, then strode the length of the room. The doves splashing in the canals outside cooed to them, but even all these paces away the hunch of the Verdaani Lord's shoulders, the prominence of his brow, reminded her of the brute that he was. Even so far away, she could tell both men stared in silent rage. There was nothing of this liberal realm about them: nothing of a fountain's merriment in their step; nothing of evening's lassitude in their pose. Nothing. And Mariano, emissary in a foreign court, had forgone the open vest and kamarband he favoured for Terlaani turban, baggy shalvar, and long kurta, burgundy to represent the Crown.

They stopped at the bottom of the dais and accorded Ordosteen a tense bow.

Ordosteen cleared his throat. The formal greetings, the false welcome stretched interminable, though the stilted words did not last a warbler's entire song. And then it came.

"Prince Mariano, Lord Ahkdul, I deliver Princess Kordahla into your care. She has been treated well. Neither Terlaan nor Verdaan can take issue with our hospitality or our cooperation."

"Your compliance in the matter of the Princess is duly noted," Mariano said. His eyes locked on her. They held nothing of their usual affection. "But there is another matter. She carried with her two valuable items from our Realm. Terlaan demands their return."

"The Princess did not bestow any gifts upon members of this household," Ordosteen said. "I am given to understand from my captain that she arrived at our border with nothing. If she brought items with her, they remain in her possession."

Mariano cast cold eyes over her. "Minoria, are they on her person?"

Only then did she notice the mahktashaan behind her brother. Were it not for the cerulean crystal around his neck, she would not have identified him. What betrayal had he suffered to lose the calm confidence that distinguished him in an instant from the horde of the hated soldier-magicians.

Clutching his crystal, Arun spoke a magic word. "The crystal is not in this room," he said.

Mariano turned to Ordosteen. "We request permission to search the palace."

"The mage guild is a likely to have appropriated them," Arun said to Mariano. Her brother added it to his request.

"My permission is withheld." Ordosteen said. "You may search Princess Kordahla's room, if you wish. Beyond that, the palace is denied you."

Mariano would not have expected another answer, bearing the tidings he did, but neither would he capitulate with so valuable an item at stake. Even a closeted Terlaani princess understood this. "The return of these item is not negotiable," her brother said, predictable, unbendable. "We leave here with them, or consider your intentions hostile."

The wretched situation was degenerating into naked threat. It had never been her intention to start a war. "I lost the crystals," Kordahla said. "In the scums." Let Myklaan keep them. Vae'oeldin, let the mages even find a way to employ them. If they saved another Ilyam the loss of his father, prevented even one citizen succumbing to addiction, let the Myklaani have them. Vae'oenka knew this realm had been kind to her for a time.

"It seems the matter is settled," Ordosteen said.

Far from it. Even a closeted princess denied access to her father's counsel could guess at that. Those crystals were sacred to Terlaan. They were the secret to the realm's magical and military prowess. Her word was worthless. The Crown Prince and Minoria knew it. For now, Mariano chose to remain silent, flicking his eyes across her in contemptuous dismissal.

"I have acted in good faith." Ordosteen rose, though he remained upon the dais. "To further demonstrate our goodwill, I relinquish three of our citizens to you, prisoners who sought to despoil the princess."

Both Mariano and Ahkdul snapped around to face him at that.

Mariano's face was the colour of a beet. Ahkdul was turning back to her, a look of such loathing on him that she knew she would pay for this too.

"How can you be sure she was not sullied?" the brute asked. His fingers formed claws by his side as though he longed to throttle her for enticing men to violate her.

Ordosteen held up a forestalling hand. "They were prevented from their crime by a captain, but they ravaged a young girl the princess travelled with. They are yours to deal with as you see fit."

"In Terlaan, they would pay with their lives."

"As you see fit," Ordosteen reiterated, walking down the steps. "As an indication of our goodwill."

"We wish first to question the princess," Mariano said, leaving no doubt as to her status.

"You may use her chamber. The guards will escort you," Ordosteen replied. He was peering at her, a worried frown on her face.

"She travelled with my page," Ahkdul said. "I have use for him."

Ordosteen's eyes grew defiant. "Princess Kordahla arrived with Akerin guides, a man and a girl."

Ahkdul drew his bushy brows together. When it was clear he would make no challenge, Ordosteen turned to her with an unwelcome look of pity. Between them, these men had robbed her of every decision. They had treated her as a bargaining tool. There was but one choice left to her, and she intended to take it because, by the Vae, she would not allow them to turn her into that brute of a man's trophy wife. Ordosteen's pity would only stand in her way. She stepped away from it to find Arun blocking her way. Prisoners did not take the lead.

No matter. It was almost over.

Matisse pounded on the side door to the court.

Jordayne sighed. "You may as well give up. It is clear our uncle seeks neither our opinion nor our advice."

Two guards stepped forward as Matisse raised his fist again, crossing their raised swords in front of the door. "No one is to be admitted," one said.

"I command you to stand aside."

"His Majesty's orders," the guard amended, as if it had not occurred to them Ordosteen was the only personage with the authority to countermand the heir.

Matisse turned to her. The strain on his face was a novel sight. Jordayne would wager their stunning Terlaani guest had made more of an impression than he cared to admit. "Did Ordosteen intimate what he was going to do?"

"I should think that rather obvious," she replied. She intended to give their neglectful uncle an earful for admitting highborn guests into the court without the chance for refreshment. It was highly irregular, and of course a deliberate plan to exclude her from negotiations.

"Who summoned me?" Drucilamere asked. The Master Magus was standing hands on hips, contemplating the wooden door. "Was it you or the Shah?"

"The three of us were of one mind," she replied. "Shah Wilshem saw fit to send a mahktashaan with Crown Prince Mariano. The real question is how Ordosteen managed to orchestrate our exclusion from the meeting. I was at the hospice this morning when I received word the emissaries had arrived." She turned to her brother. "Where were you?"

Matisse strode away without answering. She would have to seek Kordahla out and ask, though the girl would need a delicate touch to divulge that titillating titbit.

"Where are you going?" she called after him. If he was ever to make the shah their dear uncle believed he could be, he was going to have to put the realm above his liaisons. Although last night's, if it had occurred, was one of which she wholeheartedly approved.

"The main entrance. At some point, they will need to leave."

True, though at that point events would be outside their influence. She touched Druce lightly on the arm to indicate they should follow. The retreating backs of their Terlaani guests as they moved into the palace proper was not what she had hoped to see. Sparing a scathing remark for the guards who blocked their access to Kordahla, she swept across the front of the palace, through the irritating brightness of the left *pistaq*, beneath the oak-and-bear mosaic of the *iwan*, and into the now open court. Ordosteen, sitting crooked on his throne, was staring at the marble floor. His posture did rather spoil the care he had taken with his regal coat.

"I take it you were expecting us," she said, as the others piled in.

"You turned her over," Matisse accused, pointing his sword at Ordosteen's heart. The guards did not wait for orders to draw theirs, nor did Matisse acknowledge the threat. His face puce, Ordosteen rose.

"Stop this nonsense," Jordayne said, moving to embrace her uncle. For his ears alone, she said, "I hope whatever prize the djinn offered was worth the guilt."

Grabbing her arms, Ordosteen growled, "What do you know of it?"

She fought hard to bury her surprise and her hurt. "Unhand me. I will not stand for this."

"You forget who is Shah."

"Release her, Uncle. Your quarrel is with me."

Ordosteen strode down the court, stopping within reach of the sword. "Lower it before I find you guilty of treason."

"I will not till you explain your actions."

"Oh do grow up, both of you. Men are such boys when it comes to women."

Matisse stepped forward. The point of his sword pressed into Ordosteen's kurta. In a blur of reaction, the guards were upon him. He slashed left and right, disarmed one then another, parried and thrust. And their guilty, lovesick Uncle just stood there, not even watching.

"Lord Matisse, you forget yourself," Drucilamere said, stepping in and eliciting a curse from Matisse as he jerked an upswing short to avoid cutting the mage. He brought the point of the sword down.

"You barter your life, mage. And I am not the one who forgets my duty."

"This helps no one. *You* cannot slake your lust from the dungeon, and *you*," Jordayne said, turning to Ordosteen, "cannot hope to govern this realm without the assistance of an heir."

Matisse threw Ordosteen a look of disgust, then belted his sword.

"That's better, brother dear. Now why the sudden genuine interest in the Princess? I was sure she was merely the prospect of a good bedding before today."

"Did you lie with her?" Drucilamere asked, urgent.

Matisse stared across the court at the double doors Kordahla had exited.

"Did you bed her?"

"She intended to give herself to you last night. I hope she experienced one night in the arms of someone who could pleasure her," Jordayne said.

Ordosteen gurgled. A storm cloud had settled about him. The decision to hand Kordahla over to her family sat ill, it seemed, with her dear, honourable uncle, who was not so honourable after all. "Rochelle was not in her room last night."

"Rochelle was entertaining me."

"My poor Princess. I was counting on you seducing her, Matisse. You have rather let me down. A man should never doom a girl to a life of loveless beddings without first educating her as to how delightful the intimacy she fears can be." Ordosteen, she decided, was a pig if he could hand a woman over to the likes of Ahkdul. And that went double for the Crown Prince of Terlaan.

Matisse flushed. How interesting. She would not have thought mere words could ever embarrass her womanising brother. His guilt did make her reconsider. "Oh?" she said. "Have I misjudged the pair of you?"

"I ask you yet again. Did you lie with the Princess?"

"Enough, Drucilamere. It is not your place," Matisse said.

"He did," she said. "I can see it in his face."

Drucilamere's hands formed fists by his side. "You callous boil on the butt of a hairy djinn. They will put her to the sword if they find out."

"She has only to keep her mouth quiet," Jordayne said.

"Which will buy her time only until Lord Ahkdul deigns to take her to his bed. What do you imagine his justice will be like then?"

The thought shocked them all to silence. Ordosteen was looking pale.

Drucilamere turned on the Shah. "Do you intend to return the crystals?"

"Myklaan has no crystals."

"She gifted them to you in exchange for protection."

"Everywhere we turn, portents of a grim future bear down upon us. If such a talisman were in Myklaan I would not relinquish it."

"Then you do nothing to avert a war. Why? Why did you surrender her when it brings you no gain?"

Poor Drucilamere. He was not in possession of all the facts. Her fault. No one had taken the time to inform him of the djinn plaguing the Shah these forty years. Or the night-time visit she had heard the Princess received.

"It is not your place to question my decisions. It is done," Ordosteen said. He rounded on Matisse. "Though I expected better of you. Was this any way to treat a guest?"

"I did not think the girl would seek me out. By the Vae, I thought she might enjoy the respite."

"You mean she caught you cheating on her?" Jordayne asked. The conversation was getting more intriguing by the minute.

"My door was locked. I swear. I don't know how she entered."

That did not require much effort of thought. "Felt many still winds lately?"

Ordosteen blanched to a peculiar translucence. "She did not object to my decision," he said, his voice tremulous. "She did not object," he shouted, regaining colour too fast. It did sound like he was trying to convince himself. The problem was Jordayne suspected he was reasoning in much the same way she was. Smarting from a rejection and faced with a life of abuse, the foolish, naive girl was likely to do something stupid. The Vae knew *she* would.

"They are still in the palace grounds. It is not too late to change your mind. Or regain your honour," Jordayne said.

"I will not sacrifice the good of Myklaan for a single Terlaani girl."

"A Terlaani princess, Uncle. Who could help us acquire more of those crystals you are enamoured of if the right union were made." She shot Matisse a pointed look.

Ordosteen mounted the dais and sat on his throne with the deliberate authority of a ruler about to make a binding decree. "Princess Kordahla claims she lost the crystals in the scums. Her brother will have to accept that. I command you all to make no mention of her gift."

"There was a mahktashaan with them," Drucilamere said. The vein at his temple was throbbing with the strain of keeping his anger in check.

"There was," Ordosteen said, rising, "though I fail to see..."

"Slow on the uptake, today, aren't we?" she couldn't help saying. Her disgust was growing by the second.

"The Crown's decision is sound. Anyone who opposes it is guilty of treason."

Well it wouldn't be the first time. "Where are they?" she asked, feigning a languid disinterest. "The least we can do is bid the princess goodbye."

"They have taken her to her room. After that, they go to the dungeons. With my blessing. With my blessing, do you hear?" Ordosteen looked at them each in turn, daring them to oppose his will before he stormed from the room.

Jordayne sighed. "Come along, Matisse. I doubt there is a way to put this to rights, but you will at least try. I might need you too, darling."

"How nice, Jordayne. You just might need me to fix another of your messes."

"Don't take that tone with me. This is hardly my mess."

"Oh no? Don't tell me you didn't encourage her. Don't tell me you didn't flaunt your sexuality in her face."

"As I recall, you were a rather willing participant."

Matisse strode from the room, his sword in his hand. At that precise instant, they both stopped arguing. With a knowing look at each other, they hurried after him.

Chapter Fifty

THE MAHKTASHAAN WITH THE saffron crystal, whose name Vinsant still did not know, unlocked his chains, led him by the same rocky route they had walked each morning since he arrived, and delivered him to Mahktashaan Fenz. The silent minekeeper pointed to a practice sword among the weapons and armour stored around the sides of the small cavern. Vinsant picked it up, warmed up with a few swings, and stepped over the edge of the training ring which had been scraped into the levelled floor. Minekeeper Fenz launched straight into a bruising attack before somehow managing to instruct Vinsant in a new manoeuvre without uttering a single word. The malicious man was deliberating aiming for his chaffed wrists and sore leg. Bitter experience over the last three days had taught Vinsant the sooner he shut up and mastered the strokes, the sooner he could devour the tasteless slop they served him for breakfast. The only saving grace of the meals in this dismal, dusty pit lay in the quantity of food at each, but with the forced labour he was bound to endure he suffered a constant gnawing in his stomach.

The swordplay over, he followed Saffron Crystal through more rough-hewn tunnels to the rough crystal-lit chamber Levi used to instruct him. Not that he needed an escort. The chambers were labelled in much the same way as the lair under the palace. This chamber was not much different from the one he practiced swordplay in, really, except here the room was bare.

"All praise to Mahktos. All honour to you, Majoria," Vinsant intoned with a bow before his magic lesson began. This was by far the most enjoyable part of the day, even if Levi had reverted to his no question approach. In fact, the Majoria had even stopped giving lectures. The only words that came out of his mouth were those necessary to avert calamity as Vinsant messed up one magic feat or the other. It made for a lonely life. His muscles ached from his labours. His hands were becoming calloused. And he smelt. Three days without a bath in the grime of the stinking dungeon was inhuman.

Today's lessons involved opening locks. Easy since he had already stumbled on success in the dungeons back home. He mastered the trick in minutes, spent many more perfecting magicks from previous days and sighed as Levi pointed at the exit. He had tried to mess up the magic yesterday, just so he would not be forced to the mines and the tedious, backbreaking digging so soon. Summoning water just outside the bowl or in such minute quantities it simply seeped into the ground was not difficult to arrange even while convincing Levi he was concentrating. His brilliant plan had failed. When his allotted time was up, Levi had sent him on anyway.

So he followed Saffron Crystal, his supervisor for the remainder of the day, down and along narrow caves, out of the area where the mahktashaan conducted their daily business to the excavation tunnels. Resigned to another day of torture, he held out his wrists for the shackles that prevented the use of magic to aid in the gruelling task, picked up his pick and set to striking the craggy rock in the hope of finding a buried crystal. At least he had this evening's swordplay and magic lesson to look forward to before they chained him to the wall in his barred cell for the night. Well, for one hour of it, anyway. Which was almost more than he could bear.

Thank Mahktos there were only three and a half more days to serve. Vinsant was sure he could last that long, and then he would treat himself to a feast, a bath and a long earned rest, whatever Levi tried to demand. He was still a prince after all.

"I've never met anyone who enjoyed being abused so much."

In his surprise at hearing someone strike up a conversation, Vinsant almost drove the pick into his foot. He looked around. Saffron Crystal had retreated down the tunnel to consult with another mahktashaan. There was no one else in sight. That sent a prickle of warning down his spine because the voice had been strangely familiar. Worse, goosebumps were erupting over his arms.

"You really are a speck of dirt on the behind of a flea," the indigo djinn said, emerging from the rock. He pointed at Vinsant's shackles and they fell off his wrist.

"Oh no," Vinsant said, desperately trying to fasten them back on because an extension of his punishment was the last thing he needed. Just his luck they would not lock. "Put them back."

"Don't you want to see what predicament your delicious sister faces? Is all your concern for her an act?"

Vinsant froze. It was a goad and he knew it, but he was suffering this humiliation for Kordahla.

"It only takes a small amount of water."

What harm could there be? The mahktashaan were moving further away. *Acquos*, Vinsant thought, because Levi had taught him while spoken words helped focus the magic, a good mahktashaan would eventually learn to think them. He hadn't succeeded at it yet but the last thing he needed was Saffron Crystal investigating the sound of his voice. Well, how was that? A sliver of rock in the wall he was hacking turned damp. *Acquos. Acquos.* A shallow pool trickled into the shallow depression he was concentrating on. Heart beating fast, he looked in. Vermillion eyes blazing, the djinn pointed a finger at the pool and blew. Vinsant gagged on his fishy breath. The breath misted the surface of the water, then evaporated. Kordahla's face appeared on the water. Her left eye was swollen, her cheek inflamed. Even as he watched, her head jerked as a punch connected with her face.

"No!" Vinsant said, gripping a couple of crags.

"Your precious sister is no longer pure. She has given herself to a man like a common whore. The swine is going to kill her."

"Stop him." The djinn floated to the ceiling. Lying on his stomach he looked down at the image in the pool. "Stop him," Vinsant pleaded.

The djinn sighed and held out a hand. Vinsant backed away.

"She thinks you want to be a mahktashaan to protect her. What good will quartz or crystal be if she is dead?"

"You're lying."

The djinn yawned and rolled onto this back. "Cunning, yes. Duplicitous, certainly. Devious, without a doubt. But where is it written djinn lie?"

"Now you're splitting hairs."

"So be it." The creature's lower body dissolved into indigo smoke.

Vinsant hesitated. He glanced at the pool. Kordahla's face was a mess. "Take something else. Anything else. They'll kill me if I lose this quartz." His voice was barely above a whisper.

"Oh very well. I'll throw your puny, worthless life into the bargain. Now give me the quartz."

"My life?" Vinsant asked, not entirely convinced the djinn could do that. His life belonged to Mahktos and Mahktos was a god. God trumped djinn any day. In the pool, Kordahla was weeping like the end of her life was near. It shamed him. Scared him.

"Wait!" Vinsant cried, yanking the crimson quartz off his neck. He wasn't supposed to be crying, but he could never live with himself if Kordahla died. Being a mahktashaan would mean nothing. The djinn began solidifying once more. Vinsant closed his eyes. *Forgive me, Mahktos.* Trembling, he held out the quartz.

"Apprentice, no!" Fenz cried, racing towards him, Saffron Crystal at his heels.

❖ ❖ ❖

As soon as they entered her chamber, Kordahla dropped to her knees. She stared straight ahead, through the sunlit balcony the maids must have opened, to the lazy cascade of fiery lantana over the terraces in the hanging garden. She would not empower these men by looking up.

"My lords, I have dishonoured your families. I have given myself to another man. I submit to your justice. I submit to your sword."

Ahkdul's reaction came quick as a djinn. He punched her in the face. "Is it true, whore?" he demanded.

Her eye watering, she yet found the dignity to raise her face, refusing to either look at him or answer.

"Is it true?" he repeated, punching her again.

This time she cried out as a ring sliced open the skin under her puffy eye. Still she gathered the courage to bring her head up. "Blood honour demands only my life. Mete out your justice, and let it be swift."

Ahkdul grabbed her by the arms and shook her until she thought the teeth would rattle out of her gums. "Who? Who-did-you-bed, you-despicable-slut?"

"Enough," Mariano said, pushing the swine off her, though he looked like he might hit her himself. The sympathy she had come to trust was gone from his eyes. That betrayal melted through her frozen heart. Weeping, she sank down, her poise gone.

"IS IT TRUE?" Ahkdul roared.

Her sobs were pure misery against a warbler's joyous trill.

He slapped her. "It is a ruse," he said, rounding on Mariano. "She seeks to avoid a marriage. She has already proven the depths to which she will fall to get her way."

"That can be ascertained," Mariano said. "I will demand a physic."

"No man may touch her if she is indeed a virgin. That act will soil her in itself."

"Minoria," Mariano commanded.

Hooded and hunched, Arun came forward.

She shook her head. "I will not suffer his touch. I confess."

"You have forfeited your integrity. We have a right to the truth." Mariano turned to Ahkdul. "Will you accept the pronouncement of the mahktashaan?"

"Who is this one sworn to?" Ahkdul asked.

"To the Crown, and so to my father before me."

"Yes. Let him search her."

So she must suffer another indignity. Arun reached for her. The jerk of her head was involuntary. She flicked her eyes away, refusing to look at him, another violator of her person.

"This will not hurt, Princess," he reassured, too gentle in this violent mess. His bare hands went to her temples. His mind nudged the edges of her own, and his voice sounded inside her head.

Let me help you, Kordahla.

She closed her mind to it, threw up a blank wall. Vae'oenka forgive her, for she did not have the strength to fend him off. It was a small blessing his search was more reminiscent of the Master Magus's touch than the brute slap Levi had planted upon her. For that she was grateful. She offered the least embarrassing memories of her lovemaking freely, willing this nightmare to end. Arun skipped past her offering, on and down through the corridors, and into the recesses of her mind. Heart pounding, she waited for the verdict that would end her life.

"She is pure," Arun said, the worst betrayal of all.

"Why are you lying?" she asked. She looked into his hood to his shadowed, cerulean eyes. Sank beneath their pity further into despair.

He made no reply.

"There remains the matter of her flight," Mariano said to Ahkdul. "Do you wish to renounce her?"

Ahkdul narrowed his calculating eyes. "I do not. She will be my wife, and her punishment shall be mine to mete out."

And when he forced her to his bed? When he discovered the lie perpetrated on him? What would become of her then?

"Your Highness, she is lying about more than her chastity," Arun said. How could she have once thought him a friend?

Mariano's eyes narrowed. At that moment, he reminded her of Ahkdul. "Speak," he commanded.

"The crystal and quartz are in Myklaan."

Now her brother slapped her. His lips pursed as he attempted to reign in his temper. She dropped her head. No quarter, no compassion from any man.

"And my page?" Ahkdul asked. His tongue ran over his fat lips. He had thrown back the cover on her bed, as if searching for evidence of her dishonour.

"Perished in the scums," Arun said.

"Bring her," Mariano said to Arun, drawing his sword.

He opened the door. Seeing him armed, the four guards outside drew their weapons.

"You will take us to the dungeons," Mariano said. "Then I demand another audience with the Shah."

Arun lifted her to her feet. Stiff and numb, she tried to pull away. Would she could take refuge in the merry court and country scenes painted on bed and dresser.

Hush, came the thought within her mind.

Why did you betray me? she shot back, a hysterical scream, that belied her impassive exterior.

She sensed surprise, then a grief, deep, but nowhere near as bottomless as her own. He sent a burst of calm her way. She fought it tooth and nail, though to look at her vacant eyes Mariano and Ahkdul would never know.

The intrusion in her mind eased. *At least let me take your pain*, Arun said.

She made no reply. Refused to look at him, even. How could she have known it would not stop him dampening the sting in her face? A small mercy that gave her the courage to frame the one question that mattered. *How is Vinsant?*

His surprise this time was mild, but still it was there. He chose to speak to her, a low murmur that covered his words from the others. "Prince Vinsant is being punished for aiding you, but it is nothing that will not strengthen him on his path to becoming the powerful mahktashaan he dreams of being."

Arun dropped his hands. They had stayed at her temple while he spoke, stroking her errant hairs back. She put a finger on the watermelon gem tucked into her choli, gave it a fleeting press. Let it serve as a constant reminder of her folly.

The wary guards flanked them as they walked vaulted halls etched with lauded lines from the histories, of betrayal, and of treason. She was careful to avoid contact with anyone, and with Arun most of all. His justice, not his pity, was what she craved.

They passed into the fragrant gardens, into the tingling caress of the sun, and on to a courtyard with walls stretching up to the second terrace, ivy clinging to one wall, and a calligraphy of prayers leaping from another. Their guards spoke to comrades at the entrance to the dungeon, and the two descended into the gloom. In this regard Ordosteen was to remain true to his word. But that was not fair. He had never promised her she might remain in this wonderful, treacherous realm.

She readily sank to her knees when Mariano pushed her down. His grip on her shoulders as they awaited the prisoners was iron. The brutes emerged chained hand and foot, growling about a trial. It was as well they balked when they saw the three armed men, and her kneeling before them, else it may not have been the guards forcing them to their knees, the one with the red beard, the one who yet had a bandage across his shoulder, and the shaggy third. She fought down the bitter taste of bile. Even in her dishonour Mariano sought justice for her. And yet this witnessing served only to compound her feeling of filth.

"Which one despoiled your companion?" Mariano asked.

"He is dead," she answered, not caring about the fate of these remorseless men, "but the last one tried to hurt...another," she said, catching herself at the last moment. If Ahkdul's preoccupation with her honour had deflected his attention from Timak, she would bite her tongue off before she diverted it back.

Mariano pulled the shaggy man's head back by the hair. "What manner of man are you?"

"What is this?" the man asked, eyes bulging with fear. "We have had no trial."

"Terlaani justice," Mariano said, releasing him. He swung his sword. The man's head rolled off his shoulders and bounced on the floor. Blood splattered over his companions, and across her face. The stench of his bowels spread across the stone of the courtyard. The other two were hollering now.

Ahkdul squatted beside her, gripped her chin in his hand, and put his lips to her good cheek. "Which one tried to divest you of your honour?"

"The bearded one," she said, looking through a dangling noose near the far wall. She felt nothing. Thought nothing, even when a peculiar apricot ball of light flitted through the loop.

Ahkdul walked around the prisoner. The man was a coward to close his eyes. His blindness served neither to still his trembles nor stave off his death. Ahkdul raised his sword and drove it into his stomach. The man's eyes popped open in surprise. "Verdaani justice," Ahkdul said as the brute keeled over, hands clutching at the wound. "A quick death is too good for the likes of you." He jerked the sword free and turned to her, standing close so that her breath spread over his middle. "For all I know, their crude attentions may have awakened sinful lust in the Princess."

"Prin-ce-ss-ss," the dying man gurgled.

The bandaged man was shaking his head. "Condemn me, but you've no honour to leave a man to die like that."

"Arun," Mariano said.

The Minoria bowed his head and executed the final prisoner with a clean strike of the sword. Glancing at her, he raised his sword over the dying man. Once, his compassion would have endeared him to her; now, it failed to rouse the glimmer of an emotion.

"Hold," Ahkdul commanded. "He deserves no mercy."

"Your Highness," Arun appealed.

"His death is Lord Ahkdul's to determine." Mariano replied. He wiped his sword upon the dead man's kurta before sheathing it.

"What occurred here?" a voice demanded from the archway.

Now there was a stirring, the echo of a deep hurt. Before she could guard against it, it pulled her face around to Matisse, fair as Mariano was dark.

"Oh, my dear," Jordayne said, hurrying out from behind him, hurrying to her, embracing her. "What have they done to you?"

Matisse was with her a moment later, nudging his sister aside so he could wipe the blood from her cheek with his thumb. He pulled her up, another man she could not face, would not look in the eye. Leaving her to Jordayne, he placed a hand on the hilt of his sword. His eyes travelled to each of her captors. "Which of you is responsible for this?"

You, her insides screamed at him, though she knew it was unjust. *You are responsible for this.* Her hand gripped at her bodice, closing tight around the watermelon gem.

"Shah Ordosteen sanctioned these executions," Mariano said, gripping the pommel of his sword.

"Which of you would hit a woman?" Matisse's stance was ready for the attack.

There was a moment of silence, accentuated by the scrape of the dying man's body on the paving as he dragged himself from the centre of the courtyard. Along the far wall, the apricot ball of light wove through the ivy, stalking his progress, a strange magic unnoticed or ignored by all save she.

"It was you." Ahkdul sneered, too controlled in his aggression. He raised his weapon and ran at Matisse. "You filthy, dishonouring scumsucker."

The speed with which Matisse drew his sword belied belief, but Mariano had his own sword in hand a mere moment later. Calm, Kordahla stepped away from Jordayne's encircling arm; stepped between the men, waiting for one of the three blades to pierce her, to bring back the pain that had deserted her. They came fast, and aimed true.

"*Retracktos,*" came Arun's command. The swords sailed out of their wielder's hands, into the azure where their tips touched above her head before they arced over to twang point down in the narrow gap between the pavers at the edges of the courtyard. The stunned men stared at her, standing within reach. Then Ahkdul shoved her out his way.

"You forced her to consider debasing herself," the swine accused.

She suffered Jordayne to herd her to the prayer wall as Ahkdul swung a punch. Was she the more wanton for being glad Matisse dodged it? Was her soul lost for hoping Matisse's fist connected with Ahkdul's chin?

"*Imbolil,*" Drucilamere said, holding out a hand, fingers spread wide. Ahkdul froze. The mage would not have thought ill of her, when he worked such magic on the Verdaani lord. But it was Lord Matisse he sought to protect, and the strain on his face mirrored that on the swine's as Ahkdul fought to break free of the spell. Sweat dripped from Drucilamere's brow, and the vein in his forehead throbbed. Would that Matisse consider them all and walk away instead of pull the corner of his lip into a twisted smile and pummel Ahkdul in the stomach. Ahkdul,

Lord Swine, honoured guest of her father's realm. Even a sheltered princess understood the Minoria was honour bound to raise a hand, to point a finger at the Myklaani heir. Not so bound he need prevent Matisse landing a hit on Ahkdul's jaw.

"*Imbolil,*" Arun said as Matisse let fly with a third punch. His crystal glowed. Matisse stiffened mid swing.

"Can he hear me?" Mariano asked, walking around the man she had thought she loved. His boots squelched in congealing blood.

"Yes, Your Highness," Arun replied.

Kordahla shifted her weight. Jordayne sized her up, took one look at Drucilamere, and went to her lover. "Ahkdul is the greater threat, I think," she said.

Drucilamere managed a single nod.

Mariano ignored the master mage. No threat he, when the Minoria stood guard. He stepped in close to Matisse. Two pairs of lifeless eyes, two pairs of mute lips, two severed necks bore witness to his right. "If you have laid even an inappropriate eye on my sister, if you are responsible for marring her innocence enough for her to claim she gave herself to a man, I will exact a blood price on you." Stepping back, he clasped his hands behind his back. "However, if you behaved with honour, you will understand her discipline is my prerogative."

"Mo-re po-prin," Drucilamere gasped, his face white.

"Druce," Jordayne said, quiet and concerned.

His magic faltered; Ahkdul fell free. The glow in Arun's crystal dimmed, and Matisse stumbled past Mariano. Beyond them, mahktashaan and mage faced each other, bound by magic, split by might.

Jordayne should not have bothered to come back to her, anklets tinkling urgent, skirts rustling her unease. "What did you tell your brother?" the lady whispered. "Matisse has admitted you took pleasure in each other."

Kordahla stared at the noose. She wanted to be free of this nightmare. The rope might provide a way, but the Minoria would never let it tighten, even if she evaded them all long enough to reach it. And the crackling ball of light zig-zagged near that wall, scaring her more than death. It hovered near the dying man, vibrating with furious, pent up energy. The renegade must have sensed its ominous presence, for he turned his head. With the last of his breath he emitted a desperate gurgle, tried to force his failing body back. The light dove for his chest, plunging inside as though his flesh posed no barrier. A racking spasm lifted his chest from the ground, dragging his flaccid head along the paving as his arms and legs thrashed. Seconds later, he lay inert, eyes wide.

Kordahla's heart thumped. An archaic power lay within this possession, something which should not be abroad in the world of living men. She stared at the gutted corpse.

"My dear," Jordayne said.

Her silence drove Jordayne back to Drucilamere.

"How dare you talk about honour when you hit a woman," Matisse said, finding himself free. He lunged at Mariano. Matisse jerked, crying out in pain, before their bodies connected.

Ahkdul laughed. "Your puny drug addict of a mage can't protect you." He drew a knife from his boot, tilting it to reflect the sun into Matisse's eyes. A cruel curve played about his lips as he thrust. Yelped. Dropped the blade before it could cut kurta or skin. He grimaced as it clattered on the stone at his feet.

Mariano smirked. "For daring to lay a hand on a Crown Prince, you pretender to a throne," he said. But he too, cried out before he could land a punch. He was facing away from Arun, and would not have seen the crystal glow blue at the Minoria's neck; would not, in his anger have noticed Jordayne squeeze Drucilamere's arm, or the mage breathe calm.

The Minoria's hood turned her way. His head dipped, a gesture Kordahla would have taken as respect were they any other place at any other time. Here and now, respect was not a virtue she deserved.

"Your Highness, there is business to attend," Arun said in his usual steady voice, though mahktashaan and mage were eyeing each other off.

"What further business could you possibly have in Myklaan?" Matisse said, and despite the casual way he dropped the words, it was obvious he wanted his sword in his hand.

"I demand the return of the crystal and quartz," Mariano said.

Matisse flicked a glance at the Minoria, dismissed him by returning to his appraisal of Mariano. Kordahla stepped toward the noose. For all his languid manner, Matisse would not fight to free her from Ahkdul's grasp. A stable throne was too great a treasure, and she a diversion, a minor prize at most.

"A deal then. Princess Kordahla will remain in Myklaan. In return, I will talk to the mages. They will return the crystals, if they have them."

Ahkdul clenched fists and jaw. "She is pledged to me, you conceited –"

Mariano raised a hand to forestall him. "Neither the Princess–"

"– pig."

"– nor the crystals are yours to bargain with."

Matisse folded his arms. "Is that how you regard her life? A commodity to trade for your success?" Danger lurked behind his light tone.

"She is a Princess. She was born to duty, and it is mine to ensure hers is fulfilled."

The heir to the Myklaani throne picked up the bearded, disembodied head by the hair and made a display of examining it. "Your sense of honour is strong," he said at last. He fixed Mariano with a look of challenge. "Yet you would entrust your sister to a man who regards her with contempt."

Drucilamere leant forward to plant a cautionary word in Matisse's ear. His words were fast and clipped, his eyes were bright with sobriety. The pair of them played a dangerous game.

"Neither our politics nor our family business are your concern," Mariano said.

Matisse tossed the head to Ahkdul's feet. "He got what he deserved. But since politics are not our business, it will not distress you to learn Shah Ordosteen denies the existence of the crystals."

"Then tell your Shah Terlaan considers his actions an act of war." Mariano gestured and they filed out of the courtyard. Never again would gardens smell so sweet with frangipani, jasmine, and rose. Never again would the sun sparkle on canals rippling with fountain-fall, or parrots with ruffled plumes delight in their bath. Never again would she see that confidence-destroying smile on her lover's face. He was shaking off Drucilamere's hand, striding fast toward her where she walked, trapped between her brother and Ahkdul, while a wary Arun brought up the rear. A soft glow of the crystal and one raised finger was all Arun needed to warn him off as Jordayne, her face frozen in shock, stared after her.

They were allowed to leave the grounds and join their guards unmolested. History would not record Myklaan as starting this war, nor would the Vae mark the realm as dishonourable during the lead up to a battle. Mounted on fresh horses, armed, provisioned, and under escort, Mariano, Ahkdul, Arun and scared Kahlmed flanked her as they began the journey north.

Outside the city gates, Kordahla turned her head to the northeast. Brooding Faradil Forest was the only sight to behold, but Tarana lay in that direction, her home despite her foolish flight. Vinsant too, the one person she longed to see. And Father, who would chastise her till her insides were raw before embracing her like a young child and kissing her despair into reluctant acceptance.

She shuddered as Ahkdul caught her wistful gaze and brought his horse alongside hers. Shuddered as he spoke. "Oh no, my wicked wife. You are coming with me to Verdaan. Your father has agreed. We are to wed without delay."

About the Author

Tia Reed lives in Australia with her bossy cat and boisterous dog, both of whom believe her writing takes far too much of her attention away from them. Much of the inspiration for her stories has come from the experiences thrown at her while travelling. When she is not teaching or writing, she enjoys taking her dog for walks, and trying to tame her beast of a garden.

33275711R00331

Printed in Great Britain
by Amazon